THE BEST

OF

H. P. LOVECRAFT

BLOODCURDLING TALES OF HORROR AND THE MACABRE

THE BEST
OF
H.P. LOVECRAFT

BLOODCURDLING TALES
OF HORROR AND THE MACABRE

H.P. Lovecraft

Introduction by
Robert Bloch

DEL REY

The Ballantine Publishing Group
New York

A Del Rey® Book
Published by The Ballantine Publishing Group

Copyright © 1963 by August Derleth
Published by arrangement with Arkham House Publishers, Inc.
Introduction copyright © 1982 by Robert Bloch

http://www.randomhouse.com/delrey/

Library of Congress Catalog Card Number: 82-90468
ISBN: 0-345-35080-4

Manufactured in the United States of America

Cover design by Michelle T. Gengaro
Cover painting by Michael Whelan

First Edition: October 1982

26   27   28   29   30

Contents

Heritage of Horror

Robert Bloch

"The oldest and strongest emotion of mankind is fear, and the oldest and strongest kind of fear is fear of the unknown."

This is the opening sentence of "Supernatural Horror in Literature," one of the finest essays on horror fiction ever written. Its author, H. P. Lovecraft, is considered by many to be one of the finest writers of such fiction.

Howard Phillips Lovecraft was born in Providence, Rhode Island, on August 20, 1890. He was the last lineal descendant of an old New England family that had seen better days. His father died of paresis in 1898; his mother survived until 1921, but her own mental instability increased as the family fortunes declined.

Lovecraft wrote, "As a child I was very peculiar and sensitive, always preferring the society of grown persons to that of other children." Actually it was his neurotic mother who labelled him peculiar and "protected" him from contact with other youngsters. A precocious child, he learned to read when he was four and soon experimented with writing. Poor health kept him from college and economic necessity eventually caused him to neglect amateur journalism in favor of ghostwriting or revising the work of others for professional publication. Gradually he began to produce poetry and fiction of his own.

After his mother's death he lived for a time in New York, married an older woman from whom he separated amicably two years later, then returned to Providence. Here he made his home with two elderly aunts. One of them died in 1932; he and his surviving relative resided together until his own death on March 15, 1937.

Robert Bloch was a teenage protégé of H. P. Lovecraft. He since has become one of the masters of modern horror fiction. Bloch is perhaps best known for his novel *Psycho*, on which the popular film was based. After an interval of twenty-two years, Bloch returned to the world of Norman Bates, and *Psycho II* was published in September 1982.

Lovecraft's career as a professional writer was largely compressed into a span of about sixteen years. He remained virtually unknown except to the limited readership of pulp magazines such as *Weird Tales* in which his work appeared. It earned only a pitiful pittance to supplement the income from a meager inheritance, and he continued his anonymous chores for other writers. At the same time he brightened and broadened his uneventful existence with a widespread correspondence among fellow writers and readers of fantastic fiction. The most constant and devoted members of this group formed what would later be called "the Lovecraft Circle"; his lengthy letters of comment, criticism, and literary advice encouraged them to write or attempt writing in the genre. When a combination of cancer and Bright's disease claimed his life at the age of forty-six the loss was mourned by far-off friends, many of whom had known him only as a correspondent.

Lovecraft's literary style was distinctive and frequently imitated by protégés. With his approval, they and others borrowed the imaginary settings of his stories, together with the weird books and grotesque gods he created to heighten horror.

At the time of his death he had already become what would now be called a "cult figure." But the cult was comparatively small and had absolutely no influence on contemporary critics or publishers. It took long years to bring the man and his work to the attention of a larger audience.

Today Lovecraft is established as a major American fantasy writer, frequently ranked as the equal of Poe. His work is in print here and abroad and the mild-mannered, old-fashioned, conservative New England gentleman has become an acknowledged master of horror fiction.

But certain critics disagree. Perhaps the earliest negative verdict was pronounced by Edmund Wilson, writing in *The New Yorker* in 1945 to accuse Lovecraft of "bad taste and bad art." Other nonadmirers broadened their attacks to include the man as well as his work. In recent years Ted White, former editor of *Amazing* and *Fantastic*, expressed the belief that this sort of "sick" writing is the product of a "sick" mind—and suggested that anyone attracted to it is also "sick."

The notion is interesting, but its revisionist attitude toward literature could have far-reaching implications. If safeguarding our mental health requires us to avoid the work of those whose life-styles depart from the accepted norm, then our bookshelves would soon be stripped bare. The literary efforts of chronic alcoholics, drug addicts, sexual deviants, and victims of psychosis with suicidal tendencies can indeed be dismissed, but we must be prepared to accept the consequences.

We will, of course, lose the efforts of Poe, Hawthorne, de Maupassant, and Kafka. But we will also be deprived of *Alice's Adventures in Wonderland*, *Huckleberry Finn*, *Moby-Dick*, *Crime and Punishment*, *A Farewell to Arms*, *The Great Gatsby*, *Remembrance of Things Past*, and hundreds of other titles that some regard as literary masterpieces. We must avoid O Henry, Katherine Mansfield, Sherwood Anderson, Virginia Woolf, Jack London, André Gide, Thomas Wolfe, Somerset Maugham, Sinclair Lewis, Jean Cocteau, Christopher Isherwood, William Faulkner, and Oscar Wilde, to name only a few. The same applies to such diverse talents as Dashiell Hammett, Nietzsche, Brendan Behan, Raymond Chandler, Schopenhauer, and Hans Christian Andersen. Poets would vanish; Byron, Auden, Baudelaire, Rimbaud, Dylan Thomas, Edna St. Vincent Millay, Swinburne, Verlaine, Hart Crane, Walt Whitman. We would also cast into oblivion the plays of Marlowe, Genet, Tennessee Williams, Eugene O'Neill, Noel Coward and—according to some authorities—the complete works of William Shakespeare.

It seems a high price to pay for our mental hygiene, particularly in the case of Lovecraft. After all, the man didn't drink, smoke or do drugs. His sex life was apparently limited to a brief marriage but his wife pronounced him an "adequately excellent lover" and even his most ardent detractors have failed to find any evidence of homosexual activity. Although he admittedly suffered from psychological handicaps, his sedentary existence was unmarred by antisocial behavior.

"Sickness," like beauty, is often in the eye of the beholder. Sometimes it takes the form of personal convictions; Arthur Conan Doyle really believed in fairies and Emanuel Swedenborg had literal visions of heaven and hell. Both wrote earnestly about their unorthodox concepts but neither are generally regarded as "sick."

In terms of pure imagination, what are we to make of someone who devotes much of his adult life to writing about hobbits, or the land of Oz? Despite the upbeat content of works by Tolkien and L. Frank Baum, there are dark and dreadful creatures lurking in the caverns beneath the sunny worlds they created; gnomes and monsters, evil entities with demoniac powers of sorcery and witchcraft. Were these men also "sick"?

And what of those who placed their horrors in the context of contemporary reality? Was little Mary Shelley unbalanced when she wrote *Frankenstein*? Does mental illness account for Stevenson's *The Strange Case of Dr. Jekyll and Mr. Hyde*? How crazy must you be to destroy the world, like H. G. Wells, or alter its future as morbidly and mercilessly as did Huxley and Orwell?

"Sick" or healthy, all creative activity—including writing—is the product of individual imagination, colored by personal viewpoint, an attitude toward life. And it seems generated by an intense desire or need to communicate with others.

Most of us satisfy such urges in a simpler fashion. The physically attractive and the energetically aggressive seldom find a need to become "creative" in order to enjoy the rewards of our society. The losers and loners escape from competitive situations as "dropouts" or members of the counterculture; even the criminal element enjoys a shadowy status of its own. Rebellion and misbehavior become ways of attracting attention, even admiration.

Before society became so openly permissive the introvert had to find other solutions to his problems. If no one responded to a child's need for favorable attention—if no one answered the cry of "Look at me!"—then perhaps the pleas could be rephrased. "Look at my pictures—hear my music—listen to my story." In that context all writers can be called "sick," including those who assume the superior role of critic.

Not all creative artists are physically unattractive or without charm and social graces. But for one reason or another most possess feelings of inadequacy or insecurity that they are impelled to overcome—and thus it must have been since time immemorial.

Hence the artists who decorated the walls of caves in our distant past, the singers who chanted and played upon primitive instruments in those echoing caverns, the tellers of tales who squatted beside the flickering campfires. And though means and methods changed, the impulse and conditions generating creativity remain constant; hence today's talent.

Hence Lovecraft, the child who was sickly and studious; the growing boy whose own mother inculcated a belief in his "ugliness"; the young man who found himself ill at ease and ill-equipped to compete socially or economically with his peer group. Like others not naturally endowed with qualities to make them easy winners but who are not satisfied to abandon the contest entirely, he had to find a vehicle for recognition. Writing solved the problem of communication, of gaining notice. If he found difficulty going out into the world he could send his writing out instead, and perhaps the world would come to him.

But what sort of writing? He tried his hand at many things— juvenile imitations of Poe, which he destroyed in his late teens; astronomy articles for local newspapers; scientific and literary essays self-published as a member of amateur journalism societies; poetry; criticism; then the ghostwriting and revision. None of this brought him the recognition he craved. He rationalized the lack by claiming to despise commercial success; a true gentleman wrote only as an amateur, free of all restrictions. Nevertheless he gradually resumed production of his own fiction.

Fiction, as we know, takes many forms, from gritty realism to far-fetched fantasy. In recognizing categories we can also recognize the reasons why certain writers choose to work within them. Their efforts establish an image—often as wish-fulfillment—of the brawny he-man, the unshockable sophisticate, the romantic lover, the keen and objective analyst of human behavior, the cynical realist, the compassionate idealist, the wise philosopher, the sexual athlete, the poet, the carefree adventurer, and every possible persona in the Jungian pantheon of archetypes.

Writers are role players, but the role is not the man, even though it may incorporate certain of his beliefs and attitudes.

Lovecraft's work offers obvious examples of this. His lifelong aversion to cold is apparent in stories such as "Cool Air" and his short novel, "At the Mountains of Madness." An allergy to seafood is embodied in "The Shadow Over Innsmouth," and a tone-deaf distaste for music as dissonance echoes in "The Music of Erich Zann." A love of cats is obvious in many tales; so is a fondness for colonial architecture and outrage over its gradual destruction.

The literary detective will have no trouble finding clues pointing to Lovecraft's lifelong Anglophilia; it surfaces even in his preference for English modes of spelling, as in "The Colour Out of Space." His style betrays a bias in favor—or *favour*, as he would put it—for the language, literary forms, and life-styles of the eighteenth century that he professed to find superior to our own. Privately he often declared a longing to have lived as a loyal colonial subject of King George III in pre-Revolutionary days, and perhaps he truly believed this.

With tongue more obviously in cheek he began referring to himself as an "old gentleman" and signing his letters "Grandpa" while still in his thirties. But the pose reveals a preoccupation with age and aging that is omnipresent in his work. Old houses and old tombs are abundantly in evidence and often their presence is unpleasant, even unnatural. Ancient edifices hold monstrous secrets in "The Rats in the Walls," "The Lurking Fear," "The Shadow Over Innsmouth," "The Shadow Out of Time," "The Shunned House," "The Dreams in the Witch-House" and a dozen other tales. Old people are often equally evil; Wizard Whateley in "The Dunwich Horror" is not exactly the sort of farmer the Department of Agriculture would approve of, nor would nutritionists endorse the diet of the elderly owner of "The Picture in the House." Other oldsters in "He," "The Case of Charles Dexter Ward," and "The Terrible Old Man" do not represent advances in geriatrics, while both dwelling and dweller are equally disturbing in "The Strange High House in the Mist." And the Elder Gods—the "Great Old Ones" of his later stories—are hardly qualified to bridge the generation gap. At best, Lovecraft's attitude toward age is ambivalent, but his obsession with the subject is literally mirrored in "The Outsider."

So is his interest in astronomy and the physical sciences; the avowed antiquarian was also a lifelong student of developments in modern research. Generally regarded only as a writer of fantasy, a good share of his output contains more of a scientific element than much of what today is classified as science fiction or—at higher word rates—"speculative fiction."

"The Colour Out of Space," "At the Mountains of Madness," and "The Shadow Out of Time" were first published in science fiction magazines, and rightly so. But most of his work saw print in *Weird Tales*, and its appearance there blinded readers to its actual content. "Cool Air" anticipates cryogenic research; "The Dreams in the Witch-House" suggests that advanced physics will recapitulate the discoveries of powers used in witchcraft. "The Whisperer in Darkness" is an outstanding early example of one of science fiction's major motifs—the "aliens among us" theme. "The Shadow Over Innsmouth" offers its own portraits of architectural decay and dirty old men, together with a perverted worship of perverted beings, but the main thrust of the story doesn't depend upon anything supernatural. Its grotesque monstrosities are the product of biological mutation rather than black magic.

Degenerative mutation also figures in "The Outsider," "The Lurking Fear," "The Rats in the Walls," and in the grotesque miscegenations of "The Dunwich Horror" and "Arthur Jermyn." Some critics cite this as a disguised example of the racism they find evident in "He," "The Horror at Red Hook," "The Call of Cthulhu," and other stories.

If Lovecraft was a racist we must recognize that the term was not generally considered pejorative during his own time. In the twenties and thirties, Anglo-Saxon superiority was virtually taken for granted not only in literature but in daily life. And nowhere was this belief more pronounced than in New England. Here the D.A.R. held sway, and the inhabitants of the self-styled Shrine of Liberty shuddered as their communities were invaded by immigrants. Ignoring the fact that most of these "foreigners" had been imported by blue-blooded, 100 percent Americans to provide cheap labor for their factories, they watched in dismay as cities became crowded, old landmarks gave way to new construction, and their political, economic, and social control gradually vanished.

To Lovecraft these changes were anathema, and he expressed his attitude both privately and in print. But his views were not inflexible. As he matured he gradually came out of his shell and his outlook broadened; the racist element of earlier efforts is muted or absent in later tales. And what sort of anti-Semitic author marries a Jewess, associates with Jews as friends and correspondents, and retains one as his literary agent?

The one theme incontrovertibly constant in both his life and his work is a preoccupation with dreams.

From earliest childhood on, Lovecraft's sleep ushered him into a world filled with vivid visions of alien and exotic landscapes that at times formed a background for terrifying nightmares.

His earlier fiction often utilized the strange settings glimpsed in these dreamworlds; they were ideal for the prose poems he fashioned in the manner of Poe or Dunsany. Later, as his own style evolved, he confronted the nightmare elements as well and translated them into chilling, convincing realities. Many of the characters in his tales are dominated by their dreams. His alter ego in several stories, Randolph Carter, is a dreamer; "The Silver Key" and "Through the Gates of the Silver Key" (written in collaboration with E. Hoffman Price) both emphasize Carter's nocturnal fantasies. The novel-length *The Dream-Quest of Unknown Kadath* enters Carter's dreamworld and the first story in which he figures, "The Statement of Randolph Carter," derives directly from one of Lovecraft's nightmares. Dreams figure in "The Rats in the Walls," "The Dreams in the Witch-House" and many other tales. In "The Call of Cthulhu," the first story to deal fully with what later came to be known as the "Cthulhu Mythos," the dreams of a neurotic artist and his counterparts all over the world herald the resurrection of a hideous Elder God from his lair beneath the sea.

The so-called "Cthulhu Mythos" represents Lovecraft's chief claim to fame and the stories in which it evolves bring together all of his major influences and interests.

An affinity for colonial New England and fears regarding its decadence both found embodiment in fictional settings for those tales. Kingsport and Innsmouth are ancient seaports; Arkham is an old city steeped in traditions of the witchcraft craze and now the site of Miskatonic University. In this milieu dwell the sensitive scholars who serve as narrators or protagonists of the stories. At Miskatonic some of them find access to one of six known remaining copies of a strange book containing the secrets of a race older than mankind—the Great Old Ones. Invaders from other dimensions and other worlds, they once ruled earth but were vanquished and expelled by other cosmic forces. In some cases they were merely imprisoned, like Cthulhu in the sunken city of R'lyeh, or in subterranea beneath deserts and polar ice caps. But their legend survives, as does their telepathic influence, and they are still worshiped by certain primitive people as well as more sophisticated members of cults dedicated to bringing about their return and reign.

"When the stars are right" the Great Old Ones could plunge from world to world through the sky or rise again from deathless sleep. And the blasphemous book, *The Necronomicon*, contained incantations that would aid their advent, as well as other spells and ceremonies designed to defeat them.

The original Arabic version had been lost, but the text was translated into Greek, then Latin, and the volume was sought after by both those who worshiped and those who opposed the Ancient Ones. It is these entities—creatures like Yog-Sothoth and Nyarlathotep—who haunt the "Cthulhu Mythos" tales.

Nyarlathotep emerged directly from Lovecraft's dreams, as did some of the weird locales he mentions—the plateau of Leng, and Kadath in the Cold Waste. Yuggoth, the dwelling place of certain terrifying extraterrestial beings, was another name for the planet Pluto; in a poem cycle, "Fungi From Yuggoth," there are allusions to many more fantastic figures and places referred to in his prose.

Some of these were borrowed from the work of other writers and the basic concept of the "Cthulhu Mythos" probably owes a great deal to Arthur Machen, who wrote about a stunted and debased race of primitive beings still secretly existing beneath the lonely Welsh hills. Lovecraft was much impressed with this concept but he alone expanded the notion of a localized prehuman survival into a vast cosmology of his own creation.

Gradually he built up a rationale for both reality and dreams, nothing less than a history of the entire universe. As such, the "Cthulhu Mythos" is a literary creation far surpassing the word-worlds of Cabell, C. S. Lewis, or Tolkien in breadth and scope.

While imaginary worlds abound in modern fantasy, few of today's writers set their sagas in Poictesme, Perelanda, or Middle-earth. But stories and novels based on the Mythos continue to proliferate. In terms of imitation and inspiration, Lovecraft may well have had more influence on other writers than any contemporary except Ernest Hemingway.

It didn't happen overnight. As noted, he received scant critical attention during his lifetime. The annual "best" short-story collections list only two of his tales as "also-rans"; they printed none. And in *Weird Tales*, the lowly pulp magazine where most of his output appeared, he was never even granted a cover illustration for anything he wrote. Such honors were reserved for more popular authors and their creations—Seabury Quinn's French detective, Jules de Grandin, or Robert E. Howard's barbarian adventurer, Conan.

During the latter years of Lovecraft's life the most successful purveyors of short fiction found a hospitable and high-paying market in the weekly "slicks"—*Collier's, Liberty, The Saturday Evening Post*—and the big-circulation monthly magazines. Authors with "serious" aspirations often opted for *The Atlantic Monthly, The American Mercury, The New Yorker, Story,* or regional periodicals. The world's greatest short-story writer was William Saroyan; we knew, because he told us so.

Lovecraft made no such claims. At the time of his death glowing tributes graced the letter column of *Weird Tales* and some of the amateur "fanzines" privately circulated among a few devotees of fantasy or science fiction. But their readership was minimal and their influence nugatory.

Aside from a small Canadian edition of *Weird Tales*, Lovecraft's efforts had appeared abroad only in Christine Campbell Thompson's sleazily printed British "Not at Night" series. One story was reprinted in an American anthology but attempts to publish two of his novellas in hardcover had failed. There were no foreign translations at all. In the years that followed, a single tale was adapted for radio. Filmmakers weren't interested; television didn't exist, nor paperback books. Lovecraft was dead, and to all intents and purposes, so was his work.

But the "Lovecraft Circle" of correspondents remained. Two of them, fellow-writers August Derleth and Donald Wandrei, tried to interest publishers in putting out a collection of his stories. Meeting with no success, they then founded a company of their own called Arkham House and announced the publication of *The Outsider and Others*. This imposing volume of over three hundred thousand words would sell for $5, but could be purchased at a prepublication price of $3.50. Despite wide advance publicity throughout the fantasy and science fiction field, only 150 orders were received, and the remaining 1,118 copies took more than four years to sell out.

Determined to overcome indifference, Arkham House went on to print a companion volume, *Beyond the Wall of Sleep*, then gradually extended its list to include the work of other contemporary fantasy authors. A series of complications subsequently arose, involving royalty bequests from Lovecraft's aunt who died in 1941, the suicide of his literary executor ten years later, plus legal disputes between Wandrei and Derleth.

Lovecraft's work survived it all. It even survived Derleth's imitations of his style and subject matter, which he began writing in the forties. Derleth had won deserved praise for his "Solar Pons" pastiches, based on the Sherlock Holmes stories of Conan Doyle. But his pseudo-Lovecraft efforts were less convincing. Using a line or two from Lovecraft's commonplace book scarcely justified calling the total work a "posthumous collaboration." And when he abandoned this pretext his attempts to convey the essence of Lovecraft's style didn't come off; he sounded the notes but lost the music.

It was Derleth who constantly used the term "Cthulhu Mythos" to describe Lovecraft's cosmic concepts. Unfortunately, his own writing involved a distortion of its meaning that may have derived from his own status as a lapsed or lax Catholic. In any case, he divided Lovecraft's Great Old Ones into what in effect were the Good Guys and the Bad Guys, fighting over possession of the earth instead of the ranch. Some later imitators picked up on this, straying far from Lovecraftian logic.

But when considering Derleth's influence, one single fact remains all-important—he championed the revival of interest in Lovecraft's work. After Donald Wandrei's service in World War II his Arkham House activity was largely limited to editing Lovecraft's letters, eventually published in five volumes. Derleth, however, continued to keep the stories in print, reissuing portions of the original collections under other titles. When fantasy anthologies began to flourish, he sold one-time reprint rights to various stories, including those in public domain, and until his death in 1961 he claimed control of the literary estate. As early as 1945 he compiled a paperback Lovecraft collection for an Armed Services edition. Its unexpected popularity with a wide readership encouraged later reprinting efforts by other paperback publishers here and abroad. Gradually this continued exposure led to the formation of a new fandom, enthusiasts interested in every aspect of the man and the work. Following recognition on the part of foreign critics, Lovecraft—like his predecessor, Edgar Allan Poe—finally came to the attention of the American literary establishment.

Shortly after L. Frank Baum began writing, certain guardians of young minds and morals instigated a campaign to keep his Oz books off public library shelves. Today it is evident that this ban-the-Baum movement has failed. That it did so is in no small part due to the success of the 1939 film *The Wizard of Oz*. But although a number of Lovecraft's stories have been adapted for television and motion pictures, no first-rate film has yet seen release. As a result, Cthulhu is scarcely a household word.

Nevertheless, the writing of theses and serious critiques increases with each passing year. Lovecraft has been the subject of several book-length biographies and memoirs, plus innumerable scholarly disquisitions. His books are on the library shelves. There is a Lovecraft Collection at Brown University in Providence. The prose, verse, and a significant portion of his letters are in print and seem destined to remain so, while recognition and reputation continues to soar. The fame that eluded him in his lifetime has come to Lovecraft almost half a century after his death.

Why did interest in horror fiction lay dormant for so long a time? And what brought about its present popularity?

Perhaps the answer lies buried in Lovecraft's own work. Great Cthulhu and the Elder Gods never truly died, but they could be aroused from their slumbers only when "the stars were right." And what Lovecraft described as the oldest and strongest kind of fear—fear of the unknown—lay deathless but dormant in the years following his birth.

The age of materialism had dawned and science was hailed as a savior, freeing the world from those ancient fears of the unknown. Even those who still believed in the supernatural now engaged in psychic research to explain such phenomena on a scientific basis.

Emphasis on rationality dominated the fiction of the day. Dr. Jekyll's transformation was the result of laboratory chemicals rather than demonic possession. And even if a few creatures like Dracula existed, they could be detected and defeated by scientists like Van Helsing.

The few horror stories approved by the literary establishment dealt almost exclusively with polite antiquarians and retired English gentlemen encountering a ghost. Fear was an isolated phenomenon born of some unusual individual experience.

World War I changed that concept. Catastrophe became common property, horror invaded the daily lives—and deaths—of millions. Rationalists sought to combat fear by denying those deaths; interest in spiritualism and psychic investigation became a popular preoccupation in the next decade.

But the depiction of legendary dread was another matter; such vulgarities were relegated to the pages of obscure publications such as *Weird Tales*. At the time Lovecraft penned his stories, no self-styled sophisticate dared presume to take them seriously, either as literature or as a metaphor for contemporary reality.

During the same period the printed page faced growing competition from film and radio. With the advent of sound in cinema the mass audience shifted allegiance to the new form.

In the economic and social upheaval following the war, German studios produced a number of supernatural fantasy films that reflected the doubts and fears obsessing European audiences. Americans, in the boom years of expansion and material prosperity, spurned such subject matter. Their mystery movies and the horror pictures of Lon Chaney offered realistic explanations.

It was not until this country faced its own financial depression that the supernatural finally found a degree of acceptance. Radio shows like *Lights Out* and *Inner Sanctum* gained popularity, largely with the young. And it was their response that insured success for the horror films that became regular fare in the thirties; their king was Kong, Count Dracula their dark and noble lord. Frankenstein's monster served as surrogate for their own self-image as unwanted outcasts, victims of authority figures in a competitive society where their elders maintained rigid control.

But the majority of the audience still rejected such fantasies in favor of other forms of escapism; "screwball" comedies involving the exploits of "madcap heiresses" and wish-fulfillment sagas of lowly shop-girls or poor-but-honest young men who rose to riches. Even the gangster films catered to such visions; their anti-heroes shared the common goal of attaining fortune, even by unorthodox methods. The American Dream had yet to die, prosperity was just around the corner; individual effort, aided by scientific advances, would still bring success. Doubters and dissenters might read the new "proletarian literature" or even espouse the cause of communism, but they continued to believe in their own power to remold the world to their heart's desire. Like the conservative upholders of the status quo, they continued to firmly reject the bogeymen and bugaboos of the supernatural.

World War II decimated American Dreamers and dissenters alike. Those who survived were faced with terrifying truths. Vast power *can* fall into evil hands—the world *can* be destroyed—science, armed with biological and nuclear weaponry of its own creation, is not our savior but an omnipresent enemy.

There was a growing distrust of every ideology in the age of "ism"—fascism, communism, militarism, sectarianism, McCarthyism, racism, terrorism, even misguided idealism, proved no protection against corrupt leadership. In the light of such attitudes the movie monsters of the thirties frightened no one in the forties. Even Abbott and Costello could easily outwit them. Their place was taken by mad scientists, prehistoric beasts, or creatures from outer space. Such menaces came in many forms, but with a choice of only two motivations—to take over the world or to destroy it.

Nevertheless, the hero usually managed to triumph in the end.

The world could still be saved after all, and for a time this message was reassuring.

But revelations of personal insecurity continued to rise in the decades that followed. Depletion of natural resources, spiraling inflation, religious warfare, governmental and industrial corruption, political assassination, street crime, mass murder, and drug addiction grew and flourished. No heroes appeared on the scene to offer succor or solutions.

Like the turmoil and upheaval that preceded the return of the Great Old Ones in Lovecraft's fiction, the world seemed to be preparing for its final fate now that "the stars were right."

And it was then, in doubt, dismay, even in despair, that many turned to the one "ism" that still remained.

Exorcism.

Graffiti proclaimed, "God is dead." And a television comedian capped the concept with an explanation for subsequent behavior patterns—"The Devil made me do it."

Black humor, perhaps, but many a true word is spoken in jest. And when the book and film of *Rosemary's Baby* appeared, heralding the literal rebirth of Satan on earth, its satirical thrust was blunted by recognition of a growing reality. Cults dedicated to witchcraft and Satanism had indeed become popular and the acknowledgement of Evil as a tangible presence gained adherents. Materialists still scoffed but some of them began decorating their cars with bumper stickers announcing that "Richard Nixon is Rosemary's Baby." Again, the avowed intent was humorous—but behind the jokes could be sensed a genuine desire to personify the source of man's misfortunes. Satan became the scapegoat. And exorcism—that ancient, half-forgotten ritual to rid us of our demons—suddenly captured the imagination and attention of the masses.

Viewed in retrospect, *The Exorcist* was scarcely a literary landmark, and the film that followed was illogical and prolix. Few members of the audience could clearly explain the origin of the demon, why this entity took possession of a child, or exactly how it met its final fate. Nor was their interest a religious one. The spectacle of a little girl whose face was transformed by makeup into an unreasonable facsimile of Harpo Marx's "gookie" grimace, spewing obscenities and green pea soup or rotating her head a full 360°, seemed the chief attraction.

Nevertheless, it was clearly stated that the Devil made her do it. And the statements of box-office receipts convinced both filmmakers and publishers that doing it was profitable. Hell had become a hot property.

Now the Devil popped up again, together with his deputy demons, in a spate of fiction and film; *The Exorcist* spawned a sequel, *The Omen* became a trilogy, *The Sentinel* and a score of others advanced the notion that the Evil One was alive and well and living in your local drive-in theater.

If the Devil lives, then it would seem that other evils flourish in his wake. And so they did. Vampires rose again to refresh themselves with a sanguinary nightcap; not to be outdone by the undead, the dead themselves awakened from their graves for a midnight snack of sheep intestines that convincingly substituted for human entrails. Hirsute werewolves followed suit and a seemingly psychotic mass murderer was solemnly identified by a psychiatrist as "the Bogeyman." Ghosts, ghouls, succubi, and incubi infested earth, and even in outer space *The Alien* incubated in a human breast, emerging to create catastrophe for cat lovers on a spacecraft.

Explicit violence increased in a series of "spatter films" and the butcheries depicted in many horror novels could be described as hackwork in every sense of the word. Grand Guignol degenerated into not-so-grand gross-out.

All of which was a far cry—or shriek—from the perils presented in the work of H. P. Lovecraft. Or was it?

Consider the phenomenon of exorcism, this time from the viewpoint of the artist rather than the audience. Most writers who choose to work within the horror genre do so to exorcise their own fears by exposing and expressing them to an audience. In childhood such writers are usually gifted—or cursed—with a hyperactive imagination. As adults they translate early dread of pain, death, and the unknown into fictional form; what frightened them, they reason, will also frighten their readers. Drawing upon a common cultural heritage of myth, legend, and fairy tales, they employ a technique of conveying their visions in terms of convincing reality.

The success of such efforts depends upon learning ways to involve the reader emotionally and inducing what has been called "the temporary suspension of disbelief." It is not easily attained, and the offerings of apprentice authors in the horror field tend to be derivative and overblown.

Lovecraft was no exception to the rule. In earlier tales he often relied on the excessive use of adjectives rather than the power of suggestion, with disastrous results. But gradually he learned the value of restraint and of a more realistic approach. Refining his style, he also refined his method.

Generally speaking, most fiction can be divided into two categories, both dependent upon establishing the credibility of the supposed narrator. In simple terms, that narrator is presented as either wiser or less knowledgeable than the reader.

In the first instance, the device is used to convince the reader that anyone as intelligent as the author must know what he's talking about and is obviously telling the truth. Belief in the narrator leads to belief in the story.

The alternative approach is perhaps best illustrated in Ring Lardner's story "Haircut." Here the monologue of an ignorant small-town barber unwittingly reveals to the reader more than the narrator himself is aware of.

Lovecraft's inspiration was to combine both of these techniques into one.

His narrators are usually scientists or scholars of a high intellectual order who address the reader with obvious authority. At the same time they exhibit an equally obvious flaw—not stupidity per se, but an overcautious tendency to voice unreasonable reservations regarding the fantastic facts they so convincingly and objectively present. As a result the reader soon becomes convinced that what they doubt is actually a dreadful reality. And when, at the end of the story, the narrator is forced to recognize the existence of what lurks behind his hints of horror, the reader shares the ultimate terror of truth.

The source of a writer's personal fantasies is to a great extent colored by what he reads or views during his impressionable early years. Today's fictioneers and filmmakers often come late to an acquaintance with literary traditions. Their youthful influences were more often the science fiction films and the comic books of the fifties and sixties. As a result, a great deal of what they present as horror relies on crude and explicit violence. Dwelling on gruesome detail in print and utilizing special effects for shock on the screen, they opt for the easy out of evoking nausea and revulsion instead of genuine fear. Even their lighter efforts, involving the renascence of "superheroes," betray an intellectual dependency on the comics of their childhood. As such, their efforts find greatest favor with juvenile audiences today.

Lovecraft had a thorough grounding in the classics of the genre, presented in their original form. In this lies the enduring strength of his own work, and its continuing power to capture a mature following after a half-century of change and chaos.

In "Supernatural Horror in Literature" he wrote, "Children will always be afraid of the dark, and men with minds sensitive to hereditary impulses will always tremble at the thought of the hidden and fathomless worlds of strange life which may pulsate in the gulfs beyond the stars or press hideously upon our own globe in unholy dimensions which only the dead and the moonstruck may glimpse."

Couched in this florid prose, Lovecraft intended to present an explanation of why horror fiction appealed to certain types of readers. And in so doing he unconsciously revealed his own reasons for writing—as attempts to come to grips with a lifelong fear of the unknown.

What he said about the readers of fifty years ago is still valid. In a time of turmoil there is a widespread intimation—not based on hereditary impulse but on today's realities—that the evils abroad in the world may come from without as well as from within ourselves. While we may consciously reject his cosmology as absurd, a part of us finds in it a chilling confirmation of secret fears.

At the time Lovecraft created it, the "Cthulhu Mythos" and its threat of Elder Gods rising and returning to rule over earth could be easily dismissed as merely a paranoid fable of the future. Today there is a growing suspicion that this future may become our present.

If so, H. P. Lovecraft has indeed bequeathed us a heritage of horror.

THE BEST

OF

H. P. LOVECRAFT

BLOODCURDLING TALES OF HORROR AND THE MACABRE

The Rats In The Walls

On July 16, 1923, I moved into Exham Priory after the last work-man had finished his labors. The restoration had been a stupendous task, for little had remained of the deserted pile but a shell-like ruin; yet because it had been the seat of my ancestors, I let no expense deter me. The place had not been inhabited since the reign of James the First, when a tragedy of intensely hideous, though largely unex-plained, nature had struck down the master, five of his children, and several servants; and driven forth under a cloud of suspicion and ter-ror the third son, my lineal progenitor and the only survivor of the abhorred line.

With this sole heir denounced as a murderer, the estate had re-verted to the crown, nor had the accused man made any attempt to exculpate himself or regain his property. Shaken by some horror greater than that of conscience or the law, and expressing only a fran-tic wish to exclude the ancient edifice from his sight and memory, Walter de la Poer, eleventh Baron Exham, fled to Virginia and there founded the family which by the next century had become known as Delapore.

Exham Priory had remained untenanted, though later allotted to the estates of the Norrys family and much studied because of its pe-culiarly composite architecture; an architecture involving Gothic towers resting on a Saxon or Romanesque substructure, whose foun-dation in turn was of a still earlier order or blend of orders—Roman, and even Druidic or native Cymric, if legends speak truly. This foun-dation was a very singular thing, being merged on one side with the solid limestone of the precipice from whose brink the priory over-looked a desolate valley three miles west of the village of Anchester.

Architects and antiquarians loved to examine this strange relic of forgotten centuries, but the country folk hated it. They had hated it hundreds of years before, when my ancestors lived there, and they hated it now, with the moss and mould of abandonment on it. I had not been a day in Anchester before I knew I came of an accursed house. And this week workmen have blown up Exham Priory, and are busy obliterating the traces of its foundations.

The bare statistics of my ancestry I had always known, together with the fact that my first American forbear had come to the colonies under a strange cloud. Of details, however, I had been kept wholly ignorant through the policy of reticence always maintained by the Delapores. Unlike our planter neighbors, we seldom boasted of crusading ancestors or other mediaeval and Renaissance heroes; nor was any kind of tradition handed down except what may have been recorded in the sealed envelope left before the Civil War by every squire to his eldest son for posthumous opening. The glories we cherished were those achieved since the migration; the glories of a proud and honorable, if somewhat reserved and unsocial Virginia line.

During the war our fortunes were extinguished and our whole existence changed by the burning of Carfax, our home on the banks of the James. My grandfather, advanced in years, had perished in that incendiary outrage, and with him the envelope that had bound us all to the past. I can recall that fire today as I saw it then at the age of seven, with the Federal soldiers shouting, the women screaming, and the negroes howling and praying. My father was in the army, defending Richmond, and after many formalities my mother and I were passed through the lines to join him.

When the war ended we all moved north, whence my mother had come; and I grew to manhood, middle age, and ultimate wealth as a stolid Yankee. Neither my father nor I ever knew what our hereditary envelope had contained, and as I merged into the greyness of Massachusetts business life I lost all interest in the mysteries which evidently lurked far back in my family tree. Had I suspected their nature, how gladly I would have left Exham Priory to its moss, bats, and cobwebs!

My father died in 1904, but without any message to leave to me, or to my only child, Alfred, a motherless boy of ten. It was this boy who reversed the order of family information, for although I could give him only jesting conjectures about the past, he wrote me of some very interesting ancestral legends when the late war took him to England in 1917 as an aviation officer. Apparently the Delapores had a colorful and perhaps sinister history, for a friend of my son's, Capt. Edward Norrys of the Royal Flying Corps, dwelt near the family seat at Anchester and related some peasant superstitions which few novelists could equal for wildness and incredibility. Norrys himself, of course, did not take them so seriously; but they amused my son and made good material for his letters to me. It was this legendry which definitely turned my attention to my transatlantic heritage, and made me resolve to purchase and restore the family seat which Norrys showed to Alfred in its picturesque desertion, and offered to get for him at a surprisingly reasonable figure, since his own uncle was the present owner.

I bought Exham Priory in 1918, but was almost immediately distracted from my plans of restoration by the return of my son as a maimed invalid. During the two years that he lived I thought of nothing but his care, having even placed my business under the direction of partners.

In 1921, as I found myself bereaved and aimless, a retired manufacturer no longer young, I resolved to divert my remaining years with my new possession. Visiting Anchester in December, I was entertained by Capt. Norrys, a plump, amiable young man who had thought much of my son, and secured his assistance in gathering plans and anecdotes to guide in the coming restoration. Exham Priory itself I saw without emotion, a jumble of tottering mediaeval ruins covered with lichens and honeycombed with rooks' nests, perched perilously upon a precipice, and denuded of floors or other interior features save the stone walls of the separate towers.

As I gradually recovered the image of the edifice as it had been when my ancestors left it over three centuries before, I began to hire workmen for the reconstruction. In every case I was forced to go outside the immediate locality, for the Anchester villagers had an almost unbelievable fear and hatred of the place. This sentiment was so great that it was sometimes communicated to the outside laborers, causing numerous desertions; whilst its scope appeared to include both the priory and its ancient family.

My son had told me that he was somewhat avoided during his visits because he was a de la Poer, and now I found myself subtly ostracised for a like reason until I convinced the peasants how little I knew of my heritage. Even then they sullenly disliked me, so that I had to collect most of the village traditions through the mediation of Norrys. What the people could not forgive, perhaps, was that I had come to restore a symbol so abhorrent to them; for, rationally or not, they viewed Exham Priory as nothing less than a haunt of fiends and werewolves.

Piecing together the tales which Norrys collected for me, and supplementing them with the accounts of several savants who had studied the ruins, I deduced that Exham Priory stood on the site of a prehistoric temple; a Druidical or ante-Druidical thing which must have been contemporary with Stonehenge. That indescribable rites had been celebrated there, few doubted, and there were unpleasant tales of the transference of these rites into the Cybeleworship which the Romans had introduced.

Inscriptions still visible on the subcellar bore such unmistakable letters as "DIV . . . OPS . . . MAGNA. MAT . . ." signs of the Magna Mater whose dark worship was once vainly forbidden to Roman citizens. Anchester had been the camp of the third Augustan legion, as many remains attest, and it was said that the temple of Cybele was splendid and thronged with worshippers who performed nameless ceremonies at the bidding of a Phrygian priest. Tales added that the fall of the old religion did not end the orgies at the temple, but that the priests lived on in the new faith without real change. Likewise was it said that the rites did not vanish with the Roman power, and that certain among the Saxons added to what remained of the temple, and gave it the essential outline it subsequently preserved, making it the center of a cult feared through half the heptarchy. About 1000 A.D. the place is mentioned in a chronicle as being a substantial stone priory housing a strange and powerful monastic order and surrounded by extensive gardens which needed no walls to exclude a frightened populace. It was never destroyed by the Danes, though after the Norman Conquest it must have declined tremendously; since there was no impediment when Henry the Third granted the site to my ancestor, Gilbert de la Poer, First Baron Exham, in 1261.

Of my family before this date there is no evil report, but something strange must have happened then. In one chronicle there is a reference to a de la Poer as "cursed of God" in 1307, whilst village legendry had nothing but evil and frantic fear to tell of the castle that went up on the foundations of the old temple and priory. The fireside tales were of the most grisly description, all the ghastlier because of their frightened reticence and cloudy evasiveness. They represented my ancestors as a race of hereditary daemons beside whom Gilles de Retz and the Marquis de Sade would seem the veriest tyros, and hinted whisperingly at their responsibility for the occasional disappearances of villagers through several generations.

The worst characters, apparently, were the barons and their direct heirs; at least, most was whispered about these. If of healthier inclinations, it was said, an heir would early and mysteriously die to make way for another more typical scion. There seemed to be an inner cult in the family, presided over by the head of the house, and sometimes closed except to a few members. Temperament rather than ancestry was evidently the basis of this cult, for it was entered by several who married into the family. Lady Margaret Trevor from

Cornwall, wife of Godfrey, the second son of the fifth baron, became a favorite bane of children all over the countryside, and the daemon heroine of a particularly horrible old ballad not yet extinct near the Welsh border. Preserved in balladry, too, though not illustrating the same point, is the hideous tale of Lady Mary de la Poer, who shortly after her marriage to the Earl of Shrewsfield was killed by him and his mother, both of the slayers being absolved and blessed by the priest to whom they confessed what they dared not repeat to the world.

These myths and ballads, typical as they were of crude superstition, repelled me greatly. Their persistence, and their application to so long a line of my ancestors, were especially annoying; whilst the imputations of monstrous habits proved unpleasantly reminiscent of the one known scandal of my immediate forbears—the case of my cousin, young Randolph Delapore of Carfax, who went among the negroes and became a voodoo priest after he returned from the Mexican War.

I was much less disturbed by the vaguer tales of wails and howlings in the barren, windswept valley beneath the limestone cliff; of the graveyard stenches after the spring rains; of the floundering, squealing white thing on which Sir John Clave's horse had trod one night in a lonely field; and of the servant who had gone mad at what he saw in the priory in the full light of day. These things were hackneyed spectral lore, and I was at that time a pronounced skeptic. The accounts of vanished peasants were less to be dismissed, though not especially significant in view of mediaeval custom. Prying curiosity meant death, and more than one severed head had been publicly shown on the bastions—now effaced—around Exham Priory.

A few of the tales were exceedingly picturesque, and made me wish I had learnt more of the comparative mythology in my youth. There was, for instance, the belief that a legion of batwinged devils kept witches' sabbath each night at the priory—a legion whose sustenance might explain the disproportionate abundance of coarse vegetables harvested in the vast gardens. And, most vivid of all, there was the dramatic epic of the rats—the scampering army of obscene vermin which had burst forth from the castle three months after the tragedy that doomed it to desertion—the lean, filthy, ravenous army which had swept all before it and devoured fowl, cats, dogs, hogs, sheep, and even two hapless human beings before its fury was spent. Around that unforgettable rodent army a whole separate cycle of myths revolves, for it scattered among the village homes and brought curses and horrors in its train.

Such was the lore that assailed me as I pushed to completion, with an elderly obstinacy, the work of restoring my ancestral home. It must not be imagined for a moment that these tales formed my principal psychological environment. On the other hand, I was constantly praised and encouraged by Capt. Norrys and the antiquarians who surrounded and aided me. When the task was done, over two years after its commencement, I viewed the great rooms, wainscotted walls, vaulted ceilings, mullioned windows, and broad staircases with a pride which fully compensated for the prodigious expense of the restoration.

Every attribute of the Middle Ages was cunningly reproduced, and the new parts blended perfectly with the original walls and foundations. The seat of my fathers was complete, and I looked forward to redeeming at last the local fame of the line which ended in me. I would reside here permanently, and prove that a de la Poer (for I had adopted again the original spelling of the name) need not be a fiend. My comfort was perhaps augmented by the fact that, although Exham Priory was mediaevally fitted, its interior was in truth wholly new and free from old vermin and old ghosts alike.

As I have said, I moved in on July 16, 1923. My household consisted of seven servants and nine cats, of which latter species I am particularly fond. My eldest cat, "Nigger-Man," was seven years old and had come with me from my home in Bolton, Massachusetts; the others I had accumulated whilst living with Capt. Norrys' family during the restoration of the priory.

For five days our routine proceeded with the utmost placidity, my time being spent mostly in the codification of old family data. I had now obtained some very circumstantial accounts of the final tragedy and flight of Walter de la Poer, which I conceived to be the probable contents of the hereditary paper lost in the fire at Carfax. It appeared that my ancestor was accused with much reason of having killed all the other members of his household, except four servant confederates, in their sleep, about two weeks after a shocking discovery which changed his whole demeanor, but which, except by implication, he disclosed to no one save perhaps the servants who assisted him and afterward fled beyond reach.

This deliberate slaughter, which included a father, three brothers, and two sisters, was largely condoned by the villagers, and so slackly treated by the law that its perpetrator escaped honored, unharmed, and undisguised to Virginia; the general whispered sentiment being that he had purged the land of immemorial curse. What discovery had prompted an act so terrible, I could scarcely even conjecture. Walter de la Poer must have known for years the sinister tales about his family, so that this material could have given him no fresh impulse. Had he, then, witnessed some appalling ancient rite, or stumbled upon some frightful and revealing symbol in the priory or its vicinity? He was reputed to have been a shy, gentle youth in England. In Virginia he seemed not so much hard or bitter as harassed and apprehensive. He was spoken of in the diary of another gentleman adventurer, Francis Harley of Bellview, as a man of unexampled justice, honor, and delicacy.

On July 22 occurred the first incident which, though lightly dismissed at the time, takes on a preternatural significance in relation to later events. It was so simple as to be almost negligible, and could not possibly have been noticed under the circumstances; for it must be recalled that since I was in a building practically fresh and new except for the walls, and surrounded by a well-balanced staff of servitors, apprehension would have been absurd despite the locality.

What I afterward remembered is merely this—that my old black cat, whose moods I know so well, was undoubtedly alert and anxious to an extent wholly out of keeping with his natural character. He roved from room to room, restless and disturbed, and sniffed constantly about the walls which formed part of the Gothic structure. I realize how trite this sounds—like the inevitable dog in the ghost story, which always growls before his master sees the sheeted figure—yet I cannot consistently suppress it.

The following day a servant complained of restlessness among all the cats in the house. He came to me in my study, a lofty west room on the second story, with groined arches, black oak panelling, and a triple Gothic window overlooking the limestone cliff and desolate valley; and even as he spoke I saw the jetty form of Nigger-Man creeping along the west wall and scratching at the new panels which overlaid the ancient stone.

I told the man that there must be some singular odor or emanation from the old stonework, imperceptible to human senses, but affecting the delicate organs of cats even through the new woodwork. This I truly believed, and when the fellow suggested the presence of mice or rats, I mentioned that there had been no rats there for three hundred years, and that even the field mice of the surrounding country could hardly be found in these high walls, where they had never been known to stray. That afternoon I called on Capt. Norrys, and he assured me that it would be quite incredible for field mice to infest the priory in such a sudden and unprecedented fashion.

That night, dispensing as usual with a valet, I retired in the west tower chamber which I had chosen as my own, reached from the study by a stone staircase and short gallery—the former partly ancient, the latter entirely restored. This room was circular, very high, and without wainscotting, being hung with arras which I had myself chosen in London.

Seeing that Nigger-Man was with me, I shut the heavy Gothic door and retired by the light of the electric bulbs which so cleverly counterfeited candles, finally switching off the light and sinking on the carved and canopied four-poster, with the venerable cat in his accustomed place across my feet. I did not draw the curtains, but gazed out at the narrow north window which I faced. There was a suspicion of aurora in the sky, and the delicate traceries of the window were pleasantly silhouetted.

At some time I must have fallen quietly asleep, for I recall a distinct sense of leaving strange dreams, when the cat started violently from his placid position. I saw him in the faint auroral glow, head strained forward, forefeet on my ankles, and hind feet stretched behind. He was looking intensely at a point on the wall somewhat west of the windows, a point which to my eye had nothing to mark it, but toward which all my attention was now directed.

And as I watched, I knew that Nigger-Man was not vainly excited. Whether the arras actually moved I cannot say. I think it did, very slightly. But what I can swear to is that behind it I heard a low, distinct scurrying as of rats or mice. In a moment the cat had jumped bodily on the screening tapestry, bringing the affected section to the floor with his weight, and exposing a damp, ancient wall of stone; patched here and there by the restorers, and devoid of any trace of rodent prowlers.

Nigger-Man raced up and down the floor by this part of the wall, clawing the fallen arras and seemingly trying at times to insert a paw between the wall and oaken floor. He found nothing, and after a time returned wearily to his place across my feet. I had not moved, but I did not sleep again that night.

In the morning I questioned all the servants, and found that none of them had noticed anything unusual, save that the cook remembered the actions of the cat which had rested on her windowsill. This cat had howled at some unknown hour of the night, awaking the cook in time for her to see him dart purposefully out of the open door down the stairs. I drowsed away the noontime, and in the afternoon called again on Capt. Norrys, who became exceedingly interested in what I told him. The odd incidents—so slight yet so curious—appealed to his sense of the picturesque, and elicited from him a number of reminiscences of local ghostly lore. We were genuinely perplexed at the presence of rats, and Norrys lent me some traps and Paris green, which I had the servants place in strategic localities when I returned.

I retired early, being very sleepy, but was harassed by dreams of the most horrible sort. I seemed to be looking down from an immense height upon a twilit grotto, knee-deep with filth, where a white-bearded daemon swineherd drove about with his staff a flock of fungous, flabby beasts whose appearance filled me with unutterable loathing. Then, as the swineherd paused and nodded over his task, a mighty swarm of rats rained down on the stinking abyss and fell to devouring beasts and man alike.

From this terrific vision I was abruptly awaked by the motions of Nigger-Man, who had been sleeping as usual across my feet. This time I did not have to question the source of his snarls and hisses, and of the fear which made him sink his claws into my ankle, unconscious of their effect; for on every side of the chamber the walls were alive with nauseous sound—the verminous slithering of ravenous, gigantic rats. There was now no aurora to show the state of the arras—the fallen section of which had been replaced—but I was not too frightened to switch on the light.

As the bulbs leapt into radiance I saw a hideous shaking all over the tapestry, causing the somewhat peculiar designs to execute a singular dance of death. This motion disappeared almost at once, and the sound with it. Springing out of bed, I poked at the arras with the long handle of a warming-pan that rested near, and lifted one section to see what lay beneath. There was nothing but the patched stone wall, and even the cat had lost his tense realization of abnormal presences. When I examined the circular trap that had been placed in the room, I found all of the openings sprung, though no trace remained of what had been caught and had escaped.

Further sleep was out of the question, so, lighting a candle, I opened the door and went out into the gallery toward the stairs to my study, Nigger-Man following at my heels. Before we had reached the stone steps, however, the cat darted ahead of me and vanished down the ancient flight. As I descended the stairs myself, I became suddenly aware of sounds in the great room below; sounds of a nature which could not be mistaken.

The oak-panelled walls were alive with rats, scampering and milling, whilst Nigger-Man was racing about with the fury of a baffled hunter. Reaching the bottom, I switched on the light, which did not this time cause the noise to subside. The rats continued their riot, stampeding with such force and distinctness that I could finally assign to their motions a definite direction. These creatures, in numbers apparently inexhaustible, were engaged in one stupendous migration from inconceivable heights to some depth conceivably or inconceivably below.

I now heard steps in the corridor, and in another moment two servants pushed open the massive door. They were searching the house for some unknown source of disturbance which had thrown all the cats into a snarling panic and caused them to plunge precipitately down several flights of stairs and squat, yowling, before the closed door to the sub-cellar. I asked them if they had heard the rats, but they replied in the negative. And when I turned to call their attention to the sounds in the panels, I realized that the noise had ceased.

With the two men, I went down to the door of the sub-cellar, but found the cats already dispersed. Later I resolved to explore the crypt below, but for the present I merely made a round of the traps. All were sprung, yet all were tenantless. Satisfying myself that no one had heard the rats save the felines and me, I sat in my study till morning, thinking profoundly and recalling every scrap of legend I had unearthed concerning the building I inhabited.

I slept some in the forenoon, leaning back in the one comfortable library chair which my mediaeval plan of furnishing could not banish. Later I telephoned to Capt. Norrys, who came over and helped me explore the sub-cellar.

Absolutely nothing untoward was found, although we could not repress a thrill at the knowledge that this vault was built by Roman hands. Every low arch and massive pillar was Roman—not the debased Romanesque of the bungling Saxons, but the severe and harmonious classicism of the age of the Caesars; indeed, the walls abounded with inscriptions familiar to the antiquarians who had repeatedly explored the place—things like "P. GETAE. PROP . . . TEMP . . . DONA . . ." and "L. PRAEC . . . VS . . . PONTIFI . . . ATYS. . . ."

The reference to Atys made me shiver, for I had read Catullus and knew something of the hideous rites of the Eastern god, whose worship was so mixed with that of Cybele. Norrys and I, by the light of lanterns, tried to interpret the odd and nearly effaced designs on certain irregularly rectangular blocks of stone generally held to be altars, but could make nothing of them. We remembered that one pattern, a sort of rayed sun, was held by students to imply a non-Roman origin, suggesting that these altars had merely been adopted by the Roman priests from some older and perhaps aboriginal temple on the same site. On one of these blocks were some brown stains which made me wonder. The largest, in the center of the room, had certain features on the upper surface which indicated its connection with fire—probably burnt offerings.

Such were the sights in that crypt before whose door the cats howled, and where Norrys and I now determined to pass the night. Couches were brought down by the servants, who were told not to mind any nocturnal actions of the cats, and Nigger-Man was admitted as much for help as for companionship. We decided to keep the great oak door—a modern replica with slits for ventilation—tightly closed; and, with this attended to, we retired with lanterns still burning to await whatever might occur.

The vault was very deep in the foundations of the priory, and undoubtedly far down on the face of the beetling limestone cliff overlooking the waste valley. That it had been the goal of the scuffling and unexplainable rats I could not doubt, though why, I could not tell. As we lay there expectantly, I found my vigil occasionally mixed with half-formed dreams from which the uneasy motions of the cat across my feet would rouse me.

These dreams were not wholesome, but horribly like the one I had had the night before. I saw again the twilit grotto, and the swineherd with his unmentionable fungous beasts wallowing in filth, and as I looked at these things they seemed nearer and more distinct—so distinct that I could almost observe their features. Then I did observe the flabby features of one of them—and awakened with such a scream that Nigger-Man started up, whilst Capt. Norrys, who had not slept, laughed considerably. Norrys might have laughed more—or perhaps less—had he known what it was that made me scream. But I did not remember myself till later. Ultimate horror often paralyses memory in a merciful way.

Norrys waked me when the phenomena began. Out of the same frightful dream I was called by his gentle shaking and his urging to listen to the cats. Indeed, there was much to listen to, for beyond the closed door at the head of the stone steps was a veritable nightmare of feline yelling and clawing, whilst Nigger-Man, unmindful of his kindred outside, was running excitedly around the bare stone walls, in which I heard the same babel of scurrying rats that had troubled me the night before.

An acute terror now rose within me, for here were anomalies which nothing normal could well explain. These rats, if not the creatures of a madness which I shared with the cats alone, must be burrowing and sliding in Roman walls I had thought to be of solid limestone blocks . . . unless perhaps the action of water through more than seventeen centuries had eaten winding tunnels which rodent bodies had worn clear and ample. . . . But even so, the spectral horror was no less; for if these were living vermin why did not Norrys hear their disgusting commotion? Why did he urge me to watch Nigger-Man and listen to the cats outside, and why did he guess wildly and vaguely at what could have aroused them?

By the time I had managed to tell him, as rationally as I could, what I thought I was hearing, my ears gave me the last fading impression of the scurrying; which had retreated *still downward*, far underneath this deepest of sub-cellars till it seemed as if the whole cliff below were riddled with questing rats. Norrys was not as skeptical as I had anticipated, but instead seemed profoundly moved. He motioned to me to notice that the cats at the door had ceased their clamor, as if giving up the rats for lost; whilst Nigger-Man had a burst of renewed restlessness, and was clawing frantically around the bottom of the large stone altar in the center of the room, which was nearer Norrys' couch than mine.

My fear of the unknown was at this point very great. Something astounding had occurred, and I saw that Capt. Norrys, a younger, stouter, and presumably more naturally materialistic man, was affected fully as much as myself—perhaps because of his lifelong and intimate familiarity with local legend. We could for the moment do nothing but watch the old black cat as he pawed with decreasing fervor at the base of the altar, occasionally looking up and mewing to me in that persuasive manner which he used when he wished me to perform some favor for him.

Norrys now took a lantern close to the altar and examined the place where Nigger-Man was pawing; silently kneeling and scraping away the lichens of the centuries which joined the massive pre-Roman block to the tesselated floor. He did not find anything, and was about to abandon his efforts when I noticed a trivial circumstance which made me shudder, even though it implied nothing more than I had already imagined.

I told him of it, and we both looked at its almost imperceptible manifestation with the fixedness of fascinated discovery and acknowledgement. It was only this—that the flame of the lantern set down near the altar was slightly but certainly flickering from a draught of air which it had not before received, and which came indubitably from the crevice between the floor and the altar where Norrys was scraping away the lichens.

We spent the rest of the night in the brilliantly-lighted study, nervously discussing what we should do next. The discovery that some vault deeper than the deepest known masonry of the Romans underlay this accursed pile; some vault unsuspected by the curious antiquarians of three centuries; would have been sufficient to excite us without any background of the sinister. As it was, the fascination became two-fold; and we paused in doubt whether to abandon our search and quit the priory forever in superstitious caution, or to gratify our sense of adventure and brave whatever horrors might await us in the unknown depths.

By morning we had compromised, and decided to go to London to gather a group of archaeologists and scientific men fit to cope with the mystery. It should be mentioned that before leaving the sub-cellar we had vainly tried to move the central altar which we now recognized as the gate to a new pit of nameless fear. What secret would open the gate, wiser men than we would have to find.

During many days in London Capt. Norrys and I presented our facts, conjectures, and legendary anecdotes to five eminent authorities, all men who could be trusted to respect any family disclosures which future explorations might develop. We found most of them little disposed to scoff, but, instead, intensely interested and sincerely sympathetic. It is hardly necessary to name them all, but I may say that they included Sir William Brinton, whose excavations in the Troad excited most of the world in their day. As we all took the train for Anchester I felt myself poised on the brink of frightful revelations, a sensation symbolized by the air of mourning among the many Americans at the unexpected death of the President on the other side of the world.

On the evening of August 7 we reached Exham Priory, where the servants assured me that nothing unusual had occurred. The cats, even old Nigger-Man, had been perfectly placid; and not a trap in the house had been sprung. We were to begin exploring on the following day, awaiting which I assigned well-appointed rooms to all my guests.

I myself retired in my own tower chamber, with Nigger-Man across my feet. Sleep came quickly, but hideous dreams assailed me. There was a vision of a Roman feast like that of Trimalchio, with a horror in a covered platter. Then came that damnable, recurrent thing about the swineherd and his filthy drove in the twilit grotto. Yet when I awoke it was full daylight, with normal sounds in the house below. The rats, living or spectral, had not troubled me; and Nigger-Man was still quietly asleep. On going down, I found that the same tranquility had prevailed elsewhere; a condition which one of the assembled servants—a fellow named Thornton, devoted to the psychic—rather absurdly laid to the fact that I had now been shown the thing which certain forces had wished to show me.

All was now ready, and at 11 A.M. our entire group of seven men, bearing powerful electric searchlights and implements of excavation, went down to the sub-cellar and bolted the door behind us. Nigger-Man was with us, for the investigators found no occasion to despise his excitability, and were indeed anxious that he be present in case of obscure rodent manifestations. We noted the Roman inscriptions and unknown altar designs only briefly, for three of the savants had already seen them, and all knew their characteristics. Prime attention was paid to the momentous central altar, and within an hour Sir William Brinton had caused it to tilt backward, balanced on some unknown species of counterweight.

There now lay revealed such a horror as would have overwhelmed us had we not been prepared. Through a nearly square opening in the tiled floor, sprawling on a flight of stone steps so prodigiously worn that it was little more than an inclined plane at the center, was a ghastly array of human or semi-human bones. Those which retained their collocation as skeletons showed attitudes of panic fear, and over all were the marks of rodent gnawing. The skulls denoted nothing short of utter idiocy, cretinism, or primitive semi-apedom.

Above the hellishly littered steps arched a descending passage seemingly chiseled from the solid rock, and conducting a current of air. This current was not a sudden and noxious rush as from a closed vault, but a cool breeze with something of freshness in it. We did not pause long, but shiveringly began to clear a passage down the steps. It was then that Sir William, examining the hewn walls, made the odd observation that the passage, according to the direction of the strokes, must have been chiseled *from beneath*.

I must be very deliberate now, and choose my words.

After ploughing down a few steps amidst the gnawed bones we saw that there was light ahead; not any mystic phosphorescence, but a filtered daylight which could not come except from unknown fissures in the cliff that overlooked the waste valley. That such fissures had escaped notice from outside was hardly remarkable, for not only is the valley wholly uninhabited, but the cliff is so high and beetling that only an aeuronaut could study its face in detail. A few steps more, and our breaths were literally snatched from us by what we saw; so literally that Thornton, the psychic investigator, actually fainted in the arms of the dazed man who stood behind him. Norrys, his plump face utterly white and flabby, simply cried out inarticulately; whilst I think that what I did was to gasp or hiss, and cover my eyes.

The man behind me—the only one of the party older than I—croaked the hackneyed "My God!" in the most cracked voice I ever heard. Of seven cultivated men, only Sir William Brinton retained his composure, a thing the more to his credit because he led the party and must have seen the sight first.

It was a twilit grotto of enormous height, stretching away farther than any eye could see; a subterranean world of limitless mystery and horrible suggestion. There were buildings and other architectural remains—in one terrified glance I saw a weird pattern of tumuli, a savage circle of monoliths, a low-domed Roman ruin, a sprawling Saxon pile, and an early English edifice of wood—but all these were dwarfed by the ghoulish spectacle presented by the general surface of the ground. For yards about the steps extended an insane tangle of human bones, or bones at least as human as those on the steps. Like a foamy sea they stretched, some fallen apart, but others wholly or partly articulated as skeletons; these latter invariably in postures of daemoniac frenzy, either fighting off some menace or clutching other forms with cannibal intent.

When Dr. Trask, the anthropologist, stopped to classify the skulls, he found a degraded mixture which utterly baffled him. They were mostly lower than the Piltdown man in the scale of evolution, but in every case definitely human. Many were of higher grade, and a very few were the skulls of supremely and sensitively developed types. All the bones were gnawed, mostly by rats, but somewhat by others of the half-human drove. Mixed with them were many tiny bones of rats—fallen members of the lethal army which closed the ancient epic.

I wonder that any man among us lived and kept his sanity through that hideous day of discovery. Not Hoffmann or Huysmans could conceive a scene more wildly incredible, more frenetically repellent, or more Gothically grotesque than the twilit grotto through which we seven staggered; each stumbling on revelation after revelation, and trying to keep for the nonce from thinking of the events which must have taken place there three hundred, or a thousand, or two thousand, or ten thousand years ago. It was the antechamber of hell, and poor Thornton fainted again when Trask told him that some of the skeleton things must have descended as quadrupeds through the last twenty or more generations.

Horror piled on horror as we began to interpret the architectural remains. The quadruped things—with their occasional recruits from the biped class—had been kept in stone pens, out of which they must have broken in their last delirium of hunger or rat-fear. There had been great herds of them, evidently fattened on the coarse vegetables whose remains could be found as a sort of poisonous ensilage at the bottom of huge stone bins older than Rome. I knew now why my ancestors had had such excessive gardens—would to heaven I could forget! The purpose of the herds I did not have to ask.

Sir William, standing with his searchlight in the Roman ruin, translated aloud the most shocking ritual I have ever known; and told of the diet of the antediluvian cult which the priests of Cybele found and mingled with their own. Norrys, used as he was to the trenches, could not walk straight when he came out of the English building. It was a butcher shop and kitchen—he had expected that—but it was too much to see familiar English implements in such a place, and to read familiar English *graffiti* there, some as recent as 1610. I could not go in that building—that building whose daemon activities were stopped only by the dagger of my ancestor Walter de la Poer.

What I did venture to enter was the low Saxon building whose oaken door had fallen, and there I found a terrible row of ten stone cells with rusty bars. Three had tenants, all skeletons of high grade, and on the bony forefinger of one I found a seal ring with my own coat-of-arms. Sir William found a vault with far older cells below the Roman chapel, but these cells were empty. Below them was a low crypt with cases of formally arranged bones, some of them bearing terrible parallel inscriptions carved in Latin, Greek, and the tongue of Phrygia.

Meanwhile, Dr. Trask had opened one of the prehistoric tumuli, and brought to light skulls which were slightly more human than a gorilla's, and which bore indescribably ideographic carvings. Through all this horror my cat stalked unperturbed. Once I saw him monstrously perched atop a mountain of bones, and wondered at the secrets that might lie behind his yellow eyes.

Having grasped to some slight degree the frightful revelations of this twilit area—an area so hideously foreshadowed by my recurrent dream—we turned to that apparently boundless depth of midnight cavern where no ray of light from the cliff could penetrate. We shall never know what sightless Stygian worlds yawn beyond the little distance we went, for it was decided that such secrets are not good for mankind. But there was plenty to engross us close at hand, for we had not gone far before the searchlights showed that accursed infinity of pits in which the rats had feasted, and whose sudden lack of replenishment had driven the ravenous rodent army first to turn on the living herds of starving things, and then to burst forth from the priory in that historic orgy of devastation which the peasants will never forget.

God! those carrion black pits of sawed, picked bones and opened skulls! Those nightmare chasms choked with the pithecanthropoid, Celtic, Roman, and English bones of countless unhallowed centuries! Some of them were full, and none can say how deep they had once been. Others were still bottomless to our searchlights, and peopled by unnamable fancies. What, I thought, of the hapless rats that stumbled into such traps amidst the blackness of their quests in this grisly Tartarus?

Once my foot slipped near a horribly yawning brink, and I had a moment of ecstatic fear. I must have been musing a long time, for I could not see any of the party but the plump Capt. Norrys. Then there came a sound from that inky, boundless, farther distance that I thought I knew; and I saw my old black cat dart past me like a winged Egyptian god, straight into the illimitable gulf of the unknown. But I was not far behind, for there was no doubt after another second. It was the eldritch scurrying of those fiend-born rats, always questing for new horrors, and determined to lead me on even unto those grinning caverns of earth's center where Nyarlathotep, the mad faceless god, howls blindly in the darkness to the piping of two amorphous idiot flute-players.

My searchlight expired, but still I ran. I heard voices, and yowls, and echoes, but above all there gently rose that impious, insidious scurrying; gently rising, rising, as a stiff bloated corpse gently rises above an oily river that flows under endless onyx bridges to a black, putrid sea.

Something bumped into me—something soft and plump. It must have been the rats; the viscous, gelatinous, ravenous army that feast on the dead and the living. . . . Why shouldn't rats eat a de la Poer as a de la Poer eats forbidden things? . . . The war ate my boy, damn them all . . . and the Yanks ate Carfax with flames and burnt Grandsire Delapore and the secret . . . No, no, I tell you, I am *not* that daemon swineherd in the twilit grotto! It was *not* Edward Norrys' fat face on that flabby fungous thing! Who says I am a de la Poer? He lived, but my boy died! . . . Shall a Norrys hold the lands of a de la Poer? . . . It's voodoo, I tell you . . . that spotted snake . . . Curse you, Thornton, I'll teach you to faint at what my family do! . . . 'Sblood, thou stinkard, I'll learn ye how to gust . . . wolde ye swynke me thilke wys? . . . . *Magna Mater! Magna Mater! . . . Atys . . . Dia ad aghaidh's ad aodaun . . . agus bas dunach ort! Dhonas 's dholas ort, agus leat-sa! . . . Ungl . . . ungl . . . rrlh . . . chchch . . .*

That is what they say I said when they found me in the blackness after three hours; found me crouching in the blackness over the plump, half-eaten body of Capt. Norrys, with my own cat leaping and tearing at my throat. Now they have blown up Exham Priory, taken my Nigger-Man away from me, and shut me into this barred room at Hanwell with fearful whispers about my heredity and experience. Thornton is in the next room, but they prevent me from talking to him. They are trying, too, to suppress most of the facts concerning the priory. When I speak of poor Norrys they accuse me of a hideous thing, but they must know that I did not do it. They must know it was the rats; the slithering scurrying rats whose scampering will never let me sleep; the daemon rats that race behind the padding in this room and beckon me down to greater horrors than I have ever known; the rats they can never hear; the rats, the rats in the walls.

The Picture In The House

Searchers after horror haunt strange, far places. For them are the catacombs of Ptolemais, and the carven mausolea of the nightmare countries. They climb to the moonlit towers of ruined Rhine castles, and falter down black cobwebbed steps beneath the scattered stones of forgotten cities in Asia. The haunted wood and the desolate mountain are their shrines, and they linger around the sinister monoliths on uninhabited islands. But the true epicure in the terrible, to whom a new thrill of unutterable ghastliness is the chief end and justification of existence, esteems most of all the ancient, lonely farmhouses of backwoods New England; for there the dark elements of strength, solitude, grotesqueness and ignorance combine to form the perfection of the hideous.

Most horrible of all sights are the little unpainted wooden houses remote from travelled ways, usually squatted upon some damp grassy slope or leaning against some gigantic outcropping of rock. Two hundred years and more they have leaned or squatted there, while the vines have crawled and the trees have swelled and spread. They are almost hidden now in lawless luxuriances of green and guardian shrouds of shadow; but the small-paned windows still stare shockingly, as if blinking through a lethal stupor which wards off madness by dulling the memory of unutterable things.

In such houses have dwelt generations of strange people, whose like the world has never seen. Seized with a gloomy and fanatical belief which exiled them from their kind, their ancestors sought the wilderness for freedom. There the scions of a conquering race indeed flourished free from the restrictions of their fellows, but cowered in an appalling slavery to the dismal phantasms of their own minds. Divorced from the enlightenment of civilization, the strength of these Puritans turned into singular channels; and in their isolation, morbid self-repression, and struggle for life with relentless Nature, there came to them dark furtive traits from the prehistoric depths of their cold Northern heritage. By necessity practical and by philosophy stern, these folks were not beautiful in their sins. Erring as all mortals must, they were forced by their rigid code to seek concealment above all else; so that they came to use less and less taste in what they concealed. Only the silent, sleepy, staring houses in the backwoods can tell all that has lain hidden since the early days, and they are not communicative, being loath to shake off the drowsiness which helps them forget. Sometimes one feels that it would be merciful to tear down these houses, for they must often dream.

It was to a time-battered edifice of this description that I was driven one afternoon in November, 1896, by a rain of such chilling copiousness that any shelter was preferable to exposure. I had been travelling for some time amongst the people of the Miskatonic Valley in quest of certain genealogical data; and from the remote, devious, and problematical nature of my course, had deemed it convenient to employ a bicycle despite the lateness of the season. Now I found myself upon an apparently abandoned road which I had chosen as the shortest cut to Arkham, overtaken by the storm at a point far from any town, and confronted with no refuge save the antique and repellent wooden building which blinked with bleared windows from between two huge leafless elms near the foot of a rocky hill. Distant though it is from the remnant of a road, this house none the less impressed me unfavorably the very moment I espied it. Honest, wholesome structures do not stare at travellers so slyly and hauntingly, and in my genealogical researches I had encountered legends of a century before which biased me against places of this kind. Yet the force of the elements was such as to overcome my scruples, and I did not hesitate to wheel my machine up the weedy rise to the closed door which seemed at once so suggestive and secretive.

I had somehow taken it for granted that the house was abandoned, yet as I approached it I was not so sure, for though the walks were indeed overgrown with weeds, they seemed to retain their nature a little too well to argue complete desertion. Therefore instead of trying the door I knocked, feeling as I did so a trepidation I could scarcely explain. As I waited on the rough, mossy rock which served as a doorstep, I glanced at the neighboring windows and the panes of the transom above me, and noticed that although old, rattling, and almost opaque with dirt, they were not broken. The building, then, must still be inhabited, despite its isolation and general neglect. However, my rapping evoked no response, so after repeating the summons I tried the rusty latch and found the door unfastened. Inside was a little vestibule with walls from which the plaster was falling, and through the doorway came a faint but peculiarly hateful odor. I entered, carrying my bicycle, and closed the door behind me. Ahead rose a narrow staircase, flanked by a small door probably leading to the cellar, while to the left and right were closed doors leading to rooms on the ground floor.

Leaning my cycle against the wall I opened the door at the left, and crossed into a small low-ceiled chamber but dimly lighted by its two dusty windows and furnished in the barest and most primitive possible way. It appeared to be a kind of sitting-room, for it had a table and several chairs, and an immense fireplace above which ticked an antique clock on a mantel. Books and papers were very few, and in the prevailing gloom I could not readily discern the titles. What interested me was the uniform air of archaism as displayed in every visible detail. Most of the houses in this region I had found rich in relics of the past, but here the antiquity was curiously complete; for in all the room I could not discover a single article of definitely post-revolutionary date. Had the furnishings been less humble, the place would have been a collector's paradise.

As I surveyed this quaint apartment, I felt an increase in that aversion first excited by the bleak exterior of the house. Just what it was that I feared or loathed, I could by no means define; but something in the whole atmosphere seemed redolent of unhallowed age, of unpleasant crudeness, and of secrets which should be forgotten. I felt disinclined to sit down, and wandered about examining the various articles which I had noticed. The first object of my curiosity was a book of medium size lying upon the table and presenting such an antediluvian aspect that I marvelled at beholding it outside a museum or library. It was bound in leather with metal fittings, and was in an excellent state of preservation; being altogether an unusual sort of volume to encounter in an abode so lowly. When I opened it to the title page my wonder grew even greater, for it proved to be nothing less rare than Pigafetta's account of the Congo region, written in Latin from the notes of the sailor Lopez and printed at Frankfurt in 1598. I had often heard of this work, with its curious illustrations by the brothers De Bry, hence for a moment forgot my uneasiness in my desire to turn the pages before me. The engravings were indeed interesting, drawn wholly from imagination and careless descriptions, and represented negroes with white skins and Caucasian features; nor would I soon have closed the book had not an exceedingly trivial circumstance upset my tired nerves and revived my sensation of disquiet. What annoyed me was merely the persistent way in which the volume tended to fall open of itself at Plate XII, which represented in gruesome detail a butcher's shop of the cannibal Anziques. I experienced some shame at my susceptibility to so slight a thing, but the drawing nevertheless disturbed me, especially in connection with some adjacent passages descriptive of Anzique gastronomy.

I had turned to a neighboring shelf and was examining its meagre literary contents—an eighteenth century Bible, a "Pilgrim's Progress" of like period, illustrated with grotesque woodcuts and printed by the almanack-maker Isaiah Thomas, the rotting bulk of Cotton Mather's "Magnalia Christi Americana," and a few other books of evidently equal age—when my attention was aroused by the unmistakable sound of walking in the room overhead. At first astonished and startled, considering the lack of response to my recent knocking at the door, I immediately afterward concluded that the walker had just awakened from a sound sleep, and listened with less surprise as the footsteps sounded on the creaking stairs. The tread was heavy, yet seemed to contain a curious quality of cautiousness; a quality which I disliked the more because the tread was heavy. When I had entered the room I had shut the door behind me. Now, after a moment of silence during which the walker may have been inspecting my bicycle in the hall, I heard a fumbling at the latch and saw the paneled portal swing open again.

In the doorway stood a person of such singular appearance that I should have exclaimed aloud but for the restraints of good breeding. Old, white-bearded, and ragged, my host possessed a countenance and physique which inspired equal wonder and respect. His height could not have been less than six feet, and despite a general air of age and poverty he was stout and powerful in proportion. His face, almost hidden by a long beard which grew high on the cheeks, seemed abnormally ruddy and less wrinkled than one might expect; while over a high forehead fell a shock of white hair little thinned by the years. His blue eyes, though a trifle bloodshot, seemed inexplicably keen and burning. But for his horrible unkemptness the man would have been as distinguished-looking as he was impressive. This unkemptness, however, made him offensive despite his face and figure. Of what his clothing consisted I could hardly tell, for it seemed to me no more than a mass of tatters surmounting a pair of high, heavy boots; and his lack of cleanliness surpassed description.

The appearance of this man, and the instinctive fear he inspired, prepared me for something like enmity; so that I almost shuddered through surprise and a sense of uncanny incongruity when he motioned me to a chair and addressed me in a thin, weak voice full of fawning respect and ingratiating hospitality. His speech was very curious, an extreme form of Yankee dialect I had thought long extinct; and I studied it closely as he sat down opposite me for conversation.

"Ketched in the rain, be ye?" he greeted. "Glad ye was nigh the haouse en' hed the sense ta come right in. I calc'late I was asleep, else I'd a heerd ye—I ain't as young as I uster be, an' I need a paowerful sight o' naps naowadays. Trav'lin fur? I hain't seed many folks 'long this rud sence they tuk off the Arkham stage."

I replied that I was going to Arkham, and apologized for my rude entry into his domicile, whereupon he continued.

"Glad ta see ye, young Sir—new faces is scurce arount here, an' I hain't got much ta cheer me up these days. Guess yew hail from Bosting, don't ye? I never ben thar, but I kin tell a taown man when I see 'im—we hed one fer deestrick schoolmaster in 'eighty-four, but he quit suddent an' no one never heerd on 'im sence—" here the old man lapsed into a kind of chuckle, and made no explanation when I questioned him. He seemed to be in an aboundingly good humor, yet to possess those eccentricities which one might guess from his grooming. For some time he rambled on with an almost feverish geniality, when it struck me to ask him how he came by so rare a book as Pigafetta's "Regnum Congo." The effect of this volume had not left me, and I felt a certain hesitancy in speaking of it, but curiosity overmastered all the vague fears which had steadily accumulated since my first glimpse of the house. To my relief, the question did not seem an awkward one, for the old man answered freely and volubly.

"Oh, that Afriky book? Cap'n Ebenezer Holt traded me thet in 'sixty-eight—him as was kilt in the war." Something about the name of Ebenezer Holt caused me to look up sharply. I had encountered it in my genealogical work, but not in any record since the Revolution. I wondered if my host could help me in the task at which I was laboring, and resolved to ask him about it later on. He continued.

"Ebenezer was on a Salem merchantman for years, an' picked up a sight o' queer stuff in every port. He got this in London, I guess—he uster like ter buy things at the shops. I was up ta his haouse onct, on the hill, tradin' hosses, when I see this book. I relished the picters, so he give it in on a swap. 'Tis a queer book—here, leave me git on my spectacles—" The old man fumbled among his rags, producing a pair of dirty and amazingly antique glasses with small octagonal lenses and steel bows. Donning these, he reached for the volume on the table and turned the pages lovingly.

"Ebenezer cud read a leetle o' this—'tis Latin—but I can't. I had two er three schoolmasters read me a bit, and Passon Clark, him they say got draownded in the pond—kin yew make anything outen it?" I told him that I could, and translated for his benefit a paragraph near the beginning. If I erred, he was not scholar enough to correct me; for he seemed childishly pleased at my English version. His proximity was becoming rather obnoxious, yet I saw no way to escape without offending him. I was amused at the childish fondness of this ignorant old man for the pictures in a book he could not read, and wondered how much better he could read the few books in English which adorned the room. This revelation of simplicity removed much of the ill-defined apprehension I had felt, and I smiled as my host rambled on:

"Queer haow picters kin set a body thinkin'. Take this un here near the front. Hev yew ever seed trees like thet, with big leaves a floppin' over an' daown? And them men—them can't be niggers—they dew beat all. Kinder like Injuns, I guess, even ef they be in Afriky. Some o' these here critters looks like monkeys, or half monkeys an' half men, but I never heerd o' nothin' like this un." Here he pointed to a fabulous creature of the artist, which one might describe as a sort of dragon with the head of an alligator.

"But naow I'll show ye the best un—over here nigh the middle—" The old man's speech grew a trifle thicker and his eyes assumed a brighter glow; but his fumbling hands, though seemingly clumsier than before, were entirely adequate to their mission. The book fell open, almost of its own accord and as if from frequent consultation at this place, to the repellent twelfth plate showing a butcher's shop amongst the Anzique cannibals. My sense of restlessness returned, though I did not exhibit it. The especially bizarre thing was that the artist had made his Africans look like white men—the limbs and quarters hanging about the walls of the shop were ghastly, while the butcher with his axe was hideously incongruous. But my host seemed to relish the view as much as I disliked it.

"What d'ye think o' this—ain't never see the like hereabouts, eh? When I see this I telled Eb Holt, 'That's suthin' ta stir ye up an' make yer blood tickle.' When I read in Scripture about slayin'—like them Midianites was slew—I kinder think things, but I ain't got no picter of it. Here a body kin see all they is to it—I s'pose 'tis sinful, but ain't we all born an' livin' in sin?—Thet feller bein' chopped up gives me a tickle every time I look at 'im—I hev ta keep lookin' at 'im—see whar the butcher cut off his feet? Thar's his head on thet bench, with one arm side of it, an' t'other arm's on the other side o' the meat block."

As the man mumbled on in his shocking ecstasy the expression on his hairy, spectacled face became indescribable, but his voice sank rather than mounted. My own sensations can scarcely be recorded. All the terror I had dimly felt before rushed upon me actively and vividly, and I knew that I loathed the ancient and abhorrent creature so near me with an infinite intensity. His madness, or at least his partial perversion, seemed beyond dispute. He was almost whispering now, with a huskiness more terrible than a scream, and I trembled as I listened.

"As I says, 'tis queer haow picters sets ye thinkin'. D'ye know, young Sir, I'm right sot on this un here. Arter I got the book off Eb I uster look at it a lot, especial when I'd heerd Passon Clark rant o' Sundays in his big wig. Onct I tried suthin' funny—here, young Sir, don't git skeert—all I done was ter look at the picter afore I kilt the sheep for market—killin' sheep was kinder more fun arter lookin' at it—" The tone of the old man now sank very low, sometimes becoming so faint that his words were hardly audible. I listened to the rain, and to the rattling of the bleared, small-paned windows, and marked a rumbling of approaching thunder quite unusual for the season. Once a terrific flash and peal shook the frail house to its foundations, but the whisperer seemed not to notice it.

"Killin' sheep was kinder more fun—but d'ye know, 'twan't quite *satisfyin'*. Queer haow a cravin' gits a holt on ye—As ye love the Almighty, young man, don't tell nobody, but I swar ter Gawd thet picter begun to make me *hungry fer victuals I couldn't raise nor buy*—here, set still, what's ailin' ye?—I didn't do nothin', only I wondered haow 'twud be ef I *did*—They say meat makes blood an' flesh, an' gives ye new life, so I wondered ef 'twudn't make a man live longer an' longer ef 'twas *more the same*—" But the whisperer never continued. The interruption was not produced by my fright, nor by the rapidly increasing storm amidst whose fury I was presently to open my eyes on a a smoky solitude of blackened ruins. It was produced by a very simple though somewhat unusual happening.

The open book lay flat between us, with the picture staring repulsively upward. As the old man whispered the words *"more the same"* a tiny splattering impact was heard, and something showed on the yellowed paper of the upturned volume. I thought of the rain and of a leaky roof, but rain is not red. On the butcher's shop of the Anzique cannibals a small red splattering glistened picturesquely, lending vividness to the horror of the engraving. The old man saw it, and stopped whispering even before my expression of horror made it necessary; saw it and glanced quickly toward the floor of the room he had left an hour before. I followed his glance, and beheld just above us on the loose plaster of the ancient ceiling a large irregular spot of wet crimson which seemed to spread even as I viewed it. I did not shriek or move, but merely shut my eyes. A moment later came the titanic thunderbolt of thunderbolts; blasting that accursed house of unutterable secrets and bringing the oblivion which alone saved my mind.

The Outsider

That night the Baron dreamt of many a wo;
And all his warrior-guests, with shade and form
Of witch, and demon, and large coffin-worm,
Were long be-nightmared.

—KEATS

Unhappy is he to whom the memories of childhood bring only fear and sadness. Wretched is he who looks back upon lone hours in vast and dismal chambers with brown hangings and maddening rows of antique books, or upon awed watches in twilight groves of grotesque, gigantic, and vine-encumbered trees, that silently wave twisted branches far aloft. Such a lot the gods gave to me—to me, the dazed, the disappointed; the barren, the broken. And yet I am strangely content and cling desperately to those sere memories, when my mind momentarily threatens to reach beyond to *the other.*

I know not where I was born, save that the castle was infinitely old and infinitely horrible, full of dark passages and having high ceilings where the eye could find only cobwebs and shadows. The stones in the crumbling corridors seemed always hideously damp, and there was an accursed smell everywhere, as of the piled-up corpses of dead generations. It was never light, so that I used sometimes to light candles and gaze steadily at them for relief, nor was there any sun outdoors, since the terrible trees grew high above the topmost accessible tower. There was one black tower which reached above the trees into the unknown outer sky, but that was partly ruined and could not be ascended save by a well-nigh impossible climb up the sheer wall, stone by stone.

I must have lived years in this place, but I can not measure the time. Beings must have cared for my needs, yet I can not recall any person except myself, or anything alive but the noiseless rats and bats and spiders. I think that whoever nursed me must have been shockingly aged; since my first conception of a living person was that of something mockingly like myself, yet distorted, shriveled, and decaying like the castle. To me there was nothing grotesque in the bones and skeletons that strewed some of the stone crypts deep down among the foundations. I fantastically associated these things with everyday events, and thought them more natural than the colored pictures of living beings which I found in many of the moldy books. From such books I learned all that I know. No teacher urged or guided me, and I do not recall hearing any human voice in all those years— not even my own, for although I had read of speech, I had never thought to try to speak aloud. My aspect was a matter equally unthought of, for there were no mirrors in the castle, and I merely regarded myself by instinct as akin to the youthful figures I saw drawn and painted in the books. I felt conscious of youth because I remembered so little.

Outside, across the putrid moat and under the dark mute trees, I would often lie and dream for hours about what I read in the books; and would longingly picture myself amidst gay crowds in the sunny world beyond the endless forests. Once I tried to escape from the forest, but as I went farther from the castle the shade drew denser and the air more filled with brooding fear; so that I ran frantically back lest I lose my way in a labyrinth of nighted silence.

So through endless twilights I dreamed and waited, though I knew not what I waited for. Then in the shadowy solitude my longing for light grew so frantic that I could rest no more, and I lifted entreating hands to the single black ruined tower that reached above the forest into the unknown outer sky. And at last I resolved to scale that tower, fall though I might; since it were better to glimpse the sky and perish, than to live without ever beholding day.

In the dank twilight I climbed the worn and aged stone stairs till I reached the level where they ceased, and thereafter clung perilously to small footholds leading upward. Ghastly and terrible was that dead, stairless cylinder of rock; black, ruined, and deserted, and sinister with startled bats whose wings made no noise. But more ghastly and terrible still was the slowness of my progress; for climb as I might, the darkness overhead grew no thinner, and a new chill as of haunted and venerable mold assailed me. I shivered as I wondered why I did not reach the light, and would have looked down had I dared. I fancied that night had come suddenly upon me, and vainly groped with one free hand for a window embrasure, that I might peer out and above, and try to judge the height I had attained.

All at once, after an infinity of awesome, sightless crawling up that concave and desperate precipice, I felt my head touch a solid thing, and knew I must have gained the roof, or at least some kind of floor. In the darkness I raised my free hand and tested the barrier, finding it stone and immovable. Then came a deadly circuit of the tower, clinging to whatever holds the slimy wall could give; till finally my testing hand found the barrier yielding, and I turned upward again, pushing the slab or door with my head as I used both hands in my fearful ascent. There was no light revealed above, and as my hands went higher I knew that my climb was for the nonce ended; since the slab was the trap-door of an aperture leading to a level stone surface of greater circumference than the lower tower, no doubt the floor of some lofty and capacious observation chamber. I crawled through carefully, and tried to prevent the heavy slab from falling back into place, but failed in the latter attempt. As I lay exhausted on the stone floor I heard the eery echoes of its fall, but hoped when necessary to pry it up again.

Believing I was now at prodigious height, far above the accursed branches of the wood, I dragged myself up from the floor and fumbled about for windows, that I might look for the first time upon the sky, and the moon and stars of which I had read. But on every hand I was disappointed; since all that I found were vast shelves of marble, bearing odious oblong boxes of disturbing size. More and more I reflected, and wondered what hoary secrets might abide in this high apartment so many eons cut off from the castle below. Then unexpectedly my hands came upon a doorway, where hung a portal of stone, rough with strange chiseling. Trying it, I found it locked; but with a supreme burst of strength I overcame all obstacles and dragged it open inward. As I did so there came to me the purest ecstasy I have ever known; for shining tranquilly through an ornate grating of iron, and down a short stone passageway of steps that ascended from the newly found doorway, was the radiant full moon, which I had never before seen save in dreams and in vague visions I dared not call memories.

Fancying now that I had attained the very pinnacle of the castle, I commenced to rush up the few steps beyond the door; but the sudden veiling of the moon by a cloud caused me to stumble, and I felt my way more slowly in the dark. It was still very dark when I reached the grating—which I tried carefully and found unlocked, but which I did not open for fear of falling from the amazing height to which I had climbed. Then the moon came out.

Most demoniacal of all shocks is that of the abysmally unexpected and grotesquely unbelievable. Nothing I had before undergone could compare in terror with what I now saw; with the bizarre marvels that sight implied. The sight itself was as simple as it was stupefying, for it was merely this: instead of a dizzying prospect of treetops seen from a lofty eminence, there stretched around me on the level through the grating nothing less than *the solid ground*, decked and diversified by marble slabs and columns, and overshadowed by an ancient stone church, whose ruined spire gleamed spectrally in the moonlight.

Half unconscious, I opened the grating and staggered out upon the white gravel path that stretched away in two directions. My mind, stunned and chaotic as it was, still held the frantic craving for light; and not even the fantastic wonder which had happened could stay my course. I neither knew nor cared whether my experience was insanity, dreaming, or magic; but was determined to gaze on brilliance and gayety at any cost. I knew not who I was or what I was, or what my surroundings might be; though as I continued to stumble along I became conscious of a kind of fearsome latent memory that made my progress not wholly fortuitous. I passed under an arch out of that region of slabs and columns, and wandered through the open country; sometimes following the visible road, but sometimes leaving it curiously to tread across meadows where only occasional ruins bespoke the ancient presence of a forgotten road. Once I swam across a swift river where crumbling, mossy masonry told of a bridge long vanished.

Over two hours must have passed before I reached what seemed to be my goal, a venerable ivied castle in a thickly wooded park, maddeningly familiar, yet full of perplexing strangeness to me. I saw that the moat was filled in, and that some of the well-known towers were demolished; whilst new wings existed to confuse the beholder. But what I observed with chief interest and delight were the open windows—gorgeously ablaze with light and sending forth sound of the gayest revelry. Advancing to one of these I looked in and saw an oddly dressed company, indeed; making merry, and speaking brightly to one another. I had never, seemingly, heard human speech before and could guess only vaguely what was said. Some of the faces seemed to hold expressions that brought up incredibly remote recollections, others were utterly alien.

I now stepped through the low window into the brilliantly lighted room, stepping as I did so from my single bright moment of hope to my blackest convulsion of despair and realization. The nightmare was quick to come, for as I entered, there occurred immediately one of the most terrifying demonstrations I had ever conceived. Scarcely had I crossed the sill when there descended upon the whole company a sudden and unheralded fear of hideous intensity, distorting every face and evoking the most horrible screams from nearly every throat. Flight with universal, and in the clamor and panic several fell in a swoon and were dragged away by their madly fleeing companions. Many covered their eyes with their hands, and plunged blindly and awkwardly in their race to escape, overturning furniture and stumbling against the walls before they managed to reach one of the many doors.

The cries were shocking; and as I stood in the brilliant apartment alone and dazed, listening to their vanishing echoes, I trembled at the thought of what might be lurking near me unseen. At a casual inspection the room seemed deserted, but when I moved toward one of the alcoves I thought I detected a presence there—a hint of motion beyond the golden-arched doorway leading to another and somewhat similar room. As I approached the arch I began to perceive the presence more clearly; and then, with the first and last sound I ever uttered—a ghastly ululation that revolted me almost as poignantly as its noxious cause—I beheld in full, frightful vividness the inconceivable, indescribable, and unmentionable monstrosity which had by its simple appearance changed a merry company to a herd of delirious fugitives.

I can not even hint what it was like, for it was a compound of all that is unclean, uncanny, unwelcome, abnormal, and detestable. It was the ghoulish shade of decay, antiquity, and desolation; the putrid, dripping eidolon of unwholesome revelation, the awful baring of that which the merciful earth should always hide. God knows it was not of this world—or no longer of this world—yet to my horror I saw in its eaten-away and bone-revealing outlines a leering, abhorrent travesty on the human shape; and in its moldy, disintegrating apparel an unspeakable quality that chilled me even more.

I was almost paralyzed, but not too much so to make a feeble effort toward flight; a backward stumble which failed to break the spell in which the nameless, voiceless monster held me. My eyes, bewitched by the glassy orbs which stared loathsomely into them, refused to close; though they were mercifully blurred, and showed the terrible object but indistinctly after the first shock. I tried to raise my hand to shut out the light, yet so stunned were my nerves that my arm could not fully obey my will. The attempt, however, was enough to disturb my balance; so that I had to stagger forward several steps to avoid falling. As I did so I became suddenly and agonizingly aware of the *nearness* of the carrion thing, whose hideous hollow breathing I half fancied I could hear. Nearly mad, I found myself yet able to throw out a hand to ward off the fetid apparition which pressed so close; when in one cataclysmic second of cosmic nightmarishness and hellish accident *my fingers touched the rotting outstretched paw of the monster beneath the golden arch.*

I did not shriek, but all the fiendish ghouls that ride the nightwind shrieked for me as in that same second there crashed down upon my mind a single and fleeting avalanche of soul-annihilating memory. I knew in that second all that had been; I remembered beyond the frightful castle and the trees, and recognized the altered edifice in which I now stood; I recognized, most terrible of all, the unholy abomination that stood leering before me as I withdrew my sullied fingers from its own.

But in the cosmos there is balm as well as bitterness, and that balm is nepenthe. In the supreme horror of that second I forgot what had horrified me, and the burst of black memory vanished in a chaos of echoing images. In a dream I fled from that haunted and accursed pile, and ran swiftly and silently in the moonlight. When I returned to the churchyard place of marble and went down the steps I found the stone trap-door immovable; but I was not sorry, for I had hated the antique castle and the trees. Now I ride with the mocking and friendly ghouls on the night wind, and play by day amongst the catacombs of Nephren-Ka in the sealed and unknown valley of Hadoth by the Nile. I know that light is not for me, save that of the moon over the rock tombs of Neb, nor any gayety save the unnamed feasts of Nitokris beneath the Great Pyramid; yet in my new wildness and freedom I almost welcome the bitterness of alienage.

For although nepenthe has calmed me, I know always that I am an outsider; a stranger in this century and among those who are still men. This I have known ever since I stretched out my fingers to the abomination within the great gilded frame; stretched out my fingers and touched *a cold and unyielding surface of polished glass.*

Pickman's Model

You needn't think I'm crazy, Eliot—plenty of others have queerer prejudices than this. Why don't you laugh at Oliver's grandfather, who won't ride in a motor? If I don't like that damned subway, it's my own business; and we got here more quickly anyhow in the taxi. We'd have had to walk up the hill from Park Street if we'd taken the car.

I know I'm more nervous than I was when you saw me last year, but you don't need to hold a clinic over it. There's plenty of reason, God knows, and I fancy I'm lucky to be sane at all. Why the third degree? You didn't use to be so inquisitive.

Well, if you must hear it, I don't know why you shouldn't. Maybe you ought to know, anyhow, for you kept writing me like a grieved parent when you heard I'd begun to cut the Art Club and keep away from Pickman. Now that he's disappeared I go around to the club once in a while, but my nerves aren't what they were.

No, I don't know what's become of Pickman, and I don't like to guess. You might have surmised I had some inside information when I dropped him—and that's why I don't want to think where he's gone. Let the police find what they can—it won't be much, judging from the fact that they don't know yet of the old North End place he hired under the name of Peters. I'm not sure that I could find it again myself—not that I'd ever try, even in broad daylight! Yes, I do know, or am afraid I know, why he maintained it. I'm coming to that. And I think you'll understand before I'm through why I don't tell the police. They would ask me to guide them, but I couldn't go back there even if I knew the way. There was something there—and now I can't use the subway or (and you may as well have your laugh at this, too) go down into cellars any more.

I should think you'd have known I didn't drop Pickman for the same silly reasons that fussy old women like Dr. Reid or Joe Minot or

Rosworth did. Morbid art doesn't shock me, and when a man has the genius Pickman had I feel it an honour to know him, no matter what direction his work takes. Boston never had a greater painter than Richard Upton Pickman. I said it at first and I say it still, and I never swerved an inch, either, when he showed that "Ghoul Feeding." That, you remember, was when Minot cut him.

You know, it takes profound art and profound insight into Nature to turn out stuff like Pickman's. Any magazine-cover hack can splash paint around wildly and call it a nightmare or a Witches' Sabbath or a portrait of the devil, but only a great painter can make such a thing really scare or ring true. That's because only a real artist knows the actual anatomy of the terrible or the physiology of fear—the exact sort of lines and proportions that connect up with latent instincts or hereditary memories of fright, and the proper colour contrasts and lighting effects to stir the dormant sense of strangeness. I don't have to tell you why a Fuseli really brings a shiver while a cheap ghost-story frontispiece merely makes us laugh. There's something those fellows catch—beyond life—that they're able to make us catch for a second. Doré had it. Sime has it. Angarola of Chicago has it. And Pickman had it as no man ever had it before or—I hope to Heaven—ever will again.

Don't ask me what it is they see. You know, in ordinary art, there's all the difference in the world between the vital, breathing things drawn from Nature or models and the artificial truck that commercial small fry reel off in a bare studio by rule. Well, I should say that the really weird artist has a kind of vision which makes models, or summons up what amounts to actual scenes from the spectral world he lives in. Anyhow, he manages to turn out results that differ from the pretender's mince-pie dreams in just about the same way that the life painter's results differ from the concoctions of a correspondence-school cartoonist. If I had ever seen what Pickman saw—but no! Here, let's have a drink before we get any deeper. Gad, I wouldn't be alive if I'd ever seen what that man—if he was a man—saw!

You recall that Pickman's forte was faces. I don't believe anybody since Goya could put so much of sheer hell into a set of features or a twist of expression. And before Goya you have to go back to the mediaeval chaps who did the gargoyles and chimaeras on Notre Dame and Mont Saint-Michel. They believed all sorts of things—and maybe they saw all sorts of things, too, for the Middle Ages had some curious phases. I remember your asking Pickman yourself once, the year before you went away, wherever in thunder he got such ideas and visions. Wasn't that a nasty laugh he gave you? It was partly because of that laugh that Reid dropped him. Reid, you know, had just taken up comparative pathology, and was full of pompous "inside stuff" about the biological or evolutionary significance of this or that mental or physical symptom. He said Pickman repelled him more and more every day, and almost frightened him toward the last—that the fellow's features and expression were slowly developing in a way he didn't like; in a way that wasn't human. He had a lot of talk about diet, and said Pickman must be abnormal and eccentric to the last degree. I suppose you told Reid, if you and he had any correspondence over it, that he'd let Pickman's paintings get on his nerves or harrow up his imagination. I know I told him that myself—then.

But keep in mind that I didn't drop Pickman for anything like this. On the contrary, my admiration for him kept growing; for that "Ghoul Feeding" was a tremendous achievement. As you know, the club wouldn't exhibit it, and the Museum of Fine Arts wouldn't accept it as a gift; and I can add that nobody would buy it, so Pickman had it right in his house till he went. Now his father has it in Salem—you know Pickman comes of old Salem stock, and had a witch ancestor hanged in 1692.

I got into the habit of calling on Pickman quite often, especially after I began making notes for a monograph on weird art. Probably it was his work which put the idea into my head, any anyhow, I found him a mine of data and suggestions when I came to develop it. He showed me all the paintings and drawings he had about; including some pen-and-ink sketches that would, I verily believe, have got him kicked out of the club if many of the members had seen them. Before long I was pretty nearly a devotee, and would listen for hours like a schoolboy to art theories and philosophic speculations wild enough to qualify him for the Danvers asylum. My hero-worship, coupled with the fact that people generally were commencing to have less and less to do with him, made him get very confidential with me; and one evening he hinted that if I were fairly close-mouthed and none too squeamish, he might show me something rather unusual— something a bit stronger than anything he had in the house.

"You know," he said, "there are things that won't do for Newbury Street—things that are out of place here, and that can't be conceived here, anyhow. It's my business to catch the overtones of the soul, and you won't find those in a parvenu set of artificial streets on made land. Back Bay isn't Boston—it isn't anything yet, because it's had no time to pick up memories and attract local spirits. If there are any ghosts here, they're the tame ghosts of a salt marsh and a shallow cove; and I want human ghosts—the ghosts of beings highly organised enough to have looked on hell and known the meaning of what they saw.

"The place for an artist to live is the North End. If any aesthete were sincere, he'd put up with the slums for the sake of the massed traditions. God, man! Don't you realise that places like that weren't merely *made*, but actually *grew*? Generation after generation lived and felt and died there, and in days when people weren't afraid to live and feel and die. Don't you know there was a mill on Copp's Hill in 1632, and that half the present streets were laid out by 1650? I can show you houses that have stood two centuries and a half and more; houses that have witnessed what would make a modern house crumble into powder. What do moderns know of life and the forces behind it? You call the Salem witchcraft a delusion, but I'll wager my four-times-great-grandmother could have told you things. They hanged her on Gallows Hill, with Cotton Mather looking sanctimoniously on. Mather, damn him, was afraid somebody might succeed in kicking free of this accursed cage of monotony—I wish someone had laid a spell on him or sucked his blood in the night!

"I can show you a house he lived in, and I can show you another one he was afraid to enter in spite of all his fine bold talk. He knew things he didn't dare put into that stupid *Magnalia* or that puerile *Wonders of the Invisible World*. Look here, do you know the whole North End once had a set of tunnels that kept certain people in touch with each other's houses, and the burying ground, and the sea? Let them prosecute and persecute above ground—things went on every day that they couldn't reach, and voices laughed at night that they couldn't place!

"Why, man, out of ten surviving houses built before 1700 and not moved since I'll wager that in eight I can show you something queer in the cellar. There's hardly a month that you don't read of workmen finding bricked-up arches and wells leading nowhere in this or that old place as it comes down—you could see one near Henchman Street from the elevated last year. There were witches and what their spells summoned; pirates and what they brought in from the sea; smugglers; privateers—and I tell you, people knew how to live, and how to enlarge the bounds of life, in the old time! This wasn't the only world a bold and wise man could know—faugh! And to think of today in contrast, with such pale-pink brains that even a club of supposed artists gets shudders and convulsions if a picture goes beyond the feelings of a Beacon Street teatable!

"The only saving grace of the present is that it's too damned stupid to question the past very closely. What do maps and records and guidebooks really tell of the North End? Bah! At a guess I'll guarantee to lead you to thirty or forty alleys and networks of alleys north of Prince Street that aren't suspected by ten living beings outside of the foreigners that swarm them. And what do those Dagoes know of their meaning? No, Thurber, these ancient places are dreaming gorgeously and overflowing with wonder and terror and escapes from the commonplace, and yet there's not a living soul to understand or profit by them. Or rather, there's only one living soul—for I haven't been digging around in the past for nothing!

"See here, you're interested in this sort of thing. What if I told you that I've got another studio up there, where I can catch the night-spirit of antique horror and paint things that I couldn't even think of in Newbury Street? Naturally I don't tell those cursed old maids at the club—with Reid, damn him, whispering even as it is that I'm a sort of monster bound down the toboggan of reverse evolution. Yes, Thurber, I decided long ago that one must paint terror as well as beauty from life, so I did some exploring in places where I had reason to know terror lives.

"I've got a place that I don't believe three living Nordic men besides myself have ever seen. It isn't so very far from the elevated as distance goes, but it's centuries away as the soul goes. I took it because of the queer old brick well in the cellar—one of the sort I told you about. The shack's almost tumbling down, so that nobody else would live there, and I'd hate to tell you how little I pay for it. The windows are boarded up, but I like that all the better, since I don't want daylight for what I do. I paint in the cellar, where the inspiration is thickest, but I've other rooms furnished on the ground floor. A Sicilian owns it, and I've hired it under the name of Peters.

"Now if you're game, I'll take you there tonight. I think you'd enjoy the pictures, for as I said, I've let myself go a bit there. It's no vast tour—I sometimes do it on foot, for I don't want to attract attention with a taxi in such a place. We can take the shuttle at the South Station for Battery Street, and after that the walk isn't much."

Well, Eliot, there wasn't much for me to do after that harangue but to keep myself from running instead of walking for the first vacant cab we could sight. We changed to the elevated at the South Station, and at about twelve o'clock had climbed down the steps at Battery Street and struck along the old waterfront past Constitution Wharf. I didn't keep track of the cross streets, and can't tell you yet which it was we turned up, but I know it wasn't Greenough Lane.

When we did turn, it was to climb through the deserted length of the oldest and dirtiest alley I ever saw in my life, with crumbling-looking gables, broken small-paned windows, and archaic chimneys that stood out half-disintegrated against the moonlit sky. I don't believe there were three houses in sight that hadn't been standing in Cotton Mather's time—certainly I glimpsed at least two with an overhang, and once I thought I saw a peaked roof-line of the almost forgotten pre-gambrel type, though antiquarians tell us there are none left in Boston.

From that alley, which had a dim light, we turned to the left into an equally silent and still narrower alley with no light at all: and in a minute made what I think was an obtuse-angled bend toward the right in the dark. Not long after this Pickman produced a flashlight and revealed an antediluvian ten-panelled door that looked damnably worm-eaten. Unlocking it, he ushered me into a barren hallway with what was once splendid dark-oak panelling—simple, of course, but thrillingly suggestive of the times of Andros and Phipps and the Witchcraft. Then he took me through a door on the left, lighted an oil lamp, and told me to make myself at home.

Now, Eliot, I'm what the man in the street would call fairly "hard-boiled," but I'll confess that what I saw on the walls of that room gave me a bad turn. They were his pictures, you know—the ones he couldn't paint or even show in Newbury Street—and he was right when he said he had "let himself go." Here—have another drink—I need one anyhow!

There's no use in my trying to tell you what they were like, because the awful, the blasphemous horror, and the unbelievable loathsomeness and moral foetor came from simple touches quite beyond the power of words to classify. There was none of the exotic technique you see in Sidney Sime, none of the trans-Saturnian landscapes and lunar fungi that Clark Ashton Smith uses to freeze the blood. The backgrounds were mostly old churchyards, deep woods, cliffs by the sea, brick tunnels, ancient panelled rooms, or simple vaults of masonry. Copp's Hill Burying Ground, which could not be many blocks away from this very house, was a favourite scene.

The madness and monstrosity lay in the figures in the foreground— for Pickman's morbid art was preëminently one of daemoniac portraiture. These figures were seldom completely human, but often approached humanity in varying degree. Most of the bodies, while roughly bipedal, had a forward slumping, and a vaguely canine cast. The texture of the majority was a kind of unpleasant rubberiness. Ugh! I can see them now! Their occupations—well, don't ask me to be too precise. They were usually feeding—I won't say on what. They were sometimes shown in groups in cemeteries or underground passages, and often appeared to be in battle over their prey—or rather, their treasure-trove. And what damnable expressiveness Pickman sometimes gave the sightless faces of this charnel booty! Occasionally the things were shown leaping through open windows at night, or squatting on the chests of sleepers, worrying at their throats. One canvas showed a ring of them baying about a hanged witch on Gallows Hill, whose dead face held a close kinship to theirs.

But don't get the idea that it was all this hideous business of theme and setting which struck me faint. I'm not a three-year-old kid, and I'd seen much like this before. It was the *faces*, Eliot, those accursed *faces*, that leered and slavered out of the canvas with the very breath of life! By God, man, I verily believe they *were* alive! That nauseous wizard had waked the fires of hell in pigment, and his brush had been a nightmare-spawning wand. Give me that decanter, Eliot!

There was one thing called "The Lesson"—Heaven pity me, that I ever saw it! Listen—can you fancy a squatting circle of nameless dog-like things in a churchyard teaching a small child how to feed like themselves? The price of a changeling, I suppose—you know the old myth about how the weird people leave their spawn in cradles in exchange for the human babes they steal. Pickman was showing what happens to those stolen babes—how they grow up—and then I began to see a hideous relationship in the faces of the human and non-human figures. He was, in all his gradations of morbidity between the frankly nonhuman and the degradedly human, establishing a sardonic linkage and evolution. The dog-things were developed from mortals!

And no sooner had I wondered what he made of their own young as left with mankind in the form of changelings, than my eye caught a picture embodying that very thought. It was that of an ancient Puritan interior—a heavily beamed room with lattice windows, a settle, and clumsy seventeenth-century furniture, with the family sitting about while the father read from the Scriptures. Every face but one showed nobility and reverence, but that one reflected the mockery of the pit. It was that of a young man in years, and no doubt belonged to a supposed son of that pious father, but in essence it was the kin of the unclean things. It was their changeling—and in a spirit of supreme irony Pickman had given the features a very perceptible resemblance to his own.

By this time Pickman had lighted a lamp in an adjoining room and was politely holding open the door for me; asking me if I would care to see his "modern studies." I hadn't been able to give him much of my opinions—I was too speechless with fright and loathing—but I think he fully understood and felt highly complimented. And now I want to assure you again, Eliot, that I'm no mollycoddle to scream at anything which shows a bit of departure from the usual. I'm middle-aged and decently sophisticated, and I guess you saw enough of me in France to know I'm not easily knocked out. Remember, too, that I'd just about recovered my wind and gotten used to those frightful pictures which turned colonial New England into a kind of annex of hell. Well, in spite of all this, that next room forced a real scream out of me, and I had to clutch at the doorway to keep from keeling over. The other chamber had shown a pack of ghouls and witches overrunning the world of our forefathers, but this one brought the horror right into our own daily life!

Gad, how that man could paint! There was a study called "Subway Accident," in which a flock of the vile things were clambering up from some unknown catacomb through a crack in the floor of the Boylston Street subway and attacking a crowd of people on the platform. Another showed a dance on Copp's Hill among the tombs with the background of today. Then there were any number of cellar views, with monsters creeping in through holes and rifts in the masonry and grinning as they squatted behind barrels or furnaces and waited for their first victim to descend the stairs.

One disgusting canvas seemed to depict a vast cross-section of Beacon Hill, with ant-like armies of the mephitic monsters squeezing themselves through burrows that honeycombed the ground. Dances in the modern cemeteries were freely pictured, and another conception somehow shocked me more than all the rest—a scene in an unknown vault, where scores of the beasts crowded about one who held a well-known Boston guidebook and was evidently reading aloud. All were pointing to a certain passage, and every face seemed so distorted with epileptic and reverberant laughter that I almost thought I heard the fiendish echoes. The title of the picture was, "Holmes, Lowell, and Longfellow Lie Buried in Mount Auburn."

As I gradually steadied myself and got readjusted to this second room of deviltry and morbidity, I began to analyse some of the points in my sickening loathing. In the first place, I said to myself, these things repelled because of the utter inhumanity and callous cruelty they showed in Pickman. The fellow must be a relentless enemy of all mankind to take such glee in the torture of brain and flesh and the degradation of the mortal tenement. In the second place, they terrified because of their very greatness. Their art was the art that convinced—when we saw the pictures we saw the daemons themselves and were afraid of them. And the queer part was, that Pickman got none of his power from the use of selectiveness or bizarrerie. Nothing was blurred, distorted, or conventionalised; outlines were sharp and lifelike, and details were almost painfully defined. And the faces!

It was not any mere artist's interpretation that we saw; it was pandaemonium itself, crystal clear in stark objectivity. That was it, by Heaven! The man was not a fantaisiste or romanticist at all—he did not even try to give us the churning, prismatic ephemera of dreams, but coldly and sardonically reflected some stable, mechanistic, and well-established horror-world which he saw fully, brilliantly, squarely, and unfalteringly. God knows what that world can have been, or where he ever glimpsed the blasphemous shapes that loped and trotted and crawled through it; but whatever the baffling source of his images, one thing was plain. Pickman was in every sense— in conception and in execution—a thorough, painstaking, and almost scientific *realist*.

My host was now leading the way down cellar to his actual studio, and I braced myself for some hellish effects among the unfinished canvases. As we reached the bottom of the damp stairs he turned his flashlight to a corner of the large open space at hand, revealing the circular brick curb of what was evidently a great well in the earthen floor. We walked nearer, and I saw that it must be five feet across, with walls a good foot thick and some six inches above the ground level—solid work of the seventeenth century, or I was much mistaken. That, Pickman said, was the kind of thing he had been talking about—an aperture of the network of tunnels that used to undermine the hill. I noticed idly that it did not seem to be bricked up, and that a heavy disc of wood formed the apparent cover. Thinking of the things this well must have been connected with if Pickman's wild hints had not been mere rhetoric, I shivered slightly; then turned to follow him up a step and through a narrow door into a room of fair size, provided with a wooden floor and furnished as a studio. An acetylene gas outfit gave the light necessary for work.

The unfinished pictures on easels or propped against the walls were as ghastly as the finished ones upstairs, and showed the painstaking methods of the artist. Scenes were blocked out with extreme care, and pencilled guide lines told of the minute exactitude which Pickman used in getting the right perspective and proportions. The man was great—I say it even now, knowing as much as I do. A large camera on a table excited my notice, and Pickman told me that he used it in taking scenes for backgrounds, so that he might paint them from photographs in the studio instead of carting his outfit around the town for this or that view. He thought a photograph quite as good as an actual scene or model for sustained work, and declared he employed them regularly.

There was something very disturbing about the nauseous sketches and half-finished monstrosities that leered around from every side of the room, and when Pickman suddenly unveiled a huge canvas on the side away from the light I could not for my life keep back a loud scream—the second I had emitted that night. It echoed and echoed through the dim vaultings of that ancient and nitrous cellar, and I had to choke back a flood of reaction that threatened to burst out as hysterical laughter. Merciful Creator! Eliot, but I don't know how much was real and how much was feverish fancy. It doesn't seem to me that earth can hold a dream like that!

It was a colossal and nameless blasphemy with glaring red eyes, and it held in bony claws a thing that had been a man, gnawing at the head as a child nibbles at a stick of candy. Its position was a kind of crouch, and as one looked one felt that at any moment it might drop its present prey and seek a jucier morsel. But damn it all, it wasn't even the fiendish subject that made it such an immortal fountainhead of all panic—not that, nor the dog face with its pointed ears, bloodshot eyes, flat nose, and drooling lips. It wasn't the scaly claws nor the mould-caked body nor the half-hooved feet—none of these, though any one of them might well have driven an excitable man to madness.

It was the technique, Eliot—the cursed, the impious, the unnatural technique! As I am a living being, I never elsewhere saw the actual breath of life so fused into a canvas. The monster was there—it glared and gnawed and gnawed and glared—and I knew that only a suspension of Nature's laws could ever let a man paint a thing like that without a model—without some glimpse of the nether world which no mortal unsold to the Fiend has ever had.

Pinned with a thumb-tack to a vacant part of the canvas was a piece of paper now badly curled up—probably, I thought, a photograph from which Pickman meant to paint a background as hideous as the nightmare it was to enhance. I reached out to uncurl and look at it, when suddenly I saw Pickman start as if shot. He had been listening with peculiar intensity ever since my shocked scream had waked unaccustomed echoes in the dark cellar, and now he seemed struck with a fright which, though not comparable to my own, had in it more of the physical than of the spiritual. He drew a revolver and motioned me to silence, then stepped out into the main cellar and closed the door behind him.

I think I was paralysed for an instant. Imitating Pickman's listening, I fancied I heard a faint scurrying sound somewhere, and a series of squeals or bleats in a direction I couldn't determine. I thought of huge rats and shuddered. Then there came a subdued sort of clatter which somehow set me all in gooseflesh—a furtive, groping kind of clatter, though I can't attempt to convey what I mean in words. It was like heavy wood falling on stone or brick—wood on brick—what did that make me think of?

It came again, and louder. There was a vibration as if the wood had fallen farther than it had fallen before. After that followed a sharp grating noise, a shouted gibberish from Pickman, and the deafening discharge of all six chambers of a revolver, fired spectacularly as a lion-tamer might fire in the air for effect. A muffled squeal or squawk, and a thud. Then more wood and brick grating, a pause, and the opening of the door—at which I'll confess I started violently. Pickman reappeared with his smoking weapon, cursing the bloated rats that infested the ancient well.

"The deuce knows what they eat, Thurber," he grinned, "for those archaic tunnels touched graveyard and witch-den and sea-coast. But whatever it is, they must have run short, for they were devilish anxious to get out. Your yelling stirred them up, I fancy. Better be cautious in these old places—our rodent friends are the one drawback, though I sometimes think they're a positive asset by way of atmosphere and colour."

Well, Eliot, that was the end of the night's adventure. Pickman had promised to show me the place, and Heaven knows he had done it. He led me out of that tangle of alleys in another direction, it seems, for when we sighted a lamp post we were in a half-familiar street with monotonous rows of mingled tenement blocks and old houses. Charter Street, it turned out to be, but I was too flustered to notice just where we hit it. We were too late for the elevated, and walked back downtown through Hanover Street. I remember that walk. We switched from Tremont up Beacon, and Pickman left me at the corner of Joy, where I turned off. I never spoke to him again.

Why did I drop him? Don't be impatient. Wait till I ring for coffee. We've had enough of the other stuff, but I for one need something. No—it wasn't the paintings I saw in that place; though I'll swear they were enough to get him ostracised in nine-tenths of the homes and clubs of Boston, and I guess you won't wonder now why I have to steer clear of subways and cellars. It was—something I found in my coat the next morning. You know, the curled-up paper tacked to that frightful canvas in the cellar; the thing I thought was a photograph of some scene he meant to use as a background for that monster. That last scare had come while I was reaching to uncurl it, and it seems I had vacantly crumpled it into my pocket. But here's the coffee—take it black, Eliot, if you're wise.

Yes, that paper was the reason I dropped Pickman; Richard Upton Pickman, the greatest artist I have ever known—and the foulest being that ever leaped the bounds of life into the pits of myth and madness. Eliot—old Reid was right. He wasn't strictly human. Either he was born in strange shadow, or he'd found a way to unlock the forbidden gate. It's all the same now, for he's gone—back into the fabulous darkness he loved to haunt. Here, let's have the chandelier going.

Don't ask me to explain or even conjecture about what I burned. Don't ask me, either, what lay behind that mole-like scrambling Pickman was so keen to pass off as rats. There are secrets, you know, which might have come down from old Salem times, and Cotton Mather tells even stranger things. You know how damned lifelike Pickman's paintings were—how we all wondered where he got those faces.

Well—that paper wasn't a photograph of any background, after all. What is showed was simply the monstrous being he was painting on that awful canvas. It was the model he was using—and its background was merely the wall of the cellar studio in minute detail. But by God, Eliot, *it was a photograph from life.*

In The Vault

❧

There is nothing more absurd, as I view it, than that conventional association of the homely and the wholesome which seems to pervade the psychology of the multitude. Mention a bucolic Yankee setting, a bungling and thick-fibered village undertaker, and a careless mishap in a tomb, and no average reader can be brought to expect more than a hearty albeit grotesque phase of comedy. God knows, though, that the prosy tale which George Birch's death permits me to tell has in it aspects beside which some of our darkest tragedies are light.

Birch acquired a limitation and changed his business in 1881, yet never discussed the case when he could avoid it. Neither did his old physician, Doctor Davis, who died years ago. It was generally stated that the affliction and shock were results of an unlucky slip whereby Birch had locked himself for nine hours in the receiving-tomb of Peck Valley Cemetery, escaping only by crude and disastrous mechanical means; but while this much was undoubtedly true, there were other and blacker things which the man used to whisper to me in his drunken delirium toward the last. He confided in me because I was his doctor, and because he probably felt the need of confiding in some one else after Davis died. He was a bachelor, wholly without relatives.

Birch, before 1881, had been the village undertaker of Peck Valley, and was a very calloused and primitive specimen even as such specimens go. The practises I heard attributed to him would be unbelievable today, at least in a city; and even Peck Valley would have shuddered a bit had it known the easy ethics of its mortuary artist in such matters as the ownership of costly "laying-out" apparel invisible beneath the casket's lid, and the degrees of dignity to be maintained in posing and adapting the unseen members of lifeless tenants to containers not always calculated with sublimest accuracy. Most distinctly Birch was lax, insensitive, and professionally undesirable; yet I still think he was not an evil man. He was merely crass of fiber and function—thoughtless, careless, and liquorish, as his easily avoidable accident proves, and without that modicum of imagination which holds the average citizen within certain limits fixed by taste.

Just where to begin Birch's story I can hardly decide, since I am no practised teller of tales. I suppose one should start in the cold December of 1880, when the ground froze and the cemetery delvers found they could dig no more graves till spring. Fortunately the village was small and the death rate low, so that it was possible to give all of Birch's inanimate charges a temporary haven in the single antiquated receiving-tomb. The undertaker grew doubly lethargic in the bitter weather, and seemed to outdo even himself in carelessness. Never did he knock together flimsier and ungainlier caskets, nor disregard more flagrantly the needs of the rusty lock on the tomb door which he slammed open and shut with such nonchalant abandon.

At last the spring thaw came, and graves were laboriously prepared for the nine silent harvests of the grim reaper which waited in the tomb. Birch, though dreading the bother of removal and interment, began his task of transference one disagreeable April morning, but ceased before noon because of a heavy rain that seemed to irritate his horse, after having laid but one body to its permanent rest. That was Darius Peck, the nonagenarian, whose grave was not far from the tomb. Birch decided that he would begin the next day with little old Matthew Fenner, whose grave was also near by; but actually postponed the matter for three days, not getting to work until Good Friday, the fifteenth. Being without superstition, he did not heed the day at all; though ever afterward he refused to do anything of importance on that fateful sixth day of the week. Certainly, the events of that evening greatly changed George Birch.

On the afternoon of Friday, April fifteenth, then, Birch set out for the tomb with horse and wagon to transfer the body of Matthew Fenner. That he was not perfectly sober, he subsequently admitted; though he had not then taken to the wholesale drinking by which he later tried to forget certain things. He was just dizzy and careless enough to annoy his sensitive horse, which as he drew it viciously up at the tomb, neighed and pawed and tossed its head, much as on that former occasion when the rain had seemingly vexed it. The day was clear, but a high wind had sprung up; and Birch was glad to get to shelter, as he unlocked the iron door and entered the side-hill vault. Another might not have relished the damp, odorous chamber with the eight carelessly placed coffins; but Birch in those days was insensitive, and was concerned only in getting the right coffin for the right grave. He had not forgotten the criticism aroused when Hannah Bixby's relatives, wishing to transport her body to the cemetery in the city whither they had moved, found the casket of Judge Capwell beneath her headstone.

The light was dim, but Birch's sight was good, and he did not get Asaph Sawyer's coffin by mistake, although it was very similar. He had, indeed, made that coffin for Matthew Fenner; but had cast it aside at last as too awkward and flimsy, in a fit of curious sentimentality aroused by recalling how kindly and generous the little old man had been to him during his bankruptcy five years before. He gave old Matt the very best his skill could produce, but was thrifty enough to save the rejected specimen, and to use it when Asaph Sawyer died of a malignant fever. Sawyer was not a lovable man, and many stories were told of his almost inhuman vindictiveness and tenacious memory for wrongs real or fancied. To him Birch had felt no compunction in assigning the carelessly made coffin which he now pushed out of the way in his quest for the Fenner casket.

It was just as he had recognized old Matt's coffin that the door slammed to in the wind, leaving him in a dusk even deeper than before. The narrow transom admitted only the feeblest rays, and the overhead ventilation funnel virtually none at all; so that he was reduced to a profane fumbling as he made his halting way among the long boxes toward the latch. In this funereal twilight he rattled the rusty handles, pushed at the iron panels, and wondered why the massive portal had grown so suddenly recalcitrant. In this twilight, too, he began to realize the truth and to shout loudly as if his horse outside could do more than neigh an unsympathetic reply. For the long-neglected latch was obviously broken, leaving the careless undertaker trapped in the vault, a victim of his own oversight.

The thing must have happened at about three-thirty in the afternoon. Birch, being by temperament phlegmatic and practical, did not shout long; but proceeded to grope about for some tools which he recalled seeing in a corner of the tomb. It is doubtful whether he was touched at all by the horror and exquisite weirdness of his position, but the bald fact of imprisonment so far from the daily paths of men was enough to exasperate him thoroughly. His day's work was sadly interrupted, and unless chance presently brought some rambler hither, he might have to remain all night or longer. The pile of tools soon reached, and a hammer and chisel selected, Birch returned over the coffins to the door. The air had begun to be exceedingly unwholesome, but to this detail he paid no attention as he toiled, half by feeling, at the heavy and corroded metal of the latch. He would have given much for a lantern or bit of candle; but, lacking these, bungled semi-sightlessly as best he might.

When he perceived that the latch was hopelessly unyielding, at least to such meager tools and under such tenebrous conditions as these, Birch glanced about for other possible points of escape. The vault had been dug from a sidehill, so that the narrow ventilation tunnel in the top ran through several feet of earth, making this direction utterly useless to consider. Over the door, however, the high, slit-like transom in the brick façade gave promise of possible enlargement to a diligent worker; hence upon this his eyes long rested as he racked his brains for means to reach it. There was nothing like a ladder in the tomb, and the coffin niches on the sides and rear, which Birch seldom took the trouble to use, afforded no ascent to the space above the door. Only the coffins themselves remained as potential stepping-stones, and as he considered these he speculated on the best mode of arranging them. Three coffin-heights, he reckoned, would permit him to reach the transom; but he could do better with four. The boxes were fairly even, and could be piled up like blocks; so he began to compute how he might most stably use the eight to rear a scalable platform four deep. As he planned, he could not but wish that the units of his contemplated staircase had been more securely made. Whether he had imagination enough to wish they were empty, is strongly to be doubted.

Finally he decided to lay a base of three parallel with the wall, to place upon this two layers of two each, and upon these a single box to serve as the platform. This arrangement could be ascended with a minimum of awkwardness, and would furnish the desired height. Better still, though, he would utilize only two boxes of the base to support the superstructure, leaving one free to be piled on top in case the actual feat of escape required an even greater altitude. And so the prisoner toiled in the twilight, heaving the unresponsive remnants of mortality with little ceremony as his miniature Tower of Babel rose course by course. Several of the coffins began to split under the stress of handling, and he planned to save the stoutly built casket of little Matthew Fenner for the top, in order that his feet might have as certain a surface as possible. In the semi-gloom he trusted mostly to touch to select the right one, and indeed came upon it almost by accident, since it tumbled into his hands as if through some odd volition after he had unwittingly placed it beside another on the third layer.

The tower at length finished, and his aching arms rested by a pause during which he sat on the bottom step of his grim device, Birch cautiously ascended with his tools and stood abreast of the narrow transom. The borders of the space were entirely of brick, and there seemed little doubt but that he could shortly chisel away enough to allow his body to pass. As his hammer blows began to fall, the horse outside whinnied in a tone which may have been encouraging and may have been mocking. In either case, it would have been appropriate, for the unexpected tenacity of the easy-looking brickwork was surely a sardonic commentary on the vanity of mortal hopes, and the source of a task whose performance deserved every possible stimulus.

Dusk fell and found Birch still toiling. He worked largely by feeling now, since newly-gathered clouds hid the moon; and though progress was still slow, he felt heartened at the extent of his encroachments on the top and bottom of the aperture. He could, he was sure, get out by midnight; though it is characteristic of him that this thought was untinged with eery implications. Undisturbed by oppressive reflections on the time, the place, and the company beneath his feet, he philosophically chipped away the stony brickwork, cursing when a fragment hit him in the face, and laughing when one struck the increasingly excited horse that pawed near the cypress tree. In time the hole grew so large that he ventured to try his body in it now and then, shifting about so that the coffins beneath him rocked and creaked. He would not, he found, have to pile another on his platform to make the proper height, for the hole was on exactly the right level to use as soon as its size would permit.

It must have been midnight at least when Birch decided he could get through the transom. Tired and perspiring despite many rests, he descended to the floor and sat a while on the bottom box to gather strength for the final wriggle and leap to the ground outside. The hungry horse was neighing repeatedly and almost uncannily, and he vaguely wished it would stop. He was curiously unelated over his impending escape, and almost dreaded the exertion, for his form had the idolent stoutness of early middle age. As he remounted the splitting coffins he felt his weight very poignantly; especially when, upon reaching the topmost one, he heard that aggravated crackle which bespeaks the wholesale rending of wood. He had, it seems, planned in vain when choosing the stoutest coffin for the platform; for no sooner was his full bulk again upon it than the rotting lid gave way, jouncing him two feet down on a surface which even he did not care to imagine. Maddened by the sound, or by the stench which billowed forth even to the open air, the waiting horse gave a scream that was too frantic for a neigh, and plunged madly off through the night, the wagon rattling crazily behind it.

Birch, in his ghastly situation, was now too low for an easy scramble out of the enlarged transom, but gathered his energies for a determined try. Clutching the edges of the aperture, he sought to pull himself up, when he noticed a queer retardation in the form of an apparent drag on both his ankles. In another moment he knew fear for the first time that night; for struggle as he would, he could not shake clear of the unknown grasp which held his feet in relentless captivity. Horrible pains, as of savage wounds, shot through his calves; and in his mind was a vortex of fright mixed with an unquenchable materialism that suggested splinters, loose nails, or some other attribute of a breaking wooden box. Perhaps he screamed. At any rate, he kicked and squirmed frantically and automatically whilst his consciousness was almost eclipsed in a half-swoon.

Instinct guided him in his wriggle through the transom, and in the crawl which followed his jarring thud on the damp ground. He could not walk, it appeared, and the emerging moon must have witnessed a horrible sight as he dragged his bleeding ankles toward the cemetery lodge, his fingers clawing the black mold in brainless haste, and his body responding with that maddening slowness from which one suffers when chased by the phantoms of nightmare. There was evidently, however, no pursuer; for he was alone and alive when Armington, the lodge-keeper, responded to his feeble clawing at the door.

Armington helped Birch to the outside of a spare bed and sent his little son Edwin for Doctor Davis. The afflicted man was fully conscious, but would say nothing of any consequence, merely muttering such things as "Oh, my ankles!", "Let go!", or ". . . shut in the tomb." Then the doctor came with his medicine-case and asked crisp questions, and removed the patient's outer clothing, shoes and socks. The wounds—for both ankles were frightfully lacerated about the Achilles tendons—seemed to puzzle the old physician greatly, and finally almost to frighten him. His questioning grew more than medically tense, and his hands shook as he dressed the mangled members, binding them as if he wished to get the wounds out of sight as quickly as possible.

For an impersonal doctor, Davis's ominous and awestruck cross-examination became very strange indeed as he sought to drain from the weakened undertaker every last detail of his horrible experience. He was oddly anxious to know if Birch were sure—absolutely sure—of the identity of that top coffin of the pile, how he had chosen it, how he had been certain of it as the Fenner coffin in the dark, and how he had distinguished it from the inferior duplicate coffin of vicious Asaph Sawyer. Would the firm Fenner casket have caved in so readily? Davis, an old-time village practitioner, had of course seen both at the respective funerals, as indeed he had attended both Fenner and Sawyer in their last illnesses. He had even wondered, at Sawyer's funeral, how the vindictive farmer had managed to lie straight in a box so closely akin to that of the diminutive Fenner.

After a full two hours Doctor Davis left, urging Birch to insist at all times that his wounds were due entirely to loose nails and splintering wood. What else, he added, could ever in any case be proved or believed? But it would be well to say as little as could be said, and to let no other doctor treat the wounds. Birch heeded this advice all the rest of his life until he told me his story, and when I saw the scars—ancient and whitened as they then were—I agreed that he was wise in so doing. He always remained lame, for the great tendons had been severed; but I think the greatest lameness was in his soul. His thinking processes, once so phlegmatic and logical, had become ineffaceably scarred, and it was pitiful to note his reaction to certain chance allusions such as "Friday," "tomb," "coffin," and words of less obvious concatenation. His frightened horse had gone home, but his frightened wits never quite did that. He changed his business, but something always preyed upon him. It may have been just fear, and it may have been fear mixed with a queer belated sort of remorse for bygone crudities. His drinking, of course, only aggravated what he sought to alleviate.

When Doctor Davis left Birch that night, he had taken a lantern and gone to the old receiving-tomb. The moon was shining on the scattered brick fragments and marred façade, and the latch of the great door yielded readily to a touch from the outside. Steeled by old ordeals in dissecting-rooms, the doctor entered and looked about, stifling the nausea of mind and body that everything in sight and smell induced. He cried aloud once, and a little later gave a gasp that was more terrible than a cry. Then he fled back to the lodge and broke all the rules of his calling by rousing and shaking his patient, and hurling at him a succession of shuddering whispers that seared into the bewildered ears like the hissing of a vitriol.

"It was Asaph's coffin, Birch, just as I thought! I knew his teeth, with the front ones missing on the upper jaw—never, for God's sake, show those wounds! The body was pretty badly gone, but if ever I saw vindictiveness on any face—or former face! . . . You know what a fiend he was for revenge—how he ruined old Raymond thirty years after their boundary suit, and how he stepped on the puppy that snapped at him a year ago last August. . . . He was the devil incarnate, Birch, and I believe his eye-for-an-eye fury could beat time and death! God, his rage—I'd hate to have it aimed at me!

"Why did you do it, Birch? He was a scoundrel, and I don't blame you for giving him a cast-aside coffin, but you always did go too damned far! Well enough to skimp on the thing in some way, but you knew what a little man old Fenner was.

"I'll never get the picture out of my head as long as I live. You kicked hard, for Asaph's coffin was on the floor. His head was broken in, and everything was tumbled about. I've seen sights before, but there was one thing too much here. An eye for an eye! Great heavens, Birch, but you got what you deserved! The skull turned my stomach, but the other was worse—*those ankles cut neatly off to fit Matt Fenner's cast-aside coffin!*"

The Silver Key

When Randolph Carter was thirty he lost the key of the gate of dreams. Prior to that time he had made up for the prosiness of life by nightly excursions to strange and ancient cities beyond space, and lovely, unbelievable garden lands across ethereal seas; but as middle age hardened upon him he felt those liberties slipping away little by little, until at last he was cut off altogether. No more could his galleys sail up the river Oukranos past the gilded spires of Thran, or his elephant caravans tramp through perfumed jungles in Kled, where forgotten palaces with veined ivory columns sleep lovely and unbroken under the moon.

He had read much of things as they are, and talked with too many people. Well-meaning philosophers had taught him to look into the logical relations of things, and analyse the processes which shaped his thoughts and fancies. Wonder had gone away, and he had forgotten that all life is only a set of pictures in the brain, among which there is no difference betwixt those born of real things and those born of inward dreamings, and no cause to value the one above the other. Custom had dinned into his ears a superstitious reverence for that which tangibly and physically exists, and had made him secretly ashamed to dwell in visions. Wise men told him his simple fancies were inane and childish, and even more absurd because their actors persist in fancying them full of meaning and purpose as the blind cosmos grinds aimlessly on from nothing to something and from something back to nothing again, neither heeding nor knowing the wishes or existence of the minds that flicker for a second now and then in the darkness.

They had chained him down to things that are, and had then explained the workings of those things till mystery had gone out of the world. When he complained, and longed to escape into twilight realms where magic moulded all the little vivid fragments and prized

associations of his mind into vistas of breathless expectancy and unquenchable delight, they turned him instead toward the newfound
prodigies of science, bidding him find wonder in the atom's vortex
and mystery in the sky's dimensions. And when he had failed to find
these boons in things whose laws are known and measurable, they
told him he lacked imagination, and was immature because he preferred dream-illusions to the illusions of our physical creation.

So Carter had tried to do as others did, and pretended that the
common events and emotions of earthy minds were more important
than the fantasies of rare and delicate souls. He did not dissent when
they told him that the animal pain of a stuck pig or dyspeptic plough-
man in real life is a greater thing than the peerless beauty of Narath
with its hundred carven gates and domes of chalcedony, which he
dimly remembered from his dreams; and under their guidance he cultivated a painstaking sense of pity and tragedy.

Once in a while, though, he could not help seeing how shallow,
fickle, and meaningless all human aspirations are, and how emptily
our real impulses contrast with those pompous ideals we profess
to hold. Then he would have recourse to the polite laughter they
had taught him to use against the extravagance and artificiality of
dreams; for he saw that the daily life of our world is every inch as extravagant and artificial, and far less worthy of respect because of its
poverty in beauty and its silly reluctance to admit its own lack of reason and purpose. In this way he became a kind of humorist, for he did
not see that even humour is empty in a mindless universe devoid of
any true standard of consistency or inconsistency.

In the first days of his bondage he had turned to the gentle
churchly faith endeared to him by the naive trust of his fathers, for
thence stretched mystic avenues which seemed to promise escape
from life. Only on closer view did he mark the starved fancy and
beauty, the stale and prosy triteness, and the owlish gravity and
grotesque claims of solid truth which reigned boresomely and over-
whelmingly among most of its professors; or feel to the full the
awkwardness with which it sought to keep alive as literal fact the
outgrown fears and guesses of a primal race confronting the unknown. It wearied Carter to see how solemnly people tried to make
earthly reality out of old myths which every step of their boasted science confuted, and this misplaced seriousness killed the attachment
he might have kept for the ancient creeds had they been content to
offer the sonorous rites and emotional outlets in their true guise of
ethereal fantasy.

But when he came to study those who had thrown off the old
myths, he found them even more ugly than those who had not. They

did not know that beauty lies in harmony, and that loveliness of life has no standard amidst an aimless cosmos save only its harmony with the dreams and the feelings which have gone before and blindly moulded our little spheres out of the rest of chaos. They did not see that good and evil and beauty and ugliness are only ornamental fruits of perspective, whose sole value lies in their linkage to what chance made our fathers think and feel, and whose finer details are different for every race and culture. Instead, they either denied these things altogether or transferred them to the crude, vague instincts which they shared with the beasts and peasants; so that their lives were dragged malodorously out in pain, ugliness, and disproportion, yet filled with a ludicrous pride at having escaped from something no more unsound than that which still held them. They had traded the false gods of fear and blind piety for those of license and anarchy.

Carter did not taste deeply of these modern freedoms; for their cheapness and squalor sickened a spirit loving beauty alone while his reason rebelled at the flimsy logic with which their champions tried to gild brute impulse with a sacredness stripped from the idols they had discarded. He saw that most of them, in common with their cast-off priestcraft, could not escape from the delusion that life has a meaning apart from that which men dream into it; and could not lay aside the crude notion of ethics and obligations beyond those of beauty, even when all Nature shrieked of its unconsciousness and impersonal unmorality in the light of their scientific discoveries. Warped and bigoted with preconceived illusions of justice, freedom, and consistency, they cast off the old lore and the old way with the old beliefs; nor ever stopped to think that that lore and those ways were the sole makers of their present thoughts and judgments, and the sole guides and standards in a meaningless universe without fixed aims or stable points of reference. Having lost these artificial settings, their lives grew void of direction and dramatic interest; till at length they strove to drown their ennui in bustle and pretended usefulness, noise and excitement, barbaric display and animal sensation. When these things palled, disappointed, or grew nauseous through revulsion, they cultivated irony and bitterness, and found fault with the social order. Never could they realize that their brute foundations were as shifting and contradictory as the gods of their elders, and that the satisfaction of one moment is the bane of the next. Calm, lasting beauty comes only in a dream, and this solace the world had thrown away when in its worship of the real it threw away the secrets of childhood and innocence.

Amidst this chaos of hollowness and unrest Carter tried to live as befitted a man of keen thought and good heritage. With his dreams fading under the ridicule of the age he could not believe in anything, but the love of harmony kept him close to the ways of his race and station. He walked impassive through the cities of men, and sighed because no vista seemed fully real; because every flash of yellow sunlight on tall roofs and every glimpse of balustraded plazas in the first lamps of evening served only to remind him of dreams he had once known, and to make him homesick for ethereal lands he no longer knew how to find. Travel was only a mockery; and even the Great War stirred him but little, though he served from the first in the Foreign Legion of France. For a while he sought friends, but soon grew weary of the crudeness of their emotions, and the sameness and earthiness of their visions. He felt vaguely glad that all his relatives were distant and out of touch with him, for they would not have understood his mental life. That is, none but his grandfather and great-uncle Christopher could, and they were long dead.

Then he began once more the writing of books, which he had left off when dreams first failed him. But here, too, was there no satisfaction or fulfillment; for the touch of earth was upon his mind, and he could not think of lovely things as he had done of yore. Ironic humor dragged down all the twilight minarets he reared, and the earthy fear of improbability blasted all the delicate and amazing flowers in his faery gardens. The convention of assumed pity spilt mawkishness on his characters, while the myth of an important reality and significant human events and emotions debased all his high fantasy into thin-veiled allegory and cheap social satire. His new novels were successful as his old ones had never been; and because he knew how empty they must be to please an empty herd, he burned them and ceased his writing. They were very graceful novels, in which he urbanely laughed at the dreams he lightly sketched; but he saw that their sophistication had sapped all their life away.

It was after this that he cultivated deliberate illusion, and dabbled in the notions of the bizarre and the eccentric as an antidote for the commonplace. Most of these, however, soon showed their poverty and barrenness; and he saw that the popular doctrines of occultism are as dry and inflexible as those of science, yet without even the slender palliative of truth to redeem them. Gross stupidity, falsehood, and muddled thinking are not dream; and form no escape from life to a mind trained above their own level. So Carter bought stranger books and sought out deeper and more terrible men of fantastic erudition; delving into arcana of consciousness that few have trod, and learning things about the secret pits of life, legend, and immemorial antiquity which disturbed him ever afterward. He decided to live on a rarer plane, and furnished his Boston home to suit his changing moods; one room for each, hung in appropriate colours, furnished with befitting books and objects, and provided with sources of the proper sensations of light, heat, sound, taste, and odour.

Once he heard of a man in the south, who was shunned and feared for the blasphemous things he read in prehistoric books and clay tablets smuggled from India and Arabia. Him he visited living with him and sharing his studies for seven years, till horror overtook them one midnight in an unknown and archaic graveyard, and only one emerged where two had entered. Then he went back to Arkham, the terrible witch-haunted old town of his forefathers in New England, and had experiences in the dark, amidst the hoary willows and tottering gambrel roofs, which made him seal forever certain pages in the diary of a wild-minded ancestor. But these horrors took him only to the edge of reality, and were not of the true dream country he had known in youth; so that at fifty he despaired of any rest or contentment in a world grown too busy for beauty and too shrewd for dreams.

Having perceived at last the hollowness and futility of real things, Carter spent his days in retirement, and in wistful disjointed memories of his dream-filled youth. He thought it rather silly that he bothered to keep on living at all, and got from a South American acquaintance a very curious liquid to take him to oblivion without suffering. Inertia and force of habit, however, caused him to defer action; and he lingered indecisively among thoughts of old times, taking down the strange hangings from his walls and refitting the house as it was in his early boyhood—purple panes, Victorian furniture, and all.

With the passage of time he became almost glad he had lingered, for his relics of youth and his cleavage from the world made life and sophistication seem very distant and unreal; so much so that a touch of magic and expectancy stole back into his nightly slumbers. For years those slumbers had known only such twisted reflections of every-day things as the commonest slumbers know, but now there returned a flicker of something stranger and wilder; something of vaguely awesome imminence which took the form of tensely clear pictures from his childhood days, and made him think of little inconsequential things he had long forgotten. He would often awake calling for his mother and grandfather, both in their graves a quarter of a century.

Then one night his grandfather reminded him of the key. The grey old scholar, as vivid as in life, spoke long and earnestly of their ancient line, and of the strange visions of the delicate and sensitive men who composed it. He spoke of the flame-eyed Crusader who learnt wild secrets of the Saracens that held him captive; and of the first Sir

Randolph Carter who studied magic when Elizabeth was queen. He spoke, too, of that Edmund Carter who had just escaped hanging in the Salem witchcraft, and who had placed in an antique box a great silver key handed down from his ancestors. Before Carter awaked, the gentle visitant had told him where to find that box; that carved oak box of archaic wonder whose grotesque lid no hand had raised for two centuries.

In the dust and shadows of the great attic he found it, remote and forgotten at the back of a drawer in a tall chest. It was about a foot square, and its Gothic carvings were so fearful that he did not marvel no person since Edmund Carter had dared to open it. It gave forth no noise when shaken, but was mystic with the scent of unremembered spices. That it held a key was indeed only a dim legend, and Randolph Carter's father had never known such a box existed. It was bound in rusty iron, and no means was provided for working the formidable lock. Carter vaguely understood that he would find within it some key to the lost gate of dreams, but of where and how to use it his grandfather had told him nothing.

An old servant forced the carven lid, shaking as he did so at the hideous faces leering from the blackened wood, and at some unplaced familiarity. Inside, wrapped in a discoloured parchment, was a huge key of tarnished silver covered with cryptical arabesques; but of any legible explanation there was none. The parchment was voluminous, and held only the strange hieroglyphs of an unknown tongue written with an antique reed. Carter recognized the characters as those he had seen on a certain papyrus scroll belonging to that terrible scholar of the South who had vanished one midnight in a nameless cemetery. The man had always shivered when he read this scroll, and Carter shivered now.

But he cleaned the key, and kept it by him nightly in its aromatic box of ancient oak. His dreams were meanwhile increasing in vividness, and though showing him none of the strange cities and incredible gardens of the old days, were assuming a definite cast whose purpose could not be mistaken. They were calling him back along the years, and with the mingled wills of all his fathers were pulling him toward some hidden and ancestral source. Then he knew he must go into the past and merge himself with old things, and day after day he thought of the hills to the north where haunted Arkham and the rushing Miskatonic and the lonely rustic homestead of his people lay.

In the brooding fire of autumn Carter took the old remembered way past graceful lines of rolling hill and stone-walled meadow, distant vale and hanging woodland, curving road and nestling farmstead, and the crystal windings of the Miskatonic, crossed here and there by rustic bridges of wood or stone. At one bend he saw the group of giant elms among which an ancestor had oddly vanished a century and a half before, and shuddered as the wind blew meaningly through them. Then there was the crumbling farmhouse of old Goody Fowler the witch, with its little evil windows and great roof sloping nearly to the ground on the north side. He speeded up his car as he passed it, and did not slacken till he had mounted the hill where his mother and her fathers before her were born, and where the old white house still looked proudly across the road at the breathlessly lovely panorama of rocky slope and verdant valley, with the distant spires of Kingsport on the horizon, and hints of the archaic, dream-laden sea in the farthest background.

Then came the steeper slope that held the old Carter place he had not seen in over forty years. Afternoon was far gone when he reached the foot, and at the bend half way up he paused to scan the outspread countryside golden and glorified in the slanting floods of magic poured out by a western sun. All the strangeness and expectancy of his recent dreams seemed present in this hushed and unearthly landscape, and he thought of the unknown solitudes of other planets as his eyes traced out the velvet and deserted lawns shining undulant between their tumbled walls, and clumps of faery forest setting off far lines of purple hills beyond hills, and the spectral wooded valley dipping down in shadow to dank hollows where trickling waters crooned and gurgled among swollen and distorted roots.

Something made him feel that motors did not belong in the realm he was seeking, so he left his car at the edge of the forest, and putting the great key in his coat pocket walked on up the hill. Woods now engulfed him utterly, though he knew the house was on a high knoll that cleared the trees except to the north. He wondered how it would look, for it had been left vacant and untended through his neglect since the death of his strange great-uncle Christopher thirty years before. In his boyhood he had revelled through long visits there, and had found weird marvels in the woods beyond the orchard.

Shadows thickened around him, for the night was near. Once a gap in the trees opened up to the right, so that he saw off across leagues of twilight meadow and spied the old Congregational steeple on Central Hill in Kingsport; pink with the last flush of day, the panes of the little round windows blazing with reflected fire. Then, when he was in deep shadow again, he recalled with a start that the glimpse must have come from childish memory alone, since the old white church had long been torn down to make room for the Congregational Hospital. He had read of it with interest, for the paper had told about some strange burrows or passages found in the rocky hill beneath.

Through his puzzlement a voice piped, and he started again at its familiarity after long years. Old Benijah Corey had been his Uncle Christopher's hired man, and was aged even in those far-off times of his boyhood visits. Now he must be well over a hundred, but that piping voice could come from no one else. He could distinguish no words, yet the tone was haunting and unmistakable. To think that "Old Benijy" should still be alive!

"Mister Randy! Mister Randy! Wharbe ye? D'ye want to skeer yer Aunt Marthy plumb to death? Hain't she tuld ye to keep nigh the place in the arternoon an' git back afur dark? Randy! Ran . . . dee! . . . He's the beatin'est boy fer runnin' off in the woods I ever see; haff the time asettin' moonin' raound that snake-den in the upper timber-lot! . . . Hey yew, Ran . . . dee!"

Randolph Carter stopped in the pitch darkness and rubbed his hand across his eyes. Something was queer. He had been somewhere he ought not to be; had strayed very far away to places where he had not belonged, and was now inexcusably late. He had not noticed the time on the Kingsport steeple, though he could easily have made it out with his pocket telescope; but he knew his lateness was something very strange and unprecedented. He was not sure he had his little telescope with him, and put his hand in his blouse pocket to see. No, it was not there, but there was the big silver key he had found in a box somewhere. Uncle Chris had told him something odd once about an old unopened box with a key in it, but Aunt Martha had stopped the story abruptly, saying it was no kind of thing to tell a child whose head was already too full of queer fancies. He tried to recall just where he had found the key, but something seemed very confused. He guessed it was in the attic at home in Boston, and dimly remembered bribing Parks with half his week's allowance to help him open the box and keep quiet about it; but when he remembered this, the face of Parks came up very strangely, as if the wrinkles of long years had fallen upon the brisk little Cockney.

"Ran . . . dee! Ran . . . dee! Hi! Hi! Randy!"

A swaying lantern came around the black bend, and old Benijah pounced on the silent and bewildered form of the pilgrim.

"Durn ye, boy, so thar ye be! Ain't ye got a tongue in yer head, that ye can't answer a body! I ben callin' this haff hour, an' ye must a heerd me long ago! Dun't ye know yer Aunt Marthy's all a-fidget over yer bein' off arter dark? Wait till I tell yer Uncle Chris when he gits hum! Ye'd orta know these here woods ain't no fitten place to be traipsin' this hour! They's things abroad what dun't do nobody no good, as my gran'sir' knowed afur me. Come, Mister Randy, or Hannah wunt keep supper no longer!"

So Randolph Carter was marched up the road where wondering stars glimmered through high autumn boughs. And dogs barked as the yellow light of small-paned windows shone out at the farther turn, and the Pleiades twinkled across the open knoll where a great gambrel roof stood black against the dim west. Aunt Martha was in the doorway, and did not scold too hard when Benijah shoved the truant in. She knew Uncle Chris well enough to expect such things of the Carter blood. Randolph did not show his key, but ate his supper in silence and protested only when bedtime came. He sometimes dreamed better when awake, and he wanted to use that key.

In the morning Randolph was up early, and would have run off to the upper timber-lot if Uncle Chris had not caught him and forced him into his chair by the breakfast table. He looked impatiently around the low-pitched room with the rag carpet and exposed beams and corner-posts, and smiled only when the orchard boughs scratched at the leaded panes of the rear window. The trees and the hills were close to him, and formed the gates of that timeless realm which was his true country.

Then, when he was free, he felt in his blouse pocket for the key; and being reassured, skipped off across the orchard to the rise beyond, where the wooded hill climbed again to heights above even the treeless knoll. The floor of the forest was mossy and mysterious, and great lichened rocks rose vaguely here and there in the dim light like Druid monoliths among the swollen and twisted trunks of a sacred grove. Once in his ascent Randolph crossed a rushing stream whose falls a little way off sang runic incantations to the lurking fauns and aegipans and dryads.

Then he came to the strange cave in the forest slope, the dreaded "snake-den" which country folk shunned, and away from which Benijah had warned him again and again. It was deep; far deeper than anyone but Randolph suspected, for the boy had found a fissure in the farthermost black corner that led to a loftier grotto beyond—a haunting sepulchral place whose granite walls held a curious illusion of conscious artifice. On this occasion he crawled in as usual, lighting his way with matches filched from the sitting-room match-safe, and edging through the final crevice with an eagerness hard to explain even to himself. He could not tell why he approached the farther wall so confidently, or why he instinctively drew forth the great silver key as he did so. But on he went, and when he danced back to the house that night he offered no excuses for his lateness, nor heeded in the least the reproofs he gained for ignoring the noontide dinner-horn altogether.

Now it is agreed by all the distant relatives of Randolph Carter that something occurred to heighten his imagination in his tenth year. His cousin, Ernest B. Aspinwall, Esq., of Chicago, is fully ten years his senior; and distinctly recalls a change in the boy after the autumn of 1883. Randolph had looked on scenes of fantasy that few others can ever have beheld, and stranger still were some of the qualities which he showed in relation to very mundane things. He seemed, in fine, to have picked up an odd gift of prophecy; and reacted unusually to things which, though at the time without meaning, were later found to justify the singular impressions. In subsequent decades as new inventions, new names, and new events appeared one by one in the book of history, people would now and then recall wonderingly how Carter had years before let fall some careless word of undoubted connection with what was then far in the future. He did not himself understand these words, or know why certain things made him feel certain emotions; but fancied that some unremembered dream must be responsible. It was as early as 1897 that he turned pale when some traveller mentioned the French town of Belloy-en-Santerre, and friends remembered it when he was almost mortally wounded there in 1916, while serving with the Foreign Legion in the Great War.

Carter's relatives talk much of these things because he has lately disappeared. His little old servant Parks, who for years bore patiently with his vagaries, last saw him on the morning he drove off alone in his car with a key he had recently found. Parks had helped him get the key from the old box containing it, and had felt strangely affected by the grotesque carvings on the box, and by some other odd quality he could not name. When Carter left, he had said he was going to visit his old ancestral country around Arkham.

Half way up Elm Mountain, on the way to the ruins of the old Carter place, they found his motor set carefully by the roadside; and in it was a box of fragrant wood with carvings that frightened the countrymen who stumbled on it. The box held only a queer parchment whose characters no linguist or palaeographer has been able to decipher or identify. Rain had long effaced any possible footprints, though Boston investigators had something to say about evidences of disturbances among the fallen timbers of the Carter place. It was, they averred, as though someone had groped about the ruins at no distant period. A common white handkerchief found among forest rocks on the hillside beyond cannot be identified as belonging to the missing man.

There is talk of apportioning Randolph Carter's estate among his heirs, but I shall stand firmly against this course because I do not believe he is dead. There are twists of time and space, of vision and reality, which only a dreamer can divine; and from what I know of Carter I think he has merely found a way to traverse these mazes. Whether or not he will ever come back, I cannot say. He wanted the lands of dream he had lost, and yearned for the days of his childhood. Then he found a key, and I somehow believe he was able to use it to strange advantage.

I shall ask him when I see him, for I expect to meet him shortly in a certain dream-city we both used to haunt. It is rumoured in Ulthar, beyond the River Skai, that a new king reigns on the opal throne of Ilek-Vad, that fabulous town of turrets atop the hollow cliffs of glass overlooking the twilight sea wherein the bearded and finny Gnorri build their singular labyrinths, and I believe I know how to interpret this rumour. Certainly, I look forward impatiently to the sight of that great silver key, for in its cryptical arabesques there may stand symbolised all the aims and mysteries of a blindly impersonal cosmos.

The Music of Erich Zann

I have examined maps of the city with the greatest care, yet have never again found the Rue d'Auseil. These maps have not been modern maps alone, for I know that names change. I have, on the contrary, delved deeply into all the antiquities of the place, and have personally explored every region, of whatever name, which could possibly answer to the street I knew as the Rue d'Auseil. But despite all I have done, it remains an humiliating fact that I cannot find the house, the street, or even the locality, where, during the last months of my impoverished life as a student of metaphysics at the university, I heard the music of Erich Zann.

That my memory is broken, I do not wonder; for my health, physical and mental, was gravely disturbed throughout the period of my residence in the Rue d'Auseil, and I recall that I took none of my few acquaintances there. But that I cannot find the place again is both singular and perplexing; for it was within a half-hour's walk of the university and was distinguished by peculiarities which could hardly be forgotten by any one who had been there. I have never met a person who has seen the Rue d'Auseil.

The Rue d'Auseil lay across a dark river bordered by precipitous brick blear-windowed warehouses and spanned by a ponderous bridge of dark stone. It was always shadowy along that river, as if the smoke of neighboring factories shut out the sun perpetually. The river was also odorous with evil stenches which I have never smelled elsewhere, and which may some day help me to find it, since I should recognize them at once. Beyond the bridge were narrow cobbled streets with rails; and then came the ascent, at first gradual, but incredibly steep as the Rue d'Auseil was reached.

I have never seen another street as narrow and steep as the Rue d'Auseil. It was almost a cliff, closed to all vehicles, consisting in several places of flights of steps, and ending at the top in a lofty ivied wall. Its paving was irregular, sometimes stone slabs, sometimes cobblestones, and sometimes bare earth with struggling greenish-grey vegetation. The houses were tall, peaked-roofed, incredibly old, and crazily leaning backward, forward, and sidewise. Occasionally an opposite pair, both leaning forward, almost met across the street like an arch; and certainly they kept most of the light from the ground below. There were a few overhead bridges from house to house across the street.

The inhabitants of that street impressed me peculiarly. At first I thought it was because they were all silent and reticent; but later decided it was because they were all very old. I do not know how I came to live on such a street, but I was not myself when I moved there. I had been living in many poor places, always evicted for want of money; until at last I came upon that tottering house in the Rue d'Auseil kept by the paralytic Blandot. It was the third house from the top of the street, and by far the tallest of them all.

My room was on the fifth story; the only inhabited room there, since the house was almost empty. On the night I arrived I heard strange music from the peaked garret overhead, and the next day asked old Blandot about it. He told me it was an old German viol-player, a strange dumb man who signed his name as Erich Zann, and who played evenings in a cheap theater orchestra; adding that Zann's desire to play in the night after his return from the theater was the reason he had chosen this lofty and isolated garret room, whose single gable window was the only point on the street from which one could look over the terminating wall at the declivity and panorama beyond.

Thereafter I heard Zann every night, and although he kept me awake, I was haunted by the weirdness of his music. Knowing little of the art myself, I was yet certain that none of his harmonies had any relation to music I had heard before; and concluded that he was a composer of highly original genius. The longer I listened, the more I was fascinated, until after a week I resolved to make the old man's acquaintance.

One night as he was returning from his work, I intercepted Zann in the hallway and told him that I would like to know him and be with him when he played. He was a small, lean, bent person, with shabby clothes, blue eyes, grotesque, satyrlike face, and nearly bald head; and at my first words seemed both angered and frightened. My obvious friendliness, however, finally melted him; and he grudgingly motioned to me to follow him up the dark, creaking and rickety attic stairs. His room, one of only two in the steeply pitched garret, was on the west side, toward the high wall that formed the upper end of the street. Its size was very great, and seemed the greater because of its extraordinary barrenness and neglect. Of furniture there was only a narrow iron bedstead, a dingy wash-stand, a small table, a large bookcase, an iron music-rack, and three old-fashioned chairs. Sheets of music were piled in disorder about the floor. The walls were of bare boards, and had probably never known plaster; whilst the abundance of dust and cobwebs made the place seem more deserted than inhabited. Evidently Erich Zann's world of beauty lay in some far cosmos of the imagination.

Motioning me to sit down, the dumb man closed the door, turned the large wooden bolt, and lighted a candle to augment the one he had brought with him. He now removed his viol from its motheaten covering, and taking it, seated himself in the least uncomfortable of the chairs. He did not employ the music-rack, but, offering no choice and playing from memory, enchanted me for over an hour with strains I had never heard before; strains which must have been of his own devising. To describe their exact nature is impossible for one unversed in music. They were a kind of fugue, with recurrent passages of the most captivating quality, but to me were notable for the absence of any of the weird notes I had overheard from my room below on other occasions.

Those haunting notes I had remembered, and had often hummed and whistled inaccurately to myself, so when the player at length laid down his bow I asked him if he would render some of them. As I began my request the wrinkled satyrlike face lost the bored placidity it had possessed during the playing, and seemed to show the same curious mixture of anger and fright which I had noticed when first I accosted the old man. For a moment I was inclined to use persuasion, regarding rather lightly the whims of senility; and even tried to awaken my host's weirder mood by whistling a few of the strains to which I had listened the night before. But I did not pursue this course for more than a moment; for when the dumb musician recognized the whistled air his face grew suddenly distorted with an expression wholly beyond analysis, and his long, cold, bony right hand reached out to stop my mouth and silence the crude imitation. As he did this he further demonstrated his eccentricity by casting a startled glance toward the lone curtained window, as if fearful of some intruder—a glance doubly absurd, since the garret stood high and inaccessible above all the adjacent roofs, this window being the only point on the steep street, as the concierge had told me, from which one could see over the wall at the summit.

The old man's glance brought Blandot's remark to my mind, and with a certain capriciousness I felt a wish to look out over the wide and dizzying panorama of moonlit roofs and city lights beyond the hilltop, which of all the dwellers in the Rue d'Auseil only this crabbed musician could see. I moved toward the window and would have drawn aside the nondescript curtains, when with a frightened rage even greater than before, the dumb lodger was upon me again; this time motioning with his head toward the door as he nervously strove to drag me thither with both hands. Now thoroughly disgusted with my host, I ordered him to release me, and told him I would go at once. His clutch relaxed, and as he saw my disgust and offense, his own anger seemed to subside. He tightened his relaxing grip, but this time in a friendly manner, forcing me into a chair; then with an appearance of wistfulness crossing to the littered table, where he wrote many words with a pencil, in the labored French of a foreigner.

The note which he finally handed me was an appeal for tolerance and forgiveness. Zann said that he was old, lonely, and afflicted with strange fears and nervous disorders connected with his music and with other things. He had enjoyed my listening to his music, and wished I would come again and not mind his eccentricities. But he could not play to another his weird harmonies, and could not bear hearing them from another; nor could he bear having anything in his room touched by another. He had not known until our hallway conversation that I could overhear his playing in my room, and now asked me if I would arrange with Blandot to take a lower room where I could not hear him in the night. He would, he wrote, defray the difference in rent.

As I sat deciphering the execrable French, I felt more lenient toward the old man. He was a victim of physical and nervous suffering, as was I; and my metaphysical studies had taught me kindness. In the silence there came a slight sound from the window—the shutter must have rattled in the night wind, and for some reason I started almost as violently as did Erich Zann. So when I had finished reading, I shook my host by the hand, and departed as a friend.

The next day Blandot gave me a more expensive room on the third floor, between the apartments of an aged money-lender and the room of a respectable upholsterer. There was no one on the fourth floor.

It was not long before I found that Zann's eagerness for my company was not as great as it had seemed while he was persuading me to move down from the fifth story. He did not ask me to call on him, and when I did call he appeared uneasy and played listlessly. This was always at night—in the day he slept and would admit no one. My liking for him did not grow, though the attic room and the weird music seemed to hold an odd fascination for me. I had a curious desire to look out of that window, over the wall and down the unseen slope at the glittering roofs and spires which must lie outspread there. Once I went up to the garret during theater hours, when Zann was away, but the door was locked.

What I did succeed in doing was to overhear the nocturnal playing of the dumb old man. At first I would tip-toe up to my old fifth floor, then I grew bold enough to climb the last creaking staircase to the peaked garret. There in the narrow hall, outside the bolted door with the covered keyhole, I often heard sounds which filled me with an indefinable dread—the dread of vague wonder and brooding mystery. It was not that the sounds were hideous, for they were not; but that they held vibrations suggesting nothing on this globe of earth, and that at certain intervals they assumed a symphonic quality which I could hardly conceive as produced by one player. Certainly, Erich Zann was a genius of wild power. As the weeks passed, the playing grew wilder, whilst the old musician acquired an increasing haggardness and furtiveness pitiful to behold. He now refused to admit me at any time, and shunned me whenever we met on the stairs.

Then one night as I listened at the door, I heard the shrieking viol swell into a chaotic babel of sound; a pandemonium which would have led me to doubt my own shaking sanity had there not come from behind that barred portal a piteous proof that the horror was real—the awful, inarticulate cry which only a mute can utter, and which rises only in moments of the most terrible fear or anguish. I knocked repeatedly at the door, but received no response. Afterward I waited in the black hallway, shivering with cold and fear, till I heard the poor musician's feeble effort to rise from the floor by the aid of a chair. Believing him just conscious after a fainting fit, I renewed my rapping, at the same time calling out my name reassuringly. I heard Zann stumble to the window and close both shutter and sash, then stumble to the door, which he falteringly unfastened to admit me. This time his delight at having me present was real; for his distorted face gleamed with relief while he clutched at my coat as a child clutches at its mother's skirts.

Shaking pathetically, the old man forced me into a chair whilst he sank into another, beside which his viol and bow lay carelessly on the floor. He sat for some time inactive, nodding oddly, but having a paradoxical suggestion of intense and frightened listening. Subsequently he seemed to be satisfied, and crossing to a chair by the table wrote a brief note, handed it to me, and returned to the table, where he began to write rapidly and incessantly. The note implored me in the name of mercy, and for the sake of my own curiosity, to wait where I was while he prepared a full account in German of all the marvels and terrors which beset him. I waited, and the dumb man's pencil flew.

It was perhaps an hour later, while I still waited and while the old musician's feverishly written sheets still continued to pile up, that I saw Zann start as from the hint of a horrible shock. Unmistakably he was looking at the curtained window and listening shudderingly. Then I half fancied I heard a sound myself; though it was not a horrible sound, but rather an exquisitely low and infinitely distant musical note, suggesting a player in one of the neighboring houses, or in some abode beyond the lofty wall over which I had never been able to look. Upon Zann the effect was terrible, for, dropping his pencil, suddenly he rose, seized his viol, and commenced to rend the night with the wildest playing I had ever heard from his bow save when listening at the barred door.

It would be useless to describe the playing of Erich Zann on that dreadful night. It was more horrible than anything I had ever overheard, because I could now see the expression of his face, and could realize that this time the motive was stark fear. He was trying to make a noise; to ward something off or drown something out—what, I could not imagine, awesome though I felt it must be. The playing grew fantastic, delirious, and hysterical, yet kept to the last the qualities of supreme genius which I knew this strange old man possessed. I recognized the air—it was a wild Hungarian dance popular in the theaters, and I reflected for a moment that this was the first time I had ever heard Zann play the work of another composer.

Louder and louder, wilder and wilder, mounted the shrieking and whining of that desperate viol. The player was dripping with an uncanny perspiration and twisted like a monkey, always looking frantically at the curtained window. In his frenzied strains I could almost see shadowy satyrs and bacchanals dancing and whirling insanely through seething abysses of clouds and smoke and lightning. And then I thought I heard a shriller, steadier note that was not from the viol; a calm, deliberate, purposeful, mocking note from far away in the West.

At this juncture the shutter began to rattle in a howling night wind which had sprung up outside as if in answer to the mad playing within. Zann's screaming viol now outdid itself emitting sounds I had never thought a viol could emit. The shutter rattled more loudly, unfastened, and commenced slamming against the window. Then the glass broke shiveringly under the persistent impacts, and the chill wind rushed in, making the candles sputter and rustling the sheets of paper on the table where Zann had begun to write out his horrible secret. I looked at Zann, and saw that he was past conscious observation. His blue eyes were bulging, glassy and sightless, and the frantic playing had become a blind, mechanical, unrecognizable orgy that no pen could even suggest.

A sudden gust, stronger than the others, caught up the manuscript and bore it toward the window. I followed the flying sheets in desperation, but they were gone before I reached the demolished panes. Then I remembered my old wish to gaze from this window, the only window in the Rue d'Auseil from which one might see the slope beyond the wall, and the city outspread beneath. It was very dark, but the city's lights always burned, and I expected to see them there amidst the rain and wind. Yet when I looked from that highest of all gable windows, looked while the candles sputtered and the insane viol howled with the night-wind, I saw no city spread below, and no friendly lights gleamed from remembered streets, but only the blackness of space illimitable; unimagined space alive with motion and music, and having no semblance of anything on earth. And as I stood there looking in terror, the wind blew out both the candles in that ancient peaked garret, leaving me in savage and impenetrable darkness with chaos and pandemonium before me, and the demon madness of that night-baying viol behind me.

I staggered back in the dark, without the means of striking a light, crashing against the table, overturning a chair, and finally groping my way to the place where the blackness screamed with shocking music. To save myself and Erich Zann I could at least try, whatever the powers opposed to me. Once I thought some chill thing brushed me, and I screamed, but my scream could not be heard above that hideous viol. Suddenly out of the blackness the madly sawing bow struck me, and I knew I was close to the player. I felt ahead, touched the back of Zann's chair, and then found and shook his shoulder in an effort to bring him to his senses.

He did not respond, and still the viol shrieked on without slackening. I moved my hand to his head, whose mechanical nodding I was able to stop, and shouted in his ear that we must both flee from the unknown things of the night. But he neither answered me nor abated the frenzy of his unutterable music, while all through the garret strange currents of wind seemed to dance in the darkness and babel. When my hand touched his ear I shuddered, though I knew not why—knew not why till I felt the still face; the ice-cold, stiffened, unbreathing face whose glassy eyes bulged uselessly into the void. And then, by some miracle, finding the door and the large wooden bolt, I plunged wildly away from that glassy-eyed thing in the dark, and from the ghoulish howling of that accursed viol whose fury increased even as I plunged.

Leaping, floating, flying down those endless stairs through the dark house; racing mindlessly out into the narrow, steep, and ancient street of steps and tottering houses; clattering down steps and over cobbles to the lower streets and the putrid canyon-walled river; panting across the great dark bridge to the broader, healthier streets and boulevards we know; all these are terrible impressions that linger with me. And I recall that there was no wind, and that the moon was out, and that all the lights of the city twinkled.

Despite my most careful searches and investigations, I have never since been able to find the Rue d'Auseil. But I am not wholly sorry; either for this or for the loss in undreamable abysses of the closely-written sheets which alone could have explained the music of Erich Zann.

The Call of Cthulhu

Of such great powers or beings there may be conceivably a survival . . . a survival of a hugely remote period when . . . consciousness was manifested, perhaps, in shapes and forms long since withdrawn before the tide of advancing humanity . . . forms of which poetry and legend alone have caught a flying memory and called them gods, monsters, mythical beings of all sorts and kinds . . .

—ALGERNON BLACKWOOD

I. THE HORROR IN THE CLAY

The most merciful thing in the world, I think, is the inability of the human mind to correlate all its contents. We live on a placid island of ignorance in the midst of black seas of infinity, and it was not meant that we should voyage far. The sciences, each straining in its own direction, have hitherto harmed us little; but some day the piecing together of dissociated knowledge will open up such terrifying vistas of reality, and of our frightful position therein, that we shall either go mad from the revelation or flee from the deadly light into the peace and safety of a new dark age.

Theosophists have guessed at the awesome grandeur of the cosmic cycle wherein our world and human race form transient incidents. They have hinted at strange survivals in terms which would freeze the blood if not masked by a bland optimism. But it is not from them that there came the single glimpse of forbidden eons which chills me when I think of it and maddens me when I dream of it. That glimpse, like all dread glimpses of truth, flashed out from an accidental piecing together of separated things—in this case an old newspaper item and

---

(Found among the papers of the late Francis Wayland Thurston, of Boston.)

the notes of a dead professor. I hope that no one else will accomplish this piecing out; certainly, if I live, I shall never knowingly supply a link in so hideous a chain. I think that the professor, too, intended to keep silent regarding the part he knew, and that he would have destroyed his notes had not sudden death seized him.

My knowledge of the thing began in the winter of 1926–27 with the death of my granduncle, George Gammell Angell, Professor Emeritus of Semitic Languages in Brown University, Providence, Rhode Island. Professor Angell was widely known as an authority on ancient inscriptions, and had frequently been resorted to by the heads of prominent museums; so that his passing at the age of ninety-two may be recalled by many. Locally, interest was intensified by the obscurity of the cause of death. The professor had been stricken whilst returning from the Newport boat; falling suddenly, as witnesses said, after having been jostled by a nautical-looking negro who had come from one of the queer dark courts on the precipitous hillside which formed a short cut from the waterfront to the deceased's home in Williams Street. Physicians were unable to find any visible disorder, but concluded after perplexed debate that some obscure lesion of the heart, induced by the brisk ascent of so steep a hill by so elderly a man, was responsible for the end. At the time I saw no reason to dissent from this dictum, but latterly I am inclined to wonder—and more than wonder.

As my granduncle's heir and executor, for he died a childless widower, I was expected to go over his papers with some thoroughness; and for that purpose moved his entire set of files and boxes to my quarters in Boston. Much of the material which I correlated will be later published by the American Archaeological Society, but there was one box which I found exceedingly puzzling, and which I felt much averse from showing to other eyes. It had been locked, and I did not find the key till it occurred to me to examine the personal ring which the professor carried always in his pocket. Then, indeed, I succeeded in opening it, but when I did so seemed only to be confronted by a greater and more closely locked barrier. For what could be the meaning of the queer clay bas-relief and the disjointed jottings, ramblings, and cuttings which I found? Had my uncle, in his latter years, become credulous of the most superficial impostures? I resolved to search out the eccentric sculptor responsible for this apparent disturbance of an old man's peace of mind.

The bas-relief was a rough rectangle less than an inch thick and about five by six inches in area; obviously of modern origin. Its designs, however, were far from modern in atmosphere and suggestion; for, although the vagaries of cubism and futurism are many and wild, they do not often reproduce that cryptic regularity which lurks in prehistoric writing. And writing of some kind the bulk of these designs seemed certainly to be; though my memory, despite much familiarity with the papers and collections of my uncle, failed in any way to identify this particular species, or even hint at its remotest affiliations.

Above these apparent hieroglyphics was a figure of evidently pictorial intent, though its impressionistic execution forbade a very clear idea of its nature. It seemed to be a sort of monster, or symbol representing a monster, of a form which only a diseased fancy could conceive. If I say that my somewhat extravagant imagination yielded simultaneous pictures of an octopus, a dragon, and a human caricature, I shall not be unfaithful to the spirit of the thing. A pulpy, tentacled head surmounted a grotesque and scaly body with rudimentary wings; but it was the *general outline* of the whole which made it most shockingly frightful. Behind the figure was a vague suggestion of a Cyclopean architectural background.

The writing accompanying this oddity was, aside from a stack of press cuttings, in Professor Angell's most recent hand; and made no pretense to literary style. What seemed to be the main document was headed "CTHULHU CULT" in characters painstakingly printed to avoid the erroneous reading of a word so unheard-of. This manuscript was divided into two sections, the first of which was headed "1925—Dream and Dream Work of H. A. Wilcox, 7 Thomas St., Providence, R. I.," and the second, "Narrative of Inspector John R. Legrasse, 121 Bienville St., New Orleans, La., at 1908 A. A. S. Mtg.— Notes on Same, & Prof. Webb's Acct." The other manuscript papers were all brief notes, some of them accounts of the queer dreams of different persons, some of them citations from theosophical books and magazines (notably W. Scott-Elliott's *Atlantis and the Lost Lemuria*), and the rest comments on long-surviving secret societies and hidden cults, with references to passages in such mythological and anthropological source-books as Frazer's *Golden Bough* and Miss Murray's *Witch-Cults in Western Europe*. The cuttings largely alluded to outré mental illness and outbreaks of group folly or mania in the spring of 1925.

The first half of the principal manuscript told a very peculiar tale. It appears that on March 1st, 1925, a thin, dark young man of neurotic and excited aspect had called upon Professor Angell bearing the singular clay bas-relief, which was then exceedingly damp and fresh. His card bore the name of Henry Anthony Wilcox, and my uncle had recognized him as the youngest son of an excellent family slightly known to him, who had latterly been studying sculpture at the

Rhode Island School of Design and living alone at the Fleur-de-Lys Building near that institution. Wilcox was a precocious youth of known genius but great eccentricity, and had from childhood excited attention through the strange stories and odd dreams he was in the habit of relating. He called himself "psychically hypersensitive," but the staid folk of the ancient commercial city dismissed him as merely "queer." Never mingling much with his kind, he had dropped gradually from social visibility, and was now known only to a small group of esthetes from other towns. Even the Providence Art Club, anxious to preserve its conservatism, had found him quite hopeless.

On the occasion of the visit, ran the professor's manuscript, the sculptor abruptly asked for the benefit of his host's archeological knowledge in identifying the hieroglyphics on the bas-relief. He spoke in a dreamy, stilted manner which suggested pose and alienated sympathy; and my uncle showed some sharpness in replying, for the conspicuous freshness of the tablet implied kinship with anything but archeology. Young Wilcox's rejoinder, which impressed my uncle enough to make him recall and record it verbatim, was of a fantastically poetic cast which must have typified his whole conversation, and which I have since found highly characteristic of him. He said, "It is new, indeed, for I made it last night in a dream of strange cities; and dreams are older than brooding Tyre, or the contemplative Sphinx, or garden-girdled Babylon."

It was then that he began that rambling tale which suddenly played upon a sleeping memory and won the fevered interest of my uncle. There had been a slight earthquake tremor the night before, the most considerable felt in New England for some years; and Wilcox's imagination had been keenly affected. Upon retiring, he had had an unprecedented dream of great Cyclopean cities of Titan blocks and sky-flung monoliths, all dripping with green ooze and sinister with latent horror. Hieroglyphics had covered the walls and pillars, and from some undetermined point below had come a voice that was not a voice; a chaotic sensation which only fancy could transmute into sound, but which he attempted to render by the almost unpronounceable jumble of letters, *"Cthulhu fhtagn."*

This verbal jumble was the key to the recollection which excited and disturbed Professor Angell. He questioned the sculptor with scientific minuteness; and studied with almost frantic intensity the bas-relief on which the youth had found himself working, chilled and clad only in his nightclothes, when waking had stolen bewilderingly over him. My uncle blamed his old age, Wilcox afterward said, for his slowness in recognizing both hieroglyphics and pictorial design. Many of his questions seemed highly out of place to his visitor, especially those which tried to connect the latter with strange cults or societies; and Wilcox could not understand the repeated promises of silence which he was offered in exchange for an admission of membership in some widespread mystical or paganly religious body. When Professor Angell became convinced that the sculptor was indeed ignorant of any cult or system of cryptic lore, he besieged his visitor with demands for future reports of dreams. This bore regular fruit, for after the first interview the manuscript records daily calls of the young man, during which he related startling fragments of nocturnal imagery whose burden was always some terrible Cyclopean vista of dark and dripping stone, with a subterrene voice or intelligence shouting monotonously in enigmatical sense-impacts uninscribable save as gibberish. The two sounds most frequently repeated are those rendered by the letters "Cthulhu" and "R'lyeh."

On March 23, the manuscript continued, Wilcox failed to appear; and inquiries at his quarters revealed that he had been stricken with an obscure sort of fever and taken to the home of his family in Waterman Street. He had cried out in the night, arousing several other artists in the building, and had manifested since then only alternations of unconsciousness and delirium. My uncle at once telephoned the family, and from that time forward kept close watch of the case; calling often at the Thayer Street office of Dr. Tobey, whom he learned to be in charge. The youth's febrile mind, apparently, was dwelling on strange things; and the doctor shuddered now and then as he spoke of them. They included not only a repetition of what he had formerly dreamed, but touched wildly on a gigantic thing "miles high" which walked or lumbered about. He at no time fully described this object but occasional frantic words, as repeated by Dr. Tobey, convinced the professor that it must be identical with the nameless monstrosity he had sought to depict in his dream-sculpture. Reference to this object, the doctor added, was invariably a prelude to the young man's subsidence into lethargy. His temperature, oddly enough, was not greatly above normal; but the whole condition was otherwise such as to suggest true fever rather than mental disorder.

On April 2 at about 3 P.M. every trace of Wilcox's malady suddenly ceased. He sat upright in bed, astonished to find himself at home and completely ignorant of what had happened in dream or reality since the night of March 22. Pronounced well by his physician, he returned to his quarters in three days; but to Professor Angell he was of no further assistance. All traces of strange dreaming had vanished with his recovery, and my uncle kept no record of his night-thoughts after a week of pointless and irrelevant accounts of thoroughly usual visions.

Here the first part of the manuscript ended, but references to certain of the scattered notes gave me much material for thought—so much, in fact, that only the ingrained skepticism then forming my philosophy can account for my continued distrust of the artist. The notes in question were those descriptive of the dreams of various persons covering the same period as that in which young Wilcox had had his strange visitations. My uncle, it seems, had quickly instituted a prodigiously far-flung body of inquiries amongst nearly all the friends whom he could question without impertinence, asking for nightly reports of their dreams, and the dates of any notable visions for some time past. The reception of his request seems to have been varied; but he must, at the very least, have received more responses than any ordinary man could have handled without a secretary. This original correspondence was not preserved, but his notes formed a thorough and really significant digest. Average people in society and business—New England's traditional "salt of the earth"—gave an almost completely negative result, though scattered cases of uneasy but formless nocturnal impressions appear here and there, always between March 23 and April 2—the period of young Wilcox's delirium. Scientific men were little more affected, though four cases of vague description suggest fugitive glimpses of strange landscapes, and in one case there is mentioned a dread of something abnormal.

It was from the artists and poets that the pertinent answers came, and I know that panic would have broken loose had they been able to compare notes. As it was, lacking their original letters, I half suspected the compiler of having asked leading questions, or of having edited the correspondence in corroboration of what he had latently resolved to see. That is why I continued to feel that Wilcox, somehow cognizant of the old data which my uncle had possessed, had been imposing on the veteran scientist. These responses from esthetes told a disturbing tale. From February 28 to April 2 a large proportion of them had dreamed very bizarre things, the intensity of the dreams being immeasurably the stronger during the period of the sculptor's delirium. Over a fourth of those who reported anything, reported scenes and half-sounds not unlike those which Wilcox had described; and some of the dreamers confessed acute fear of the gigantic nameless thing visible toward the last. One case, which the note describes with emphasis, was very sad. The subject, a widely known architect with leanings toward theosophy and occultism, went violently insane on the date of young Wilcox's seizure, and expired several months later after incessant screamings to be saved from some escaped denizen of hell. Had my uncle referred to these cases by name instead of merely by number, I should have attempted some corroboration and personal investigation; but as it was, I succeeded in tracing down only a few. All of these, however, bore out the notes in full. I have often wondered if all the objects of the professor's questioning felt as puzzled as did this fraction. It is well that no explanation shall ever reach them.

The press cuttings, as I have intimated, touched on cases of panic, mania, and eccentricity during the given period. Professor Angell must have employed a cutting bureau, for the number of extracts was tremendous, and the sources scattered throughout the globe. Here was a nocturnal suicide in London, where a lone sleeper had leaped from a window after a shocking cry. Here likewise a rambling letter to the editor of a paper in South America, where a fanatic deduces a dire future from visions he has seen. A dispatch from California describes a theosophist colony as donning white robes en masse for some "glorious fulfillment" which never arrives, whilst items from India speak guardedly of serious native unrest toward the end of March. Voodoo orgies multiply in Haiti, and African outposts report ominous mutterings. American officers in the Philippines find certain tribes bothersome about this time, and New York policemen are mobbed by hysterical Levantines on the night of March 22–23. The west of Ireland, too, is full of wild rumour and legendry, and a fantastic painter named Ardois-Bonnot hangs a blasphemous *Dream Landscape* in the Paris spring salon of 1926. And so numerous are the recorded troubles in insane asylums that only a miracle can have stopped the medical fraternity from noting strange parallelisms and drawing mystified conclusions. A weird bunch of cuttings, all told; and I can at this date scarcely envisage the callous rationalism with which I set them aside. But I was then convinced that young Wilcox had known of the older matters mentioned by the professor.

II. THE TALE OF INSPECTOR LEGRASSE

The older matters which had made the sculptor's dream and bas-relief so significant to my uncle formed the subject of the second half of his long manuscript. Once before, it appears, Professor Angell had seen the hellish outlines of the nameless monstrosity, puzzled over the unknown hieroglyphics, and heard the ominous syllables which can be rendered only as "*Cthulhu*"; and all this in so stirring and horrible a connection that it is small wonder he pursued young Wilcox with queries and demands for data.

This earlier experience had come in 1908, seventeen years before, when the American Archaeological Society held its annual meeting in St. Louis. Professor Angell, as befitted one of his authority and attainments, had had a prominent part in all the deliberations; and was one of the first to be approached by the several outsiders who took advantage of the convocation to offer questions for correct answering and problems for expert solution.

The chief of these outsiders, and in a short time the focus of interest for the entire meeting, was a commonplace-looking middle-aged man who had travelled all the way from New Orleans for certain special information unobtainable from any local source. His name was John Raymond Legrasse, and he was by profession an inspector of police. With him he bore the subject of his visit, a grotesque, repulsive, and apparently very ancient stone statuette whose origin he was at a loss to determine.

It must not be fancied that Inspector Legrasse had the least interest in archeology. On the contrary, his wish for enlightenment was prompted by purely professional considerations. The statuette, idol, fetish, or whatever it was, had been captured some months before in the wooded swamps south of New Orleans during a raid on a supposed voodoo meeting; and so singular and hideous were the rites connected with it, that the police could not but realize that they had stumbled on a dark cult totally unknown to them, and infinitely more diabolic than even the blackest of the African voodoo circles. Of its origin, apart from the erratic and unbelievable tales extorted from the captured members, absolutely nothing was to be discovered; hence the anxiety of the police for any antiquarian lore which might help them to place the frightful symbol, and through it track down the cult to its fountain-head.

Inspector Legrasse was scarcely prepared for the sensation which his offering created. One sight of the thing had been enough to throw the assembled men of science into a state of tense excitement, and they lost no time in crowding around him to gaze at the diminutive figure whose utter strangeness and air of genuinely abysmal antiquity hinted so potently at unopened and archaic vistas. No recognized school of sculpture had animated this terrible object, yet centuries and even thousands of years seemed recorded in its dim and greenish surface of unplaceable stone.

The figure, which was finally passed slowly from man to man for close and careful study, was between seven and eight inches in height, and of exquisitely artistic workmanship. It represented a monster of vaguely anthropoid outline, but with an octopuslike head whose face was a mass of feelers, a scaly, rubbery-looking body, prodigious claws on hind and fore feet, and long, narrow wings behind. This thing, which seemed instinct with a fearsome and unnatural malignancy, was of a somewhat bloated corpulence, and squatted evilly on a rectangular block or pedestal covered with undecipherable characters. The tips of the wings touched the back edge of the block, the seat occupied the center, whilst the long, curved claws of the doubled-up, crouching hind legs gripped the front edge and extended a quarter of the way down toward the bottom of the pedestal. The cephalopod head was bent forward, so that the ends of the facial feelers brushed the backs of huge forepaws which clasped the croucher's elevated knees. The aspect of the whole was abnormally lifelike, and the more subtly fearful because its source was so totally unknown. Its vast, awesome, and incalculable age was unmistakable; yet not one link did it show with any known type of art belonging to civilization's youth—or indeed to any other time.

Totally separate and apart, its very material was a mystery; for the soapy, greenish-black stone with its golden or iridescent flecks and striations resembled nothing familiar to geology or mineralogy. The characters along the base were equally baffling; and no member present, despite a representation of half the world's expert learning in this field, could form the least notion of even their remotest linguistic kinship. They, like the subject and material, belonged to something horribly remote and distinct from mankind as we know it; something frightfully suggestive of old and unhallowed cycles of life in which our world and our conceptions have no part.

And yet, as the members severally shook their heads and confessed defeat at the inspector's problem, there was one man in that gathering who suspected a touch of bizarre familiarity in the monstrous shape and writing, and who presently told with some diffidence of the odd trifle he knew. This person was the late William Channing Webb, professor of anthropology in Princeton University, and an explorer of no slight note.

Professor Webb had been engaged, forty-eight years before, in a tour of Greenland and Iceland in search of some Runic inscriptions which he failed to unearth; and whilst high up on the West Greenland coast had encountered a singular tribe or cult of degenerate Eskimos whose religion, a curious form of devil-worship, chilled him with its deliberate bloodthirstiness and repulsiveness. It was a faith of which other Eskimos knew little, and which they mentioned only with shudders, saying that it had come down from horribly ancient eons before ever the world was made. Besides nameless rites and human sacrifices there were certain queer hereditary rituals addressed to a supreme elder devil or *tornasuk*; and of this Professor Webb had taken a careful phonetic copy from an aged *angekok* or wizard-priest, expressing the sounds in Roman letters as best he knew how. But just now of prime significance was the fetish which this cult had cherished, and around which they danced when the aurora leaped high over the ice cliffs. It was, the professor stated, a very crude bas-relief of stone, comprising a hideous picture and some cryptic writing. And as far as he could tell, it was a rough parallel in all essential features of the bestial thing now lying before the meeting.

These data, received with suspense and astonishment by the assembled members, proved doubly exciting to Inspector Legrasse; and he began at once to ply his informant with questions. Having noted and copied an oral ritual among the swamp cult-worshippers his men had arrested, he besought the professor to remember as best he might the syllables taken down amongst the diabolist Eskimos. There then followed an exhaustive comparison of details, and a moment of really awed silence when both detective and scientist agreed on the virtual identity of the phrase common to two hellish rituals so many worlds of distance apart. What, in substance, both the Eskimo wizards and the Louisiana swamp-priests had chanted to their kindred idols was something very like this—the word-divisions being guessed at from traditional breaks in the phrase as chanted aloud:

"Ph-nglui mglw'nafh Cthulhu R'lyeh wgah'nagl fhtagn."

Legrasse had one point in advance of Professor Webb, for several among his mongrel prisoners had repeated to him what older celebrants had told them the words meant. This text, as given, ran something like this:

"In his house at R'lyeh dead Cthulhu waits dreaming."

And now, in response to a general urgent demand, Inspector Legrasse related as fully as possible his experience with the swamp worshippers; telling a story to which I could see my uncle attached profound significance. It savored of the wildest dreams of mythmaker and theosophist, and disclosed an astonishing degree of cosmic imagination among such half-castes and pariahs as might be least expected to possess it.

On November 1, 1907, there had come to New Orleans police a frantic summons from the swamp and lagoon country to the south. The squatters there, mostly primitive but good-natured descendants of Lafitte's men, were in the grip of stark terror from an unknown thing which had stolen upon them in the night. It was voodoo, apparently, but voodoo of a more terrible sort than they had ever known; and some of their women and children had disappeared since the malevolent tom-tom had begun its incessant beating far within the black haunted woods where no dweller ventured. There were insane shouts and harrowing screams, soul-chilling chants and dancing devil-flames; and, the frightened messenger added, the people could stand it no more.

So a body of twenty police, filling two carriages and an automobile, had set out in the late afternoon with the shivering squatter as a guide. At the end of the passable road they alighted, and for miles splashed on in silence through the terrible cypress woods where day never came. Ugly roots and malignant hanging nooses of Spanish moss beset them, and now and then a pile of dank stones or fragments of a rotting wall intensified by its hint of morbid habitation a depression which every malformed tree and every fungous islet combined to create. At length the squatter settlement, a miserable huddle of huts, hove in sight; and hysterical dwellers ran out to cluster around the group of bobbing lanterns. The muffled beat of tom-toms was now faintly audible far, far ahead; and a curdling shriek came at infrequent intervals when the wind shifted. A reddish glare, too, seemed to filter through the pale undergrowth beyond endless avenues of forest night. Reluctant even to be left alone again, each one of the cowed squatters refused point-blank to advance another inch toward the scene of unholy worship, so Inspector Legrasse and his nineteen colleagues plunged on unguided into black arcades of horror that none of them had ever trod before.

The region now entered by the police was one of traditionally evil repute, substantially unknown and untraversed by white men. There were legends of a hidden lake unglimpsed by mortal sight, in which dwelt a huge, formless white polypous thing with luminous eyes; and squatters whispered that bat-winged devils flew up out of caverns in inner earth to worship it at midnight. They said it had been there before D'Iberville, before La Salle, before the Indians, and before even the wholesome beasts and birds of the woods. It was nightmare itself, and to see it was to die. But it made men dream, and so they knew enough to keep away. The present voodoo orgy was, indeed, on the merest fringe of this abhorred area, but that location was bad enough; hence perhaps the very place of the worship had terrified the squatters more than the shocking sounds and incidents.

Only poetry or madness could do justice to the noises heard by Legrasse's men as they plowed on through the black morass toward the red glare and the muffled tom-toms. There are vocal qualities peculiar to men, and vocal qualities peculiar to beasts; and it is terrible to hear the one when the source should yield the other. Animal fury and orgiastic license here whipped themselves to demoniac heights by howls and squawking ecstasies that tore and reverberated through those nighted woods like pestilential tempests from the gulfs of hell. Now and then the less organized ululations would cease, and from what seemed a well-drilled chorus of hoarse voices would rise in singsong chant that hideous phrase or ritual:

"Ph'nglui mglw'nafh Cthulhu R'lyeh wgah'nagl fhtagn."

Then the men, having reached a spot where the trees were thinner, came suddenly in sight of the spectacle itself. Four of them reeled, one fainted, and two were shaken into a frantic cry which the mad cacophony of the orgy fortunately deadened. Legrasse dashed swamp water on the face of the fainting man, and all stood trembling and nearly hypnotized with horror.

In a natural glade of the swamp stood a grassy island of perhaps an acre's extent, clear of trees and tolerably dry. On this now leaped and twisted a more indescribable horde of human abnormality than any but a Sime or an Angarola could paint. Void of clothing, this hybrid spawn were braying, bellowing and writhing about a monstrous ring-shaped bonfire; in the center of which, revealed by occasional rifts in the curtain of flame, stood a great granite monolith some eight feet in height; on top of which, incongruous in its diminutiveness, rested the noxious carven statuette. From a wide circle of ten scaffolds set up at regular intervals with the flame-girt monolith as a center hung, head downward, the oddly marred bodies of the helpess squatters who had disappeared. It was inside this circle that the ring of wor-shipers jumped and roared, the general direction of the mass motion being from left to right in endless bacchanale between the ring of bodies and the ring of fire.

It may have been only imagination and it may have been only echoes which induced one of the men, an excitable Spaniard, to fancy he heard antiphonal responses to the ritual from some far and unillu-mined spot deeper within the wood of ancient legendry and horror. This man, Joseph D. Galvez, I later met and questioned; and he proved distractingly imaginative. He indeed went so far as to hint of the faint beating of great wings, and of a glimpse of shining eyes and mountainous white bulk beyond the remotest trees—but I suppose he had been hearing too much native superstition.

Actually, the horrified pause of the men was of comparatively brief duration. Duty came first; and although there must have been nearly a hundred mongrel celebrants in the throng, the police relied on their firearms and plunged determinedly into the nauseous rout. For five minutes the resultant din and chaos were beyond descrip-tion. Wild blows were struck, shots were fired, and escapes were made; but in the end Legrasse was able to count some forty-seven sullen prisoners, whom he forced to dress in haste and fall into line between two rows of policemen. Five of the worshipers lay dead, and two severely wounded ones were carried away on improvised stretch-ers by their fellow-prisoners. The image on the monolith, of course, was carefully removed and carried back by Legrasse.

Examined at headquarters after a trip of intense strain and weari-ness, the prisoners all proved to be men of a very low, mixed-blooded, and mentally aberrant type. Most were seamen, and a sprinkling of negroes and mulattoes, largely West Indians or Brava Portuguese from the Cape Verde Islands, gave a coloring of voodooism to the heterogeneous cult. But before many questions were asked, it became manifest that something far deeper and older than negro fetishism was involved. Degraded and ignorant as they were, the creatures held with surprising consistency to the central idea of their loathsome faith.

They worshiped, so they said, the Great Old Ones who lived ages before there were any men, and who came to the young world out of the sky. These Old Ones were gone now, inside the earth and under the sea; but their dead bodies had told their secrets in dreams to the first man, who formed a cult which had never died. This was that cult, and the prisoners said it had always existed and always would exist, hidden in distant wastes and dark places all over the world until the time when the great priest Cthulhu, from his dark house in the mighty city of R'lyeh under the waters, should rise and bring the earth again beneath his sway. Some day he would call, when the stars were ready, and the secret cult would always be waiting to liber-ate him.

Meanwhile no more must be told. There was a secret which even torture could not extract. Mankind was not absolutely alone among the conscious things of earth, for shapes came out of the dark to visit the faithful few. But these were not the Great Old Ones. No man had ever seen the Old Ones. The carven idol was great Cthulhu, but none might say whether or not the others were precisely like him. No one could read the old writing now, but things were told by word of mouth. The chanted ritual was not the secret—that was never spo-ken aloud, only whispered. The chant meant only this: "In his house at R'lyeh dead Cthulhu waits dreaming."

Only two of the prisoners were found sane enough to be hanged, and the rest were committed to various institutions. All denied a part in the ritual murders, and averred that the killing had been done by Black-winged Ones which had come to them from their immemorial meeting-place in the haunted wood. But of those mysterious allies no coherent account could ever be gained. What the police did extract came mainly from an immensely aged mestizo named Castro, who claimed to have sailed to strange ports and talked with undying lead-ers of the cult in the mountains of China.

Old Castro remembered bits of hideous legend that paled the speculations of theosophists and made man and the world seem recent and transient indeed. There had been eons when other Things ruled on the earth, and They had had great cities. Remains of Them, he said the deathless Chinamen had told him, were still to be found as Cyclopean stones on islands in the Pacific. They all died vast epochs of time before man came, but there were arts which could revive Them when the stars had come round again to the right positions in the cycle of eternity. They had, indeed, come themselves from the stars, and brought Their images with Them.

These Great Old Ones, Castro continued, were not composed altogether of flesh and blood. They had shape—for did not this star-fashioned image prove it?—but that shape was not made of matter. When the stars were right, They could plunge from world to world through the sky; but when the stars were wrong, They could not live. But although They no longer lived, They would never really die. They all lay in stone houses in Their great city of R'lyeh, preserved by the spells of mighty Cthulhu for a glorious resurrection when the stars and the earth might once more be ready for Them. But at that time some force from outside must serve to liberate Their bodies. The spells that preserved Them intact likewise prevented Them from making an initial move, and They could only lie awake in the dark and think whilst uncounted millions of years rolled by. They knew all that was occurring in the universe, for Their mode of speech was transmitted thought. Even now They talked in Their tombs. When, after infinities of chaos, the first men came, the Great Old Ones spoke to the sensitive among them by molding their dreams; for only thus could Their language reach the fleshy minds of mammals.

Then, whispered Castro, those first men formed the cult around small idols which the Great Ones showed them; idols brought in dim eras from dark stars. That cult would never die till the stars came right again, and the secret priests would take great Cthulhu from His tomb and revive His subjects and resume His rule of earth. The time would be easy to know, for then mankind would have become as the Great Old Ones; free and wild and beyond good and evil, with laws and morals thrown aside and all men shouting and killing and reveling in joy. Then the liberated Old Ones would teach them new ways to shout and kill and revel and enjoy themselves, and all the earth would flame with a holocaust of ecstasy and freedom. Meanwhile the cult, by appropriate rites, must keep alive the memory of those ancient ways and shadow forth the prophecy of their return.

In the elder time chosen men had talked with the entombed Old Ones in dreams, but then something had happened. The great stone city R'lyeh, with its monoliths and sepulchers, had sunk beneath the waves; and the deep waters, full of the one primal mystery through which not even thought can pass, had cut off the spectral intercourse. But memory never died, and high priests said that the city would rise again when the stars were right. Then came out of the earth the black spirits of earth, moldy and shadowy, and full of dim rumors picked up in caverns beneath forgotten sea-bottoms. But of them old Castro dared not speak much. He cut himself off hurriedly, and no amount of persuasion or subtlety could elicit more in this direction. The *size* of the Old Ones, too, he curiously declined to mention. Of the cult, he said that he thought the center lay amid the pathless deserts of Arabia, where Irem, the City of Pillars, dreams hidden and untouched. It was not allied to the European witch-cult, and was virtually unknown beyond its members. No book had ever really hinted of it, though the deathless Chinamen said that there were double meanings in the *Necronomicon* of the mad Arab Abdul Alhazred which the initiated might read as they chose, especially the much-discussed couplet:

That is not dead which can eternal lie,
And with strange eons even death may die.

Legrasse, deeply impressed and not a little bewildered, had inquired in vain concerning the historic affiliations of the cult. Castro, apparently, had told the truth when he said that it was wholly secret. The authorities at Tulane University could shed no light upon either cult or image, and now the detective had come to the highest authorities in the country and met with no more than the Greenland tale of Professor Webb.

The feverish interest aroused at the meeting by Legrasse's tale, corroborated as it was by the statuette, is echoed in the subsequent correspondence of those who attended; although scant mention occurs in the formal publication of the society. Caution is the first care of those accustomed to face occasional charlatanry and imposture. Legrasse for some time lent the image to Professor Webb, but at the latter's death it was returned to him and remains in his possession, where I viewed it not long ago. It is truly a terrible thing, and unmistakably akin to the dream-sculpture of young Wilcox.

That my uncle was excited by the tale of the sculptor I did not wonder, for what thoughts must arise upon hearing, after a knowledge of what Legrasse had learned of the cult, of a sensitive young man who had *dreamed* not only the figure and exact hieroglyphics of the swamp-found image and the Greenland devil tablet, but had come *in his dreams* upon at least three of the precise words of the formula uttered alike by Eskimo diabolists and mongrel Louisianans?

Professor Angell's instant start on an investigation of the utmost thoroughness was eminently natural; though privately I suspected young Wilcox of having heard of the cult in some indirect way, and of having invented a series of dreams to heighten and continue the mystery at my uncle's expense. The dream-narratives and cuttings collected by the professor were, of course, strong corroboration; but the rationalism of my mind and the extravagance of the whole subject led me to adopt what I thought the most sensible conclusions. So, after thoroughly studying the manuscript again and correlating the theosophical and anthropological notes with the cult narrative of Legrasse, I made a trip to Providence to see the sculptor and give him the rebuke I thought proper for so boldly imposing upon a learned and aged man.

Wilcox still lived alone in the Fleur-de-Lys Building in Thomas Street, a hideous Victorian imitation of Seventeenth Century Breton architecture which flaunts its stuccoed front amidst the lovely Colonial houses on the ancient hill, and under the very shadow of the finest Georgian steeple in America. I found him at work in his rooms, and at once conceded from the specimens scattered about that his genius is indeed profound and authentic. He will, I believe, be heard from sometime as one of the great decadents; for he has crystallized in clay and will one day mirror in marble those nightmares and fantasies which Arthur Machen evokes in prose, and Clark Ashton Smith makes visible in verse and in painting.

Dark, frail, and somewhat unkempt in aspect, he turned languidly at my knock and asked me my business without rising. When I told him who I was, he displayed some interest; for my uncle had excited his curiosity in probing his strange dreams, yet had never explained the reason for the study. I did not enlarge his knowledge in this regard, but sought with some subtlety to draw him out.

In a short time I became convinced of his absolute sincerity for he spoke of the dreams in a manner none could mistake. They and their subconscious residuum had influenced his art profoundly, and he showed me a morbid statue whose contours almost made me shake with the potency of its black suggestion. He could not recall having seen the original of this thing except in his own dream bas-relief, but the outlines had formed themselves insensibly under his hands. It was, no doubt, the giant shape he had raved of in delirium. That he really knew nothing of the hidden cult, save from what my uncle's relentless catechism had let fall, he soon made clear; and again I strove to think of some way in which he could possibly have received the weird impressions.

He talked of his dreams in a strangely poetic fashion; making me see with terrible vividness the damp Cyclopean city of slimy green stone—whose *geometry*, he oddly said, was *all wrong*—and hear with frightened expectancy the ceaseless, half-mental calling from underground: *"Cthulhu fhtagn," "Cthulhu fhtagn."*

These words had formed part of that dread ritual which told of dead Cthulhu's dream-vigil in his stone vault at R'lyeh, and I felt deeply moved despite my rational beliefs. Wilcox, I was sure, had heard of the cult in some casual way, and had soon forgotten it amidst the mass of his equally weird reading and imagining. Later, by virtue of its sheer impressiveness, it had found subconscious expression in dreams, in the bas-relief, and in the terrible statue I now beheld; so that his imposture upon my uncle had been a very innocent one. The youth was of a type, at once slightly affected and slightly ill-mannered, which I could never like; but I was willing enough now to admit both his genius and his honesty. I took leave of him amicably, and wish him all the success his talent promises.

The matter of the cult still remained to fascinate me, and at times I had visions of personal fame from researches into its origin and connections. I visited New Orleans, talked with Legrasse and others of that old-time raiding-party, saw the frightful image, and even questioned such of the mongrel prisoners as still survived. Old Castro, unfortunately, had been dead for some years. What I now heard so graphically at first hand, though it was really no more than a detailed confirmation of what my uncle had written, excited me afresh; for I felt sure that I was on the track of a very real, very secret, and very ancient religion whose discovery would make me an anthropologist of note. My attitude was still one of absolute materialism *as I wish it still were*, and I discounted with a most inexplicable perversity the coincidence of the dream notes and odd cuttings collected by Professor Angell.

One thing which I began to suspect, and which I now fear I *know*, is that my uncle's death was far from natural. He fell on a narrow hill street leading up from an ancient waterfront swarming with foreign mongrels, after a careless push from a negro sailor. I did not forget the mixed blood and marine pursuits of the cult-members in Louisiana, and would not be surprised to learn of secret methods and poison needles as ruthless and as anciently known as the cryptic rites and beliefs. Legrasse and his men, it is true, have been let alone; but in Norway a certain seaman who saw things is dead. Might not the deeper inquiries of my uncle after encountering the sculptor's data have come to sinister ears? I think Professor Angell died because he knew too much, or because he was likely to learn too much. Whether I shall go as he did remains to be seen, for I have learned much now.

III. THE MADNESS FROM THE SEA

If heaven ever wishes to grant me a boon, it will be a total effacing of the results of a mere chance which fixed my eye on a certain stray piece of shelf-paper. It was nothing on which I would naturally have stumbled in the course of my daily round, for it was an old number of an Australian journal, *Sydney Bulletin* for April 18, 1925. It had escaped even the cutting bureau which had at the time of its issuance been avidly collecting material for my uncle's research.

I had largely given over my inquiries into what Professor Angell called the "Cthulhu Cult," and was visiting a learned friend of Paterson, New Jersey; the curator of a local museum and a mineralogist of note. Examining one day the reserve specimens roughly set on the storage shelves in a rear room of the museum, my eye was caught by an odd picture in one of the old papers spread beneath the stones. It was the *Sydney Bulletin* I have mentioned, for my friend has wide affiliations in all conceivable foreign parts; and the picture was a half-tone cut of a hideous stone image almost identical with that which Legrasse had found in the swamp.

Eagerly clearing the sheet of its precious contents, I scanned the item in detail; and was disappointed to find it of only moderate length. What it suggested, however, was of portentous significance to my flagging quest; and I carefully tore it out for immediate action. It read as follows:

MYSTERY DERELICT FOUND AT SEA

Vigilant Arrives with Helpless Armed New Zealand Yacht in Tow. One Survivor and Dead Man Found Aboard. Tale of Desperate Battle and Deaths at Sea. Rescued Seaman Refuses Particulars of Strange Experience. Odd Idol Found in His Possession. Inquiry to Follow.

The Morrison Co.'s freighter *Vigilant*, bound from Valparaiso, arrived this morning at its wharf in Darling Harbour, having in tow the battled and disabled but heavily armed steam yacht *Alert* of Dunedin, N. Z., which was sighted April 12th in S. Latitude 34° 21', W. Longitude 152° 17', with one living and one dead man aboard.

The *Vigilant* left Valparaiso March 25th, and on April 2d was driven considerably south of her course by exceptionally heavy storms and monster waves. On April 12th the derelict was sighted; and though apparently deserted, was found upon boarding to contain one survivor in a half-delirious condition and one man who had evidently been dead for more than a week.

The living man was clutching a horrible stone idol of unknown origin, about a foot in height, regarding whose nature authorities at Sydney University, the Royal Society, and the Museum in College

Street all profess complete bafflement, and which the survivor says he found in the cabin of the yacht, in a small carved shrine of common pattern.

This man, after recovering his senses, told an exceedingly strange story of piracy and slaughter. He is Gustaf Johansen, a Norwegian of some intelligence, and had been second mate of the two-masted schooner *Emma* of Auckland, which sailed for Callao February 20th, with a complement of eleven men.

The *Emma*, he says, was delayed and thrown widely south of her course by the great storm of March 1st, and on March 22d, in S. Latitude 49° 51', W. Longitude 128° 34', encountered the *Alert*, manned by a queer and evil-looking crew of Kanakas and half-castes. Being ordered peremptorily to turn back, Capt. Collins refused; whereupon the strange crew began to fire savagely and without warning upon the schooner with a peculiarly heavy battery of brass cannon forming part of the yacht's equipment.

The *Emma*'s men showed fight, says the survivor, and though the schooner began to sink from shots beneath the waterline they managed to heave alongside their enemy and board her, grappling with the savage crew on the yacht's deck, and being forced to kill them all, the number being slightly superior, because of their particularly abhorrent and desperate though rather clumsy mode of fighting.

Three of the *Emma*'s men, including Capt. Collins and First Mate Green, were killed; and the remaining eight under Second Mate Johansen proceeded to navigate the captured yacht, going ahead in their original direction to see if any reason for their ordering back had existed.

The next day, it appears, they raised and landed on a small island, although none is known to exist in that part of the ocean; and six of the men somehow died ashore, though Johansen is queerly reticent about this part of his story and speaks only of their falling into a rock chasm.

Later, it seems, he and one companion boarded the yacht and tried to manage her, but were beaten about by the storm of April 2d.

From that time till his rescue on the 12th, the man remembers little, and he does not even recall when William Briden, his companion, died. Briden's death reveals no apparent cause, and was probably due to excitement or exposure.

Cable advices from Dunedin report that the *Alert* was well known there as an island trader, and bore an evil reputation along the waterfront. It was owned by a curious group of half-castes whose frequent meetings and night trips to the woods attracted no little curiosity; and it had set sail in great haste just after the storm and earth tremors of March 1st.

Our Auckland correspondent gives the *Emma* and her crew an

excellent reputation, and Johansen is described as a sober and worthy man.

The admiralty will institute an inquiry on the whole matter beginning tomorrow, at which every effort will be made to induce Johansen to speak more freely than he has done hitherto.

This was all, together with the picture of the hellish image; but what a train of ideas it started in my mind! Here were new treasuries of data on the Cthulhu Cult, and evidence that it had strange interests at sea as well as on land. What motive prompted the hybrid crew to order back the *Emma* as they sailed about with their hideous idol? What was the unknown island on which six of the *Emma*'s crew had died, and about which the mate Johansen was so secretive? What had the vice-admiralty's investigation brought out, and what was known of the noxious cult in Dunedin? And most marvelous of all, what deep and more than natural linkage of dates was this which gave a malign and now undeniable significance to the various turns of event so carefully noted by my uncle?

March 1st—our February 28th according to the International Date Line—the earthquake and storm had come. From Dunedin the *Alert* and her noisome crew had darted eagerly forth as if imperiously summoned, and on the other side of the earth poets and artists had begun to dream of a strange, dank Cyclopean city whilst a young sculptor had molded in his sleep the form of the dreaded Cthulhu. March 23rd the crew of the *Emma* landed on an unknown island and left six men dead; and on that date the dreams of sensitive men assumed a heightened vividness and darkened with dread of a giant monster's malign pursuit, whilst an architect had gone mad and a sculptor had lapsed suddenly into delirium! And what of this storm of April 2d—the date on which all dreams of the dank city ceased, and Wilcox emerged unharmed from the bondage of strange fever? What of all this—and of those hints of old Castro about the sunken, star-born Old Ones and their coming reign; their faithful cult *and their mastery of dreams*? Was I tottering on the brink of cosmic horrors beyond man's power to bear? If so, they must be horrors of the mind alonefo in some way the second of April had put a stop to whatever monstrous menace had begun its siege of mankind's soul.

That evening, after a day of hurried cabling and arranging, I bade my host adieu and took a train for San Francisco. In less than a month I was in Dunedin: where, however, I found that little was known of the strange cult-members who had lingered in the old sea taverns. Waterfront scum was far too common for special mention; though there was vague talk about one inland trip these mongrels had made, during which faint drumming and red flame were noted on the distant hills.

In Auckland I learned that Johansen had returned *with yellow hair turned white* after a perfunctory and inconclusive questioning at Sydney, and had thereafter sold his cottage in West Street and sailed with his wife to his old home in Oslo. Of his stirring experience he would tell his friends no more than he had told the admiralty officials, and all they could do was to give me his Oslo address.

After that I went to Sydney and talked profitlessly with seamen and members of the vice-admiralty court. I saw the *Alert*, now sold and in commercial use, at Circular Quay in Sydney Cove, but gained nothing from its noncommittal bulk. The crouching image with its cuttlefish head, dragon body, scaly wings, and hieroglyphed pedestal, was preserved in the Museum at Hyde Park; and I studied it long and well, finding it a thing of balefully exquisite workmanship, and with the same utter mystery, terrible antiquity, and unearthly strangeness of material which I had noted in Legrasse's smaller specimen. Geologists, the curator told me, had found it a monstrous puzzle; for they vowed that the world held no rock like it. Then I thought with a shudder of what old Castro had told Legrasse about the primal Great Ones: "They had come from the stars, and had brought Their images with Them."

Shaken with such a mental revolution as I had never before known, I now resolved to visit Mate Johansen in Oslo. Sailing for London, I re-embarked at once for the Norwegian capital; and one autumn day landed at the trim wharves in the shadow of the Egeberg.

Johansen's address, I discovered, lay in the Old Town of King Harold Haardrada, which kept alive the name of Oslo during all the centuries that the greater city masqueraded as "Christiania." I made the brief trip by taxicab, and knocked with palpitant heart at the door of a neat and ancient building with plastered front. A sad-faced woman in black answered my summons, and I was stung with disappointment when she told me in halting English that Gustaf Johansen was no more.

He had not long survived his return, said his wife, for the doings at sea in 1925 had broken him. He had told her no more than he had told the public, but had left a long manuscript—of "technical matters" as he said—written in English, evidently in order to safeguard her from the peril of casual perusal. During a walk through a narrow lane near the Gothenburg dock, a bundle of papers falling from an attic window had knocked him down. Two Lascar sailors at once helped him to his feet, but before the ambulance could reach him he was dead. Physicians found no adequate cause for the end, and laid it to heart trouble and a weakened constitution.

I now felt gnawing at my vitals that dark terror which will never leave me till I, too, am at rest; "accidentally" or otherwise. Persuading the widow that my connection with her husband's "technical matters" was sufficient to entitle me to his manuscript, I bore the document away and began to read it on the London boat.

It was a simple, rambling thing—a naïve sailor's effort at a post-facto diary—and strove to recall day by day that last awful voyage. I can not attempt to translate it verbatim in all its cloudiness and redundance, but I will tell its gist enough to show why the sound of the water against the vessel's sides became so unendurable to me that I stopped my ears with cotton.

Johansen, thank God, did not know quite all, even though he saw the city and the Thing, but I shall never sleep calmly again when I think of the horrors that lurk ceaselessly behind life in time and in space, and of those unhallowed blasphemies from elder stars which dream beneath the sea, known and favored by a nightmare cult ready and eager to loose them on the world whenever another earthquake shall heave their monstrous stone city again to the sun and air.

Johansen's voyage had begun just as he told it to the vice-admiralty. The *Emma*, in ballast, had cleared Auckland on February 20th, and had felt the full force of that earthquake-born tempest which must have heaved up from the sea-bottom the horrors that filled men's dreams. Once more under control, the ship was making good progress when held up by the *Alert* on March 22nd, and I could feel the mate's regret as he wrote of her bombardment and sinking. Of the swarthy cult-fiends on the *Alert* he speaks with significant horror. There was some peculiarly abominable quality about them which made their destruction seem almost a duty, and Johansen shows ingenuous wonder at the charge of ruthlessness brought against his party during the proceedings of the court of inquiry. Then, driven ahead by curiosity in their captured yacht under Johansen's command, the men sight a great stone pillar sticking out of the sea, and in S. Latitude 47° 9', W. Longitude 126° 43', come upon a coast-line of mingled mud, ooze, and weedy Cyclopean masonry which can be nothing less than the tangible substance of earth's supreme terror—the nightmare corpse-city of R'lyeh, that was built in measureless eons behind history by the vast, loathsome shapes that seeped down from the dark stars. There lay great Cthulhu and his hordes, hidden in green slimy vaults and sending out at last, after cycles incalculable, the thoughts that spread fear to the dreams of the sensitive and called imperiously to the faithful to come on a pilgrimage of liberation and restoration. All this Johansen did not suspect, but God knows he soon saw enough!

I suppose that only a single mountain-top, the hideous monolith-crowned citadel whereon great Cthulhu was buried, actually emerged from the waters. When I think of the *extent* of all that may be brooding down there I almost wish to kill myself forthwith. Johansen and his men were awed by the cosmic majesty of this dripping Babylon of elder demons, and must have guessed without guidance that it was nothing of this or of any sane planet. Awe at the unbelievable size of the greenish stone blocks, at the dizzying height of the great carven monolith, and at the stupefying identity of the colossal statues and bas-reliefs with the queer image found in the shrine on the *Alert*, is poignantly visible in every line of the mate's frightened description.

Without knowing what futurism is like, Johansen achieved something very close to it when he spoke of the city; for instead of describing any definite structure of building, he dwells only on the broad impressions of vast angles and stone surfaces—surfaces too great to belong to any thing right or proper for this earth, and impious with horrible images and hieroglyphs. I mention his talk about *angles* because it suggests something Wilcox had told me of his awful dreams. He had said that the *geometry* of the dream-place he saw was abnormal, non-Euclidean, and loathsomely redolent of spheres and dimensions apart from ours. Now an unlettered seaman felt the same thing whilst gazing at the terrible reality.

Johansen and his men landed at a sloping mud-bank on this monstrous acropolis, and clambered slipperily up over titan oozy blocks which could have been no mortal staircase. The very sun of heaven seemed distorted when viewed through the polarizing miasma welling out from this sea-soaked perversion, and twisted menace and suspense lurked leeringly in those crazily elusive angles of carven rock where a second glance showed concavity after the first showed convexity.

Something very like fright had come over all the explorers before anything more definite than rock and ooze and weed was seen. Each would have fled had he not feared the scorn of the others, and it was only half-heartedly that they searched—vainly, as it proved—for some portable souvenir to bear away.

It was Rodriguez the Portuguese who climbed up the foot of the monolith and shouted of what he had found. The rest followed him, and looked curiously at the immense carved door with the now familiar squid-dragon bas-relief. It was, Johansen said, like a great barn-door; and they all felt that it was a door because of the ornate lintel, threshold, and jambs around it, though they could not decide whether it lay flat like a trap door or slantwise like an outside cellar-door. As Wilcox would have said, the geometry of the place was all wrong. One could not be sure that the sea and the ground were hori-

zontal, hence the relative position of everything else seemed fantas-
mally variable.

Briden pushed at the stone in several places without result. Then
Donovan felt over it delicately around the edge, pressing each point
separately as he went. He climbed interminably along the grotesque
stone molding—that is, one would call it climbing if the thing was
not after all horizontal—and the men wondered how any door in
the universe could be so vast. Then, very softly and slowly, the acre-
great panel began to give inward at the top; and they saw that it was
balanced.

Donovan slid or somehow propelled himself down or along the
jamb and rejoined his fellows, and everyone watched the queer reces-
sion of the monstrously carven portal. In this fantasy of prismatic
distortion it moved anomalously in a diagonal way, so that all the
rules of matter and perspective seemed upset.

The aperture was black with a darkness almost material. That
tenebrousness was indeed a *positive quality*; for it obscured such
parts of the inner walls as ought to have been revealed, and actually
burst forth like smoke from its eon-long imprisonment, visibly dark-
ening the sun as it slunk away into the shrunken and gibbous sky on
flapping membranous wings. The odor arising from the newly opened
depths was intolerable, and at length the quick-eared Hawkins thought
he heard a nasty, slopping sound down there. Everyone listened,
and everyone was listening still when It lumbered slobberingly into
sight and gropingly squeezed Its gelatinous green immensity through
the black doorway into the tainted outside air of that poison city of
madness.

Poor Johansen's handwriting almost gave out when he wrote of
this. Of the six men who never reached the ship, he thinks two perished of pure fright in that accursed instant. The Thing can not be
described—there is no langauge for such abysms of shrieking and immemorial lunacy, such eldritch contradictions of all matter, force,
and cosmic order. A mountain walked or stumbled. God! What wonder that across the earth a great architect went mad, and poor Wilcox
raved with fever in that telepathic instant? The Thing of the idols,
the green, sticky spawn of the stars, had awaked to claim his own.
The stars were right again, and what an age-old cult had failed to
do by design, a band of innocent sailors had done by accident. After
vigintillions of years great Cthulhu was loose again, and ravening for
delight.

Three men were swept up by the flabby claws before anybody
turned. God rest them, if there be any rest in the universe. They were
Donovan, Guerrera and Angstrom. Parker slipped as the other three

were plunging frenziedly over endless vistas of green-crusted rock to the boat, and Johansen swears he was swallowed up by an angle of masonry which shouldn't have been there; an angle which was acute, but behaved as if it were obtuse. So only Briden and Johansen reached the boat, and pulled desperately for the *Alert* as the mountainous monstrosity flopped down the slimy stones and hesitated, floundering at the edge of the water.

Steam had not been suffered to go down entirely, despite the departure of all hands for the shore; and it was the work of only a few moments of feverish rushing up and down between wheels and engines to get the *Alert* under way. Slowly, amidst the distorted horrors of that indescribable scene, she began to churn the lethal waters; whilst on the masonry of that charnel shore that was not of earth the titan Thing from the stars slavered and gibbered like Polypheme cursing the fleeing ship of Odysseus. Then, bolder than the storied Cyclops, great Cthulhu slid greasily into the water and began to pursue with vast wave-raising strokes of cosmic potency. Briden looked back and went mad, laughing at intervals till death found him one night in the cabin whilst Johansen was wandering deliriously.

But Johansen had not given out yet. Knowing that the Thing could surely overtake the *Alert* until steam was fully up, he resolved on a desperate chance; and, setting the engine for full speed, ran lightning-like on deck and reversed the wheel. There was a mighty eddying and foaming in the noisome brine, and as the steam mounted higher and higher the brave Norwegian drove his vessel head on against the pursuing jelly which rose above the unclean froth like the stern of a demon galleon. The awful squid-head with writhing feelers came nearly up to the bowsprit of the sturdy yacht, but Johansen drove on relentlessly.

There was a bursting as of an exploding bladder, a slushy nastiness as of a cloven sunfish, a stench as of a thousand opened graves, and a sound that the chronicler would not put on paper. For an instant the ship was befouled by an acrid and blinding green cloud, and then there was only a venomous seething astern; where—God in heaven!—the scattered plasticity of that nameless sky-spawn was nebulously *recombining* in its hateful original form, whilst its distance widened every second as the *Alert* gained impetus from its mounting steam.

That was all. After that Johansen only brooded over the idol in the cabin and attended to a few matters of food for himself and the laughing maniac by his side. He did not try to navigate after the first bold flight; for the reaction had taken something out of his soul. Then came the storm of April 2nd, and a gathering of the clouds about his consciousness. There is a sense of spectral whirling through liquid gulfs of infinity, of dizzying rides through reeling universes on a comet's tail, and of hysterical plunges from the pit to the moon and from the moon back again to the pit, all livened by a cachinnating chorus of the distorted, hilarious elder gods and the green, bat-winged mocking imps of Tartarus.

Out of that dream came rescue—the *Vigilant*, the vice-admiralty court, the streets of Dunedin, and the long voyage back home to the old house by the Egeberg. He could not tell—they would think him mad. He would write of what he knew before death came, but his wife must not guess. Death would be a boon if only it could blot out the memories.

That was the document I read, and now I have placed it in the tin box beside the bas-relief and the papers of Professor Angell. With it shall go this record of mine—this test of my own sanity, wherein is pieced together that which I hope may never be pieced together again. I have looked upon all that the universe has to hold of horror, and even the skies of spring and the flowers of summer must ever afterward be poison to me. But I do not think my life will be long. As my uncle went, as poor Johansen went, so I shall go. I know too much, and the cult still lives.

Cthulhu still lives, too, I suppose, again in that chasm of stone which has shielded him since the sun was young. His accursed city is sunken once more, for the *Vigilant* sailed over the spot after the April storm; but his ministers on earth still bellow and prance and slay around idol-capped monoliths in lonely places. He must have been trapped by the sinking whilst within his black abyss, or else the world would by now be screaming with fright and frenzy. Who knows the end? What has risen may sink, and what has sunk may rise. Loathsomeness waits and dreams in the deep, and decay spreads over the tottering cities of men. A time will come—but I must not and can not think! Let me pray that, if I do not survive this manuscript, my executors may put caution before audacity and see that it meets no other eye.

The Dunwich Horror

Gorgons, and Hydras, and Chimaeras—dire stories of Celaeno
and the Harpies—may reproduce themselves in the brain of
superstition—but they were there before. They are transcripts, types—the archetypes are in us, and eternal. How else
should the recital of that which we know in a waking sense
to be false come to affect us at all? Is it that we naturally conceive terror from such objects, considered in their capacity of
being able to inflict upon us bodily injury? O, least of all!
These terrors are of older standing. They date beyond body—
or without the body, they would have been the same. . . .
That the kind of fear here treated is purely spiritual—that it
is strong in proportion as it is objectless on earth, that it pre-
dominates in the period of our sinless infancy—are difficulties the solution of which might afford some probable insight
into our ante-mundane condition, and a peep at least into the
shadowland of pre-existence.
— CHARLES LAMB: Witches and Other Night-Fears

When a traveller in north central Massachusetts takes the wrong
fork at the junction of the Aylesbury pike just beyond Dean's Corners
he comes upon a lonely and curious country. The ground gets higher,
and the brier-bordered stone walls press closer and closer against the
ruts of the dusty, curving road. The trees of the frequent forest belts
seem too large, and the wild weeds, brambles, and grasses attain a
luxuriance not often found in settled regions. At the same time the
planted fields appear singularly few and barren; while the sparsely
scattered houses wear a surprisingly uniform aspect of age, squalor,
and dilapidation. Without knowing why, one hesitates to ask directions from the gnarled, solitary figures spied now and then on crum-

bling doorsteps or on the sloping, rock-strewn meadows. Those figures are so silent and furtive that one feels somehow confronted by forbidden things, with which it would be better to have nothing to do. When a rise in the road brings the mountains in view above the deep woods, the feeling of strange uneasiness is increased. The summits are too rounded and symmetrical to give a sense of comfort and naturalness, and sometimes the sky silhouettes with especial clearness the queer circles of tall stone pillars with which most of them are crowned.

Gorges and ravines of problematical depth intersect the way, and the crude wooden bridges always seem of dubious safety. When the road dips again there are stretches of marshland that one instinctively dislikes, and indeed almost fears at evening when unseen whippoorwills chatter and the fireflies come out in abnormal profusion to dance to the raucous, creepily insistent rhythms of stridently piping bull-frogs. The thin, shining line of the Miskatonic's upper reaches has an oddly serpent-like suggestion as it winds close to the feet of the domed hills among which it rises.

As the hills draw nearer, one heeds their wooded sides more than their stone-crowned tops. Those sides loom up so darkly and precipitously that one wishes they would keep their distance, but there is no road by which to escape them. Across a covered bridge one sees a small village huddled between the stream and the vertical slope of Round Mountain, and wonders at the cluster of rotting gambrel roofs bespeaking an earlier architectural period than that of the neighbouring region. It is not reassuring to see, on a closer glance, that most of the houses are deserted and falling to ruin, and that the broken-steepled church now harbours the one slovenly mercantile establishment of the hamlet. One dreads to trust the tenebrous tunnel of the bridge, yet there is no way to avoid it. Once across, it is hard to prevent the impression of a faint, malign odour about the village street, as of the massed mould and decay of centuries. It is always a relief to get clear of the place, and to follow the narrow road around the base of the hills and across the level country beyond till it rejoins the Aylesbury pike. Afterward one sometimes learns that one has been through Dunwich.

Outsiders visit Dunwich as seldom as possible, and since a certain season of horror all the signboards pointing toward it have been taken down. The scenery, judged by any ordinary aesthetic canon, is more than commonly beautiful; yet there is no influx of artists or summer tourists. Two centuries ago, when talk of witch-blood, Satan-worship, and strange forest presences was not laughed at, it was the custom to give reasons for avoiding the locality. In our sensible age—since the

Dunwich horror of 1928 was hushed up by those who had the town's and the world's welfare at heart—people shun it without knowing exactly why. Perhaps one reason—though it cannot apply to uninformed strangers—is that the natives are now repellently decadent, having gone far along that path of retrogression so common in many New-England backwaters. They have come to form a race by themselves, with the well-defined mental and physical stigmata of degeneracy and inbreeding. The average of their intelligence is woefully low, whilst their annals reek of overt viciousness and of half-hidden murders, incests, and deeds of almost unnamable violence and perversity. The old gentry, representing the two or three armigerous families which came from Salem in 1692, have kept somewhat above the general level of decay; though many branches are sunk into the sordid populace so deeply that only their names remain as a key to the origin they disgrace. Some of the Whateleys and Bishops still send their eldest sons to Harvard and Miskatonic, though those sons seldom return to the mouldering gambrel roofs under which they and their ancestors were born.

No one, even those who have the facts concerning the recent horror, can say just what is the matter with Dunwich; though old legends speak of unhallowed rites and conclaves of the Indians, amidst which they called forbidden shapes of shadow out of the great rounded hills, and made wild orgiastic prayers that were answered by loud crackings and rumblings from the ground below. In 1747 the Reverend Abijah Hoadley, newly come to the Congregational Church at Dunwich Village, preached a memorable sermon on the close presence of Satan and his imps; in which he said:

> It must be allow'd, that these Blasphemies of an infernall Train of Daemons are Matters of too common Knowledge to be deny'd; the cursed Voices of *Azazel* and *Buzrael*, of *Beelzebub* and *Belial*, being heard now from under Ground by above a Score of credible Witnesses now living. I my self did not more than a Fortnight ago catch a very plain Discourse of evill Powers in the Hill behind my House; wherein there were a Rattling and Rolling, Groaning, Screeching, and Hissing, such as no Things of this Earth cou'd raise up, and which must needs have come from those Caves that only black Magick can discover, and only the Divell unlock.

Mr. Hoadley disappeared soon after delivering this sermon; but the text, printed in Springfield, is still extant. Noises in the hills continued to be reported from year to year, and still form a puzzle to geologists and physiographers.

Other traditions tell of foul odours near the hill-crowning circles of stone pillars, and of rushing airy presences to be heard faintly at certain hours from stated points at the bottom of the great ravines; while still others try to explain the Devil's Hop Yard—a bleak, blasted hillside where no tree, shrub, or grass-blade will grow. Then too, the natives are mortally afraid of the numerous whippoorwills which grow vocal on warm nights. It is vowed that the birds are psychopomps lying in wait for the souls of the dying, and that they time their eery cries in unison with the sufferer's struggling breath. If they can catch the fleeing soul when it leaves the body, they instantly flutter away chittering in daemoniac laughter; but if they fail, they subside gradually into a disappointed silence.

These tales, of course, are obsolete and ridiculous; because they come down from very old times. Dunwich is indeed ridiculously old—older by far than any of the communities within thirty miles of it. South of the village one may still spy the cellar walls and chimney of the ancient Bishop house, which was built before 1700; whilst the ruins of the mill at the falls, built in 1806, form the most modern piece of architecture to be seen. Industry did not flourish here, and the nineteenth century factory movement proved short-lived. Oldest of all are the great rings of rough-hewn stone columns on the hilltops, but these are more generally attributed to the Indians than to the settlers. Deposits of skulls and bones, found within these circles and around the sizeable table-like rock on Sentinel Hill, sustain the popular belief that such spots were once the burial-places of the Pocumtucks; even though many ethnologists, disregarding the absurd improbability of such a theory, persist in believing the remains Caucasian.

II

It was in the township of Dunwich, in a large and partly inhabited farmhouse set against a hillside four miles from the village and a mile and a half from any other dwelling, that Wilbur Whateley was born at 5 A.M. on Sunday, the second of February, 1913. This date was recalled because it was Candlemas, which people in Dunwich curiously observe under another name; and because the noises in the hills had sounded, and all the dogs of the countryside had barked persistently, throughout the night before. Less worthy of notice was the fact that the mother was one of the decadent Whateleys, a somewhat deformed, unattractive albino woman of 35, living with an aged and half-insane father about whom the most frightful tales of wizardry had been whispered in his youth. Lavinia Whateley had no known husband, but according to the custom of the region made no attempt to disavow the child; concerning the other side of whose ancestry the country folk might—and did—speculate as widely as they chose. On the contrary, she seemed strangely proud of the dark, goatish-looking infant who formed such a contrast to her own sickly and pink-eyed albinism, and was heard to mutter many curious prophecies about its unusual powers and tremendous future.

Lavinia was one who would be apt to mutter such things, for she was a lone creature given to wandering amidst thunderstorms in the hills and trying to read the great odorous books which her father had inherited through two centuries of Whateleys, and which were fast falling to pieces with age and worm-holes. She had never been to school, but was filled with disjointed scraps of ancient lore that Old Whateley had taught her. The remote farmhouse had always been feared because of Old Whateley's reputation for black magic, and the unexplained death by violence of Mrs. Whateley when Lavinia was twelve years old had not helped to make the place popular. Isolated among strange influences, Lavinia was fond of wild and grandiose daydreams and singular occupations; nor was her leisure much taken up by household cares in a home from which all standards of order and cleanliness had long since disappeared.

There was a hideous screaming which echoed above even the hill noises and the dogs' barking on the night Wilbur was born, but no known doctor or midwife presided at his coming. Neighbors knew nothing of him till a week afterward, when Old Whateley drove his sleigh through the snow into Dunwich Village and discoursed incoherently to the group of loungers at Osborn's general store. There seemed to be a change in the old man—an added element of furtiveness in the clouded brain which subtly transformed him from an object to a subject of fear—though he was not one to be perturbed by any common family event. Amidst it all he shewed some trace of the pride later noticed in his daughter, and what he said of the child's paternity was remembered by many of his hearers years afterward.

"I dun't keer what folks think—ef Lavinny's boy looked like his pa, he wouldn't look like nothin' ye expeck. Ye needn't think the only folks is the folks hereabouts. Lavinny's read some, an' has seed some things the most o' ye only tell abaout. I calc'late her man is as good a husban' as ye kin' find this side of Aylesbury; an' if ye knowed as much abaout the hills as I dew, ye wouldn't ast no better church weddin' nor her'n. Let me tell ye suthin'—*some day yew folks'll hear a child o' Lavinny's a-callin' its father's name on the top o' Sentinel Hill!*"

The only persons who saw Wilbur during the first month of his life were old Zechariah Whateley, of the undecayed Whateleys, and Earl Sawyer's common-law wife, Mamie Bishop. Mamie's visit was frankly one of curiosity, and her subsequent tales did justice to her observations; but Zechariah came to lead a pair of Alderney cows which Old Whateley had bought of his son Curtis. This marked the beginning of a course of cattle-buying on the part of small Wilbur's family which ended only in 1928, when the Dunwich horror came and went; yet at no time did the ramshackle Whateley barn seem overcrowded with livestock. There came a period when people were curious enough to steal up and count the herd that grazed precariously on the steep hillside above the old farmhouse, and they could never find more than ten or twelve anaemic, bloodless-looking specimens. Evidently some blight or distemper, perhaps sprung from the unwholesome pasturage or the diseased fungi and timbers of the filthy barn, caused a heavy mortality amongst the Whateley animals. Odd wounds or sores, having something of the aspect of incisions, seemed to afflict the visible cattle; and once or twice during the earlier months certain callers fancied they could discern similar sores about the throats of the grey, unshaven old man and his slatternly, crinkly-haired albino daughter.

In the spring after Wilbur's birth Lavinia resumed her customary rambles in the hills, bearing in her misproportioned arms the swarthy child. Public interest in the Whateleys subsided after most of the country folk had seen the baby, and no one bothered to comment on the swift development which that newcomer seemed every day to exhibit. Wilbur's growth was indeed phenomenal, for within three months of his birth he had attained a size and muscular power not usually found in infants under a full year of age. His motions and even his vocal sounds shewed a restraint and deliberateness highly peculiar in an infant, and no one was really unprepared when, at seven months, he began to walk unassisted, with falterings which another month was sufficient to remove.

It was somewhat after this time—on Hallowe'en—that a great blaze was seen at midnight on the top of Sentinel Hill where the old table-like stone stands amidst its tumulus of ancient bones. Considerable talk was started when Silas Bishop—of the undecayed Bishops—mentioned having seen the boy running sturdily up that hill ahead of his mother about an hour before the blaze was remarked. Silas was rounding up a stray heifer, but he nearly forgot his mission when he fleetingly spied the two figures in the dim light of his lantern. They darted almost noiselessly through the underbrush, and the astonished watcher seemed to think they were entirely unclothed. Afterward he could not be sure about the boy, who may have had some kind of a fringed belt and a pair of dark trunks or trousers on. Wilbur was never subsequently seen alive and conscious without complete and tightly buttoned attire, the disarrangement or threatened disarrangement of which always seemed to fill him with anger and alarm. His contrast with his squalid mother and grandfather in this respect was thought very notable until the horror of 1928 suggested the most valid of reasons.

The next January gossips were mildly interested in the fact that "Lavviny's black brat" had commenced to talk, and at the age of only eleven months. His speech was somewhat remarkable both because of its difference from the ordinary accents of the region, and because it displayed a freedom from infantile lisping of which many children of three or four might well be proud. The boy was not talkative, yet when he spoke he seemed to reflect some elusive element wholly unpossessed by Dunwich and its denizens. The strangeness did not reside in what he said, or even in the simple idioms he used; but seemed vaguely linked with his intonation or with the internal organs that produced the spoken sounds. His facial aspect, too, was remarkable for its maturity; for though he shared his mother's and grandfather's chinlessness, his firm and precociously shaped nose united with the expression of his large, dark, almost Latin eyes to give him an air of quasi-adulthood and well-nigh preternatural intelligence. He was, however, exceedingly ugly despite his appearance of brilliancy; there being something almost goatish or animalistic about his thick lips, large-pored, yellowish skin, coarse crinkly hair, and oddly elongated ears. He was soon disliked even more decidedly than his mother and grandsire, and all conjectures about him were spiced with references to the bygone magic of Old Whateley, and how the hills once shook when he shrieked the dreadful name of *Yog-Sothoth* in the midst of a circle of stones with a great book open in his arms before him. Dogs abhorred the boy, and he was always obliged to take various defensive measures against their barking menace.

III

Meanwhile Old Whateley continued to buy cattle without measurably increasing the size of his herd. He also cut timber and began to repair the unused parts of his house—a spacious, peaked-roofed affair whose rear end was buried entirely in the rocky hillside, and whose three least-ruined ground-floor rooms had always been sufficient for himself and his daughter. There must have been prodigious reserves of strength in the old man to enable him to accomplish so much hard labour; and though he still babbled dementedly at times, his carpen-

try seemed to shew the effects of sound calculation. It had already begun as soon as Wilbur was born, when one of the many tool sheds had
been put suddenly in order, clapboarded, and fitted with a stout fresh
lock. Now, in restoring the abandoned upper story of the house, he
was a no less thorough craftsman. His mania shewed itself only in his
tight boarding-up of all the windows in the reclaimed section—
though many declared that it was a crazy thing to bother with the
reclamation at all. Less inexplicable was his fitting up of another
downstairs room for his new grandson—a room which several callers
saw, though no one was ever admitted to the closely-boarded upper
story. This chamber he lined with tall, firm shelving; along which he
began gradually to arrange, in apparently careful order, all the rotting
ancient books and parts of books which during his own day had been
heaped promiscuously in odd corners of the various rooms.

"I made some use of 'em," he would say as he tried to mend a torn
black-letter page with paste prepared on the rusty kitchen stove, "but
the boy's fitten to make better use of 'em. He'd orter hev 'em as well
so as he kin, for they're goin' to be all of his larnin'."

When Wilbur was a year and seven months old—in September
of 1914—his size and accomplishments were almost alarming. He
had grown as large as a child of four, and was a fluent and incredibly
intelligent talker. He ran freely about the fields and hills, and accompanied his mother on all her wanderings. At home he would pore diligently over the queer pictures and charts in his grandfather's books,
while Old Whateley would instruct and catechise him through long,
hushed afternoons. By this time the restoration of the house was finished, and those who watched it wondered why one of the upper windows had been made into a solid plank door. It was a window in the
rear of the east gable end, close against the hill; and no one could
imagine why a clated wooden runway was built up to it from the
ground. About the period of this work's completion people noticed
that the old tool-house, tightly locked and windowlessly clapboarded
since Wilbur's birth, had been abandoned again. The door swung listlessly open, and when Earl Sawyer once stepped within after a cattle-
selling call on Old Whateley he was quite discomposed by the singular
odour he encountered—such a stench, he averred, as he had never before smelt in all his life except near the Indian circles on the hills,
and which could not come from anything sane or of this earth. But
then, the homes and sheds of Dunwich's folk have never been remarkable for olfactory immaculateness.

The following months were void of visible events, save that everyone swore to a slow but steady increase in the mysterious hill noises.
On May Eve of 1915 there were tremors which even the Aylesbury

people felt, whilst the following Hallowe'en produced an underground rumbling queerly synchronised with bursts of flame—"them witch Whateleys' doin's"—from the summit of Sentinel Hill. Wilbur was growing up uncannily, so that he looked like a boy of ten as he entered his fourth year. He read avidly by himself now; but talked much less than formerly. A settled taciturnity was absorbing him, and for the first time people began to speak specifically of the dawning look of evil in his goatish face. He would sometimes mutter an unfamiliar jargon, and chant in bizarre rhythms which chilled the listener with a sense of unexplainable terror. The aversion displayed toward him by dogs had now become a matter of wide remark, and he was obliged to carry a pistol in order to traverse the countryside in safety. His occasional use of the weapon did not enhance his popularity amongst the owners of canine guardians.

The few callers at the house would often find Lavinia alone on the ground floor, while odd cries and footsteps resounded in the boarded-up second story. She would never tell what her father and the boy were doing up there, though once she turned pale and displayed an abnormal degree of fear when a jocose fish-peddler tried the locked door leading to the stairway. That peddler told the store loungers at Dunwich Village that he thought he heard a horse stamping on that floor above. The loungers reflected, thinking of the door and runway, and of the cattle that so swiftly disappeared. Then they shuddered as they recalled tales of Old Whateley's youth, and of the strange things that are called out of the earth when a bullock is sacrificed at the proper time to certain heathen gods. It had for some time been noticed that dogs had begun to hate and fear the whole Whateley place as violently as they hated and feared young Wilbur personally.

In 1917 the war came, and Squire Sawyer Whateley, as chairman of the local draft board, had hard work finding a quota of young Dunwich men fit even to be sent to development camp. The government, alarmed at such signs of wholesale regional decadence, sent several officers and medical experts to investigate; conducting a survey which New England newspaper readers may still recall. It was the publicity attending this investigation which set reporters on the track of the Whateleys, and caused the *Boston Globe* and *Arkham Advertiser* to print flamboyant Sunday stories of young Wilbur's precociousness, Old Whateley's black magic, and the shelves of strange books, the sealed second story of the ancient farmhouse, and the weirdness of the whole region and its hill noises. Wilbur was four and a half then, and looked like a lad of fifteen. His lips and cheeks were fuzzy with a coarse dark down, and his voice had begun to break.

Earl Sawyer went out to the Whateley place with both sets of reporters and camera men, and called their attention to the queer stench which now seemed to trickle down from the sealed upper spaces. It was, he said, exactly like a smell he had found in the tool-shed abandoned when the house was finally repaired; and like the faint odours which he sometimes thought he caught near the stone circle on the mountains. Dunwich folk read the stories when they appeared, and grinned over the obvious mistakes. They wondered, too, why the writers made so much of the fact that Old Whateley always paid for his cattle in gold pieces of extremely ancient date. The Whateleys had received their visitors with ill-concealed distaste, though they did not dare court further publicity by a violent resistance or refusal to talk.

IV

For a decade the annals of the Whateleys sink indistinguishably into the general life of a morbid community used to their queer ways and hardened to their May Eve and All-Hallows orgies. Twice a year they would light fires on the top of Sentinel Hill, at which times the mountain rumblings would recur with greater and greater violence; while at all seasons there were strange and portentous doings at the lonely farmhouse. In the course of time callers professed to hear sounds in the sealed upper story even when all the family were downstairs, and they wondered how swiftly or how lingeringly a cow or bullock was usually sacrificed. There was talk of a complaint to the Society for the Prevention of Cruelty to Animals; but nothing ever came of it, since Dunwich folk are never anxious to call the outside world's attention to themselves.

About 1923, when Wilbur was a boy of ten whose mind, voice, stature, and bearded face gave all the impressions of maturity, a second great siege of carpentry went on at the old house. It was all inside the sealed upper part, and from bits of discarded lumber people concluded that the youth and his grandfather had knocked out all the partitions and even removed the attic floor, leaving only one vast open void between the ground story and the peaked roof. They had torn down the great central chimney, too, and fitted the rusty range with a flimsy outside tin stovepipe.

In the spring after this event Old Whateley noticed the growing number of whippoorwills that would come out of Cold Spring Glen to chirp under his window at night. He seemed to regard the circumstance as one of great significance, and told the loungers at Osborn's that he thought his time had almost come.

"They whistle jest in tune with my breathin' naow," he said, "an' I guess they're gittin' ready to ketch my soul. They know it's a-goin' aout, an' dun't calc'late to miss it. Yew'll know, boys, arter I'm gone, whether they git me er not. Ef they dew, they'll keep up a-singin' an' laffin' till break o' day. Ef they dun't they'll kinder quiet daown like. I expeck them an' the souls they hunts fer hev some pretty tough tussles sometimes."

On Lammas Night, 1924, Dr. Houghton of Aylesbury was hastily summoned by Wilbur Whateley, who had lashed his one remaining horse through the darkness and telephoned from Osborn's in the village. He found Old Whatelely in a very grave state, with a cardiac action and stertorous breathing that told of an end not far off. The shapeless albino daughter and oddly bearded grandson stood by the bedside, whilst from the vacant abyss overhead there came a disquieting suggestion of rhythmical surging or lapping, as of the waves on some level beach. The doctor, though, was chiefly disturbed by the chattering night birds outside; a seemingly limitless legion of whippoorwills that cried their endless message in repetitions timed diabolically to the wheezing gasps of the dying man. It was uncanny and unnatural—too much, thought Dr. Houghton, like the whole of the region he had entered so reluctantly in response to the urgent call.

Toward one o'clock Old Whateley gained consciousness, and interrupted his wheezing to choke out a few words to his grandson.

"More space, Willy, more space soon. Yew grows—an' *that* grows faster. It'll be ready to sarve ye soon, boy. Open up the gates to Yog-Soloth with the long chant that ye'll find on page 751 *of the complete edition*, an' *then* put a match to the prison. Fire from airth can't burn it nohaow."

He was obviously quite mad. After a pause, during which the flock of whippoorwills outside adjusted their cries to the altered tempo while some indications of the strange hill noises came from afar off, he added another sentence or two.

"Feed it reg'lar, Willy, an' mind the quantity; but dun't let it grow too fast fer the place, fer ef it busts quarters or gits aout afore ye opens to Yog-Sothoth, it's all over an' no use. Only them from beyont kin make it multiply an' work. . . . Only them, the old uns as wants to come back. . . ."

But speech gave place to gasps again, and Lavinia screamed at the way the whippoorwills followed the change. It was the same for more than an hour, when the final throaty rattle came. Dr. Houghton drew shrunken lids over the glazing grey eyes as the tumult of birds faded imperceptibly to silence. Lavinia sobbed, but Wilbur only chuckled whilst the hill noises rumbled faintly.

"They didn't git him," he muttered in his heavy bass voice.

Wilbur was by this time a scholar of really tremendous erudition in his one-sided way, and was quietly known by correspondence to many librarians in distant places where rare and forbidden books of old days are kept. He was more and more hated and dreaded around Dunwich because of certain youthful disappearances which suspicion laid vaguely at his door; but was always able to silence inquiry through fear or through use of that fund of old-time gold which still, as in his grandfather's time, went forth regularly and increasingly for cattle-buying. He was now tremendously mature of aspect, and his height, having reached the normal adult limit, seemed inclined to wax beyond that figure. In 1925, when a scholarly correspondent from Miskatonic University called upon him one day and departed pale and puzzled, he was fully six and three-quarters feet tall.

Through all the years Wilbur had treated his half-deformed albino mother with a growing contempt, finally forbidding her to go to the hills with him on May Eve and Hallowmass; and in 1926 the poor creature complained to Mamie Bishop of being afraid of him.

"They's more abaout him as I knows than I kin tell ye, Mamie," she said, "an' naowadays they's more nor what I know myself. I vaow afur Gawd, I dun't know what he wants nor what he's a-tryin' to dew."

That Hallowe'en the hill noises sounded louder than ever, and fire burned on Sentinel Hill as usual; but people paid more attention to the rhythmical screaming of vast flocks of unnaturally belated whippoorwills which seemed to be assembled near the unlighted Whateley farmhouse. After midnight their shrill notes burst into a kind of pandaemoniac cachinnation which filled all the countryside, and not until dawn did they finally quiet down. Then they vanished, hurrying southward where they were fully a month overdue. What this meant, no one could quite be certain till later. None of the countryfolk seemed to have died—but poor Lavinia Whateley, the twisted albino, was never seen again.

In the summer of 1927 Wilbur repaired two sheds in the farmyard and began moving his books and effects out to them. Soon afterward Earl Sawyer told the loungers at Osborn's that more carpentry was going on in the Whateley farmhouse. Wilbur was closing all the doors and windows on the ground floor, and seemed to be taking out partitions as he and his grandfather had done upstairs four years before. He was living in one of the sheds, and Sawyer thought he seemed unusually worried and tremulous. People generally suspected him of knowing something about his mother's disappearance, and very few ever approached his neighbourhood now. His height had increased to more than seven feet, and shewed no signs of ceasing its development.

V

The following winter brought an event no less strange than Wilbur's first trip outside the Dunwich region. Correspondence with the Widener Library at Harvard, the Bibliotheque Nationale in Paris, the British Museum, the University of Buenos Aires, and the Library of Miskatonic University at Arkham had failed to get him the loan of a book he desperately wanted; so at length he set out in person, shabby, dirty, bearded, and uncouth of dialect, to consult the copy at Miskatonic, which was the nearest to him geographically. Almost eight feet tall, and carrying a cheap new valise from Osborn's general store, this dark and goatish gargoyle appeared one day in Arkham in quest of the dreaded volume kept under lock and key at the college library—the hideous *Necronomicon* of the mad Arab Abdul Alhazred in Olaus Wormius' Latin version, as printed in Spain in the seventeenth century. He had never seen a city before, but had no thought save to find his way to the university grounds; where, indeed, he passed heedlessly by the great white-fanged watchdog that barked with unnatural fury and enmity, and tugged frantically at its stout chain.

Wilbur had with him the priceless but imperfect copy of Dr. Dee's English version which his grandfather had bequeathed him, and upon receiving access to the Latin copy he at once began to collate the two texts with the aim of discovering a certain passage which would have come on the 751st page of his own defective volume. This much he could not civilly refrain from telling the librarian—the same erudite Henry Armitage (A. M. Miskatonic, Ph. D. Princeton, Litt.D. Johns Hopkins) who had once called at the farm, and who now politely plied him with questions. He was looking, he had to admit, for a kind of formula or incantation containing the frightful name *Yog-Sothoth*, and it puzzled him to find discrepancies, duplications, and ambiguities which made the matter of determination far from easy. As he copied the formula he finally chose, Dr. Armitage looked involuntarily over his shoulder at the open pages; the left-hand one of which, in the Latin version, contained such monstrous threats to the peace and sanity of the world.

Nor is it to be thought, [ran the text as Armitage mentally translated it] that man is either the oldest or the last of earth's masters, or that the common bulk of life and substance walks alone. The Old Ones were, the Old Ones are, and the Old Ones shall be. Not in the spaces we know, but *between* them. They walk serene and primal, undimensioned and to us unseen. *Yog-Sothoth* knows the gate. *Yog-Sothoth* is the gate. *Yog-Sothoth* is the key and guardian of the gate. Past, present, future, all are one in *Yog-Sothoth*. He knows where the Old Ones broke through of old, and where They shall break through again. He knows where They have trod earth's fields, and where They still tread them, and why no one can behold Them as They tread. By Their smell can men sometimes know Them near, but of Their semblance can no man know, *saving only in the features of those They have begotten on mankind;* and of those are there many sorts, differing in likeness from man's truest eidolon to that shape without sight or substance which is *Them*. They walk unseen and foul in lonely places where the Words have been spoken and the Rites howled through at their Seasons. The wind gibbers with Their voices, and the earth mutters with Their consciousness. They bend the forest and crush the city, yet may not forest or city behold the hand that smites. Kadath in the cold waste hath known Them, and what man knows Kadath? The ice desert of the South and the sunken isles of Ocean hold stones whereon Their seal is engraven, but who hath seen the deep frozen city or the sealed tower long garlanded with seaweed and barnacles? Great Cthulhu is Their cousin, yet can he spy Them only dimly. *Iä! Shub-Niggurath!* As a foulness shall ye know Them. Their hand is at your throats, yet ye see Them not; and Their habitation is even one with your guarded threshold. *Yog-Sothoth* is the key to the gate, whereby the spheres meet. Man rules now where They ruled once; They shall soon rule where man rules now. After summer is winter, and after winter summer. They wait patient and potent, for here shall They reign again.

Dr. Armitage, associating what he was reading with what he had heard of Dunwich and its brooding presences, and of Wilbur Whateley and his dim, hideous aura that stretched from a dubious birth to a cloud of probable matricide, felt a wave of fright as tangible as a draught of the tomb's cold clamminess. The bent, goatish giant before him seemed like the spawn of another planet or dimension; like something only partly of mankind, and linked to black gulfs of essence and entity that stretch like titan phantasms beyond all spheres of force and matter, space and time. Presently Wilbur raised his head and began speaking in that strange, resonant fashion which hinted at sound-producing organs unlike the run of mankind's.

"Mr. Armitage," he said, "I calc'late I've got to take that book home. They's things in it I've got to try under sarten conditions that I can't git here, an' it 'ud be a mortal sin to let a red-tape rule hold me up. Let me take it along, Sir, an' I'll swar they wun't nobody know the difference. I dun't need to tell ye I'll take good keer of it. It wan't me that put this Dee copy in the shape it is. . . ."

He stopped as he saw firm denial on the librarian's face, and his own goatish features grew crafty. Armitage, half-ready to tell him he might make a copy of what parts he needed, thought suddenly of the possible consequences and checked himself. There was too much responsibility in giving such a being the key to such blasphemous outer spheres. Whateley saw how things stood, and tried to answer lightly.

"Wal, all right, ef ye feel that way abaout it. Maybe Harvard wun't be so fussy as yew be." And without saying more he rose and strode out of the building, stooping at each doorway.

Armitage heard the savage yelping of the great watchdog, and studied Whateley's gorilla-like lope as he crossed the bit of campus visible from the window. He thought of the wild tales he had heard, and recalled the old Sunday stories in the *Advertiser*; these things, and the lore he had picked up from Dunwich rustics and villagers during his one visit there. Unseen things not of earth—or at least not of tri-dimensional earth—rushed foetid and horrible through New England's glens, and brooded obscenely on the mountaintops. Of this he had long felt certain. Now he seemed to sense the close presence of some terrible part of the intruding horror, and to glimpse a hellish advance in the black dominion of the ancient and once passive nightmare. He locked away the *Necronomicon* with a shudder of disgust, but the room still reeked with an unholy and unidentifiable stench. "As a foulness shall ye know them," he quoted. Yes—the odour was the same as that which had sickened him at the Whateley farmhouse less than three years before. He thought of Wilbur, goatish and ominous, once again, and laughed mockingly at the village rumours of his parentage.

"Inbreeding?" Armitage muttered half-aloud to himself. "Great God, what simpletons! Shew them Arthur Machen's Great God Pan and they'll think it a common Dunwich scandal! But what thing—what cursed shapeless influence on or off this three-dimensioned earth—was Wilbur Whateley's father? Born on Candlemas—nine months after May Eve of 1912, when the talk about the queer earth noises reached clear to Arkham—what walked on the mountains that May night? What Roodmas horror fastened itself on the world in half-human flesh and blood?"

During the ensuing weeks Dr. Armitage set about to collect all possible data on Wilbur Whateley and the formless presences around Dunwich. He got in communication with Dr. Houghton of Aylesbury, who had attended Old Whateley in his last illness, and found much to ponder over in the grandfather's last words as quoted by the physician. A visit to Dunwich Village failed to bring out much that was new; but a close survey of the *Necronomicon*, in those parts which Wilbur had sought so avidly, seemed to supply new and terrible clues to the nature, methods, and desires of the strange evil so vaguely threatening this planet. Talks with several students of archaic lore in Boston, and letters to many others elsewhere, gave him a growing amazement which passed slowly through varied degrees of alarm to a state of really acute spiritual fear. As the summer drew on he felt dimly that something ought to be done about the lurking terrors of the upper Miskatonic valley, and about the monstrous being known to the human world as Wilbur Whateley.

VI

The Dunwich horror itself came between Lammas and the equinox in 1928, and Dr. Armitage was among those who witnessed its monstrous prologue. He had heard, meanwhile, of Whateley's grotesque trip to Cambridge, and of his frantic efforts to borrow or copy from the *Necronomicon* at the Widener Library. Those efforts had been in vain, since Armitage had issued warnings of the keenest intensity to all librarians having charge of the dreaded volume. Wilbur had been shockingly nervous at Cambridge; anxious for the book, yet almost equally anxious to get home again, as if he feared the results of being away long.

Early in August the half-expected outcome developed, and in the small hours of the third Dr. Armitage was awakened suddenly by the wild, fierce cries of the savage watchdog on the college campus. Deep and terrible, the snarling, half-mad growls and barks continued; always in mounting volume, but with hideously significant pauses. Then there rang out a scream from a wholly different throat—such a scream as roused half the sleepers of Arkham and haunted their dreams ever afterward—such a scream as could come from no being born of earth, or wholly of earth.

Armitage, hastening into some clothing and rushing across the street and lawn to the college buildings, saw that others were ahead of him; and heard the echoes of a burglar-alarm still shrilling from the library. An open window shewed black and gaping in the moonlight. What had come had indeed completed its entrance; for the barking and the screaming, now fast fading into a mixed low growling and moaning, proceeded unmistakably from within. Some instinct warned Armitage that what was taking place was not a thing for unfortified eyes to see, so he brushed back the crowd with authority as he unlocked the vestibule door. Among the others he saw Professor Warren Rice and Dr. Francis Morgan, men to whom he had told some of his conjectures and misgivings; and these two he motioned to accompany him inside. The inward sounds, except for a watchful, droning whine from the dog, had by this time quite subsided; but Armitage now perceived with a sudden start that a loud chorus of whippoorwills among the shrubbery had commenced a damnably rhythmical piping, as if in unison with the last breaths of a dying man.

The building was full of a frightful stench which Dr. Armitage knew too well, and the three men rushed across the hall to the small genealogical reading-room whence the low whining came. For a second nobody dared to turn on the light, then Armitage summoned up his courage and snapped the switch. One of the three—it is not certain which—shrieked aloud at what sprawled before them among disordered tables and overturned chairs. Professor Rice declares that he wholly lost consciousness for an instant, though he did not stumble or fall.

The thing that lay half-bent on its side in a foetid pool of greenish-yellow ichor and tarry stickiness was almost nine feet tall, and the dog had torn off all the clothing and some of the skin. It was not quite dead, but twitched silently and spasmodically while its chest heaved in monstrous unison with the mad piping of the expectant whippoorwills outside. Bits of shoe-leather and fragments of apparel were scattered about the room, and just inside the window an empty canvas sack lay where it had evidently been thrown. Near the central desk a revolver had fallen, a dented but undischarged cartridge later explaining why it had not been fired. The thing itself, however, crowded out all other images at the time. It would be trite and not wholly accurate to say that no human pen could describe it, but one may properly say that it could not be vividly visualised by anyone whose ideas of aspect and contour are too closely bound up with the common life-forms of this planet and of the three known dimensions. It was partly human, beyond a doubt, with very manlike hands and head, and the goatish, chinless face had the stamp of the Whateleys upon it. But the torso and lower parts of the body were teratologically fabulous, so that only generous clothing could ever have enabled it to walk on earth unchallenged or uneradicated.

Above the waist it was semi-anthropomorphic; though its chest, where the dog's rending paws still rested watchfully, had the leathery, reticulated hide of a crocodile or alligator. The back was piebald with yellow and black, and dimly suggested the squamous covering of certain snakes. Below the waist, though, it was the worst; for here all human resemblance left off and sheer phantasy began. The skin was thickly covered with coarse black fur, and from the abdomen a score of long greenish-grey tentacles with red sucking mouths protruded limply. Their arrangement was odd, and seemed to follow the symmetries of some cosmic geometry unknown to earth or the solar system. On each of the hips, deep set in a kind of pinkish, ciliated orbit, was what seemed to be a rudimentary eye; whilst in lieu of a tail there depended a kind of trunk or feeler with purple annular markings, and with many evidences of being an undeveloped mouth or throat. The limbs, save for their black fur, roughly resembled the hind legs of prehistoric earth's giant saurians; and terminated in ridgy-veined pads that were neither hooves nor claws. When the thing breathed, its tail and tentacles rhythmically changed colour, as if from some circulatory cause normal to the non-human side of its ancestry. In the tentacles this was observable as a deepening of the greenish tinge, whilst in the tail it was manifest as a yellowish appearance which alternated with a sickly greyish-white in the spaces between the purple rings. Of genuine blood there was none; only the foetid greenish-yellow ichor which trickled along the painted floor beyond the radius of the stickiness, and left a curious discolouration behind it.

As the presence of the three men seemed to rouse the dying thing, it began to mumble without turning or raising its head. Dr. Armitage made no written record of its mouthings, but asserts confidently that nothing in English was uttered. At first the syllables defied all correlation with any speech of earth, but toward the last there came some disjointed fragments evidently taken from the *Necronomicon*, that monstrous blasphemy in quest of which the thing had perished. These fragments, as Armitage recalls them, ran something like "*N'-gai, n'gha'ghaa, bugg-shoggog, y'hah; Yog-Sothoth, Yog-Sothoth . . .*" They trailed off into nothingness as the whippoorwills shrieked in rhythmical crescendoes of unholy anticipation.

Then came a halt in the gasping, and the dog raised its head in a long, lugubrious howl. A change came over the yellow, goatish face of the prostrate thing, and the great black eyes fell in appallingly. Outside the window the shrilling of the whippoorwills had suddenly ceased, and above the murmurs of the gathering crowd there came the sound of a panic-struck whirring and fluttering. Against the moon vast clouds of feathery watchers rose and raced from sight, frantic at that which they had sought for prey.

All at once the dog started up abruptly, gave a frightened bark, and leaped nervously out of the window by which it had entered. A cry rose from the crowd, and Dr. Armitage shouted to the men outside that no one must be admitted till the police or medical examiner came. He was thankful that the windows were just too high to permit of peering in, and drew the dark curtains carefully down over each one. By this time two policemen had arrived; and Dr. Morgan, meeting them in the vestibule, was urging them for their own sakes to postpone entrance to the stench-filled reading-room till the examiner came and the prostrate thing could be covered up.

Meanwhile frightful changes were taking place on the floor. One need not describe the *kind* and *rate* of shrinkage and disintegration that occurred before the eyes of Dr. Armitage and Professor Rice; but it is permissible to say that, aside from the external appearance of face and hands, the really human element in Wilbur Whateley must have been very small. When the medical examiner came, there was only a sticky whitish mass on the painted boards, and the monstrous odour had nearly disappeared. Apparently Whateley had had no skull or bony skeleton; at least, in any true or stable sense. He had taken somewhat after his unknown father.

VII

Yet all this was only the prologue of the actual Dunwich horror. Formalities were gone through by bewildered officials, abnormal details were duly kept from press and public, and men were sent to Dunwich and Aylesbury to look up property and notify any who might be heirs of the late Wilbur Whateley. They found the countryside in great agitation, both because of the growing rumblings beneath the domed hills, and because of the unwonted stench and the surging, lapping sounds which came increasingly from the great empty shell formed by Whateley's boarded-up farmhouse. Earl Sawyer, who tended the horse and cattle during Wilbur's absence, had developed a woefully acute case of nerves. The officials devised excuses not to enter the noisome boarded place; and were glad to confine their survey of the deceased's living quarters, the newly mended sheds, to a single visit. They filed a ponderous report at the courthouse in Aylesbury, and litigations concerning heirship are said to be still in progress amongst the innumerable Whateleys, decayed and undecayed, of the upper Miskatonic valley.

An almost interminable manuscript in strange characters, written in a huge ledger and adjudged a sort of diary because of the spacing and the variations in ink and penmanship, presented a baffling puzzle to those who found it on the old bureau which served as its owner's desk. After a week of debate it was sent to Miskatonic University, together with the deceased's collection of strange books, for study and possible translation; but even the best linguists soon saw that it was not likely to be unriddled with ease. No trace of the ancient gold with which Wilbur and Old Whateley had always paid their debts has yet been discovered.

It was in the dark of September ninth that the horror broke loose. The hill noises had been very pronounced during the evening, and dogs barked frantically all night. Early risers on the tenth noticed a peculiar stench in the air. About seven o'clock Luther Brown, the hired boy at George Corey's, between Cold Spring Glen and the village, rushed frenziedly back from his morning trip to Ten-Acre Meadow with the cows. He was almost convulsed with fright as he stumbled into the kitchen; and in the yard outside the no less frightened herd were pawing and lowing pitifully, having followed the boy back in the panic they shared with him. Between gasps Luther tried to stammer out his tale to Mrs. Corey.

"Up thar in the rud beyont the glen, Mis' Corey—they's suthin' ben thar! It smells like thunder, an' all the bushes an' little trees is pushed back from the rud like they'd a haouse ben moved along of it. An' that ain't the wust, nuther. They's *prints* in the rud, Mis' Corey— great raound prints as big as barrel-heads, all sunk daown deep like a elephant had ben along, *only they's a sight more nor four feet could make!* I looked at one or two afore I run, an' I see every one was covered with lines spreadin' aout from one place, like as if big palm-leaf fans—twict or three times as big as any they is—hed of ben paounded daown into the rud. An' the smell was awful, like what it is around Wizard Whatelay's ol' haouse. . . ."

Here he faltered, and seemed to shiver afresh with the fright that had sent him flying home. Mrs. Corey, unable to extract more information, began telephoning the neighbours; thus starting on its rounds the overture of panic that heralded the major terrors. When she got Sally Sawyer, housekeeper at Seth Bishop's, the nearest place to Whateley's, it became her turn to listen instead of transmit; for Sally's boy Chauncey, who slept poorly, had been up on the hill toward Whateley's, and had dashed back in terror after one look at the place, and at the pasturage where Mr. Bishop's cows had been left out all night.

"Yes, Mis' Corey," came Sally's tremulous voice over the party wire, "Cha'ncey he just come back a-postin', and couldn't haff talk fer bein' scairt! He says Ol' Whateley's house is all blowed up, with timbers scattered raound like they'd ben dynamite inside; only the bottom floor ain't through, but is all covered with a kind o' tar-like stuff that smells awful an' drips daown offen the aidges onto the graoun' whar the side timbers is blowed away. An' they's awful kinder marks in the yard, tew—great raound marks bigger raound than a hogshead, an' all sticky with stuff like is on the blowed-up haouse. Cha'ncey he says they leads off into the medders, whar a great swath wider'n a barn is matted daown, an' all the stun walls tumbled every whichway wherever it goes.

"An' he says, says he, Mis' Corey, as haow he sot to look fer Seth's caows, frighted ez he was; an' faound 'em in the upper pasture nigh the Devil's Hop Yard in an awful shape. Haff on 'em's clean gone, an' nigh haff o' them that's left is sucked most dry o' blood, with sores on 'em like they's ben on Whateley's cattle ever senct Lavinny's black brat was born. Seth he's gone aout naow to look at 'em, though I'll vaow he wun't keer ter git very nigh Wizard Whateley's! Cha'ncey didn't look keerful ter see whar the big matted-daown swath led arter it lef the pasturage, but he says he thinks it p'inted towards the glen rud to the village.

"I tell ye, Mis' Corey, they's suthin' abroad as hadn't orter be abroad, an' I for one think that black Wilbur Whateley, as come to the bad end he desarved, is at the bottom of the breedin' of it. He wa'n't all human hisself, I allus says to everybody; an' I think he an' Ol' Whateley must a raised suthin' in that there nailed-up haouse as ain't even so human as he was. They's allus ben unseen things araound Dunwich—livin' things—as ain't human an' ain't good fer human folks.

"The graoun' was a'talkin' las' night, an' towards mornin' Cha'ncey he heered the whippoorwills so laoud in Col' Spring Glen he couldn't sleep nun. Then he thought he heerd another faint-like saound over toward Wizard Whateley's—a kinder rippin' or tearin' o' wood, like some big box er crate was bin' opened fur off. What with this an' that, he didn't git to sleep at all till sunup, an' no sooner was he up this mornin', but he's got to go over to Whateley's an' see what's the matter. He see enough, I tell ye, Mis' Corey! This dun't mean no good, an' I think as all the men-folks ought to git up a party an' do suthin'. I know suthin' awful's abaout, an' feel my time is nigh, though only Gawd knows jest what it is.

"Did your Luther take accaount o' whar them big tracks led tew? No? Wal, Mis' Corey, ef they was on the glen rud this side o' the glen, an' ain't got to your haouse yet, I calc'late they must go into the glen itself. They would do that. I allus says Col' Spring Glen ain't no healthy nor decent place. The whippoorwills an' fireflies there never did act like they was creaters o' Gawd, an' they's them as says ye kin hear strange things a-rushin' an' a-talkin' in the air daown thar ef ye stand in the right place, atween the rock falls an' Bear's Den."

By that noon fully three-quarters of the men and boys of Dunwich were trooping over the roads and meadows between the new-made Whateley ruins and Cold Spring Glen, examining in horror the vast, monstrous prints, the maimed Bishop cattle, the strange, noisome wreck of the farmhouse, and the bruised, matted vegetation of the fields and roadsides. Whatever had burst loose upon the world had assuredly gone down into the great sinister ravine; for all the trees on the banks were bent and broken, and a great avenue had been gouged in the precipice-hanging underbrush. It was as though a house, launched by an avalanche, had slid down through the tangled growths of the almost vertical slope. From below no sound came, but only a distant, undefinable foeter; and it is not to be wondered at that the men preferred to stay on the edge and argue, rather than descend and beard the unknown Cyclopean horror in its lair. Three dogs that were with the party had barked furiously at first, but seemed cowed and reluctant when near the glen. Someone telephoned the news to the *Aylesbury Transcript*; but the editor, accustomed to wild tales from Dunwich, did no more than concoct a humorous paragraph about it; an item soon afterward reproduced by the Associated Press.

That night everyone went home, and every house and barn was barricaded as stoutly as possible. Needless to say, no cattle were allowed to remain in open pasturage. About two in the morning a frightful stench and the savage barking of the dogs awakened the household at Elmer Frye's, on the eastern edge of Cold Spring Glen, and all agreed that they could hear a sort of muffled swishing or lapping sound from somewhere outside. Mrs. Frye proposed telephoning the neighbours, and Elmer was about to agree when the noise of splintering wood burst in upon their deliberation. It came, apparently, from the barn; and was quickly followed by a hideous screaming and stamping amongst the cattle. The dogs slavered and crouched close to the feet of the fear-numbed family. Frye lit a lantern through force of habit, but knew it would be death to go out into that black farmyard. The children and the women-folk whimpered, kept from screaming by some obscure, vestigial instinct of defence which told them their lives depended on silence. At last the noise of the cattle subsided to a pitiful moaning, and a great snapping, crashing, and crackling ensued. The Fryes, huddled together in the sitting-room, did not dare to move until the last echoes died away far down in Cold Spring Glen. Then, amidst the dismal moans from the stable and the daemoniac piping of late whippoorwills in the glen, Selina Frye tottered to the telephone and spread what news she could of the second phase of the horror.

The next day all the countryside was in a panic; and cowed,

uncommunicative groups came and went where the fiendish thing had occurred. Two titan swaths of destruction stretched from the glen to the Frye farmyard, monstrous prints covered the bare patches of ground, and one side of the old red barn had completely caved in. Of the cattle, only a quarter could be found and identified. Some of these were in curious fragments, and all that survived had to be shot. Earl Sawyer suggested that help be asked from Aylesbury or Arkham, but others maintained it would be of no use. Old Zebulon Whateley, of a branch that hovered about halfway between soundness and decadence, made darkly wild suggestions about rites that ought to be practiced on the hill-tops. He came of a line where tradition ran strong, and his memories of chantings in the great stone circles were not altogether connected with Wilbur and his grandfather.

Darkness fell upon a stricken countryside too passive to organise for real defence. In a few cases closely related families would band together and watch in the gloom under one roof; but in general there was only a repetition of the barricading of the night before, and a futile, ineffective gesture of loading muskets and setting pitchforks handily about. Nothing, however, occurred except some hill noises; and when the day came there were many who hoped that the new horror had gone as swiftly as it had come. There were even bold souls who proposed an offensive expedition down in the glen, though they did not venture to set an actual example to the still reluctant majority.

When night came again the barricading was repeated, though there was less huddling together of families. In the morning both the Frye and the Seth Bishop households reported excitement among the dogs and vague sounds and stenches from afar, while early explorers noted with horror a fresh set of the monstrous tracks in the road skirting Sentinel Hill. As before, the sides of the road showed a bruising indicative of the blasphemously stupendous bulk of the horror; whilst the conformation of the tracks seemed to argue a passage in two directions, as if the moving mountain had come from Cold Spring Glen and returned to it along the same path. At the base of the hill a thirty-foot swath of crushed shrubbery saplings led steeply upward, and the seekers gasped when they saw that even the most perpendicular places did not deflect the inexorable trail. Whatever the horror was, it could scale a sheer stony cliff of almost complete verticality; and as the investigators climbed around to the hill's summit by safer routes they saw that the trail ended—or rather, reversed—there.

It was here that the Whateleys used to build their hellish fires and chant their hellish rituals by the table-like stone on May Eve and Hallowmass. Now that very stone formed the centre of a vast space thrashed around by the mountainous horror, whilst upon its slightly concave surface was a thick and foetid deposit of the same tarry stickiness observed on the floor of the ruined Whateley farmhouse when the horror escaped. Men looked at one another and muttered. Then they looked down the hill. Apparently the horror had descended by a route much the same as that of its ascent. To speculate was futile. Reason, logic, and normal ideas of motivation stood confounded. Only old Zebulon who was not with the group, could have done justice to the situation or suggested a plausible explanation.

Thursday night began much like the others, but it ended less happily. The whippoorwills in the glen had screamed with such unusual persistence that many could not sleep, and about 3 A.M. all the party telephones rang tremulously. Those who took down their receivers heard a fright-mad voice shriek out, "Help, oh, my Gawd! . . ." and some thought a crashing sound followed the breaking off of the exclamation. There was nothing more. No one dared do anything, and no one knew till morning whence the call came. Then those who had heard it called everyone on the line, and found that only the Frye's did not reply. The truth appeared an hour later, when a hastily assembled group of armed men trudged out to the Frye place at the head of the glen. It was horrible, yet hardly a surprise. There were more swaths and monstrous prints, but there was no longer any house. It had caved in like an eggshell, and amongst the ruins nothing living or dead could be discovered. Only a stench and a tarry stickiness. The Elmer Fryes had been erased from Dunwich.

VIII

In the meantime a quieter yet even more spiritually poignant phase of the horror had been blackly unwinding itself behind the closed door of a shelf-lined room in Arkham. The curious manuscript record or diary of Wilbur Whateley, delivered to Miskatonic University for translation, had caused much worry and bafflement among the experts in languages both ancient and modern; its very alphabet, notwithstanding a general resemblance to the heavily-shaded Arabic used in Mesopotamia, being absolutely unknown to any available authority. The final conclusion of the linguists was that the text represented an artificial alphabet, giving the effect of a cipher; though none of the usual methods of cryptographic solution seemed to furnish any clue, even when applied on the basis of every tongue the writer might conceivably have used. The ancient books taken from Whateley's quarters, while absorbingly interesting and in several cases promising to open up new and terrible lines of research among philosophers and men of science, were of no assistance whatever in this matter. One of them, a heavy tome with an iron clasp, was in another unknown alphabet—this one of a very different cast, and resembling Sanskrit more than anything else. The old ledger was at length given wholly into the charge of Dr. Armitage, both because of his peculiar interest in the Whateley matter, and because of his wide linguistic learning and skill in the mystical formulae of antiquity and the middle ages.

Armitage had an idea that the alphabet might be something esoterically used by certain forbidden cults which have come down from old times, and which have inherited many forms and traditions from the wizards of the Saracenic world. That question, however, he did not deem vital; since it would be unnecessary to know the origin of the symbols if, as he suspected, they were used as a cipher in a modern language. It was his belief that, considering the great amount of text involved, the writer would scarcely have wished the trouble of using another speech than his own, save perhaps in certain special formulae and incantations. Accordingly he attacked the manuscript with the preliminary assumption that the bulk of it was in English.

Dr. Armitage knew, from the repeated failures of his colleagues, that the riddle was a deep and complex one; and that no simple mode of solution could merit even a trial. All through late August he fortified himself with the mass lore of cryptography; drawing upon the fullest resources of his own library, and wading night after night amidst the arcana of Trithemius' *Poligraphia*, Giambattista Porta's *De Furtivis Literarum Notis*, De Vigenere's *Traite des Chiffres*, Falconer's *Cryptomenysis Patefacta*, Davys' and Thicknesse's eighteenth-century treatises, and such fairly modern authorities as Blair, von Marten, and Klüber's *Kryptographik*. He interspersed his study of the books with attacks on the manuscript itself, and in time became convinced that he had to deal with one of those subtlest and most ingenious of cryptograms, in which many separate lists of corresponding letters are arranged like the multiplication table, and the message built up with arbitrary key-words known only to the initiated. The older authorities seemed rather more helpful than the newer ones, and Armitage concluded that the code of the manuscript was one of great antiquity, no doubt handed down through a long line of mystical experimenters. Several times he seemed near daylight, only to be set back by some unforeseen obstacle. Then, as September approached, the clouds began to clear. Certain letters, as used in certain parts of the manuscript, emerged definitely and unmistakably; and it became obvious that the text was indeed in English.

On the evening of September second the last major barrier gave way, and Dr. Armitage read for the first time a continuous passage of Wilbur Whateley's annals. It was in truth a diary, as all had thought; and it was couched in a style clearly shewing the mixed occult erudition and general illiteracy of the strange being who wrote it. Almost the first long passage that Armitage deciphered, an entry dated November 26, 1916, proved highly startling and disquieting. It was written, he remembered, by a child of three and a half who looked like a lad of twelve or thirteen.

> Today learned the Aklo for the Sabaoth (it ran), which did not like, it being answerable from the hill and not from the air. That upstairs more ahead of me than I had thought it would be, and is not like to have much earth brain. Shot Elam Hutchins's collie Jack when he went to bite me, and Elam says he would kill me if he dast. I guess he won't. Grandfather kept me saying the Dho formula last night, and I think I saw the inner city at the 2 magnetic poles. I shall go to those poles when the earth is cleared off, if I can't break through with the Dho-Hna formula when I commit it. They from the air told me at Sabbat that it will be years before I can clear off the earth, and I guess grandfather will be dead then, so I shall have to learn all the angles of the planes and all the formulas between the Yr and the Nhhngr. They from outside will help, but they cannot take body without human blood. That upstairs looks it will have the right cast. I can see it a little when I make the Voorish sign or blow the powder of Ibn Ghazi at it, and it is near like them at May Eve on the Hill. The other face may wear off some. I wonder how I shall look when the earth is cleared and there are no earth beings on it. He that came with the Aklo Sabaoth said I may be transfigured there being much of outside to work on.

Morning found Dr. Armitage in a cold sweat of terror and a frenzy of wakeful concentration. He had not left the manuscript all night, but sat at his table under the electric light turning page after page with shaking hands as fast as he could decipher the cryptic text. He had nervously telephoned his wife he would not be home, and when she brought him a breakfast from the house he could scarcely dispose of a mouthful. All the day he read on, now and then halted maddeningly as a reapplication of the complex key became necessary. Lunch and dinner were brought him, but he ate only the smallest fraction of either. Toward the middle of the next night he drowsed off in his chair, but soon woke out of a tangle of nightmares almost as hideous as the truths and menaces to man's existence that he had uncovered.

On the morning of September fourth Professor Rice and Dr. Morgan insisted on seeing him for a while, and departed trembling and ashen-grey. That evening he went to bed, but slept only fitfully. Wednesday—the next day—he was back at the manuscript, and began to take copious notes both from the current sections and from those he had already deciphered. In the small hours of that night he slept a little in an easy-chair in his office, but was at the manuscript again before dawn. Some time before noon his physician, Dr. Hartwell, called to see him and insisted that he cease work. He refused; intimating that it was of the most vital importance for him to complete the reading of the diary and promising an explanation in due course of time. That evening, just as twilight fell, he finished his terrible perusal and sank back exhausted. His wife, bringing his dinner, found him in a half-comatose state; but he was conscious enough to warn her off with a sharp cry when he saw her eyes wander toward the notes he had taken. Weakly rising, he gathered up the scribbled papers and sealed them all in a great envelope, which he immediately placed in his inside coat pocket. He had sufficient strength to get home, but was so clearly in need of medical aid that Dr. Hartwell was summoned at once. As the doctor put him to bed he could only mutter over and over again, *"But what, in God's name, can we do?"*

Dr. Armitage slept, but was partly delirious the next day. He made no explanations to Hartwell, but in his calmer moments spoke of the imperative need of a long conference with Rice and Morgan. His wilder wanderings were very startling indeed, including frantic appeals that something in a boarded-up farmhouse be destroyed, and fantastic references to some plan for the extirpation of the entire human race and all animal and vegetable life from the earth by some terrible elder race of beings from another dimension. He would shout that the world was in danger, since the Elder Things wished to strip it and drag it away from the solar system and cosmos of matter into some other plane or phase of entity from which it had once fallen, vigintillions of aeons ago. At other times he would call for the dreaded *Necronomicon* and the *Daemonolatreia* of Remigius, in which he seemed hopeful of finding some formula to check the peril he conjured up.

"Stop them, stop them!" he would shout. "Those Whateleys meant to let them in, and the worst of all is left! Tell Rice and Morgan we must do something—it's a blind business, but I know how to make the powder. . . . It hasn't been fed since the second of August, when Wilbur came here to his death, and at that rate. . . ."

But Armitage had a sound physique despite his seventy-three years, and slept off his disorder that night without developing any real fever. He woke late Friday, clear of head, though sober with a gnawing fear and tremendous sense of responsibility. Saturday afternoon he felt able to go over to the library and summon Rice and Morgan for a conference, and the rest of that day and evening the three men tortured their brains in the wildest speculation and the most desperate debate. Strange and terrible books were drawn voluminously from the stack shelves and from secure places of storage; and diagrams and formulae were copied with feverish haste and in bewildering abundance. Of skepticism there was none. All three had seen the body of Wilbur Whateley as it lay on the floor in a room of that very building, and after that not one of them could feel even slightly inclined to treat the diary as a madman's raving.

Opinions were divided as to notifying the Massachusetts State Police, and the negative finally won. There were things involved which simply could not be believed by those who had not seen a sample, as indeed was made clear during certain subsequent investigations. Late at night the conference disbanded without having developed a definite plan, but all day Sunday Armitage was busy comparing formulae and mixing chemicals obtained from the college laboratory. The more he reflected on the hellish diary, the more he was inclined to doubt the efficacy of any material agent in stamping out the entity which Wilbur Whateley had left behind him—the earth-threatening entity which, unknown to him, was to burst forth in a few hours and become the memorable Dunwich horror.

Monday was a repetition of Sunday with Dr. Armitage, for the task in hand required an infinity of research and experiment. Further consultations of the monstrous diary brought about various changes of plan, and he knew that even in the end a large amount of uncertainty must remain. By Tuesday he had a definite line of action mapped out, and believed he would try a trip to Dunwich within a week. Then, on Wednesday, the great shock came. Tucked obscurely away in a corner of the *Arkham Advertiser* was a facetious little item from the Associated Press, telling what a record-breaking monster the bootleg whiskey of Dunwich had raised up. Armitage, half stunned, could only telephone for Rice and Morgan. Far into the night they discussed, and the next day was a whirlwind of preparation on the part of them all. Armitage knew he would be meddling with terrible powers, yet saw that there was no other way to annul the deeper and more malign muddling which others had done before him.

IX

Friday morning Armitage, Rice, and Morgan set out by motor for Dunwich, arriving at the village about one in the afternoon. The day was pleasant, but even in the brightest sunlight a kind of quiet dread and portent seemed to hover about the strangely domed hills and the deep, shadowy ravines of the stricken region. Now and then on some mountain top a gaunt circle of stones could be glimpsed against the sky. From the air of hushed fright at Osborn's store they knew something hideous had happened, and soon learned of the annihilation of the Elmer Frye house and family. Throughout that afternoon they rode around Dunwich; questioning the natives concerning all that had occurred, and seeing for themselves with rising pangs of horror the drear Frye ruins with their lingering traces of the tarry stickiness, the blasphemous tracks in the Frye yard, the wounded Seth Bishop cattle, and the enormous swaths of disturbed vegetation in various places. The trail up and down Sentinel Hill seemed to Armitage of almost cataclysmic significance, and he looked long at the sinister altar-like stone on the summit.

At length the visitors, apprised of a party of State Police which had come from Aylesbury that morning in response to the first telephone reports of the Frye tragedy, decided to seek out the officers and compare notes as far as practicable. This, however, they found more easily planned than performed; since no sign of the party could be found in any direction. There had been five of them in a car, but now the car stood empty near the ruins in the Frye yard. The natives, all of whom had talked with the policemen, seemed at first as perplexed as Armitage and his companions. Then old Sam Hutchins thought of something and turned pale, nudging Fred Farr and pointing to the dank, deep hollow that yawned close by.

"Gawd," he gasped, "I told 'em not ter go daown into the glen, an' I never thought nobody'd dew it with them tracks an' that smell an' the whippoorwills a-screechin' daown thar in the dark o' noonday. . . ."

A cold shudder ran through natives and visitors alike, and every ear seemed strained in a kind of instinctive, unconscious listening. Armitage, now that he had actually come upon the horror and its monstrous work, trembled with the responsibility he felt to be his. Night would soon fall, and it was then that the mountainous blasphemy lumbered upon its eldritch course. *Negotium perambulans in tenebris.* . . . The old librarian rehearsed the formulae he had memorized, and clutched the paper containing the alternative one he had not memorized. He saw that his electric flashlight was in working order. Rice, beside him, took from a valise a metal sprayer of the sort used in combating insects; whilst Morgan uncased the big-game rifle on which he relied despite his colleague's warnings that no material weapon would be of help.

Armitage, having read the hideous diary, knew painfully well what kind of manifestation to expect; but he did not add to the fright of the Dunwich people by giving any hints or clues. He hoped that it might be conquered without any revelation to the world of the monstrous thing it had escaped. As the shadows gathered, the natives commenced to disperse homeward, anxious to bar themselves indoors despite the present evidence that all human locks and bolts were useless before a force that could bend trees and crush houses when it chose. They shook their heads at the visitors' plan to stand guard at the Frye ruins near the glen; and as they left, had little expectancy of ever seeing the watchers again.

There were rumblings under the hills that night, and the whippoorwills piped threateningly. Once in a while a wind, sweeping up out of Cold Spring Glen, would bring a touch of ineffable foetor to the heavy night air; such a foetor as all three of the watchers had smelled once before, when they stood above a dying thing that had passed for fifteen years and a half as a human being. But the looked-for terror did not appear. Whatever was down there in the glen was biding its time, and Armitage told his colleagues it would be suicidal to try to attack it in the dark.

Morning came wanly, and the night-sounds ceased. It was a grey, bleak day, with now and then a drizzle of rain; and heavier and heavier clouds seemed to be piling themselves up beyond the hills to the northwest. The men from Arkham were undecided what to do. Seeking shelter from the increasing rainfall beneath one of the few undestroyed Frye outbuildings, they debated the wisdom of waiting, or of taking the aggressive and going down into the glen in quest of their nameless, monstrous quarry. The downpour waxed in heaviness, and distant peals of thunder sounded from far horizons. Sheet lightning shimmered, and then a forky bolt flashed near at hand, as if descending into the accursed glen itself. The sky grew very dark, and the watchers hoped that the storm would prove a short, sharp one followed by clear weather.

It was still gruesomely dark when, not much over an hour later, a confused babel of voices sounded down the road. Another moment brought to view a frightened group of more than a dozen men, running, shouting, and even whimpering hysterically. Someone in the lead began sobbing out words, and the Arkham men started violently when those words developed a coherent form.

"Oh, my Gawd, my Gawd," the voice choked out. "It's a-goin' agin, *an' this time by day!* It's aout—it's aout an' a-movin' this very minute, an' only the Lord knows when it'll be on us all!"

The speaker panted into silence, but another took up his message.

"Nigh on a haour ago Zeb Whateley here heerd the 'phone a-ringin', an' it was Mis' Corey, George's wife, that lives daown by the junc-tion. She says the hired boy Luther was aout drivin' in the caows from the storm arten the big bolt, when he see all the trees a-bendin' at the maouth o' the glen—opposite side ter this—an' smelt the same awful smell like he smelt when he faound the big tracks las' Monday mornin'. An' she says he says they was a swishin', lappin' saound, more nor what the bendin' trees an' bushes could make, an' all on a suddent the trees along the rud begun ter git pushed one side, an' they was a awful stompin' an' splashin' in the mud. But mind ye, Luther he didn't see nothin' at all, only just the bendin' trees an' underbrush.

"Then fur ahead where Bishop's Brook goes under the rud he heerd a awful creakin' an' strainin' on the bridge, an' says he could tell the saound o' wood a-startin' to crack an' split. An' all the whiles he never see a thing, only them trees an' bushes a-bendin'. An' when the swishin' Sentinel Hill—Luther he had the guts ter step up whar he'd heerd it fust an' look at the graound. It was all mud an' water, an' the sky was dark, an' the rain was wipin' aout all tracks abaout as fast as could be; but beginnin' at the glen maouth, whar the trees hed moved, they was still some o' them awful prints big as bar'ls like he seen Monday."

At this point the first excited speaker interrupted.

"But *that* ain't the trouble naow—that was only the start. Zeb here was callin' folks up an' everybody was a-listenin' in when a call from Seth Bishop's cut in. His haousekeeper Sally was carryin' on fit to kill—she'd jest seed the trees a'bendin' beside the rud, an' says they was a kind o' mushy saound, like a elephant puffin' an' treadin', a-headin' fer the haouse. Then she up an' spoke suddent of a fearful smell, an' says her boy Cha'ncey was a-screamin' as haow it was jest like what he smelt up to the Whateley rewins Monday mornin'. An' the dogs was all barkin' an' whinin' awful.

"An' then she let aout a turrible yell, an' says the shed daown the rud had jest caved in like the storm hed blowed it over, only the wind wa'n't strong enough to dew that. Everybody was a-listenin', an' we could hear lots o' folks on the wire a-gaspin'. All to onct Sally she yelled again, an' says the front yard picket fence hed just crumbled up, though they wa'n't no sign o' what done it. Then everybody on the line could hear Cha'ncey an' old' Seth Bishop a-yellin' tew', an' Sally was shriekin' aout that suthin' heavy hed struck the haouse—not lightnin' nor nothin', but suthin' heavy again the front, that kep' a-launchin' itself agin an' agin, though ye couldn't see nothin' aout the front winders. An' then . . . an' then. . . ."

Lines of fright deepened on every face; and Armitage, shaken as he was, had barely poise enough to prompt the speaker.

"An' then . . . Sally she yelled aout, 'O help, the haouse is a-cavin' in' . . . an' on the wire we could hear a turrible crashin' an' a hull flock o' screamin' . . . jes like when Elmer Frye's place was took, only wuss. . . ."

The man paused, and another of the crowd spoke.

"That's all—not a saound nor squeak over the 'phone arter that. Jest still-like. We that heerd it got aout Fords an' wagons an' rounded up as many able-bodied men-folks as we could git, at Corey's place, an' come up here ter see what yew thought best ter dew. Not but what I think it's the Lord's jedgment fer our iniquities, that no mortal kin ever set aside."

Armitage saw that the time for positive action had come, and spoke decisively to the faltering group of frightened rustics.

"We must follow it, boys." He made his voice as reassuring as possible. "I believe there's a chance of putting it out of business. You men know that those Whateleys were wizards—well, this thing is a thing of wizardry, and must be put down by the same means. I've seen Wilbur Whateley's diary and read some of the strange old books he used to read; and I think I know the right kind of spell to recite to make the thing fade away. Of course, one can't be sure, but we can always take a chance. It's invisible—I knew it would be—but there's powder in this long-distance sprayer that might make it show up for a second. Later on we'll try it. It's a frightful thing to have alive, but it isn't as bad as what Wilbur would have let in if he'd lived longer. You'll never know what the world escaped. Now we've only this one thing to fight, and it can't multiply. It can, though, do a lot of harm; so we mustn't hesitate to rid the community of it.

"We must follow it—and the way to begin is to go to the place that has just been wrecked. Let somebody lead the way—I don't know your roads very well, but I've an idea there might be a shorter cut across lots. How about it?"

The men shuffled about a moment, and then Earl Sawyer spoke softly, pointing with a grimy finger through the steadily lessening rain.

"I guess ye kin git to Seth Bishop's quickest by cuttin' acrost the lower medder here, wadin' the brook at the low place, an' climbin' through Carrier's mowin' an' the timber-lot beyont. That comes aout on the upper rud mighty nigh Seth's—a leetle t'other side."

Armitage, with Rice and Morgan, started to walk in the direction indicated; and most of the natives followed slowly. The sky was growing lighter, and there were signs that the storm had worn itself away. When Armitage inadvertently took a wrong direction, Joe Osborn warned him and walked ahead to show the right one. Courage and confidence were mounting; though the twilight of the almost perpendicular wooded hill which lay toward the end of their short cut, and among whose fantastic ancient trees they had to scramble as if up a ladder, put these qualities to a severe test.

At length they emerged on a muddy road to find the sun coming out. They were a little beyond the Seth Bishop place, but bent trees and hideously unmistakable tracks shewed what had passed by. Only a few moments were consumed in surveying the ruins just around the bend. It was the Frye incident all over again, and nothing dead or living was found in either of the collapsed shells which had been the Bishop house and barn. No one cared to remain there amidst the stench and tarry stickiness, but all turned instinctively to the line of horrible prints leading on toward the wrecked Whateley farmhouse and the altar-crowned slopes of Sentinel Hill.

As the men passed the site of Wilbur Whateley's abode they shuddered visibly, and seemed again to mix hesitancy with their zeal. It was no joke tracking down something as big as a house that one could not see, but that had all the vicious malevolence of a daemon. Opposite the base of Sentinel Hill the tracks left the road, and there was a fresh bending and matting visible along the broad swath marking the monster's former route to and from the summit.

Armitage produced a pocket telescope of considerable power and scanned the steep green side of the hill. Then he handed the instrument to Morgan, whose sight was keener. After a moment of gazing Morgan cried out sharply, passing the glass to Earl Sawyer and indicating a certain spot on the slope with his finger. Sawyer, as clumsy as most non-users of optical devices are, fumbled a while; but eventually focussed the lenses with Armitage's aid. When he did so his cry was less restrained than Morgan's had been.

"Gawd almighty, the grass an' bushes is a-movin'! It's a-goin' up— slow-like—creepin'—up ter the top this minute, heaven only knows what fur!"

Then the germ of panic seemed to spread among the seekers. It was one thing to chase the nameless entity, but quite another to find it. Spells might be all right—but suppose they weren't? Voices began questioning Armitage about what he knew of the thing, and no reply seemed quite to satisfy. Everyone seemed to feel himself in close proximity to phases of Nature and of being utterly forbidden, and wholly outside the sane experience of mankind.

X

In the end the three men from Arkham—old, white-bearded Dr. Armitage, stocky, iron-grey Professor Rice, and lean, youngish Dr. Morgan, ascended the mountain alone. After much patient instruction regarding its focussing and use, they left the telescope with the frightened group that remained in the road; and as they climbed they were watched closely by those among whom the glass was passed around. It was hard going, and Armitage had to be helped more than once. High above the toiling group the great swath trembled as its hellish maker repassed with snail-like deliberateness. Then it was obvious that the pursuers were gaining.

Curtis Whateley—of the undecayed branch—was holding the telescope when the Arkham party detoured radically from the swath. He told the crowd that the men were evidently trying to get to a subordinate peak which overlooked the swath at a point considerably ahead of where the shrubbery was now bending. This, indeed, proved to be true; and the party were seen to gain the minor elevation only a short time after the invisible blasphemy had passed it.

Then Wesley Corey, who had taken the glass, cried out that Armitage was adjusting the sprayer which Rice held, and that something must be about to happen. The crowd stirred uneasily, recalling that his sprayer was expected to give the unseen horror a moment of visibility. Two or three men shut their eyes, but Curtis Whateley snatched back the telescope and strained his vision to the utmost. He saw that Rice, from the party's point of vantage above and behind the entity, had an excellent chance of spreading the potent powder with marvelous effect.

Those without the telescope saw only an instant's flash of grey cloud—a cloud about the size of a moderately large building—near the top of the mountain. Curtis, who held the instrument, dropped it with a piercing shriek into the ankle-deep mud of the road. He reeled, and would have crumpled to the ground had not two or three others seized and steadied him. All he could do was moan half-inaudibly.

"Oh, oh, great Gawd . . . *that* . . . *that*. . . ."

There was a pandemonium of questioning, and only Henry Wheeler thought to rescue the fallen telescope and wipe it clean of mud. Curtis was past all coherence, and even isolated replies were almost too much for him.

"Bigger'n a barn . . . all made o' squirmin' ropes . . . hull thing sort o' shaped like a hen's egg bigger'n anything with dozens o' legs like hogsheads that haff shut up when they step . . . nothin' solid abaout it—all like jelly, an' made o' sep'rit wrigglin' ropes pushed clost together . . . great bulgin' eyes all over it . . . ten or twenty maouths or trunks a-stickin' aout all along the sides, big as stove-pipes, an' all a-tossin' an' openin' an' shuttin' . . . all grey, with kinder blue or purple rings . . . *an' Gawd in Heaven—that haff face on top!* . . ."

This final memory, whatever it was, proved too much for poor Curtis; and he collapsed completely before he could say more. Fred Farr and Will Hutchins carried him to the roadside and laid him on the damp grass. Henry Wheeler, trembling, turned the rescued telescope on the mountain to see what he might. Through the lenses were discernible three tiny figures, apparently running toward the summit as fast as the steep incline allowed. Only these—nothing more. Then everyone noticed a strangely unseasonable noise in the deep valley behind, and even in the underbrush of Sentinel Hill itself. It was the piping of unnumbered whippoorwills, and in their shrill chorus there seemed to lurk a note of tense and evil expectancy.

Earl Sawyer now took the telescope and reported the three figures as standing on the topmost ridge, virtually level with the altarstone but at a considerable distance from it. One figure, he said, seemed to be raising its hands above its head at rhythmic intervals; and as Sawyer mentioned the circumstance the crowd seemed to hear a faint, half-musical sound from the distance, as if a loud chant were accompanying the gestures. The weird silhouette on that remote peak must have been a spectacle of infinite grotesqueness and impressiveness, but no observer was in a mood for aesthetic appreciation. "I guess he's sayin' the spell," whispered Wheeler as he snatched back the telescope. The whippoorwills were piping wildly, and in a singularly curious irregular rhythm quite unlike that of the visible ritual.

Suddenly the sunshine seemed to lessen without the intervention of any discernible cloud. It was a very peculiar phenomenon, and was plainly marked by all. A rumbling sound seemed brewing beneath the hills, mixed strangely with a concordant rumbling which clearly came from the sky. Lightning flashed aloft, and the wondering crowd looked in vain for the portents of storm. The chanting of the men from Arkham now became unmistakable, and Wheeler saw through the glass that they were all raising their arms in the rhythmic incantation. From some farmhouse far away came the frantic barking of dogs.

The change in the quality of the daylight increased, and the crowd gazed about the horizon in wonder. A purplish darkness, born of nothing more than a spectral deepening of the sky's blue, pressed down upon the rumbling hills. Then the lightning flashed again, somewhat brighter than before, and the crowd fancied that it had shewed a certain mistiness around the altar-stone on the distant height. No one, however, had been using the telescope at that instant. The whippoorwills continued their irregular pulsation, and the men of Dunwich braced themselves tensely against some imponderable menace with which the atmosphere seemed surcharged.

Without warning came those deep, cracked, raucous vocal sounds which will never leave the memory of the stricken group who heard them. Not from any human throat were they born, for the organs of man can yield no such acoustic perversions. Rather would one have said they came from the pit itself, had not their source been so unmistakably the altar-stone on the peak. It is almost erroneous to call them *sounds* at all, since so much of their ghastly, infra-bass timbre spoke to dim seats of consciousness and terror far subtler than the ear; yet one must do so, since their form was indisputably though vaguely that of half-articulate *words*. They were loud—loud as the rumblings and the thunder above which they echoed—yet did they come from no visible being. And because imagination might suggest a conjectural source in the world of non-visible beings, the huddled crowd at the mountain's base huddled still closer, and winced as if in expectation of a blow.

"Ygnaiih . . . ygnaiih . . . thflthkh'ngha . . . Yog-Sothoth . . ." rang the hideous croaking out of space. "Y'bthnk . . . h'ehye—n'grkdl'lh . . ."

The speaking impulse seemed to falter here, as if some frightful psychic struggle were going on. Henry Wheeler strained his eye at the telescope, but saw only the three grotesquely silhouetted human figures on the peak, all moving their arms furiously in strange gestures as their incantation drew near its culmination. From what black wells of Acherontic fear or feeling, from what unplumbed gulfs of extra-cosmic consciousness or obscure, long-latent heredity, were those half-articulate thunder-croakings drawn? Presently they began to gather renewed force and coherence as they grew in stark, utter, ultimate frenzy.

"Eh-ya-ya-ya-yahaah—e'yayayayaaaa . . . ngh'aaaaa . . . ngh'aaa . . . h'yuh . . . h'yuh . . . HELP! HELP! . . . ff—ff—ff—FATHER! FATHER! YOG-SOTHOTH! . . ."

But that was all. The pallid group in the road, still reeling at the *indisputably English* syllables that had poured thickly and thunderously down from the frantic vacancy beside that shocking altar-stone, were never to hear such syllables again. Instead, they jumped violently at the terrific report which seemed to rend the hills; the deafening, cataclysmic peal whose source, be it inner earth or sky, no hearer was ever able to place. A single lightning bolt shot from the purple zenith to the altar-stone, and a great tidal wave of viewless force and indescribable stench swept down from the hill to all the countryside. Trees, grass, and underbrush were whipped into a fury; and the frightened crowd at the mountain's base, weakened by the lethal foetor that seemed about to asphyxiate them, were almost hurled off their feet. Dogs howled from the distance, green grass and foliage wilted to a curious, sickly yellow-grey, and over field and forest were scattered the bodies of dead whippoorwills.

The stench left quickly, but the vegetation never came right again. To this day there is something queer and unholy about the growths on and around that fearsome hill. Curtis Whateley was only just regaining consciousness when the Arkham men came slowly down the mountain in the beams of a sunlight once more brilliant and untainted. They were grave and quiet, and seemed shaken by memories and reflections even more terrible than those which had reduced the group of natives to a state of cowed quivering. In reply to a jumble of questions they only shook their heads and reaffirmed one vital fact.

"The thing has gone for ever," Armitage said. "It has been split up into what it was originally made of, and can never exist again. It was an impossibility in a normal world. Only the least fraction was really matter in any sense we know. It was like its father—and most of it has gone back to him in some vague realm or dimension outside our material universe; some vague abyss out of which only the most accursed rites of human blasphemy could ever have called him for a moment on the hills."

There was a brief silence, and in that pause the scattered senses of poor Curtis Whateley began to knit back into a sort of continuity; so that he put his hands to his head with a moan. Memory seemed to pick itself up where it had left off, and the horror of the sight that had prostrated him burst in upon him again.

"Oh, oh, my Gawd, that haff face—that haff face on top of it . . . that face with the red eyes an' crinkly albino hair, an' no chin, like the Whateleys. . . . It was a octopus, centipede, spider kind o' thing, but they was a haff-shaped man's face on top of it, an' it looked like Wizard Whateley's, only it was yards an' yards acrost. . . ."

He paused exhausted, as the whole group of natives stared in a bewilderment not quite crystallized into fresh terror. Only old Zebulon Whateley, who wanderingly remembered ancient things but who had been silent heretofore, spoke aloud.

"Fifteen year' gone," he rambled, "I heerd Ol' Whateley say as haow some day we'd hear a child o' Lavinny's a-callin its father's name on the top o' Sentinel Hill. . . ."

But Joe Osborn interrupted him to question the Arkham men anew.

"What was it, anyahow, an' haowever did young Wizard Whateley call it aout o' the air it come from?"

Armitage chose his words very carefully.

"It was—well, it was mostly a kind of force that doesn't belong in our part of space; a kind of force that acts and grows and shapes itself by other laws than those of our sort of Nature. We have no business calling in such things from outside, and only very wicked people and very wicked cults ever try to. There was some of it in Wilbur Whateley himself—enough to make a devil and a precocious monster of him, and to make his passing out a pretty terrible sight. I'm going to burn his accursed diary, and if you men are wise you'll dynamite that altar-stone up there, and pull down all the rings of standing stones on the other hills. Things like that brought down the beings those Whateleys were so fond of—the beings they were going to let in tangibly to wipe out the human race and drag the earth off to some nameless place for some nameless purpose.

"But as to this thing we've just sent back—the Whateleys raised it for a terrible part in the doings that were to come. It grew fast and big from the same reason that Wilbur grew fast and big—but it beat him because it had a greater share of the *outsideness* in it. You needn't ask how Wilbur called it out of the air. He didn't call it out. *It was his twin brother, but it looked more like the father than he did."*

The Whisperer in Darkness

Bear in mind closely that I did not see any actual visual horror at the end. To say that a mental shock was the cause of what I inferred—that last straw which sent me racing out of the lonely Akeley farmhouse and through the wild domed hills of Vermont in a commandeered motor at night—is to ignore the plainest facts of my final experience. Notwithstanding the deep things I saw and heard, and the admitted vividness of the impression produced on me by these things, I cannot prove even now whether I was right or wrong in my hideous inference. For after all, Akeley's disappearance establishes nothing. People found nothing amiss in his house despite the bullet-marks on the outside and inside. It was just as though he had walked out casually for a ramble in the hills and failed to return. There was not even a sign that a guest had been there, or that those horrible cylinders and machines had been stored in the study. That he had mortally feared the crowded green hills and endless trickle of brooks among which he had been born and reared, means nothing at all, either; for thousands are subject to just such morbid fears. Eccentricity, moreover, could easily account for his strange acts and apprehensions toward the last.

The whole matter began, so far as I am concerned, with the historic and unprecedented Vermont floods of November 3, 1927. I was then, as now, an instructor of literature at Miskatonic University in Arkham, Massachusetts, and an enthusiastic amateur student of New England folklore. Shortly after the flood, amidst the varied reports of hardship, suffering, and organized relief which filled the press, there appeared certain odd stories of things found floating in some of the swollen rivers; so that many of my friends embarked on curious discussions and appealed to me to shed what light I could on the subject. I felt flattered at having my folklore study taken so seriously, and did what I could to belittle the wild, vague tales which seemed so clearly an outgrowth of old rustic superstitions. It amused me to find several persons of education who insisted that some stratum of obscure, distorted fact might underlie the rumors.

The tales thus brought to my notice came mostly through newspaper cuttings; though one yarn had an oral source and was repeated to a friend of mine in a letter from his mother in Hardwick, Vermont. The type of thing described was essentially the same in all cases, though there seemed to be three separate instances involved—one connected with the Winooski River near Montpelier, another attached to the West River in Windham County beyond Newfane, and a third centering in the Passumpsic in Caledonia County above Lyndonville. Of course many of the stray items mentioned other instances, but on analysis they all seemed to boil down to these three. In each case country folk reported seeing one or more very bizarre and disturbing objects in the surging waters that poured down from the unfrequented hills, and there was a widespread tendency to connect these sights with a primitive, half-forgotten cycle of whispered legend which old people resurrected for the occasion.

What people thought they saw were organic shapes not quite like any they had ever seen before. Naturally, there were many human bodies washed along by the streams in that tragic period; but those who described these strange shapes felt quite sure that they were not human, despite some superficial resemblances in size and general outline. Nor, said the witnesses, could they have been any kind of animal known to Vermont. They were pinkish things about five feet long; with crustaceous bodies bearing vast pairs of dorsal fins or membranous wings and several sets of articulated limbs, and with a sort of convoluted ellipsoid, covered with multitudes of very short antennae, where a head would ordinarily be. It was really remarkable how closely the reports from different sources tended to coincide; though the wonder was lessened by the fact that the old legends, shared at one time throughout the hill country, furnished a morbidly vivid picture which might well have coloured the imaginations of all the witnesses concerned. It was my conclusion that such witnesses— in every case naïve and simple backwoods folk—had glimpsed the battered and bloated bodies of human beings or farm animals in the whirling currents; and had allowed the half-remembered folklore to invest these pitiful objects with fantastic attributes.

The ancient folklore, while cloudy, evasive, and largely forgotten by the present generation, was of a highly singular character, and obviously reflected the influence of still earlier Indian tales. I knew it well, though I had never been in Vermont, through the exceedingly rare monograph of Eli Davenport, which embraces material orally obtained prior to 1839 among the oldest people of the state. This material, moreover, closely coincided with tales which I had personally heard from elderly rustics in the mountains of New Hampshire. Briefly summarized, it hinted at a hidden race of monstrous beings which lurked somewhere among the remoter hills—in the deep woods of the highest peaks, and the dark valleys where streams trickle from unknown sources. These beings were seldom glimpsed, but evidences of their presence were reported by those who had ventured farther than usual up the slopes of certain mountains or into certain deep, steep-sided gorges that even the wolves shunned.

There were queer footprints or claw-prints in the mud of brook-margins and barren patches, and curious circles of stones, with the grass around them worn away, which did not seem to have been placed or entirely shaped by Nature. There were, too, certain caves of problematical depth in the sides of the hills; with mouths closed by boulders in a manner scarcely accidental, and with more than an average quota of the queer prints leading both toward and away from them—if indeed the direction of these prints could be justly estimated. And worst of all, there were the things which adventurous people had seen very rarely in the twilight of the remotest valleys and the dense perpendicular woods above the limits of normal hill-climbing.

It would have been less uncomfortable if the stray accounts of these things had not agreed so well. As it was, nearly all the rumors had several points in common; averring that the creatures were a sort of huge, light-red crab with many pairs of legs and with two great bat-like wings in the middle of the back. They sometimes walked on all their legs, and sometimes on the hindmost pair only, using the others to convey large objects of indeterminate nature. On one occasion they were spied in considerable numbers, a detachment of them wading along a shallow woodland watercourse three abreast in evidently disciplined formation. Once a specimen was seen flying—launching itself from the top of a bald, lonely hill at night and vanishing in the sky after its great flapping wings had been silhouetted an instant against the full moon.

These things seemed content, on the whole, to let mankind alone; though they were at times held responsible for the disappearance of venturesome individuals—especially persons who built houses too close to certain valleys or too high up on certain mountains. Many localities came to be known as inadvisable to settle in, the feeling persisting long after the cause was forgotten. People would look up at some of the neighbouring mountain-precipices with a shudder, even when not recalling how many settlers had been lost, and how many farmhouses burnt to ashes, on the lower slopes of those grim, green sentinels.

But while according to the earliest legends the creatures would appear to have harmed only those trespassing on their privacy; there were later accounts of their curiosity respecting men, and of their attempts to establish secret outposts in the human world. There were tales of the queer claw-prints seen around farmhouse windows in the morning, and of occasional disappearances in regions outside the obviously haunted areas. Tales, besides, of buzzing voices in imitation of human speech which made surprising offers to lone travelers on roads and cart-paths in the deep woods, and of children frightened out of their wits by things seen or heard where the primal forest pressed close upon their dooryards. In the final layer of legends—the layer just preceding the decline of superstition and the abandonment of close contact with the dreaded places—there are shocked references to hermits and remote farmers who at some period of life appeared to have undergone a repellent mental change, and who were shunned and whispered about as mortals who had sold themselves to the strange beings. In one of the northeastern counties it seemed to be a fashion about 1800 to accuse eccentric and unpopular recluses of being allies or representatives of the abhorred things.

As to what the things were—explanations naturally varied. The common name applied to them was "those ones," or "the old ones," though other terms had a local and transient use. Perhaps the bulk of the Puritan settlers set them down bluntly as familiars of the devil, and made them a basis of awed theological speculation. Those with Celtic legendry in their heritage—mainly the Scotch-Irish element of New Hampshire, and their kindred who had settled in Vermont on Governor Wentworth's colonial grants—linked them vaguely with the malign fairies and "little people" of the bogs and raths, and protected themselves with scraps of incantation handed down through many generations. But the Indians had the most fantastic theories of all. While different tribal legends differed, there was a marked consensus of belief in certain vital particulars; it being unanimously agreed that the creatures were not native to this earth.

The Pennacook myths, which were the most consistent and picturesque, taught that the Winged Ones came from the Great Bear in the sky, and had mines in our earthly hills whence they took a kind of stone they could not get on any other world. They did not live here, said the myths, but merely maintained outposts and flew back with vast cargoes of stone to their own stars in the north.

They harmed only those earth-people who got too near them or spied upon them. Animals shunned them through instinctive hatred, not because of being hunted. They could not eat the things and animals of earth, but brought their own food from the stars. It was bad to get near them, and sometimes young hunters who went into their hills never came back. It was not good, either, to listen to what they whispered at night in the forest with voices like a bee's that tried to be like the voices of men. They knew the speech of all kinds of men—Pennacooks, Hurons, men of the Five Nations—but did not seem to have or need any speech of their own. They talked with their heads, which changed colour in different ways to mean different things.

All the legendry, of course, white and Indian alike, died down during the nineteenth century, except for occasional atavistical flareups. The ways of the Vermonters became settled; and once their habitual paths and dwellings were established according to a certain fixed plan, they remembered less and less what fears and avoidances had determined that plan, and even that there had been any fears or avoidances. Most people simply knew that certain hilly regions were considered as highly unhealthy, unprofitable, and generally unlucky to live in, and that the farther one kept from them the better off one usually was. In time the ruts of custom and economic interest became so deeply cut in approved places that there was no longer any reason for going outside them, and the haunted hills were left deserted by accident rather than by design. Save during infrequent local scares, only wonder-loving grandmothers and retrospective nonagenarians ever whispered of beings dwelling in those hills; and even such whispers admitted that there was not much to fear from those things now that they were used to the presence of houses and settlements, and now that human beings let their chosen territory severely alone.

All this I had long known from my reading, and from certain folk tales picked up in New Hampshire; hence when the flood-time rumours began to appear, I could easily guess what imaginative background had evolved them. I took great pains to explain this to my friends, and was correspondingly amused when several contentious souls continued to insist on a possible element of truth in the reports. Such persons tried to point out that the early legends had a significant persistence and uniformity, and that the virtually unexplored nature of the Vermont hills made it unwise to be dogmatic about what might or might not dwell among them; nor could they be silenced by my assurance that all the myths were of a well-known pattern common to most of mankind and determined by early phases of imaginative experience which always produced the same type of delusion.

It was of no use to demonstrate to such opponents that the Vermont myths differed but little in essence from those universal legends of natural personification which filled the ancient world with fauns and dryads and satyrs, suggested the *kallikanzarai* of modern Greece, and gave to wild Wales and Ireland their dark hints of strange, small, and terrible hidden races of troglodytes and burrowers. No use, either, to point out the even more startlingly similar belief of the Nepalese hill tribes in the dreaded *Mi-Go* or "Abominable Snow-Men" who lurk hideously amidst the ice and rock pinnacles of the Himalayan summits. When I brought up this evidence, my opponents turned it against me by claiming that it must imply some actual historicity for the ancient tales; that it must argue the real existence of some queer elder earth-race, driven to hiding after the advent and dominance of mankind, which might very conceivably have survived in reduced numbers to relatively recent times—or even to the present.

The more I laughed at such theories, the more these stubborn friends asseverated them; adding that even without the heritage of legend the recent reports were too clear, consistent, detailed, and sanely prosaic in manner of telling, to be completely ignored. Two or three fanatical extremists went so far as to hint at possible meanings in the ancient Indian tales which gave the hidden beings a nonterrestrial origin; citing the extravagant books of Charles Fort with their claims that voyagers from other worlds and outer space have often visited the earth. Most of my foes, however, were merely romanticists who insisted on trying to transfer to real life the fantastic lore of lurking "little people" made popular by the magnificent horror-fiction of Arthur Machen.

II

As was only natural under the circumstances, this piquant debating finally got into print in the form of letters to the *Arkham Advertiser*; some of which were copied in the press of those Vermont regions whence the flood-stories came. The *Rutland Herald* gave half a page of extracts from the letters on both sides, while the *Brattleboro Reformer* reprinted one of my long historical and mythological summaries in full, with some accompanying comments in "The Pendrifter's" thoughtful column which supported and applauded my skeptical conclusions. By the spring of 1928 I was almost a well-known figure in Vermont, notwithstanding the fact that I had never set foot in the state. Then came the challenging letters from Henry Akeley which impressed me so profoundly, and which took me for the first and last time to that fascinating realm of crowded green precipices and muttering forest streams.

Most of what I know of Henry Wentworth Akeley was gathered by correspondence with his neighbours, and with his only son in California, after my experience in his lonely farmhouse. He was, I discovered, the last representative on his home soil of a long, locally distinguished line of jurists, administrators, and gentlemen-agriculturists. In him, however, the family mentally had veered away from practical affairs to pure scholarship; so that he had been a notable student of mathematics, astronomy, biology, anthropology, and folklore at the University of Vermont. I had never previously heard of him, and he did not give many autobiographical details in his communications; but from the first I saw he was a man of character, education, and intelligence, albeit a recluse with very little worldly sophistication.

Despite the incredible nature of what he claimed, I could not help at once taking Akeley more seriously than I had taken any of the other challengers of my views. For one thing, he was really close to the actual phenomena—visible and tangible—that he speculated so grotesquely about; and for another thing, he was amazingly willing to leave his conclusions in a tentative state like a true man of science. He had no personal preferences to advance, and was always guided by what he took to be solid evidence. Of course I began by considering him mistaken, but gave him credit for being intelligently mistaken; and at no time did I emulate some of his friends in attributing his ideas, and his fear of the lonely green hills, to insanity. I could see that there was a great deal to the man, and knew that what he reported must surely come from strange circumstance deserving investigation, however little it might have to do with the fantastic causes he assigned. Later on I received from him certain material proofs which placed the matter on a somewhat different and bewilderingly bizarre basis.

I cannot do better than transcribe in full, so far as is possible, the long letter in which Akeley introduced himself, and which formed such an important landmark in my own intellectual history. It is no longer in my possession, but my memory holds almost every word of its portentous message; and again I affirm my confidence in the sanity of the man who wrote it. Here is the text—a text which reached me in the cramped, archaic-looking scrawl of one who had obviously not mingled much with the world during his sedate, scholarly life.

R.F.D. #2,
Townshend, Windham Co., Vermont.
May 5, 1928

Albert N. Wilmarth, Esq.,
118 Saltonstall St.,
Arkham, Mass.

My Dear Sir:—

I have read with great interest the *Brattleboro Reformer*'s reprint
(Apr. 23, '28) of your letter on the recent stories of strange bodies seen
floating in our flooded streams last fall, and on the curious folklore
they so well agree with. It is easy to see why an outlander would take
the position you take, and even why "Pendrifter" agrees with you.
That is the attitude generally taken by educated persons both in
and out of Vermont, and was my own attitude as a young man (I am
now 57) before my studies, both general and in Davenport's book, led
me to do some exploring in parts of the hills hereabouts not usually
visited.

I was directed toward such studies by the queer old tales I used to
hear from elderly farmers of the more ignorant sort, but now I wish I
had let the whole matter alone. I might say, with all proper modesty,
that the subject of anthropology and folklore is by no means strange
to me. I took a good deal of it at college, and am familiar with most of
the standard authorities such as Tylor, Lubbock, Frazer, Quatrefages,
Murray, Osborn, Keith, Boule, G. Elliott Smith, and so on. It is no
news to me that tales of hidden races are as old as all mankind. I have
seen the reprints of letters from you, and those agreeing with you, in
the *Rutland Herald*, and guess I know about where your controversy
stands at the present time.

What I desire to say now is, that I am afraid your adversaries are
nearer right than yourself, even though all reason seems to be on your
side. They are nearer right than they realise themselves—for of
course they go only by theory, and cannot know what I know. If I
knew as little of the matter as they, I would feel justified in believing
as they do. I would be wholly on your side.

You can see that I am having a hard time getting to the point,
probably because I really dread getting to the point; but the upshot of
the matter is that *I have certain evidence that monstrous things do
indeed live in the woods on the high hills which nobody visits*. I
have not seen any of the things floating in the rivers, as reported, *but
I have seen things like them* under circumstances I dread to repeat. I
have seen footprints, and of late have seen them nearer my own
home (I live in the old Akeley place south of Townshend Village, on

the side of Dark Mountain) than I dare tell you now. And I have over-heard voices in the woods at certain points that I will not even begin to describe on paper.

At one place I heard them so much that I took a phonograph there—with a dictaphone attachment and wax blank—and I shall try to arrange to have you hear the record I got. I have run it on the machine for some of the old people up here, and one of the voices had nearly scared them paralysed by reason of its likeness to a certain voice (that buzzing voice in the woods which Davenport mentions) that their grandmothers have told about and mimicked for them. I know what most people think of a man who tells about "hearing voices"—but before you draw conclusions just listen to this record and ask some of the older backwoods people what they think of it. If you can account for it normally, very well; but there must be something behind it. *Ex nihilo nihil fit*, you know.

Now my object in writing you is not to start an argument but to give you information which I think a man of your tastes will find deeply interesting. *This is private. Publicly I am on your side*, for certain things show me that it does not do for people to know too much about these matters. My own studies are now wholly private, and I would not think of saying anything to attract people's attention and cause them to visit the places I have explored. It is true—terribly true—that there are *non-human creatures watching us all the time*; with spies among us gathering information. It is from a wretched man who, if he was sane (as I think he was) *was one of those spies*, that I got a large part of my clues to the matter. He later killed himself, but I have reason to think there are others now.

The things come from another planet, being able to live in interstellar space and fly through it on clumsy, powerful wings which have a way of resisting the aether but which are too poor at steering to be of much use in helping them about on earth. I will tell you about this later if you do not dismiss me at once as a madman. They come here to get metals from mines that go deep under the hills, *and I think I know where they come from*. They will not hurt us if we let them alone, but no one can say what will happen if we get too curious about them. Of course a good army of men could wipe out their mining colony. That is what they are afraid of. But if that happened, more would come from *outside*—any number of them. They could easily conquer the earth, but have not tried so far because they have not needed to. They would rather leave things as they are to save bother.

I think they mean to get rid of me because of what I have discovered. There is a great black stone with unknown hieroglyphics half worn away which I found in the woods on Round Hill, east of here;

and after I took it home everything became different. If they think I suspect too much they will either kill me *or take me off the earth to where they come from.* They like to take away men of learning once in a while, to keep informed on the state of things in the human world.

This leads me to my secondary purpose in addressing you—namely, to urge you to hush up the present debate rather than give it more publicity. *People must be kept away from these hills,* and in order to effect this, their curiosity ought not to be aroused any further. Heaven knows there is peril enough anyway, with promoters and real estate men flooding Vermont with herds of summer people to overrun the wild places and cover the hills with cheap bungalows.

I shall welcome further communication with you, and shall try to send you that phonograph record and black stone (which is so worn that photographs don't show much) by express if you are willing. I say "try" because I think those creatures have a way of tampering with things around here. There is a sullen furtive fellow named Brown, on a farm near the village, who I think is their spy. Little by little they are trying to cut me off from our world because I know too much about their world.

They have the most amazing way of finding out what I do. You may not even get this letter. I think I shall have to leave this part of the country and go live with my son in San Diego, Cal., if things get any worse, but it is not easy to give up the place you were born in, and where your family has lived for six generations. Also, I would hardly dare sell this house to anybody now that the *creatures* have taken notice of it. They seem to be trying to get the black stone back and destroy the phonograph record, but I shall not let them if I can help it. My great police dogs always hold them back, for there are very few here as yet, and they are clumsy in getting about. As I have said, their wings are not much use for short flights on earth. I am on the very brink of deciphering that stone—in a very terrible way—and with your knowledge of folklore you may be able to supply the missing links enough to help me. I suppose you know all about the fearful myths antedating the coming of man to the earth—the Yog-Sothoth and Cthulhu cycles—which are hinted at in the *Necronomicon.* I had access to a copy of that once, and hear that you have one in your college library under lock and key.

To conclude, Mr. Wilmarth, I think that with our respective studies we can be very useful to each other. I don't wish to put you in any peril, and suppose I ought to warn you that possession of the stone and the record won't be very safe; but I think you will find any risks worth running for the sake of knowledge. I will drive down to Newfane or Brattleboro to send whatever you authorize me to send, for the express offices there are more to be trusted. I might say that I live quite alone now, since I can't keep hired help any more. They won't stay because of the things that try to get near the house at night, and that keep the dogs barking continually. I am glad I didn't get as deep as this into the business while my wife was alive, for it would have driven her mad.

Hoping that I am not bothering you unduly, and that you will decide to get in touch with me rather than throw this letter into the waste basket as a madman's raving, I am

Yrs. very truly,
Henry W. Akeley

P.S. I am making some extra prints of certain photographs taken by me, which I think will help to prove a number of the points I have touched on. The old people think they are monstrously true. I shall send you these very soon if you are interested.

H.W.A.

It would be difficult to describe my sentiments upon reading this strange document for the first time. By all ordinary rules, I ought to have laughed more loudly at these extravagances than at the far milder theories which had previously moved me to mirth; yet something in the tone of the letter made me take it with paradoxical seriousness. Not that I believed for a moment in the hidden race from the stars which my correspondent spoke of; but that, after some grave preliminary doubts, I grew to feel oddly sure of his sanity and sincerity, and of his confrontation by some genuine though singular and abnormal phenomenon which he could not explain except in this imaginative way. It could not be as he thought it, I reflected, yet on the other hand, it could not be otherwise than worthy of investigation. The man seemed unduly excited and alarmed about something, but it was hard to think that all cause was lacking. He was so specific and logical in certain ways—and after all, his yarn did fit in so perplexingly well with some of the old myths—even the wildest Indian legends.

That he had really overheard disturbing voices in the hills, and had really found the black stone he spoke about, was wholly possible despite the crazy inferences he had made—inferences probably suggested by the man who had claimed to be a spy of the outer beings and had later killed himself. It was easy to deduce that this man must have been wholly insane, but that he probably had a streak of perverse outward logic which made the naïve Akeley—already prepared for such things by his folklore studies—believe his tale. As for the latest developments—it appeared from his inability to keep hired help that Akeley's humbler rustic neighbours were as convinced as he that his house was besieged by uncanny things at night. The dogs really barked, too.

And then the matter of that phonograph record, which I could not but believe he had obtained in the way he said. It must mean something; whether animal noises deceptively like human speech, or the speech of some hidden, night-haunting human being decayed to a state not much above that of lower animals. From this my thoughts went back to the black hieroglyphed stone, and to speculations upon what it might mean. Then, too, what of the photographs which Akeley said he was about to send, and which the old people had found so convincingly terrible?

As I re-read the cramped handwriting I felt as never before that my credulous opponents might have more on their side than I had conceded. After all, there might be some queer and perhaps hereditarily misshapen outcasts in those shunned hills, even though no such race of star-born monsters as folklore claimed. And if there were, then the presence of strange bodies in the flooded streams would not be wholly beyond belief. Was it too presumptuous to suppose that both the old legends and the recent reports had this much of reality behind them? But even as I harboured these doubts I felt ashamed that so fantastic a piece of bizarrerie as Henry Akeley's wild letter had brought them up.

In the end I answered Akeley's letter, adopting a tone of friendly interest and soliciting further particulars. His reply came almost by return mail; and contained, true to promise, a number of Kodak views of scenes and objects illustrating what he had to tell. Glancing at these pictures as I took them from the envelope, I felt a curious sense of fright and nearness to forbidden things; for in spite of the vagueness of most of them, they had a damnably suggestive power which was intensified by the fact of their being genuine photographs—actual optical links with what they portrayed, and the product of an impersonal transmitting process without prejudice, fallibility, or mendacity.

The more I looked at them, the more I saw that my serious estimate of Akeley and his story had not been unjustified. Certainly, these pictures carried conclusive evidence of something in the Vermont hills which was at least vastly outside the radius of our common knowledge and belief. The worst thing of all was the footprint—a view taken where the sun shone on a mud patch somewhere in a deserted upland. This was no cheaply counterfeited thing, I could see at a glance; for the sharply defined pebbles and grassblades in the field of vision gave a clear index of scale and left no possibility of a tricky double exposure. I have called the thing a "footprint," but "claw-print" would be a better term. Even now I can scarcely describe it save to say that it was hideously crablike, and that there seemed to be some ambiguity about its direction. It was not a very deep or fresh print, but seemed to be about the size of an average man's foot. From a central pad, pairs of saw-toothed nippers projected in opposite directions—quite baffling as to function, if indeed the whole object were exclusively an organ of locomotion.

Another photograph—evidently a time-exposure taken in deep shadow—was of the mouth of a woodland cave, with a boulder of rounded regularity choking the aperture. On the bare ground in front of it one could just discern a dense network of curious tracks, and when I studied the picture with a magnifier I felt uneasily sure that the tracks were like the one in the other view. A third picture showed a druid-like circle of standing stones on the summit of a wild hill. Around the cryptic circle the grass was very much beaten down and worn away, though I could not detect any footprints even with the glass. The extreme remoteness of the place was apparent from the veritable sea of tenantless mountains which formed the background and stretched away toward a misty horizon.

But if the most disturbing of all the views was that of the foot-print, the most curiously suggestive was that of the great black stone found in the Round Hill woods. Akeley had photographed it on what was evidently his study table, for I could see rows of books and a bust of Milton in the background. The thing, as nearly as one might guess, had faced the camera vertically with a somewhat irregularly curved surface of one by two feet; but to say anything definite about that sur-face, or about the general shape of the whole mass, almost defies the power of language. What outlandish geometrical principles had guided its cutting—for artificially cut it surely was—I could not even begin to guess; and never before had I seen anything which struck me as so strangely and unmistakably alien to this world. Of the hiero-glyphics on the surface I could discern very few, but one or two that I did see gave rather a shock. Of course they might be fraudulent, for others besides myself had read the monstrous and abhorred *Necro-nomicon* of the mad Arab Abdul Alhazred; but it nevertheless made me shiver to recognise certain ideographs which study had taught me to link with the most blood-curdling and blasphemous whispers of things that had had a kind of mad half-existence before the earth and the other inner worlds of the solar system were made.

Of the five remaining pictures, three were of swamp and hill scenes which seemed to bear traces of hidden and unwholesome tenancy. Another was of a queer mark in the ground very near Akeley's house, which he said he had photographed the morning after a night on which the dogs had barked more violently than usual. It was very blurred, and one could really draw no certain conclusions from it; but it did seem fiendishly like that other mark or claw-print photographed on the deserted upland. The final picture was of the Akeley place itself; a trim white house of two stories and attic, about a century and a quarter old, and with a well-kept lawn and stone-bordered path leading up to a tastefully carved Georgian doorway. There were several huge police dogs on the lawn, squatting near a pleasant-faced man with a close-cropped grey beard whom I took to be Akeley himself—his own photographer, one might infer from the tube-connected bulb in his right hand.

From the pictures I turned to the bulky, closely-written letter itself; and for the next three hours was immersed in a gulf of unutterable horror. Where Akeley had given only outlines before, he now entered into minute details; presenting long transcripts of words overheard in the woods at night, long accounts of monstrous pinkish forms spied in thickets at twilight on the hills, and a terrible cosmic narrative derived from the application of profound and varied scholarship to the endless bygone discourses of the mad self-styled spy who had killed himself. I found myself faced by names and terms that I had heard elsewhere in the most hideous of connections—Yuggoth, Great Cthulhu, Tsathoggua, Yog-Sothoth, R'lyeh, Nyarlathotep, Azathoth, Hastur, Yian, Leng, the Lake of Hali, Bethmoora, the Yellow Sign, L'mur-Kathulos, Bran, and the Magnum Innominandum—and was drawn back through nameless aeons and inconceivable dimensions to worlds of elder, outer entity at which the crazed author of the *Necronomicon* had only guessed in the vaguest way. I was told of the pits of primal life, and of the streams that had trickled down therefrom; and finally, of the tiny rivulets from one of those streams which had become entangled with the destinies of our own earth.

My brain whirled; and where before I had attempted to explain things away, I now began to believe in the most abnormal and incredible wonders. The array of vital evidence was damnably vast and overwhelming; and the cool, scientific attitude of Akeley—an attitude removed as far as imaginable from the demented, the fanatical, the hysterical, or even the extravagantly speculative—had a tremendous effect on my thought and judgment. By the time I laid the frightful letter aside I could understand the fears he had come to entertain, and was ready to do anything in my power to keep people away from those wild, haunted hills. Even now, when time has dulled the impression and made me half-question my own experience and horrible doubts, there are things in that letter of Akeley's which I would not quote, or even form into words on paper. I am almost glad that the letter and record and photographs are gone now—and I wish, for reasons I shall soon make clear, that the new planet beyond Neptune had not been discovered.

With the reading of that letter my public debating about the Vermont horror permanently ended. Arguments from opponents remained unanswered or put off with promises, and eventually the controversy petered out into oblivion. During late May and June I was in constant correspondence with Akeley; though once in a while a letter would be lost, so that we would have to retrace our ground and perform considerable laborious copying. What we were trying to do, as a whole, was to compare notes in matters of obscure mythological scholarship and arrive at a clearer correlation of the Vermont horrors with the general body of primitive world legend.

For one thing, we virtually decided that these morbidities and the hellish Himalayan *Mi-Go* were one and the same order of incarnated nightmare. There was also absorbing zoölogical conjectures, which I would have referred to Professor Dexter in my own college but for Akeley's imperative command to tell no one of the matter before us. If I seem to disobey that command now, it is only because I think that at this stage a warning about those farther Vermont hills—and about those Himalayan peaks which bold explorers are more and more determined to ascend—is more conducive to public safety than silence would be. One specific thing we were leading up to was a deciphering of the hieroglyphics on that infamous black stone—a deciphering which might well place us in possession of secrets deeper and more dizzying than any formerly known to man.

III

Toward the end of June the phonograph record came—shipped from Brattleboro, since Akeley was unwilling to trust conditions on the branch line north of there. He had begun to feel an increased sense of espionage, aggravated by the loss of some of our letters; and said much about the insidious deeds of certain men whom he considered tools and agents of the hidden beings. Most of all he suspected the surly farmer Walter Brown, who lived alone on a run-down hillside place near the deep woods, and who was often seen loafing around corners in Brattleboro, Bellows Falls, Newfane, and South Londonderry in the most inexplicable and seemingly unmotivated way. Brown's voice, he felt convinced, was one of those he had overheard on a certain occasion in a very terrible conversation; and he had once found a footprint or claw-print near Brown's house which might possess the most ominous significance. It had been curiously near some of Brown's own footprints—footprints that faced toward it.

So the record was shipped from Brattleboro, whither Akeley drove in his Ford car along the lonely Vermont back roads. He confessed in an accompanying note that he was beginning to be afraid of those roads, and that he would not even go into Townshend for supplies now except in broad daylight. It did not pay, he repeated again and again, to know too much unless one were very remote from those silent and problematical hills. He would be going to California pretty soon to live with his son, though it was hard to leave a place where all one's memories and ancestral feelings centered.

Before trying the record on the commercial machine which I borrowed from the college administration building I carefully went over all the explanatory matter in Akeley's various letters. This record, he had said, was obtained about 1 A.M. on the 1st of May, 1915, near the closed mouth of a cave where the wooded west slope of Dark Mountain rises out of Lee's swamp. The place had always been unusually plagued with strange voices, this being the reason he had brought the phonograph, dictaphone, and blank in expectation of results. Former experience had told him that May Eve—the hideous Sabbat-night of underground European legend—would probably be more fruitful than any other date, and he was not disappointed. It was noteworthy, though, that he never again heard voices at that particular spot.

Unlike most of the overheard forest voices, the substance of the record was quasi-ritualistic, and included one palpably human voice which Akeley had never been able to place. It was not Brown's, but seemed to be that of a man of greater cultivation. The second voice, however, was the real crux of the thing—for this was the accursed *buzzing* which had no likeness to humanity despite the human words which it uttered in good English grammar and a scholarly accent.

The recording phonograph and dictaphone had not worked uniformly well, and had of course been at a great disadvantage because of the remote and muffled nature of the overheard ritual; so that the actual speech secured was very fragmentary. Akeley had given me a transcript of what he believed the spoken words to be, and I glanced through this again as I prepared the machine for action. The text was darkly mysterious rather than openly horrible, though a knowledge of its origin and manner of gathering gave it all the associative horror which any words could well possess. I will present it here in full as I remember it—and I am fairly confident that I know it correctly by heart, not only from reading the transcript, but from playing the record itself over and over again. It is not a thing which one might readily forget!

(Indistinguishable Sounds)

(A Cultivated Male Human Voice)

. . . is the Lord of the Wood, even to . . . and the gifts of the men of Leng . . . so from the wells of night to the gulfs of space, and from the gulfs of space to the wells of night, ever the praises of Great Cthulhu, of Tsathoggua, and of Him Who is not to be Named. Ever Their praises, and abundance to the Black Goat of the Woods. Iä! Shub-Niggurath! The Goat with a Thousand Young!

(A Buzzing Imitation of Human Speech)

Iäl Shub-Niggurath! The Black Goat of the Woods with a Thousand Young!

(Human Voice)

And it has come to pass that the Lord of the Woods, being . . . seven and nine, down the onyx steps . . . (tri)butes to Him in the Gulf, Azathoth, He of Whom Thou has taught us marv(els) . . . on the wings of night out beyond space, out beyond th . . . to That whereof Yuggoth is the youngest child, rolling alone in black aether at the rim. . . .

(Buzzing Voice)

. . . go out among men and find the ways thereof, that He in the Gulf may know. To Nyarlathotep, Mighty Messenger, must all things be told. And He shall put on the semblance of men, the waxen mask and the robe that hides, and come down from the world of Seven Suns to mock. . . .

(Human Voice)

. . . (Nyarl)athotep, Great Messenger, bringer of strange joy to Yuggoth through the void, Father of the Million Favoured Ones, Stalker among. . . .

(Speech Cut Off by End of Record)

Such were the words for which I was to listen when I started the phonograph. It was with a trace of genuine dread and reluctance that I pressed the lever and heard the preliminary scratching of the sapphire point, and I was glad that the first faint, fragmentary words were in a human voice—a mellow, educated voice which seemed vaguely

Bostonian in accent, and which was certainly not that of any native of the Vermont hills. As I listened to the tantalisingly feeble rendering, I seemed to find the speech identical with Akeley's carefully prepared transcript. On it chanted, in that mellow Bostonian voice . . . "Iä! Shub-Niggurath! The Goat with a Thousand Young! . . ."

And then I heard *the other voice*. To this hour I shudder retrospectively when I think of how it struck me, prepared though I was by Akeley's accounts. Those to whom I have since described the record profess to find nothing but cheap imposture or madness in it; but *could they have the accursed thing itself,* or read the bulk of Akeley's correspondence, (especially that terrible and encyclopaedic second letter), I know they would think differently. It is, after all, a tremendous pity that I did not disobey Akeley and play the record for others—a tremendous pity, too, that all of his letters were lost. To me, with my first-hand impression of the actual sounds, and with my knowledge of the background and surrounding circumstances, the voice was a monstrous thing. It swiftly followed the human voice in ritualistic response, but in my imagination it was a morbid echo winging its way across unimaginable abysses from unimaginable outer hells. It is more than two years now since I last ran off that blasphemous waxen cylinder; but at this moment, and at all other moments, I can still hear that feeble, fiendish buzzing as it reached me for the first time.

"Iä! Shub-Niggurath! The Black Goat of the Woods with a Thousand Young!"

But though the voice is always in my ears, I have not even yet been able to analyse it well enough for a graphic description. It was like the drone of some loathsome, gigantic insect ponderously shaped into the articulate speech of an alien species, and I am perfectly certain that the organs producing it can have no resemblance to the vocal organs of man, or indeed to those of any of the mammalia. There were singularities in timbre, range, and overtones which placed this phenomenon wholly outside the sphere of humanity and earth-life. Its sudden advent that first time almost stunned me, and I heard the rest of the record through in a sort of abstracted daze. When the longer passage of buzzing came, there was a sharp intensification of that feeling of blasphemous infinity which had struck me during the shorter and earlier passage. At last the record ended abruptly, during an unusually clear speech of the human and Bostonian voice; but I sat stupidly staring long after the machine had automatically stopped.

I hardly need say that I gave that shocking record many another playing, and that I made exhaustive attempts at analysis and comment in comparing notes with Akeley. It would be both useless and disturbing to repeat here all that we concluded; but I may hint that we agreed in believing we had secured a clue to the source of some of the most repulsive primordial customs in the cryptic elder religions of mankind. It seemed plain to us, also, that there were ancient and elaborate alliances between the hidden outer creatures and certain members of the human race. How extensive these alliances were, and how their state today might compare with their state in earlier ages, we had no means of guessing; yet at best there was room for a limitless amount of horrified speculation. There seemed to be an awful, immemorial linkage in several definite stages betwixt man and nameless infinity. The blasphemies which appeared on earth, it was hinted, came from the dark planet Yuggoth, at the rim of the solar system; but this was itself merely the populous outpost of a frightful interstellar race whose ultimate source must lie far outside even the Einsteinian space-time continuum or greatest known cosmos.

Meanwhile we continued to discuss the black stone and the best way of getting it to Arkahm—Akeley deeming it inadvisable to have me visit him at the scene of his nightmare studies. For some reason or other, Akeley was afraid to trust the thing to any ordinary or expected transportation route. His final idea was to take it across country to Bellows Falls and ship it on the Boston and Maine system through Keene and Winchendon and Fitchburg, even though this would necessitate his driving along somewhat lonelier and more forest-traversing hill roads than the main highway to Brattleboro. He said he had noticed a man around the express office at Brattleboro when he had sent the phonograph record, whose actions and expression had been far from reassuring. This man had seemed too anxious to talk with the clerks, and had taken the train on which the record was shipped. Akeley confessed that he had not felt strictly at ease about that record until he heard from me of its safe receipt.

About this time—the second week in July—another letter of mine went astray, as I learned through an anxious communication from Akeley. After that he told me to address him no more at Townshend, but to send all mail in care of the General Delivery at Brattleboro; whither he would make frequent trips either in his car or on the motor-coach line which had lately replaced passenger service on the lagging branch railway. I could see that he was getting more and more anxious, for he went into much detail about the increased barking of the dogs on moonless nights, and about the fresh claw-prints he sometimes found in the road and in the mud at the back of his farmyard when morning came. Once he told about a veritable army of prints drawn up in a line facing an equally thick and resolute line of dog-tracks, and sent a loathsomely disturbing Kodak picture to

prove it. That was after a night on which the dogs had outdone themselves in barking and howling.

On the morning of Wednesday, July 18, I received a telegram from
Bellows Falls, in which Akeley said he was expressing the black
stone over the B. & M. on Train No. 5508, leaving Bellows Falls at
12:15 P.M., standard time, and due at the North Station in Boston
at 4:12 P.M. It ought, I calculated, to get up to Arkham at least by
the next noon; and accordingly I stayed in all Thursday morning to
receive it. But noon came and went without its advent, and when I
telephoned down to the express office I was informed that no shipment for me had arrived. My next act, performed amidst a growing
alarm, was to give a long-distance call to the express agent at the
Boston North Station; and I was scarcely surprised to learn that my
consignment had not appeared. Train No. 5508 had pulled in only 35
minutes late on the day before, but had contained no box addressed to
me. The agent promised, however, to institute a searching inquiry;
and I ended the day by sending Akeley a night-letter outlining the
situation.

With commendable promptness a report came from the Boston office on the following afternoon, the agent telephoning as soon as he
learned the facts. It seemed that the railway express clerk on No.
5508 had been able to recall an incident which might have much
bearing on my loss—an argument with a very curious-voiced man,
lean, sandy, and rustic-looking, when the train was waiting at Keene,
N.H., shortly after one o'clock standard time.

The man, he said, was greatly excited about a heavy box which he
claimed to expect, but which was neither on the train nor entered on
the company's books. He had given the name of Stanley Adams, and
had had such a queerly thick droning voice, that it made the clerk
abnormally dizzy and sleepy to listen to him. The clerk could not
remember quite how the conversation had ended, but recalled starting into a fuller awakeness when the train began to move. The
Boston agent added that this clerk was a young man of wholly unquestioned veracity and reliability, of known antecedents and long
with the company.

That evening I went to Boston to interview the clerk in person,
having obtained his name and address from the office. He was a
frank, prepossessing fellow, but I saw that he could add nothing to his
original account. Oddly, he was scarcely sure that he could even
recognise the strange inquirer again. Realising that he had no more to
tell, I returned to Arkham and sat up till morning writing letters to
Akeley, to the express company and to the police department and station agent in Keene. I felt that the strange-voiced man who had so

queerly affected the clerk must have a pivotal place in the ominous business, and hoped that Keene station employees and telegraph-office records might tell something about him and about how he happened to make his inquiry when and where he did.

I must admit, however, that all my investigations came to nothing. The queer-voiced man had indeed been noticed around the Keene station in the early afternoon of July 18, and one lounger seemed to couple him vaguely with a heavy box; but he was altogether unknown, and had not been seen before or since. He had not visited the telegraph office or received any message so far as could be learned, nor had any message which might justly be considered a notice of the black stone's presence on No. 5508 come through the office for anyone. Naturally Akeley joined with me in conducting these inquiries, and even made a personal trip to Keene to question the people around the station; but his attitude toward the matter was more fatalistic than mine. He seemed to find the loss of the box a portentous and menacing fulfilment of inevitable tendencies, and had no real hope at all of its recovery. He spoke of the undoubted telepathic and hypnotic powers of the hill creatures and their agents, and in one letter hinted that he did not believe the stone was on this earth any longer. For my part, I was duly enraged, for I had felt there was at least a chance of learning profound and astonishing things from the old, blurred hieroglyphs. The matter would have rankled bitterly in my mind had not Akeley's immediately subsequent letters brought up a new phase of the whole horrible hill problem which at once seized all my attention.

IV

The unknown things, Akeley wrote in a script grown pitifully tremulous, had begun to close in on him with a wholly new degree of determination. The nocturnal barking of the dogs whenever the moon was dim or absent was hideous now, and there had been attempts to molest him on the lonely roads he had to traverse by day. On the second of August, while bound for the village in his car, he had found a tree-trunk laid in his path at a point where the highway ran through a deep patch of woods; while the savage barking of the two great dogs he had with him told all too well of the things which must have been lurking near. What would have happened had the dogs not been there, he did not dare guess—but he never went out now without at least two of his faithful and powerful pack. Other road experiences had occurred on August fifth and sixth; a shot grazing his car on one occasion, and the barking of the dogs telling of unholy woodland presences on the other.

On August fifteenth I received a frantic letter which disturbed me greatly, and which made me wish Akeley could put aside his lonely reticence and call in the aid of the law. There had been frightful happenings on the night of the 12–13th, bullets flying outside the farmhouse, and three of the twelve great dogs being found shot dead in the morning. There were myriads of claw-prints in the road, with the human prints of Walter Brown among them. Akeley had started to telephone to Brattleboro for more dogs, but the wire had gone dead before he had a chance to say much. Later he went to Brattleboro in his car, and learned there that linemen had found the main cable neatly cut at a point where it ran through the deserted hills north of Newfane. But he was about to start home with four fine new dogs, and several cases of ammunition for his big-game repeating rifle. The letter was written at the post office in Brattleboro, and came through to me without delay.

My attitude toward the matter was by this time quickly slipping from a scientific to an alarmedly personal one. I was afraid for Akeley in his remote, lonely farmhouse, and half afraid for myself because of my now definite connection with the strange hill problem. The thing was *reaching out so*. Would it suck me in and engulf me? In replying to his letter I urged him to seek help, and hinted that I might take action myself if he did not. I spoke of visiting Vermont in person in spite of his wishes, and of helping him explain the situation to the proper authorities. In return, however, I received only a telegram from Bellows Falls which read thus:

APPRECIATE YOUR POSITION BUT CAN DO NOTHING TAKE NO ACTION YOURSELF FOR IT COULD ONLY HARM BOTH WAIT FOR EXPLANATION
HENRY AKELY

But the affair was steadily deepening. Upon my replying to the telegram I received a shaky note from Akeley with the astonishing news that he had not only never sent the wire, but had not received the letter from me to which it was an obvious reply. Hasty inquiries by him at Bellows Falls had brought out that the message was deposited by a strange sandy-haired man with a curiously thick, droning voice, though more than this he could not learn. The clerk showed him the original text as scrawled in pencil by the sender, but the handwriting was wholly unfamiliar. It was noticeable that the signature was misspelled—A-K-E-L-Y, without the second "E." Certain conjectures were inevitable, but amidst the obvious crisis he did not stop to elaborate upon them.

He spoke of the death of more dogs and the purchase of still others, and of the exchange of gunfire which had become a settled feature each moonless night. Brown's prints, and the prints of at least one or two more shod human figures, were now found regularly among the claw-prints in the road, and at the back of the farmyard. It was, Akeley admitted, a pretty bad business; and before long he would probably have to go to live with his California son whether or not he could sell the old place. But it was not easy to leave the only spot one could really think of as home. He must try to hang on a little longer; perhaps he could scare off the intruders—especially if he openly gave up all further attempts to penetrate their secrets.

Writing Akeley at once, I renewed my offers of aid, and spoke again of visiting him and helping him convince the authorities of his dire peril. In his reply he seemed less set against that plan than his past attitude would have led one to predict, but said he would like to hold off a little while longer—long enough to get his things in order and reconcile himself to the idea of leaving an almost morbidly cherished birthplace. People looked askance at his studies and speculations and it would be better to get quietly off without setting the countryside in a turmoil and creating widespread doubts of his own sanity. He had had enough, he admitted, but he wanted to make a dignified exit if he could.

This letter reached me on the 28th of August, and I prepared and mailed as encouraging a reply as I could. Apparently the encouragement had effect, for Akeley had fewer terrors to report when he acknowledged my note. He was not very optimistic, though, and expressed the belief that it was only the full moon season which was holding the creatures off. He hoped there would not be many densely cloudy nights, and talked vaguely of boarding in Brattleboro when the moon waned. Again I wrote him encouragingly but on September 5th there came a fresh communication which had obviously crossed my letter in the mails; and to this I could not give any such hopeful response. In view of its importance I believe I had better give it in full— as best I can do from memory of the shaky script. It ran substantially as follows:

Monday

Dear Wilmarth—

A rather discouraging P.S. to my last. Last night was thickly cloudy—though no rain—and not a bit of moonlight got through. Things were pretty bad, and I think the end is getting near, in spite of all we have hoped. After midnight something landed on the roof of the house, and the dogs all rushed up to see what it was. I could hear them snapping and tearing around, and then one managed to get on the roof by jumping from the low ell. There was a terrible fight up there, and I heard a frightful *buzzing* which I'll never forget. And then there was a shocking smell. About the same time bullets came through the window and nearly grazed me. I think the main line of the hill creatures had got close to the house when the dogs divided because of the roof business. What was up there I don't know yet, but I'm afraid the creatures are learning to steer better with their space wings. I put out the light and used the windows for loopholes, and raked all around the house with rifle fire aimed just high enough not to hit the dogs. That seemed to end the business, but in the morning I found great pools of blood in the yard, besides pools of a green sticky stuff that had the worst odour I have ever smelled. I climbed up on the roof and found more of the sticky stuff there. Five of the dogs were killed—I'm afraid I hit one myself by aiming too low, for he was shot in the back. Now I am setting the panes the shots broke, and am going to Brattleboro for more dogs. I guess the men at the kennels think I am crazy. Will drop another note later. Suppose I'll be ready for moving in a week or two, though it nearly kills me to think of it.

Hastily—Akeley

But this was not the only letter from Akeley to cross mine. On the next morning—September 6th—still another came; this time a frantic scrawl which utterly unnerved me and put me at a loss what to say or do next. Again I cannot do better than quote the text as faithfully as memory will let me.

Tuesday

Clouds didn't break, so no moon again—and going into the wane anyhow. I'd have the house wired for electricity and put in a searchlight if I didn't know they'd cut the cables as fast as they could be mended.

I think I am going crazy. It may be that all I have ever written you is a dream or madness. It was bad enough before, but this time it is too much. *They talked to me last night*—talked in that cursed buzzing voice and told me things *that I dare not repeat to you.* I heard them plainly above the barking of the dogs, and once when they were drowned out *a human voice helped them.* Keep out of this, Wilmarth—it is worse than either you or I ever suspected. *They don't mean to let me get to California now—they want to take me off alive, or what theoretically and mentally amounts to alive*—not only to Yuggoth, but beyond that—away outside the galaxy *and possibly beyond the last curved rim of space.* I told them I wouldn't go where they wish, *or in the terrible way they propose to take me,* but

I'm afraid it will be no use. My place is so far out that they may come by day as well as by night before long. Six more dogs killed, and I felt presences all along the wooded parts of the road when I drove to Brattleboro today.

It was a mistake for me to try to send you that phonograph record and black stone. Better smash the record before it's too late. Will drop you another line tomorrow if I'm still here. Wish I could arrange to get my books and things to Brattleboro and board there. I would run off without anything if I could but something inside my mind holds me back. I can slip out to Brattleboro, where I ought to be safe, but I feel just as much a prisoner there as at the house. And I seem to know that I couldn't get much farther even if I dropped everything and tried. It is horrible—don't get mixed up in this.

Yrs—Akeley

I did not sleep at all the night after receiving this terrible thing, and was utterly baffled as to Akeley's remaining degree of sanity. The substance of the note was wholly insane, yet the manner of expression—in view of all that had gone before—had a grimly potent quality of convincingness. I made no attempt to answer it, thinking it better to wait until Akeley might have time to reply to my latest communication. Such a reply indeed came on the following day, though the fresh material in it quite overshadowed any of the points brought up by the letter nominally answered. Here is what I recall of the text, scrawled and blotted as it was in the course of a plainly frantic and hurried composition.

Wednesday

W—

Your letter came, but it's no use to discuss anything any more. I am fully resigned. Wonder that I have even enough will power left to fight them off. Can't escape even if I were willing to give up everything and run. They'll get me.

Had a letter from them yesterday—R.F.D. man brought it while I was at Brattleboro. Typed and postmarked Bellows Falls. Tells what they want to do with me—I can't repeat it. Look out for yourself, too! Smash that record. Cloudy nights keep up, and moon waning all the time. Wish I dared to get help—it might brace up my will power—but everyone who would dare to come at all would call me crazy unless there happened to be some proof. Couldn't ask people to come for no reason at all—am all out of touch with everybody and have been for years.

But I haven't told you the worst, Wilmarth. Brace up to read this,

for it will give you a shock. I am telling the truth, though. It is this—
*I have seen and touched one of the things, or part of one of the
things.* God, man, but it's awful! It was dead, of course. One of
the dogs had it, and I found it near the kennel this morning. I tried to
save it in the woodshed to convince people of the whole thing, but it
all evaporated in a few hours. Nothing left. You know, all those
things in the rivers were seen only on the first morning after the
flood. And here's the worst. I tried to photograph it for you, but when
I developed the film *there wasn't anything visible except the woodshed.* What can the thing have been made of? I saw it and felt it, and
they all leave footprints. It was surely made of matter—but what
kind of matter? The shape can't be described. It was a great crab with
a lot of pyramided fleshy rings or knots of thick, ropy stuff covered
with feelers where a man's head would be. That green sticky stuff is
its blood or juice. And there are more of them due on earth any
minute.

Walter Brown is missing—hasn't been seen loafing around any of
his usual corners in the villages hereabouts. I must have got him
with one of my shots, though the creatures always seem to try to
take their dead and wounded away.

Got into town this afternoon without any trouble, but am afraid
they're beginning to hold off because they're sure of me. Am writing
this in Brattleboro P.O. This may be goodbye—if it is, write my son
George Goodenough Akeley, 176 Pleasant St., San Diego, Cal., *but
don't come up here.* Write the boy if you don't hear from me in a
week, and watch the papers for news.

I'm going to play my last two cards now—if I have the will power
left. First to try poison gas on the things (I've got the right chemicals
and have fixed up masks for myself and the dogs) and then if that
doesn't work, tell the sheriff. They can lock me in a madhouse if they
want to—it'll be better than what the *other creatures* would do. Perhaps I can get them to pay attention to the prints around the house—
they are faint, but I can find them every morning. Suppose, though,
police would say I faked them somehow; for they all think I'm a
queer character.

Must try to have a state policeman spend a night here and see for
himself—though it would be just like the creatures to learn about it
and hold off that night. They cut my wires whenever I try to telephone in the night—the linemen think it is very queer, and may testify for me if they don't go and imagine I cut them myself. I haven't
tried to keep them repaired for over a week now.

I could get some of the ignorant people to testify for me about the
reality of the horrors, but everybody laughs at what they say, and

anyway, they have shunned my place for so long that they don't know any of the new events. You couldn't get one of those rundown farmers to come within a mile of my house for love or money. The mail-carrier hears what they say and jokes me about it—God! If I only dared tell him how real it is! I think I'll try to get him to notice the prints, but he comes in the afternoon and they're usually about gone by that time. If I kept one by setting a box or pan over it, he'd think surely it was a fake or joke.

Wish I hadn't gotten to be such a hermit, so folks don't drop around as they used to. I've never dared show the black stone or the Kodak pictures, or play that record, to anybody but the ignorant people. The others would say I faked the whole business and do nothing but laugh. But I may yet try showing the pictures. They give those claw-prints clearly, even if the things that made them can't be photographed. What a shame nobody else saw that *thing* this morning before it went to nothing!

But I don't know as I care. After what I've been through, a madhouse is as good a place as any. The doctors can help me make up my mind to get away from this house, and that is all that will save me.

Write my son George if you don't hear soon. Goodbye, smash that record, and don't mix up in this.

Yrs—Akeley

This letter frankly plunged me into the blackest of terror. I did not know what to say in answer, but scratched off some incoherent words of advice and encouragement and sent them by registered mail. I recall urging Akeley to move to Brattleboro at once, and place himself under the protection of the authorities; adding that I would come to that town with the phonograph record and help convince the courts of his sanity. It was time, too, I think I wrote, to alarm the people generally against this thing in their midst. It will be observed that at this moment of stress my own belief in all Akeley had told and claimed was virtually complete, though I did think his failure to get a picture of the dead monster was due not to any freak of Nature but to some excited slip of his own.

V

Then, apparently crossing my incoherent note and reaching me Saturday afternoon, September 8th, came that curiously different and calming letter neatly typed on a new machine; that strange letter of reassurance and invitation which must have marked so prodigious a transition in the whole nightmare drama of the lonely hills. Again I will quote from memory—seeking for special reasons to preserve as much of the flavour of the style as I can. It was postmarked Bellows Falls, and the signature as well as the body of the letter was typed—as is frequent with beginners in typing. The text, though, was marvellously accurate for a tyro's work; and I concluded that Akeley must have used a machine at some previous period—perhaps in college. To say that the letter relieved me would be only fair, yet beneath my relief lay a substratum of uneasiness. If Akeley had been sane in his terror, was he now sane in his deliverance? And the sort of "improved rapport" mentioned . . . what was it? The entire thing implied such a diametrical reversal of Akeley's previous attitude! But here is the substance of the text, carefully transcribed from a memory in which I take some pride.

Townshend, Vermont,
Thursday, Sept. 6, 1928.

My dear Wilmarth:—

It gives me great pleasure to be able to set you at rest regarding all the silly things I've been writing you. I say "silly," although by that I mean my frightened attitude rather than my descriptions of certain phenomena. Those phenomena are real and important enough; my mistake had been in establishing an anomalous attitude toward them.

I think I mentioned that my strange visitors were beginning to communicate with me, and to attempt such communication. Last night this exchange of speech became actual. In response to certain signals I admitted to the house a messenger from those outside—a fellow-human, let me hasten to say. He told me much that neither you nor I had even begun to guess, and showed clearly how totally we had misjudged and misinterpreted the purpose of the Outer Ones in maintaining their secret colony on this planet.

It seems that the evil legends about what they have offered to men, and what they wish in connection with the earth, are wholly the result of an ignorant misconception of allegorical speech—speech, of course, moulded by cultural backgrounds and thought-habits vastly different from anything we dream of. My own conjectures, I freely own, shot as widely past the mark as any of the guesses of illiterate farmers and savage Indians. What I had thought morbid and shameful and ignominious is in reality awesome and mind-expanding and even *glorious*—my previous estimate being merely a phase of man's eternal tendency to hate and fear and shrink from the *utterly different*.

Now I regret the harm I have inflicted upon these alien and

incredible beings in the course of our nightly skirmishes. If only I had consented to talk peacefully and reasonably with them in the first place! But they bear me no grudge, their emotions being organised very differently from ours. It is their misfortune to have had as their human agents in Vermont some very inferior specimens—the late Walter Brown, for example. He prejudiced me vastly against them. Actually, they have never knowingly harmed men, but have often been cruelly wronged and spied upon by our species. There is a whole secret cult of evil men (a man of your mystical erudition will understand me when I link them with Hastur and the Yellow Sign) devoted to the purpose of tracking them down and injuring them on behalf of monstrous powers from other dimensions. It is against these aggressors—not against normal humanity—that the drastic precautions of the Outer Ones are directed. Incidently, I learned that many of our lost letters were stolen not by the Outer Ones but by the emissaries of this malign cult.

All that the Outer Ones wish of man is peace and non-molestation and an increasing intellectual rapport. This latter is absolutely necessary now that our inventions and devices are expanding our knowledge and motions, and making it more and more impossible for the Outer Ones' necessary outposts to exist *secretly* on this planet. The alien beings desire to know mankind more fully, and to have a few of mankind's philosophic and scientific leaders know more about them. With such an exchange of knowledge all perils will pass, and a satisfactory *modus vivendi* be established. The very idea of any attempt to *enslave* or *degrade* mankind is ridiculous.

As a beginning of this improved rapport, the Outer Ones have naturally chosen me—whose knowledge of them is already so considerable—as their primary interpreter on earth. Much was told me last night—facts of the most stupendous and vista-opening nature—and more will be subsequently communicated to me both orally and in writing. I shall not be called upon to make any trip *outside* just yet, though I shall probably *wish* to do so later on—employing special means and transcending everything which we have hitherto been accustomed to regard as human experience. My house will be besieged no longer. Everything has reverted to normal, and the dogs will have no further occupation. In place of terror I have been given a rich boon of knowledge and intellectual adventure which few other mortals have ever shared.

The Outer Beings are perhaps the most marvellous organic things in or beyond all space and time—members of a cosmos-wide race of which all other life-forms are merely degenerate variants. They are more vegetable than animal, if these terms can be applied to the sort of matter composing them, and have a somewhat fungoid structure; though the presence of a chlorophyll-like substance and a very singular nutritive system differentiate them altogether from true cormophytic fungi. Indeed, the type is composed of a form of matter totally alien to our part of space—with electrons having a wholly different vibration-rate. That is why the beings cannot be photographed on the *ordinary* camera films and plates of our known universe, even though our eyes can see them. With proper knowledge, however, any good chemist could make a photographic emulsion which would record their images.

The genus is unique in its ability to traverse the heatless and airless interstellar void in full corporeal form, and some of its variants cannot do this without mechanical aid or curious surgical transpositions. Only a few species have the ether-resisting wings characteristic of the Vermont variety. Those inhabiting certain remote peaks in the Old World were brought in other ways. Their external resemblance to animal life, and to the sort of structure we understand as material, is a matter of parallel evolution rather than of close kinship. Their brain-capacity exceeds that of any other surviving lifeform, although the winged types of our hill country are by no means the most highly developed. Telepathy is their usual means of discourse, though we have rudimentary vocal organs which, after a slight operation (for surgery is an incredibly expert and every-day thing among them), can roughly duplicate the speech of such types of organism as still use speech.

Their main *immediate* abode is a still undiscovered and almost lightless planet at the very edge of our solar system—beyond Neptune, and the ninth in distance from the sun. It is, as we have inferred, the object mystically hinted at as "Yuggoth" in certain ancient and forbidden writings; and it will soon be the scene of a strange focussing of thought upon our world in an effort to facilitate mental rapport. I would not be surprised if astronomers become sufficiently sensitive to these thought-currents to discover Yuggoth when the Outer Ones wish them to do so. But Yuggoth, of course, is only the stepping-stone. The main body of the beings inhabits strangely organized abysses wholly beyond the utmost reach of any human imagination. The space-time globule which we recognize as the totality of all cosmic entity is only an atom in the genuine infinity which is theirs. *And as much of this infinity as any human brain can hold is eventually to be opened up to me, as it has been to not more than fifty other men since the human race has existed.*

You will probably call this raving at first, Wilmarth, but in time you will appreciate the titanic opportunity I have stumbled upon. I want you to share as much of it as is possible, and to that end must tell you thousands of things that won't go on paper. In the past I have warned you not to come to see me. Now that all is safe, I take pleasure in rescinding that warning and inviting you.

Can't you make a trip up here before your college term opens? It would be marvelously delightful if you could. Bring along the phonograph record and all my letters to you as consultative data—we shall need them in piecing together the whole tremendous story. You might bring the Kodak prints, too, since I seem to have mislaid the negatives and my own prints in all this recent excitement. But what a wealth of facts I have to add to all this groping and tentative material—*and what a stupendous device I have to supplement my additions!*

Don't hesitate—I am free from espionage now, and you will not meet anything unnatural or disturbing. Just come along and let my car meet you at the Brattleboro station—prepare to stay as long as you can, and expect many an evening of discussion of things beyond all human conjecture. Don't tell anyone about it, of course—for this matter must not get to the promiscuous public.

The train service to Brattleboro is not bad—you can get a timetable in Boston. Take the B. & M. to Greenfield, and then change for the brief remainder of the way. I suggest your taking the convenient 4:10 P.M.—standard—from Boston. This gets into Greenfield at 7:35, and at 9:19 a train leaves there which reaches Brattleboro at 10:01. That is week-days. Let me know the date and I'll have my car on hand at the station.

Pardon this typed letter, but my handwriting has grown shaky of late, as you know, and I don't feel equal to long stretches of script. I got this new Corona in Brattleboro yesterday—it seems to work very well.

Awaiting word, and hoping to see you shortly with the phonograph record and all my letters—and the Kodak prints—

I am

Yours in anticipation,

Henry W. Akeley

TO ALBERT N. WILMARTH, ESQ.,
MISKATONIC UNIVERSITY,
ARKHAM, MASS.

The complexity of my emotions upon reading, re-reading, and pondering over this strange and unlooked-for letter is past adequate description. I have said that I was at once relieved and made uneasy, but this expresses only crudely the overtones of diverse and largely subconscious feelings which comprised both the relief and the uneasiness. To begin with, the thing was so antipodally at variance with the whole chain of horrors preceding it—the change of mood from stark terror to cool complacency and even exultation was so unheralded, lightning-like, and complete! I could scarcely believe that a single day could so alter the psychological perspective of one who had written that final frenzied bulletin of Wednesday, no matter what relieving disclosures that day might have brought. At certain moments a sense of conflicting unrealities made me wonder whether this whole distantly reported drama of fantastic forces were not a kind of half-illusory dream created largely within my own mind. Then I thought of the phonograph record and gave way to still greater bewilderment.

The letter seemed so unlike anything which could have been expected! As I analysed my impression, I saw that it consisted of two distinct phases. First, granting that Akeley had been sane before and was still sane, the indicated change in the situation itself was so swift and unthinkable. And secondly, the change in Akeley's own manner, attitude, and language was so vastly beyond the normal or the predictable. The man's whole personality seemed to have undergone an insidious mutation—a mutation so deep that one could scarcely reconcile his two aspects with the supposition that both represented equal sanity. Word-choice, spelling—all were subtly different. And with my academic sensitiveness to prose style, I could trace profound divergences in his commonest reactions and rhythm-responses. Certainly, the emotional cataclysm or revelation which could produce so radical an overturn must be an extreme one indeed! Yet in another way the letter seemed quite characteristic of Akeley. The same old passion for infinity—the same old scholarly inquisitiveness. I could not a moment—or more than a moment—credit the idea of spuriousness or malign substitution. Did not the invitation—the willingness to have me test the truth of the letter in person—prove its genuineness?

I did not retire Saturday night, but sat up thinking of the shadows and marvels behind the letter I had received. My mind, aching from the quick succession of monstrous conceptions it had been forced to confront during the last four months, worked upon this startling new material in a cycle of doubt and acceptance which repeated most of the steps experienced in facing the earlier wonders; till long before dawn a burning interest and curiosity had begun to replace the original storm of perplexity and uneasiness. Mad or sane, metamorphosed or merely relieved, the chances were that Akeley had actually encountered some stupendous change of perspective in his hazardous research; some change at once diminishing his danger—real or fancied—and opening dizzy new vistas of cosmic and superhuman knowledge. My own zeal for the unknown flared up to meet his, and I felt myself touched by the contagion of the morbid barrier-breaking. To shake off the maddening and wearying limitations of time and space and natural law—to be linked with the vast *outside*—to come close to the nighted and abysmal secrets of the infinite and the ultimate—surely such a thing was worth the risk of one's life, soul, and sanity! And Akeley had said there was no longer any peril—he had invited me to visit him instead of warning me away as before. I tingled at the thought of what he might now have to tell me—there was an almost paralysing fascination in the thought of sitting in that lonely and lately-beleaguered farmhouse with a man who had talked with actual emissaries from outer space; sitting there with the terrible record and the pile of letters in which Akeley had summarised his earlier conclusions.

So late Sunday morning I telegraphed Akeley that I would meet him in Brattleboro on the following Wednesday—September 12th—if that date were convenient for him. In only one respect did I depart from his suggestions, and that concerned the choice of a train. Frankly, I did not feel like arriving in that haunted Vermont region late at night; so instead of accepting the train he chose I telephoned the station and devised another arrangement. By rising early and taking the 8:07 A.M. (standard) into Boston, I could catch the 9:25 for Greenfield; arriving there at 12:22 noon. This connected exactly with a train reaching Brattleboro at 1:08 P.M.—a much more comfortable hour than 10:01 for meeting Akeley and riding with him into the close-packed, secret-guarding hills.

I mentioned this choice in my telegram, and was glad to learn in the reply which came toward evening that it had met with my prospective host's endorsement. His wire ran thus:

ARRANGEMENT SATISFACTORY WILL MEET ONE EIGHT TRAIN WEDNES-
DAY DONT FORGET RECORD AND LETTERS AND PRINTS KEEP DESTINA-
TION QUIET EXPECT GREAT REVELATIONS

AKELEY

Receipt of this message in direct response to one sent to Akeley—and necessarily delivered to his house from the Townshend station either by official messenger or by a restored telephone service—removed any lingering subconscious doubts I may have had about the authorship of the perplexing letter. My relief was marked—indeed, it was greater than I could account for at the time; since all such doubts had been rather deeply buried. But I slept soundly and long that night, and was eagerly busy with preparations during the ensuing two days.

VI

On Wednesday I started as agreed, taking with me a valise full of simple necessities and scientific data, including the hideous phonograph record, the Kodak prints, and the entire file of Akeley's correspondence. As requested, I had told no one where I was going; for I could see that the matter demanded utmost privacy, even allowing for its most favourable turns. The thought of actual mental contact with alien, outside entities was stupefying enough to my trained and somewhat prepared mind; and this being so, what might one think of its effect on the vast masses of uninformed laymen? I do not know whether dread or adventurous expectancy was uppermost in me as I changed trains at Boston and began the long westward run out of familiar regions into those I knew less thoroughly. Waltham—Concord—Ayer—Fitchburg—Gardner—Athol—

My train reached Greenfield seven minutes late, but the north-bound connecting express had been held. Transferring in haste, I felt a curious breathlessness as the cars rumbled on through the early afternoon sunlight into territories I had always read of but had never before visited. I knew I was entering an altogether older-fashioned and more primitive New England than the mechanised, urbanised coastal and southern areas where all my life had been spent; an unspoiled, ancestral New England without the foreigners and factory-smoke, bill-boards and concrete roads, of the sections which modernity has touched. There would be odd survivals of that continuous native life whose deep roots make it the one authentic outgrowth of the landscape—the continuous native life which keeps alive strange ancient memories, and fertilises the soil for shadowy, marvellous, and seldom-mentioned beliefs.

Now and then I saw the blue Connecticut River gleaming in the sun, and after leaving Northfield we crossed it. Ahead loomed green and cryptical hills, and when the conductor came around I learned that I was at last in Vermont. He told me to set my watch back an hour, since the northern hill country will have no dealings with new-fangled daylight time schemes. As I did so it seemed to me that I was likewise turning the calendar back a century.

The train kept close to the river, and across in New Hampshire I could see the approaching slope of steep Wantastiquet, about which singular old legends cluster. Then streets appeared on my left, and a green island showed in the stream on my right. People rose and filed to the door, and I followed them. The car stopped, and I alighted beneath the long train-shed of the Brattleboro station.

Looking over the line of waiting motors I hesitated a moment to see which one might turn out to be the Akeley Ford, but my identity was divined before I could take the initiative. And yet it was clearly not Akeley himself who advanced to meet me with an outstretched hand and a mellowly phrased query as to whether I was indeed Mr. Albert N. Wilmarth of Arkham. This man bore no resemblance to the bearded, grizzled Akeley of the snapshot; but was a younger and more urbane person, fashionably dressed, and wearing only a small, dark moustache. His cultivated voice held an odd and almost disturbing hint of vague familiarity; though I could not definitely place it in my memory.

As I surveyed him I heard him explaining that he was a friend of my prospective host's who had come down from Townshend in his stead. Akeley, he declared, had suffered a sudden attack of some asthmatic trouble, and did not feel equal to making a trip in the outdoor air. It was not serious, however, and there was to be no change in plans regarding my visit. I could not make out just how much this Mr. Noyes—as he announced himself—knew of Akeley's researches and discoveries, though it seemed to me that his casual manner stamped him as a comparative outsider. Remembering what a hermit Akeley had been, I was a trifle surprised at the ready availability of such a friend; but did not let my puzzlement deter me from entering the motor to which he gestured me. It was not the small ancient car I had expected from Akeley's descriptions, but a large and immaculate specimen of recent pattern—apparently Noyes's own, and bearing Massachusetts license plates with the amusing "sacred codfish" device of that year. My guide, I concluded, must be a summer transient in the Townshend region.

Noyes climbed into the car beside me and started it at once. I was glad that he did not overflow with conversation, for some peculiar atmospheric tensity made me feel disinclined to talk. The town seemed very attractive in the afternoon sunlight as we swept up an incline and turned to the right into the main street. It drowsed like the older New England cities which one remembers from boyhood, and something in the collocation of roofs and steeples and chimneys and brick walls formed contours touching deep violstrings of ancestral emotion. I could tell that I was at the gateway of a region half-bewitched through the piling-up of unbroken time-accumulations; a region where old, strange things have had a chance to grow and linger because they have never been stirred up.

As we passed out of Brattleboro my sense of constraint and foreboding increased, for a vague quality in the hill-crowded countryside with its towering, threatening, close-pressing green and granite slopes hinted at obscure secrets and immemorial survivals which might or might not be hostile to mankind. For a time our course followed a broad, shallow river which flowed down from unknown hills in the north, and I shivered when my companion told me it was the West River. It was in this stream, I recalled from newspaper items, that one of the morbid crablike beings had been seen floating after the floods.

Gradually the country around us grew wilder and more deserted. Archaic covered bridges lingered fearsomely out of the past in pockets of the hills, and the half-abandoned railway track paralleling the river seemed to exhale a nebulously visible air of desolation. There were awesome sweeps of vivid valley where great cliffs rose, New England's virgin granite showing grey and austere through the verdure that scaled the crests. There were gorges where untamed streams leaped, bearing down toward the river the unimagined secrets of a thousand pathless peaks. Branching away now and then were narrow, half-concealed roads that bored their way through solid, luxuriant masses of forest among whose primal trees whole armies of elemental spirits might well lurk. As I saw these I thought of how Akeley had been molested by unseen agencies on his drives along this very route, and did not wonder that such things could be.

The quaint, sightly village of Newfane, reached in less than an hour, was our last link with that world which man can definitely call his own by virtue of conquest and complete occupancy. After that we cast off all allegiance to immediate, tangible, and time-touched things, and entered a fantastic world of hushed unreality in which the narrow, ribbon-like road rose and fell and curved with an almost sentient and purposeful caprice amidst the tenantless green peaks and half-deserted valleys. Except for the sound of the motor, and the faint stir of the few lonely farms we passed at infrequent intervals, the only thing that reached my ears was the gurgling, insidious trickle of strange waters from numberless hidden fountains in the shadowy woods.

The nearness and intimacy of the dwarfed, domed hills now became veritably breath-taking. Their steepness and abruptness were even greater than I had imagined from hearsay, and suggested nothing in common with the prosaic objective world we know. The dense, unvisited woods on those inaccessible slopes seemed to harbour alien and incredible things, and I felt that the very outline of the hills themselves held some strange and aeon-forgotten meaning, as if they were vast hieroglyphs left by a rumoured titan race whose glories live only in rare, deep dreams. All the legends of the past, and all the stupefying imputations of Henry Akeley's letters and exhibits, welled up in my memory to heighten the atmosphere of tension and growing menace. The purpose of my visit, and the frightful abnormalities it postulated struck at me all at once with a chill sensation that nearly over-balanced my ardour for strange delvings.

My guide must have noticed my disturbed attitude; for as the road grew wilder and more irregular, and our motion slower and more jolting, his occasional pleasant comments expanded into a steadier flow of discourse. He spoke of the beauty and weirdness of the country, and revealed some acquaintance with the folklore studies of my prospective host. From his polite questions it was obvious that he knew I had come for a scientific purpose, and that I was bringing data of some importance; but he gave no sign of appreciating the depth and awfulness of the knowledge which Akeley had finally reached.

His manner was so cheerful, normal, and urbane that his remarks ought to have calmed and reassured me; but oddly enough, I felt only the more disturbed as we bumped and veered onward into the unknown wilderness of hills and woods. At times it seemed as if he were pumping me to see what I knew of the monstrous secrets of the place, and with every fresh utterance that vague, teasing, baffling *familiarity* in his voice increased. It was not an ordinary or healthy familiarity despite the thoroughly wholesome and cultivated nature of the voice. I somehow linked it with forgotten nightmares, and felt that I might go mad if I recognised it. If any good excuse had existed, I think I would have turned back from my visit. As it was, I could not well do so—and it occurred to me that a cool, scientific conversation with Akeley himself after my arrival would help greatly to pull me together.

Besides, there was a strangely calming element of cosmic beauty in the hypnotic landscape through which we climbed and plunged fantastically. Time had lost itself in the labyrinths behind, and around us stretched only the flowering waves of faery and the recaptured loveliness of vanished centuries—the hoary groves, the untainted pastures edged with gay autumnal blossoms, and at vast intervals the small brown farmsteads nestling amidst huge trees beneath vertical precipices of fragrant brier and meadow-grass. Even the sunlight assumed a supernal glamour, as if some special atmosphere or exhalation mantled the whole region. I had seen nothing like it before save in the magic vistas that sometimes form the backgrounds of Italian primitives. Sodoma and Leonardo conceived such expanses, but only in the distance, and through the vaultings of Renaissance arcades. We were now burrowing bodily through the midst of the picture, and I seemed to find in its necromancy a thing I had innately known or inherited and for which I had always been vainly searching.

Suddenly, after rounding an obtuse angle at the top of a sharp ascent, the car came to a standstill. On my left, across a well-kept lawn which stretched to the road and flaunted a border of whitewashed stones, rose a white, two-and-a-half-story house of unusual size and elegance for the region, with a congeries of contiguous or arcade-linked barns, sheds, and windmill behind and to the right. I recognised it at once from the snapshot I had received, and was not surprised to see the name of Henry Akeley on the galvanised-iron mailbox near the road. For some distance back of the house a level stretch of marshy and sparsely-wooded land extended, beyond which soared a steep, thickly-forested hillside ending in a jagged leafy crest. This latter, I knew, was the summit of Dark Mountain, half way up which we must have climbed already.

Alighting from the car and taking my valise, Noyes asked me to wait while he went in and notified Akeley of my advent. He himself, he added, had important business elsewhere, and could not stop for more than a moment. As he briskly walked up the path to the house I climbed out of the car myself, wishing to stretch my legs a little before settling down to a sedentary conversation. My feeling of nervousness and tension had risen to a maximum again now that I was on the actual scene of the morbid beleaguering described so hauntingly in Akeley's letters, and I honestly dreaded the coming discussions which were to link me with such alien and forbidden worlds.

Close contact with the utterly bizarre is often more terrifying than inspiring, and it did not cheer me to think that this very bit of dusty road was the place where those monstrous tracks and that foetid green ichor had been found after moonless nights of fear and death. Idly I noticed that none of Akeley's dogs seemed to be about. Had he sold them all as soon as the Outer Ones made peace with him? Try as I might, I could not have the same confidence in the depth and sincerity of that peace which appeared in Akeley's final and queerly different letter. After all, he was a man of much simplicity and with little worldly experience. Was there not, perhaps, some deep and sinister undercurrent beneath the surface of the new alliance?

Led by my thoughts, my eyes turned downward to the powdery road surface which had held such hideous testimonies. The last few days had been dry, and tracks of all sorts cluttered the rutted, irregular highway despite the unfrequented nature of the district. With a vague curiosity I began to trace the outline of some of the heterogeneous impressions, trying meanwhile to curb the flights of macabre fancy which the place and its memories suggested. There was something menacing and uncomfortable in the funereal stillness, in the muffled, subtle trickle of distant brooks, and in the crowding green peaks and black-wooded precipices that choked the narrow horizon.

And then an image shot into my consciousness which made those vague menaces and flights of fancy seem mild and insignificant indeed. I have said that I was scanning the miscellaneous prints in the road with a kind of idle curiosity—but all at once that curiosity was shockingly snuffed out by a sudden and paralysing gust of active terror. For though the dust tracks were in general confused and overlapping, and unlikely to arrest any casual gaze, my restless vision had caught certain details near the spot where the path to the house joined the highway; and had recognised beyond doubt or hope the frightful significance of those details. It was not for nothing, alas, that I had pored for hours over the Kodak views of the Outer Ones' claw-prints which Akeley had sent. Too well did I know the marks of those loathsome nippers, and that hint of ambiguous direction which stamped the horrors as no creatures of this planet. No chance had been left me for merciful mistake. Here, indeed, in objective form before my own eyes, and surely made not many hours ago, were at least three marks which stood out blasphemously among the surprising plethora of blurred footprints leading to and from the Akeley farmhouse. *They were the hellish tracks of the living fungi from Yuggoth.*

I pulled myself together in time to stifle a scream. After all, what more was there than I might have expected, assuming that I had really believed Akeley's letters? He had spoken of making peace with the things. Why, then, was it strange that some of them had visited his house? But the terror was stronger than the reassurance. Could any man be expected to look unmoved for the first time upon the claw-marks of animate beings from outer depths of space? Just then I saw Noyes emerge from the door and approach with a brisk step. I must, I reflected, keep command of myself, for the chances were that this genial friend knew nothing of Akeley's profoundest and most stupendous probings into the forbidden.

Akeley, Noyes hastened to inform me, was glad and ready to see me; although his sudden attack of asthma would prevent him from being a very competent host for a day or two. These spells hit him hard when they came, and were always accompanied by a debilitating fever and general weakness. He never was good for much while they lasted—had to talk in a whisper, and was very clumsy and feeble in getting about. His feet and ankles swelled, too, so that he had to bandage them like a gouty old beef-eater. Today he was in rather bad shape, so that I would have to attend very largely to my own needs; but he was none the less eager for conversation. I would find him in the study at the left of the front hall—the room where the blinds were shut. He had to keep the sunlight out when he was ill, for his eyes were very sensitive.

As Noyes bade me adieu and rode off northward in his car I began to walk slowly toward the house. The door had been left ajar for me; but before approaching and entering I cast a searching glance around the whole place, trying to decide what had struck me as so intangibly queer about it. The barns and sheds looked trimly prosaic enough, and I noticed Akeley's battered Ford in its capacious, unguarded shelter. Then the secret of the queerness reached me. It was the total silence. Ordinarily a farm is at least moderately murmurous from its various kinds of livestock, but here all signs of life were missing. What of the hens and the dogs? The cows, of which Akeley had said he possessed several, might conceivably be out to pasture, and the dogs might possibly have been sold; but the absence of any trace of cackling or grunting was truly singular.

I did not pause long on the path, but resolutely entered the open house door and closed it behind me. It had cost me a distinct psychological effort to do so, and now that I was shut inside I had a momentary longing for precipitate retreat. Not that the place was in the least sinister in visual suggestion; on the contrary, I thought the graceful late-colonial hallway very tasteful and wholesome, and admired the evident breeding of the man who had furnished it. What made me wish to flee was something very attenuated and indefinable. Perhaps it was a certain odd odour which I thought I noticed—though I well knew how common musty odours are in even the best of ancient farmhouses.

VII

Refusing to let these cloudy qualms overmaster me, I recalled Noyes's instructions and pushed open the six-panelled, brass-latched white door on my left. The room beyond was darkened as I had known before; and as I entered it I noticed that the queer odour was stronger there. There likewise appeared to be some faint, half-imaginary rhythm or vibration in the air. For a moment the closed blinds allowed me to see very little, but then a kind of apologetic hacking or whispering sound drew my attention to a great easy-chair in the farther, darker corner of the room. Within its shadowy depths I saw the white blur of a man's face and hands; and in a moment I had crossed to greet the figure who had tried to speak. Dim though the light was, I perceived that this was indeed my host. I had studied the Kodak picture repeatedly, and there could be no mistake about this firm, weather-beaten face with the cropped, grizzled beard.

But as I looked again my recognition was mixed with sadness and anxiety; for certainly, his face was that of a very sick man. I felt that there must be something more than asthma behind that strained, rigid, immobile expression and unwinking glassy stare; and realised how terribly the strain of his frightful experiences must have told on him. Was it not enough to break any human being—even a younger man than this intrepid delver into the forbidden? The strange and sudden relief, I feared, had come too late to save him from something like a general breakdown. There was a touch of the pitiful in the limp, lifeless way his lean hands rested in his lap. He had on a loose dressing-gown, and was swathed around the head and high around the neck with a vivid yellow scarf or hood.

And then I saw that he was trying to talk in the same hacking whisper with which he had greeted me. It was a hard whisper to catch at first, since the grey moustache concealed all movements of the lips, and something in its timbre disturbed me greatly; but by concentrating my attention I could soon make out its purport surprisingly well. The accent was by no means a rustic one, and the language was even more polished than correspondence had led me to expect.

"Mr. Wilmarth, I presume? You must pardon my not rising. I am quite ill, as Mr. Noyes must have told you; but I could not resist having you come just the same. You know what I wrote in my last letter—there is so much to tell you tomorrow when I shall feel better. I can't say how glad I am to see you in person after all our many letters. You have the file with you, of course? And the Kodak prints and records? Noyes put your valise in the hall—I suppose you saw it. For tonight I fear you'll have to wait on yourself to a great extent. Your room is upstairs—the one over this—and you'll see the bathroom door open at the head of the staircase. There's a meal spread for you in the dining-room—right through this door at our right—which you can take whenever you feel like it. I'll be a better host tomorrow—but just now weakness leaves me helpless.

"Make yourself at home—you might take out the letters and pictures and records and put them on the table here before you go upstairs with your bag. It is here that we shall discuss them—you can see my phonograph on that corner stand.

"No, thanks—there's nothing you can do for me. I know these spells of old. Just come back for a little quiet visiting before night, and then go to bed when you please. I'll rest right here—perhaps sleep here all night as I often do. In the morning I'll be far better able to go into the things we must go into. You realise, of course, the utterly stupendous nature of the matter before us. To us, as to only a few men on this earth, there will be opened up gulfs of time and space and knowledge beyond anything within the conception of human science or philosophy.

"Do you know that Einstein is wrong, and that certain objects and forces *can* move with a velocity greater than that of light? With proper aid I expect to go backward and forward in time, and actually *see* and *feel* the earth of remote past and future epochs. You can't imagine the degree to which those beings have carried science. There is nothing they can't do with the mind and body of living organisms. I expect to visit other planets, and even other stars and galaxies. The first trip will be to Yuggoth, the nearest world fully peopled by the beings. It is a strange dark orb at the very rim of our solar system—unknown to earthly astronomers as yet. But I must have written you about this. At the proper time, you know, the beings there will direct thought-currents toward us and cause it to be discovered—or perhaps let one of their human allies give the scientists a hint.

"There are mighty cities on Yuggoth—great tiers of terraced towers built of black stone like the specimen I tried to send you. That came from Yuggoth. The sun shines there no brighter than a star, but the beings need no light. They have other subtler senses, and put no windows in their great houses and temples. Light even hurts and hampers and confuses them, for it does not exist at all in the black cosmos outside time and space where they came from originally. To visit Yuggoth would drive any weak man mad—yet I am going there. The black rivers of pitch that flow under those mysterious cyclopean bridges—things built by some elder race extinct and forgotten before the beings came to Yuggoth from the ultimate voids—ought to be enough to make any man a Dante or Poe if he can keep sane long enough to tell what he has seen.

"But remember—that dark world of fungoid gardens and windowless cities isn't really terrible. It is only to us that it would seem so. Probably this world seemed just as terrible to the beings when they first explored it in the primal age. You know they were here long before the fabulous epoch of Cthulhu was over, and remember all about sunken R'lyeh when it was above the waters. They've been inside the earth, too—there are openings which human beings know nothing of—some of them in these very Vermont hills—and great worlds of unknown life down there; blue-litten K'n-yan, red-litten Yoth, and black, lightless N'kai. It's from N'kai that frightful Tsathoggua came—you know, the amorphous, toad-like god-creature mentioned in the *Pnakotic Manuscripts* and the *Necronomicon* and the Commoriom myth-cycle preserved by the Atlantean high-priest Klarkash-Ton.

"But we will talk of all this later on. It must be four or five o'clock by this time. Better bring the stuff from your bag, take a bite, and then come back for a comfortable chat."

Very slowly I turned and began to obey my host; fetching my valise, extracting and depositing the desired articles, and finally ascending to the room designated as mine. With the memory of that roadside claw-print fresh in my mind, Akeley's whispered paragraphs had affected me queerly; and the hints of familiarity with this unknown world of fungous life—forbidden Yuggoth—made my flesh creep more than I cared to own. I was tremendously sorry about Akeley's illness, but had to confess that his hoarse whisper had a hateful as well as pitiful quality. If only he wouldn't gloat so about Yuggoth and its black secrets!

My room proved a very pleasant and well-furnished one, devoid alike of the musty odour and disturbing sense of vibration; and after leaving my valise there I descended again to greet Akeley and take the lunch he had set out for me. The dining-room was just beyond the study, and I saw that a kitchen ell extended still farther in the same direction. On the dining-table an ample array of sandwiches, cake, and cheese awaited me, and a Thermos-bottle beside a cup and saucer testified that hot coffee had not been forgotten. After a well-relished meal I poured myself a liberal cup of coffee, but found that the culinary standard had suffered a lapse in this one detail. My first spoonful revealed a faintly unpleasant acrid taste, so that I did not take more. Throughout the lunch I thought of Akeley sitting silently in the great chair in the darkened next room. Once I went in to beg him to share the repast, but he whispered that he could eat nothing as yet. Later on, just before he slept, he would take some malted milk—all he ought to have that day.

After lunch I insisted on clearing the dishes away and washing them in the kitchen sink—incidentally emptying the coffee which I had not been able to appreciate. Then returning to the darkened study I drew up a chair near my host's corner and prepared for such conversation as he might feel inclined to conduct. The letters, pictures, and record were still on the large centre-table, but for the nonce we did not have to draw upon them. Before long I forgot even the bizarre odour and curious suggestions of vibration.

I have said that there were things in some of Akeley's letters—especially the second and most voluminous one—which I would not dare to quote or even form into words on paper. This hesitancy applies with still greater force to the things I heard whispered that evening in the darkened room among the lonely hills. Of the extent of the cosmic horrors unfolded by that raucous voice I cannot even hint. He had known hideous things before, but what he had learned since making his pact with the Outside Things was almost too much for sanity to bear. Even now I absolutely refused to believe what he implied about the constitution of ultimate infinity, the juxtaposition of dimensions, and the frightful position of our known cosmos of space and time in the unending chain of linked cosmos-atoms which makes up the immediate super-cosmos of curves, angles, and material and semi-material electronic organisation.

Never was a sane man more dangerously close to the arcana of basic entity—never was an organic brain nearer to utter annihilation in the chaos that transcends form and force and symmetry. I learned whence Cthulhu *first* came, and why half the great temporary stars of history had flared forth. I guessed—from hints which made even my informant pause timidly—the secret behind the Magellanic Clouds and globular nebulae, and the black truth veiled by the immemorial allegory of Tao. The nature of the Doels was plainly revealed, and I was told the essence (thought not the source) of the Hounds of Tindalos. The legend of Yig, Father of Serpents, remained figurative no longer, and I started with loathing when told of the monstrous nuclear chaos beyond angled space which the *Necronomicon* had mercifully cloaked under the name of Azathoth. It was shocking to have the foulest nightmares of secret myth cleared up in concrete terms whose stark, morbid hatefulness exceeded the boldest hints of ancient and mediaeval mystics. Ineluctably I was led to believe that the first whisperers of these accursed tales must have had discourse with Akeley's Outer Ones, and perhaps have visited outer cosmic realms as Akeley now proposed visiting them.

I was told of the Black Stone and what it implied, and was glad that it had not reached me. My guesses about those hieroglyphics had been all too correct! And yet Akeley now seemed reconciled to the whole fiendish system he had stumbled upon; reconciled and eager to probe farther into the monstrous abyss. I wondered what beings he had talked with since his last letter to me, and whether many of them had been as human as that first emissary he had mentioned. The tension in my head grew insufferable, and I built up all sorts of wild theories about that queer, persistent odour and those insidious hints of vibration in the darkened room.

Night was falling now, and as I recalled what Akeley had written me about those earlier nights I shuddered to think there would be no moon. Nor did I like the way the farmhouse nestled in the lee of that colossal forested slope leading up to Dark Mountain's unvisited crest. With Akeley's permission I lighted a small oil lamp, turned it low, and set it on a distant bookcase beside the ghostly bust of Milton; but afterward I was sorry I had done so, for it made my host's strained, immobile face and listless hands look damnably abnormal and corpse-like. He seemed half-incapable of motion, though I saw him nod stiffly once in awhile.

After what he had told, I could scarcely imagine what profounder secrets he was saving for the morrow; but at last it developed that his trip to Yuggoth and beyond—*and my own possible participation in it*—was to be the next day's topic. He must have been amused by the start of horror I gave at hearing a cosmic voyage on my part proposed, for his head wabbled violently when I showed my fear. Subsequently he spoke very gently of how human beings might accomplish—and several times had accomplished—the seemingly impossible flight across the interstellar void. *It seemed that complete human bodies did not indeed make the trip,* but that the prodigious surgical, biological, chemical, and mechanical skill of the Outer Ones had found a way to convey human brains without their concomitant physical structure.

There was a harmless way to extract a brain, and a way to keep the organic residue alive during its absence. The bare, compact cerebral matter was then immersed in an occasionally replenished fluid within an ether-tight cylinder of a metal mined in Yuggoth, certain electrodes reaching through and connecting at will with elaborate instruments capable of duplicating the three vital faculties of sight, hearing, and speech. For the winged fungus-beings to carry the brain-cylinders intact through space was an easy matter. Then, on every planet covered by their civilisation, they would find plenty of adjustable faculty-instruments capable of being connected with the encased brains; so that after a little fitting these travelling intelligences could be given a full sensory and articulate life—albeit a bodiless and mechanical one—at each stage of their journeying through and beyond the space-time continuum. It was as simple as carrying a phonograph record about and playing it wherever a phonograph of corresponding make exists. Of its success there could be no question. Akeley was not afraid. Had it not been brilliantly accomplished again and again?

For the first time one of the inert, wasted hands raised itself and pointed stiffly to a high shelf on the farther side of the room. There, in a neat row, stood more than a dozen cylinders of a metal I had never seen before—cylinders about a foot high and somewhat less in diameter, with three curious sockets set in an isosceles triangle over the front convex surface of each. One of them was linked at two of the sockets to a pair of singular-looking machines that stood in the background. Of their purport I did not need to be told, and I shivered as with ague. Then I saw the hand point to a much nearer corner where some intricate instruments with attached cords and plugs, several of them much like the two devices on the shelf behind the cylinders, were huddled together.

"There are four kinds of instruments here, Wilmarth," whispered the voice. "Four kinds—three faculties each—makes twelve pieces in all. You see there are four different sorts of beings represented in those cylinders up there. Three humans, six fungoid beings who can't navigate space corporeally, two beings from Neptune (God! if you could see the body this type has on its own planet!), and the rest entities from the central caverns of an especially interesting dark star beyond the galaxy. In the principal outpost inside Round Hill you'll now and then find more cylinders and machines—cylinders of extracosmic brains with different senses from any we know—allies and explorers from the uttermost Outside—and special machines for giving them impressions and expression in the several ways suited at once to them and to the comprehensions of different types of listeners. Round Hill, like most of the beings' main outposts all through the various universes, is a very cosmopolitan place. Of course, only the more common types have been lent to me for experiment.

"Here—take the three machines I point to and set them on the table. That tall one with the two glass lenses in front—then the box with the vacuum tubes and sounding-board—and now the one with the metal disc on top. Now for the cylinder with the label 'B-67' pasted on it. Just stand in that Windsor chair to reach the shelf. Heavy? Never mind! Be sure of the number—B-67. Don't bother that fresh, shiny cylinder joined to the two testing instruments—the one with my name on it. Set B-67 on the table near where you've put the machines—and see that the dial switch on all three machines is jammed over to the extreme left.

"Now connect the cord of the lens machine with the upper socket on the cylinder—there! Join the tube machine to the lower left-hand socket, and the disc apparatus to the outer socket. Now move all the dial switches on the machine over to the extreme right—first the lens one, then the disc one, and then the tube one. That's right. I might as well tell you that this is a human being—just like any of us. I'll give you a taste of some of the others tomorrow."

To this day I do not know why I obeyed those whispers so slavishly, or whether I thought Akeley was mad or sane. After what had gone before, I ought to have been prepared for anything; but this mechanical mummery seemed so like the typical vagaries of crazed inventors and scientists that it struck a chord of doubt which even the preceding discourse had not excited. What the whisperer implied was beyond all human belief—yet were not the other things still farther beyond, and less preposterous only because of their remoteness from tangible concrete proof?

As my mind reeled amidst this chaos, I became conscious of a mixed grating and whirring from all three of the machines lately linked to the cylinder—a grating and whirring which soon subsided into a virtual noiselessness. What was about to happen? Was I to hear a voice? And if so, what proof would I have that it was not some cleverly concocted radio device talked into by a concealed but closely watched speaker? Even now I am unwilling to swear just what I heard, or just what phenomenon really took place before me. But something certainly seemed to take place.

To be brief and plain, the machine with the tubes and sound-box began to speak, and with a point and intelligence which left no doubt that the speaker was actually present and observing us. The voice was loud, metallic, lifeless, and plainly mechanical in every detail of its production. It was incapable of inflection or expressiveness, but scraped and rattled on with a deadly precision and deliberation.

"Mr. Wilmarth," it said, "I hope I do not startle you. I am a human being like yourself, though my body is now resting safely under proper vitalising treatment inside Round Hill, about a mile and a half east of here. I myself am here with you—my brain is in that cylinder and I see, hear, and speak through these electronic vibrators. In a week I am going across the void as I have been many times before, and I expect to have the pleasure of Mr. Akeley's company. I wish I might have yours as well; for I know you by sight and reputation, and have kept close track of your correspondence with our friend. I am, of course, one of the men who have become allied with the outside beings visiting our planet. I met them first in the Himalayas, and have helped them in various ways. In return they have given me experiences such as few men have ever had.

"Do you realise what it means when I say I have been on thirty-seven different celestial bodies—planets, dark stars, and less definable objects—including eight outside our galaxy and two outside the curved cosmos of space and time? All this has not harmed me in the least. My brain has been removed from my body by fissions so adroit that it would be crude to call the operation surgery. The visiting beings have methods which make these extractions easy and almost normal—and one's body never ages when the brain is out of it. The brain, I may add, is virtually immortal with its mechanical faculties and a limited nourishment supplied by occasional changes of the preserving fluid.

"Altogether, I hope most heartily that you will decide to come with Mr. Akeley and me. The visitors are eager to know men of knowledge like yourself, and to show them the great abysses that most of us have had to dream about in fanciful ignorance. It may seem strange at first to meet them, but I know you will be above minding that. I think Mr. Noyes will go along, too—the man who doubtless brought you up here in his car. He has been one of us for years—I suppose you recognised his voice as one of those on the record Mr. Akeley sent you."

At my violent start the speaker paused a moment before concluding.

"So Mr. Wilmarth, I will leave the matter to you; merely adding that a man with your love of strangeness and folklore ought never to miss such a chance as this. There is nothing to fear. All transitions are painless, and there is much to enjoy in a wholly mechanised state of sensation. When the electrodes are disconnected, one merely drops off into a sleep of especially vivid and fantastic dreams.

"And now, if you don't mind, we might adjourn our session till tomorrow. Good night—just turn all the switches back to the left; never mind the exact order, though you might let the lens machine be last. Good night, Mr. Akeley—treat our guest well! Ready now with those switches?"

That was all. I obeyed mechanically and shut off all three switches, though dazed with doubt of everything that had occurred. My head was still reeling as I heard Akeley's whispering voice telling me that I might leave all the apparatus on the table just as it was. He did not essay any comment on what had happened, and indeed no comment could have conveyed much to my burdened faculties. I heard him telling me I could take the lamp to use in my room, and deduced that he wished to rest alone in the dark. It was surely time he rested, for his discourse of the afternoon and evening had been such as to exhaust even a vigorous man. Still dazed, I bade my host good night and went upstairs with the lamp, although I had an excellent pocket flashlight with me.

I was glad to be out of that downstairs study with the queer odour and vague suggestions of vibration, yet could not of course escape a hideous sense of dread and peril and cosmic abnormality as I thought of the place I was in and the forces I was meeting. The wild, lonely region, the black, mysteriously forested slope towering so close behind the house, the footprint in the road, the sick, motionless whisperer in the dark, the hellish cylinders and machines, and above all the invitations to strange surgery and stranger voyagings—these things, all so new and in such sudden succession, rushed in on me with a cumulative force which sapped my will and almost undermined my physical strength.

To discover that my guide Noyes was the human celebrant in that monstrous bygone Sabbat-ritual on the phonograph record was a particular shock, though I had previously sensed a dim, repellant familiarity in his voice. Another special shock came from my own attitude toward my host whenever I paused to analyse it; for much as I had instinctively liked Akeley as revealed in his correspondence, I now found that he filled me with a distinct repulsion. His illness ought to have excited my pity; but instead, it gave me a kind of shudder. He was so rigid and inert and corpselike—and that incessant whispering was so hateful and un-human!

It occurred to me that this whispering was different from anything else of the kind I had ever heard; that, despite the curious motionlessness of the speaker's moustache-screened lips, it had a latent strength and carrying-power remarkable for the wheezing of an asthmatic. I had been able to understand the speaker when wholly across the room, and once or twice it had seemed to me that the faint but penetrant sounds represented not so much weakness as deliberate repression—for what reason I could not guess. From the first I had felt a disturbing quality in their timbre. Now, when I tried to weigh the matter, I thought I could trace this impression to a kind of subconscious familiarity like that which had made Noyes's voice so hazily ominous. But when or where I had encountered the thing it hinted at, was more than I could tell.

One thing was certain—I would not spend another night here. My scientific zeal had vanished amidst fear and loathing, and I felt nothing now but a wish to escape from this net of morbidity and unnatural revelation. I knew enough now. It must indeed be true that strange cosmic linkages do exist—but such things are surely not meant for normal human beings to meddle with.

Blasphemous influences seemed to surround me and press chokingly upon my senses. Sleep, I decided, would be out of the question; so I merely extinguished the lamp and threw myself on the bed fully dressed. No doubt it was absurd, but I kept ready for some unknown emergency; gripping in my right hand the revolver I had brought along, and holding the pocket flashlight in my left. Not a sound came from below, and I could imagine how my host was sitting there with cadaverous stiffness in the dark.

Somewhere I heard a clock ticking, and was vaguely grateful for the normality of the sound. It reminded me, though, of another thing about the region which disturbed me—the total absence of animal life. There were certainly no farm beasts about, and now I realised that even the accustomed night-noises of wild living things were absent. Except for the sinister trickle of distant unseen waters, that stillness was anomalous—interplanetary—and I wondered what star-spawned, intangible blight could be hanging over the region. I recalled from old legends that dogs and other beasts had always hated the Outer Ones, and thought of what those tracks in the road might mean.

VIII

Do not ask me how long my unexpected lapse into slumber lasted, or how much of what ensued was sheer dream. If I tell you that I awakened at a certain time, and heard and saw certain things, you will merely answer that I did not wake then; and that everything was a dream until the moment when I rushed out of the house, stumbled to the shed where I had seen the old Ford, and seized that ancient vehicle for a mad, aimless race over the haunted hills which at last landed me—after hours of jolting and winding through forest-threatened labyrinths—in a village which turned out to be Townshend.

You will also, of course, discount everything else in my report; and declare that all the pictures, record-sounds, cylinder-and-machine sounds, and kindred evidences were bits of pure deception practiced on me by the missing Henry Akeley. You will even hint that he conspired with other eccentrics to carry out a silly and elaborate hoax—that he had the express shipment removed at Keene, and that he had Noyes make that terrifying wax record. It is odd, though, that Noyes has not ever yet been identified; that he was unknown at any of the villages near Akeley's place, though he must have been frequently in the region. I wish I had stopped to memorize the license-number of his car—or perhaps it is better after all that I did not. For I, despite all you can say, and despite all I sometimes try to say to myself, know that loathsome outside influences must be lurking there in the half-unknown hills—and that those influences have spies and emissaries in the world of men. To keep as far as possible from such influences and such emissaries is all that I ask of life in future.

When my frantic story sent a sheriff's posse out to the farmhouse, Akeley was gone without leaving a trace. His loose dressing gown, yellow scarf, and foot-bandages lay on the study floor near his corner easy-chair, and it could not be decided whether any of his other apparel had vanished with him. The dogs and livestock were indeed missing, and there were some curious bullet-holes both on the house's exterior and on some of the walls within; but beyond this nothing unusual could be detected. No cylinders or machines, none of the evidences I had brought in my valise, no queer odour or vibration-sense, no foot-prints in the road, and none of the problematical things I glimpsed at the very last.

I stayed a week in Brattleboro after my escape, making inquiries among people of every kind who had known Akeley; and the results convince me that the matter is no figment of dream or delusion. Akeley's queer purchase of dogs and ammunition and chemicals, and the cutting of his telephone wires, are matters of record; while all who knew him—including his son in California—concede that his occasional remarks on strange studies had a certain consistency. Solid citizens believe he was mad, and unhesitatingly pronounce all reported evidences mere hoaxes devised with insane cunning and perhaps abetted by eccentric associates; but the lowlier country folk sustain his statements in every detail. He had showed some of these rustics his photographs and black stone, and had played the hideous record for them, and they all said the footprints and buzzing voice were like those described in ancestral legends.

They said, too, that suspicious sights and sounds had been noticed increasingly around Akeley's house after he found the black stone, and that the place was now avoided by everybody except the mail man and other casual, tough-minded people. Dark Mountain and Round Hill were both notoriously haunted spots, and I could find no one who had ever closely explored either. Occasional disappearances of natives throughout the district's history were well attested, and these now included the semi-vagabond Walter Brown, whom Akeley's letters had mentioned. I even came upon one farmer who thought he had personally glimpsed one of the queer bodies at floodtime in the swollen West River, but his tale was too confused to be really valuable.

When I left Brattleboro I resolved never to go back to Vermont, and I feel quite certain I shall keep my resolution. Those wild hills are surely the outpost of a frightful cosmic race—as I doubt all the less since reading that a new ninth planet has been glimpsed beyond Neptune, just as those influences had said it would be glimpsed. Astronomers, with a hideous appropriateness they little suspect, have named this thing "Pluto." I feel, beyond question, that it is nothing less than nighted Yuggoth—and I shiver when I try to figure out the real reason *why* its monstrous denizens wish it to be known in this way at this especial time. I vainly try to assure myself that these daemoniac creatures are not gradually leading up to some new policy hurtful to the earth and its normal inhabitants.

But I have still to tell of the ending of that terrible night in the farmhouse. As I have said, I did finally drop into a troubled doze; a doze filled with bits of dream which involved monstrous landscape-glimpses. Just what awaked me I cannot yet say, but that I did indeed awake at this given point I feel very certain. My first confused impression was of stealthily creaking floor-boards in the hall outside my door, and of a clumsy, muffled fumbling at the latch. This, however, ceased almost at once; so that my really clear impressions begin with the voices heard from the study below. There seemed to be several speakers, and I judged that they were controversially engaged.

By the time I had listened a few seconds I was broad awake, for the nature of the voices was such as to make all thought of sleep ridiculous. The tones were curiously varied, and no one who had listened to that accursed phonograph record could harbour any doubts about the nature of at least two of them. Hideous though the idea was, I knew that I was under the same roof with nameless things from abysmal space; for those two voices were unmistakably the blasphemous buzzings which the Outside Beings used in their communication with men. The two were individually different—different in pitch, accent, and tempo—but they were both of the same damnable general kind.

A third voice was indubitably that of a mechanical utterance-machine connected with one of the detached brains in the cylinders. There was as little doubt about that as about the buzzings; for the loud, metallic, lifeless voice of the previous evening, with its inflectionless, expressionless scraping and rattling, and its impersonal precision and deliberation, had been utterly unforgettable. For a time I did not pause to question whether the intelligence behind the scraping was the identical one which had formerly talked to me; but shortly afterward I reflected that *any* brain would emit vocal sounds of the same quality if linked to the same mechanical speech-producer; the only possible differences being in language, rhythm, speed, and pronunciation. To complete the eldritch colloquy there were two actually human voices—one the crude speech of an unknown and evidently rustic man, and the other the suave Bostonian tones of my erstwhile guide Noyes.

As I tried to catch the words which the stoutly-fashioned floor so bafflingly intercepted, I was also conscious of a great deal of stirring and scratching and shuffling in the room below; so that I could not escape the impression that it was full of living beings—many more than the few whose speech I could single out. The exact nature of this stirring is extremely hard to describe, for very few good bases of comparison exist. Objects seemed now and then to move across the room like conscious entities; the sound of their footfalls having something about it like a loose, hard-surfaced clattering—as of the contact of ill-coördinated surfaces of horn or hard rubber. It was, to use a more concrete but less accurate comparison, as if people with loose, splintery wooden shoes were shambling and rattling about on the polished board floor. Of the nature and appearance of those responsible for the sounds, I did not care to speculate.

Before long I saw that it would be impossible to distinguish any connected discourse. Isolated words—including the names of Akeley and myself—now and then floated up, especially when uttered by the mechanical speech-producer; but their true significance was lost for want of continuous context. Today I refuse to form any definite deductions from them, and even their frightful effect on me was one of *suggestion* rather than of *revelation*. A terrible and abnormal conclave, I felt certain, was assembled below me; but for what shocking deliberations I could not tell. It was curious how this unquestioned sense of the malign and the blasphemous pervaded me despite Akeley's assurances of the Outsider's friendliness.

With patient listening I began to distinguish clearly between voices, even though I could not grasp much of what any of the voices said. I seemed to catch certain typical emotions behind some of the speakers. One of the buzzing voices, for example, held an unmistakable note of authority; whilst the mechanical voice, notwithstanding its artificial loudness and regularity, seemed to be in a position of subordination and pleading. Noyes's tones exuded a kind of conciliatory atmosphere. The others I could make no attempt to interpret. I did not hear the familiar whisper of Akeley, but well knew that such a sound could never penetrate the solid flooring of my room.

I will try to set down some of the few disjointed words and other sounds I caught, labelling the speakers of the words as best I know how. It was from the speech-machine that I first picked up a few recognisable phrases.

(The Speech-Machine)

". . . brought it on myself . . . sent back the letters and the record . . . end on it . . . taken in . . . seeing and hearing . . . damn you . . . impersonal force, after all . . . fresh, shiny cylinder . . . great God. . . ."

(First Buzzing Voice)

". . . time we stopped . . . small and human . . . Akeley . . . brain . . . saying. . . ."

(Second Buzzing Voice)

". . . Nyarlathotep . . . Wilmarth . . . records and letters . . . cheap imposture. . . ."

(Noyes)

". . . (an unpronounceable word or name, possibly *N'gah-Kthun*) . . . harmless . . . peace . . . couple of weeks . . . theatrical . . . told you that before. . . ."

(First Buzzing Voice)

". . . no reason . . . original plan . . . effects . . . Noyes can watch . . .
Round Hill . . . fresh cylinder . . . Noyes's car. . . ."

(Noyes)

". . . well . . . all yours . . . down here . . . rest . . . place. . . ."

(Several Voices at Once in Indistinguishable Speech)

(Many Footsteps, Including the Peculiar Loose Stirring or Clattering)

(A Curious Sort of Flapping Sound)

(The Sound of an Automobile Starting and Receding)

(Silence)

That is the substance of what my ears brought me as I lay rigid
upon that strange upstairs bed in the haunted farmhouse among the
daemoniac hills—lay there fully dressed, with a revolver clenched in
my right hand and a pocket flashlight gripped in my left. I became, as
I have said, broad awake; but a kind of obscure paralysis nevertheless
kept me inert till long after the last echoes of the sounds had died
away. I heard the wooden, deliberate ticking of the ancient Connecticut clock somewhere far below, and at last made out the irregular
snoring of a sleeper. Akeley must have dozed off after the strange session, and I could well believe that he needed to do so.

Just what to think or what to do was more than I could decide. After
all, what *had* I heard beyond things which previous information might
have led me to expect? Had I not known that the nameless Outsiders
were now freely admitted to the farmhouse? No doubt Akeley had
been surprised by an unexpected visit from them. Yet something in
that fragmentary discourse had chilled me immeasurably, raised the
most grotesque and horrible doubts, and made me wish fervently that I
might wake up and prove everything a dream. I think my subconscious
mind must have caught something which my consciousness has not
yet recognised. But what of Akeley? Was he not my friend, and would
he not have protested if any harm were meant me? The peaceful snoring below seemed to cast ridicule on all my suddenly intensified fears.

Was it possible that Akeley had been imposed upon and used as a
lure to draw me into the hills with the letters and pictures and
phonograph record? Did those beings mean to engulf us both in a
common destruction because we had come to know too much? Again
I thought of the abruptness and unnaturalness of that change in the
situation which must have occurred between Akeley's penultimate
and final letters. Something, my instinct told me, was terribly wrong.

All was not as it seemed. The acrid coffee which I refused—had there not been an attempt by some hidden, unknown entity to drug it? I must talk to Akeley at once, and restore his sense of proportion. They had hypnotised him with their promises of cosmic revelations, but now he must listen to reason. We must get out of this before it would be too late. If he lacked the will power to make the break for liberty, I would supply it. Or if I could not persuade him to go, I could at least go myself. Surely he would let me take his Ford and leave it in a garage in Brattleboro. I had noticed it in the shed—the door being left unlocked and open now that peril was deemed past—and I believed there was a good chance of its being ready for instant use. That momentary dislike of Akeley which I had felt during and after the evening's conversation was all gone now. He was in a position much like my own, and we must stick together. Knowing his indisposed condition, I hated to wake him at this juncture, but I knew that I must. I could not stay in this place till morning as matters stood.

At last I felt able to act, and stretched myself vigorously to regain command of my muscles. Arising with a caution more impulsive than deliberate, I found and donned my hat, took my valise, and started downstairs with the flashlight's aid. In my nervousness I kept the revolver clutched in my right hand, being able to take care of both valise and flashlight with my left. Why I exerted these precautions I do not really know, since I was even then on my way to awaken the only other occupant of the house.

As I half-tiptoed down the creaking stairs to the lower hall I could hear the sleeper more plainly, and noticed that he must be in the room on my left—the living-room I had not entered. On my right was the gaping blackness of the study in which I had heard the voices. Pushing open the unlatched door of the living-room I traced a path with the flashlight toward the source of the snoring, and finally turned the beams on the sleeper's face. But in the next second I hastily turned them away and commenced a catlike retreat to the hall, my caution this time springing from reason as well as from instinct. For the sleeper on the couch was not Akeley at all, but my quondam guide Noyes.

Just what the real situation was, I could not guess; but common sense told me that the safest thing was to find out as much as possible before arousing anybody. Regaining the hall, I silently closed and latched the living-room door after me; thereby lessening the chances of awakening Noyes. I now cautiously entered the dark study, where I expected to find Akeley, whether asleep or awake, in the great corner chair which was evidently his favorite resting-place. As I advanced, the beams of my flashlight caught the great centre-table, revealing one of the hellish cylinders with sight and hearing machines attached, and with a speech machine standing close by, ready to be connected at any moment. This, I reflected, must be the encased brain I had heard talking during the frightful conference; and for a second I had a perverse impulse to attach the speech machine and see what it would say.

It must, I thought, be conscious of my presence even now; since the sight and hearing attachments could not fail to disclose the rays of my flashlight and the faint creaking of the floor beneath my feet. But in the end I did not dare meddle with the thing. I idly saw that it was the fresh shiny cylinder with Akeley's name on it, which I had noticed on the shelf earlier in the evening and which my host had told me not to bother. Looking back at that moment, I can only regret my timidity and wish that I had boldly caused the apparatus to speak. God knows what mysteries and horrible doubts and questions of identity it might have cleared up! But then, it may be merciful that I let it alone.

From the table I turned my flashlight to the corner where I thought Akeley was, but found to my perplexity that the great easy-chair was empty of any human occupant asleep or awake. From the seat to the floor there trailed voluminously the familiar old dressing-gown, and near it on the floor lay the yellow scarf and the huge foot-bandages I had thought so odd. As I hesitated, striving to conjecture where Akeley might be, and why he had so suddenly discarded his necessary sick-room garments, I observed that the queer odour and sense of vibration were no longer in the room. What had been their cause? Curiously it occurred to me that I had noticed them only in Akeley's vicinity. They had been strongest where he sat, and wholly absent except in the room with him or just outside the doors of that room. I paused, letting the flashlight wander about the dark study and racking my brain for explanations of the turn affairs had taken.

Would to Heaven I had quietly left the place before allowing that light to rest again on the vacant chair. As it turned out, I did not leave quietly; but with a muffled shriek which must have disturbed, though it did not quite awake, the sleeping sentinel across the hall. That shriek, and Noyes's still-unbroken snore, are the last sounds I ever heard in that morbidity-choked farmhouse beneath the black-wooded crest of haunted mountain—that focus of transcosmic horror amidst the lonely green hills and curse-muttering brooks of a spectral rustic land.

It is a wonder that I did not drop flashlight, valise, and revolver in my wild scramble, but somehow I failed to lose any of these. I actually managed to get out of that room and that house without making any further noise, to drag myself and my belongings safely into the old Ford in the shed, and to set that archaic vehicle in motion toward some unknown point of safety in the black, moonless night. The ride that followed was a piece of delirium out of Poe or Rimbaud or the drawings of Doré, but finally I reached Townshend. That is all. If my sanity is still unshaken, I am lucky. Sometimes I fear what the years will bring, especially since that new planet Pluto has been so curiously discovered.

As I have implied, I let my flashlight return to the vacant easy-chair after its circuit of the room; then noticing for the first time the presence of certain objects in the seat, made inconspicuous by the adjacent loose folds of the empty dressing-gown. These are the objects, three in number, which the investigators did not find when they came later on. As I said at the outset, there was nothing of actual visual horror about them. The trouble was in what they led one to infer. Even now I have my moments of half-doubt—moments in which I half-accept the scepticism of those who attribute my whole experience to dream and nerves and delusion.

The three things were damnably clever constructions of their kind, and were furnished with ingenious metallic clamps to attach them to organic developments of which I dare not form any conjecture. I hope—devoutly hope—that they were the waxen products of a master artist, despite what my inmost fears tell me. Great God! That whisperer in darkness with its morbid odour and vibrations! Sorcerer, emissary, changeling, outsider . . . that hideous repressed buzzing . . . and all the time in that fresh, shiny cylinder on the shelf . . . poor devil . . . "Prodigious surgical, biological, chemical, and mechanical skill. . . ."

For the things in the chair, perfect to the last, subtle detail of microscopic resemblance—or identity—were the face and hands of Henry Wentworth Akeley.

The Colour Out Of Space

$\twoheadleftarrow\!\!=\!\!\twoheadrightarrow$

West of Arkham the hills rise wild, and there are valleys with deep woods that no axe has ever cut. There are dark narrow glens where the trees slope fantastically, and where thin brooklets trickle without ever having caught the glint of sunlight. On the gentler slopes there are farms, ancient and rocky, with squat, moss-coated cottages brooding eternally over old New England secrets in the lee of great ledges; but these are all vacant now, the wide chimneys crumbling and the shingled sides bulging perilously beneath low gambrel roofs.

The old folk have gone away, and foreigners do not like to live there. French-Canadians have tried it, Italians have tried it, and the Poles have come and departed. It is not because of anything that can be seen or heard or handled, but because of something that is imagined. The place is not good for imagination, and does not bring restful dreams at night. It must be this which keeps the foreigners away, for old Ammi Pierce has never told them of anything he recalls from the strange days. Ammi, whose head has been a little queer for years, is the only one who still remains, or who ever talks of the strange days; and he dares to do this because his house is so near the open fields and the travelled roads around Arkham.

There was once a road over the hills and through the valleys, that ran straight where the blasted heath is now; but people ceased to use it and a new road was laid curving far toward the south. Traces of the old one can still be found amidst the weeds of a returning wilderness, and some of them will doubtless linger even when half the hollows are flooded for the new reservoir. Then the dark woods will be cut down and the blasted heath will slumber far below blue waters whose surface will mirror the sky and ripple in the sun. And the secrets of the strange days will be one with the deep's secrets; one with the hidden lore of old ocean, and all the mystery of primal earth.

When I went into the hills and vales to survey for the new

reservoir they told me the place was evil. They told me this in Arkham, and because that is a very old town full of witch legends I thought the evil must be something which grandams had whispered to children through centuries. The name "blasted heath" seemed to me very odd and theatrical, and I wondered how it had come into the folklore of a Puritan people. Then I saw that dark westward tangle of glens and slopes for myself, and ceased to wonder at anything beside its own elder mystery. It was morning when I saw it, but shadow lurked always there. The trees grew too thickly, and their trunks were too big for any healthy New England wood. There was too much silence in the dim alleys between them, and the floor was too soft with the dank moss and mattings of infinite years of decay.

In the open spaces, mostly along the line of the old road, there were little hillside farms; sometimes with all the buildings standing, sometimes with only one or two, and sometimes with only a lone chimney or fast-filling cellar. Weeds and briers reigned, and furtive wild things rustled in the undergrowth. Upon everything was a haze of restlessness and oppression; a touch of the unreal and the grotesque, as if some vital element of perspective or chiaroscuro were awry. I did not wonder that the foreigners would not stay, for this was no region to sleep in. It was too much like a landscape of Salvator Rosa; too much like some forbidden woodcut in a tale of terror.

But even all this was not so bad as the blasted heath. I knew it the moment I came upon it at the bottom of a spacious valley; for no other name could fit such a thing, or any other thing fit such a name. It was as if the poet had coined the phrase from having seen this one particular region. It must, I thought as I viewed it, be the outcome of a fire; but why had nothing new ever grown over those five acres of grey desolation that sprawled open to the sky like a great spot eaten by acid in the woods and fields? It lay largely to the north of the ancient road line, but encroached a little on the other side. I felt an odd reluctance about approaching, and did so at last only because my business took me through and past it. There was no vegetation of any kind on that broad expanse, but only a fine grey dust or ash which no wind seemed ever to blow about. The trees near it were sickly and stunted, and many dead trunks stood or lay rotting at the rim. As I walked hurriedly by I saw the tumbled bricks and stones of an old chimney and cellar on my right, and the yawning black maw of an abandoned well whose stagnant vapours played strange tricks with the hues of the sunlight. Even the long, dark woodland climb beyond seemed welcome in contrast, and I marvelled no more at the frightened whispers of Arkham people. There had been no house or ruin near; even in the old days the place must have been lonely and remote. And at twilight, dreading to repass that ominous spot, I walked circuitously back to the town by the curving road on the south. I vaguely wished some clouds would gather, for an odd timidity about the deep skyey voids above had crept into my soul.

In the evening I asked old people in Arkham about the blasted heath, and what was meant by that phrase "strange days" which so many evasively muttered. I could not, however, get any good answers, except that all the mystery was much more recent than I had dreamed. It was not a matter of old legendry at all, but something within the lifetime of those who spoke. It had happened in the 'eighties, and a family had disappeared or was killed. Speakers would not be exact; and because they all told me to pay no attention to old Ammi Pierce's crazy tales, I sought him out the next morning, having heard that he lived alone in the ancient tottering cottage where the trees first begin to get very thick. It was a fearsomely ancient place, and had begun to exude the faint miasmal odour which clings about houses that have stood too long. Only with persistent knocking could I rouse the aged man, and when he shuffled timidly to the door I could tell he was not glad to see me. He was not so feeble as I had expected; but his eyes drooped in a curious way, and his unkempt clothing and white beard made him seem very worn and dismal.

Not knowing just how he could best be launched on his tales, I feigned a matter of business; told him of my surveying, and asked vague questions about the district. He was far brighter and more educated than I had been led to think, and before I knew it had grasped quite as much of the subject as any man I had talked with in Arkham. He was not like other rustics I had known in the sections where reservoirs were to be. From him there were no protests at the miles of old wood and farmland to be blotted out, though perhaps there would have been had not his home lain outside the bounds of the future lake. Relief was all that he showed; relief at the doom of the dark ancient valleys through which he had roamed all his life. They were better under water now—better under water since the strange days. And with this opening his husky voice sank low, while his body leaned forward and his right forefinger began to point shakily and impressively.

It was then that I heard the story, and as the rambling voice scraped and whispered on I shivered again and again despite the summer day. Often I had to recall the speaker from ramblings, piece out scientific points which he knew only by a fading parrot memory of professors' talk, or bridge over gaps, where his sense of logic and continuity broke down. When he was done I did not wonder that his mind had snapped a trifle, or that the folk of Arkham would not speak much of the blasted heath. I hurried back before sunset to my hotel, unwilling to have the stars come out above me in the open; and the next day returned to Boston to give up my position. I could not go into that dim chaos of old forest and slope again, or face another time that grey blasted heath where the black well yawned deep beside the tumbled bricks and stones. The reservoir will soon be built now, and all those elder secrets will be safe forever under watery fathoms. But even then I do not believe I would like to visit that country by night—at least not when the sinister stars are out; and nothing could bribe me to drink the new city water of Arkham.

It all began, old Ammi said, with the meteorite. Before that time there had been no wild legends at all since the witch trials, and even then these western woods were not feared half so much as the small island in the Miskatonic where the devil held court beside a curious stone altar older than the Indians. These were not haunted woods, and their fantastic dusk was never terrible till the strange days. Then there had come that white noontide cloud, that string of explosions in the air, and that pillar of smoke from the valley far in the wood. And by night all Arkham had heard of the great rock that fell out of the sky and bedded itself in the ground beside the well at the Nahum Gardner place. That was the house which had stood where the blasted heath was to come—the trim white Nahum Gardner house amidst its fertile gardens and orchards.

Nahum had come to town to tell people about the stone, and dropped in at Ammi Pierce's on the way. Ammi was forty then, and all the queer things were fixed very strongly in his mind. He and his wife had gone with the three professors from Miskatonic University who hastened out the next morning to see the weird visitor from unknown stellar space, and had wondered why Nahum had called it so large the day before. It had shrunk, Nahum said as he pointed out the big brownish mound above the ripped earth and charred grass near the archaic well-sweep in his front yard; but the wise men answered that stones do not shrink. Its heat lingered persistently, and Nahum declared it had glowed faintly in the night. The professors tried it with a geologist's hammer and found it was oddly soft. It was, in truth, so soft as to be almost plastic; and they gouged rather than chipped a specimen to take back to the college for testing. They took it in an old pail borrowed from Nahum's kitchen, for even the small piece refused to grow cool. On the trip back they stopped at Ammi's to rest, and seemed thoughtful when Mrs. Pierce remarked that the fragment was growing smaller and burning the bottom of the pail. Truly, it was not large, but perhaps they had taken less than they thought.

The day after that—all this was in June of '82—the professors had
trooped out again in a great excitement. As they passed Ammi's they
told him what queer things the specimen had done, and how it had
faded wholly away when they put it in a glass beaker. The beaker had
gone, too, and the wise men talked of the strange stone's affinity for
silicon. It had acted quite unbelievably in that well-ordered laboratory; doing nothing at all and showing no occluded gases when
heated on charcoal, being wholly negative in the borax bead, and
soon proving itself absolutely non-volatile at any producible temperature, including that of the oxy-hydrogen blowpipe. On an anvil it appeared highly malleable, and in the dark its luminosity was very
marked. Stubbornly refusing to grow cool, it soon had the college in a
state of real excitement; and when upon heating before the spectroscope it displayed shining bands unlike any known colours of the
normal spectrum there was much breathless talk of new elements,
bizarre optical properties, and other things which puzzled men of science are wont to say when faced by the unknown.

Hot as it was, they tested it in a crucible with all the proper
reagents. Water did nothing. Hydrochloric acid was the same. Nitric
acid and even aqua regia merely hissed and spattered against its torrid
invulnerability. Ammi had difficulty in recalling all these things, but
recognized some solvents as I mentioned them in the usual order of
use. There were ammonia and caustic soda, alcohol and ether, nauseous carbon disulphide and a dozen others; but although the weight
grew steadily less as time passed, and the fragment seemed to be
slightly cooling, there was no change in the solvents to show that
they had attacked the substance at all. It was a metal, though, beyond
a doubt. It was magnetic, for one thing; and after its immersion in the
acid solvents there seemed to be faint traces of the Widmänstätten
figures found on meteoric iron. When the cooling had grown very
considerable, the testing was carried on in glass; and it was in a glass
beaker that they left all the chips made of the original fragment during the work. The next morning both chips and beaker were gone
without trace, and only a charred spot marked the place on the
wooden shelf where they had been.

All this the professors told Ammi as they paused at his door, and
once more he went with them to see the stony messenger from the
stars, though this time his wife did not accompany him. It had now
most certainly shrunk, and even the sober professors could not doubt
the truth of what they saw. All around the dwindling brown lump
near the well was a vacant space, except where the earth had caved
in; and whereas it had been a good seven feet across the day before,
it was now scarcely five. It was still hot, and the sages studied its

surface curiously as they detached another and larger piece with hammer and chisel. They gouged deeply this time, and as they pried away the smaller mass they saw that the core of the thing was not quite homogeneous.

They had uncovered what seemed to be the side of a large coloured globule embedded in the substance. The colour, which resembled some of the bands in the meteor's strange spectrum, was almost impossible to describe; and it was only by analogy that they called it colour at all. Its texture was glossy, and upon tapping it appeared to promise both brittleness and hollowness. One of the professors gave it a smart blow with a hammer, and it burst with a nervous little pop. Nothing was emitted, and all trace of the thing vanished with the puncturing. It left behind a hollow spherical space about three inches across, and all thought it probable that others would be discovered as the enclosing substance wasted away.

Conjecture was vain; so after a futile attempt to find additional globules by drilling, the seekers left again with their new specimen—which proved, however, as baffling in the laboratory as its predecessor. Aside from being almost plastic, having heat, magnetism, and slight luminosity, cooling slightly in powerful acids, possessing an unknown spectrum, wasting away in air, and attacking silicon compounds with mutual destruction as a result, it presented no identifying features whatsoever; and at the end of the tests the college scientists were forced to own that they could not place it. It was nothing of this earth, but a piece of the great outside; and as such dowered with outside properties and obedient to outside laws.

That night there was a thunderstorm, and when the professors went out to Nahum's the next day they met with a bitter disappointment. The stone, magnetic as it had been, must have had some peculiar electrical property; for it had "drawn the lightning," as Nahum said, with a singular persistence. Six times within an hour the farmer saw the lightning strike the furrow in the front yard, and when the storm was over nothing remained but a ragged pit by the ancient well-sweep, half-choked with a caved-in earth. Digging had borne no fruit, and the scientists verified the fact of the utter vanishment. The failure was total; so that nothing was left to do but go back to the laboratory and test again the disappearing fragment left carefully cased in lead. That fragment lasted a week, at the end of which nothing of value had been learned of it. When it had gone, no residue was left behind, and in time the professors felt scarcely sure they had indeed seen with waking eyes that cryptic vestige of the fathomless gulfs outside; that lone, weird message from other universes and other realms of matter, force, and entity.

As was natural, the Arkham papers made much of the incident with its collegiate sponsoring, and sent reporters to talk with Nahum Gardner and his family. At least one Boston daily also sent a scribe, and Nahum quickly became a kind of local celebrity. He was a lean, genial person of about fifty, living with his wife and three sons on the pleasant farmstead in the valley. He and Ammi exchanged visits frequently, as did their wives; and Ammi had nothing but praise for him after all these years. He seemed slightly proud of the notice his place had attracted, and talked often of the meteorite in the succeeding weeks. That July and August were hot; and Nahum worked hard at his haying in the ten-acre pasture across Chapman's Brook; his rattling wain wearing deep ruts in the shadowy lanes between. The labour tired him more than it had in other years, and he felt that age was beginning to tell on him.

Then fell the time of fruit and harvest. The pears and apples slowly ripened, and Nahum vowed that his orchards were prospering as never before. The fruit was growing to phenomenal size and unwonted gloss, and in such abundance that extra barrels were ordered to handle the future crop. But with the ripening came sore disappointment, for of all that gorgeous array of specious lusciousness not one single jot was fit to eat. Into the fine flavour of the pears and apples had crept a stealthy bitterness and sickishness, so that even the smallest bites induced a lasting disgust. It was the same with the melons and tomatoes, and Nahum sadly saw that his entire crop was lost. Quick to connect events, he declared that the meteorite had poisoned the soil, and thanked Heaven that most of the other crops were in the upland lot along the road.

Winter came early, and was very cold. Ammi saw Nahum less often than usual, and observed that he had begun to look worried. The rest of his family too, seemed to have grown taciturn; and were far from steady in their church-going or their attendance at the various social events of the countryside. For this reserve or melancholy no cause could be found, though all the household confessed now and then to poorer health and a feeling of vague disquiet. Nahum himself gave the most definite statement of anyone when he said he was disturbed about certain footprints in the snow. They were the usual winter prints of red squirrels, white rabbits, and foxes, but the brooding farmer professed to see something not quite right about their nature and arrangement. He was never specific, but appeared to think that they were not as characteristic of the anatomy and habits of squirrels and rabbits and foxes as they ought to be. Ammi listened without interest to this talk until one night when he drove past Nahum's house in his sleigh on the way back from Clark's Corner.

There had been a moon, and a rabbit had run across the road, and the leaps of that rabbit were longer than either Ammi or his horse liked. The latter, indeed, had almost run away when brought up by a firm rein. Thereafter Ammi gave Nahum's tales more respect, and wondered why the Gardner dogs seemed so cowed and quivering every morning. They had, it developed, nearly lost the spirit to bark.

In February the McGregor boys from Meadow Hill were out shooting woodchucks, and not far from the Gardner place bagged a very peculiar specimen. The proportions of its body seemed slightly altered in a queer way impossible to describe, while its face had taken on an expression which no one ever saw in a woodchuck before. The boys were genuinely frightened, and threw the thing away at once, so that only their grotesque tales of it ever reached the people of the countryside. But the shying of horses near Nahum's house had now become an acknowledged thing, and all the basis for a cycle of whispered legend was fast taking form.

People vowed that the snow melted faster around Nahum's than it did anywhere else, and early in March there was an awed discussion in Potter's general store at Clark's Corners. Stephen Rice had driven past Gardner's in the morning, and had noticed the skunk-cabbages coming up through the mud by the woods across the road. Never were things of such size seen before, and they held strange colours that could not be put into any words. Their shapes were monstrous, and the horse had snorted at an odour which struck Stephen as wholly unprecedented. That afternoon several persons drove past to see the abnormal growth, and all agreed that plants of that kind ought never to sprout in a healthy world. The bad fruit of the fall before was freely mentioned, and it went from mouth to mouth that there was poison in Nahum's ground. Of course it was the meteorite; and remembering how strange the men from the college had found that stone to be, several farmers spoke about the matter to them.

One day they paid Nahum a visit; but having no love of wild tales and folklore were very conservative in what they inferred. The plants were certainly odd, but all skunk-cabbages are more or less odd in shape and hue. Perhaps some mineral element from the stone had entered the soil, but it would soon be washed away. And as for the footprints and frightened horses—of course this was mere country talk which such a phenomenon as the aerolite would be certain to start. There was really nothing for serious men to do in cases of wild gossip, for superstitious rustics will say and believe anything. And so all through the strange days the professors stayed away in contempt. Only one of them, when given two phials of dust for analysis in a police job over a year and half later, recalled that the queer colour of that skunk-cabbage had been very like one of the anomalous bands of light shown by the meteor fragment in the college spectroscope, and like the brittle globule found imbedded in the stone from the abyss. The samples in this analysis case gave the same odd bands at first, though later they lost the property.

The trees budded prematurely around Nahum's, and at night they swayed ominously in the wind. Nahum's second son Thaddeus, a lad of fifteen, swore that they swayed also when there was no wind; but even the gossips would not credit this. Certainly, however, restlessness was in the air. The entire Gardner family developed the habit of stealthy listening, though not for any sound which they could consciously name. The listening was, indeed, rather a product of moments when consciousness seemed half to slip away. Unfortunately such moments increased week by week, till it became common speech that "something was wrong with all Nahum's folks." When the early saxifrage came out it had another strange colour; not quite like that of the skunk-cabbage, but plainly related and equally unknown to anyone who saw it. Nahum took some blossoms to Arkham and showed them to the editor of the *Gazette*, but that dignitary did no more than write a humorous article about them, in which the dark fears of rustics were held up to polite ridicule. It was a mistake of Nahum's to tell a stolid city man about the way the great, overgrown mourning-cloak butterflies behaved in connection with these saxifrages.

April brought a kind of madness to the country folk, and began that disuse of the road past Nahum's which led to its ultimate abandonment. It was the vegetation. All the orchard trees blossomed forth in strange colours, and through the stony soil of the yard and adjacent pasturage there sprang up a bizarre growth which only a botanist could connect with the proper flora of the region. No sane wholesome colours were anywhere to be seen except in the green grass and leafage; but everywhere were those hectic and prismatic variants of some diseased, underlying primary tone without a place among the known tints of earth. The "Dutchman's breeches" became a thing of sinister menace, and the bloodroots grew insolent in their chromatic perversion. Ammi and the Gardners thought that most of the colours had a sort of haunting familiarity, and decided that they reminded one of the brittle globule in the meteor. Nahum ploughed and sowed the ten-acre pasture and the upland lot, but did nothing with the land around the house. He knew it would be of no use, and hoped that the summer's strange growths would draw all the poison from the soil. He was prepared for almost anything now, and had grown used to the sense of something near him waiting to be heard. The shunning of his house by neighbors told on him, of course; but it told on his wife more. The boys were better off, being at school each day; but they could not help being frightened by the gossip. Thaddeus, an especially sensitive youth, suffered the most.

In May the insects came, and Nahum's place became a nightmare of buzzing and crawling. Most of the creatures seemed not quite usual in their aspects and motions, and their nocturnal habits contradicted all former experience. The Gardners took to watching at night—watching in all directions at random for something—they could not tell what. It was then that they owned that Thaddeus had been right about the trees. Mrs. Gardner was the next to see it from the window as she watched the swollen boughs of a maple against a moonlit sky. The boughs surely moved, and there was no wind. It must be the sap. Strangeness had come into everything growing now. Yet it was none of Nahum's family at all who made the next discovery. Familiarity had dulled them, and what they could not see was glimpsed by a timid windmill salesman from Bolton who drove by one night in ignorance of the country legends. What he told in Arkham was given a short paragraph in the *Gazette*; and it was there that all the farmers, Nahum included, saw it first. The night had been dark and the buggy-lamps faint, but around a farm in the valley which everyone knew from the account must be Nahum's, the darkness had been less thick. A dim though distinct luminosity seemed to inhere in all the vegetation, grass, leaves, and blossoms alike, while at one moment a detached piece of the phosphorescence appeared to stir furtively in the yard near the barn.

The grass had so far seemed untouched, and the cows were freely pastured in the lot near the house, but toward the end of May the milk began to be bad. Then Nahum had the cows driven to the uplands, after which this trouble ceased. Not long after this the change in grass and leaves became apparent to the eye. All the verdure was going grey, and was developing a highly singular quality of brittleness. Ammi was now the only person who ever visited the place, and his visits were becoming fewer and fewer. When school closed the Gardners were virtually cut off from the world, and sometimes let Ammi do their errands in town. They were failing curiously both physically and mentally, and no one was surprised when the news of Mrs. Gardner's madness stole around.

It happened in June, about the anniversary of the meteor's fall, and the poor woman screamed about things in the air which she could not describe. In her raving there was not a single specific noun, but only verbs and pronouns. Things moved and changed and fluttered, and ears tingled to impulses which were not wholly sounds. Something was taken away—she was being drained of something—

something was fastening itself on her that ought not to be—someone must make it keep off—nothing was ever still in the night—the walls and windows shifted. Nahum did not send her to the county asylum, but let her wander about the house as long as she was harmless to herself and others. Even when her expression changed he did nothing. But when the boys grew afraid of her, and Thaddeus nearly fainted at the way she made faces at him, he decided to keep her locked in the attic. By July she had ceased to speak and crawled on all fours, and before that month was over Nahum got the mad notion that she was slightly luminous in the dark, as he now clearly saw was the case with the nearby vegetation.

It was a little before this that the horses had stampeded. Something had aroused them in the night, and their neighing and kicking in their stalls had been terrible. There seemed virtually nothing to do to calm them, and when Nahum opened the stable door they all bolted out like frightened woodland deer. It took a week to track all four, and when found they were seen to be quite useless and unmanageable. Something had snapped in their brains, and each one had to be shot for its own good. Nahum borrowed a horse from Ammi for his haying, but found it would not approach the barn. It shied, balked, and whinnied, and in the end he could do nothing but drive it into the yard while the men used their own strength to get the heavy wagon near enough the hayloft for convenient pitching. And all the while the vegetation was turning grey and brittle. Even the flowers whose hues had been so strange were greying now, and the fruit was coming out grey and dwarfed and tasteless. The asters and golden-rod bloomed grey and distorted, and the roses and zinneas and hollyhocks in the front yard were such blasphemous-looking things that Nahum's oldest boy Zenas cut them down. The strangely puffed insects died about that time, even the bees that had left their hives and taken to the woods.

By September all the vegetation was fast crumbling to a greyish powder, and Nahum feared that the trees would die before the poison was out of the soil. His wife now had spells of terrific screaming, and he and the boys were in a constant state of nervous tension. They shunned people now, and when school opened the boys did not go. But it was Ammi, on one of his rare visits, who first realised that the well water was no longer good. It had an evil taste that was not exactly fetid nor exactly salty, and Ammi advised his friend to dig another well on higher ground to use till the soil was good again. Nahum, however, ignored the warning, for he had by that time become calloused to strange and unpleasant things. He and the boys continued to use the tainted supply, drinking it as listlessly and mechanically as they ate their meagre and ill-cooked meals and did their thankless and monotonous chores through the aimless days. There was something of stolid resignation about them all, as if they walked half in another world between lines of nameless guards to a certain and familiar doom.

Thaddeus went mad in September after a visit to the well. He had gone with a pail and had come back empty-handed, shrieking and waving his arms, and sometimes lapsing into an inane titter or a whisper about "the moving colours down there." Two in one family was pretty bad, but Nahum was very brave about it. He let the boy run about for a week until he began stumbling and hurting himself, and then he shut him in an attic room across the hall from his mother's. The way they screamed at each other from behind their locked doors was very terrible, especially to little Merwin, who fancied they talked in some terrible language that was not of earth. Merwin was getting frightfully imaginative, and his restlessness was worse after the shutting away of the brother who had been his greatest playmate.

Almost at the same time the mortality among the livestock commenced. Poultry turned greyish and died very quickly, their meat being found dry and noisome upon cutting. Hogs grew inordinately fat, then suddenly began to undergo loathsome changes which no one could explain. Their meat was of course useless, and Nahum was at his wit's end. No rural veterinary would approach his place, and the city veterinary from Arkham was openly baffled. The swine began growing grey and brittle and falling to pieces before they died, and their eyes and muzzles developed singular alterations. It was very inexplicable, for they had never been fed from the tainted vegetation. Then something struck the cows. Certain areas or sometimes the whole body would be uncannily shrivelled or compressed, and atrocious collapses or disintegrations were common. In the last stages— and death was always the result—there would be a greying and turning brittle like that which beset the hogs. There could be no question of poison, for all the cases occurred in a locked and undisturbed barn. No bites of prowling things could have brought the virus, for what live beast of earth can pass through solid obstacles? It must be only natural disease—yet what disease could wreak such results was beyond any mind's guessing. When the harvest came there was not an animal surviving on the place, for the stock and poultry were dead and the dogs had run away. These dogs, three in number, had all vanished one night and were never heard of again. The five cats had left some time before, but their going was scarcely noticed since there now seemed to be no mice, and only Mrs. Gardner had made pets of the graceful felines.

On the nineteenth of October Nahum staggered into Ammi's house with hideous news. The death had come to poor Thaddeus in his attic room, and it had come in a way which could not be told. Nahum had dug a grave in the railed family plot behind the farm, and had put therein what he found. There could have been nothing from outside, for the small barred window and locked door were intact; but it was much as it had been in the barn. Ammi and his wife consoled the stricken man as best they could, but shuddered as they did so. Stark terror seemed to cling round the Gardners and all they touched, and the very presence of one in the house was a breath from regions unnamed and unnamable. Ammi accompanied Nahum home with the greatest reluctance, and did what he might to calm the hysterical sobbing of little Merwin. Zenas needed no calming. He had come of late to do nothing but stare into space and obey what his father told him; and Ammi thought that his fate was very merciful. Now and then Merwin's screams were answered faintly from the attic, and in response to an inquiring look Nahum said that his wife was getting very feeble. When night approached, Ammi managed to get away; for not even friendship could make him stay in that spot when the faint glow of the vegetation began and the trees may or may not have swayed without wind. It was really lucky for Ammi that he was not more imaginative. Even as things were, his mind was bent ever so slightly; but had he been able to connect and reflect upon all the portents around him he must inevitably have turned a total maniac. In the twilight he hastened home, the screams of the mad woman and the nervous child ringing horribly in his ears.

Three days later Nahum burst into Ammi's kitchen in the early morning, and in the absence of his host stammered out a desperate tale once more, while Mrs. Pierce listened in a clutching fright. It was little Merwin this time. He was gone. He had gone out late at night with a lantern and pail for water, and had never come back. He'd been going to pieces for days, and hardly knew what he was about. Screamed at everything. There had been a frantic shriek from the yard then, but before the father could get to the door the boy was gone. There was no glow from the lantern he had taken, and of the child himself no trace. At the time Nahum thought the lantern and pail were gone too; but when dawn came, and the man had plodded back from his all-night search of the woods and fields, he had found some very curious things near the well. There was a crushed and apparently somewhat melted mass of iron which had certainly been the lantern; while a bent handle and twisted iron hoops beside it, both half-fused, seemed to hint at the remnants of the pail. That was all. Nahum was past imagining, Mrs. Pierce was blank, and Ammi, when he had reached home and heard the tale, could give no guess. Merwin was gone, and there would be no use in telling the people around, who shunned all Gardners now. No use, either, in telling the city people at Arkham who laughed at everything. Thad was gone, and now Merwin was gone. Something was creeping and creeping and waiting to be seen and heard. Nahum would go soon, and he wanted Ammi to look after his wife and Zenas if they survived him. It must all be a judgment of some sort; though he could not fancy what for, since he had always walked uprightly in the Lord's ways so far as he knew.

For over two weeks Ammi saw nothing of Nahum; and then, worried about what might have happened, he overcame his fears and paid the Gardner place a visit. There was no smoke from the great chimney, and for a moment the visitor was apprehensive of the worst. The aspect of the whole farm was shocking—greyish withered grass and leaves on the ground, vines falling in brittle wreckage from archaic walls and gables, and great bare trees clawing up at the grey November sky with a studied malevolence which Ammi could not but feel had come from some subtle change in the tilt of the branches. But Nahum was alive, after all. He was weak, and lying on a couch in the low-ceiled kitchen, but perfectly conscious and able to give simple orders to Zenas. The room was deadly cold; and as Ammi visibly shivered, the host shouted huskily to Zenas for more wood. Wood, indeed, was sorely needed; since the cavernous fireplace was unlit and empty, with a cloud of soot blowing about in the chill wind that came down the chimney. Presently Nahum asked him if the extra wood had made him any more comfortable, and then Ammi saw what had happened. The stoutest cord had broken at last, and the hapless farmer's mind was proof against more sorrow.

Questioning tactfully, Ammi could get no clear data at all about the missing Zenas. "In the well—he lives in the well—" was all that the clouded father would say. Then there flashed across the visitor's mind a sudden thought of the mad wife, and he changed his line of inquiry. "Nabby? Why, here she is!" was the surprised response of poor Nahum, and Ammi soon saw that he must search for himself. Leaving the harmless babbler on the couch, he took the keys from their nail beside the door and climbed the creaking stairs to the attic. It was very close and noisome up there, and no sound could be heard from any direction. Of the four doors in sight, only one was locked, and on this he tried various keys of the ring he had taken. The third key proved the right one, and after some fumbling Ammi threw open the low white door.

It was quite dark inside, for the window was small and half-obscured by the crude wooden bars; and Ammi could see nothing at all on the wide-planked floor. The stench was beyond enduring, and before proceeding further he had to retreat to another room and return with his lungs filled with breathable air. When he did enter he saw something dark in the corner, and upon seeing it more clearly he screamed outright. While he screamed he thought a momentary cloud eclipsed the window, and a second later he felt himself brushed as if by some hateful current of vapour. Strange colours danced before his eyes; and had not a present horror numbed him he would have thought of the globule in the meteor that the geologist's hammer had shattered, and of the morbid vegetation that had sprouted in the spring. As it was he thought only of the blasphemous monstrosity which confronted him, and which all too clearly had shared the nameless fate of young Thaddeus and the livestock. But the terrible thing about the horror was that it very slowly and perceptibly moved as it continued to crumble.

Ammi would give me no added particulars of this scene, but the shape in the corner does not reappear in his tale as a moving object. There are things which cannot be mentioned, and what is done in common humanity is sometimes cruelly judged by the law. I gathered that no moving thing was left in that attic room, and that to leave anything capable of motion there would have been a deed so monstrous as to damn any accountable being to eternal torment. Anyone but a stolid farmer would have fainted or gone mad, but Ammi walked conscious through that low doorway and locked the accursed secret behind him. There would be Nahum to deal with now; he must be fed and tended, and removed to some place where he could be cared for.

Commencing his descent of the dark stairs, Ammi heard a thud below him. He even thought a scream had been suddenly choked off, and recalled nervously the clammy vapour which had brushed by him in that frightful room above. What presence had his cry and entry started up? Halted by some vague fear, he heard still further sounds below. Indubitably there was a sort of heavy dragging, and a most detestably sticky noise as of some fiendish and unclean species of suction. With an associative sense goaded to feverish heights, he thought unaccountably of what he had seen upstairs. Good God! What eldritch dream-world was this into which he had blundered? He dared move neither backward nor forward, but stood there trembling at the black curve of the boxed-in staircase. Every trifle of the scene burned itself into his brain. The sounds, the sense of dread expectancy, the darkness, the steepness of the narrow steps—and merciful Heaven!—the faint but unmistakable luminosity of all the woodwork in sight; steps, sides, exposed laths, and beams alike.

Then there burst forth a frantic whinny from Ammi's horse outside, followed at once by a clatter which told of a frenzied runaway. In another moment horse and buggy had gone beyond earshot, leaving the frightened man on the dark stairs to guess what had sent them. But that was not all. There had been another sound out there. A sort of liquid splash—water—it must have been the well. He had left Hero untied near it, and a buggywheel must have brushed the coping a knocked in a stone. And still the pale phosphorescence glowed in that detestably ancient woodwork. God! how old the house was! Most of it built before 1670, and the gambrel roof no later than 1730.

A feeble scratching on the floor downstairs now sounded distinctly, and Ammi's grip tightened on a heavy stick he had picked up in the attic for some purpose. Slowly nerving himself, he finished his descent and walked boldly toward the kitchen. But he did not complete the walk, because what he sought was no longer there. It had come to meet him, and it was still alive after a fashion. Whether it had crawled or whether it had been dragged by any external forces, Ammi could not say; but the death had been at it. Everything had happened in the last half-hour, but collapse, greying, and disintegration were already far advanced. There was a horrible brittleness, and dry fragments were scaling off. Ammi could not touch it, but looked horrifiedly into the distorted parody that had been a face. "What was it, Nahum—what was it?" He whispered, and the cleft, bulging lips were just able to crackle out a final answer.

"Nothin' . . . nothin' . . . the colour . . . it burns . . . cold an' wet, but it burns . . . it lived in the well . . . I seen it . . . a kind of smoke . . . jest like the flowers last spring . . . the well shone at night . . . Thad an' Merwin an' Zenas . . . everything alive . . . suckin' the life out of everything . . . in that stone . . . it must a' come in that stone . . . pizened the whole place . . . dun't know what it wants . . . that round thing them men from the college dug outen the stone . . . they smashed it . . . it was the same colour . . . jest the same, like the flowers an' plants . . . must a' ben more of 'em . . . seeds . . . seeds . . . they growed . . . I seen it the fust time this week . . . must a' got strong on Zenas . . . he was a big boy, full o' life . . . it beats down your mind an' then gets ye . . . burns ye up . . . in the well water . . . you was right about that . . . evil water . . . Zenas never come back from the well . . . can't git away . . . draws ye . . . ye know summ'at's comin' but tain't no use . . . I seen it time an' agin senct Zenas was took . . . whar's Nabby, Ammi? . . . my head's no good . . . dun't know how long sense I fed her . . . it'll git her ef we ain't keerful . . . jest a colour . . . her face is gittin' to hev that colour sometimes towards night . . . an' it burns an' sucks . . . it come from some place whar things ain't as

they is here . . . one o' them professors said so . . . he was right . . .
look out, Ammi, it'll do suthin' more . . . sucks the life out . . ."

But that was all. That which spoke could speak no more because it
had completely caved in. Ammi laid a red checked tablecloth over
what was left and reeled out the back door into the fields. He climbed
the slope to the ten-acre pasture and stumbled home by the north
road and the woods. He could not pass that well from which his
horses had run away. He had looked at it through the window, and
had seen that no stone was missing from the rim. Then the lurching
buggy had not dislodged anything after all—the splash had been
something else—something which went into the well after it had
done with poor Nahum. . . .

When Ammi reached his house the horses and buggy had arrived
before him and thrown his wife into fits of anxiety. Reassuring her
without explanations, he set out at once for Arkham and notified the
authorities that the Gardner family was no more. He indulged in no
details, but merely told of the deaths of Nahum and Nabby, that of
Thaddeus being already known, and mentioned that the cause
seemed to be the same strange ailment which had killed the livestock. He also stated that Merwin and Zenas had disappeared. There
was considerable questioning at the police station, and in the end
Ammi was compelled to take three officers to the Gardner farm, together with the coroner, the medical examiner, and the veterinary
who had treated the diseased animals. He went much against his
will, for the afternoon was advancing and he feared the fall of night
over that accursed place, but it was some comfort to have so many
people with him.

The six men drove out in a democrat-wagon, following Ammi's
buggy, and arrived at the pest-ridden farmhouse about four o'clock.
Used as the officers were to gruesome experiences, not one remained
unmoved at what was found in the attic and under the red checked
tablecloth on the floor below. The whole aspect of the farm with its
grey desolation was terrible enough, but those two crumbling objects
were beyond all bounds. No one could look long at them, and even
the medical examiner admitted that there was very little to examine.
Specimens could be analysed, of course, so he busied himself in ob-
taining them—and here it develops that a very puzzling aftermath occurred at the college laboratory where the two phials of dust were
finally taken. Under the spectroscope both samples gave off an unknown spectrum, in which many of the baffling bands were precisely
like those which the strange meteor had yielded in the previous year.
The property of emitting this spectrum vanished in a month, the dust
thereafter consisting mainly of alkaline phosphates and carbonates.

Ammi would not have told the men about the well if he had

thought they meant to do anything then and there. It was getting toward sunset, and he was anxious to be away. But he could not help glancing nervously at the stony curb by the great sweep, and when a detective questioned him he admitted that Nahum had feared something down there—so much so that he had never even thought of searching it for Merwin or Zenas. After that nothing would do but that they empty and explore the well immediately, so Ammi had to wait trembling while pail after pail of rank water was hauled up and splashed on the soaking ground outside. The men sniffed in disgust at the fluid, and toward the last held their noses against the foetor they were uncovering. It was not so long a job as they had feared it would be, since the water was phenomenally low. There is no need to speak too exactly of what they found. Merwin and Zenas were both there, in part, though the vestiges were mainly skeletal. There were also a small deer and a large dog in about the same state, and a number of bones of small animals. The ooze and slime at the bottom seemed inexplicably porous and bubbling, and a man who descended on hand-holds with a long pole found that he could sink the wooden shaft to any depth in the mud of the floor without meeting any solid obstruction.

Twilight had now fallen, and lanterns were brought from the house. Then, when it was seen that nothing further could be gained from the well, everyone went indoors and conferred in the ancient sitting-room while the intermittent light of a spectral half-moon played wanly on the grey desolation outside. The men were frankly nonplussed by the entire case, and could find no convincing common element to link the strange vegetable conditions, the unknown disease of live-stock and humans, and the unaccountable deaths of Merwin and Zenas in the tainted well. They had heard the common country talk, it is true; but could not believe that anything contrary to natural law had occurred. No doubt the meteor had poisoned the soil, but the illness of persons and animals who had eaten nothing grown in that soil was another matter. Was it the well water? Very possibly. It might be a good idea to analyze it. But what peculiar madness could have made both boys jump into the well? Their deeds were so similar—and the fragments showed that they had both suffered from the grey brittle death. Why was everything so grey and brittle?

It was the coroner, seated near a window overlooking the yard, who first noticed the glow about the well. Night had fully set in, and all the abhorrent grounds seemed faintly luminous with more than the fitful moonbeams; but this new glow was something definite and distinct, and appeared to shoot up from the black pit like a softened ray from a searchlight, giving dull reflections in the little ground pools where the water had been emptied. It had a very queer colour, and as all the men clustered round the window Ammi gave a violent start. For this strange beam of ghastly miasma was to him of no unfamiliar hue. He had seen that colour before, and feared to think what it might mean. He had seen it in the nasty brittle globule in that aerolite two summers ago, had seen it in the crazy vegetation of the springtime, and had thought he had seen it for an instant that very morning against the small barred window of that terrible attic room where nameless things had happened. It had flashed there a second, and a clammy and hateful current of vapour had brushed past him— and then poor Nahum had been taken by something of that colour. He had said so at the last—said it was like the globule and the plants. After that had come the runaway in the yard and the splash in the well—and now that well was belching forth to the night a pale insidious beam of the same demoniac tint.

It does credit to the alertness of Ammi's mind that he puzzled even at that tense moment over a point which was essentially scientific. He could not but wonder at his gleaning of the same impression from a vapour glimpsed in the daytime, against a window opening on the morning sky, and from a nocturnal exhalation seen as a phosphorescent mist against the black and blasted landscape. It wasn't right— it was against Nature—and he thought of those terrible last words of his stricken friend, "It come from some place whar things ain't as they is here . . . one o' them professors said so. . . ."

All three horses outside, tied to a pair of shrivelled saplings by the road, were now neighing and pawing frantically. The wagon driver started for the door to do something, but Ammi laid a shaky hand on his shoulder. "Dun't go out thar," he whispered. "They's more to this nor what we know. Nahum said somethin' lived in the well that sucks your life out. He said it must be some'at growed from a round ball like one we all seen in the meteor stone that fell a year ago June. Sucks an' burns, he said, an' is jest a cloud of colour like that light out thar now, that ye can hardly see an' can't tell what it is. Nahum thought it feeds on everything livin' an' gits stronger all the time. He said he seen it this last week. It must be somethin' from away off in the sky like the men from the college last year says the meteor stone was. The way it's made an' the way it works ain't like no way o' God's world. It's some'at from beyond."

So the men paused indecisively as the light from the well grew stronger and the hitched horses pawed and whinnied in increasing frenzy. It was truly an awful moment; with terror in that ancient and accursed house itself, four monstrous sets of fragments—two from the house and two from the well—in the woodshed behind, and that shaft of unknown and unholy iridescence from the slimy depths in front. Ammi had restrained the driver on impulse, forgetting how uninjured he himself was after the clammy brushing of that coloured vapour in the attic room, but perhaps it is just as well that he acted as he did. No one will ever know what was abroad that night; and though the blasphemy from beyond had not so far hurt any human of unweakened mind, there is no telling what it might not have done at that last moment, and with its seemingly increased strength and the special signs of purpose it was soon to display beneath the half-clouded moonlit sky.

All at once one of the detectives at the window gave a short, sharp gasp. The others looked at him, and then quickly followed his own gaze upward to the point at which its idle straying had been suddenly arrested. There was no need for words. What had been disputed in country gossip was disputable no longer, and it is because of the thing which every man of that party agreed in whispering later on, that the strange days are never talked about in Arkham. It is necessary to premise that there was no wind at that hour of the evening. One did arise not long afterward, but there was absolutely none then. Even the dry tips of the lingering hedge-mustard, grey and blighted, and the fringe on the roof of the standing democrat-wagon were unstirred. And yet amid that tense godless calm the high bare boughs of all the trees in the yard were moving. They were twitching morbidly and spasmodically, clawing in convulsive and epileptic madness at the moonlit clouds; scratching impotently in the noxious air as if jerked by some allied and bodiless line of linkage with subterrene horrors writhing and struggling below the black roots.

Not a man breathed for several seconds. Then a cloud of darker depth passed over the moon, and the silhouette of clutching branches faded out momentarily. At this there was a general cry; muffled with awe, but husky and almost identical from every throat. For the terror had not faded with the silhouette, and in a fearsome instant of deeper darkness the watchers saw wriggling at that tree top height a thousand tiny points of faint and unhallowed radiance, tipping each bough like the fire of St. Elmo or the flames that come down on the apostles' heads at Pentecost. It was a monstrous constellation of unnatural light, like a glutted swarm of corpse-fed fireflies dancing hellish sarabands over an accursed marsh, and its colour was that same nameless intrusion which Ammi had come to recognize and dread. All the while the shaft of phosphorescence from the well was getting brighter and brighter, bringing to the minds of the huddled men, a sense of doom and abnormality which far outraced any image their conscious minds could form. It was no longer *shining* out; it was *pouring* out; and as the shapeless stream of unplaceable colour left the well it seemed to flow directly into the sky.

The veterinary shivered, and walked to the front door to drop the heavy extra bar across it. Ammi shook no less, and had to tug and point for lack of controllable voice when he wished to draw notice to the growing luminosity of the trees. The neighing and stamping of the horses had become utterly frightful, but not a soul of that group in the old house would have ventured forth for any earthly reward. With the moments the shining of the trees increased, while their restless branches seemed to strain more and more toward verticality. The wood of the well-sweep was shining now, and presently a policeman dumbly pointed to some wooden sheds and bee-hives near the stone wall on the west. They were commencing to shine, too, though the tethered vehicles of the visitors seemed so far unaffected. Then there was a wild commotion and clopping in the road, and as Ammi quenched the lamp for better seeing they realized that the span of frantic greys had broken their sapling and run off with the democrat-wagon.

The shock served to loosen several tongues, and embarrassed whispers were exchanged. "It spreads on everything organic that's been around here," muttered the medical examiner. No one replied, but the man who had been in the well gave a hint that his long pole must have stirred up something intangible. "It was awful," he added. "There was no bottom at all. Just ooze and bubbles and the feeling of something lurking under there." Ammi's horse still pawed and screamed deafeningly in the road outside, and nearly drowned its owner's faint quaver as he mumbled his formless reflections. "It come from that stone—it growed down thar—it got everything livin'—it fed itself on 'em, mind and body—Thad an' Merwin, Zenas an' Nabby—Nahum was the last—they all drunk the water—it got strong on 'em—it come from beyond, whar things ain't like they be here—now it's goin' home—"

At this point, as the column of unknown colour flared suddenly stronger and began to weave itself into fantastic suggestions of shape which each spectator described differently, there came from poor tethered Hero such a sound as no man before or since ever heard from a horse. Every person in that low-pitched sitting room stopped his ears, and Ammi turned away from the window in horror and nausea. Words could not convey it—when Ammi looked out again the hapless beast lay huddled inert on the moonlit ground between the splintered shafts of the buggy. That was the last of Hero till they buried him next day. But the present was no time to mourn, for almost at this instant a detective silently called attention to something terrible in the very room with them. In the absence of the lamplight it was clear that a faint phosphorescence had begun to pervade the entire apartment. It glowed on the broad-planked floor and the fragment of rag carpet, and shimmered over the sashes of the small-paned windows. It ran up and down the exposed corner-posts, coruscated about the shelf and mantel, and infected the very doors and furniture. Each minute saw it strengthen, and at last it was very plain that healthy living things must leave that house.

Ammi showed them the back door and the path up through the fields to the ten-acre pasture. They walked and stumbled as in a dream, and did not dare look back till they were far away on the high ground. They were glad of the path, for they could not have gone the front way, by that well. It was bad enough passing the glowing barn and sheds, and those shining orchard trees with their gnarled, fiendish contours; but thank Heaven the branches did their worst twisting high up. The moon went under some very black clouds as they crossed the rustic bridge over Chapman's Brook, and it was blind groping from there to the open meadows.

When they looked back toward the valley and the distant Gardner place at the bottom they saw a fearsome sight. All the farm was shining with the hideous unknown blend of colour; trees, buildings, and even such grass and herbage as had not been wholly changed to lethal grey brittleness. The boughs were all straining skyward, tipped with tongues of foul flame, and lambent tricklings of the same monstrous fire were creeping about the ridgepoles of the house, barn and sheds. It was a scene from a vision of Fuseli, and over all the rest reigned that riot of luminous amorphousness, that alien and undimensioned rainbow of cryptic poison from the well—seething, feeling, lapping, reaching, scintillating, straining, and malignly bubbling in its cosmic and unrecognizable chromaticism.

Then without warning the hideous thing shot vertically up toward the sky like a rocket or meteor, leaving behind no trail and disappearing through a round and curiously regular hole in the clouds before any man could gasp or cry out. No watcher can ever forget that sight, and Ammi stared blankly at the stars of Cygnus, Deneb twinkling above the others, where the unknown colour had melted into the Milky Way. But his gaze was the next moment called swiftly to earth by the crackling in the valley. It was just that. Only a wooden ripping and crackling, and not an explosion, as so many others of the party vowed. Yet the outcome was the same, for in one feverish kaleidoscopic instant there burst up from that doomed and accursed farm a gleamingly eruptive cataclysm of unnatural sparks and substance;

blurring the glance of the few who saw it, and sending forth to the zenith a bombarding cloudburst of such coloured and fantastic fragments as our universe must needs disown. Through quickly re-closing vapours they followed the great morbidity that had vanished, and in another second they had vanished too. Behind and below was only a darkness to which the men dared not return, and all about was a mounting wind which seemed to sweep down in black, frore gusts from interstellar space. It shrieked and howled, and lashed the fields and distorted woods in a mad cosmic frenzy, till soon the trembling party realized it would be no use waiting for the moon to show what was left down there at Nahum's.

Too awed even to hint theories, the seven shaking men trudged back toward Arkham by the north road. Ammi was worse than his fellows, and begged them to see him inside his own kitchen, instead of keeping straight on to town. He did not wish to cross the blighted, wind-whipped woods alone to his home on the main road. For he had had an added shock that the others were spared, and was crushed for-ever with a brooding fear he dared not even mention for many years to come. As the rest of the watchers on that tempestuous hill had stolidly set their faces toward the road, Ammi had looked back an in-stant at the shadowed valley of desolation so lately sheltering his ill-starred friend. And from that stricken, far-away spot he had seen something feebly rise, only to sink down again upon the place from which the great shapeless horror had shot into the sky. It was just a colour—but not any colour of our earth or heavens. And because Ammi recognized that colour, and knew that this last faint remnant must still lurk down there in the well, he has never been quite right since.

Ammi would never go near the place again. It is forty-four years now since the horror happened, but he has never been there, and will be glad when the new reservoir blots it out. I shall be glad, too, for I do not like the way the sunlight changed colour around the mouth of that abandoned well I passed. I hope the water will always be very deep—but even so, I shall never drink it. I do not think I shall visit the Arkham country herafter. Three of the men who had been with Ammi returned the next morning to see the ruins by daylight, but there were not any real ruins. Only the bricks of the chimney, the stones of the cellar, some mineral and metallic litter here and there, and the rim of that nefandous well. Save for Ammi's dead horse, which they towed away and buried, and the buggy which they shortly returned to him, everything that had ever been living had gone. Five eldritch acres of dusty grey desert remained, nor has anything ever grown there since. To this day it sprawls open to the sky like a great spot eaten by acid in the woods and fields, and the few who have ever dared glimpse it in spite of the rural tales have named it "the blasted heath."

The rural tales are queer. They might be even queerer if city men and college chemists could be interested enough to analyze the water from that disused well, or the grey dust that no wind seems to disperse. Botanists, too, ought to study the stunted flora on the borders of that spot, for they might shed light on the country notion that the blight is spreading—little by little, perhaps an inch a year. People say the colour of the neighboring herbage is not quite right in the spring, and that wild things leave queer prints in the light winter snow. Snow never seems quite so heavy on the blasted heath as it is elsewhere. Horses—the few that are left in this motor age—grow skittish in the silent valley; and hunters cannot depend on their dogs too near the splotch of greyish dust.

They say the mental influences are very bad, too; numbers went queer in the years after Nahum's taking, and always they lacked the power to get away. Then the stronger-minded folk all left the region, and only the foreigners tried to live in the crumbling old homesteads. They could not stay, though; and one sometimes wonders what insight beyond ours their wild, weird stories of whispered magic have given them. Their dreams at night, they protest, are very horrible in that grotesque country; and surely the very look of the dark realm is enough to stir a morbid fancy. No traveler has ever escaped a sense of strangeness in those deep ravines, and artists shiver as they paint thick woods whose mystery is as much of the spirits as of the eye. I myself am curious about the sensation I derived from my one lone walk before Ammi told me his tale. When twilight came I had vaguely wished some clouds would gather, for an odd timidity about the deep skyey voids above had crept into my soul.

Do not ask me for my opinion. I do not know—that is all. There was no one but Ammi to question; for Arkham people will not talk about the strange days, and all three professors who saw the aerolite and its coloured globule are dead. There were other globules—depend upon that. One must have fed itself and escaped, and probably there was another which was too late. No doubt it is still down the well—I know there was something wrong with the sunlight I saw above the miasmal brink. The rustics say the blight creeps an inch a year, so perhaps there is a kind of growth or nourishment even now. But whatever demon hatchling is there, it must be tethered to something or else it would quickly spread. Is it fastened to the roots of those trees that claw the air? One of the current Arkham tales is about fat oaks that shine and move as they ought not to do at night.

What it is, only God knows. In terms of matter I suppose the thing Ammi described would be called a gas, but this gas obeyed the laws that are not of our cosmos. This was no fruit of such worlds and suns as shine on the telescopes and photographic plates of our observatories. This was no breath from the skies whose motions and dimensions our astronomers measure or deem too vast to measure. It was just a colour out of space—a frightful messenger from unformed realms of infinity beyond all Nature as we know it; from realms whose mere existence stuns the brain and numbs us with the black extra-cosmic gulfs it throws open before our frenzied eyes.

I doubt very much if Ammi consciously lied to me, and I do not think his tale was all a freak of madness as the townsfolk had forewarned. Something terrible came to the hills and valleys on that meteor, and something terrible—though I know not in what proportion—still remains. I shall be glad to see the water come. Meanwhile I hope nothing will happen to Ammi. He saw so much of the thing—and its influence was so insidious. Why has he never been able to move away? How clearly he recalled those dying words of Nahum's—"can't git away—draws ye—ye know summ'at's comin' but tain't no use—" Ammi is such a good old man—when the reservoir gang gets to work I must write the chief engineer to keep a sharp watch on him. I would hate to think of him as the grey, twisted, brittle monstrosity which persists more and more in troubling my sleep.

The Haunter Of The Dark

(DEDICATED TO ROBERT BLOCH)

> *I have seen the dark universe yawning*
> *Where the dark planets roll without aim—*
> *Where they roll in their horror unheeded,*
> *Without knowledge or luster or name.*
> —NEMESIS.

Cautious investigators will hesitate to challenge the common belief that Robert Blake was killed by lightning, or by some profound nervous shock derived from an electrical discharge. It is true that the window he faced was unbroken, but nature has shown herself capable of many freakish performances. The expression on his face may easily have arisen from some obscure muscular source unrelated to anything he saw, while the entries in his diary are clearly the result of a fantastic imagination aroused by certain local superstitions and by certain old matters he had uncovered. As for the anomalous conditions at the deserted church of Federal Hill—the shrewd analyst is not slow in attributing them to some charlatanry, conscious or unconscious, with at least some of which Blake was secretly connected.

For after all, the victim was a writer and painter wholly devoted to the field of myth, dream, terror, and superstition, and avid in his quest for scenes and effects of a bizarre, spectral sort. His earlier stay in the city—a visit to a strange old man as deeply given to occult and forbidden lore as he—had ended amidst death and flame, and it must have been some morbid instinct which drew him back from his home in Milwaukee. He may have known of the old stories despite his statements to the contrary in the diary, and his death may have nipped in the bud some stupendous hoax destined to have a literary reflection.

Among those, however, who have examined and correlated all this evidence, there remain several who cling to less rational and common-place theories. They are inclined to take much of Blake's diary at its face value, and point significantly to certain facts such as the un-doubted genuineness of the old church record, the verified existence of the disliked and unorthodox Starry Wisdom sect prior to 1877, the recorded disappearance of an inquisitive reporter named Edwin M. Lillibridge in 1893, and—above all—the look of monstrous, transfig-uring fear on the face of the young writer when he died. It was one of these believers who, moved to fanatical extremes, threw into the bay the curiously angled stone and its strangely adorned metal box found in the old church steeple—the black windowless steeple, and not the tower where Blake's diary said those things originally were. Though widely censured both officially and unofficially, this man—a repu-table physician with a taste for odd folklore—averred that he had rid the earth of something too dangerous to rest upon it.

Between these two schools of opinion the reader must judge for himself. The papers have given the tangible details from a skeptical angle, leaving for others the drawing of the picture as Robert Blake saw it—or thought he saw it—or pretended to see it. Now, studying the diary closely, dispassionately, and at leisure, let us summarize the dark chain of events from the expressed point of view of their chief actor.

Young Blake returned to Providence in the winter of 1834–5, tak-ing the upper floor of a venerable dwelling in a grassy court off Col-lege Street—on the crest of the great eastward hill near the Brown University campus and behind the marble John Hay Library. It was a cozy and fascinating place, in a little garden oasis of village-like an-tiquity where huge, friendly cats sunned themselves atop a conve-nient shed. The square Georgian house had a monitor roof, classic doorway with fan carving, small-paned windows, and all the other earmarks of early nineteenth century workmanship. Inside were six-paneled doors, wide floorboards, a curving colonial staircase, white Aram-period mantels, and a rear set of rooms three steps below the general level.

Blake's study, a large southwest chamber, overlooked the front gar-den on one side, while its west windows—before one of which he had his desk—faced off from the brow of the hill and commanded a splen-did view of the lower town's outspread roofs and of the mystical sun-sets that flamed behind them. On the far horizon were the open countryside's purple slopes. Against these, some two miles away, rose the spectral hump of Federal Hill, bristling with huddled roofs and steeples whose remote outlines wavered mysteriously, taking fantastic forms as the smoke of the city swirled up and enmeshed them. Blake had a curious sense that he was looking upon some unknown, ethereal world which might or might not vanish in dream if ever he tried to seek it out and enter it in person.

Having sent home for most of his books, Blake bought some antique furniture suitable to his quarters and settled down to write and paint—living alone, and attending to the simple housework himself. His studio was in a north attic room, where the panes of the monitor roof furnished admirable lighting. During that first winter he produced five of his best-known short stories—*The Burrower Beneath, The Stairs in the Crypt, Shaggai, In the Vale of Pnath,* and *The Feaster from the Stars*—and painted seven canvases; studies of nameless, unhuman monsters, and profoundly alien, non-terrestrial landscapes.

At sunset he would often sit at his desk and gaze dreamily off at the outspread west—the dark towers of Memorial Hall just below, the Georgian courthouse belfry, the lofty pinnacles of the downtown section, and that shimmering, spire-crowned mound in the distance whose unknown streets and labyrinthine gables so potently provoked his fancy. From his few local acquaintances he learned that the far-off slope was a vast Indian quarter, though most of the houses were remnants of older Yankee and Irish days. Now and then he would train his field-glasses on that spectral, unreachable world beyond the curling smoke; picking out individual roofs and chimneys and steeples, and speculating upon the bizarre and curious mysteries they might house. Even with optical aid Federal Hill seemed somehow alien, half fabulous, and linked to the unreal, intangible marvels of Blake's own tales and pictures. The feeling would persist long after the hill had faded into the violet, lamp-starred twilight, and the court-house floodlights and the red Industrial Trust beacon had blazed up to make the night grotesque.

Of all the distant objects on Federal Hill, a certain huge, dark church most fascinated Blake. It stood out with especial distinctness at certain hours of the day, and at sunset the great tower and tapering steeple loomed blackly against the flaming sky. It seemed to rest on especially high ground; for the grimy façade, and the obliquely seen north side with sloping roof and the tops of great pointed windows, rose boldly above the tangle of surrounding ridgepoles and chimney-pots. Peculiarly grim and austere, it appeared to be built of stone, stained and weathered with the smoke and storms of a century and more. The style, so far as the glass could show, was that earliest experimental form of Gothic revival which preceded the stately Upjohn period and held over some of the outlines and proportions of the Georgian age. Perhaps it was reared around 1810 or 1815.

As months passed, Blake watched the far-off, forbidding structure with an oddly mounting interest. Since the vast windows were never lighted, he knew that it must be vacant. The longer he watched, the more his imagination worked, till at length he began to fancy curious things. He believed that a vague, singular aura of desolation hovered over the place, so that even the pigeons and swallows shunned its smoky eaves. Around other towers and belfries his glass would reveal great flocks of birds, but here they never rested. At least, that is what he thought and set down in his diary. He pointed the place out to several friends, but none of them had even been on Federal Hill or possessed the faintest notion of what the church was or had been.

In the spring a deep restlessness gripped Blake. He had begun his long-planned novel—based on a supposed survival of the witch-cult in Maine—but was strangely unable to make progress with it. More and more he would sit at his westward window and gaze at the distant hill and the black, frowning steeple shunned by the birds. When the delicate leaves came out on the garden boughs the world was filled with a new beauty, but Blake's restlessness was merely increased. It was then that he first thought of crossing the city and climbing bodily up that fabulous slope into the smoke-wreathed world of dream.

Late in April, just before the eon-shadowed Walpurgis time, Blake made his first trip into the unknown. Plodding through the endless downtown streets and the bleak, decayed squares beyond, he came finally upon the ascending avenue of century-worn steps, sagging Doric porches, and blear-paned cupolas which he felt must lead up to the long-known, unreachable world beyond the mists. There were dingy blue-and-white street signs which meant nothing to him, and presently he noted the strange, dark faces of the drifting crowds, and the foreign signs over curious shops in brown, decade-weathered buildings. Nowhere could he find any of the objects he had seen from afar; so that once more he half fancied that the Federal Hill of that distant view was a dream-world never to be trod by living human feet.

Now and then a battered church façade or crumbling spire came in sight, but never the blackened pile that he sought. When he asked a shopkeeper about a great stone church the man smiled and shook his head, though he spoke English freely. As Blake climbed higher, the region seemed stranger and stranger, with bewildering mazes of brooding brown alleys leading eternally off to the south. He crossed two or three broad avenues, and once thought he glimpsed a familiar tower. Again he asked a merchant about the massive church of stone, and this time he could have sworn that the plea of ignorance was feigned.

The dark man's face had a look of fear which he tried to hide, and Blake saw him make a curious sign with his right hand.

Then suddenly a black spire stood out against the cloudy sky on his left, above the tiers of brown roofs lining the tangled southerly alleys. Blake knew at once what it was, and plunged toward it through the squalid, unpaved lanes that climbed from the avenue. Twice he lost his way, but he somehow dared not ask any of the patriarchs or housewives who sat on their door-steps, or any of the children who shouted and played in the mud of the shadowy lanes.

At last he saw the tower plain against the southwest, and a huge stone bulk rose darkly at the end of an alley. Presently he stood in a windswept open square, quaintly cobblestoned, with a high bank wall on the farther side. This was the end of his quest; for upon the wide, iron-railed, weed-grown plateau which the wall supported—a separate, lesser world raised fully six feet above the surrounding streets—there stood a grim, titan bulk whose identity, despite Blake's new perspective, was beyond dispute.

The vacant church was in a state of great decrepitude. Some of the high stone buttresses had fallen, and several delicate finials lay half lost among the brown, neglected weeds and grasses. The sooty Gothic windows were largely unbroken, though many of the stone mullions were missing. Blake wondered how the obscurely painted panes could have survived so well, in view of the known habits of small boys the world over. The massive doors were intact and tightly closed. Around the top of the bank wall, fully enclosing the grounds, was a rusty iron fence whose gate—at the head of a flight of steps from the square—was visibly padlocked. The path from the gate to the building was completely overgrown. Desolation and decay hung like a pall above the place, and in the birdless eaves and black, ivyless walls Blake felt a touch of the dimly sinister beyond his power to define.

There were very few people in the square, but Blake saw a policeman at the northerly end and approached him with questions about the church. He was a great wholesome Irishman, and it seemed odd that he would do little more than make the sign of the cross and mutter that people never spoke of that building. When Blake pressed him he said very hurriedly that the Italian priests warned everybody against it, vowing that a monstrous evil had once dwelt there and left its mark. He himself had heard dark whispers of it from his father, who recalled certain sounds and rumors from his boyhood.

There had been a bad sect there in the old days—an outlaw sect that called up awful things from some unknown gulf of night. It had taken a good priest to exorcise what had come, though there did be those who said that merely the light could do it. If Father O'Malley were alive there would be many the thing he could tell. But now there was nothing to do but let it alone. It hurt nobody now, and those that owned it were dead or far away. They had run away like rats after the threatening talk in '77, when people began to mind the way folks vanished now and then in the neighborhood. Some day the city would step in and take the property for lack of heirs, but little good would come of anybody's touching it. Better it be left alone for the years to topple, lest things be stirred that ought to rest for ever in their black abyss.

After the policeman had gone Blake stood staring at the sullen steepled pile. It excited him to find that the structure seemed as sinister to others as to him, and he wondered what grain of truth might lie behind the old tales the bluecoat had repeated. Probably they were mere legends evoked by the evil look of the place, but even so, they were like a strange coming to life of one of his own stories.

The afternoon sun came out from behind dispersing clouds, but seemed unable to light up the stained, sooty walls of the old temple that towered on its high plateau. It was odd that the green of spring had not touched the brown, withered growths in the raised, iron-fenced yard. Blake found himself edging nearer the raised area and examining the blank wall and rusted fence for possible avenues of ingress. There was a terrible lure about the blackened fane which was not to be resisted. The fence had no opening near the steps, but around on the north side were some missing bars. He could go up the steps and walk around on the narrow coping outside the fence till he came to the gap. If the people feared the place so wildly, he would encounter no interference.

He was on the embankment and almost inside the fence before anyone noticed him. Then, looking down, he saw the few people in the square edging away and making the same sign with their right hands that the shopkeeper in the avenue had made. Several windows were slammed down, and a fat woman darted into the street and pulled some small children inside a rickety, unpainted house. The gap in the fence was very easy to pass through, and before long Blake found himself wading amidst the rotting, tangled growths of the deserted yard. Here and there the worn stump of a headstone told him that there had once been burials in this field; but that, he saw, must have been very long ago. The sheer bulk of the church was oppressive now that he was close to it, but he conquered his mood and approached to try the three great doors in the façade. All were securely locked, so he began a circuit of the Cyclopean building in quest of some minor and more penetrable opening. Even then he could not be sure that he wished to enter that haunt of desertion and shadow, yet the pull of its strangeness dragged him on automatically.

A yawning and unprotected cellar window in the rear furnished the needed aperture. Peering in, Blake saw a subterrene gulf of cobwebs and dust faintly litten by the western sun's filtered rays. Debris, old barrels, and ruined boxes and furniture of numerous sorts met his eye, though over everything lay a shroud of dust which softened all sharp outlines. The rusted remains of a hot-air furnace showed that the building had been used and kept in shape as late as Mid-Victorian times.

Acting almost without conscious initiative, Blake crawled through the window and let himself down to the dust-carpeted and debris-strewn concrete floor. The vaulted cellar was a vast one, without partitions; and in a corner far to the right, amid dense shadows, he saw a black archway evidently leading upstairs. He felt a peculiar sense of oppression at being actually within the great spectral building, but kept it in check as he cautiously scouted about—finding a still-intact barrel amid the dust, and rolling it over to the open window to provide for his exit. Then, bracing himself, he crossed the wide, cobweb-festooned space toward the arch. Half choked with the omnipresent dust, and covered with ghostly gossamer fibers, he reached and began to climb the worn stone steps which rose into the darkness. He had no light, but groped carefully with his hands. After a sharp turn he felt a closed door ahead, and a little fumbling revealed its ancient latch. It opened inward, and beyond it he saw a dimly illumined corridor with worm-eaten paneling.

Once on the ground floor, Blake began exploring in a rapid fashion. All the inner doors were unlocked, so that he freely passed from room to room. The colossal nave was an almost eldritch place with its drifts and mountains of dust over box pews, altar, hour-glass pulpit, and sounding-board, and its titanic ropes of cobweb stretching among the pointed arches of the gallery and entwining the clustered Gothic columns. Over all this hushed desolation played a hideous leaden light as the declining afternoon sun sent its rays through the strange, half-blackened panes of the great apsidal windows.

The paintings on those windows were so obscured by soot that Blake could scarcely decipher what they had represented, but from the little he could make out he did not like them. The designs were largely conventional, and his knowledge of obscure symbolism told him much concerning some of the ancient patterns. The few saints depicted bore expressions distinctly open to criticism, while one of the windows seemed to show merely a dark space with spirals of curious luminosity scattered about in it. Turning away from the windows, Blake noticed that the cobwebbed cross above the altar was not of the ordinary kind, but resembled the primordial ankh or crux ansata of shadowy Egypt.

In a rear vestry room beside the apse Blake found a rotting desk and ceiling-high shelves of mildewed, disintegrating books. Here for the first time he received a positive shock of objective horror, for the title of those books told him much. They were the black, forbidden things which most sane people have never even heard of, or have heard of only in furtive, timorous whispers; the banned and dreaded repositories of equivocal secrets and immemorial formulae which have trickled down the stream of time from the days of man's youth, and the dim, fabulous days before man was. He had himself read many of them—a Latin version of the abhorred *Necronomicon*, the sinister *Liber Ivonis*, the infamous *Cultes des Goules* of Comte d'Erlette, the *Unaussprechlichen Kulten* of von Junzt, and old Ludvig Prinn's hellish *De Vermis Mysteriis*. But there were others he had known merely by reputation or not at all—the *Pnakotic Manuscripts*, the *Book of Dzyan*, and a crumbling volume in wholly unidentifiable characters yet with certain symbols and diagrams shudderingly recognizable to the occult student. Clearly, the lingering local rumors had not lied. This place had once been the seat of an evil older than mankind and wider than the known universe.

In the ruined desk was a small leatherbound record-book filled with entries in some odd cryptographic medium. The manuscript writing consisted of the common traditional symbols used today in astronomy and anciently in alchemy, astrology, and other dubious arts—the devices of the sun, moon, planets, aspects, and zodiacal signs—here massed in solid pages of text, with divisions and paragraphings suggesting that each symbol answered to some alphabetical letter.

In the hope of later solving the cryptogram, Blake bore off this volume in his coat pocket. Many of the great tomes on the shelves fascinated him unutterably, and he felt tempted to borrow them at some later time. He wondered how they could have remained undisturbed so long. Was he the first to conquer the clutching, pervasive fear which had for nearly sixty years protected this deserted place from visitors?

Having now thoroughly explored the ground floor, Blake plowed again through the dust of the spectral nave to the front vestibule, where he had seen a door and staircase presumably leading up to the blackened tower and steeple—objects so long familiar to him at a distance. The ascent was a choking experience, for dust lay thick, while the spiders had done their worst in this constricted place. The staircase was a spiral with high, narrow wooden treads, and now and then Blake passed a clouded window looking dizzily out over the city. Though he had seen no ropes below, he expected to find a bell or peal of bells in the towers whose narrow, louver-boarded lancet windows his field-glass had studied so often. Here he was doomed to disappointment; for when he attained the top of the stairs he found the tower chamber vacant of chimes, and clearly devoted to vastly different purposes.

The room, about fifteen feet square, was faintly lighted by four lancet windows, one on each side, which were glazed within their screening of decayed louver-boards. These had been further fitted with tight, opaque screens, but the latter were now largely rotted away. In the center of the dust-laden floor rose a curiously angled stone pillar some four feet in height and two in average diameter, covered on each side with bizarre, crudely incised and wholly unrecognizable hieroglyphs. On this pillar rested a metal box of peculiarly asymmetrical form; its hinged lid thrown back, and its interior holding what looked beneath the decade-deep dust to be an egg-shaped or irregularly spherical object some four inches through. Around the pillar in a rough circle were seven high-backed Gothic chairs still largely intact, while behind them, ranging along the dark-paneled walls, were seven colossal images of crumbling, black-painted plaster, resembling more than anything else the cryptic carven megaliths of mysterious Easter Island. In one corner of the cobwebbed chamber a ladder was built into the wall, leading up to the closed trap door of the windowless steeple above.

As Blake grew accustomed to the feeble light he noticed odd basreliefs on the strange open box of yellowish metal. Approaching, he tried to clear the dust away with his hands and handkerchief, and saw that the figurings were of a monstrous and utterly alien kind; depicting entities which, though seemingly alive, resembled no known lifeform ever evolved on this planet. The four-inch seeming sphere turned out to be a nearly black, red-striated polyhedron with many irregular flat surfaces; either a very remarkable crystal of some sort, or an artificial object of carved and highly polished mineral matter. It did not touch the bottom of the box, but was held suspended by means of a metal band around its center, with seven queerly-designed supports extending horizontally to angles of the box's inner wall near the top. This stone, once exposed, exerted upon Blake an almost alarming fascination. He could scarcely tear his eyes from it, and as he looked at its glistening surfaces he almost fancied it was transparent, with half-formed worlds of wonder within. Into his mind floated pictures of alien orbs with great stone towers, and other orbs with titan mountains and no mark of life, and still remoter spaces where only a stirring in vague blackness told of the presence of consciousness and will.

When he did look away, it was to notice a somewhat singular mound of dust in the far corner near the ladder to the steeple. Just why it took his attention he could not tell, but something in its contours carried a message to his unconscious mind. Plowing toward it, and brushing aside the hanging cobwebs as he went, he began to discern something grim about it. Hand and handkerchief soon revealed the truth, and Blake gasped with a baffling mixture of emotions. It was a human skeleton, and it must have been there for a very long time. The clothing was in shreds, but some buttons and fragments of cloth bespoke the man's grey suit. There were other bits of evidence—shoes, metal clasps, huge buttons for round cuffs, a stickpin of bygone pattern, a reporter's badge with the name of the old *Providence Telegram*, and a crumbling leather pocket-book. Blake examined the latter with care, finding within it several bills of antiquated issue, a celluloid advertising calendar for 1893, some cards with the name "Edwin M. Lillibridge," and a paper covered with penciled memoranda.

This paper held much of a puzzling nature, and Blake read it carefully at the dim westward window. Its disjointed text included such phrases as the following:

"Prof. Enoch Bowen home from Egypt May 1844—buys old Free-Will Church in July—his archaeological work & studies in occult well known."

"Dr. Drowne of 4th Baptist warns against Starry Wisdom in sermon Dec. 29, 1844."

"Congregation 97 by end of '45."

"1846—3 disappearances—first mention of Shining Trapezohedron."

"7 disappearances 1848—stories of blood sacrifice begin."

"Investigation 1853 comes to nothing—stories of sounds."

"Fr. O'Malley tells of devil-worship with box found in great Egyptian ruins—says they call up something that can't exist in light. Flees a little light, and banished by strong light. Then has to be summoned again. Probably got this from deathbed confession of Francis X. Feeney, who had joined Starry Wisdom in '49. These people say the Shining Trapezohedron shows them heaven & other worlds, & that the Haunter of the Dark tells them secrets in some way."

"Story of Orrin B. Eddy 1857. They call it up by gazing at the crystal, & have a secret language of their own."

"200 or more in cong. 1863, exclusive of men at front."

"Irish boys mob church in 1869 after Patrick Regan's disappearance."

"Veiled article in J. March 14, '72, but people don't talk about it."

"6 disappearances 1876—secret committee calls on Mayor Doyle."

"Action promised Feb. 1877—church closes in April."

"Gang—Federal Hill Boys—threaten Dr.—— and vestrymen in May."

"181 persons leave city before end of '77—mention no names."

"Ghost stories begin around 1880—try to ascertain truth of report that no human being has entered church since 1877."

"Ask Lanigan for photograph of place taken 1851." . . .

Restoring the paper to the pocketbook and placing the latter in his coat, Blake turned to look down at the skeleton in the dust. The implications of the notes were clear, and there could be no doubt but that this man had come to the deserted edifice forty-two years before in quest of a newspaper sensation which no one else had been bold enough to attempt. Perhaps no one else had known of his plan—who could tell? But he had never returned to his paper. Had some bravely-suppressed fear risen to overcome him and bring on sudden heart-failure? Blake stooped over the gleaming bones and noted their peculiar state. Some of them were badly scattered, and a few seemed oddly *dissolved* at the ends. Others were strangely yellowed, with vague suggestions of charring. This charring extended to some of the fragments of clothing. The skull was in a very peculiar state—stained yellow, and with a charred aperture in the top as if some powerful acid had eaten through the solid bone. What had happened to the skeleton during its four decades of silent entombment here Blake could not imagine.

Before he realized it, he was looking at the stone again, and letting its curious influence call up a nebulous pageantry in his mind. He saw processions of robed, hooded figures whose outlines were not human, and looked on endless leagues of desert lined with carved, sky-reaching monoliths. He saw towers and walls in nighted depths under the sea, and vortices of space where wisps of black mist floated before thin shimmerings of cold purple haze. And beyond all else he glimpsed an infinite gulf of darkness, where solid and semi-solid forms were known only by their windy stirrings, and cloudy patterns of force seemed to superimpose order on chaos and hold forth a key to all the paradoxes and arcana of the worlds we know.

Then all at once the spell was broken by an access of gnawing, indeterminate panic fear. Blake choked and turn away from the stone, conscious of some formless alien presence close to him and watching him with horrible intentness. He felt entangled with something—something which was not in the stone, but which had looked through it at him—something which would ceaselessly follow him with a cognition that was not physical sight. Plainly, the place was getting on his nerves—as well it might in view of his gruesome find. The light was waning, too, and since he had no illuminant with him he knew he would have to be leaving soon.

It was then, in the gathering twilight, that he thought he saw a faint trace of luminosity in the crazily angled stone. He had tried to look away from it, but some obscure compulsion drew his eyes back. Was there a subtle phosphorescence of radio-activity about the thing? What was it that the dead man's notes had said concerning a *Shining Trapezohedron*? What, anyway, was this abandoned lair of cosmic evil? What had been done here, and what might still be lurking in the bird-shunned shadows? It seemed now as if an elusive touch of fetor had arisen somewhere close by, though its source was not apparent. Blake seized the cover of the long-open box and snapped it down. It moved easily on its alien hinges, and closed completely over the unmistakably glowing stone.

At the sharp click of that closing a soft stirring sound seemed to come from the steeple's eternal blackness overhead, beyond the trapdoor. Rats, without question—the only living things to reveal their presence in this accursed pile since he had entered it. And yet that stirring in the steeple frightened him horribly, so that he plunged almost wildly down the spiral stairs, across the ghoulish nave, into the vaulted basement, out amidst the gathering dusk of the deserted square, and down through the teeming, fear-haunted alleys and avenues of Federal Hill toward the sane central streets and the home-like brick sidewalks of the college district.

During the days which followed, Blake told no one of his expedition. Instead, he read much in certain books, examined long years of newspaper files downtown, and worked feverishly at the cryptogram in that leather volume from the cobwebbed vestry room. The cipher, he soon saw, was no simple one; and after a long period of endeavor he felt sure that its language could not be English, Latin, Greek, French, Spanish, Italian, or German. Evidently he would have to draw upon the deepest wells of his strange erudition.

Every evening the old impulse to gaze westward returned, and he saw the black steeple as of yore amongst the bristling roofs of a distant and half-fabulous world. But now it held a fresh note of terror for him. He knew the heritage of evil lore it masked, and with the knowledge his vision ran riot in queer new ways. The birds of spring were returning, and as he watched their sunset flights he fancied they avoided the gaunt, lone spire as never before. When a flock of them approached it, he thought, they would wheel and scatter in panic confusion—and he could guess at the wild twitterings which failed to reach him across the intervening miles.

It was in June that Blake's diary told of his victory over the cryptogram. The text was, he found, in the dark Aklo language used by certain cults of evil antiquity, and known to him in a halting way through previous researches. The diary is strangely reticent about what Blake deciphered, but he was patently awed and disconcerted by his results. There are references to a Haunter of the Dark awaked by gazing into the Shining Trapezohedron, and insane conjectures about the black gulfs of chaos from which it was called. The being is spoken of as holding all knowledge, and demanding monstrous sacrifices. Some of Blake's entries show fear lest the thing, which he seemed to regard as summoned, stalk abroad; though he adds that the streetlights form a bulwark which cannot be crossed.

Of the Shining Trapezohedron he speaks often, calling it a window on all time and space, and tracing its history from the days it was fashioned on dark Yuggoth, before ever the Old Ones brought it to earth. It was treasured and placed in its curious box by the crinoid things of Antarctica, salvaged from their ruins by the serpent-men of Valusia, and peered at eons later in Lemuria by the first human beings. It crossed strange lands and stranger seas, and sank with Atlantis before a Minoan fisher meshed it in his net and sold it to swarthy merchants from nighted Khem. The Pharaoh Nephren-Ka built around it a temple with a windowless crypt, and did that which caused his name to be stricken from all monuments and records. Then it slept in the ruins of that evil fane which the priests and the new Pharaoh destroyed, till the delver's spade once more brought it forth to curse mankind.

Early in July the newspapers oddly supplement Blake's entries, though in so brief and casual a way that only the diary has called general attention to their contribution. It appears that a new fear had been growing on Federal Hill since a stranger had entered the dreaded church. The Italians whispered of unaccustomed stirrings and bumpings and scrapings in the dark windowless steeple, and called on their priests to banish an entity which haunted their dreams. Something, they said, was constantly watching at a door to see if it were dark enough to venture forth. Press items mentioned the longstanding local superstitions, but failed to shed much light on the earlier background of the horror. It was obvious that the young reporters of today are no antiquarians. In writing of these things in his diary, Blake expresses a curious kind of remorse, and talks of the duty of burying the Shining Trapezohedron and of banishing what he had evoked by letting daylight into the hideous jutting spire. At the same time, however, he displays the dangerous extent of his fascination, and admits a morbid longing—pervading even his dreams—to visit the accursed tower and gaze again into the cosmic secrets of the glowing stone.

Then something in the *Journal* on the morning of July 17 threw the diarist into a veritable fervor of horror. It was only a variant of the other half-humorous items about the Federal Hill restlessness, but to Blake it was somehow very terrible indeed. In the night a thunderstorm had put the city's lighting-system out of commission for a full hour, and in that black interval the Italians had nearly gone mad with fright. Those living near the dreaded church had sworn that the thing in the steeple had taken advantage of the street lamps' absence and gone down into the body of the church, flopping and bumping around in a viscous, altogether dreadful way. Toward the last it had bumped up to the tower, where there were sounds of the shattering of glass. It could go wherever the darkness reached, but light would always send it fleeing.

When the current blazed on again there had been a shocking commotion in the tower, for even the feeble light trickling through the grime-blackened, louver-boarded windows was too much for the thing. It had bumped and slithered up into its tenebrous steeple just in time—for a long dose of light would have sent it back into the abyss whence the crazy stranger had called it. During the dark hour praying crowds had clustered round the church in the rain with lighted candles and lamps somehow shielded with folded paper and umbrellas—a guard of light to save the city from the nightmare that stalks in darkness. Once, those nearest the church declared, the outer door had rattled hideously.

But even this was not the worst. That evening in the *Bulletin* Blake read of what the reporters had found. Aroused at last to the whimsical news value of the scare, a pair of them had defied the frantic crowds of Italians and crawled into the church through the cellar window after trying the doors in vain. They found the dust of the vestibule and of the spectral nave plowed up in a singular way, with pits of rotted cushions and satin pew-linings scattered curiously around. There was a bad odor everywhere, and here and there were bits of yellow stain and patches of what looked like charring. Opening the door to the tower, and pausing a moment at the suspicion of a scraping sound above, they found the narrow spiral stairs wiped roughly clean.

In the tower itself a similarly half-swept condition existed. They spoke of the heptagonal stone pillar, the overturned Gothic chairs, and the bizarre plaster images; though strangely enough the metal box and the old mutilated skeleton were not mentioned. What disturbed Blake the most—except for the hints of stains and charring and bad odors—was the final detail that explained the crashing glass. Every one of the tower's lancet windows was broken, and two of them had been darkened in a crude and hurried way by the stuffing of satin pew-linings and cushion-horsehair into the spaces between the slanting exterior louver-boards. More satin fragments and bunches of horsehair lay scattered around the newly swept floor, as if someone had been interrupted in the act of restoring the tower to the absolute blackness of its tightly curtained days.

Yellowish stains and charred patches were found on the ladder to the windowless spire, but when a reporter climbed up, opened the horizontally-sliding trapdoor and shot a feeble flashlight beam into the black and strangely fetid space, he saw nothing but darkness, and an heterogeneous litter of shapeless fragments near the aperture. The verdict, of course, was charlatanry. Somebody had played a joke on the superstitious hill-dwellers, or else some fanatic had striven to bolster up their fears for their own supposed good. Or perhaps some of the younger and more sophisticated dwellers had staged an elaborate hoax on the outside world. There was an amusing aftermath when the police sent an officer to verify the reports. Three men in succession found ways of evading the assignment, and the fourth went very reluctantly and returned very soon without adding to the account given by the reporters.

From this point onward Blake's diary shows a mounting tide of insidious horror and nervous apprehension. He upbraids himself for not doing something, and speculates wildly on the consequences of another electrical breakdown. It has been verified that on three occasions—during thunderstorms—he telephoned the electric light company in a frantic vein and asked that desperate precautions against a lapse of power be taken. Now and then his entries show concern over the failure of the reporters to find the metal box and stone, and the strangely marred old skeleton, when they explored the shadowy tower room. He assumed that these things had been removed—whither, and by whom or what, he could only guess. But his worst fears concerned himself, and the kind of unholy rapport he felt to exist between his mind and that lurking horror in the distant steeple—that monstrous thing of night which his rashness had called out of the ultimate black spaces. He seemed to feel a constant tugging at his will, and callers of that period remember how he would sit abstractedly at his desk and stare out of the west window at that far-off spire-bristling mound beyond the swirling smoke of the city. His entries dwell monotonously on certain terrible dreams, and of a strengthening of the unholy rapport in his sleep. There is mention of a night when he awakened to find himself fully dressed, outdoors, and headed automatically down College Hill toward the west. Again and again he dwells on the fact that the thing in the steeple knows where to find him.

The week following July 30 is recalled as the time of Blake's partial breakdown. He did not dress, and ordered all his food by telephone. Visitors remarked the cords he kept near his bed, and he said that sleep-walking had forced him to bind his ankles every night with knots which would probably hold or else waken him with the labor of untying.

In his diary he told of the hideous experience which had brought the collapse. After retiring on the night of the 30th he had suddenly found himself groping about in an almost black space. All he could see were short, faint, horizontal streaks of bluish light, but he could smell an overpowering fetor and hear a curious jumble of soft, furtive sounds above him. Whenever he moved he stumbled over something, and at each noise there would come a sort of answering sound from above—a vague stirring, mixed with the cautious sliding of wood on wood.

Once his groping hands encountered a pillar of stone with a vacant top, whilst later he found himself clutching the rungs of a ladder built into the wall, and fumbling his uncertain way upward toward some region of intenser stench where a hot, searing blast beat down against him. Before his eyes a kaleidoscopic range of fantasmal images played, all of them dissolving at intervals into the picture of a vast, unplumbed abyss of night wherein whirled suns and worlds of an even profounder blackness. He thought of the ancient legends of Ultimate Chaos, at whose center sprawls the blind idiot god Azathoth, Lord of All Things, encircled by his flopping horde of mindless and amorphous dancers, and lulled by the thin monotonous piping of a demoniac flute held in nameless paws.

Then a sharp report from the outer world broke through his stupor and roused him to the unutterable horror of his position. What it was, he never knew—perhaps it was some belated peal from the fireworks heard all summer on Federal Hill as the dwellers hail their various patron saints, or the saints of their native villages in Italy. In any event he shrieked aloud, dropped frantically from the ladder, and stumbled blindly across the obstructed floor of the almost lightless chamber that encompassed him.

He knew instantly where he was, and plunged recklessly down the narrow spiral staircase, tripping and bruising himself at every turn. There was a nightmare flight through a vast cobwebbed nave whose ghostly arches reached up to realms of leering shadow, a sightless scramble through a littered basement, a climb to regions of air and street lights outside, and a mad racing down a spectral hill of gibbering gables, across a grim, silent city of tall black towers, and up the steep eastward precipice to his own ancient door.

On regaining consciousness in the morning he found himself lying on his study floor fully dressed. Dirt and cobwebs covered him, and every inch of his body seemed sore and bruised. When he faced the mirror he saw that his hair was badly scorched, while a trace of strange, evil odor seemed to cling to his upper outer clothing. It was then that his nerves broke down. Thereafter, lounging exhaustedly about in a dressing-gown, he did little but stare from his west window, shiver at the threat of thunder, and make wild entries in his diary.

The great storm broke just before midnight on August 8th. Lightning struck repeatedly in all parts of the city, and two remarkable fireballs were reported. The rain was torrential, while a constant fusillade of thunder brought sleeplessness to thousands. Blake was utterly frantic in his fear for the lighting system, and tried to telephone the company around one A.M., though by that time service had been temporarily cut off in the interest of safety. He recorded everything in his diary—the large, nervous, and often undecipherable hieroglyphs telling their own story of growing frenzy and despair, and of entries scrawled blindly in the dark.

He had to keep the house dark in order to see out the window, and it appears that most of his time was spent at his desk, peering anxiously through the rain across the glistening miles of downtown roofs at the constellation of distant lights marking Federal Hill. Now and then he would fumblingly make an entry in his diary, so that detached phrases such as "The lights must not go"; "It knows where I am"; "I must destroy it"; and "It is calling to me, but perhaps it means no injury this time"; are found scattered down two of the pages.

Then the lights went out all over the city. It happened at 2:12 A.M. according to power-house records, but Blake's diary gives no indication of the time. The entry is merely, "Lights out—God help me." On Federal Hill there were watchers as anxious as he, and rainsoaked knots of men paraded the square and alleys around the evil church with umbrella-shaded candles, electric flashlights, oil lanterns, crucifixes, and obscure charms of the many sorts common to southern Italy. They blessed each flash of lightning, and made cryptical signs of fear with their right hands when a turn in the storm caused the flashes to lessen and finally to cease altogether. A rising wind blew out most of the candles, so that the scene grew threatening dark.

Someone roused Father Merluzzo of Spirito Santo Church, and he hastened to the dismal square to pronounce whatever helpful syllables he could. Of the restless and curious sounds in the blackened tower, there could be no doubt whatever.

For what happened at 2:35 we have the testimony of the priest, a young, intelligent, and well-educated person; of Patrolman William J. Monohan of the Central Station, an officer of the highest reliability who had paused at that part of his beat to inspect the crowd; and of most of the seventy-eight men who had gathered around the church's high bank wall—especially those in the square where the eastward façade was visible. Of course there was nothing which can be proved as being outside the order of nature. The possible causes of such an event are many. No one can speak with certainty of the obscure chemical processes arising in a vast, ancient, ill-aired, and long-deserted building of heterogeneous contents. Mephitic vapors—spontaneous combustion—pressure of gases born of long decay—any one of numberless phenomena might be responsible. And then, of course, the factor of conscious charlatanry can by no means be excluded. The thing was really quite simple in itself, and covered less then three minutes of actual time. Father Merluzzo, always a precise man, looked at his watch repeatedly.

It started with a definite swelling of the dull fumbling sounds inside the black tower. There had for some time been a vague exhalation of strange, evil odors from the church, and this had now become emphatic and offensive. Then at last there was a sound of splintering wood, and a large, heavy object crashed down in the yard beneath the frowning easterly façade. The tower was invisible now that the candles would not burn, but as the object neared the ground the people knew that it was the smoke-grimed louver-boarding of that tower's east window.

Immediately afterward an utterly unbearable fetor welled forth from the unseen heights, choking and sickening the trembling watchers, and almost prostrating those in the square. At the same time the air trembled with a vibration as of flapping wings, and a sudden east-blowing wind more violent than any previous blast snatched off the hats and wrenched the dripping umbrellas of the crowd. Nothing definite could be seen in the candleless night, though some upward-looking spectators thought they glimpsed a great spreading blur of denser blackness against the inky sky—something like a formless cloud of smoke that shot with meteorlike speed toward the east.

That was all. The watchers were half numbed with fright, awe, and discomfort, and scarcely knew what to do, or whether to do anything at all. Not knowing what had happened, they did not relax their vigil; and a moment later they sent up a prayer as a sharp flash of belated lightning, followed by an earsplitting crash of sound, rent the flooded heavens. Half an hour later the rain stopped, and in fifteen minutes more the street lights sprang on again, sending the weary, bedraggled watchers relievedly back to their homes.

The next day's papers gave these matters minor mention in connection with the general storm reports. It seems that the great lightning flash and deafening explosion which followed the Federal Hill occurrence were even more tremendous farther east, where a burst of the singular fetor was likewise noticed. The phenomenon was most marked over College Hill, where the crash awaked all the sleeping inhabitants and led to a bewildered round of speculations. Of those who were already awake only a few saw the anomalous blaze of light near the top of the hill, or noticed the inexplicable upward rush of air which almost stripped the leaves from the trees and blasted the plants in the gardens. It was agreed that the lone, sudden lightning-bolt must have struck somewhere in this neighborhood, though no trace of its striking could afterward be found. A youth in the Tau Omega fraternity house thought he saw a grotesque and hideous mass of smoke in the air just as the preliminary flash burst, but his observation has not been verified. All of the few observers, however, agree as to the violent gust from the west and the flood of intolerable stench which preceded the belated stroke; whilst evidence concerning the momentary burned odor after the stroke is equally general.

These points were discussed very carefully because of their probable connection with the death of Robert Blake. Students in the Psi Delta house, whose upper rear windows looked into Blake's study, noticed the blurred white face at the westward window on the morning of the ninth, and wondered what was wrong with the expression. When they saw the same face in the same position that evening, they felt worried, and watched for the lights to come up in his apartment. Later they rang the bell of the darkened flat, and finally had a policeman force the door.

The rigid body sat bolt upright at the desk by the window, and when the intruders saw the glassy, bulging eyes, and the marks of stark, convulsive fright on the twisted features, they turned away in sickened dismay. Shortly afterward the coroner's physician made an examination, and despite the unbroken window reported electrical shock, or nervous tension induced by electrical discharge, as the cause of death. The hideous expression he ignored altogether, deeming it a not improbable result of the profound shock as experienced by a person of such abnormal imagination and unbalanced emotions. He deduced these latter qualities from the books, paintings, and manuscripts found in the apartment, and from the blindly scrawled entries in the diary on the desk. Blake had prolonged his frenzied jottings to the last, and the broken-pointed pencil was found clutched in his spasmodically contracted right hand.

The entries after the failure of the lights were highly disjointed, and legible only in part. From them certain investigators have drawn conclusions differing greatly from the materialistic official verdict, but such speculations have little chance for belief among the conservative. The case of these imaginative theorists has not been helped by the action of superstitious Doctor Dexter, who threw the curious box and angled stone—an object certainly self-luminous as seen in the black windowless steeple where it was found—into the deepest channel of Narragansett Bay. Excessive imagination and neurotic unbalance on Blake's part, aggravated by knowledge of the evil bygone cult whose startling traces he had uncovered, form the dominant interpretation given those final frenzied jottings. These are the entries—or all that can be made of them.

"Lights still out—must be five minutes now. Everything depends on lightning. Yaddith grant it will keep up! . . . Some influence seems beating through it. . . . Rain and thunder and wind deafen. . . The thing is taking hold of my mind. . . .

"Trouble with memory. I see things I never knew before. Other worlds and other galaxies. . . . Dark. . . . The lightning seems dark and the darkness seems light. . . .

"It cannot be the real hill and church that I see in the pitch-darkness. Must be retinal impression left by flashes. Heaven grant the Italians are out with their candles if the lightning stops!

"What am I afraid of? Is it not an avatar of Nyarlathotep, who in antique and shadowy Khem even took the form of man? I remember Yuggoth, and more distant Shaggai, and the ultimate void of the black planets. . . .

"The long, winging flight through the void . . . cannot cross the universe of light . . . re-created by the thoughts caught in the Shining Trapezohedron . . . send it through the horrible abysses of radiance. . . .

"My name is Blake—Robert Harrison Blake of 620 East Knapp Street, Milwaukee, Wisconsin. . . . I am on this planet. . . .

"Azathoth have mercy!—the lightning no longer flashes—horrible—I can see everything with a monstrous sense that is not sight—light is dark and dark is light . . . those people on the hill . . . guard . . . candles and charms . . . their priests. . . .

"Sense of distance gone—far is near and near is far. No light—no glass—see that steeple—that tower—window—can hear—Roderick

Usher—am mad or going mad—the thing is stirring and fumbling in the tower—I am it and it is I—I want to get out . . . must get out and unify the forces. . . . It knows where I am. . . .

"I am Robert Blake, but I see the tower in the dark. There is a monstrous odor . . . senses transfigured . . . boarding at that tower window cracking and giving way. . . . Iä . . . ngai . . . ygg. . . .

"I see it—coming here—hell-wind—titan blur—black wings— Yog-Sothoth save me—the three-lobed burning eye. . . ."

The Thing On The Doorstep

It is true that I have sent six bullets through the head of my best friend, and yet I hope to show by this statement that I am not his murderer. At first I shall be called a madman—madder than the man I shot in his cell at the Arkham Sanitarium. Later some of my readers will weigh each statement, correlate it with the known facts, and ask themselves how I could have believed otherwise than I did after facing the evidence of that horror—that thing on the doorstep.

Until then I also saw nothing but madness in the wild tales I have acted on. Even now I ask myself whether I was misled—or whether I am not mad after all. I do not know—but others have strange things to tell of Edward and Asenath Derby, and even the stolid police are at their wits' ends to account for that last terrible visit. They have tried weakly to concoct a theory of a ghastly jest or warning by discharged servants, yet they know in their hearts that the truth is something infinitely more terrible and incredible.

So I say that I have not murdered Edward Derby. Rather have I avenged him, and in so doing purged the earth of a horror whose survival might have loosed untold terrors on all mankind. There are black zones of shadow close to our daily paths, and now and then some evil soul breaks a passage through. When that happens, the man who knows must strike before reckoning the consequences.

I have known Edward Pickman Derby all his life. Eight years my junior, he was so precocious that we had much in common from the time he was eight and I was sixteen. He was the most phenomenal child scholar I have ever known, and at seven was writing verse of a sombre, fantastic, almost morbid cast which astonished the tutors surrounding him. Perhaps his private education and coddled seclusion had something to do with his premature flowering. An only child, he had organic weaknesses which startled his doting parents and caused them to keep him closely chained to their side. He was never allowed out without his nurse, and seldom had a chance to play unconstrainedly with other children. All this doubtless fostered a strange secretive life in the boy, with imagination as his one avenue of freedom.

At any rate, his juvenile learning was prodigious and bizarre; and his facile writings such as to captivate me despite my greater age. About that time I had leanings toward art of a somewhat grotesque cast, and I found in this younger child a rare kindred spirit. What lay behind our joint love of shadows and marvels was, no doubt, the ancient, mouldering, and subtly fearsome town in which we lived— witch-cursed, legend-haunted Arkham, whose huddled, sagging gambrel roofs and crumbling Georgian balustrades brood out the centuries beside the darkly muttering Miskatonic.

As time went by I turned to architecture and gave up my design of illustrating a book of Edward's demoniac poems, yet our comradeship suffered no lessening. Young Derby's odd genius developed remarkably, and in his eighteenth year his collected nightmare-lyrics made a real sensation when issued under the title *Azathoth and Other Horrors*. He was a close correspondent of the notorious Baudelairean poet Justin Geoffrey, who wrote *The People of the Monolith* and died screaming in a madhouse in 1926 after a visit to a sinister, ill-regarded village in Hungary.

In self-reliance and practical affairs, however, Derby was greatly retarded because of his coddled existence. His health had improved, but his habits of childish dependence were fostered by over-careful parents, so that he never travelled alone, made independent decisions, or assumed responsibilities. It was early seen that he would not be equal to a struggle in the business or professional arena, but the family fortune was so ample that this formed no tragedy. As he grew to years of manhood he retained a deceptive aspect of boyishness. Blond and blue-eyed, he had the fresh complexion of a child; and his attempt to raise a moustache were discernible only with difficulty. His voice was soft and light, and his unexercised life gave him a juvenile chubbiness rather than a paunchiness of premature middle age. He was of good height, and his handsome face would have made him a notable gallant had not his shyness held him to seclusion and bookishness.

Derby's parents took him abroad every summer, and he was quick to seize on the surface aspects of European thought and expression. His Poe-like talents turned more and more toward the decadent, and other artistic sensitiveness and yearnings were half-aroused in him. We had great discussions in those days. I had been through Harvard, had studied in a Boston architect's office, had married, and had finally returned to Arkham to practise my profession—settling in the family homestead in Saltonstall Street since my father had moved to Florida for his health. Edward used to call almost every evening, till I came to regard him as one of the household. He had a characteristic way of ringing the doorbell or sounding the knocker that grew to be a veritable code signal, so that after dinner I always listened for the familiar three brisk strokes followed by two more after a pause. Less frequently I would visit at his house and note with envy the obscure volumes in his constantly growing library.

Derby went through Miskatonic University in Arkahm since his parents would not let him board away from them. He entered at sixteen and completed his course in three years, majoring in English and French literature and receiving high marks in everything but mathematics and the sciences. He mingled very little with the other students, though looking enviously at the "daring" or "Bohemian" set—whose superficially "smart" language and meaningless ironic pose he aped, and whose dubious conduct he wished he dared adopt.

What he did do was to become an almost fanatical devotee of subterranean magical lore, for which Miskatonic's library was and is famous. Always a dweller on the surface of phantasy and strangeness, he now delved deep into the actual runes and riddles left by a fabulous past for the guidance or puzzlement of posterity. He read things like the frightful *Book of Eibon*, the *Unaussprechlichen Kulten* of von Junzt, and the forbidden *Necronomicon* of the mad Arab Abdul Alhazred, though he did not tell his parents he had seen them. Edward was twenty when my son and only child was born, and seemed pleased when I named the newcomer Edward Derby Upton, after him.

By the time he was twenty-five Edward Derby was a prodigiously learned man and a fairly well-known poet and fantaisiste, though his lack of contacts and responsibilities had slowed down his literary growth by making his products derivative and over-bookish. I was perhaps his closest friend—finding him an inexhaustible mine of vital theoretical topics, while he relied on me for advice in whatever matters he did not wish to refer to his parents. He remained single—more through shyness, inertia, and parental protectiveness than through inclination—and moved in society only to the slightest and most perfunctory extent. When the war came both health and ingrained timidity kept him at home. I went to Plattsburg for a commission, but never got overseas.

So the years wore on. Edward's mother died when he was thirty-four, and for months he was incapacitated by some odd psychological malady. His father took him to Europe, however, and he managed to pull out of his trouble without visible effects. Afterward he seemed to feel a sort of grotesque exhilaration, as if of partial escape from some unseen bondage. He began to mingle in the more "advanced" college set despite his middle age, and was present at some extremely wild doings—on one occasion paying heavy blackmail (which he borrowed of me) to keep his presence at a certain affair from his father's notice. Some of the whispered rumors about the wild Miskatonic set were extremely singular. There was even talk of black magic and of happenings utterly beyond credibility.

II

Edward was thirty-eight when he met Asenath Waite. She was, I judge, about twenty-three at the time; and was taking a special course in mediaeval metaphysics at Miskatonic. The daughter of a friend of mine had met her before—in the Hall School at Kingsport—and had been inclined to shun her because of her odd reputation. She was dark, smallish, and very good-looking except for overprotuberant eyes; but something in her expression alienated extremely sensitive people. It was, however, largely her origin and conversation which caused average folk to avoid her. She was one of the Innsmouth Waites, and dark legends have clustered for generations about crumbling, half-deserted Innsmouth and its people. There are tales of horrible bargains about the year 1850, and of a strange element "not quite human" in the ancient families of the run-down fishing port—tales such as only old-time Yankees can devise and repeat with proper awesomeness.

Asenath's case was aggravated by the fact that she was Ephraim Waite's daughter—the child of his old age by an unknown wife who always went veiled. Ephraim lived in a half-decayed mansion in Washington Street, Innsmouth, and those who had seen the place (Arkham folk avoid going to Innsmouth whenever they can) declared that the attic windows were always boarded, and that strange sounds sometimes floated from within as evening drew on. The old man was known to have been a prodigious magical student in his day, and legend averred that he could raise or quell storms at sea according to his whim. I had seen him once or twice in my youth as he came to Arkham to consult forbidden tomes at the college library, and had hated his wolfish, saturnine face with its tangle of iron-grey beard. He had died insane—under rather queer circumstances—just before his daughter (by his will made a nominal ward of the principal) entered the Hall School, but she had been his morbidly avid pupil and looked fiendishly like him at times.

The friend whose daughter had gone to school with Asenath Waite repeated many curious things when the news of Edward's acquaintance with her began to spread about. Asenath, it seemed, had posed as a kind of magician at school; and had really seemed able to accomplish some highly baffling marvels. She professed to be able to raise thunderstorms, though her seeming success was generally laid to some uncanny knack at prediction. All animals markedly disliked her, and she could make any dog howl by certain motions of her right hand. There were times when she displayed snatches of knowledge and language very singular—and very shocking—for a young girl; when she would frighten her school-mates with leers and winks of an inexplicable kind, and would seem to extract an obscene zestful irony from her present situation.

Most unusual, though, were the well-attested cases of her influence over other persons. She was, beyond question, a genuine hypnotist. By gazing peculiarly at a fellow-student she would often give the latter a distinct feeling of *exchanged personality*—as if the subject were placed momentarily in the magician's body and able to stare half across the room at her real body, whose eyes blazed and protruded with an alien expression. Asenath often made wild claims about the nature of consciousness and about its independence of the physical frame—or at least from the life-processes of the physical frame. Her crowning rage, however, was that she was not a man; since she believed a male brain had certain unique and far-reaching cosmic powers. Given a man's brain, she declared, she could not only equal but surpass her father in mastery of unknown forces.

Edward met Asenath at a gathering of "intelligentsia" held in one of the students' rooms, and could talk of nothing else when he came to see me the next day. He had found her full of the interests and erudition which engrossed him most, and was in addition wildly taken with her appearance. I had never seen the young woman, and recalled casual references only faintly, but I knew who she was. It seemed rather regrettable that Derby should become so upheaved about her; but I said nothing to discourage him, since infatuation thrives on opposition. He was not, he said, mentioning her to his father.

In the next few weeks I heard of very little but Asenath from young Derby. Others now remarked Edward's autumnal gallantry, though they agreed that he did not look even nearly his actual age, or seem at all inappropriate as an escort for his bizarre divinity. He was only a trifle paunchy despite his indolence and self-indulgence, and his face was absolutely without lines. Asenath, on the other hand, had the premature crow's feet which come from the exercises of an intense will.

About this time Edward brought the girl to call on me, and I at once saw that his interest was by no means one-sided. She eyed him continually with an almost predatory air, and I perceived that their intimacy was beyond untangling. Soon afterward I had a visit from old Mr. Derby, whom I had always admired and respected. He had heard the tales of his son's new friendship, and had wormed the whole truth out of "the boy." Edward meant to marry Asenath, and had even been looking at houses in the suburbs. Knowing my usually great influence with his son, the father wondered if I could help to break the ill-advised affair off; but I regretfully expressed my doubts. This time it was not a question of Edward's weak will but of the woman's strong will. The perennial child had transferred his dependence from the parental image to a new and stronger image, and nothing could be done about it.

The wedding was performed a month later—by a justice of the peace, according to the bride's request. Mr. Derby, at my advice, offered no opposition, and he, my wife, my son, and I attended the brief ceremony—the other guests being wild young people from the college. Asenath had bought the old Crowninshield place in the country at the end of High Street, and they proposed to settle there after a short trip to Innsmouth, whence three servants and some books and household goods were to be brought. It was probably not so much consideration for Edward and his father as a personal wish to be near the college, its library, and its crowd of "sophisticates," that made Asenath settle in Arkham instead of returning permanently home.

When Edward called on me after the honeymoon I thought he looked slightly changed. Asenath had made him get rid of the undeveloped moustache, but there was more than that. He looked soberer and more thoughtful, his habitual pout of childish rebelliousness being exchanged for a look almost of genuine sadness. I was puzzled to decide whether I liked or disliked the change. Certainly he seemed for the moment more normally adult than ever before. Perhaps the marriage was a good thing—might not the *change* of dependence form a start toward actual *neutralisation*, leading ultimately to responsible independence? He came alone, for Asenath was very busy. She had brought a vast store of books and apparatus from Innsmouth (Derby shuddered as he spoke the name), and was finishing the restoration of the Crowninshield house and grounds.

Her home—in that town—was a rather disgusting place, but certain objects in it had taught him some surprising things. He was progressing fast in esoteric lore now that he had Asenath's guidance. Some of the experiments she proposed were very daring and radical— he did not feel at liberty to describe them—but he had confidence in her powers and intentions. The three servants were very queer—an incredibly aged couple who had been with old Ephraim and referred occasionally to him and to Asenath's dead mother in a cryptic way, and a swarthy young wench who had marked anomalies of feature and seemed to exude a perpetual odour of fish.

III

For the next two years I saw less and less of Derby. A fortnight would sometimes slip by without the familiar three-and-two strokes at the front door; and when he did call—or when, as happened with increasing infrequency, I called on him—he was very little disposed to converse on vital topics. He had become secretive about those occult studies which he used to describe and discuss so minutely, and preferred not to talk of his wife. She had aged tremendously since her marriage, till now—oddly enough—she seemed the elder of the two. Her face held the most concentratedly determined expression I had ever seen, and her whole aspect seemed to gain a vague, unplaceable repulsiveness. My wife and son noticed it as much as I, and we all ceased gradually to call on her—for which, Edward admitted in one of his boyishly tactless moments, she was unmitigatedly grateful. Occasionally the Derbys would go on long trips—ostensibly to Europe, though Edward sometimes hinted at obscurer destinations.

It was after the first year that people began talking about the change in Edward Derby. It was very casual talk, for the change was purely psychological; but it brought up some interesting points. Now and then, it seemed Edward was observed to wear an expression and to do things wholly incompatible with his usual flabby nature. For example—although in the old days he could not drive a car, he was now seen occasionally to dash into or out of the old Crowninshield driveway with Asenath's powerful Packard, handling it like a master, and meeting traffic entanglements with a skill and determination utterly alien to his accustomed nature. In such cases he seemed always to be just back from some trip or just starting on one—what sort of trip, no one could guess, although he mostly favoured the Innsmouth road.

Oddly, the metamorphosis did not seem altogether pleasing. People said he looked too much like his wife, or like old Ephraim Waite himself, in these moments—or perhaps these moments seemed unnatural because they were so rare. Sometimes, hours after starting out in this way, he would return listlessly sprawled on the rear seat of the car while an obviously hired chauffeur or mechanic drove. Also, his preponderant aspect on the streets during his decreasing round of social contacts (including, I may say, his calls on me) was the old-time indecisive one—its irresponsible childishness even more marked than in the past. While Asenath's face aged, Edward's—aside from those exceptional occasions—actually relaxed into a kind of exaggerated immaturity, save when a trace of the new sadness or understanding would flash across it. It was really very puzzling. Meanwhile the Derbys almost dropped out of the gay college circle—not through their own disgust, we heard, but because something about their present studies shocked even the most callous of the other decadents.

It was in the third year of the marriage that Edward began to hint openly to me of a certain fear and dissatisfaction. He would let fall remarks about things "going too far," and would talk darkly about the need of "gaining his identity." At first I ignored such references, but in time I began to question him guardedly, remembering what my friend's daughter had said about Asenath's hypnotic influence over the other girls at school—the cases where students had thought they were in her body looking across the room at themselves. This questioning seemed to make him at once alarmed and grateful, and once he mumbled something about having a serious talk with me later.

About this time old Mr. Derby died, for which I was afterward very thankful. Edward was badly upset, though by no means disorganized. He had seen astonishingly little of his parent since his marriage, for Asenath had concentrated in herself all his vital sense of family linkage. Some called him callous in his loss—especially since those jaunty and confident moods in the car began to increase. He now wished to move back into the old family mansion, but Asenath insisted on staying in the Crowninshield house to which she had become well adjusted.

Not long afterward my wife heard a curious thing from a friend—one of the few who had not dropped the Derbys. She had been out to the end of High Street to call on the couple, and had seen a car shoot briskly out of the drive with Edward's oddly confident and almost sneering face above the wheel. Ringing the bell, she had been told by the repulsive wench that Asenath was also out; but had chanced to look at the house in leaving. There, at one of Edward's library windows, she had glimpsed a hastily withdrawn face—a face whose expression of pain, defeat, and wistful hopelessness was poignant beyond description. It was—incredibly enough in view of its usual domineering cast—Asenath's; yet the caller had vowed that in that instant the sad, muddled eyes of poor Edward were gazing out from it.

Edward's calls now grew a trifle more frequent, and his hints occasionally became concrete. What he said was not to be believed, even in centuried and legend-haunted Arkham; but he threw out his dark lore with a sincerity and convincingness which made one fear for his sanity. He talked about terrible meetings in lonely places, of cyclopean ruins in the heart of the Maine woods beneath which vast staircases led down to abysses of nighted secrets, of complex angles that led through invisible walls to other regions of space and time, and of hideous exchanges of personality that permitted explorations in remote and forbidden places, on other worlds, and in different space-time continua.

He would now and then back up certain crazy hints by exhibiting objects which utterly nonplussed me—elusively coloured and bafflingly textured objects like nothing ever heard of on earth, whose insane curves and surfaces answered no conceivable purpose, and followed no conceivable geometry. These things, he said, came "from outside"; and his wife knew how to get them. Sometimes—but always in frightened and ambiguous whispers—he would suggest things about old Ephraim Waite, whom he had seen occasionally at the college library in the old days. These adumbrations were never specific, but seemed to revolve around some especially horrible doubt as to whether the old wizard were really dead—in a spiritual as well as corporeal sense.

At times Derby would halt abruptly in his revelations, and I wondered whether Asenath could possibly have divined his speech at a distance and cut him off through some unknown sort of telepathic mesmerism—some power of the kind she had displayed at school. Certainly, she suspected that he told me things, for as the weeks passed she tried to stop his visits with words and glances of a most inexplicable potency. Only with difficulty could he get to see me, for although he would pretend to be going somewhere else, some invisible force would generally clog his motions or make him forget his destination for the time being. His visits usually came when Asenath was way—"away in her own body," as he once oddly put it. She always found out later—the servants watched his goings and comings—but evidently she thought it inexpedient to do anything drastic.

IV

Derby had been married more than three years on that August day when I got that telegram from Maine. I had not seen him for two months, but had heard he was away "on business." Asenath was supposed to be with him, though watchful gossip declared there was someone upstairs in the house behind the doubly curtained windows.

They had watched the purchases made by the servants. And now the town marshal of Chesuncook had wired of the draggled madman who stumbled out of the woods with delirious ravings and screamed to me for protection. It was Edward—and he had been just able to recall his own name and address.

Chesuncook is close to the wildest, deepest, and least explored forest belt in Maine, and it took a whole day of feverish jolting through fantastic and forbidding scenery to get there in a car. I found Derby in a cell at the town farm, vacillating between frenzy and apathy. He knew me at once, and began pouring out a meaningless, half-incoherent torrent of words in my direction.

"Dan—for God's sake! The pit of the shoggoths! Down the six thousand steps . . . the abomination of abominations . . . I never would let her take me, and then I found myself there—Iä! Shub-Niggurath!—The shape rose up from the altar, and there were five hundred that howled—The Hooded Thing bleated 'Kamog! Kamog!'— that was old Ephraim's secret name in the coven—I was there, where she promised she wouldn't take me—A minute before I was locked in the library, and then I was there where she had gone with my body— in the place of utter blasphemy, the unholy pit where the black realm begins and the watcher guards the gate—I saw a shoggoth—it changed shape—I can't stand it—I'll kill her if she ever sends me there again— I'll kill that entity—her, him, it—I'll kill it! I'll kill it with my own hands!"

It took me an hour to quiet him, but he subsided at last. The next day I got him decent clothes in the village, and set out with him for Arkham. His fury of hysteria was spent, and he was inclined to be silent, though he began muttering darkly to himself when the car passed through Augusta—as if the sight of a city aroused unpleasant memories. It was clear that he did not wish to go home; and considering the fantastic delusions he seemed to have about his wife— delusions undoubtedly springing from some actual hypnotic ordeal to which he had been subjected—I thought it would be better if he did not. I would, I resolved, put him up myself for a time; no matter what unpleasantness it would make with Asenath. Later I would help him get a divorce, for most assuredly there were mental factors which made this marriage suicidal for him. When we struck open country again Derby's muttering faded away, and I let him nod and drowse on the seat beside me as I drove.

During our sunset dash through Portland the muttering commenced again, more distinctly than before, and as I listened I caught a stream of utterly insane drivel about Asenath. The extent to which she had preyed on Edward's nerves was plain, for he had woven a whole set of hallucinations around her. His present predicament, he mumbled furtively, was only one of a long series. She was getting hold of him, and he knew that some day she would never let go. Even now she probably let him go only when she had to, because she couldn't hold on long at a time. She constantly took his body and went to nameless places for nameless rites, leaving him in her body and locking him upstairs—but sometimes she couldn't hold on, and he would find himself suddenly in his own body again in some far-off, horrible, and perhaps unknown place. Sometimes she'd get hold of him again and sometimes she couldn't. Often he was left stranded somewhere as I had found him—time and again he had to find his way home from frightful distances, getting somebody to drive the car after he found it.

The worst thing was that she was holding on to him longer and longer at a time. She wanted to be a man—to be fully human—that was why she got hold of him. She had sensed the mixture of fine-wrought brain and weak will in him. Some day she would crowd him out and disappear with his body—disappear to become a great magician like her father and leave him marooned in that female shell that wasn't even quite human. Yes, he knew about the Innsmouth blood now. There had been traffik with things from the sea—it was horrible. . . . And old Ephraim—he had known the secret, and when he grew old did a hideous thing to keep alive—he wanted to live forever—Asenath would succeed—one successful demonstration had taken place already.

As Derby muttered on I turned to look at him closely, verifying the impression of change which an earlier scrutiny had given me. Paradoxically, he seemed in better shape than usual—harder, more normally developed, and without the trace of sickly flabbiness caused by his indolent habits. It was as if he had been really active and properly exercised for the first time in his coddled life, and I judged that Asenath's force must have pushed him into unwonted channels of motion and alertness. But just now his mind was in a pitiable state; for he was mumbling wild extravagances about his wife, about black magic, about old Ephraim, and about some revelation which would convince even me. He repeated names which I recognized from bygone browsings in forbidden volumes, and at times made me shudder with a certain thread of mythological consistency—or convincing coherence—which ran through his maundering. Again and again he would pause, as if to gather courage for some final and terrible disclosure.

"Dan, Dan, don't you remember him—wild eyes and the unkempt beard that never turned white? He glared at me once, and I never forgot it. Now *she* glares that way. *And I know why!* He found it in the *Necronomicon*—the formula. I don't dare tell you the page yet, but when I do you can read and understand. Then you will know what has engulfed me. On, on, on, on—body to body to body— he means never to die. The life-glow—he knows how to break the link . . . it can flicker on a while even when the body is dead. I'll give you hints and maybe you'll guess. Listen, Dan—do you know why my wife always takes such pains with that silly backhand writing? Have you ever seen a manuscript of old Ephraim's? Do you want to know why I shivered when I saw some hasty notes Asenath had jotted down?

"Asenath—*is there such a person?* Why did they half-think there was poison in old Ephraim's stomach? Why do the Gilmans whisper about the way he shrieked—like a frightened child—when he went mad and Asenath locked him up in the padded attic room where—the other—had been? *Was it old Ephraim's soul that was locked in? Who locked in whom?* Why had he been looking for months for someone with a fine mind and a weak will?—Why did he curse that his daughter wasn't a son? Tell me, Daniel Upton—*what devilish exchange was perpetrated in the house of horror where that blasphemous monster had his trusting, weak-willed half-human child at his mercy?* Didn't he make it permanent—as she'll do in the end with me? Tell me why that thing that calls itself Asenath writes differently off guard, *so that you can't tell its script from—*"

Then the thing happened. Derby's voice was rising to a thin treble scream as he raved, when suddenly it was shut off with an almost mechanical click. I thought of those other occasions at my home when his confidences had abruptly ceased—when I had half-fancied that some obscure telepathic wave of Asenath's mental force was intervening to keep him silent. This, though, was something altogether different—and, I felt, infinitely more horrible. The face beside me was twisted almost unrecognizably for a moment, while through the whole body there passed a shivering motion—as if all the bones, organs, muscles, nerves, and glands were adjusting themselves to a radically different posture, set of stresses, and general personality.

Just where the supreme horror lay, I could not for my life tell; yet there swept over me such a swamping wave of sickness and repulsion—such a freezing, petrifying sense of utter alienage and abnormality—that my grasp of the wheel grew feeble and uncertain. The figure beside me seemed less like a life-long friend than like some monstrous intrusion from outer space—some damnable, utterly accursed focus of unknown and malign cosmic forces.

I had faltered only a moment, but before another moment was

over my companion had seized the wheel and forced me to change places with him. The dusk was now very thick, and the lights of Portland far behind, so I could not see much of his face. The blaze of his eyes, though, was phenomenal; and I knew that he must now be in that queerly energized state—so unlike his usual self—which so many people had noticed. It seemed odd and incredible that listless Edward Derby—he who could never assert himself, and who had never learned to drive—should be ordering me about and taking the wheel of my own car, yet that was precisely what had happened. He did not speak for some time, and in my inexplicable horror I was glad he did not.

In the lights of Biddeford and Saco I saw his firmly set mouth, and shivered at the blaze of his eyes. The people were right—he did look damnably like his wife and like old Ephraim when in these moods. I did not wonder that the moods were disliked—there was certainly something unnatural in them, and I felt the sinister element all the more because of the wild ravings I had been hearing. This man, for all my lifelong knowledge of Edward Pickman Derby, was a stranger—an intrusion of some sort from the black abyss.

He did not speak until we were on a dark stretch of road, and when he did his voice seemed utterly unfamiliar. It was deeper, firmer, and more decisive than I had ever known it to be; while its accent and pronunciation were altogether changed—though vaguely, remotely, and rather disturbingly recalling something I could not quite place. There was, I thought, a trace of very profound and very genuine irony in the timbre—not the flashy, meaninglessly jaunty pseudo-irony of the callow "sophisticate," which Derby had habitually affected, but something brim, basic, pervasive, and potentially evil. I marvelled at the self-possession so soon following the spell of panic-struck muttering.

"I hope you'll forget my attack back there, Upton," he was saying. "You know what my nerves are, and I guess you can excuse such things. I'm enormously grateful, of course, for this lift home.

"And you must forget, too, any crazy things I may have been saying about my wife—and about things in general. That's what comes from overstudy in a field like mine. My philosophy is full of bizarre concepts, and when the mind gets worn out it cooks up all sorts of imaginary concrete applications. I shall take a rest from now on—you probably won't see me for some time, and you needn't blame Asenath for it.

"This trip was a bit queer, but it's really very simple. There are certain Indian relics in the north woods—standing stones, and all that—which mean a good deal in folklore, and Asenath and I are following that stuff up. It was a hard search, so I seem to have gone off my head. I must send somebody for the car when I get home. A month's relaxation will put me on my feet."

I do not recall just what my own part of the conversation was, for the baffling alienage of my seatmate filled all my consciousness. With every moment my feeling of elusive cosmic horror increased, till at length I was in a virtual delirium of longing for the end of the drive. Derby did not offer to relinquish the wheel, and I was glad of the speed with which Portsmouth and Newburyport flashed by.

At the junction where the main highway runs inland and avoids Innsmouth, I was half-afraid my driver would take the bleak shore road that goes through that damnable place. He did not, however, but darted rapidly past Rowley and Ipswich toward our destination. We reached Arkham before midnight, and found the lights still on at the old Crowninshield house. Derby left the car with a hasty repetition of his thanks, and I drove home alone with a curious feeling of relief. It had been a terrible drive—all the more terrible because I could not quite tell why—and I did not regret Derby's forecast of a long absence from my company.

The next two months were full of rumours. People spoke of seeing Derby more and more in his new energized state, and Asenath was scarcely ever in to her callers. I had only one visit from Edward, when he called briefly in Asenath's car—duly reclaimed from wherever he had left it in Maine—to get some books he had lent me. He was in his new state, and paused only long enough for some evasively polite remarks. It was plain that he had nothing to discuss with me when in this condition—and I noticed that he did not even trouble to give the old three-and-two signal when ringing the doorbell. As on that evening in the car, I felt a faint, infinitely deep horror which I could not explain; so that his swift departure was a prodigious relief.

In mid-September Derby was away for a week, and some of the decadent college set talked knowingly of the matter—hinting at a meeting with a notorious cult-leader, lately expelled from England, who had established headquarters in New York. For my part I could not get that strange ride from Maine out of my head. The transformation I had witnessed had affected me profoundly, and I caught myself again and again trying to account for the thing—and for the extreme horror it had inspired in me.

But the oddest rumours were those about the sobbing in the old Crowninshield house. The voice seemed to be a woman's, and some of the younger people thought it sounded like Asenath's. It was heard only at rare intervals, and would sometimes be choked off as if by force. There was talk of an investigation, but this was dispelled one day when Asenath appeared in the streets and chatted in a sprightly way with a large number of acquaintances—apologizing for her recent absence and speaking incidentally about the nervous breakdown and hysteria of a guest from Boston. The guest was never seen, but Asenath's appearance left nothing to be said. And then someone complicated matters by whispering that the sobs had once or twice been in a man's voice.

One evening in mid-October, I heard the familiar three-and-two ring at the front door. Answering it myself, I found Edward on the steps, and saw in a moment that his personality was the old one which I had not encountered since the day of his ravings on that terrible ride from Chesuncook. His face was twitching with a mixture of odd emotions in which fear and triumph seemed to share dominion, and he looked furtively over his shoulder as I closed the door behind him.

Following me clumsily to the study, he asked for some whiskey to steady his nerves. I forbore to question him, but waited till he felt like beginning whatever he wanted to say. At length he ventured some information in a choking voice.

"Asenath has gone, Dan. We had a long talk last night while the servants were out, and I made her promise to stop preying on me. Of course I had certain—certain occult defences I never told you about. She had to give in, but got frightfully angry. Just packed up and started for New York—walked right out to catch the eight-twenty in to Boston. I suppose people will talk, but I can't help that. You needn't mention that there was any trouble—just say she's gone on a long research trip.

"She's probably going to stay with one of her horrible groups of devotees. I hope she'll go west and get a divorce—anyhow, I've made her promise to keep away and let me alone. It was horrible, Dan—she was stealing my body—crowding me out—making a prisoner of me. I lay low and pretended to let her do it, but I had to be on the watch. I could plan if I was careful, for she can't read my mind literally, or in detail. All she could read of my planning was a sort of general mood of rebellion—and she always thought I was helpless. Never thought I could get the best of her . . . but I had a spell or two that worked."

Derby looked over his shoulder and took some more whiskey.

"I paid off those damned servants this morning when they got back. They were ugly about it, and asked questions, but they went. They're her kind—Innsmouth people—and were hand and glove with her. I hope they'll let me alone—I didn't like the way they laughed when they walked away. I must get as many of Dad's old servants again as I can. I'll move back home now.

"I suppose you think I'm crazy, Dan—but Arkham history ought to hint at things that back up what I've told you—and what I'm going to tell you. You've seen one of the changes, too—in your car after I told you about Asenath that day coming home from Maine. That was when she got me—drove me out of my body. The last thing I remember was when I was all worked up trying to tell you *what that she-devil is.* Then she got me, and in a flash I was back at the house—in the library where those damned servants had me locked up—and in that cursed fiend's body . . . that isn't even human. . . .You know it was she you must have ridden home with—that preying wolf in my body—You ought to have known the difference!"

I shuddered as Derby paused. Surely, I *had* known the difference—yet could I accept an explanation as insane as this? But my distracted caller was growing even wilder.

"I had to save myself—I had to, Dan! She'd have got me for good at Hallowmass—they hold a Sabbat up there beyond Chesuncook, and the sacrifice would have clinched things. She'd have got me for good—she'd have been I, and I'd have been she—forever—too late—My body'd have been hers for good—She'd have been a man, and fully human, just as she wanted to be—I suppose she'd have put me out of the way—killed her own ex-body with me in it, damn her, *just as she did before*—just as she did, or it did before—" Edward's face was now atrociously distorted, and he bent it uncomfortably close to mine as his voice fell to a whisper.

"You must know what I hinted in the car—*that she isn't Asenath at all, but really old Ephraim himself.* I suspected it a year and a half ago, and I know it now. Her handwriting shows it when she goes off guard—sometimes she jots down a note in writing that's just like her father's manuscripts, stroke for stroke—and sometimes she says things that nobody but an old man like Ephraim could say. He changed forms with her when he felt death coming—she was the only one he could find with the right kind of brain and a weak enough will—he got her body permanently, just as she almost got mine, and then poisoned the old body he'd put her into. Haven't you seen old Ephraim's soul glaring out of that she-devil's eyes dozens of times—and out of mine when she has control of my body?"

The whisperer was panting, and paused for breath. I said nothing; and when he resumed his voice was nearer normal. This, I reflected, was a case for the asylum, but I would not be the one to send him there. Perhaps time and freedom from Asenath would do its work. I could see that he would never wish to dabble in morbid occultism again.

"I'll tell you more later—I must have a long rest now. I'll tell you something of the forbidden horrors she led me into—something of the age-old horrors that even now are festering in out-of-the-way corners with a few monstrous priests to keep them alive. Some people know things about the universe that nobody ought to know, and can do things that nobody ought to be able to do. I've been in it up to my neck, but that's the end. Today I'd burn that damned *Necronomicon* and all the rest if I were librarian at Miskatonic.

"But she can't get me now. I must get out of that accursed house as soon as I can, and settle down at home. You'll help me, I know, if I need help. Those devilish servants, you know—and if people should get too inquisitive about Asenath. You see, I can't give them her address. . . . Then there are certain groups of searchers—certain cults, you know—that might misunderstand our breaking up . . . some of them have damnably curious ideas and methods. I know you'll stand by me if anything happens—even if I have to tell you a lot that will shock you. . . ."

I had Edward stay and sleep in one of the guest-chambers that night, and in the morning he seemed calmer. We discussed certain possible arrangements for his moving back into the Derby mansion, and I hoped he would lose no time in making the change. He did not call the next evening, but I saw him frequently during the ensuing weeks. We talked as little as possible about strange and unpleasant things, but discussed the renovation of the old Derby house, and the travels which Edward promised to take with my son and me the following summer.

Of Asenath we said almost nothing, for I saw that the subject was a peculiarly disturbing one. Gossip, of course, was rife; but that was no novelty in connection with the strange menage at the old Crowninshield house. One thing I did not like was what Derby's banker let fall in an over-expansive mood at the Miskatonic Club—about the cheques Edward was sending regularly to a Moses and Abigail Sargent and a Eunice Babson in Innsmouth. That looked as if those evil-faced servants were extorting some kind of tribute from him—yet he had not mentioned the matter to me.

I wished that the summer—and my son's Harvard vacation—would come, so that we could get Edward to Europe. He was not, I soon saw, mending as rapidly as I had hoped he would; for there was something a bit hysterical in his occasional exhilaration, while his moods of fright and depression were altogether too frequent. The old Derby house was ready by December, yet Edward constantly put off moving. Though he hated and seemed to fear the Crowninshield place, he was at the same time queerly enslaved by it. He could not seem to begin dismantling things, and invented every kind of excuse to postpone action. When I pointed this out to him he appeared unaccountably frightened. His father's old butler—who was there with other reacquired servants—told me one day that Edward's occasional prowlings about the house, and especially down cellar, looked odd and unwholesome to him. I wondered if Asenath had been writing disturbing letters, but the butler said there was no mail which could have come from her.

It was about Christmas that Derby broke down one evening while calling on me. I was steering the conversation toward next summer's travels when he suddenly shrieked and leaped up from his chair with a look of shocking, uncontrollable fright—a cosmic panic and loathing such as only the nether gulfs of nightmare could bring to any sane mind.

"My brain! My brain! God, Dan—it's tugging—from beyond—knocking—clawing—that she-devil—even now—Ephraim—Kamog! Kamog!—The pit of the shoggoths—Iä! Shub-Niggurath! The Goat with a Thousand Young! . . .

"The flame—the flame—beyond body, beyond life—in the earth—oh, God! . . ."

I pulled him back to his chair and poured some wine down his throat as his frenzy sank to a dull apathy. He did not resist, but kept his lips moving as if talking to himself. Presently I realized that he was trying to talk to me, and bent my ear to his mouth to catch the feeble words.

"—Again, again—she's trying—I might have known—nothing can stop that force; not distance nor magic, nor death—it comes and comes, mostly in the night—I can't leave—it's horrible—oh, God, Dan, *if you only knew as I do just how horrible it is. . . .*"

When he had slumped down into a stupor I propped him with pillows and let normal sleep overtake him. I did not call a doctor, for I knew what would be said of his sanity, and wished to give nature a chance if I possibly could. He waked at midnight, and I put him to bed upstairs, but he was gone by morning. He had let himself quietly out of the house—and his butler, when called on the wire, said he was at home pacing about the library.

Edward went to pieces rapidly after that. He did not call again, but I went daily to see him. He would always be sitting in his library, staring at nothing and having an air of abnormal *listening*. Sometimes he talked rationally, but always on trivial topics. Any mention of his trouble, of future plans, or of Asenath would send him into a frenzy. His butler said he had frightful seizures at night, during which he might eventually do himself harm.

I had a long talk with his doctor, banker, and lawyer, and finally took the physician with two specialist colleagues to visit him. The spasms that resulted from the first questions were violent and pitiable—and that evening a closed car took his poor struggling body to the Arkham Sanitarium. I was made his guardian and called on him twice weekly—almost weeping to hear his wild shrieks, awesome whispers, and dreadful, droning repetitions of such phrases as "I had to do it—I had to do it—it'll get me—it'll get me—down there—down there in the dark—Mother! Mother! Dan! Save me—save me—"

How much hope of recovery there was, no one could say, but I tried my best to be optimistic. Edward must have a home if he emerged, so I transferred his servants to the Derby mansion, which would surely be his sane choice. What to do about the Crowninshield place with its complex arrangements and collections of utterly inexplicable objects I could not decide, so left it momentarily untouched—telling the Derby household to go over and dust the chief rooms once a week, and ordering the furnace man to have a fire on those days.

The final nightmare came before Candlemas—heralded, in cruel irony, by a false gleam of hope. One morning late in January the sanitarium telephoned to report that Edward's reason had suddenly come back. His continuous memory, they said, was badly impaired; but sanity itself was certain. Of course he must remain some time for observation, but there could be little doubt of the outcome. All going well, he would surely be free in a week.

I hastened over in a flood of delight, but stood bewildered when a nurse took me to Edward's room. The patient rose to greet me, extending his hand with a polite smile; but I saw in an instant that he bore the strangely energized personality which had seemed so foreign to his own nature—the competent personality I had found so vaguely horrible, and which Edward himself had once vowed was the intruding soul of his wife. There was the same blazing vision—so like Asenath's and old Ephraims'—and the same firm mouth; and when he spoke I could sense the same grim, pervasive irony in his voice—the deep irony so redolent of potential evil. This was the person who had driven my car through the night five months before—the person I had not seen since that brief call when he had forgotten the oldtime doorbell signal and stirred such nebulous fears in me—and now he filled me with the same dim feeling of blasphemous alienage and ineffable cosmic hideousness.

He spoke affably of arrangements for release—and there was nothing for me to do but assent, despite some remarkable gaps in his recent memories. Yet I felt that something was terribly, inexplicably wrong and abnormal. There were horrors in this thing that I could not reach. This was a sane person—but was it indeed the Edward Derby I had known? If not, who or what was it—and where was Edward? Ought it to be free or confined—or ought it to be extirpated from the face of the earth? There was a hint of the abysmally sardonic in everything the creature said—the Asenath-like eyes lent a special and baffling mockery to certain words about the early liberty earned by an *especially close confinement*! I must have behaved very awkwardly, and was glad to beat a retreat.

All that day and the next I racked my brain over the problem. What had happened? What sort of mind looked out through those alien eyes in Edward's face? I could think of nothing but this dimly terrible enigma, and gave up all efforts to perform my usual work. The second morning the hospital called up to say that the recovered patient was unchanged, and by evening I was close to a nervous collapse—a state I admit, though others will vow it coloured my subsequent vision. I have nothing to say on this point except that no madness of mine could account for *all* the evidence.

V

It was in the night—after that second evening—that stark, utter horror burst over me and weighted my spirit with a black, clutching panic from which it can never shake free. It began with a telephone call just before midnight. I was the only one up, and sleepily took down the receiver in the library. No one seemed to be on the wire, and I was about to hang up and go to bed when my ear caught a very faint suspicion of sound at the other end. Was someone trying under great difficulties to talk? As I listened I thought I heard a sort of half-liquid bubbling noise—"glub . . . glub . . . glub"—which had an odd suggestion of inarticulate, unintelligible word and syllable divisions. I called "Who is it?" But the only answer was "glub . . . glub . . . glub-glub." I could only assume that the noise was mechanical; but fancying that it might be a case of a broken instrument able to receive but not to send, I added, "I can't hear you. Better hang up and try Information." Immediately I heard the receiver go on the hook at the other end.

This, I say, was just about midnight. When the call was traced afterward it was found to come from the old Crowninshield house, though it was fully half a week from the housemaid's day to be there. I shall only hint what was found at that house—the upheaval in a remote cellar storeroom, the tracks, the dirt, the hastily rifled wardrobe, the baffling marks on the telephone, the clumsily used sta-

tionery, and the detestable stench lingering over everything. The police, poor fools, have their smug little theories, and are still searching
for those sinister discharged servants—who have dropped out of sight
amidst the present furore. They speak of a ghoulish revenge for
things that were done, and say I was included because I was Edward's
best friend and adviser.

Idiots! Do they fancy those brutish clowns could have forged that
handwriting? Do they fancy they could have brought what later
came? Are they blind to the changes in that body that was Edward's?
As for me, *I now believe all that Edward Derby ever told me.* There
are horrors beyond life's edge that we do not suspect, and once in a
while man's evil prying calls them just within our range. Ephraim—
Asenath—that devil called them in, and they engulfed Edward as
they are engulfing me.

Can I be sure that I am safe? Those powers survive the life of the
physical form. The next day—in the afternoon, when I pulled out of
my prostration and was able to walk and talk coherently—I went to
the madhouse and shot him dead for Edward's and the world's sake,
but can I be sure till he is cremated? They are keeping the body for
some silly autopsies by different doctors—but I say he must be cremated. *He must be cremated—he who was not Edward Derby when
I shot him.* I shall go mad if he is not, for I may be the next. But my
will is not weak—and I shall not let it be undermined by the terrors
I know are seething around it. One life—Ephraim, Asenath, and
Edward—who now? I *will not* be driven out of my body . . . I *will not*
change souls with that bullet-ridden lich in the madhouse!

But let me try to tell coherently of that final horror. I will not
speak of what the police persistently ignored—the tales of that
dwarfed, grotesque, malodorous thing met by at least three wayfarers
in High Street just before two o'clock, and the nature of the single
footprints in certain places. I will say only that just about two the
doorbell and knocker waked me—doorbell and knocker both, plied
alternately and uncertainly in a kind of weak desperation, *and each
trying to keep Edward's old signal of three-and-two strokes.*

Roused from sound sleep, my mind leaped into a turmoil. Derby at
the door—and remembering the old code! That new personality had
not remembered it . . . was Edward suddenly back in his rightful
state? Why was he here in such evident stress and haste? Had he been
released ahead of time, or had he escaped? Perhaps, I thought as I
flung on a robe and bounded downstairs, his return to his own self
had brought raving and violence, revoking his discharge and driving
him to a desperate dash for freedom. Whatever had happened, he was
good old Edward again, and I would help him!

When I opened the door into the elm-arched blackness a gust of insufferably foetid wind almost flung me prostrate. I choked in nausea, and for a second scarcely saw the dwarfed, humped figure on the steps. The summons had been Edward's, but who was this foul, stunted parody? Where had Edward had time to go? His ring had sounded only a second before the door opened.

The caller had on one of Edward's overcoats—its bottom almost touching the ground, and its sleeves rolled back yet still covering the hands. On the head was a slouch hat pulled low, while a black silk muffler concealed the face. As I stepped unsteadily forward, the figure made a semi-liquid sound like that I had heard over the telephone—"glub . . . glub . . ."—and thrust at me a large, closely written paper impaled on the end of a long pencil. Still reeling from the morbid and unaccountable foetor, I seized the paper and tried to read it in the light from the doorway.

Beyond question, it was in Edward's script. But why had he written when he was close enough to ring—and why was the script so awkward, coarse and shaky? I could make out nothing in the dim half light, so edged back into the hall, the dwarf figure clumping mechanically after but pausing on the inner door's threshold. The odour of this singular messenger was really appalling, and I hoped (not in vain, thank God!) that my wife would not wake and confront it.

Then, as I read the paper, I felt my knees give under me and my vision go black. I was lying on the floor when I came to, that accursed sheet still clutched in my fear-rigid hand. This is what it said.

"Dan—go to the sanitarium and kill it. Exterminate it. It isn't Edward Derby any more. She got me—it's Asenath—*and she has been dead three months and a half.* I lied when I said she had gone away. I killed her. I had to. It was sudden, but we were alone and I was in my right body. I saw a candlestick and smashed her head in. She would have got me for good at Hallowmass.

"I buried her in the farther cellar storeroom under some old boxes and cleaned up all the traces. The servants suspected next morning, but they have such secrets that they dare not tell the police. I sent them off, but God knows what they—and others of the cult—will do.

"I thought for a while I was all right, and then I felt the tugging at my brain. I knew what it was—I ought to have remembered. A soul like hers—or Ephraim's—is half detached, and keeps right on after death as long as the body lasts. She was getting me—making me change bodies with her—*seizing my body and putting me in that corpse of hers buried in the cellar.*

"I knew what was coming—that's why I snapped and had to go to the asylum. Then it came—I found myself choked in the dark—in

Asenath's rotting carcass down there in the cellar under the boxes where I put it. And I knew she must be in my body at the sanitarium—permanently, for it was after Hallowmass, and the sacrifice would work even without her being there—sane, and ready for release as a menace to the world. I was desperate, *and in spite of everything I clawed my way out.*

"I'm too far gone to talk—I couldn't manage to telephone—but I can still write. I'll get fixed up somehow and bring this last word and warning. *Kill that fiend* if you value the peace and comfort of the world. *See that it is cremated.* If you don't, it will live on and on, body to body forever, and I can't tell you what it will do. Keep clear of black magic, Dan, it's the devil's business. Goodbye—you've been a great friend. Tell the police whatever they'll believe—and I'm damnably sorry to drag all this on you. I'll be at peace before long—this thing won't hold together much more. Hope you can read this. *And kill that thing—kill it.*

Yours—Ed."

It was only afterward that I read the last half of this paper, for I had fainted at the end of the third paragraph. I fainted again when I saw and smelled what cluttered up the threshold where the warm air had struck it. The messenger would not move or have consciousness any more.

The butler, tougher-fibred than I, did not faint at what met him in the hall in the morning. Instead, he telephoned the police. When they came I had been taken upstairs to bed, but the—other mass—lay where it had collapsed in the night. The men put handkerchiefs to their noses.

What they finally found inside Edward's oddly-assorted clothes was mostly liquescent horror. There were bones, too—and a crushed-in skull. Some dental work positively identified the skull as Asenath's.

The Shadow Over Innsmouth

$\dagger\!\!=\!\!\!\succ\!\!=\!\!\dagger$

During the winter of 1927–28 officials of the Federal government made a strange and secret investigation of certain conditions in the ancient Massachusetts seaport of Innsmouth. The public first learned of it in February, when a vast series of raids and arrests occurred, followed by the deliberate burning and dynamiting—under suitable precautions—of an enormous number of crumbling, worm-eaten, and supposedly empty houses along the abandoned waterfront. Uninquiring souls let this occurrence pass as one of the major clashes in a spasmodic war on liquor.

Keener news-followers, however, wondered at the prodigious number of arrests, the abnormally large force of men used in making them, and the secrecy surrounding the disposal of the prisoners. No trials, or even definite charges, were reported; nor were any of the captives seen thereafter in the regular gaols of the nation. There were vague statements about disease and concentration camps, and later about dispersal in various naval and military prisons, but nothing positive ever developed. Innsmouth itself was left almost depopulated, and it is even now only beginning to show signs of a sluggishly revived existence.

Complaints from many liberal organisations were met with long confidential discussions, and representatives were taken on trips to certain camps and prisons. As a result, these societies became surprisingly passive and reticent. Newspaper men were harder to manage, but seemed largely to cooperate with the government in the end. Only one paper—a tabloid always discounted because of its wild policy—mentioned the deep-diving submarine that discharged torpedoes downward in the marine abyss just beyond Devil Reef. That item, gathered by chance in a haunt of sailors, seemed indeed rather far-fetched; since the low, black reef lies a full mile and a half out from Innsmouth Harbour.

People around the country and in the nearby towns muttered a great deal among themselves, but said very little to the outer world. They had talked about dying and half-deserted Innsmouth for nearly a century, and nothing new could be wilder or more hideous than what they had whispered and hinted years before. Many things had taught them secretiveness, and there was no need to exert pressure on them. Besides, they really knew little; for wide salt marshes, desolate and unpeopled, kept neighbours off from Innsmouth on the landward side.

But at last I am going to defy the ban on speech about this thing. Results, I am certain, are so thorough that no public harm save a shock of repulsion could ever accrue from a hinting of what was found by those horrified raiders at Innsmouth. Besides, what was found might possibly have more than one explanation. I do not know just how much of the whole tale has been told even to me, and I have many reasons for not wishing to probe deeper. For my contact with this affair has been closer than that of any other layman, and I have carried away impressions which are yet to drive me to drastic measures.

It was I who fled frantically out of Innsmouth in the early morning hours of July 16, 1927, and whose frightened appeals for government inquiry and action brought on the whole reported episode. I was willing enough to stay mute while the affair was fresh and uncertain; but now that it is an old story, with public interest and curiosity gone, I have an odd craving to whisper about those few frightful hours in that ill-rumoured and evilly-shadowed seaport of death and blasphemous abnormality. The mere telling helps me to restore confidence in my own faculties; to reassure myself that I was not simply the first to succumb to a contagious nightmare hallucination. It helps me, too, in making up my mind regarding a certain terrible step which lies ahead of me.

I never heard of Innsmouth till the day before I saw it for the first and—so far—last time. I was celebrating my coming of age by a tour of New England—sightseeing, antiquarian, and genealogical—and had planned to go directly from ancient Newburyport to Arkham, whence my mother's family was derived. I had no car, but was travelling by train, trolley and motor-coach, always seeking the cheapest possible route. In Newburyport they told me that the steam train was the thing to take to Arkham; and it was only at the station ticket-office, when I demurred at the high fare, that I learned about Innsmouth. The stout, shrewd-faced agent, whose speech shewed him to be no local man, seemed sympathetic toward my efforts at economy, and made a suggestion that none of my other informants had offered.

"You could take that old bus, I suppose," he said with a certain hesitation, "but it ain't thought much of hereabouts. It goes through Innsmouth—you may have heard about that—and so the people don't like it. Run by an Innsmouth fellow—Joe Sargent—but never gets any custom from here, or Arkham either, I guess. Wonder it keeps running at all. I s'pose it's cheap enough, but I never see mor'n two or three people in it—nobody but those Innsmouth folks. Leaves the Square—front of Hammond's Drug Store—at 10 A.M. and 7 P.M. unless they've changed lately. Looks like a terrible rattletrap—I've never ben on it."

That was the first I ever heard of shadowed Innsmouth. Any reference to a town not shown on common maps or listed in recent guidebooks would have interested me, and the agent's odd manner of allusion roused something like real curiosity. A town able to inspire such dislike in its neighbours, I thought, must be at least rather unusual, and worthy of a tourist's attention. If it came before Arkham I would stop off there—and so I asked the agent to tell me something about it. He was very deliberate, and spoke with an air of feeling slightly superior to what he said.

"Innsmouth? Well, it's a queer kind of a town down at the mouth of the Manuxet. Used to be almost a city—quite a port before the War of 1812—but all gone to pieces in the last hundred years or so. No railroad now—B. and M. never went through, and the branch line from Rowley was given up years ago.

"More empty houses than there are people, I guess, and no business to speak of except fishing and lobstering. Everybody trades mostly either here or in Arkham or Ipswich. Once they had quite a few mills, but nothing's left now except one gold refinery running on the leanest kind of part time.

"That refinery, though, used to a big thing, and old man Marsh, who owns it, must be richer'n Croesus. Queer old duck, though, and sticks mighty close in his home. He's supposed to have developed some skin disease or deformity late in life that makes him keep out of sight. Grandson of Captain Obed Marsh, who founded the business. His mother seems to've ben some kind of foreigner—they say a South Sea islander—so everybody raised Cain when he married an Ipswich girl fifty years ago. They always do that about Innsmouth people, and folks here and hereabouts always try to cover up any Innsmouth blood they have in 'em. But Marsh's children and grandchildren look just like anyone else so far's I can see. I've had 'em pointed out to me here—though, come to think of it, the elder children don't seem to be around lately. Never saw the old man.

"And why is everybody so down on Innsmouth? Well, young fellow, you mustn't take too much stock in what people around here say. They're hard to get started, but once they do get started they never let up. They've been telling things about Innsmouth—whispering 'em, mostly—for the last hundred years, I guess, and I gather they're more scared than anything else. Some of the stories would make you laugh—about old Captain Marsh driving bargains with the devil and bringing imps out of hell to live in Innsmouth, or about some kind of devil-worship and awful sacrifices in some place near the wharves that people stumbled on around 1845 or thereabouts—but I come from Panton, Vermont, and that kind of story don't go down with me.

"You ought to hear, though, what some of the old-timers tell about the black reef off the coast—Devil Reef, they call it. It's well above water a good part of the time, and never much below it, but at that you could hardly call it an island. The story is that there's a whole legion of devils seen sometimes on that reef—sprawled about, or darting in and out of some kind of caves near the top. It's a rugged, uneven thing, a good bit over a mile out, and toward the end of shipping days sailors used to make big detours just to avoid it.

"That is, sailors that didn't hail from Innsmouth. One of the things they had against old Captain Marsh was that he was supposed to land on it sometimes at night when the tide was right. Maybe he did, for I dare say the rock formation was interesting, and it's just barely possible he was looking for pirate loot and maybe finding it; but there was talk of his dealing with demons there. Fact is, I guess on the whole it was really the Captain that gave the bad reputation to the reef.

"That was before the big epidemic of 1846, when over half the folks in Innsmouth was carried off. They never did quite figure out what the trouble was, but it was probably some foreign kind of disease brought from China or somewhere by the shipping. It surely was bad enough—there were riots over it, and all sorts of ghastly doings that I don't believe ever got outside of town—and it left the place in awful shape. Never came back—there can't be more'n 300 or 400 people living there now.

"But the real thing behind the way folks feel is simply race prejudice—and I don't say I'm blaming those that hold it. I hate those Innsmouth folks myself, and I wouldn't care to go to their town. I s'pose you know—though I can see you're a Westerner by your talk—what a lot our New England ships used to have to do with queer ports in Africa, Asia, the South Seas, and everywhere else, and what queer kinds of people they sometimes brought back with 'em. You've probably heard about the Salem man that came home with a Chinese wife, and maybe you know there's still a bunch of Fiji Islanders some-where around Cape Cod.

"Well, there must be something like that back of the Innsmouth people. The place always was badly cut off from the rest of the country by marshes and creeks, and we can't be sure about the ins and outs of the matter; but it's pretty clear that old Captain Marsh must have brought home some odd specimens when he had all three of his ships in commission back in the twenties and thirties. There certainly is a strange kind of streak in the Innsmouth folks today—I don't know how to explain it, but it sort of makes you crawl. You'll notice a little in Sargent if you take his bus. Some of 'em have queer narrow heads with flat noses and bulgy, stary eyes that never seem to shut, and their skin ain't quite right. Rough and scabby, and the sides of their necks are all shrivelled or creased up. Get bald, too, very young. The older fellows look the worst—fact is, I don't believe I've ever seen a very old chap of that kind. Guess they must die of looking in the glass! Animals hate 'em—they used to have lots of horse trouble before autos came in.

"Nobody around here or in Arkham or Ipswich will have anything to do with 'em, and they act kind of offish themselves when they come to town or when anyone tries to fish on their grounds. Queer how fish are always thick off Innsmouth Harbour when there ain't any anywhere else around—but just try to fish there yourself and see how the folks chase you off! Those people used to come here on the railroad—walking and taking the train at Rowley after the branch was dropped—but now they use that bus.

"Yes, there's a hotel in Innsmouth—called the Gilman House—but I don't believe it can amount to much. I wouldn't advise you to try it. Better stay over here and take the ten o'clock bus tomorrow morning; then you can get an evening bus there for Arkham at eight o'clock. There was a factory inspector who stopped at the Gilman a couple of years ago and he had a lot of unpleasant hints about the place. Seems they get a queer crowd there, for this fellow heard voices in other rooms—though most of 'em was empty—that gave him the shivers. It was foreign talk, he thought, but he said the bad thing about it was the kind of voice that sometimes spoke. It sounded so unnatural—slopping-like, he said—that he didn't dare undress and go to sleep. Just waited up and lit out the first thing in the morning. The talk went on most all night.

"This fellow—Casey, his name was—had a lot to say about how the Innsmouth folks watched him and seemed kind of on guard. He found the Marsh refinery a queer place—it's in an old mill on the lower falls of the Manuxet. What he said tallied up with what I'd heard. Books in bad shape, and no clear account of any kind of dealings. You know it's always ben a kind of mystery where the Marshes get the gold they refine. They've never seemed to do much buying in that line, but years ago they shipped out an enormous lot of ingots.

"Used to be talk of a queer foreign kind of jewellery that the sailors and refinery men sometimes sold on the sly, or that was seen once or twice on some of the Marsh women-folks. People allowed maybe old Captain Obed traded for it in some heathen port, especially since he always ordered stacks of glass beads and trinkets such as seafaring men used to get for native trade. Others thought and still think he'd found an old pirate cache out on Devil Reef. But here's a funny thing. The old Captain's ben dead these sixty years, and there ain't ben a good-sized ship out of the place since the Civil War; but just the same the Marshes still keep on buying a few of those native trade things—mostly glass and rubber gewgaws, they tell me. Maybe the Innsmouth folk like 'em to look at themselves—Gawd knows they've gotten to be about as bad as South Sea cannibals and Guinea savages.

"That plague of '46 must have taken off the best blood in the place. Anyway, they're a doubtful lot now, and the Marshes and other rich folks are as bad as any. As I told you, there probably ain't more'n 400 people in the whole town in spite of all the streets they say there are. I guess they're what they call 'white trash' down South—lawless and sly, and full of secret doings. They got a lot of fish and lobsters and do exporting by truck. Queer how the fish swarm right there and nowhere else.

"Nobody can ever keep track of these people, and state school officials and census men have a devil of a time. You can bet that prying strangers ain't welcome around Innsmouth. I've heard personally of more'n one business or government man that's disappeared there, and there's loose talk of one who went crazy and is out at Danvers now. They must have fixed up some awful scare for that fellow.

"That's why I wouldn't go at night if I was you. I've never ben there and have no wish to go, but I guess a daytime trip couldn't hurt you—even though the people hereabouts will advise you not to make it. If you're just sightseeing, and looking for old-time stuff, Innsmouth ought to be quite a place for you."

And so I spent part of that evening at the Newburyport Public Library looking up data about Innsmouth. When I had tried to question the natives in the shops, the lunchroom, the garages, and the fire station, I had found them even harder to get started than the ticket agent had predicted; and realised that I could not spare the time to overcome their first instinctive reticences. They had a kind of obscure suspiciousness, as if there were something amiss with anyone too much interested in Innsmouth. At the Y.M.C.A., where I was stopping, the clerk merely discouraged my going to such a dismal, decadent place; and the people at the library shewed much the same attitude. Clearly, in the eyes of the educated, Innsmouth was merely an exaggerated case of civic degeneration.

The Essex County histories on the library shelves had very little to say, except that the town was founded in 1643, noted for shipbuilding before the Revolution, a seat of great marine prosperity in the early 19th century, and later a minor factory centre using the Manuxet as power. The epidemic and riots of 1846 were very sparsely treated, as if they formed a discredit to the county.

References to decline were few, though the significance of the later record was unmistakable. After the Civil War all industrial life was confined to the Marsh Refining Company, and the marketing of gold ingots formed the only remaining bit of major commerce aside from the eternal fishing. That fishing paid less and less as the price of the commodity fell and large-scale corporations offered competition, but there was never a dearth of fish around Innsmouth Harbour. Foreigners seldom settled there, and there was some discreetly veiled evidence that a number of Poles and Portuguese who had tried it had been scattered in a peculiarly drastic fashion.

Most interesting of all was a glancing reference to the strange jewellery vaguely associated with Innsmouth. It had evidently impressed the whole countryside more than a little, for mention was made of specimens in the museum of Miskatonic University at Arkham, and in the display room of the Newburyport Historical Society. The fragmentary descriptions of these things were bald and prosaic, but they hinted to me an undercurrent of persistent strangeness. Something about them seemed so odd and provocative that I could not put them out of my mind, and despite the relative lateness of the hour I resolved to see the local sample—said to be a large, queerly-proportioned thing evidently meant for a tiara—if it could possibly be arranged.

The librarian gave me a note of introduction to the curator of the Society, a Miss Anna Tilton, who lived nearby, and after a brief explanation that ancient gentlewoman was kind enough to pilot me into the closed building, since the hour was not outrageously late. The collection was a notable one indeed, but in my present mood I had eyes for nothing but the bizarre object which glistened in a corner cupboard under the electric lights.

It took no excessive sensitiveness to beauty to make me literally gasp at the strange, unearthly splendour of the alien, opulent phantasy that rested there on a purple velvet cushion. Even now I can hardly describe what I saw, though it was clearly enough a sort of tiara, as the description had said. It was tall in front, and with a very large and curiously irregular periphery, as if designed for a head of almost freakishly elliptical outline. The material seemed to be predominantly gold, though a weird lighter lustrousness hinted at some strange alloy with an equally beautiful and scarcely identifiable metal. Its condition was almost perfect, and one could have spent hours in studying the striking and puzzlingly untraditional designs—some simply geometrical, and some plainly marine—chased or moulded in high relief on its surface with a craftsmanship of incredible skill and grace.

The longer I looked, the more the thing fascinated me; and in this fascination there was a curiously disturbing element hardly to be classified or accounted for. At first I decided that it was the queer otherworldly quality of the art which made me uneasy. All other art objects I had ever seen either belonged to some known racial or national stream, or else were consciously modernistic defiances of every recognised stream. The tiara was neither. It clearly belonged to some settled technique of infinite maturity and perfection, yet that technique was utterly remote from any—Eastern or Western, ancient or modern—which I had ever heard of or seen exemplified. It was as if the workmanship were that of another planet.

However, I soon saw that my uneasiness had a second and perhaps equally potent source residing in the pictorial and mathematical suggestion of the strange designs. The patterns all hinted of remote secrets and unimaginable abysses in time and space, and the monotonously aquatic nature of the reliefs became almost sinister. Among these reliefs were fabulous monsters of abhorrent grotesqueness and malignity—half ichthyic and half batrachian in suggestion—which one could not dissociate from a certain haunting and uncomfortable sense of pseudomemory, as if they called up some image from deep cells and tissues whose retentive functions are wholly primal and awesomely ancestral. At times I fancied that every contour of these blasphemous fish-frogs was overflowing with the ultimate quintessence of unknown and inhuman evil.

In odd contrast to the tiara's aspect was its brief and prosy history as related by Miss Tilton. It had been pawned for a ridiculous sum at a shop in State Street in 1873, by a drunken Innsmouth man shortly afterward killed in a brawl. The Society had acquired it directly from the pawnbroker, at once giving it a display worthy of its quality. It was labelled as of probable East-Indian or Indo-Chinese provenance, though the attribution was frankly tentative.

Miss Tilton, comparing all possible hypotheses regarding its origin and its presence in New England, was inclined to believe that it formed part of some exotic pirate hoard discovered by old Captain Obed Marsh. This view was surely not weakened by the insistent offers of purchase at a high price which the Marshes began to make as soon as they knew of its presence, and which they repeated to this day despite the Society's unvarying determination not to sell.

As the good lady shewed me out of the building she made it clear that the pirate theory of the Marsh fortune was a popular one among the intelligent people of the region. Her own attitude toward shadowed Innsmouth—which she had never seen—was one of disgust at a community slipping far down the cultural scale, and she assured me that the rumours of devil-worship were partly justified by a peculiar secret cult which had gained force there and engulfed all the orthodox churches.

It was called, she said, "The Esoteric Order of Dagon," and was undoubtedly a debased, quasi-pagan thing imported from the East a century before, at a time when the Innsmouth fisheries seemed to be going barren. Its persistence among a simple people was quite natural in view of the sudden and permanent return of abundantly fine fishing, and it soon came to be the greatest influence in the town, replacing Freemasonry altogether and taking up headquarters in the old Masonic Hall on New Church Green.

All this, to the pious Miss Tilton, formed an excellent reason for shunning the ancient town of decay and desolation; but to me it was merely a fresh incentive. To my architectural and historical anticipations was now added an acute anthropological zeal, and I could scarcely sleep in my small room at the "Y" as the night wore away.

II

Shortly before ten the next morning I stood with one small valise in front of Hammond's Drug Store in old Market Square waiting for the Innsmouth bus. As the hour for its arrival drew near I noticed a general drift of the loungers to other places up the street, or to the Ideal Lunch across the square. Evidently the ticket-agent had not exaggerated the dislike which local people bore toward Innsmouth and its denizens. In a few moments a small motor-coach of extreme decrepitude and dirty grey colour rattled down State Street, made a turn, and drew up at the curb beside me. I felt immediately that it was the right one; a guess which the half-legible sign on the windshield—*Arkham-Innsmouth-Newb'port*—soon verified.

There were only three passengers—dark, unkempt men of sullen visage and somewhat youthful cast—and when the vehicle stopped they clumsily shambled out and began walking up State Street in a silent, almost furtive fashion. The driver also alighted, and I watched him as he went into the drug store to make some purchase. This, I reflected, must be the Joe Sargent mentioned by the ticket-agent; and even before I noticed any details there spread over me a wave of spontaneous aversion which could be neither checked nor explained. It suddenly struck me as very natural that the local people should not wish to ride on a bus owned and driven by this man, or to visit any oftener than possible the habitat of such a man and his kinsfolk.

When the driver came out of the store I looked at him more carefully and tried to determine the source of my evil impression. He was a thin, stoop-shouldered man not much under six feet tall, dressed in shabby blue civilian clothes and wearing a frayed golf cap. His age was perhaps thirty-five, but the odd, deep creases in the sides of his neck made him seem older when one did not study his dull, expressionless face. He had a narrow head, bulging, watery-blue eyes that seemed never to wink, a flat nose, a receding forehead and chin, and singularly undeveloped ears. His long thick lip and coarse-pored, greyish cheeks seemed almost beardless except for some sparse yellow hairs that straggled and curled in irregular patches; and in places the surface seemed queerly irregular, as if peeling from some cutaneous disease. His hands were large and heavily veined, and had a very unusual greyish-blue tinge. The fingers were strikingly short in proportion to the rest of the structure, and seemed to have a tendency to curl closely into the huge palm. As he walked toward the bus I observed his peculiarly shambling gait and saw that his feet were inordinately immense. The more I studied them the more I wondered how he could buy any shoes to fit them.

A certain greasiness about the fellow increased my dislike. He was evidently given to working or lounging around the fish docks, and carried with him much of their characteristic smell. Just what foreign blood was in him I could not even guess. His oddities certainly did not look Asiatic, Polynesian, Levantine or negroid, yet I could see why the people found him alien. I myself would have thought of biological degeneration rather than alienage.

I was sorry when I saw there would be no other passengers on the bus. Somehow I did not like the idea of riding alone with this driver. But as leaving time obviously approached I conquered my qualms and followed the man aboard, extending him a dollar bill and murmuring the single word "Innsmouth." He looked curiously at me for a second as he returned forty cents change without speaking. I took a seat far behind him, but on the same side of the bus, since I wished to watch the shore during the journey.

At length the decrepit vehicle started with a jerk, and rattled noisily past the old brick buildings of State Street amidst a cloud of vapour from the exhaust. Glancing at the people on the sidewalks, I thought I detected in them a curious wish to avoid looking at the bus—or at least a wish to avoid seeming to look at it. Then we turned to the left into High Street, where the going was smoother; flying by stately old mansions of the early republic and still older colonial farmhouses, passing the Lower Green and Parker River, and finally emerging into a long, monotonous stretch of open shore country.

The day was warm and sunny, but the landscape of sand, sedge-grass, and stunted shrubbery became more and more desolate as we proceeded. Out the window I could see the blue water and the sandy line of Plum Island, and we presently drew very near the beach as our narrow road veered off from the main highway to Rowley and Ipswich. There were no visible houses, and I could tell by the state of the road that traffic was very light hereabouts. The small, weather-worn telephone poles carried only two wires. Now and then we crossed crude wooden bridges over tidal creeks that wound far inland and promoted the general isolation of the region.

Once in a while I noticed dead stumps and crumbling foundation-walls above the drifting sand, and recalled the old tradition quoted in one of the histories I had read, that this was once a fertile and thickly-settled countryside. The change, it was said, came simultaneously with the Innsmouth epidemic of 1846, and was thought by simple folk to have a dark connexion with hidden forces of evil. Actually, it was caused by the unwise cutting of woodlands near the shore, which robbed the soil of its best protection and opened the way for waves of wind-blown sand.

At last we lost sight of Plum Island and saw the vast expanse of the open Atlantic on our left. Our narrow course began to climb steeply, and I felt a singular sense of disquiet in looking at the lonely crest ahead where the rutted roadway met the sky. It was as if the bus were about to keep on its ascent, leaving the sane earth altogether and merging with the unknown arcana of upper air and cryptical sky. The smell of the sea took on ominous implications, and the silent driver's bent, rigid back and narrow head became more and more hateful. As I looked at him I saw that the back of his head was almost as hairless as his face, having only a few straggling yellow strands upon a grey scabrous surface.

Then we reached the crest and beheld the outspread valley beyond, where the Manuxet joins the sea just north of the long line of cliffs that culminate in Kingsport Head and veer off toward Cape

Ann. On the far misty horizon I could just make out the dizzy profile of the Head, topped by the queer ancient house of which so many legends are told; but for the moment all my attention was captured by the nearer panorama just below me. I had, I realised, come face to face with rumour-shadowed Innsmouth.

It was a town of wide extent and dense construction, yet one with a portentous dearth of visible life. From the tangle of chimney-pots scarcely a wisp of smoke came, and the three tall steeples loomed stark and unpainted against the seaward horizon. One of them was crumbling down at the top, and in that and another there were only black gaping holes where clock-dials should have been. The vast huddle of sagging gambrel roofs and peaked gables conveyed with offensive clearness the idea of wormy decay, and as we approached along the now descending road I could see that many roofs had wholly caved in. There were some large square Georgian houses, too, with hipped roofs, cupolas, and railed "widow's walks." These were mostly well back from the water, and one or two seemed to be in moderately sound condition. Stretching inland from among them I saw the rusted, grass-grown line of the abandoned railway, with leaning telegraph-poles now devoid of wires, and the half-obscured lines of the old carriage roads to Rowley and Ipswich.

The decay was worst close to the waterfront, though in its very midst I could spy the white belfry of a fairly well-preserved brick structure which looked like a small factory. The harbour, long clogged with sand, was enclosed by an ancient stone breakwater; on which I could begin to discern the minute forms of a few seated fishermen, and at whose end were what looked like the foundations of a bygone lighthouse. A sandy tongue had formed inside this barrier, and upon it I saw a few decrepit cabins, moored dories, and scattered lobster-pots. The only deep water seemed to be where the river poured out past the belfried structure and turned southward to join the ocean at the breakwater's end.

Here and there the ruins of wharves jutted out from the shore to end in indeterminate rottenness, those farthest south seeming the most decayed. And far out at sea, despite a high tide, I glimpsed a long, black line scarcely rising above the water yet carrying a suggestion of odd latent malignancy. This, I knew, must be Devil Reef. As I looked, a subtle, curious sense of beckoning seemed superadded to the grim repulsion; and oddly enough, I found this overtone more disturbing than the primary impression.

We met no one on the road, but presently began to pass deserted farms in varying stages of ruin. Then I noticed a few inhabited houses with rags stuffed in the broken windows and shells and dead fish lying about the littered yards. Once or twice I saw listless-looking people working in barren gardens or digging clams on the fishy-smelling beach below, and groups of dirty, simian-visaged children playing around weed-grown doorsteps. Somehow these people seemed more disquieting than the dismal buildings, for almost everyone had certain peculiarities of face and motions which I instinctively disliked without being able to define or comprehend them. For a second I thought this typical physique suggested some picture I had seen, perhaps in a book, under circumstances of particular horror or melancholy; but this pseudo-recollection passed very quickly.

As the bus reached a lower level I began to catch the steady note of a waterfall through the unnatural stillness. The leaning, unpainted houses grew thicker, lined both sides of the road, and displayed more urban tendencies than did those we were leaving behind. The panorama ahead had contracted to a street scene, and in spots I could see where a cobblestone pavement and stretches of brick sidewalk had formerly existed. All the houses were apparently deserted, and there were occasional gaps where tumbledown chimneys and cellar walls told of buildings that had collapsed. Pervading everything was the most nauseous fishy odour imaginable.

Soon cross streets and junctions began to appear; those on the left leading to shoreward realms of unpaved squalor and decay, while those on the right shewed vistas of departed grandeur. So far I had seen no people in the town, but there now came signs of a sparse habitation—curtained windows here and there, and an occasional battered motorcar at the curb. Pavement and sidewalks were increasingly well-defined, and though most of the houses were quite old—wood and brick structures of the early 19th century—they were obviously kept fit for habitation. As an amateur antiquarian I almost lost my olfactory disgust and my feeling of menace and repulsion amidst this rich, unaltered survival from the past.

But I was not to reach my destination without one very strong impression of poignantly disagreeable quality. The bus had come to a sort of open concourse or radial point with churches on two sides and the bedraggled remains of a circular green in the centre, and I was looking at a large pillared hall on the right-hand junction ahead. The structure's once white paint was now grey and peeling, and the black and gold sign on the pediment was so faded that I could only with difficulty make out the words "Esoteric Order of Dagon." This, then was the former Masonic Hall now given over to a degraded cult. As I strained to decipher this inscription my notice was distracted by the raucous tones of a cracked bell across the street, and I quickly turned to look out the window on my side of the coach.

The sound came from a squat-towered stone church of manifestly later date than most of the houses, built in a clumsy Gothic fashion and having a disproportionately high basement with shuttered windows. Though the hands of its clock were missing on the side I glimpsed, I knew that those hoarse strokes were tolling the hour of eleven. Then suddenly all thoughts of time were blotted out by an onrushing image of sharp intensity and unaccountable horror which had seized me before I knew what it really was. The door of the church basement was open, revealing a rectangle of blackness inside. And as I looked, a certain object crossed or seemed to cross that dark rectangle; burning into my brain a momentary conception of nightmare which was all the more maddening because analysis could not shew a single nightmarish quality in it.

It was a living object—the first except the driver that I had seen since entering the compact part of the town—and had I been in a steadier mood I would have found nothing whatever of terror in it. Clearly, as I realised a moment later, it was the pastor; clad in some peculiar vestments doubtless introduced since the Order of Dagon had modified the ritual of the local churches. The thing which had probably caught my first subconscious glance and supplied the touch of bizarre horror was the tall tiara he wore; an almost exact duplicate of the one Miss Tilton had shown me the previous evening. This, acting on my imagination, had supplied namelessly sinister qualities to the indeterminate face and robed, shambling form beneath it. There was not, I soon decided, any reason why I should have felt that shuddering touch of evil pseudo-memory. Was it not natural that a local mystery cult should adopt among its regimentals an unique type of head-dress made familiar to the community in some strange way—perhaps as treasure-trove?

A very thin sprinkling of repellent-looking youngish people now became visible on the sidewalks—lone individuals, and silent knots of two or three. The lower floors of the crumbling houses sometimes harboured small shops with dingy signs, and I noticed a parked truck or two as we rattled along. The sound of waterfalls became more and more distinct, and presently I saw a fairly deep river-gorge ahead, spanned by a wide, iron-railed highway bridge beyond which a large square opened out. As we clanked over the bridge I looked out on both sides and observed some factory buildings on the edge of the grassy bluff or part way down. The water far below was very abundant, and I could see two vigorous sets of falls upstream on my right and at least one downstream on my left. From this point the noise was quite deafening. Then we rolled into the large semicircular square across the river and drew up on the right-hand side in front of a tall, cupola-crowned building with remnants of yellow paint and with a half-effaced sign proclaiming it to be the Gilman House.

I was glad to get out of that bus, and at once proceeded to check my valise in the shabby hotel lobby. There was only one person in sight—an elderly man without what I had come to call the "Innsmouth look"—and I decided not to ask him any of the questions which bothered me; remembering that odd things had been noticed in this hotel. Instead, I strolled out on the square, from which the bus had already gone, and studied the scene minutely and appraisingly.

One side of the cobblestoned open space was the straight line of the river; the other was a semicircle of slant-roofed brick buildings of about the 1800 period, from which several streets radiated away to the southeast, south, and southwest. Lamps were depressingly few and small—all low-powered incandescents—and I was glad that my plans called for departure before dark, even though I knew the moon would be bright. The buildings were all in fair condition, and included perhaps a dozen shops in current operation; of which one was a grocery of the First National chain, others a dismal restaurant, a drug store, and a wholesale fish-dealer's office, and still another, at the eastward extremity of the square near the river an office of the town's only industry—the Marsh Refining Company. There were perhaps ten people visible, and four or five automobiles and motor trucks stood scattered about. I did not need to be told that this was the civic centre of Innsmouth. Eastward I could catch blue glimpses of the harbour, against which rose the decaying remains of three once beautiful Georgian steeples. And toward the shore on the opposite bank of the river I saw the white belfry surmounting what I took to be the Marsh refinery.

For some reason or other I chose to make my first inquiries at the chain grocery, whose personnel was not likely to be native to Innsmouth. I found a solitary boy of about seventeen in charge, and was pleased to note the brightness and affability which promised cheerful information. He seemed exceptionally eager to talk, and I soon gathered that he did not like the place, its fishy smell, or its furtive people. A word with any outsider was a relief to him. He hailed from Arkham, boarded with a family who came from Ipswich, and went back whenever he got a moment off. His family did not like him to work in Innsmouth, but the chain had transferred him there and he did not wish to give up his job.

There was, he said, no public library or chamber of commerce in Innsmouth, but I could probably find my way about. The street I had come down was Federal. West of that were the fine old residence streets—Broad, Washington, Lafayette, and Adams—and east of it were the shoreward slums. It was in these slums—along Main Street—that I would find the old Georgian churches, but they were all long abandoned. It would be well not to make oneself too conspicuous in such neighbourhoods—especially north of the river—since the people were sullen and hostile. Some strangers had even disappeared.

Certain spots were almost forbidden territory, as he had learned at considerable cost. One must not, for example, linger much around the Marsh refinery, or around any of the still used churches, or around the pillared Order of Dagon Hall at New Church Green. Those churches were very odd—all violently disavowed by their respective denominations elsewhere, and apparently using the queerest kind of ceremonials and clerical vestments. Their creeds were heterodox and mysterious, involving hints of certain marvellous transformations leading to bodily immortality—of a sort—on this earth. The youth's own pastor—Dr. Wallace of Asbury M. E. Church in Arkham—had gravely urged him not to join any church in Innsmouth.

As for the Innsmouth people—the youth hardly knew what to make of them. They were as furtive and seldom seen as animals that live in burrows, and one could hardly imagine how they passed the time apart from their desultory fishing. Perhaps—judging from the quantities of bootleg liquor they consumed—they lay for most of the daylight hours in an alcoholic stupor. They seemed sullenly banded together in some sort of fellowship and understanding—despising the world as if they had access to other and preferable spheres of entity. Their appearance—especially those staring, unwinking eyes which one never saw shut—was certainly shocking enough; and their voices were disgusting. It was awful to hear them chanting in their churches at night, and especially during their main festivals or revivals, which fell twice a year on April 30th and October 31st.

They were very fond of the water, and swam a great deal in both river and harbour. Swimming races out to Devil Reef were very common, and everyone in sight seemed well able to share in this arduous sport. When one came to think of it, it was generally only rather young people who were seen about in public, and of these the oldest were apt to be the most tainted-looking. When exceptions did occur, they were mostly persons with no trace of aberrancy, like the old clerk at the hotel. One wondered what became of the bulk of the older folk, and whether the "Innsmouth look" were not a strange and insidious disease-phenomenon which increased its hold as years advanced.

Only a very rare affliction, of course, could bring about such vast and radical anatomical changes in a single individual after maturity—changes involving osseous factors as basic as the shape of the skull—but then, even this aspect was no more baffling and unheard-of than the visible features of the malady as a whole. It would be hard, the youth implied, to form any real conclusions regarding such a matter; since one never came to know the natives personally no matter how long one might live in Innsmouth.

The youth was certain that many specimens even worse than the worst visible ones were kept locked indoors in some places. People sometimes heard the queerest kind of sounds. The tottering waterfront hovels north of the river were reputedly connected by hidden tunnels, being thus a veritable warren of unseen abnormalities. What kind of foreign blood—if any—these beings had, it was impossible to tell. They sometimes kept certain especially repulsive characters out of sight when government agents and others from the outside world came to town.

It would be of no use, my informant said, to ask the natives anything about the place. The only one who would talk was a very aged but normal-looking man who lived at the poorhouse on the north rim of the town and spent his time walking about or lounging around the fire station. This hoary character, Zadok Allen, was 96 years old and somewhat touched in the head, besides being the town drunkard. He was a strange, furtive creature who constantly looked over his shoulder as if afraid of something, and when sober could not be persuaded to talk at all with strangers. He was, however, unable to resist any offer of his favourite poison; and once drunk would furnish the most astonishing fragments of whispered reminiscence.

After all, though, little useful data could be gained from him; since his stories were all insane, incomplete hints of impossible marvels and horrors which could have no source save in his own disordered fancy. Nobody ever believed him, but the natives did not like him to drink and talk with strangers; and it was not always safe to be seen questioning him. It was probably from him that some of the wildest popular whispers and delusions were derived.

Several non-native residents had reported monstrous glimpses from time to time, but between old Zadok's tales and the malformed inhabitants it was no wonder such illusions were current. None of the non-natives ever stayed out late at night, there being a widespread impression that it was not wise to do so. Besides, the streets were loathsomely dark.

As for business—the abundance of fish was certainly almost uncanny, but the natives were taking less and less advantage of it. Moreover, prices were falling and competition was growing. Of course the town's real business was the refinery, whose commercial office was on the square only a few doors east of where we stood. Old Man Marsh was never seen, but sometimes went to the works in a closed, curtained car.

There were all sorts of rumours about how Marsh had come to look. He had once been a great dandy, and people said he still wore the frock-coated finery of the Edwardian age curiously adapted to certain deformities. His sons had formerly conducted the office in the square, but latterly they had been keeping out of sight a good deal and leaving the brunt of affairs to the younger generation. The sons and their sisters had come to look very queer, especially the elder ones; and it was said that their health was failing.

One of the Marsh daughters was a repellent, reptilian-looking woman who wore an excess of weird jewellery clearly of the same exotic tradition as that to which the strange tiara belonged. My informant had noticed it many times, and had heard it spoken of as coming from some secret hoard, either of pirates or of demons. The clergymen—or priests, or whatever they were called nowadays—also wore this kind of ornament as a head-dress; but one seldom caught glimpses of them. Other specimens the youth had not seen, though many were rumoured to exist around Innsmouth.

The Marshes, together with the other three gently bred families of the town—the Waites, the Gilmans, and the Eliots—were all very retiring. They lived in immense houses along Washington Street, and several were reputed to harbour in concealment certain living kinsfolk whose personal aspect forbade public view, and whose deaths had been reported and recorded.

Warning me that many of the street signs were down, the youth drew for my benefit a rough but ample and painstaking sketch map of the town's salient features. After a moment's study I felt sure that it would be of great help, and pocketed it with profuse thanks. Disliking the dinginess of the single restaurant I had seen, I bought a fair supply of cheese crackers and ginger wafers to serve as a lunch later on. My programme, I decided, would be to thread the principal streets, talk with any non-natives I might encounter, and catch the eight o'clock coach for Arkham. The town, I could see, formed a significant and exaggerated example of communal decay; but being no sociologist I would limit my serious observations to the field of architecture.

Thus I began my systematic though half-bewildered tour of Innsmouth's narrow, shadow-blighted ways. Crossing the bridge and turning toward the roar of the lower falls, I passed close to the Marsh refinery, which seemed to be oddly free from the noise of industry. This building stood on the steep river bluff near a bridge and an open confluence of streets which I took to be the earliest civic centre, displaced after the Revolution by the present Town Square.

Re-crossing the gorge on the Main Street bridge, I struck a region of utter desertion which somehow made me shudder. Collapsing huddles of gambrel roofs formed a jagged and fantastic skyline, above which rose the ghoulish, decapitated steeple of an ancient church. Some houses along Main Street were tenanted, but most were tightly boarded up. Down unpaved side streets I saw the black, gaping windows of deserted hovels, many of which leaned at perilous and incredible angles through the sinking of part of the foundations. Those windows stared so spectrally that it took courage to turn eastward toward the waterfront. Certainly, the terror of a deserted house swells in geometrical rather than arithmetical progression as houses multiply to form a city of stark desolation. The sight of such endless avenues of fishy-eyed vacancy and death, and the thought of such linked infinities of black, brooding compartments given over to cobwebs and memories and the conqueror worm, start up vestigial fears and aversions that not even the stoutest philosophy can disperse.

Fish Street was as deserted as Main, though it differed in having many brick and stone warehouses still in excellent shape. Water Street was almost its duplicate, save that there were great seaward gaps where wharves had been. Not a living thing did I see except for the scattered fishermen on the distant break-water, and not a sound did I hear save the lapping of the harbour tides and the roar of the falls in the Manuxet. The town was getting more and more on my nerves, and I looked behind me furtively as I picked my way back over the tottering Water Street bridge. The Fish Street bridge, according to the sketch, was in ruins.

North of the river there were traces of squalid life—active fish-packing houses in Water Street, smoking chimneys and patched roofs here and there, occasional sounds from indeterminate sources, and infrequent shambling forms in the dismal streets and unpaved lanes—but I seemed to find this even more oppressive than the southerly desertion. For one thing, the people were more hideous and abnormal than those near the centre of the town; so that I was several times evilly reminded of something utterly fantastic which I could not quite place. Undoubtedly the alien strain in the Innsmouth folk was stronger here than farther inland—unless, indeed, the "Innsmouth look" were a disease rather than a blood strain, in which case this district might be held to harbour the more advanced cases.

One detail that annoyed me was the distribution of the few faint sounds I heard. They ought naturally to have come wholly from the visibly inhabited houses, yet in reality were often strongest inside the most rigidly boarded-up facades. There were creakings, scurryings, and hoarse doubtful noises; and I thought uncomfortably about the hidden tunnels suggested by the grocery boy. Suddenly I found myself wondering what the voices of those denizens would be like. I had heard no speech so far in this quarter, and was unaccountably anxious not to do so.

Pausing only long enough to look at two fine but ruinous old churches at Main and Church Streets, I hastened out of that vile waterfront slum. My next logical goal was New Church Green, but somehow or other I could not bear to repass the church in whose basement I had glimpsed the inexplicably frightening form of that strangely diademed priest or pastor. Besides, the grocery youth had told me that churches, as well as the Order of Dagon Hall, were not advisable neighbourhoods for strangers.

Accordingly I kept north along Main to Martin, then turning inland, crossing Federal Street safely north of the Green, and entering the decayed patrician neighbourhood of northern Broad, Washington, Lafayette, and Adams Streets. Though these stately old avenues were ill-surfaced and unkempt, their elm-shaded dignity had not entirely departed. Mansion after mansion claimed my gaze, most of them decrepit and boarded up amidst neglected grounds, but one or two in each street shewing signs of occupancy. In Washington Street there was a row of four or five in excellent repair and with finely-tended lawns and gardens. The most sumptuous of these—with wide terraced parterres extending back the whole way to Lafayette Street—I took to be the home of Old Man Marsh, the afflicted refinery owner.

In all these streets no living thing was visible, and I wondered at the complete absence of cats and dogs from Innsmouth. Another thing which puzzled and disturbed me, even in some of the best-preserved mansions, was the tightly shuttered condition of many third-storey and attic windows. Furtiveness and secretiveness seemed universal in this hushed city of alienage and death, and I could not escape the sensation of being watched from ambush on every hand by sly, staring eyes that never shut.

I shivered as the cracked stroke of three sounded from a belfry on my left. Too well did I recall the squat church from which those notes came. Following Washington Street toward the river, I now faced a new zone of former industry and commerce; noting the ruins of a factory ahead, and seeing others, with the traces of an old railway station and covered railway bridge beyond, up the gorge on my right.

The uncertain bridge now before me was posted with a warning sign, but I took the risk and crossed again to the south bank where traces of life reappeared. Furtive, shambling creatures stared cryptically in my direction, and more normal faces eyed me coldly and curiously. Innsmouth was rapidly becoming intolerable, and I turned down Paine Street toward the Square in the hope of getting some vehicle to take me to Arkham before the still-distant starting-time of that sinister bus.

It was then that I saw the tumbledown fire station on my left, and noticed the red-faced, bushy-bearded, watery-eyed old man in nondescript rags who sat on a bench in front of it talking with a pair of unkempt but not abnormal-looking firemen. This, of course, must be Zadok Allen, the half-crazed, liquorish nonagenarian whose tales of old Innsmouth and its shadows were so hideous and incredible.

III

It must have been some imp of the perverse—or some sardonic pull from dark, hidden sources—which made me change my plans as I did. I had long before resolved to limit my observations to architecture alone, and I was even then hurrying toward the Square in an effort to get quick transportation out of this festering city of death and decay; but the sight of old Zadok Allen set up new currents in my mind and made me slacken my pace uncertainly.

I had been assured that the old man could do nothing but hint at wild, disjointed, and incredible legends, and I had been warned that the natives made it unsafe to be seen talking with him; yet the thought of this aged witness to the town's decay, with memories going back to the early days of ships and factories, was a lure that no amount of reason could make me resist. After all, the strangest and maddest of myths are often merely symbols or allegories based upon truth—and old Zadok must have seen everything which went on around Innsmouth for the last ninety years. Curiosity flared up beyond sense and caution, and in my youthful egotism I fancied I might be able to sift a nucleus of real history from the confused, extravagant outpouring I would probably extract with the aid of raw whiskey.

I knew that I could not accost him then and there, for the firemen would surely notice and object. Instead, I reflected, I would prepare by getting some bootleg liquor at a place where the grocery boy had told me it was plentiful. Then I would loaf near the fire station in apparent casualness, and fall in with old Zadok after he had started on one of his frequent rambles. The youth had said that he was very restless, seldom sitting around the station for more than an hour or two at a time.

A quart bottle of whiskey was easily, though not cheaply, obtained in the rear of a dingy variety-store just off the Square in Eliot Street. The dirty-looking fellow who waited on me had a touch of the staring "Innsmouth look," but was quite civil in his way; being perhaps used to the custom of such convivial strangers—truckmen, gold-buyers, and the like—as were occasionally in town.

Reentering the Square I saw that luck was with me; for—shuffling out of Paine Street around the corner of the Gilman House—I glimpsed nothing less than the tall, lean, tattered form of old Zadok Allen himself. In accordance with my plan, I attracted his attention by brandishing my newly-purchased bottle; and soon realised that he had begun to shuffle wistfully after me as I turned into Waite Street on my way to the most deserted region I could think of.

I was steering my course by the map the grocery boy had prepared, and was aiming for the wholly abandoned stretch of southern waterfront which I had previously visited. The only people in sight there had been the fishermen on the distant breakwater; and by going a few squares south I could get beyond the range of these, finding a pair of seats on some abandoned wharf and being free to question old Zadok unobserved for an indefinite time. Before I reached Main Street I could hear a faint and wheezy "Hey, Mister!" behind me, and I presently allowed the old man to catch up and take copious pulls from the quart bottle.

I began putting out feelers as we walked amidst the omnipresent desolation and crazily tilted ruins, but found that the aged tongue did not loosen as quickly as I had expected. At length I saw a grass-grown opening toward the sea between crumbling brick walls, with the weedy length of an earth-and-masonry wharf projecting beyond. Piles of moss-covered stones near the water promised tolerable seats, and the scene was sheltered from all possible view by a ruined warehouse on the north. Here, I thought, was the ideal place for a long secret colloquy; so I guided my companion down the lane and picked out spots to sit in among the mossy stones. The air of death and desertion was ghoulish, and the smell of fish almost insufferable; but I was resolved to let nothing deter me.

About four hours remained for conversation if I were to catch the eight o'clock coach for Arkham, and I began to dole out more liquor to the ancient tippler; meanwhile eating my own frugal lunch. In my donations I was careful not to overshoot the mark, for I did not wish Zadok's vinous garrulousness to pass into a stupor. After an hour his furtive taciturnity shewed signs of disappearing, but much to my disappointment he still sidetracked my questions about Innsmouth and its shadow-haunted past. He would babble of current topics, revealing a wide acquaintance with newspapers and a great tendency to philosophise in a sententious village fashion.

Toward the end of the second hour I feared my quart of whiskey would not be enough to produce results, and was wondering whether

I had better leave old Zadok and go back for more. Just then, however, chance made the opening which my questions had been unable to make; and the wheezing ancient's rambling took a turn that caused me to lean forward and listen alertly. My back was toward the fishy-smelling sea, but he was facing it, and something or other had caused his wandering gaze to light on the low, distant line of Devil Reef, then shewing plainly and almost fascinatingly above the waves. The sight seemed to displease him, for he began a series of weak curses which ended in a confidential whisper and a knowing leer. He bent toward me, took hold of my coat lapel, and hissed out some hints that could not be mistaken.

"Thar's whar it all begun—that cursed place of all wickedness whar the deep water starts. Gate o' hell—sheer drop daown to a bottom no soundin'-line kin tech. Ol' Cap'n Obed done it—him that faound aout more'n was good fer him in the Saouth Sea islands.

"Everybody was in a bad way them days. Trade fallin' off, mills losin' business—even the new ones—an' the best of our menfolks kilt a-privaterin' in the War of 1812 or lost with the *Elizy* brig an' the *Ranger* scow—both on 'em Gilman venters. Obed Marsh he had three ships afloat—brigantine *Columby*, brig *Hetty*, an' barque *Sumatry Queen*. He was the only one as kep' on with the East-Injy an' Pacific trade, though Esdras Martin's barkentine *Malay Bride* made a venter as late as twenty-eight.

"Never was nobody like Cap'n Obed—old limb o' Satan! Heh, heh! I kin mind him a-tellin' abaout furren parts, an' callin' all the folks stupid fer goin' to Christian meetin' an' bearin' their burdens meek an' lowly. Says they'd orter git better gods like some o' the folks in the Injies—gods as ud bring 'em good fishin' in return for their sacrifices, an' ud reely answer folks's prayers.

"Matt Eliot, his fust mate, talked a lot too, only he was agin' folks's doin' any heathen things. Told abaout an island east of Otha-heite whar they was a lot o' stone ruins older'n anybody knew anything abaout, kind o' like them on Ponape, in the Carolines, but with carvin's of faces that looked like the big statues on Easter Island. Thar was a little volcanic island near thar, too, whar they was other ruins with diff'rent carvin's—ruins all wore away like they'd ben under the sea onct, an' with picters of awful monsters all over 'em.

"Wal, Sir, Matt he says the natives araound thar had all the fish they cud ketch, an' sported bracelets an' armlets an' head rigs made aout o' a queer kind o' gold an' covered with picters o' monsters jest like the ones carved over the ruins on the little island—sorter fish-like frogs or frog-like fishes that was drawed in all kinds o' positions like they was human bein's. Nobody cud git aout o' them whar they got all the stuff, an' all the other natives wondered haow they managed to find fish in plenty even when the very next islands had lean pickin's. Matt he got to wonderin' too an' so did Cap'n Obed. Obed he notices, besides, that lots of the han'some young folks ud drop aout o' sight fer good from year to year, an' that they wan't many old folks araound. Also, he thinks some of the folks looked durned queer even for Kanakys.

"It took Obed to git the truth aout o' them heathen. I dun't know haow he done it, but he begun by tradin' fer the gold-like things they wore. Ast 'em whar they come from, an' ef they cud git more, an' finally wormed the story aout o' the old chief—Walakea, they called him. Nobody but Obed ud ever a believed the old yeller devil, but the Cap'n cud read folks like they was books. Heh, heh! Nobody never believes me naow when I tell 'em, an' I dun't s'pose you will, young feller—though come to look at ye, ye hev kind o' got them sharp-readin' eyes like Obed had."

The old man's whisper grew fainter, and I found myself shuddering at the terrible and sincere portentousness of his intonation, even though I knew his tale could be nothing but drunken phantasy.

"Wal, Sir, Obed he larnt that they's things on this arth as most folks never heerd about—an' wouldn't believe ef they did hear. It seems these Kanakys was sacrificin' heaps o' their young men an' maidens to some kind o' god-things that lived under the sea, an' gittin' all kinds o' favour in return. They met the things on the little islet with the queer ruins, an' it seems them awful picters o' frog-fish monsters was supposed to be picters o' these things. Mebbe they was the kind o' critters as got all the mermaid stories an' sech started. They had all kinds o' cities on the sea-bottom, an' this island was heaved up from thar. Seems they was some of the things alive in the stone buildin's when the island come up sudden to the surface. That's haow the Kanakys got wind they was daown thar. Made sign-talk as soon as they got over bein' skeert, an' pieced up a bargain afore long.

"Them things liked human sacrifices. Had had 'em ages afore, but lost track o' the upper world arter a time. What they done to the victims it ain't fer me to say, an' I guess Obed wa'n't none too sharp abaout askin'. But it was all right with the heathens, because they'd ben havin' a hard time an' was desp'rate abaout everything. They give a sarten number o' young folks to the sea-things twice every year—May-Eve an' Hallowe'en—reg'lar as cud be. Also give some o' the carved knick-knacks they made. What the things agreed to give in return was plenty o' fish—they druv 'em in from all over the sea—an' a few gold-like things naow an' then.

"Wal, as I says, the natives met the things on the little volcanic islet—goin' thar in canoes with the sacrifices et cet'ry, and bringin' back any of the gold-like jools as was comin' to 'em. At fust the things didn't never go onto the main island, but arter a time they come to want to. Seems they hankered arter mixin' with the folks, an' havin' j'int ceremonies on the big days—May-Eve an' Hallowe'en. Ye see, they was able to live both in an' aout o' water—what they call amphibians, I guess. The Kanakys told 'em as haow folks from the other islands might wanta wipe 'em aout ef they got wind 'o their bein' thar, but they says they dun't keer much, because they cud wipe aout the hull brood o' humans ef they was willin' to bother—that is, any as didn't hev sarten signs sech as was used onct by the lost Old Ones, whoever they was. But not wantin' to bother, they'd lay low when anybody visited the island.

"When it come to matin' with them toad-lookin' fishes, the Kanakys kind o' balked, but finally they larnt something as put a new face on the matter. Seems that human folks has got a kind o' relation to sech water-beasts—that everything alive come aout o' the water onct, an' only needs a little change to go back agin. Them things told the Kanakys that ef they mixed bloods there'd be children as ud look human at fust, but later turn more'n more like the things, till finally they'd take to the water an' jine the main lot o' things daown har. An' this is the important part, young feller—them as turned into fish things an' went into the water wouldn't never die. Them things never died excep' they was kilt violent.

"Wal, Sir, it seems by the time Obed knowed them islanders they was all full o' fish blood from them deep water things. When they got old an begun to shew it, they was kep' hid until they felt like takin' to the water an quittin' the place. Some was more teched than others, an' some never did change quite enough to take to the water; but mostly they turned out jest the way them things said. Them as was born more like the things changed arly, but them as was nearly human sometimes stayed on the island till they was past seventy, though they'd usually go daown under for trial trips afore that. Folks as had took to the water gen'rally come back a good deal to visit, so's a man ud often be a-talkin' to his own five-times-great-grandfather who'd left the dry land a couple o' hundred years or so afore.

"Everybody got aout o' the idee o' dyin'—excep' in canoe wars with the other islanders, or as sacrifices to the sea-gods daown below, or from snake-bite or plague or sharp gallopin' ailments or somethin' afore they cud take to the water—but simply looked forrad to a kind o' change that wa'n't a bit horrible arter a while. They thought what they'd got was well wuth all they'd had to give up—an' I guess Obed kind o' come to think the same hisself when he'd chewed over old

Walakea's story a bit. Walakea, though, was one of the few as hadn't got none of the fish blood—bein' of a royal line that intermarried with royal lines on other islands.

"Walakea he shewed Obed a lot o' rites an' incantations as had to do with the sea things, an' let him see some o' the folks in the village as had changed a lot from human shape. Somehaow or other, though, he never would let him see one of the reg'lar things from right aout o' the water. In the end he give him a funny kind o' thingumajig made aout o' lead or something, that he said ud bring up the fish things from any place in the water whar they might be a nest o' 'em. The idee was to drop it daown with the right kind o' prayers an' sech. Walakea allaowed as the things was scattered all over the world, so's anybody that looked abaout cud find a nest an' bring 'em up ef they was wanted.

"Matt he didn't like this business at all, an' wanted Obed shud keep away from the island; but the Cap'n was sharp fer gain, an' faound he cud git them gold-like things so cheap it ud pay him to make a specialty of 'em. Things went on that way for years, an' Obed got enough o' that gold-like stuff to make him start the refinery in Waite's old run-daown fullin' mill. He didn't dass sell the pieces like they was, for folks ud be all the time askin' questions. All the same his crews ud git a piece an' dispose of it naow and then, even though they was swore to keep quiet; an' he let his womenfolks wear some o' the pieces as was more humanlike than most.

"Wal, come abaout 'thutty-eight—when I was seven year' old— Obed he faound the island people all wiped aout between v'yages. Seems the other islanders had got wind o' what was goin' on, and had took matters into their own hands. S'pose they must a had, after all, them old magic signs as the sea things says was the only things they was afeard of. No tellin' what any o' them Kanakys will chance to git a holt of when the sea-bottom throws up some island with ruins older'n the deluge. Pious cusses, these was—they didn't leave nothin' standin' on either the main island or the little volcanic islet excep' what parts of the ruins was too big to knock daown. In some places they was little stones strewed abaout—like charms—with somethin' on 'em like what ye call a swastika naowadays. Prob'ly them was the Old Ones' signs. Folks all wiped aout, no trace o' no gold-like things, an' none o' the nearby Kanakys ud breathe a word abaout the matter. Wouldn't even admit they'd ever ben any people on that island.

"That naturally hit Obed pretty hard, seein' as his normal trade was doin' very poor. It hit the whole of Innsmouth, too, because in seafarin' days what profited the master of a ship gen'lly profited the crew proportionate. Most of the folks araound the taown took the hard times kind o' sheeplike an' resigned, but they was in bad shape because the fishin' was peterin' aout an' the mills wan't doin' none too well.

"Then's the time Obed he begun a-cursin' at the folks fer bein' dull sheep an' prayin' to a Christian heaven as didn't help 'em none. He told 'em he'd knowed o' folks as prayed to gods that give somethin' ye reely need, an' says ef a good bunch o' men ud stand by him, he cud mebbe git a holt o' sarten paowers as ud bring plenty o' fish an' quite a bit o' gold. O' course them a sarved on the *Sumatry Queen*, an' seed the island knowed what he meant, an' wa'n't none too anxious to git clost to sea-things like they'd heerd tell on, but them a didn't know what 'twas all abaout got kind o' swayed by what Obed had to say, and begun to ast him what he cud do to set 'em on the way to the faith as ud bring 'em results."

Here the old man faltered, mumbled, and lapsed into a moody and apprehensive silence; glancing nervously over his shoulder and then turning back to stare fascinatedly at the distant black reef. When I spoke to him he did not answer, so I knew I would have to let him finish the bottle. The insane yarn I was hearing interested me profoundly, for I fancied there was contained within it a sort of crude allegory based upon the strangeness of Innsmouth and elaborated by an imagination at once creative and full of scraps of exotic legend. Not for a moment did I believe that the tale had any really substantial foundation; but none the less the account held a hint of genuine terror if only because it brought in references to strange jewels clearly akin to the malign tiara I had seen at Newburyport. Perhaps the ornaments had, after all, come from some strange island; and possibly the wild stories were lies of the bygone Obed himself rather than of this antique toper.

I handed Zadok the bottle, and he drained it to the last drop. It was curious how he could stand so much whiskey, for not even a trace of thickness had come into his high, wheezy voice. He licked the nose of the bottle and slipped it into his pocket, then beginning to nod and whisper softly to himself. I bent close to catch any articulate words he might utter, and thought I saw a sardonic smile behind the stained bushy whiskers. Yes—he was really forming words, and I could grasp a fair proportion of them.

"Poor Matt—Matt he allus was agin it—tried to line up the folks on his side, an' had long talks with the preachers—no use—they run the Congregational parson aout o' taown, an' the Methodist feller quit—never did see Resolved Babcock, the Baptist parson, agin—Wrath o' Jehovy—I was a mightly little critter, but I heerd what I heerd an' seen what I seen—Dagon an' Ashtoreth—Belial an' Beelzebub—Golden Caff

an' the idols o' Canaan an' the Philistines—Babylonish abominations—
Mene, mene tekel, upharsin—."

He stopped again, and from the look in his watery blue eyes I
feared he was close to a stupor after all. But when I gently shook his
shoulder he turned on me with astonishing alertness and snapped out
some more obscure phrases.

"Dun't believe me, hey? Heh, heh, heh—then jest tell me, young
feller, why Cap'n Obed an' twenty odd other folks used to row aout to
Devil Reef in the dead o' night an' chant things so laoud ye cud hear
'em all over taown when the wind was right? Tell me that, hey? An'
tell me why Obed was allus droppin' heavy things daown into the
deep water t'other side o' the reef whar the bottom shoots daown like
a cliff lower'n ye kin saound? Tell me what he done with that funny-
shaped lead thingumajig as Walakea give him? Hey, boy? An' what
did they all haowl on May-Eve, an' agin the next Hallowe'en? An'
why'd the new church parsons—fellers as used to be sailors—wear
them queer robes an' cover theirselves with them gold-like things
Obed brung? Hey?"

The watery blue eyes were almost savage and maniacal now, and
the dirty white beard bristled electrically. Old Zadok probably saw
me shrink back, for he began to cackle evilly.

"Heh, heh, heh, heh! Beginnin' to see hey? Mebbe ye'd like to a
ben me in them days, when I seed things at night aout to sea from the
cupalo top o' my haouse. Oh, I kin tell ye' little pitchers hev big ears,
an' I wa'n't missin' nothin' o' what was gossiped abaout Cap'n Obed
an' the folks aout to the reef! Heh, heh, heh! Haow abaout the night I
took my pa's ship's glass up to the cupalo an' seed the reef a-bristlin'
thick with shapes that dove off quick soon's the moon riz? Obed an
the folks was in a dory, but them shapes dove off the far side into the
deep water an' never come up. . . . Haow'd ye like to be a little shaver
alone up in a cupalo a-watchin' *shapes as wa'n't human shapes?* . . .
Hey? Heh, heh, heh. . . ."

The old man was getting hysterical, and I began to shiver with a
nameless alarm. He laid a gnarled claw on my shoulder, and it
seemed to me that its shaking was not altogether that of mirth.

"S'pose one night ye seed somethin' heavy heaved offen Obed's
dory beyond the reef, and then learned nex' day a young feller was
missin' from home. Hey! Did anybody ever see hide or hair o' Hiram
Gilman agin. Did they? An' Nick Pierce, an' Luelly Waite, an'
Adoniram Saouthwick, an' Henry Garrison. Hey? Heh, heh, heh,
heh. . . . Shapes talkin' sign language with their hands. . . . them as
had reel hands. . . .

"Wal, Sir, that was the time Obed begun to git on his feet agin.

Folks see his three darters a-wearin' gold-like things as nobody'd never see on 'em afore, an' smoke started comin' aout o' the refin'ry chimbly. Other folks was prosp'rin', too—fish begun to swarm into the harbour fit to kill, an' heaven knows what sized cargoes we begun to ship aout to Newb'ryport, Arkham, an' Boston. 'Twas then Obed got the ol' branch railrud put through. Some Kingsport fishermen heerd abaout the ketch an' come up in sloops, but they was all lost. Nobody never see 'em agin. An' jest then our folks organised the Eso-teric Order o' Dagon, an' bought Masonic Hall offen Calvary Com-mandery for it.... Heh, heh, heh! Matt Eliot was a Mason an' agin the sellin', but he dropped aout o' sight jest then.

"Remember, I ain't sayin' Obed was set on hevin' things jest like they was on that Kanaky isle. I dun't think he aimed at fust to do no mixin', nor raise no younguns to take to the water an' turn into fishes with eternal life. He wanted them gold things, an' was willin' to pay heavy, an' I guess the others was satisfied fer a while....

"Come in 'forty-six the taown done some lookin' an' thinkin' fer itself. Too many folks missin'—too much wild preachin' at meetin' of a Sunday—too much talk abaout that reef. I guess I done a bit by tellin' Selecman Mowry what I see from the cupalo. They was a party one night as follered Obed's craowd aout to the reef, an' I heerd shots betwixt the dories. Nex' day Obed and thutty-two others was in gaol, with everybody a-wonderin' jest what was afoot and jest what charge agin 'em cud be got to holt. God, ef anybody'd look'd ahead ... cou-ple o' weeks later, when nothin' had ben throwed into the sea fer thet long...."

Zadok was shewing signs of fright and exhaustion, and I let him keep silence for a while, though glancing apprehensively at my watch. The tide had turned and was coming in now, and the sound of the waves seemed to arouse him. I was glad of that tide, for at high water the fishy smell might not be so bad. Again I strained to catch his whispers.

"That awful night ... I seed 'em. I was up in the cupalo ... hordes of 'em ... swarms of 'em ... all over the reef an' swimmin' up the harbour into the Manuxet ... God, what happened in the streets of Innsmouth that night ... they rattled our door, but pa wouldn't open ... then he clumb aout the kitchen winder with his musket to find Selecman Mowry an' see what he cud do.... Maounds o' the dead an' the dyin' ... shots and screams ... shaoutin' in Ol' Squar an' Taown Squar an' New Church Green—gaol throwed open ... — proclamation.... treason ... called it the plague when folks come in an' faound haff our people missin' ... nobody left but them as ud jine in with Obed an' them things or else keep quiet.... never heerd o' my pa no more...."

The old man was panting, and perspiring profusely. His grip on my shoulder tightened.

"Everything cleaned up in the mornin'—but they was *traces* ... Obed he kinder takes charge an' says things is goin' to be changed.... *others'll* worship with us at meetin'-time, an' sarten haouses hez got to entertain *guests*.... they wanted to mix like they done with the Kanakys, an' he fer one didn't feel baound to stop 'em. Far gone, was Obed.... jest like a crazy man on the subjeck. He says they brung us fish an' treasure, an' shud hev what they hankered after....

"Nothin' was to be diff'runt on the aoutside, only we was to keep shy o' strangers ef we knowed what was good fer us. We all hed to take the Oath o' Dagon, an' later on they was secon' an' third Oaths that some on us took. Them as ud help special, ud git special rewards—gold an' sech—No use balkin', fer they was millions of 'em down thar. They'd ruther not start risin' an' wipin' aout human-kind, but ef they was gave away an' forced to, they cud do a lot toward jest that. We didn't hev them old charms to cut 'em off like folks in the Saouth Sea did, an' them Kanakys wudn't never give away their secrets.

"Yield up enough sacrifices an' savage knick-knacks an' har-bourage in the taown when they wanted it, an' they'd let well enough alone. Wudn't bother no strangers as might bear tales aoutside—that is, withaout they got pryin'. All in the band of the faithful—Order o' Dagon—an' the children shud never die, but go back to the Mother Hydra an' Father Dagon what we all come from onct.... *Iä! Iä! Cthulhu fhtagn! Ph'nglui mglw'nafh Cthulhu R'lyeh wgah-nagl fhtaga—*"

Old Zadok was fast lapsing into stark raving, and I held my breath. Poor old soul—to what pitiful depths of hallucination had his liquors plus his hatred of the decay, alienage, and disease around him, brought that fertile, imaginative brain! He began to moan now, and tears were coursing down his channelled cheeks into the depths of his beard.

"God, what I seen senct I was fifteen year' old—*Mene, mene, tekel, upharsin!*—the folks as was missin', an' them as kilt their-selves—them as told things in Arkham or Ipswich or sech places was all called crazy, like you're a callin' me right naow—but God, what I seen—They'd a kilt me long ago fer what I know, only I'd took the fust an' secon' Oaths o' Dagon offen Obed, so was pertected unlessen a jury of 'em proved I told things knowin' an' delib'rit.... but I wudn't take the third Oath—I'd a died ruther'n take that—

"It got wuss araound Civil War time, *when children born senct 'forty-six begun to grow up*—some of 'em, that is. I was afeared—

never did no pryin' arter that awful night, an' never see one o'—
them—clost to in all my life. That is, never no full-blooded one. I
went to the war, an' ef I'd a had any guts or sense I'd a never come
back, but settled away from here. But folks wrote me things wa'n't so
bad. That, I s'pose, was because gov'munt draft men was in taown
arter 'sixty-three. Arter the war it was jest as bad agin. People begun
to fall off—mills an' shops shet daown—shippin' stopped an' the harbour choked up—railrud give up—but *they* . . . they never stopped
swimmin' in an' aout o' the river from that cursed reef o' Satan—an'
more an' more attic winders got a-boarded up, an' more an' more noises
was heerd in haouses as wa'n't s'posed to hev nobody in 'em . . .

"Folks aoutside hev their stories abaout us—s'pose you've heerd a
plenty on 'em, seein' what questions ye ast—stories abaout things
they've seed naow an' then, an' abaout that queer joolry as still
comes in from somewhars an' ain't quite all melted up—but nothin'
never gits def'nite. Nobody'll believe nothin'. They call them gold-
like things pirate loot, an' allaow the Innsmouth folks hez furren
blood or is distempered or somethin'. Besides, them that lives here
shoo off as many strangers as they kin, an' encourage the rest not
to git very cur'ous, specially raound night time. Beasts balk at the
critters—hosses wuss'n mules—but when they got autos that was all
right.

"In 'forty-six Cap'n Obed took a second wife *that nobody in the
taown never see*—some says he didn't want to, but was made to by
them as he'd called in—had three children by her—two as disappeared young, but one gal as looked like anybody else an' was eddi-
cated in Europe. Obed finally got her married off by a trick to an
Arkham feller as didn't suspect nothin'. But nobody aoutside'll hev
nothin' to do with Innsmouth folks naow. Barnabas Marsh that runs
the refin'ry naow is Obed's grandson by his fust wife—son of One-
siphorus, his eldest son, *but his mother was another o' them as
wa'n't never seed aoutdoors.*

"Right naow Barnabas is abaout changed. Can't shet his eyes no
more, an' is all aout o' shape. They say he still wears clothes, but
he'll take to the water soon. Mebbe he's tried it already—they do
sometimes go daown fer little spells afore they go daown for good.
Ain't ben seed abaout in public fer nigh on ten year'. Dun't know
haow his poor wife kin feel—she come from Ipswich, an' they nigh
lynched Barnabas when he courted her fifty odd year' ago. Obed he
died in 'seventy-eight, an' all the next gen'ration is gone naow—the
fust wife's children dead, an' the rest . . . God knows. . . ."

The sound of the incoming tide was now very insistent, and little
by little it seemed to change the old man's mood from maudlin tear-

fulness to watchful fear. He would pause now and then to renew those nervous glances over his shoulder or out toward the reef, and despite the wild absurdity of his tale, I could not help beginning to share his vague apprehensiveness. Zadok now grew shriller, and seemed to be trying to whip up his courage with louder speech.

"Hey, yew, why dun't ye say somethin'? Haow'd ye like to be livin' in a taown like this, with everything a-rottin' an' a-dyin, an' boarded-up monsters crawlin' an' bleatin' an' barkin' an' hoppin' araoun' black cellars an' attics every way ye turn? Hey? Haow'd ye like to hear the haowlin' night arter night from the churches an' Order o' Dagon Hall, *an' know what's doin' part o' the haowlin'?* Haow'd ye like to hear what comes from that awful reef every May-Eve an' Hallowmass? Hey? Think the old man's crazy, eh? Wal, Sir, *let me tell ye that ain't the wust!*"

Zadok was really screaming now, and the mad frenzy of his voice disturbed me more than I care to own.

"Curse ye, dun't set thar a-starin' at me with them eyes—I tell Obed Marsh he's in hell, an' hez got to stay thar! Heh, heh. . . . in hell, I says! Can't git me—I hain't done nothin' nor told nobody nothin'—

"Oh, yew, young feller? Wal, even ef I hain't told nobody nothin' yet, I'm a-goin' to naow! Yew jest set still an' listen to me, boy—this is what I ain't never told nobody. . . . I says I didn't get to do no pryin' arter that night—*but I faound things aout jest the same!*

"Yew want to know what the reel horror is, hey? Wal, it's this—it aint' what them fish devils *hez done, but what they're a-goin' to do!* They're a-bringin' things up aout o' whar they come from into the taown—ben doin' it fer years, an' slackenin' up lately. Them haouses north o' the river betwixt Water an' Main Streets is full of 'em—them devils *an' what they brung*—an' when they git ready. . . . I say, *when they git ready. . . .* ever hear tell of a *shoggoth*?

"Hey, d'ye hear me? I tell ye *I know what them things be—I seen 'em one night when. . . . eh-ahhh-ah! e'yahhh . . .*"

The hideous suddenness and inhuman frightfulness of the old man's shriek almost made me faint. His eyes, looking past me toward the malodorous sea, were positively starting from his head; while his face was a mask of fear worthy of Greek tragedy. His bony claw dug monstrously into my shoulder, and he made no motion as I turned my head to look at whatever he had glimpsed.

There was nothing that I could see. Only the incoming tide, with perhaps one set of ripples more local than the long-flung line of breakers. But now Zadok was shaking me, and I turned back to watch the melting of that fear-frozen face into a chaos of twitching eyelids and mumbling gums. Presently his voice came back—albeit as a trembling whisper.

"*Git aout o' here!* Git aout o' here! *They seen us*—git aout fer your life! Dun't wait fer nothin'—*they know naow*—Run fer it—quick— *aout o' this taown*—"

Another heavy wave dashed against the loosening masonry of the bygone wharf, and changed the mad ancient's whisper to another inhuman and blood-curdling scream. "*E-yaahhhh!* . . . *yhaaaaaaa!* . . .."

Before I could recover my scattered wits he had relaxed his clutch on my shoulder and dashed wildly inland toward the street, reeling northward around the ruined warehouse wall.

I glanced back at the sea, but there was nothing there. And when I reached Water Street and looked along it toward the north there was no remaining trace of Zadok Allen.

IV

I can hardly describe the mood in which I was left by this harrowing episode—an episode at once mad and pitiful, grotesque and terrifying. The grocery boy had prepared me for it, yet the reality left me none the less bewildered and disturbed. Puerile though the story was, old Zadok's insane earnestness and horror had communicated to me a mounting unrest which joined with my earlier sense of loathing for the town and its blight of intangible shadow.

Later I might sift the tale and extract some nucleus of historic allegory; just now I wished to put it out of my head. The hour had grown perilously late—my watch said 7:15, and the Arkham bus left Town Square at eight—so I tried to give my thoughts as neutral and practical a cast as possible, meanwhile walking rapidly through the deserted streets of gaping roofs and leaning houses toward the hotel where I had checked my valise and would find my bus.

Though the golden light of late afternoon gave the ancient roofs and decrepit chimneys an air of mystic loveliness and peace, I could not help glancing over my shoulder now and then. I would surely be very glad to get out of malodorous and fear-shadowed Innsmouth, and wished there were some other vehicle than the bus driven by that sinister-looking fellow Sargent. Yet I did not hurry too precipitately, for there were architectural details worth viewing at every silent corner; and I could easily, I calculated, cover the necessary distance in a half-hour.

Studying the grocery youth's map and seeking a route I had not traversed before, I chose Marsh Street instead of State for my approach to Town Square. Near the corner of Fall Street I began to see scattered groups of furtive whisperers, and when I finally reached the Square I saw that almost all the loiterers were congregated around the door of the Gilman House. It seemed as if many bulging, watery, unwinking eyes looked oddly at me as I claimed my valise in the lobby, and I hoped that none of these unpleasant creatures would be my fellow-passengers on the coach.

The bus, rather early, rattled in with three passengers somewhat before eight, and an evil-looking fellow on the sidewalk muttered a few indistinguishable words to the driver. Sargent threw out a mail-bag and a roll of newspapers, and entered the hotel; while the passengers—the same men whom I had seen arriving in Newburyport that morning—shambled to the sidewalk and exchanged some faint guttural words with a loafer in a language I could have sworn was not English. I boarded the empty coach and took the same seat I had taken before, but was hardly settled before Sargent reappeared and began mumbling in a throaty voice of peculiar repulsiveness.

I was, it appeared, in very bad luck. There had been something wrong with the engine, despite the excellent time made from Newburyport, and the bus could not complete the journey to Arkham. No, it could not possibly be repaired that night, nor was there any other way of getting transportation out of Innsmouth either to Arkham or elsewhere. Sargent was sorry, but I would have to stop over at the Gilman. Probably the clerk would make the price easy for me, but there was nothing else to do. Almost dazed by this sudden obstacle, and violently dreading the fall of night in this decaying and half-unlighted town, I left the bus and reentered the hotel lobby; where the sullen queer-looking night clerk told me I could have Room 428 on next the top floor—large, but without running water—for a dollar.

Despite what I had heard of this hotel in Newburyport, I signed the register, paid my dollar, let the clerk take my valise, and followed that sour, solitary attendant up three creaking flights of stairs past dusty corridors which seemed wholly devoid of life. My room, a dismal rear one with two windows and bare, cheap furnishings, overlooked a dingy court-yard otherwise hemmed in by low, deserted brick blocks, and commanded a view of decrepit westward-stretching roofs with a marshy countryside beyond. At the end of the corridor was a bathroom—a discouraging relique with ancient marble bowl, tin tub, faint electric light, and musty wooden panelling around all the plumbing fixtures.

It being still daylight, I descended to the Square and looked around for a dinner of some sort; noticing as I did so the strange glances I received from the unwholesome loafers. Since the grocery was closed, I was forced to patronise the restaurant I had shunned before; a stooped, narrow-headed man with staring, unwinking eyes, and a flat-nosed wench with unbelievably thick, clumsy hands being in attendance. The service was all of the counter type, and it relieved me to find that much was evidently served from cans and packages. A bowl of vegetable soup with crackers was enough for me, and I soon headed back for my cheerless room at the Gilman; getting an evening paper and a fly-specked magazine from the evil-visaged clerk at the rickety stand beside his desk.

As twilight deepened I turned on the one feeble electric bulb over the cheap, iron-framed bed, and tried as best I could to continue the reading I had begun. I felt it advisable to keep my mind wholesomely occupied, for it would not do to brood over the abnormalities of this ancient, blight-shadowed town while I was still within its borders. The insane yarn I had heard from the aged drunkard did not promise very pleasant dreams, and I felt I must keep the image of his wild, watery eyes as far as possible from my imagination.

Also, I must not dwell on what the factory inspector had told the Newburyport ticket-agent about the Gilman House and the voices of its nocturnal tenants—not on that, nor on the face beneath the tiara in the black church doorway; the face for whose horror my conscious mind could not account. It would perhaps have been easier to keep my thoughts from disturbing topics had the room not been so gruesomely musty. As it was, the lethal mustiness blended hideously with the town's general fishy odour and persistently focussed one's fancy on death and decay.

Another thing that disturbed me was the absence of a bolt on the door of my room. One had been there, as marks clearly shewed, but there were signs of recent removal. No doubt it had become out of order, like so many other things in this decrepit edifice. In my nervousness I looked around and discovered a bolt on the clothespress which seemed to be of the same size, judging from the marks, as the one formerly on the door. To gain a partial relief from the general tension I busied myself by transferring this hardware to the vacant place with the aid of a handy three-in-one device including a screw-driver which I kept on my key-ring. The bolt fitted perfectly, and I was somewhat relieved when I knew that I could shoot it firmly upon retiring. Not that I had any real apprehension of its need, but that any symbol of security was welcome in an environment of this kind. There were adequate bolts on the two lateral doors to connecting rooms, and these I proceeded to fasten.

I did not undress, but decided to read till I was sleepy and then lie down with only my coat, collar, and shoes off. Taking a pocket flash light from my valise, I placed it in my trousers, so that I could read my watch if I woke up later in the dark. Drowsiness, however, did not come; and when I stopped to analyse my thoughts I found to my disquiet that I was really unconsciously listening for some-thing—listening for something which I dreaded but could not name. That inspector's story must have worked on my imagination more deeply than I had suspected. Again I tried to read, but found that I made no progress.

After a time I seemed to hear the stairs and corridors creak at in-tervals as if with footsteps, and wondered if the other rooms were be-ginning to fill up. There were no voices, however, and it struck me that there was something subtly furtive about the creaking. I did not like it, and debated whether I had better try to sleep at all. This town had some queer people, and there had undoubtedly been several dis-appearances. Was this one of those inns where travelers were slain for their money? Surely I had no look of excessive prosperity. Or were the townsfolk really so resentful about curious visitors? Had my ob-vious sightseeing, with its frequent map-consultations, aroused un-favourable notice? It occurred to me that I must be in a highly nervous state to let a few random creakings set me off speculating in this fashion—but I regretted none the less that I was unarmed.

At length, feeling a fatigue which had nothing of drowsiness in it, I bolted the newly outfitted hall door, turned off the light, and threw myself down on the hard, uneven bed—coat, collar, shoes, and all. In the darkness every faint noise of the night seemed magnified, and a flood of doubly unpleasant thoughts swept over me. I was sorry I had put out the light, yet was too tired to rise and turn it on again. Then, after a long, dreary interval, and prefaced by a fresh creaking of stairs and corridor, there came that soft, damnably unmistakable sound which seemed like a malign fulfilment of all my apprehensions. Without the least shadow of a doubt, the lock of my door was being tried—cautiously, furtively, tentatively—with a key.

My sensations upon recognising this sign of actual peril were per-haps less rather than more tumultuous because of my previous vague fears. I had been, albeit without definite reason, instinctively on my guard—and that was to my advantage in the new and real crisis, whatever it might turn out to be. Nevertheless the change in the menace from vague premonition to immediate reality was a profound shock, and fell upon me with the force of a genuine blow. It never once occurred to me that the fumbling might be a mere mistake. Ma-lign purpose was all I could think of, and I kept deathly quiet, await-ing the would-be intruder's next move.

After a time the cautious rattling ceased, and I heard the room to the north entered with a pass key. Then the lock of the connecting door to my room was softly tried. The bolt held, of course, and I heard the floor creak as the prowler left the room. After a moment there came another soft rattling, and I knew that the room to the south of me was being entered. Again a furtive trying of a bolted connecting door, and again a receding creaking. This time the creaking went along the hall and down the stairs, so I knew that the prowler had realised the bolted condition of my doors and was giving up his attempt for a greater or lesser time, as the future would shew.

The readiness with which I fell into a plan of action proves that I must have been subconsciously fearing some menace and considering possible avenues of escape for hours. From the first I felt that the unseen fumbler meant a danger not to be met or dealt with, but only to be fled from as precipitately as possible. The one thing to do was to get out of that hotel alive as quickly as I could, and through some channel other than the front stairs and lobby.

Rising softly and throwing my flashlight on the switch, I sought to light the bulb over my bed in order to choose and pocket some belongings for a swift, valiseless flight. Nothing, however, happened; and I saw that the power had been cut off. Clearly, some cryptic, evil movement was afoot on a large scale—just what, I could not say. As I stood pondering with my hand on the now useless switch I heard a muffled creaking on the floor below, and thought I could barely distinguish voices in conversation. A moment later I felt less sure that the deeper sounds were voices, since the apparent hoarse barkings and loose-syllabled croakings bore so little resemblance to recognised human speech. Then I thought with renewed force of what the factory inspector had heard in the night in this mouldering and pestilential building.

Having filled my pockets with the flashlight's aid, I put on my hat and tiptoed to the windows to consider chances of descent. Despite the state's safety regulations there was no fire escape on this side of the hotel, and I saw that my windows commanded only a sheer three-storey drop to the cobbled courtyard. On the right and left, however, some ancient brick business blocks abutted on the hotel; their slant roofs coming up to a reasonable jumping distance from my fourth-storey level. To reach either of these lines of buildings I would have to be in a room two doors from my own—in one case on the north and in the other case on the south—and my mind instantly set to work calculating what chances I had of making the transfer.

I could not, I decided, risk an emergence into the corridor; where my footsteps would surely be heard, and where the difficulties of entering the desired room would be insuperable. My progress, if it was to be made at all, would have to be through the less solidly-built connecting doors of the rooms; the locks and bolts of which I would have to force violently, using my shoulder as a battering-ram whenever they were set against me. This, I thought, would be possible owing to the rickety nature of the house and its fixtures; but I realised I could not do it noiselessly. I would have to count on sheer speed, and the chance of getting to a window before any hostile forces became coordinated enough to open the right door toward me with a pass-key. My own outer door I reinforced by pushing the bureau against it—little by little, in order to make a minimum of sound.

I perceived that my chances were very slender, and was fully prepared for any calamity. Even getting to another roof would not solve the problem, for there would then remain the task of reaching the ground and escaping from the town. One thing in my favour was the deserted and ruinous state of the abutting buildings, and the number of skylights gaping blackly open in each row.

Gathering from the grocery boy's map that the best route out of town was southward, I glanced first at the connecting door on the south side of the room. It was designed to open in my direction, hence I saw—after drawing the bolt and finding other fastenings in place—it was not a favorable one for forcing. Accordingly abandoning it as a route, I cautiously moved the bedstead against it to hamper any attack which might be made on it later from the next room. The door on the north was hung to open away from me, and this—though a test proved it to be locked or bolted from the other side—I knew must be my route. If I could gain the roofs of the buildings in Paine Street and descend successfully to the ground level, I might perhaps dart through the courtyard and the adjacent or opposite buildings to Washington or Bates—or else emerge in Paine and edge around southward into Washington. In any case, I would aim to strike Washington somehow and get quickly out of the Town Square region. My preference would be to avoid Paine, since the fire station there might be open all night.

As I thought of these things I looked out over the squalid sea of decaying roofs below me, now brightened by the beams of a moon not much past full. On the right the black gash of the river-gorge clove the panorama; abandoned factories and railway station clinging barnacle-like to its sides. Beyond it the rusted railway and the Rowley road led off through a flat, marshy terrain dotted with islets of higher and dryer scrub-grown land. On the left the creek-threaded countryside was nearer, the narrow road to Ipswich gleaming white in the moonlight. I could not see from my side of the hotel the southward route toward Arkham which I had determined to take.

I was irresolutely speculating on when I had better attack the northward door, and on how I could least audibly manage it, when I noticed that the vague noises underfoot had given place to a fresh and heavier creaking of the stairs. A wavering flicker of light shewed through my transom, and the boards of the corridor began to groan with a ponderous load. Muffled sounds of possible vocal origin approached, and at length a firm knock came at my outer door.

For a moment I simply held my breath and waited. Eternities seemed to elapse, and the nauseous fishy odour of my environment seemed to mount suddenly and spectacularly. Then the knocking was repeated—continuously, and with growing insistence. I knew that the time for action had come, and forthwith drew the bolt of the northward connecting door, bracing myself for the task of battering it open. The knocking waxed louder, and I hoped that its volume would cover the sound of my efforts. At last beginning my attempt, I lunged again and again at the thin panelling with my left shoulder, heedless of shock or pain. The door resisted even more than I had expected, but I did not give in. And all the while the clamour at the outer door increased.

Finally the connecting door gave, but with such a crash that I knew those outside must have heard. Instantly the outside knocking became a violent battering, while keys sounded ominously in the hall doors of the rooms on both sides of me. Rushing through the newly opened connexion, I succeeded in bolting the northerly hall door before the lock could be turned; but even as I did so I heard the hall door of the third room—the one from whose window I had hoped to reach the roof below—being tried with a pass key.

For an instant I felt absolute despair, since my trapping in a chamber with no window egress seemed complete. A wave of almost abnormal horror swept over me, and invested with a terrible but unexplainable singularity the flashlight-glimpsed dust prints made by the intruder who had lately tried my door from this room. Then, with a dazed automatism which persisted despite hopelessness, I made for the next connecting door and performed the blind motion of pushing at it in an effort to get through and—granting that fastenings might be as providentially intact as in this second room—bolt the hall door beyond before the lock could be turned from outside.

Sheer fortunate chance gave me my reprieve—for the connecting door before me was not only unlocked but actually ajar. In a second I was through, and had my right knee and shoulder against a hall door which was visibly opening inward. My pressure took the opener off guard, for the thing shut as I pushed, so that I could slip the well-conditioned bolt as I had done with the other door. As I gained this respite I heard the battering at the two other doors abate, while a confused clatter came from the connecting door I had shielded with the bedstead. Evidently the bulk of my assailants had entered the southerly room and were massing in a lateral attack. But at the same moment a pass key sounded in the next door to the north, and I knew that a nearer peril was at hand.

The northward connecting door was wide open, but there was no time to think about checking the already turning lock in the hall. All I could do was to shut and bolt the open connecting door, as well as its mate on the opposite side—pushing a bedstead against the one and a bureau against the other, and moving a washstand in front of the hall door. I must, I saw, trust to such makeshift barriers to shield me till I could get out the window and on the roof of the Paine Street block. But even in this acute moment my chief horror was something apart from the immediate weakness of my defences. I was shuddering because not one of my pursuers, despite some hideous pantings, gruntings, and subdued barkings at odd intervals, was uttering an unmuffled or intelligible vocal sound.

As I moved the furniture and rushed toward the windows I heard a frightful scurrying along the corridor toward the room north of me, and perceived that the southward battering had ceased. Plainly, most of my opponents were about to concentrate against the feeble connecting door which they knew must open directly on me. Outside, the moon played on the ridgepole of the block below, and I saw that the jump would be desperately hazardous because of the steep surface on which I must land.

Surveying the conditions, I chose the more southerly of the two windows as my avenue of escape; planning to land on the inner slope of the roof and make for the nearest skylight. Once inside one of the decrepit brick structures I would have to reckon with pursuit; but I hoped to descend and dodge in and out of yawning doorways along the shadowed courtyard, eventually getting to Washington Street and slipping out of town toward the south.

The clatter at the northerly connecting door was now terrific, and I saw that the weak panelling was beginning to splinter. Obviously, the besiegers had brought some ponderous object into play as a battering-ram. The bedstead, however, still held firm; so that I had at least a faint chance of making good my escape. As I opened the window I noticed that it was flanked by heavy velour draperies suspended from a pole by brass rings, and also that there was a large projecting catch for the shutters on the exterior. Seeing a possible means of avoiding the dangerous jump, I yanked at the hangings and brought them down, pole and all; then quickly hooking two of the rings in the shutter catch and flinging the drapery outside. The heavy folds reached fully to the abutting roof, and I saw that the rings and catch would be likely to bear my weight. So, climbing out of the window and down the improvised rope ladder, I left behind me for ever the morbid and horror-infested fabric of the Gilman House.

I landed safely on the loose slates of the steep roof, and succeeded in gaining the gaping black skylight without a slip. Glancing up at the window I had left, I observed it was still dark, though far across the crumbling chimneys to the north I could see lights ominously blazing in the Order of Dagon Hall, the Baptist church, and the Congregational church which I recalled so shiveringly. There had seemed to be no one in the courtyard below, and I hoped there would be a chance to get away before the spreading of a general alarm. Flashing my pocket lamp into the skylight, I saw that there were no steps down. The distance was slight, however, so I clambered over the brink and dropped; striking a dusty floor littered with crumbling boxes and barrels.

The place was ghoulish-looking, but I was past minding such impressions and made at once for the staircase revealed by my flashlight—after a hasty glance at my watch, which shewed the hour to be 2 A.M. The steps creaked, but seemed tolerably sound; and I raced down past a barnlike second storey to the ground floor. The desolation was complete, and only echoes answered my footfalls. At length I reached the lower hall at one end of which I saw a faint luminous rectangle marking the ruined Paine Street doorway. Heading the other way, I found the back door also open; and darted out and down five stone steps to the grass-grown cobblestones of the courtyard.

The moonbeams did not reach down here, but I could just see my way about without using the flashlight. Some of the windows on the Gilman House side were faintly glowing, and I thought I heard confused sounds within. Walking softly over to the Washington Street side I perceived several open doorways, and chose the nearest as my route out. The hallway inside was black, and when I reached the opposite end I saw that the street door was wedged immovably shut. Resolved to try another building, I groped my way back toward the courtyard, but stopped short when close to the doorway.

For out of an opened door in the Gilman House a large crowd of doubtful shapes was pouring—lanterns bobbing in the darkness, and horrible croaking voices exchanging low cries in what was certainly not English. The figures moved uncertainly, and I realised to my relief that they did not know where I had gone; but for all that they sent a shiver of horror through my frame. Their features were indistinguishable, but their crouching, shambling gait was abominably repellent. And worst of all, I perceived that one figure was strangely robed, and unmistakably surmounted by a tall tiara of a design altogether too familiar. As the figures spread throughout the courtyard, I felt my fears increase. Suppose I could find no egress from this building on the street side? The fishy odour was detestable, and I wondered I could stand it without fainting. Again groping toward the street, I opened a door off the hall and came upon an empty room with closely shuttered but sashless windows. Fumbling in the rays of my flashlight, I found I could open the shutters; and in another moment had climbed outside and was carefully closing the aperture in its original manner.

I was now in Washington Street, and for the moment saw no living thing nor any light save that of the moon. From several directions in the distance, however, I could hear the sound of hoarse voices, of footsteps, and of a curious kind of pattering which did not sound quite like footsteps. Plainly I had no time to lose. The points of the compass were clear to me, and I was glad that all the street lights were turned off, as is often the custom on strongly moonlit nights in unprosperous rural regions. Some of the sounds came from the south, yet I retained my design of escaping in that direction. There would, I knew, be plenty of deserted doorways to shelter me in case I met any person or group who looked like pursuers.

I walked rapidly, softly, and close to the ruined houses. While hatless and dishevelled after my arduous climb, I did not look especially noticeable; and stood a good chance of passing unheeded if forced to encounter any casual wayfarer. At Bates Street I drew into a yawning vestibule while two shambling figures crossed in front of me, but was soon on my way again and approaching the open space where Eliot Street obliquely crosses Washington at the intersection of South. Though I had never seen this space, it had looked dangerous to me on the grocery youth's map; since the moonlight would have free play there. There was no use trying to evade it, for any alternative course would involve detours of possibly disastrous visibility and delaying effect. The only thing to do was to cross it boldly and openly; imitating the typical shamble of the Innsmouth folk as best I could, and trusting that no one—or at least no pursuer of mine—would be there.

Just how fully the pursuit was organised—and indeed, just what its purpose might be—I could form no idea. There seemed to be unusual activity in the town, but I judged that the news of my escape from the Gilman had not yet spread. I would, or course, soon have to shift from Washington to some other southward street; for that party from the hotel would doubtless be after me. I must have left dust prints in that last old building, revealing how I had gained the street.

The open space was, as I had expected, strongly moonlit; and I saw the remains of a parklike, iron-railed green in its centre. Fortunately no one was about, though a curious sort of buzz or roar seemed to be increasing in the direction of Town Square. South Street was very wide, leading directly down a slight declivity to the waterfront and commanding a long view out at sea; and I hoped that no one would be glancing up it from afar as I crossed in the bright moonlight.

My progress was unimpeded, and no fresh sound arose to hint that I had been spied. Glancing about me, I involuntarily let my pace slacken for a second to take in the sight of the sea, gorgeous in the burning moonlight at the street's end. Far out beyond the breakwater was the dim, dark line of Devil Reef, and as I glimpsed it I could not help thinking of all the hideous legends I had heard in the last thirty-four hours—legends which portrayed this ragged rock as a veritable gateway to realms of unfathomed horror and inconceivable abnormality.

Then, without warning, I saw the intermittent flashes of light on the distant reef. They were definite and unmistakable, and awaked in my mind a blind horror beyond all rational proportion. My muscles tightened for panic flight, held in only by a certain unconscious caution and half-hypnotic fascination. And to make matters worse, there now flashed forth from the lofty cupola of the Gilman House, which loomed up to the northeast behind me, a series of analogous though differently spaced gleams which could be nothing less than an answering signal.

Controlling my muscles, and realising afresh how plainly visible I was, I resumed my brisker and feignedly shambling pace; though keeping my eyes on that hellish and ominous reef as long as the opening of South Street gave me a seaward view. What the whole proceeding meant, I could not imagine; unless it involved some strange rite connected with Devil Reef, or unless some party had landed from a ship on that sinister rock. I now bent to the left around the ruinous green; still gazing toward the ocean as it blazed in the spectral summer moonlight, and watching the cryptical flashing of those nameless, unexplainable beacons.

It was then that the most horrible impression of all was borne in upon me—the impression which destroyed my last vestige of self-control and sent me running frantically southward past the yawning black doorways and fishily staring windows of that deserted nightmare street. For at a closer glance I saw that the moonlit waters between the reef and the shore were far from empty. They were alive with a teeming horde of shapes swimming inward toward the town; and even at my vast distance and in my single moment of perception I could tell that the bobbing heads and flailing arms were alien and aberrant in a way scarcely to be expressed or consciously formulated.

My frantic running ceased before I had covered a block, for at my left I began to hear something like the hue and cry of organised pursuit. There were footsteps and guttural sounds, and a rattling motor wheezed south along Federal Street. In a second all my plans were utterly changed—for if the southward highway were blocked ahead of me, I must clearly find another egress from Innsmouth. I paused and drew into a gaping doorway, reflection—how lucky I was to have left the moonlit open space before those pursuers came down the parallel street.

A second reflection was less comforting. Since the pursuit was down another street, it was plain that the party was not following me directly. It had not seen me, but was simply obeying a general plan of cutting off my escape. This, however, implied that all roads leading out of Innsmouth were similarly patrolled; for the people could not have known what route I intended to take. If this were so, I would have to make my retreat across country away from any road; but how could I do that in view of the marshy and creek-riddled nature of all the surrounding region? For a moment my brain reeled—both from sheer hopelessness and from a rapid increase in the omnipresent fishy odour.

Then I thought of the abandoned railway to Rowley, whose solid line of ballasted, weed-grown earth still stretched off to the northwest from the crumbling station on the edge of the river-gorge. There was just a chance that the townsfolk would not think of that; since its briar-choked desertion made it half-impassable, and the unlikeliest of all avenues for a fugitive to choose. I had seen it clearly from my hotel window, and knew about how it lay. Most of its earlier length was uncomfortably visible from the Rowley road, and from high places in the town itself; but one could perhaps crawl inconspicuously through the undergrowth. At any rate, it would form my only chance of deliverance, and there was nothing to do but try it.

Drawing inside the hall of my deserted shelter, I once more consulted the grocery boy's map with the aid of the flashlight. The immediate problem was how to reach the ancient railway; and I now saw that the safest course was ahead to Babson Street, then west to Lafayette—there edging around but not crossing an open space homologous to the one I had traversed—and subsequently back northward and westward in a zigzagging line through Lafayette, Bates, Adams, and Bank Streets—the latter skirting the river gorge—to the abandoned and dilapidated station I had seen from my window. My reason for going ahead to Babson was that I wished neither to recross the earlier open space nor to begin my westward course along a cross street as broad as South.

Starting once more, I crossed the street to the right-hand side in order to edge around into Babson as inconspicuously as possible. Noises still continued in Federal Street, and as I glanced behind me I thought I saw a gleam of light near the building through which I had escaped. Anxious to leave Washington Street, I broke into a quiet dog-trot, trusting to luck not to encounter any observing eye. Next the corner of Babson Street I saw to my alarm that one of the houses was still inhabited, as attested by curtains at the window; but there were no lights within, and I passed it without disaster.

In Babson Street, which crossed Federal and might thus reveal me to the searchers, I clung as closely as possible to the sagging, uneven buildings; twice pausing in a doorway as the noises behind me momentarily increased. The open space ahead shone wide and desolate under the moon, but my route would not force me to cross it. During my second pause I began to detect a fresh distribution of vague sounds; and upon looking cautiously out from cover beheld a motor car darting across the open space, bound outward along Eliot Street, which there intersects both Babson and Lafayette.

As I watched—choked by a sudden rise in the fishy odour after a short abatement—I saw a band of uncouth, crouching shapes loping and shambling in the same direction; and knew that this must be the party guarding the Ipswich road, since that highway forms an extension of Eliot Street. Two of the figures I glimpsed were in voluminous robes, and one wore a peaked diadem which glistened whitely in the moonlight. The gait of this figure was so odd that it sent a chill through me—for it seemed to me the creature was almost hopping.

When the last of the band was out of sight I resumed my progress; darting around the corner into Lafayette Street, and crossing Eliot very hurriedly lest stragglers of the party be still advancing along that thoroughfare. I did hear some croaking and clattering sounds far off toward Town Square, but accomplished the passage without disaster. My greatest dread was in re-crossing broad and moonlit South Street—with its seaward view—and I had to nerve myself for the ordeal. Someone might easily be looking, and possible Eliot Street stragglers could not fail to glimpse me from either of two points. At the last moment I decided I had better slacken my trot and make the crossing as before in the shambling gait of an average Innsmouth native.

When the view of the water again opened out—this time on my right—I was half-determined not to look at it at all. I could not, however, resist; but cast a sidelong glance as I carefully and imitatively shambled toward the protecting shadows ahead. There was no ship visible, as I had half-expected there would be. Instead, the first thing which caught my eye was a small rowboat pulling in toward the abandoned wharves and laden with some bulky, tarpaulin-covered object. Its rowers, though distantly and indistinctly seen, were of an especially repellent aspect. Several swimmers were still discernible; while on the far black reef I could see a faint, steady glow unlike the winking beacon visible before, and of a curious colour which I could not precisely identify. Above the slant roofs ahead and to the right there loomed the tall cupola of the Gilman House, but it was completely dark. The fishy odour, dispelled for a moment by some merciful breeze, now closed in again with maddening intensity.

I had not quite crossed the street when I heard a muttering band advancing along Washington from the north. As they reached the broad open space where I had had my first disquieting glimpse of the moonlit water I could see them plainly only a block away—and was horrified by the bestial abnormality of their faces and the doglike sub-humanness of their crouching gait. One man moved in a positively simian way, with long arms frequently touching the ground; while another figure—robed and tiaraed—seemed to progress in an almost hopping fashion. I judged this party to be the one I had seen in the Gilman's courtyard—the one, therefore, most closely on my trail. As some of the figures turned to look in my direction I was transfixed with fright, yet managed to preserve the casual, shambling gait I had assumed. To this day I do not know whether they saw me or not. If they did, my stratagem must have deceived them, for they passed on across the moonlit space without varying their course—meanwhile croaking and jabbering in some hateful guttural patois I could not identify.

Once more in shadow, I resumed my former dog-trot past the leaning and decrepit houses that stared blankly into the night. Having crossed to the western sidewalk I rounded the nearest corner into Bates Street, where I kept close to the buildings on the southern side. I passed two houses shewing signs of habitation, one of which had faint lights in upper rooms, yet met with no obstacle. As I turned into Adams Street I felt measurably safer, but received a shock when a man reeled out of a black doorway directly in front of me. He proved, however, too hopelessly drunk to be a menace; so that I reached the dismal ruins of the Bank Street warehouses in safety.

No one was stirring in that dead street beside the river-gorge, and the roar of the waterfalls quite drowned my footsteps. It was a long dog-trot to the ruined station, and the great brick warehouse walls around me seemed somehow more terrifying than the fronts of private houses. At last I saw the ancient arcaded station—or what was left of it—and made directly for the tracks that started from its farther end.

The rails were rusty but mainly intact, and not more than half the ties had rotted away. Walking or running on such a surface was very difficult; but I did my best, and on the whole made very fair time. For some distance the line kept on along the gorge's brink, but at length I reached the long covered bridge where it crossed the chasm at a dizzy height. The condition of this bridge would determine my next step. If humanly possible, I would use it; if not, I would have to risk more street wandering and take the nearest intact highway bridge.

The vast, barnlike length of the old bridge gleamed spectrally in the moonlight, and I saw that the ties were safe for at least a few feet within. Entering, I began to use my flashlight, and was almost knocked down by the cloud of bats that flapped past me. About half-way across there was a perilous gap in the ties which I feared for a moment would halt me; but in the end I risked a desperate jump which fortunately succeeded.

I was glad to see the moonlight again when I emerged from that macabre tunnel. The old tracks crossed River Street at grade, and at once veered off into a region increasingly rural and with less and less of Innsmouth's abhorrent fishy odour. Here the dense growth of weeds and briers hindered me and cruelly tore my clothes, but I was none the less glad that they were there to give me concealment in case of peril. I knew that much of my route must be visible from the Rowley road.

The marshy region began very shortly, with the single track on a low, grassy embankment where the weedy growth was some-what thinner. Then came a sort of island of higher ground, where the line passed through a shallow open cut choked with bushes and brambles. I was very glad of this partial shelter, since at this point the Rowley road was uncomfortably near according to my win-dow view. At the end of the cut it would cross the track and swerve off to a safer distance; but meanwhile I must be exceedingly careful. I was by this time thankfully certain that the railway itself was not patrolled.

Just before entering the cut I glanced behind me, but saw no pur-suer. The ancient spires and roofs of decaying Innsmouth gleamed lovely and ethereal in the magic yellow moonlight, and I thought of how they must have looked in the old days before the shadow fell. Then, as my gaze circled inland from the town, something less tranquil arrested my notice and held me immobile for a second.

What I saw—or fancied I saw—was a disturbing suggestion of un-dulant motion far to the south; a suggestion which made me con-clude that a very large horde must be pouring out of the city along the level Ipswich road. The distance was great, and I could distinguish nothing in detail; but I did not at all like the look of that moving column. It undulated too much, and glistened too brightly in the rays of the now westering moon. There was a suggestion of sound, too, though the wind was blowing the other way—a suggestion of bestial scraping and bellowing even worse than the muttering of the parties I had lately overheard.

All sorts of unpleasant conjectures crossed my mind. I thought of those very extreme Innsmouth types said to be hidden in crumbling, centuried warrens near the waterfront. I thought, too, of those nameless swimmers I had seen. Counting the parties so far glimpsed, as well as those presumably covering other roads, the number of my pursuers must be strangely large for a town as depopulated as Innsmouth.

Whence could come the dense personnel of such a column as I now beheld? Did those ancient, unplumbed warrens teem with a twisted, uncatalogued, and unsuspected life? Or had some unseen ship indeed landed a legion of unknown outsiders on that hellish reef? Who were they? Why were they here? And if such a column of them was scouring the Ipswich road, would the patrols on the other roads be likewise augmented?

I had entered the brush-grown cut and was struggling along at a very slow pace when that damnable fishy odour again waxed dominant. Had the wind suddenly changed eastward, so that it blew in from the sea and over the town? It must have, I concluded, since I now began to hear shocking guttural murmurs from that hitherto silent direction. There was another sound, too—a kind of wholesale, colossal flopping or pattering which somehow called up images of the most detestable sort. It made me think illogically of that unpleasantly undulating column on the far-off Ipswich road.

And then both stench and sounds grew stronger, so that I paused shivering and grateful for the cut's protection. It was here, I recalled, that the Rowley road drew so close to the old railway before crossing westward and diverging. Something was coming along that road, and I must lie low till its passage and vanishment in the distance. Thank heaven these creatures employed no dogs for tracking—though perhaps that would have been impossible amidst the omnipresent regional odour. Crouched in the bushes of that sandy cleft I felt reasonably safe, even though I knew the searchers would have to cross the track in front of me not much more than a hundred yards away. I would be able to see them, but they could not, except by a malign miracle, see me.

All at once I began dreading to look at them as they passed. I saw the close moonlit space where they would surge by, and had curious thoughts about the irredeemable pollution of that space. They would perhaps be the worst of all Innsmouth types—something one would not care to remember.

The stench waxed overpowering, and the noises swelled to a bestial babel of croaking, baying and barking without the least suggestion of human speech. Were these indeed the voices of my pursuers? Did they have dogs after all? So far I had seen none of the lower animals in Innsmouth. That flopping or pattering was monstrous—I could not look upon the degenerate creatures responsible for it. I would keep my eyes shut till the sound receded toward the west. The horde was very close now—the air foul with their hoarse snarlings, and the ground almost shaking with their alien-rhythmed footfalls. My breath nearly ceased to come, and I put every ounce of will-power into the task of holding my eyelids down.

I am not even yet willing to say whether what followed was a hideous actuality or only a nightmare hallucination. The later action of the government, after my frantic appeals, would tend to confirm it as a monstrous truth; but could not an hallucination have been repeated under the quasi-hypnotic spell of that ancient, haunted, and shadowed town? Such places have strange properties, and the legacy of insane legend might well have acted on more than one human imagination amidst those dead, stench-cursed streets and huddles of rotting roofs and crumbling steeples. Is it not possible that the germ of an actual contagious madness lurks in the depths of that shadow over Innsmouth? Who can be sure of reality after hearing things like the tale of old Zadok Allen? The government men never found poor Zadok, and have no conjectures to make as to what became of him. Where does madness leave off and reality begin? Is it possible that even my latest fear is sheer delusion?

But I must try to tell what I thought I saw that night under the mocking yellow moon—saw surging and hopping down the Rowley road in plain sight in front of me as I crouched among the wild brambles of that desolate railway cut. Of course my resolution to keep my eyes shut had failed. It was foredoomed to failure—for who could crouch blindly while a legion of croaking, baying entities of unknown source flopped noisomely past, scarcely more than a hundred yards away?

I thought I was prepared for the worst, and I really ought to have been prepared considering what I had seen before. My other pursuers had been accursedly abnormal—so should I not have been ready to face a strengthening of the abnormal element; to look upon forms in which there was no mixture of the normal at all? I did not open my eyes until the raucous clamour came loudly from a point obviously straight ahead. Then I knew that a long section of them must be plainly in sight where the sides of the cut flattened out and the road crossed the track—and I could no longer keep myself from sampling whatever horror that leering yellow moon might have to shew.

It was the end, for whatever remains to me of life on the surface of this earth, of every vestige of mental peace and confidence in the integrity of nature and of the human mind. Nothing that I could have imagined—nothing, even, that I could have gathered had I credited old Zadok's crazy tale in the most literal way—would be in any way comparable to the demoniac, blasphemous reality that I saw—or believe I saw. I have tried to hint what it was in order to postpone the horror of writing it down baldly. Can it be possible that this planet has actually spawned such things; that human eyes have truly seen, as objective flesh, what man has hitherto known only in febrile phantasy and tenuous legend?

And yet I saw them in a limitless stream—flopping, hopping, croaking, bleating—surging inhumanly through the spectral moonlight in a grotesque, malignant saraband of fantastic nightmare. And some of them had tall tiaras of that nameless whitish-gold metal. . . . and some were strangely robed. . . . and one, who led the way, was clad in a ghoulishly humped black coat and striped trousers, and had a man's felt hat perched on the shapeless thing that answered for a head.

I think their predominant colour was a greyish-green, though they had white bellies. They were mostly shiny and slippery, but the ridges of their backs were scaly. Their forms vaguely suggested the anthropoid, while their heads were the heads of fish, with prodigious bulging eyes that never closed. At the sides of their necks were palpitating gills, and their long paws were webbed. They hopped irregularly, sometimes on two legs and sometimes on four. I was somehow glad that they had no more than four limbs. Their croaking, baying voices, clearly used for articulate speech, held all the dark shades of expression which their staring faces lacked.

But for all of their monstrousness they were not unfamiliar to me. I knew too well what they must be—for was not the memory of the evil tiara at Newburyport still fresh? They were the blasphemous fish-frogs of the nameless design—living and horrible—and as I saw them I knew also of what that humped, tiaraed priest in the black church basement had fearsomely reminded me. Their number was past guessing. It seemed to me that there were limitless swarms of them—and certainly my momentary glimpse could have shewn only the least fraction. In another instant everything was blotted out by a merciful fit of fainting; the first I had ever had.

V

It was gentle daylight rain that awaked me from my stupor in the brush-grown railway cut, and when I staggered out to the roadway ahead I saw no trace of any prints in the fresh mud. The fishy odour, too, was gone, Innsmouth's ruined roofs and toppling steeples loomed up greyly toward the southeast, but not a living creature did I spy in all the desolate salt marshes around. My watch was still going, and told me that the hour was past noon.

The reality of what I had been through was highly uncertain in my mind, but I felt that something hideous lay in the background. I must get away from evil-shadowed Innsmouth—and accordingly I began to test my cramped, wearied powers of locomotion. Despite weakness, hunger, horror, and bewilderment I found myself after a time able to walk; so started slowly along the muddy road to Rowley. Before evening I was in the village, getting a meal and providing myself with presentable clothes. I caught the night train to Arkham, and the next day talked long and earnestly with government officials there; a process I later repeated in Boston. With the main result of these colloquies the public is now familiar—and I wish, for normality's sake, there were nothing more to tell. Perhaps it is madness that is overtaking me—yet perhaps a greater horror—or a greater marvel—is reaching out.

As may well be imagined, I gave up most of the foreplanned features of the rest of my tour—the scenic, architectural, and antiquarian diversions on which I had counted so heavily. Nor did I dare look for that piece of strange jewellery said to be in the Miskatonic University Museum. I did, however, improve my stay in Arkham by collecting some genealogical notes I had long wished to possess; very rough and hasty data, it is true, but capable of good use later on when I might have time to collate and codify them. The curator of the historical society there—Mr. E. Lapham Peabody—was very courteous about assisting me, and expressed unusual interest when I told him I was a grandson of Eliza Orne of Arkham, who was born in 1867 and had married James Williamson of Ohio at the age of seventeen.

It seemed that a maternal uncle of mine had been there many years before on a quest much like my own; and that my grandmother's family was a topic of some local curiosity. There had, Mr. Peabody said, been considerable discussion about the marriage of her father, Benjamin Orne, just after the Civil War; since the ancestry of the bride was peculiarly puzzling. That bride was understood to have been an orphaned Marsh of New Hampshire—a cousin of the Essex County Marshes—but her education had been in France and she knew very little of her family. A guardian had deposited funds in a Boston bank to maintain her and her French governess; but that guardian's name was unfamiliar to Arkham people, and in time he dropped out of sight, so that the governess assumed his role by court appointment. The Frenchwoman—now long dead—was very taciturn, and there were those who said she could have told more than she did.

But the most baffling thing was the inability of anyone to place the recorded parents of the young woman—Enoch and Lydia (Meserve) Marsh—among the known families of New Hampshire. Possibly, many suggested, she was the natural daughter of some Marsh of prominence—she certainly had the true Marsh eyes. Most of the puzzling was done after her early death, which took place at the birth of my grandmother—her only child. Having formed some disagreeable impressions connected with the name of Marsh, I did not welcome the news that it belonged on my own ancestral tree; nor was I pleased by Mr. Peabody's suggestion that I had the true Marsh eyes myself. However, I was grateful for data which I knew would prove valuable; and took copious notes and lists of book references regarding the well-documented Orne family.

I went directly home to Toledo from Boston, and later spent a month at Maumee recuperating from my ordeal. In September I entered Oberlin for my final year, and from then till the next June was busy with studies and other wholesome activities—reminded of the bygone terror only by occasional official visits from government men in connexion with the campaign which my pleas and evidence had started. Around the middle of July—just a year after the Innsmouth experience—I spent a week with my late mother's family in Cleveland; checking some of my new genealogical data with the various notes, traditions, and bits of heirloom material in existence there, and seeing what kind of a connected chart I could construct.

I did not exactly relish this task, for the atmosphere of the Williamson home had always depressed me. There was a strain of morbidity there, and my mother had never encouraged my visiting her parents as a child, although she always welcomed her father when he came to Toledo. My Arkham-born grandmother had seemed strange and almost terrifying to me, and I do not think I grieved when she disappeared. I was eight years old then, and it was said that she had wandered off in grief after the suicide of my uncle Douglas, her eldest son. He had shot himself after a trip to New England—the same trip, no doubt, which had caused him to be recalled at the Arkham Historical Society.

This uncle had resembled her, and I had never liked him either.

Something about the staring, unwinking expression of both of them had given me a vague, unaccountable uneasiness. My mother and uncle Walter had not looked like that. They were like their father, though poor little cousin Lawrence—Walter's son—had been an almost perfect duplicate of his grandmother before his condition took him to the permanent seclusion of a sanitarium at Canton. I had not seen him in four years, but my uncle once implied that his state, both mental and physical, was very bad. This worry had probably been a major cause of his mother's death two years before.

My grandfather and his widowed son Walter now comprised the Cleveland household, but the memory of older times hung thickly over it. I still disliked the place, and tried to get my researches done as quickly as possible. Williamson records and traditions were supplied in abundance by my grandfather; though for Orne material I had to depend on my uncle Walter, who put at my disposal the contents of all his files, including notes, letters, cuttings, heirlooms, photographs, and miniatures.

It was in going over the letters and pictures on the Orne side that I began to acquire a kind of terror of my own ancestry. As I have said, my grandmother and uncle Douglas had always disturbed me. Now, years after their passing, I gazed at their pictured faces with a measurably heightened feeling of repulsion and alienation. I could not at first understand the change, but gradually a horrible sort of comparison began to obtrude itself on my unconscious mind despite the steady refusal of my consciousness to admit even the least suspicion of it. It was clear that the typical expression of these faces now suggested something it had not suggested before—something which would bring stark panic if too openly thought of.

But the worst shock came when my uncle shewed me the Orne jewellery in a downtown safe-deposit vault. Some of the items were delicate and inspiring enough, but there was one box of strange old pieces descended from my mysterious great-grandmother which my uncle was almost reluctant to produce. They were, he said, of very grotesque and almost repulsive design, and had never to his knowledge been publicly worn; though my grandmother used to enjoy looking at them. Vague legends of bad luck clustered around them, and my great-grandmother's French governess had said they ought not to be worn in New England, though it would be quite safe to wear them in Europe.

As my uncle began slowly and grudgingly to unwrap the things he urged me not to be shocked by the strangeness and frequent hideousness of the designs. Artists and archaeologists who had seen them pronounced their workmanship superlatively and exotically exquisite, though no one seemed able to define their exact material or assign them to any specific art tradition. There were two armlets, a tiara, and a kind of pectoral; the latter having in high relief certain figures of almost unbearable extravagance.

During this description I had kept a tight rein on my emotions, but my face must have betrayed my mounting fears. My uncle looked concerned, and paused in his unwrapping to study my countenance. I motioned to him to continue, which he did with renewed signs of reluctance. He seemed to expect some demonstration when the first piece—the tiara—became visible, but I doubt if he expected quite what actually happened. I did not expect it, either, for I thought I was thoroughly forewarned regarding what the jewellery would turn out to be. What I did was to faint silently away, just as I had done in that brier choked railway cut a year before.

From that day on my life has been a nightmare of brooding and apprehension, nor do I know how much is hideous truth and how much madness. My great-grandmother had been a Marsh of unknown source whose husband lived in Arkham—and did not old Zadok say that the daughter of Obed Marsh by a monstrous mother was married to an Arkham man through a trick? What was it the ancient toper had muttered about the likeness of my eyes to Captain Obed's? In Arkham, too, the curator had told me I had the true Marsh eyes. Was Obed Marsh my own great-great-grandfather? Who—or what—then, was my great-great-grandmother? But perhaps this was all madness. Those whitish-gold ornaments might easily have been bought from some Innsmouth sailor by the father of my great-grandmother, whoever he was. And that look in the staring-eyed faces of my grandmother and self-slain uncle might be sheer fancy on my part—sheer fancy, bolstered up by the Innsmouth shadow which had so darkly coloured my imagination. But why had my uncle killed himself after an ancestral quest in New England?

For more than two years I fought off these reflections with partial success. My father secured me a place in an insurance office, and I buried my self in routine as deeply as possible. In the winter of 1930–31, however, the dreams began. They were very sparse and insidious at first, but increased in frequency and vividness as the weeks went by. Great watery spaces opened out before me, and I seemed to wander through titanic sunken porticos and labyrinths of weedy cyclopean walls with grotesque fishes as my companions. Then the other shapes began to appear, filling me with nameless horror the moment I awoke. But during the dreams they did not horrify me at all—I was one with them; wearing their unhuman trappings, treading their aqueous ways, and praying monstrously at their evil sea-bottom temples.

There was much more than I could remember, but even what I did remember each morning would be enough to stamp me as a madman or a genius if ever I dared write it down. Some frightful influence, I felt, was seeking gradually to drag me out of the sane world of wholesome life into unnamable abysses of blackness and alienage; and the process told heavily on me. My health and appearance grew steadily worse, till finally I was forced to give up my position and adopt the static, secluded life of an invalid. Some odd nervous affliction had me in its grip, and I found myself at times almost unable to shut my eyes.

It was then that I began to study the mirror with mounting alarm. The slow ravages of disease are not pleasant to watch, but in my case there was something subtler and more puzzling in the background. My father seemed to notice it, too, for he began looking at me curiously and almost affrightedly. What was taking place in me? Could it be that I was coming to resemble my grandmother and uncle Douglas?

One night I had a frightful dream in which I met my grandmother under the sea. She lived in a phosphorescent palace of many terraces, with gardens of strange leprous corals and grotesque brachiate efflorescences, and welcomed me with a warmth that may have been sardonic. She had changed—as those who take to the water change—and told me she had never died. Instead, she had gone to a spot her dead son had learned about and had leaped to a realm whose wonders—destined for him as well—he had spurned with a smoking pistol. This was to be my realm, too—I could not escape it. I would never die, but would live with those who had lived since before man ever walked the earth.

I met also that which had been her grandmother. For eighty thousand years Pht'thya-l'y had lived in Y'ha-nthlei, and thither she had gone back after Obed Marsh was dead. Y'ha-nthlei was not destroyed when the upper-earth men shot death into the sea. It was hurt, but not destroyed. The Deep Ones could never be destroyed, even though the palaeogean magic of the forgotten Old Ones might sometimes check them. For the present they would rest; but some day, if they remembered, they would rise again for the tribute Great Cthulhu craved. It would be a city greater than Innsmouth next time. They had planned to spread, and had brought up that which would help them, but now they must wait once more. For bringing the upperearth men's death I must do a penance, but that would not be heavy. This was the dream in which I saw a *shoggoth* for the first time, and the sight set me awake in a frenzy of screaming. That morning the mirror definitely told me I had acquired *the Innsmouth look*.

So far I have not shot myself as my uncle Douglas did. I bought an automatic and almost took the step, but certain dreams deterred me. The tense extremes of horror are lessening, and I feel queerly drawn toward the unknown sea-deeps instead of fearing them. I hear and do strange things in sleep, and awake with a kind of exaltation instead of terror. I do not believe I need to wait for the full change as most have waited. If I did, my father would probably shut me up in a sanitarium as my poor little cousin is shut up. Stupendous and unheard-of splendours await me below, and I shall seek them soon. *Iä-R'lyeh! Cthulhu fhtagn! Iä! Iä!* No, I shall not shoot myself—I cannot be made to shoot myself!

I shall plan my cousin's escape from that Canton madhouse, and together we shall go to marvel-shadowed Innsmouth. We shall swim out to that brooding reef in the sea and dive down through black abysses to Cyclopean and many-columned Y'ha-nthlei, and in that lair of the Deep Ones we shall dwell amidst wonder and glory for ever.

The Dreams in the Witch-House

Whether the dreams brought on the fever or the fever brought on the dreams Walter Gilman did not know. Behind everything crouched the brooding, festering horror of the ancient town, and of the moldy, un-hallowed garret gable where he wrote and studied and wrestled with figures and formulae when he was not tossing on the meager iron bed. His ears were growing sensitive to a preternatural and intolera-ble degree, and he had long ago stopped the cheap mantel clock whose ticking had come to seem like a thunder of artillery. At night the subtle stirring of the black city outside, the sinister scurrying of rats in the wormy partitions, and the creaking of hidden timbers in the centuried house, were enough to give him a sense of strident pan-demonium. The darkness always teemed with unexplained sound—and yet he sometimes shook with fear lest the noises he heard should subside and allow him to hear certain other fainter noises which he suspected were lurking behind them.

He was in the changeless, legend-haunted city of Arkham, with its clustering gambrel roofs that sway and sag over attics where witches hid from the King's men in the dark, olden days of the Province. Nor was any spot in that city more steeped in macabre memory than the gable room which harbored him—for it was this house and this room which had likewise harbored old Keziah Mason, whose flight from Salem Gaol at the last no one was ever able to explain. That was in 1692—the gaoler had gone mad and babbled of a small white-fanged furry thing which scuttled out of Keziah's cell, and not even Cotton Mather could explain the curves and angles smeared on the gray stone walls with some red, sticky fluid.

Possibly Gilman ought not to have studied so hard. Non-Euclidean calculus and quantum physics are enough to stretch any brain; and when one mixes them with folklore, and tries to trace a strange back-ground of multi-dimensional reality behind the ghoulish hints of the

Gothic tales and the wild whispers of the chimney-corner, one can hardly expect to be wholly free from mental tension. Gilman came from Haverhill, but it was only after he had entered college in Arkham that he began to connect his mathematics with the fantastic legends of elder magic. Something in the air of the hoary town worked obscurely on his imagination. The professors at Miskatonic had urged him to slacken up, and had voluntarily cut down his course at several points. Moreover, they had stopped him from consulting the dubious old books on forbidden secrets that were kept under lock and key in a vault at the university library. But all these precautions came late in the day, so that Gilman had some terrible hints from the dreaded *Necronomicon* of Abdul Alhazred, the fragmentary *Book of Eibon*, and the suppressed *Unaussprechlichen Kulten* of von Junzt to correlate with his abstract formulae on the properties of space and the linkage of dimensions known and unknown.

He knew his room was in the old Witch-House—that, indeed, was why he had taken it. There was much in the Essex County records about Keziah Mason's trial, and what she had admitted under pressure to the Court of Oyer and Terminer had fascinated Gilman beyond all reason. She had told Judge Hathorne of lines and curves that could be made to point out directions leading through walls of space to other spaces beyond, and had implied that such lines and curves were frequently used at certain midnight meetings in the dark valley of the white stone beyond Meadow Hill and on the unpeopled island in the river. She had spoken also of the Black Man, of her oath, and of her new secret name of Nahab. Then she had drawn those devices on the walls of her cell and vanished.

Gilman believed strange things about Keziah, and had felt a queer thrill on learning that her dwelling was still standing after more than two hundred thirty-five years. When he heard the hushed Arkham whispers about Keziah's persistent presence in the old house and the narrow streets, about the irregular human tooth-marks left on certain sleepers in that and other houses, about the childish cries heard near May-Eve, and Hallowmass, about the stench often noted in the old house's attic just after those dreaded seasons, and about the small, furry, sharp-toothed thing which haunted the moldering structure and the town and nuzzled people curiously in the black hours before dawn, he resolved to live in the place at any cost. A room was easy to secure; for the house was unpopular, hard to rent, and long given over to cheap lodgings. Gilman could not have told what he expected to find there, but he knew he wanted to be in the building where some circumstance had more or less suddenly given a mediocre old woman of the seventeenth century an insight into mathematical depths perhaps beyond the utmost modern delvings of Planck, Heisenberg, Einstein, and de Sitter.

He studied the timber and plaster walls for traces of cryptic designs at every accessible spot where the paper had peeled, and within a week managed to get the eastern attic room where Keziah was held to have practised her spells. It had been vacant from the first—for no one had ever been willing to stay there long—but the Polish landlord had grown wary about renting it. Yet nothing whatever had happened to Gilman till about the time of the fever. No ghostly Keziah flitted through the somber halls and chambers, no small furry thing crept into his dismal eyrie to nuzzle him, and no record of the witch's incantations rewarded his constant search. Sometimes he would take walks through shadowy tangles of unpaved musty-smelling lanes where eldritch brown houses of unknown age leaned and tottered and leered mockingly through narrow, small-paned windows. Here he knew strange things had happened once, and there was a faint suggestion behind the surface that everything of that monstrous past might not—at least in the darkest, narrowest, and most intricately crooked alleys—have utterly perished. He also rowed out twice to the ill-regarded island in the river, and made a sketch of the singular angles described by the moss-grown rows of gray standing stones whose origin was so obscure and immemorial.

Gilman's room was of good size but queerly irregular shape; the north wall slanting perceptibly inward from the outer to the inner end, while the low ceiling slanted gently downward in the same direction. Aside from an obvious rat-hole and the signs of other stopped-up ones, there was no access—nor any appearance of a former avenue of access—to the space which must have existed between the slanting wall and the straight outer wall on the house's north side, though a view from the exterior showed where a window had been boarded up at a very remote date. The loft above the ceiling—which must have had a slanting floor—was likewise inaccessible. When Gilman climbed up a ladder to the cobwebbed level loft above the rest of the attic he found vestiges of a bygone aperture tightly and heavily covered with ancient planking and secured by the stout wooden pegs common in Colonial carpentry. No amount of persuasion, however, could induce the stolid landlord to let him investigate either of these two closed spaces.

As time wore along, his absorption in the irregular wall and ceiling of his room increased; for he began to read into the odd angles a mathematical significance which seemed to offer vague clues regarding their purpose. Old Keziah, he reflected, might have had excellent reasons for living in a room with peculiar angles; for was it not through certain angles that she claimed to have gone outside the boundaries of the world of space we know? His interest gradually veered away from the unplumbed voids beyond the slanting surfaces, since it now appeared that the purpose of those surfaces concerned the side he was on.

The touch of brain-fever and the dreams began early in February. For some time, apparently, the curious angles of Gilman's room had been having a strange, almost hypnotic effect on him; and as the bleak winter advanced he had found himself staring more and more intently at the corner where the down-slanting ceiling met the inward-slanting wall. About this period his inability to concentrate on his formal studies worried him considerably, his apprehensions about the mid-year examinations being very acute. But the exaggerated sense of hearing was scarcely less annoying. Life had become an insistent and almost unendurable cacophony, and there was that constant, terrifying impression of *other* sounds—perhaps from regions beyond life—trembling on the very brink of audibility. So far as concrete noises went, the rats in the ancient partitions were the worst. Sometimes their scratching seemed not only furtive but deliberate. When it came from beyond the slanting north wall it was mixed with a sort of dry rattling; and when it came from the century-closed loft above the slanting ceiling Gilman always braced himself as if expecting some horror which only bided its time before descending to engulf him utterly.

The dreams were wholly beyond the pale of sanity, and Gilman felt that they must be a result, jointly, of his studies in mathematics and in folklore. He had been thinking too much about the vague regions which his formulae told him must lie beyond the three dimensions we know, and about the possibility that old Keziah Mason—guided by some influence past all conjecture—had actually found the gate to those regions. The yellowed country records containing her testimony and that of her accusers were so damnably suggestive of things beyond human experience—and the descriptions of the darting little furry object which served as her familiar were so painfully realistic despite their incredible details.

That object—no larger than a good-sized rat and quaintly called by the townspeople "Brown Jenkin"—seemed to have been the fruit of a remarkable case of sympathetic herd-delusion, for in 1692 no less than eleven persons had testified to glimpsing it. There were recent rumors, too, with a baffling and disconcerting amount of agreement. Witnesses said it had long hair and the shape of a rat, but that its sharp-toothed, bearded face was evilly human while its paws were like tiny human hands. It took messages betwixt old Keziah and the devil, and he was nursed on the witch's blood, which it sucked like a vampire. Its voice was a kind of loathsome titter, and it could speak all languages. Of all the bizarre monstrosities in Gilman's dreams, nothing filled him with greater panic and nausea than this blasphemous and diminutive hybrid, whose image flitted across his vision in a form a thousandfold more hateful than anything his waking mind had deduced from the ancient records and the modern whispers.

Gilman's dreams consisted largely in plunges through limitless abysses of inexplicably colored twilight and bafflingly disordered sound; abysses whose material and gravitational properties, and whose relation to his own entity, he could not even begin to explain. He did not walk or climb, fly or swim, crawl or wriggle; yet always experienced a mode of motion partly voluntary and partly involuntary. Of his own condition he could not well judge, for sight of his arms, legs, and torso seemed always cut off by some odd disarrangement of perspective; but he felt that his physical organization and faculties were somehow marvelously transmuted and obliquely projected— though not without a certain grotesque relationship to his normal proportions and properties.

The abysses were by no means vacant, being crowded with indescribably angled masses of alien-hued substance, some of which appeared to be organic while others seemed inorganic. A few of the organic objects tended to awake vague memories in the back of his mind, though he could form no conscious idea of what they mockingly resembled or suggested. In the later dreams he began to distinguish separate categories into which the organic objects appeared to be divided, and which seemed to involve in each case a radically different species of conduct-pattern and basic motivation. Of these categories one seemed to him to include objects slightly less illogical and irrelevant in their motions than the members of the other categories.

All the objects—organic and inorganic alike—were totally beyond description or even comprehension. Gilman sometimes compared the inorganic matter to prisms, labyrinths, clusters of cubes and planes, and cyclopean buildings; and the organic things struck him variously as groups of bubbles, octopi, centipedes, living Hindoo idols, and intricate arabesques roused into a kind of ophidian animation. Everything he saw was unspeakably menacing and horrible; and whenever one of the organic entities appeared by its motions to be noticing him, he felt a stark, hideous fright which generally jolted him awake. Of how the organic entities moved, he could tell no more than of how he moved himself. In time he observed a further mystery—the tendency of certain entities to appear suddenly out of empty space, or to disappear totally with equal suddenness. The shrieking, roaring confusion of sound which permeated the abysses was past all analysis as to pitch, timbre or rhythm, but seemed to be synchronous with vague visual changes in all the indefinite objects, organic and inorganic alike. Gilman had a constant sense of dread that it might rise to some unbearable degree of intensity during one or another of its obscure, relentlessly inevitable fluctuations.

But it was not in these vortices of complete alienage that he saw Brown Jenkin. That shocking little horror was reserved for certain lighter, sharper dreams which assailed him just before he dropped into the fullest depths of sleep. He would be lying in the dark fighting to keep awake when a faint lambent glow would seem to shimmer around the centuried room, showing in a violet mist the convergence of angled planes which had seized his brain so insidiously. The horror would appear to pop out of the rat-hole in the corner and patter toward him over the sagging, wide-planked floor with evil expectancy in its tiny, bearded human face; but mercifully, this dream always melted away before the object got close enough to nuzzle him. It had hellishly long, sharp, canine teeth. Gilman tried to stop up the rat-hole every day, but each night the real tenants of the partitions would gnaw away the obstruction, whatever it might be. Once he had the landlord nail tin over it, but the next night the rats gnawed a fresh hole, in making which they pushed or dragged out into the room a curious little fragment of bone.

Gilman did not report his fever to the doctor, for he knew he could not pass the examinations if ordered to the college infirmary when every moment was needed for cramming. As it was, he failed in Calculus D and Advanced General Psychology, though not without hope of making up lost ground before the end of the term.

It was in March when the fresh element entered his lighter preliminary dreaming, and the nightmare shape of Brown Jenkin began to be companioned by the nebulous blur which grew more and more to resemble a bent old woman. This addition disturbed him more than he could account for, but finally he decided that it was like an ancient crone whom he had twice actually encountered in the dark tangle of lanes near the abandoned wharves. On those occasions the evil, sardonic, and seemingly unmotivated stare of the beldame had set him almost shivering—especially the first time when an overgrown rat darting across the shadowed mouth of a neighboring alley had made him think irrationally of Brown Jenkin. Now, he reflected, those nervous fears were being mirrored in his disordered dreams.

That the influence of the old house was unwholesome he could not deny, but traces of his early morbid interest still held him there. He argued that the fever alone was responsible for his nightly fantasies, and that when the touch abated he would be free from the monstrous visions. Those visions, however, were of absorbing vividness and convincingness, and whenever he awaked he retained a vague sense of having undergone much more than he remembered. He was hideously sure that in unrecalled dreams he had talked with both Brown Jenkin and the old woman, and that they had been urging him to go somewhere with them and to meet a third being of greater potency.

Toward the end of March he began to pick up in his mathmatics, though other studies bothered him increasingly. He was getting an intuitive knack for solving Riemannian equations, and astonished Professor Upham by his comprehension of fourth-dimensional and other problems which had floored all the rest of the class. One afternoon there was a discussion of possible freakish curvatures in space, and of theoretical points of approach or even contact between our part of the cosmos and various other regions as distant as the farthest stars or the transgalactic gulfs themselves—or even as fabulously remote as the tentatively conceivable cosmic units beyond the whole Einsteinian space-time continuum. Gilman's handling of this theme filled everyone with admiration, even though some of his hypothetical illustrations caused an increase in the always plentiful gossip about his nervous and solitary eccentricity. What made the students shake their heads was his sober theory that a man might—given mathematical knowledge admittedly beyond all likelihood of human acquirement—step deliberately from the earth to any other celestial body which might lie at one of an infinity of specific points in the cosmic pattern.

Such a step, he said, would require only two stages; first, a passage out of the three-dimensional sphere we know, and second, a passage back to the three-dimensional sphere at another point, perhaps one of infinite remoteness. That this could be accomplished without loss of life was in many cases conceivable. Any being from any part of three-dimensional space could probably survive in the fourth dimension; and its survival of the second stage would depend upon what alien part of three-dimensional space it might select for its re-entry. Denizens of some planets might be able to live on certain others—even planets belonging to other galaxies, or to similar dimensional phases of other space-time continua—though of course there must be vast numbers of mutually uninhabitable even though mathematically juxtaposed bodies or zones of space.

It was also possible that the inhabitants of a given dimensional realm could survive entry to many unknown and incomprehensible realms of additional or indefinitely multiplied dimensions—be they within or outside the given space-time continuum—and that the converse would be likewise true. This was a matter for speculation, though one could be fairly certain that the type of mutation involved in a passage from any given dimensional plane to the next higher plane would not be destructive of biological integrity as we understand it. Gilman could not be very clear about his reasons for this last assumption, but his haziness here was more than overbalanced by his clearness on other complex points. Professor Upham especially liked his demonstration of the kinship of higher mathematics to certain phases of magical lore transmitted down the ages from an ineffable antiquity—human or pre-human—whose knowledge of the cosmos and its laws was greater than ours.

Around the first of April Gilman worried considerably because his slow fever did not abate. He was also troubled by what some of his fellow-lodgers said about his sleep-walking. It seemed that he was often absent from his bed, and that the creaking of his floor at certain hours of the night was remarked by the man in the room below. This fellow also spoke of hearing the tread of shot feet in the night; but Gilman was sure he must have been mistaken in this, since shoes as well as other apparel were always precisely in place in the morning. One could develop all sorts of aural delutions in this morbid old house—for did not Gilman himself, even in daylight, now feel certain that noises other than rat-scratching came from the black voids beyond the slanting wall and above the slanting ceiling? His pathologically sensitive ears began to listen for faint footfalls in the immemorially sealed loft overhead, and sometimes the illusion of such things was agonizingly realistic.

However, he knew that he had actually become a somnambulist; for twice at night his room had been found vacant, though with all his clothing in place. Of this he had been assured by Frank Elwood, the one fellow-student whose poverty forced him to room in this squalid and unpopular house. Elwood had been studying in the small hours and had come up for help on a differential equation, only to find Gilman absent. It had been rather presumptuous of him to open the unlocked door after knocking had failed to rouse a response, but he had needed the help very badly and thought that his host would not mind a gentle prodding awake. On neither occasion, though, had Gilman been there; and when told of the matter he wondered where he could have been wandering, barefoot and with only his nightclothes on. He resolved to investigate the matter if reports of his sleep-walking continued, and thought of sprinkling flour on the floor of the corridor to see where his footsteps might lead. The door was the only conceivable egress, for there was no possible foothold outside the narrow window.

As April advanced, Gilman's fever-sharpened ears were disturbed by the whining prayers of a superstitious loom-fixer named Joe Mazurewicz, who had a room on the ground floor. Mazurewicz had told long, rambling stories about the ghost of old Keziah and the furry sharp-fanged, nuzzling thing, and had said he was so badly haunted at times that only his silver crucifix—given him for the purpose by Father Iwanicki of St. Stanislaus' Church—could bring him relief. Now he was praying because the Witches' Sabbath was drawing near. May Eve was Walpurgis Night, when hell's blackest evil roamed the earth and all the slaves of Satan gathered for nameless rites and deeds. It was always a very bad time in Arkham, even though the fine folks up in Miskatonic Avenue and High and Saltonstall streets pretended to know nothing about it. There would be bad doings, and a child or two would probably be missing. Joe knew about such things, for his grandmother in the old country had heard tales from her grandmother. It was wise to pray and count one's beads at this season. For three months Keziah and Brown Jenkin had not been near Joe's room, nor near Paul Choynski's room, nor anywhere else—and it meant no good when they held off like that. They must be up to something.

Gilman dropped in at the doctor's office on the sixteenth of the month, and was surprised to find his temperature was not as high as he had feared. The physician questioned him sharply, and advised him to see a nerve specialist. On reflection, he was glad he had not consulted the still more inquisitive college doctor. Old Waldron, who had curtailed his activities before, would have made him take a rest—an impossible thing now that he was so close to great results in his equations. He was certainly near the boundary between the known universe and the fourth dimension, and who could say how much father he might go?

But even as these thoughts came to him he wondered at the source of his strange confidence. Did all of this perilous sense of imminence come from the formulae on the sheets he covered day by day? The soft, stealthy, imaginary footsteps in the sealed loft above were unnerving. And now, too, there was a growing feeling that somebody was constantly persuading him to do something terrible which he could not do. How about the somnambulism? Where did he go sometimes in the night? And what was that faint suggestion of sound which once in a while seemed to trickle through the confusion of identifiable sounds even in broad daylight and full wakefulness? Its rhythm did not correspond to anything on earth, unless perhaps to the cadence of one or two unmentionable Sabbat-chants, and sometimes he feared it corresponded to certain attributes of the vague shrieking or roaring in those wholly alien abysses of dream.

The dreams were meanwhile getting to be atrocious. In the lighter preliminary phase the evil old woman was now of fiendish distinctness, and Gilman knew she was the one who had frightened him in the slums. Her bent back, long nose, and shrivelled chin were unmistakable, and her shapeless brown garments were like those he remembered. The expression on her face was one of hideous malevolence and exultation, and when he awaked he could recall a croaking voice that persuaded and threatened. He must meet the Black Man and go with them all to the throne of Azathoth at the center of ultimate chaos. That was what she said. He must sign the book of Azathoth in his own blood and take a new secret name now that his independent delvings had gone so far. What kept him from going with her and Brown Jenkin and the other to the throne of Chaos where the thin flutes pipe mindlessly was the fact that he had seen the name "Azathoth" in the *Necronomicon*, and knew it stood for a primal evil too horrible for description.

The old woman always appeared out of thin air near the corner where the downward slant met the inward slant. She seemed to crystallize at a point closer to the ceiling than to the floor, and every night she was a little nearer and more distinct before the dream shifted. Brown Jenkin, too, was always a little nearer at the last, and his yellowish-white fangs glistened shockingly in that unearthly violet phosphorescence. Its shrill loathsome tittering stuck more and more in Gilman's head, and he could remember in the morning how it had pronounced the words "Azathoth" and "Nyarlathotep."

In the deeper dreams everything was likewise more distinct, and Gilman felt that the twilight abysses around him were those of the fourth dimension. Those organic entities whose motions seemed least flagrantly irrelevant and unmotivated were probably projections of life-forms from our own planet, including human beings. What the others were in their own dimensional sphere or spheres he dared not try to think. Two of the less irrelevantly moving things—a rather large congeries of iridescent, prolately spheroidal bubbles and a very much smaller polyhedron of unknown colours and rapidly shifting surface angles—seemed to take notice of him and follow him about or float ahead as he changed position among the titan prisms, labyrinths, cube-and-plane clusters and quasi-buildings; and all the while the vague shrieking and roaring waxed louder and louder, as if approaching some monstrous climax of utterly unendurable intensity.

During the night of April 19–20 the new development occurred. Gilman was half involuntarily moving about in the twilight abysses with the bubble-mass and the small polyhedron floating ahead, when he noticed the peculiarly regular angles formed by the edges of some gigantic neighboring prism-clusters. In another second he was out of the abyss and standing tremulously on a rocky hillside bathed in intense, diffused green light. He was barefooted and in his nightclothes, and when he tried to walk discovered that he could scarcely lift his feet. A swirling vapor hid everything but the immediate sloping terrain from sight, and he shrank from the thought of the sounds that might surge out of that vapor.

Then he saw the two shapes laboriously crawling toward him— the old woman and the little furry thing. The crone strained up to her knees and managed to cross her arms in a singular fashion, while Brown Jenkin pointed in a certain direction with a horribly anthropoid forepaw which it raised with evident difficulty. Spurred by an impulse he did not originate, Gilman dragged himself forward along a course determined by the angle of the old woman's arms and the direction of the small monstrosity's paw, and before he had shuffled three steps he was back in the twilight abysses. Geometrical shapes seethed around him, and he fell dizzily and interminably. At last he woke in his bed in the crazily angled garret of the eldritch old house.

He was good for nothing that morning, and stayed away from all his classes. Some unknown attraction was pulling his eyes in a seemingly irrelevant direction, for he could not help staring at a certain vacant spot on the floor. As the day advanced, the focus of his unseeing eyes changed position, and by noon he had conquered the impulse to stare at vacancy. About two o'clock he went out for lunch and as he threaded the narrow lanes of the city he found himself turning always to the southeast. Only an effort halted him at a cafeteria in Church Street, and after the meal he felt the unknown pull still more strongly.

He would have to consult a nerve specialist after all—perhaps there was a connection with his somnambulism—but meanwhile he might at least try to break the morbid spell himself. Undoubtedly he could still manage to walk away from the pull; so with great resolution he headed against it and dragged himself deliberately north along Garrison Street. By the time he had reached the bridge over the Miskatonic he was in a cold perspiration, and he clutched at the iron railing as he gazed upstream at the ill-regarded island whose regular lines of ancient standing stones brooded sullenly in the afternoon sunlight.

Then he gave a start. For there was a clearly visible living figure on that desolate island, and a second glance told him it was certainly the strange old woman whose sinister aspect had worked itself so disastrously into his dreams. The tall grass near her was moving, too, as if some other living thing were crawling close to the ground. When the old woman began to turn toward him he fled precipitately off the bridge and into the shelter of the town's labyrinthine waterfront alleys. Distant though the island was, he felt that a monstrous and invincible evil could flow from the sardonic stare of that bent, ancient figure in brown.

The southeastward pull still held, and only with tremendous resolution could Gilman drag himself into the old house and up the rickety stairs. For hours he sat silent and aimless, with his eyes shifting gradually westward. About six o'clock his sharpened ears caught the whining prayers of Joe Mazurewicz two floors below, and in desperation he seized his hat and walked out into the sunset-golden streets, letting the now directly southward pull carry him where it might. An hour later darkness found him in the open fields beyond Hangman's Brook, with the glimmering spring stars shining ahead. The urge to walk was gradually changing to an urge to leap mystically into space, and suddenly he realized just where the source of the pull lay.

It was in the sky. A definite point among the stars had a claim on him and was calling him. Apparently it was a point somewhere between Hydra and Argo Navis, and he knew that he had been urged toward it ever since he had awaked soon after dawn. In the morning it had been underfoot, and now it was roughly south but stealing toward the west. What was the meaning of this new thing? Was he going mad? How long would it last? Again mustering his resolution, Gilman turned and dragged himself back to the sinister old house.

Mazurewicz was waiting for him at the door, and seemed both anxious and reluctant to whisper some fresh bit of superstition. It was about the witch-light. Joe had been out celebrating the night before—it was Patriots' Day in Massachusetts—and had come home after midnight. Looking up at the house from outside, he had thought at first that Gilman's window was dark, but then he had seen the faint violet glow within. He wanted to warn the gentleman about that glow, for everybody in Arkham knew it was Keziah's witch-light which played near Brown Jenkin and the ghost of the old crone herself. He had not mentioned this before, but now he must tell about it because it meant that Keziah and her long-toothed familiar were haunting the young gentleman. Sometimes he and Paul Choynski and Landlord Dombrowski thought they saw that light seeping out of cracks in the sealed loft above the young gentleman's room, but they had all agreed not to talk about that. However, it would be better for the gentleman to take another room and get a crucifix from some good priest like Father Iwanicki.

As the man rambled on, Gilman felt a nameless panic clutch at his throat. He knew that Joe must have been half drunk when he came home the night before; yet the mention of a violet light in the garret window was of frightful import. It was a lambent glow of this sort which always played about the old woman and the small furry thing in those lighter, sharper dreams which prefaced his plunge into unknown abysses, and the thought that a wakeful second person could see the dream-luminance was utterly beyond sane harborage. Yet where had the fellow got such an odd notion? Had he himself talked as well as walked around the house in his sleep? No, Joe said, he had not—but he must check up on this. Perhaps Frank Elwood could tell him something, though he hated to ask.

Fever—wild dreams—somnambulism—illusions of sounds—a pull toward a point in the sky—and now a suspicion of insane sleep-talking! He must stop studying, see a nerve specialist, and take himself in hand. When he climbed to the second story he paused at Elwood's door but saw that the other youth was out. Reluctantly he continued up to his garret room and sat down in the dark. His gaze was still pulled to the southward, but he also found himself listening intently for some sound in the closed loft above, and half imagining that an evil violet light seeped down through an infinitesimal crack in the low, slanting ceiling.

That night as Gilman slept, the violet light broke upon him with heightened intensity, and the old witch and small furry thing, getting closer than ever before, mocked him with inhuman squeals and devilish gestures. He was glad to sink into the vaguely roaring twilight abysses, though the pursuit of that iridescent bubble-congeries and that kaleidoscopic little polyhedron was menacing and irritating. Then came the shift as vast converging planes of a slippery-looking substance loomed above and below him—a shift which ended in a flash of delirium and a blaze of unknown, alien light in which yellow, carmine, and indigo were madly and inextricably blended.

He was half lying on a high, fantastically balustraded terrace above a boundless jungle of outlandish, incredible peaks, balanced planes, domes, minarets, horizontal disks poised on pinnacles, and numberless forms of still greater wildness—some of stone and some of metal—which glittered gorgeously in the mixed, almost blistering glare from a polychromatic sky. Looking upward he saw three stupendous disks of flame, each of a different hue, and at a different height above an infinitely distant curving horizon of low mountains. Behind him tiers of higher terraces towered aloft as far as he could see. The city below stretched away to the limits of vision, and he hoped that no sound would well up from it.

The pavement from which he easily raised himself was a veined, polished stone beyond his power to identify, and the tiles were cut in bizarre-angled shapes which struck him as less asymmetrical than based on some unearthly symmetry whose laws he could not comprehend. The balustrade was chest-high, delicate, and fantastically wrought, while along the rail were ranged at short intervals little figures of grotesque design and exquisite workmanship. They, like the whole balustrade, seemed to be made of some sort of shining metal whose color could not be guessed in the chaos of mixed effulgences, and their nature utterly defied conjecture. They represented some ridged barrel-shaped object with thin horizontal arms radiating spoke-like from a central ring and with vertical knobs or bulbs projecting from the head and base of the barrel. Each of these knobs was the hub of a system of five long, flat, triangularly tapering arms arranged around it like the arms of a starfish—nearly horizontal, but curving slightly away from the central barrel. The base of the bottom knob was fused to the long railing with so delicate a point of contact that several figures had been broken off and were missing. The figures were about four and a half inches in height, while the spiky arms gave them a maximum diameter of about two and a half inches.

When Gilman stood up, the tiles felt hot to his bare feet. He was wholly alone, and his first act was to walk to the balustrade and look dizzily down at the endless, cyclopean city almost two thousand feet below. As he listened he thought a rhythmic confusion of faint musical pipings covering a wide tonal range welled up from the narrow streets beneath, and he wished he might discern the denizens of the place. The sight turned him giddy after a while, so that he would have fallen to the pavement had he not clutched instinctively at the lustrous balustrade. His right hand fell on one of the projecting figures, the touch seeming to steady him slightly. It was too much, however, for the exotic delicacy of the metal-work, and the spiky figure snapped off under his grasp. Still half dazed, he continued to clutch it as his other hand seized a vacant space on the smooth railing.

But now his over-sensitive ears caught something behind him, and he looked back across the level terrace. Approaching him softly though without apparent furtiveness were five figures, two of which were the sinister old woman and the fanged, furry little animal. The other three were what sent him unconscious; for they were living entities about eight feet high, shaped precisely like the spiky images on the balustrade, and propelling themselves by a spider-like wriggling of their lower set of starfish-arms.

Gilman awoke in his bed, drenched by a cold perspiration and with a smarting sensation in his face, hands and feet. Springing to the floor, he washed and dressed in frantic haste, as if it were necessary for him to get out of the house as quickly as possible. He did not know where he wished to go, but felt that once more he would have to sacrifice his classes. The odd pull toward that spot in the sky between Hydra and Argo had abated, but another of even greater strength had taken its place. Now he felt that he must go north—infinitely north. He dreaded to cross the bridge that gave a view of the desolate island in the Miskatonic, so went over the Peabody Avenue bridge. Very often he stumbled, for his eyes and ears were chained to an extremely lofty point in the blank blue sky.

After about an hour he got himself under better control, and saw that he was far from the city. All around him stretched the bleak emptiness of salt marshes, while the narrow road ahead led to Innsmouth—that ancient, half-deserted town which Arkham people were so curiously unwilling to visit. Though the northward pull had not diminished, he resisted it as he had resisted the other pull, and finally found that he could almost balance the one against the other. Plodding back to town and getting some coffee at a soda fountain, he dragged himself into the public library and browsed aimlessly among the lighter magazines. Once he met some friends who remarked how oddly sunburned he looked, but he did not tell them of his walk. At three o'clock he took some lunch at a restaurant, noting meanwhile that the pull had either lessened or divided itself. After that he killed the time at a cheap cinema show, seeing the inane performance over and over again without paying any attention to it.

About nine at night he drifted homeward and shuffled into the ancient house. Joe Mazurewicz was whining unintelligible prayers, and Gilman hastened up to his own garret chamber without pausing to see if Elwood was in. It was when he turned on the feeble electric light that the shock came. At once he saw there was something on the table which did not belong there, and a second look left no room for doubt. Lying on its side—for it could not stand up alone—was the exotic spiky figure which in his monstrous dream he had broken off the fantastic balustrade. No detail was missing. The ridged, barrel-shaped center, the thin radiating arms, the knobs at each end, and the flat, slightly outward-curving starfish-arms spreading from those knobs—all were there. In the electric light the color seemed to be a kind of iridescent gray veined with green; and Gilman could see amidst his horror and bewilderment that one of the knobs ended in a jagged break, corresponding to its former point of attachment to the dream-railing.

Only his tendency toward a dazed stupor prevented him from screaming aloud. This fusion of dream and reality was too much to bear. Still dazed, he clutched at the spiky thing and staggered downstairs to Landlord Dombrowski's quarters. The whining prayers of the superstitious loom-fixer were still sounding through the moldy halls, but Gilman did not mind them now. The landlord was in, and greeted him pleasantly. No, he had not seen that thing before and did not know anything about it. But his wife had said she found a funny tin thing in one of the beds when she fixed the rooms at noon, and maybe that was it. Dombrowski called her, and she waddled in. Yes, that was the thing. She had found it in the young gentleman's bed— on the side next the wall. It had looked very queer to her, but of course the young gentleman had lots of queer things in his room— books and curios and pictures and markings on paper. She certainly knew nothing about it.

So Gilman climbed upstairs again in mental turmoil, convinced that he was either still dreaming or that his somnambulism had run to incredible extremes and led him to depredations in unknown places. Where had he got this outré thing? He did not recall seeing it in any museum in Arkham. It must have been somewhere, though; and the sight of it as he snatched it in his sleep must have caused the odd dream-picture of the balustraded terrace. Next day he would make some very guarded inquiries—and perhaps see the nerve specialist.

Meanwhile he would try to keep track of his somnambulism. As he went upstairs and across the garret hall he sprinkled about some flour which he had borrowed—with a frank admission as to its purpose—from the landlord. He had stopped at Elwood's door on the way, but had found all dark within. Entering his room, he placed the spiky thing on the table, and lay down in complete mental and physical exhaustion without pausing to undress. From the closed loft above the slanting ceiling he thought he heard a faint scratching and padding, but he was too disorganized even to mind it. That cryptical pull from the north was getting very strong again, though it seemed now to come from a lower place in the sky.

In the dazzling violet light of dream the old woman and the fanged, furry thing came again and with a greater distinctness than on any former occasion. This time they actually reached him, and he felt the crone's withered claws clutching at him. He was pulled out of bed and into empty space, and for a moment he heard a rhythmic roaring and saw the twilight amorphousness of the vague abysses seething around him. But that moment was very brief, for presently he was in a crude, windowless little space with rough beams and planks rising to a peak just above his head, and with a curious slanting floor underfoot. Propped level on that floor were low cases full of books of every degree of antiquity and disintegration, and in the center were a table and bench, both apparently fastened in place. Small objects of unknown shape and nature were ranged on the tops of the cases, and in the flaming violet light Gilman thought he saw a counterpart of the spiky image which had puzzled him so horribly. On the left the floor fell abruptly away, leaving a black triangular gulf out of which, after a second's dry rattling, there presently climbed the hateful little furry thing with the yellow fangs and bearded human face.

The evilly grinning beldame still clutched him, and beyond the table stood a figure he had never seen before—a tall, lean man of dead black coloration but without the slightest sign of negroid features; wholly devoid of either hair or beard, and wearing as his only garment a shapeless robe of some heavy black fabric. His feet were indistinguishable because of the table and bench, but he must have been shod, since there was a clicking whenever he changed position. The man did not speak, and bore no trace of expression on his small, regular features. He merely pointed to a book of prodigious size which lay open on the table, while the beldame thrust a huge gray quill into Gilman's right hand. Over everything was a pall of intensely maddening fear, and the climax was reached when the furry thing ran up the dreamer's clothing to his shoulders and then down his left arm, finally biting him sharply in the wrist just below his cuff. As the blood spurted from this wound Gilman lapsed into a faint.

He awaked on the morning of the twenty-second with a pain in his left wrist, and saw that his cuff was brown with dried blood. His recollections were very confused, but the scene with the black man in the unknown space stood out vividly. The rats must have bitten him as he slept, giving rise to the climax of that frightful dream. Opening the door, he saw that the flour on the corridor floor was undisturbed except for the huge prints of the loutish fellow who roomed at the other end of the garret. So he had not been sleep-walking this time. But something would have to be done about those rats. He would speak to the landlord about them. Again he tried to stop up the hole at the base of the slanting wall, wedging in a candlestick which seemed of about the right size. His ears were ringing horribly, as if with the residual echoes of some horrible noise heard in dreams.

As he bathed and changed clothes he tried to recall what he had dreamed after the scene in the violet-litten space, but nothing definite would crystallize in his mind. That scene itself must have corresponded to the sealed loft overhead, which had begun to attack his imagination so violently, but later impressions were faint and hazy. There were suggestions of the vague, twilight abysses, and of still vaster, blacker abysses beyond them—abysses in which all fixed suggestions were absent. He had been taken there by the bubble-congeries and the little polyhedron which always dogged him; but they, like himself, had changed to wisps of mist in this farther void of ultimate blackness. Something else had gone on ahead—a larger wisp which now and then condensed into nameless approximations of form—and he thought that their progress had not been in a straight line, but rather along the alien curves and spirals of some ethereal vortex which obeyed laws unknown to the physics and mathematics of any conceivable cosmos. Eventually there had been a hint of vast, leaping shadows, of a monstrous, half-acoustic pulsing, and of the thin, monotonous piping of an unseen flute—but that was all. Gilman decided he had picked up that last conception from what he had read in the *Necronomicon* about the mindless entity Azathoth, which rules all time and space from a black throne at the center of Chaos.

When the blood was washed away the wrist wound proved very slight, and Gilman puzzled over the location of the two tiny punctures. It occurred to him that there was no blood on the bedspread where he had lain—which was very curious in view of the amount on his skin and cuff. Had he been sleep-walking within his room, and had the rat bitten him as he sat in some chair or paused in some less rational position? He looked in every corner for brownish drops or stains, but did not find any. He had better, he thought, sprinkle flour within the room as well as outside the door—though after all no further proof of his sleepwalking was needed. He knew he did walk—and the thing to do now was to stop it. He must ask Frank Elwood for help. This morning the strange pulls from space seemed lessened, though they were replaced by another sensation even more inexplicable. It was a vague, insistent impulse to fly away from his present situation, but held not a hint of the specific direction in which he wished to fly. As he picked up the strange spiky image on the table he thought the older northward pull grew a trifle stronger, but even so, it was wholly overruled by the newer and more bewildering urge.

He took the spiky image down to Elwood's room, steeling himself against the whines of the loom-fixer which welled up from the ground floor. Elwood was in, thank heaven, and appeared to be stirring about. There was time for a little conversation before leaving for breakfast and college; so Gilman hurriedly poured forth an account of his recent dreams and fears. His host was very sympathetic, and agreed that something ought to be done. He was shocked by his guest's drawn, haggard aspect, and noticed the queer, abnormal-looking sunburn which others had remarked during the past week. There was not much, though, that he could say. He had not seen Gilman on any sleep-walking expedition, and had no idea what the curious image could be. He had, though, heard the French-Canadian who lodged just under Gilman talking to Mazurewicz one evening. They were telling each other how badly they dreaded the coming of

Walpurgis Night, now only a few days off; and were exchanging pitying comments about the poor, doomed young gentleman. Desrochers, the fellow under Gilman's room, had spoken of nocturnal footsteps shod and unshod, and of the violet light he saw one night when he had stolen fearfully up to peer through Gilman's keyhole. He had not dared to peer, he told Mazurewicz, after he had glimpsed that light through the cracks around the door. There had been soft talking, too—and as he began to describe it his voice had sunk to an inaudible whisper.

Elwood could not imagine what had set these superstitious creatures gossiping, but supposed their imaginations had been roused by Gilman's late hours and somnolent walking and talking on the one hand, and by the nearness of traditionally-feared May Eve on the other hand. That Gilman talked in his sleep was plain, and it was obviously from Desrochers' keyhole-listenings that the delusive notion of the violet dream-light had got abroad. These simple people were quick to imagine they had seen any odd thing they had heard about. As for a plan of action—Gilman had better move down to Elwood's room and avoid sleeping alone. Elwood would, if awake, rouse him whenever he began to talk or rise in his sleep. Very soon, too, he must see the specialist. Meanwhile they would take the spiky image around to the various museums and to certain professors; seeking identification and stating that it had been found in a public rubbish-can. Also, Dombrowski must attend to the poisoning of those rats in the walls.

Braced up by Elwood's companionship, Gilman attended classes that day. Strange urges still tugged at him, but he could sidetrack them with considerable success. During a free period he showed the queer image to several professors, all of whom were intensely interested, though none of them could shed any light upon its nature or origin. That night he slept on a couch which Elwood had had the landlord bring to the second-story room, and for the first time in weeks was wholly free from disquieting dreams. But the feverishness still hung on, and the whines of the loom-fixer were an unnerving influence.

During the next few days Gilman enjoyed an almost perfect immunity from morbid manifestations. He had, Elwood said, showed no tendency to talk or rise in his sleep; and meanwhile the landlord was putting rat-poison everywhere. The only disturbing element was the talk among the superstitious foreigners, whose imaginations had become highly excited. Mazurewicz was always trying to make him get a crucifix, and finally forced one upon him which he said had been blessed by the good Father Iwanicki. Desrochers, too, had something to say; in fact, he insisted that cautious steps had sounded in the now vacant room above him on the first and second nights of Gilman's absence from it. Paul Choynski thought he heard sounds in the halls and on the stairs at night, and claimed that his door had been softly tried, while Mrs. Dombrowski vowed she had seen Brown Jenkin for the first time since All-Hallows. But such naïve reports could mean very little, and Gilman let the cheap metal crucifix hang idly from a knob on his host's dresser.

For three days Gilman and Elwood canvassed the local museums in an effort to identify the strange spiky image, but always without success. In every quarter, however, interest was intense; for the utter alienage of the thing was a tremendous challenge to scientific curiosity. One of the small radiating arms was broken off and subjected to chemical analysis. Professor Ellery found platinum, iron and tellurium in the strange alloy; but mixed with these were at least three other apparent elements of high atomic weight which chemistry was absolutely powerless to classify. Not only did they fail to correspond with any known element, but they did not even fit the vacant places reserved for probable elements in the periodic system. The mystery remains unsolved to this day, though the image is on exhibition at the museum of Miskatonic University.

On the morning of April twenty-seventh a fresh rat-hole appeared in the room where Gilman was a guest, but Dombrowski tinned it up during the day. The poison was not having much effect, for scratchings and scurryings in the walls were virtually undiminished.

Elwood was out late that night, and Gilman waited up for him. He did not wish to go to sleep in a room alone—especially since he thought he had glimpsed in the evening twilight the repellent old woman whose image had become so horribly transferred to his dreams. He wondered who she was, and what had been near her rattling the tin can in a rubbish-heap at the mouth of a squalid courtyard. The crone had seemed to notice him and leer evilly at him—though perhaps this was merely his imagination.

The next day both youths felt very tired, and knew they would sleep like logs when night came. In the evening they drowsily discussed the mathematical studies which had so completely and perhaps harmfully engrossed Gilman, and speculated about the linkage with ancient magic and folklore which seemed so darkly probable. They spoke of old Keziah Mason, and Elwood agreed that Gilman had good scientific grounds for thinking she might have stumbled on strange and significant information. The hidden cults to which these witches belonged often guarded and handed down surprising secrets from elder, forgotten eons; and it was by no means impossible that

Keziah had actually mastered the art of passing through dimensional gates. Tradition emphasizes the uselessness of material barriers in halting a witch's motions, and who can say what underlies the old tales of broomstick rides through the night?

Whether a modern student could ever gain similar powers from mathematical research alone, was still to be seen. Success, Gilman added, might lead to dangerous and unthinkable situations; for who could foretell the conditions pervading an adjacent but normally inaccessible dimension? On the other hand, the picturesque possibilities were enormous. Time could not exist in certain belts of space, and by entering and remaining in such a belt one might preserve one's life and age indefinitely; never suffering organic metabolism or deterioration except for slight amounts incurred during visits to one's own or similar planes. One might, for example, pass into a timeless dimension and emerge at some remote period of the earth's history as young as before.

Whether anybody had ever managed to do this, one could hardly conjecture with any degree of authority. Old legends are hazy and ambiguous, and in historic times all attempts at crossing forbidden gaps seem complicated by strange and terrible alliances with beings and messengers from outside. There was the immemorial figure of the deputy or messenger of hidden and terrible powers—the "Black Man" of the witch-cult, and the "Nyarlathotep" of the *Necronomicon*. There was, too, the baffling problem of the lesser messengers or intermediaries—the quasi-animals and queer hybrids which legend depicts as witches' familiars. As Gilman and Elwood retired, too sleepy to argue further, they heard Joe Mazurewicz reel into the house half drunk, and shuddered at the desperate wildness of his whining prayers.

That night Gilman saw the violet light again. In his dream he had heard a scratching and gnawing in the partitions, and thought that some one fumbled clumsily at the latch. Then he saw the old woman and the small furry thing advancing toward him over the carpeted floor. The beldame's face was alight with inhuman exultation, and the little yellow-toothed morbidity tittered mockingly as it pointed at the heavily-sleeping form of Elwood on the other couch across the room. A paralysis of fear stifled all attempts to cry out. As once before, the hideous crone seized Gilman by the shoulders, yanking him out of bed and into empty space. Again the infinitude of the shrieking abysses flashed past him, but in another second he thought he was in a dark, muddy, unknown alley of foetid odors with the rotting walls of ancient houses towering up on every hand.

Ahead was the robed black man he had seen in the peaked space in the other dream, while from a lesser distance the old woman was beckoning and grimacing imperiously. Brown Jenkin was rubbing itself with a kind of affectionate playfulness around the ankles of the black man, which the deep mud largely concealed. There was a dark open doorway on the right, to which the black man silently pointed. Into this the grinning crone started, dragging Gilman after her by his pajama sleeves. There were evil-smelling staircases which creaked ominously, and on which the old woman seemed to radiate a faint violet light; and finally a door leading off a landing. The crone fumbled with the latch and pushed the door open, motioning to Gilman to wait, and disappearing inside the black aperture.

The youth's over-sensitive ears caught a hideous strangled cry, and presently the beldame came out of the room bearing a small, senseless form which she thrust at the dreamer as if ordering him to carry it. The sight of this form, and the expression on its face, broke the spell. Still too dazed to cry out, he plunged recklessly down the noisome staircase and into the mud outside; halting only when seized and choked by the waiting black man. As consciousness departed he heard the faint, shrill tittering of the fanged, rat-like abnormality.

On the morning of the twenty-ninth Gilman awaked into a maelstrom of horror. The instant he opened his eyes he knew something was terribly wrong, for he was back in his old garret room with the slanting wall and ceiling, sprawled on the now unmade bed. His throat was aching inexplicably, and as he struggled to a sitting posture he saw with growing fright that his feet and pajama bottoms were brown with caked mud. For the moment his recollections were hopelessly hazy, but he knew at least that he must have been sleepwalking. Elwood had been lost too deeply in slumber to hear and stop him. On the floor were confused muddy prints, but oddly enough they did not extend all the way to the door. The more Gilman looked at them, the more peculiar they seemed; for in addition to those he could recognize as his there were some smaller, almost round markings—such as the legs of a large chair or a table might make, except that most of them tended to be divided into halves. There were also some curious muddy rat-tracks leading out of a fresh hole and back into it again. Utter bewilderment and the fear of madness racked Gilman as he staggered to the door and saw that there were no muddy prints outside. The more he remembered of his hideous dream the more terrified he felt, and it added to his desperation to hear Joe Mazurewicz chanting mournfully two floors below.

Descending to Elwood's room he roused his still-sleeping host and began telling of how he had found himself, but Elwood could form no idea of what might really have happened. Where Gilman could have been, how he got back to his room without making tracks in the hall, and how the muddy, furniture-like prints came to be mixed with his in the garret chamber, were wholly beyond conjecture. Then there were those dark, livid marks on his throat, as if he had tried to strangle himself. He put his hands up to them, but found that they did not even approximately fit. While they were talking, Desrochers dropped in to say that he had heard a terrific clattering overhead in the dark small hours. No, there had been no one on the stairs after midnight, though just before midnight he had heard faint footfalls in the garret, and cautiously descending steps he did not like. It was, he added, a very bad time of year for Arkham. The young gentleman had better be sure to wear the crucifix Joe Mazurewicz had given him. Even the daytime was not safe, for after dawn there had been strange sounds in the house—especially a thin, childish wail hastily choked off.

Gilman mechanically attended classes that morning, but was wholly unable to fix his mind on his studies. A mood of hideous apprehension and expectancy had seized him, and he seemed to be awaiting the fall of some annihilating blow. At noon he lunched at the University Spa, picking up a paper from the next seat as he waited for dessert. But he never ate that dessert; for an item on the paper's first page left him limp, wild-eyed, and able only to pay his check and stagger back to Elwood's room.

There had been a strange kidnapping the night before in Orne's Gangway, and the two-year-old child of a clod-like laundry worker named Anastasia Wolejko had completely vanished from sight. The mother, it appeared, had feared the event for some time; but the reasons she assigned for her fear was so grotesque that no one took them seriously. She had, she said, seen Brown Jenkin about the place now and then ever since early in March, and knew from its grimaces and titterings that little Ladislas must be marked for sacrifice at the awful Sabbat on Walpurgis Night. She had asked her neighbor Mary Czanek to sleep in the room and try to protect the child, but Mary had not dared. She could not tell the police, for they never believed such things. Children had been taken that way every year ever since she could remember. And her friend Pete Stowacki would not help because he wanted the child out of the way.

But what threw Gilman into a cold perspiration was the report of a pair of revellers who had been walking past the mouth of the gangway just after midnight. They admitted they had been drunk, but both vowed they had seen a crazily dressed trio furtively entering the dark passageway. There had, they said, been a huge robed negro, a little old woman in rags, and a young white man in his night-clothes. The old woman had been dragging the youth, while around the feet of the negro a tame rat was rubbing and weaving in the brown mud.

Gilman sat in a daze all the afternoon, and Elwood—who had meanwhile seen the papers and formed terrible conjectures from them—found him thus when he came home. This time neither could doubt but that something hideously serious was closing in around them. Between the phantasms of nightmare and the realities of the objective world a monstrous and unthinkable relationship was crystallizing, and only stupendous vigilance could avert still more direful developments. Gilman must see a specialist sooner or later, but not just now, when all the papers were full of this kidnapping business.

Just what had really happened was maddeningly obscure, and for a moment both Gilman and Elwood exchanged whispered theories of the wildest kind. Had Gilman unconsciously succeeded better than he knew in his studies of space and its dimensions? Had he actually slipped outside our sphere to points unguessed and unimaginable? Where—if anywhere—had he been on those nights of demoniac alienage? The roaring twilight abysses—the green hillside—the blistering terrace—the pulls from the stars—the ultimate black vortex—the black man—the muddy alley and the stairs—the old witch and the fanged, furry horror—the bubble-congeries and the little polyhedron—the strange sunburn—the wrist-wound—the unexplained image—the muddy feet—the throat-marks—the tales and fears of the superstitious foreigners—what did all this mean? To what extent could the laws of sanity apply to such a case?

There was no sleep for either of them that night, but next day they both cut classes and drowsed. This was April thirtieth, and with the dusk would come the hellish Sabbat-time which all the foreigners and the superstitious old folk feared. Mazurewicz came home at six o'clock and said people at the mill were whispering that the Walpurgis-revels would be held in the dark ravine beyond Meadow Hill where the old white stone stands in a place queerly devoid of all plant life. Some of them had even told the police and advised them to look there for the missing Wolejko child, but they did not believe anything would be done. Joe insisted that the poor young gentleman wear his nickel-chained crucifix, and Gilman put it on and dropped it inside his shirt to humor the fellow.

Late at night the two youths sat drowsing in their chairs, lulled by the praying of the loom-fixer on the floor below. Gilman listened as he nodded, his preternaturally sharpened hearing seeming to strain for some subtle, dreaded murmur beyond the noises in the ancient house. Unwholesome recollections of things in the *Necronomicon* and the *Black Book* welled up, and he found himself swaying to infandous rhythms said to pertain to the blackest ceremonies of the Sabbat and to have an origin outside the time and space we comprehend.

Presently he realized what he was listening for—the hellish chant of the celebrants in the distant black valley. How did he know so much about what they expected? How did he know the time when Nahab and her acolyte were due to bear the brimming bowl which would follow the black cock and the black goat? He saw that Elwood had dropped asleep, and tried to call out and waken him. Something, however, closed his throat. He was not his own master. Had he signed the black man's book after all?

Then his fevered, abnormal hearing caught the distant, windborne notes. Over miles of hill and field and alley they came, but he recognized them none the less. The fires must be lit, and the dancers must be starting in. How could he keep himself from going? What was it that had enmeshed him? Mathematics—folklore—the house— old Keziah—Brown Jenkin . . . and now he saw that there was a fresh rat-hole in the wall near his couch. Above the distant chanting and the nearer praying of Joe Mazurewicz came another sound—a stealthy, determined scratching in the partitions. He hoped the electric lights would not go out. Then he saw the fanged, bearded little face in the rat-hole—the accursed little face which he at last realized bore such a shocking, mocking resemblance to old Keziah's—and heard the faint fumbling at the door.

The screaming twilight abysses flashed before him, and he felt himself helpless in the formless grasp of the iridescent bubble-congeries. Ahead raced the small, kaleidoscopic polyhedron and all through the churning void there was a heightening and acceleration of the vague tonal pattern which seemed to foreshadow some unutterable and unendurable climax. He seemed to know what was coming—the monstrous burst of Walpurgis-rhythm in whose cosmic timbre would be concentrated all the primal, ultimate space-time seethings which lie behind the massed spheres of matter and some-times break forth in measured reverberations that penetrate faintly to every layer of entity and give hideous significance throughout the worlds to certain dreaded periods.

But all this vanished in a second. He was again in the cramped, violet-litten peaked space with the slanting floor, the low case of an-cient books, the bench and table, the queer objects, and the triangular gulf at one side. On the table lay a small white figure—an infant boy, unclothed and unconscious—while on the other side stood the mon-strous, leering old woman with a gleaming, grotesque-hafted knife in her right hand, and a queerly proportioned pale metal bowl covered with curiously chased designs and having delicate lateral handles in her left. She was intoning some croaking ritual in a language which Gilman could not understand, but which seemed like something guardedly quoted in the *Necronomicon*.

As the scene grew clearer he saw the ancient crone bend forward and extend the empty bowl across the table—and unable to control his own emotions, he reached far forward and took it in both hands, noticing as he did so its comparative lightness. At the same moment the disgusting form of Brown Jenkin scrambled up over the brink of the triangular black gulf on his left. The crone now motioned him to hold the bowl in a certain position while she raised the huge, grotesque knife above the small white victim as high as her right hand could reach. The fanged, furry thing began tittering a continuation of the unknown ritual, while the witch croaked loathsome responses. Gilman felt a gnawing poignant abhorrence shoot through his mental and emotional paralysis, and the light metal bowl shook in his grasp. A second later the downward motion of the knife broke the spell completely, and he dropped the bowl with a resounding bell-like clangor while his hands darted out frantically to stop the monstrous deed.

In an instant he had edged up the slanting floor around the end of the table and wrenched the knife from the old woman's claws; sending it clattering over the brink of the narrow triangular gulf. In another instant, however, matters were reversed; for those murderous claws had locked themselves tightly around his own throat, while the wrinkled face was twisted with insane fury. He felt the chain of the cheap crucifix grinding into his neck, and in his peril wondered how the sight of the object itself would affect the evil creature. Her strength was altogether superhuman, but as she continued her choking he reached feebly in his shirt and drew out the metal symbol, snapping the chain and pulling it free.

At sight of the device the witch seemed struck with panic, and her grip relaxed long enough to give Gilman a chance to break it entirely. He pulled the steel-like claws from his neck, and would have dragged the beldame over the edge of the gulf had not the claws received a fresh access of strength and closed in again. This time he resolved to reply in kind, and his own hands reached out for the creature's throat. Before she saw what he was doing he had the chain of the crucifix twisted about her neck, and a moment later he had tightened it enough to cut off her breath. During her last struggle he felt something bite at his ankle, and saw that Brown Jenkin had come to her aid. With one savage kick he sent the morbidity over the edge of the gulf and heard it whimper on some level far below.

Whether he had killed the ancient crone he did not know, but he let her rest on the floor where she had fallen. Then, as he turned away, he saw on the table a sight which nearly snapped the last thread of his reason. Brown Jenkin, tough of sinew and with four tiny hands of demoniac dexterity, had been busy while the witch was throttling him, and his efforts had been in vain. What he had prevented the knife from doing to the victim's chest, the yellow fangs of the furry blasphemy had done to a wrist—and the bowl so lately on the floor stood full beside the small lifeless body.

In his dream-delirium Gilman heard the hellish alien-rhythmed chant of the Sabbat coming from an infinite distance, and knew the black man must be there. Confused memories mixed themselves with his mathematics, and he believed his subconscious mind held the *angles* which he needed to guide him back to the normal world alone and unaided for the first time. He felt sure he was in the immemorially sealed loft above his own room, but whether he could ever escape through the slanting floor or the long-stooped egress he doubted greatly. Besides, would not an escape from a dream-loft bring him merely into a dream-house—an abnormal projection of the actual place he sought? He was wholly bewildered as to the relation betwixt dream and reality in all his experiences.

The passage through the vague abysses would be frightful, for the Walpurgis-rhythm would be vibrating, and at last he would have to hear that hitherto-veiled cosmic pulsing which he so mortally dreaded. Even now he could detect a low, monstrous shaking whose tempo he suspected all too well. At Sabbat-time it always mounted and reached through to the worlds to summon the initiate to nameless rites. Half the chants of the Sabbat were patterned on this faintly overheard pulsing which no earthly ear could endure in its unveiled spatial fullness. Gilman wondered, too, whether he could trust his instincts to take him back to the right part of space. How could he be sure he would not land on that green-litten hillside of a far planet, on the tessellated terrace above the city of tentacled monsters somewere beyond the galaxy or in the spiral black vortices of that ultimate void of Chaos where reigns the mindless demon-sultan Azathoth?

Just before he made the plunge the violet light went out and left him in utter blackness. The witch—old Keziah—Nahab—that must have meant her death. And mixed with the distant chant of the Sabbat and the whimpers of Brown Jenkin in the gulf below he thought he heard another and wilder whine from unknown depths. Joe Mazurewicz—the prayers against the Crawling Chaos now turning to an inexplicably triumphant shriek—worlds of sardonic actuality impinging on vortices of febrile dream—Iä! Shub-Niggurath! The Goat with a Thousand Young. . . .

They found Gilman on the floor of his queerly-angled old garret room long before dawn, for the terrible cry had brought Desrochers and Choynski and Dombrowski and Mazurewicz at once, and had even wakened the soundly sleeping Elwood in his chair. He was alive, and with open, staring eyes, but seemed largely unconscious. On his throat were the marks of murderous hands, and on his left ankle was a distressing rat-bite. His clothing was badly rumpled, and Joe's crucifix was missing. Elwood trembled, afraid even to speculate what new form his friend's sleep-walking had taken. Mazurewicz seemed half dazed because of a "sign" he said he had had in response to his prayers, and he crossed himself frantically when the squealing and whimpering of a rat sounded from beyond the slanting partition.

When the dreamer was settled on his couch on Elwood's room they sent for Doctor Malkowski—a local practitioner who would repeat no tales where they might prove embarrassing—and he gave Gilman two hypodermic injections which caused him to relax in something like natural drowsiness. During the day the patient regained consciousness at times and whispered his newest dream disjointedly to Elwood. It was a painful process, and at its very start brought out a fresh and disconcerting fact.

Gilman—whose ears had so lately possessed an abnormal sensitiveness—was now stone-deaf. Doctor Malkowski, summoned again in haste, told Elwood that both ear-drums were ruptured, as if by the impact of some stupendous sound intense beyond all human conception or endurance. How such a sound could have been heard in the last few hours without arousing all the Miskatonic Valley was more than the honest physician could say.

Elwood wrote his part of the colloquy on paper, so that a fairly easy communication was maintained. Neither knew what to make of the whole chaotic business, and decided it would be better if they thought as little as possible about it. Both, though, agreed that they must leave this ancient and accursed house as soon as it could be arranged. Evening papers spoke of a police raid on some curious revellers in a ravine beyond Meadow Hill just before dawn, and mentioned that the white stone there was an object of age-long superstitious regard. Nobody had been caught, but among the scattering fugitives had been glimpsed a huge negro. In another column it was stated that no trace of the missing child Ladislas Wolejko had been found.

The crowning horror came that very night. Elwood will never forget it, and was forced to stay out of college the rest of the term because of the resulting nervous breakdown. He had thought he heard rats in the partition all the evening, but paid little attention to them. Then, long after both he and Gilman had retired, the atrocious shrieking began. Elwood jumped up, turned on the lights and rushed over to his guest's couch. The occupant was emitting sounds of veritably inhuman nature, as if racked by some torment beyond description. He

was writhing under the bedclothes, and a great red stain was beginning to appear on the blankets.

Elwood scarcely dared to touch him, but gradually the screaming and writhing subsided. By this time Dombrowski, Choynski,
Desrochers, Mazurewicz, and the top-floor lodger were all crowding
into the doorway, and the landlord had sent his wife back to telephone for Doctor Malkowski. Everybody shrieked when a large rat-
like form suddenly jumped out from beneath the ensanguined
bedclothes and scuttled across the floor to a fresh, open hole close by.
When the doctor arrived and began to pull down those frightful covers Walter Gilman was dead.

It would be barbarous to do more than suggest what had killed
Gilman. There had been virtually a tunnel through his body—
something had eaten his heart out. Dombrowski, frantic at the failure
of his rat-poisoning efforts, cast aside all thought of his lease and
within a week had moved with all his older lodgers to a dingy but less
ancient house in Walnut Street. The worst thing for a while was
keeping Joe Mazurewicz quiet; for the brooding loom-fixer would
never stay sober, and was constantly whining and muttering about
spectral and terrible things.

It seems that on that last hideous night Joe had stooped to look at
the crimson rat-tracks which led from Gilman's couch to the near-by
hole. On the carpet they were very indistinct, but a piece of open
flooring intervened between the carpet's edge and the baseboard.
There Mazurewicz had found something monstrous—or thought he
had, for no one else could quite agree with him despite the undeniable queerness of the prints. The tracks on the flooring were certainly
vastly unlike the average prints of a rat but even Choynski and
Desrochers would not admit that they were like the prints of four
tiny human hands.

The house was never rented again. As soon as Dombrowski left it
the pall of its final desolation began to descend, for people shunned it
both on account of its old reputation and because of the new foetid
odor. Perhaps the ex-landlord's rat-poison had worked after all, for
not long after his departure the place became a neighborhood nui-
sance. Health officials traced the smell to the closed spaces above and
beside the eastern garret room, and agreed that the number of dead
rats must be enormous. They decided, however, that it was not worth
their while to hew open and disinfect the long-sealed spaces; for the
foetor would soon be over, and the locality was not one which encouraged fastidious standards. Indeed, there were always vague local
tales of unexplained stenches upstairs in the Witch-House just after
May-Eve and Hallowmass. The neighbors acquiesced in the inertia—

but the foetor none the less formed an additional count against the place. Toward the last the house was condemned as a habitation by the building inspector.

Gilman's dreams and their attendant circumstances have never been explained. Elwood, whose thoughts on the entire episode are sometimes almost maddening, came back to college the next autumn and was graduated in the following June. He found the spectral gossip of the town much diminished, and it is indeed a fact that—notwithstanding certain reports of a ghostly tittering in the deserted house which lasted almost as long as that edifice itself—no fresh appearances either of Old Keziah or of Brown Jenkin have been muttered of since Gilman's death. It is rather fortunate that Elwood was not in Arkham in that later year when certain events abruptly renewed the local whispers about elder horrors. Of course he heard about the matter afterward and suffered untold torments of black and bewildered speculation; but even that was not as bad as actual nearness and several possible sights would have been.

In March, 1931, a gale wrecked the roof and great chimney of the vacant Witch-House, so that a chaos of crumbling bricks, blackened, moss-grown shingles, and rotting planks and timbers crashed down into the loft and broke through the floor beneath. The whole attic story was choked with debris from above, but no one took the trouble to touch the mess before the inevitable razing of the decrepit structure. The ultimate step came in the following December, and it was when Gilman's old room was cleared out by reluctant, apprehensive workmen that the gossip began.

Among the rubbish which had crashed through the ancient slanting ceiling were several things which made the workmen pause and call in the police. Later the police in turn called in the coroner and several professors from the university. There were bones—badly crushed and splintered, but clearly recognizable as human—whose manifestly modern date conflicted puzzlingly with the remote period at which their only possible lurking place, the low, slant-floored loft overhead, had supposedly been sealed from all human access. The coroner's physician decided that some belonged to a small child, while certain others—found mixed with shreds of rotten brownish cloth—belonged to a rather undersized, bent female of advanced years. Careful sifting of debris also disclosed many tiny bones of rats caught in the collapse, as well as older rat-bones gnawed by small fangs in a fashion now and then highly productive of controversy and reflection.

Other objects found included the mangled fragments of many books and papers, together with a yellowish dust left from the total disintegration of still older books and papers. All, without exception, appeared to deal with black magic in its most advanced and horrible forms; and the evidently recent date of certain items is still a mystery as unsolved as that of the modern human bones. An even greater mystery is the absolute homogeneity of the crabbed, archaic writing found on a wide range of papers whose conditions and watermarks suggest age differences of at least one hundred fifty to two hundred years. To some, though, the greatest mystery of all is the variety of utterly inexplicable objects—objects whose shapes, materials, types of workmanship, and purposes baffle all conjecture—found scattered amidst the wreckage in evidently diverse states of injury. One of these things—which excited several Miskatonic professors profoundly—is a badly damaged monstrosity plainly resembling the strange image which Gilman gave to the college museum, save that it is large, wrought of some peculiar bluish stone instead of metal, and possessed of a singularly angled pedestal with undecipherable hieroglyphics.

Archeologists and anthropologists are still trying to explain the bizarre designs chased on a crushed bowl of light metal whose inner side bore ominous brownish stains when found. Foreigners and credulous grandmothers are equally garrulous about the modern nickel crucifix with broken chain mixed in the rubbish and shiveringly identified by Joe Mazurewicz as that which he had given poor Gilman many years before. Some believe this crucifix was dragged up to the sealed loft by rats, while others think it must have been on the floor in some corner of Gilman's old room at the time. Still others, including Joe himself, have theories too wild and fantastic for sober credence.

When the slanting wall of Gilman's room was torn out, the once sealed triangular space between that partition and the house's north wall was found to contain much less structural debris, even in proportion to its size, than the room itself; though it had a ghastly layer of older materials which paralyzed the wreckers with horror. In brief, the floor was a veritable ossuary of the bones of small children— some fairly modern, but others extending back in infinite gradations to a period so remote that crumbling was almost complete. On this deep bony layer rested a knife of great size, obvious antiquity, and grotesque, ornate, and exotic design—above which the debris was piled.

In the midst of this debris, wedged between a fallen plank and a cluster of cemented bricks from the ruined chimney, was an object destined to cause more bafflement, veiled fright, and openly superstitious talk in Arkham than anything else discovered in the haunted and accursed building. The object was the partly crushed skeleton of a huge diseased rat, whose abnormalities of form are still a topic of debate and source of singular reticence among the members of Miskatonic's department of comparative anatomy. Very little concerning this skeleton has leaked out, but the workmen who found it whisper in shocked tones about the long, brownish hairs with which it was associated.

The bones of the tiny paws, it is rumored, imply prehensile characteristics more typical of a diminutive monkey than of a rat, while the small skull with its savage yellow fangs is of the utmost anomalousness, appearing from certain angles like a miniature, monstrously degraded parody of a human skull. The workmen crossed themselves in fright when they came upon this blasphemy, but later burned candles of gratitude in St. Stanislaus' Church because of the shrill, ghostly tittering they felt they would never hear again.

The Shadow Out of Time

✦━━✦

After twenty-two years of nightmare and terror, saved only by a desperate conviction of the mythical source of certain impressions, I am unwilling to vouch for the truth of that which I think I found in Western Australia on the night of July 17–18, 1935. There is reason to hope that my experience was wholly or partly an hallucination—for which, indeed, abundant causes existed. And yet, its realism was so hideous that I sometimes find hope impossible.

If the thing did happen, then man must be prepared to accept notions of the cosmos, and of his own place in the seething vortex of time, whose merest mention is paralyzing. He must, too, be placed on guard against a specific, lurking peril which, though it will never engulf the whole race, may impose monstrous and unguessable horrors upon certain venturesome members of it.

It is for this latter reason that I urge, with all the force of my being, a final abandonment of all the attempts at unearthing those fragments of unknown, primordial masonry which my expedition set out to investigate.

Assuming that I was sane and awake, my experience on that night was such as has befallen no man before. It was, moreover, a frightful confirmation of all I had sought to dismiss as myth and dream. Mercifully there is no proof, for in my fright I lost the awesome object which would—if real and brought out of that noxious abyss—have formed irrefutable evidence.

When I came upon the horror I was alone—and I have up to now told no one about it. I could not stop the others from digging in its direction, but chance and the shifting sand have so far saved them from finding it. Now I must formulate some definite statement—not only for the sake of my own mental balance, but to warn such others as may read it seriously.

These pages—much in whose earlier parts will be familiar to close readers of the general and scientific press—are written in the cabin of the ship that is bringing me home. I shall give them to my son, Professor Wingate Peaslee of Miskatonic University—the only member of my family who stuck to me after my queer amnesia of long ago, and the man best informed on the inner facts of my case. Of all living persons, he is least likely to ridicule what I shall tell of that fateful night.

I did not enlighten him orally before sailing, because I think he had better have the revelation in written form. Reading and rereading at leisure will leave with him a more convincing picture than my confused tongue could hope to convey.

He can do anything that he thinks best with this account— showing it, with suitable comment, in any quarters where it will be likely to accomplish good. It is for the sake of such readers as are unfamiliar with the earlier phases of my case that I am prefacing the revelation itself with a fairly ample summary of its background.

My name is Nathaniel Wingate Peaslee, and those who recall the newspaper tales of a generation back—or the letters and articles in psychological journals six or seven years ago—will know who and what I am. The press was filled with the details of my strange amnesia in 1908–13, and much was made of the traditions of horror, madness, and witchcraft which lurked behind the ancient Massachusetts town then and now forming my place of residence. Yet I would have it known that there is nothing whatever of the mad or sinister in my heredity and early life. This is a highly important fact in view of the shadow which fell so suddenly upon me from *outside* sources.

It may be that centuries of dark brooding had given to crumbling, whisper-haunted Arkham a peculiar vulnerability as regards such shadows—though even this seems doubtful in the light of those other cases which I later came to study. But the chief point is that my own ancestry and background are altogether normal. What came, came from *somewhere else*—where, I even now hesitate to assert in plain words.

I am the son of Jonathan and Hannah (Wingate) Peaslee, both of wholesome old Haverhill stock. I was born and reared in Haverhill— at the old homestead in Boardman Street near Golden Hill—and did not go to Arkham till I entered Miskatonic University as instructor of political economy in 1895.

For thirteen years more my life ran smoothly and happily. I married Alice Keezar of Haverhill in 1896, and my three children, Robert, Wingate and Hannah were born in 1898, 1900, and 1903, respectively. In 1898 I became an associate professor, and in 1902 a full professor. At no time had I the least interest in either occultism or abnormal psychology.

It was on Thursday, May 14, 1908, that the queer amnesia came. The thing was quite sudden, though later I realized that certain brief, glimmering visions of several hours previous—chaotic visions which disturbed me greatly because they were so unprecedented—must have formed premonitory symptoms. My head was aching, and I had a singular feeling—altogether new to me—that some one else was trying to get possession of my thoughts.

The collapse occurred about 10:20 A.M., while I was conducting a class in Political Economy VI—history and present tendencies of economics—for juniors and a few sophomores. I began to see strange shapes before my eyes, and to feel that I was in a grotesque room other than the classroom.

My thoughts and speech wandered from my subject, and the students saw that something was gravely amiss. Then I slumped down, unconscious, in my chair, in a stupor from which no one could arouse me. Nor did my rightful faculties again look out upon the daylight of our normal world for five years, four months, and thirteen days.

It is, of course, from others that I have learned what followed. I showed no sign of consciousness for sixteen and a half hours, though removed to my home at 27 Crane Street, and given the best of medical attention.

At 3 A.M. May 15th my eyes opened and I began to speak, but before long the doctor and my family were thoroughly frightened by the trend of my expression and language. It was clear that I had no rememberance of my identity and my past, though for some reason I seemed anxious to conceal this lack of knowledge. My eyes gazed strangely at the persons around me, and the flections of my facial muscles were altogether unfamiliar.

Even my speech seemed awkward and foreign. I used my vocal organs clumsily and gropingly, and my diction had a curiously stilted quality, as if I had laboriously learned the English language from books. The pronunciation was barbarously alien, whilst the idiom seemed to include both scraps of curious archaism and expressions of a wholly incomprehensible cast.

Of the latter, one in particular was very potently—even terrifiedly—recalled by the youngest of the physicians twenty years afterward. For at that late period such a phrase began to have an actual currency—first in England and then in the United States—and though of much complexity and indisputable newness, it reproduced in every least particular the mystifying words of the strange Arkham patient of 1908.

Physical strength returned at once, although I required an odd

amount of reeducation in the use of my hands, legs, and bodily apparatus in general. Because of this and other handicaps inherent in the
mnemonic lapse, I was for some time kept under strict medical care.

When I saw that my attempts to conceal the lapse had failed, I admitted it openly, and became eager for information of all sorts. Indeed, it seemed to the doctors that I lost interest in my proper
personality as soon as I found the case of amnesia accepted as a natural thing.

They noticed that my chief efforts were to master certain points in
history, science, art, language, and folklore—some of them tremendously abstruse, and some childishly simple—which remained, very
oddly in many cases, outside my consciousness.

At the same time they noticed that I had an inexplicable command of many almost unknown sorts of knowledge—a command
which I seemed to wish to hide rather than display. I would inadvertently refer, with casual assurance, to specific events in dim ages outside of the range of accepted history—passing off such references as a
jest when I saw the surprise they created. And I had a way of speaking
of the future which two or three times caused actual fright.

These uncanny flashes soon ceased to appear, though some observers laid their vanishment more to a certain furtive caution on my
part than to any waning of the strange knowledge behind them. Indeed, I seemed anomalously avid to absorb the speech, customs, and
perspectives of the age around me; as if I were a studious traveler
from a far, foreign land.

As soon as permitted, I haunted the college library at all hours;
and shortly began to arrange for those odd travels, and special courses
at American and European Universities, which evoked so much comment during the next few years.

I did not at any time suffer from a lack of learned contacts, for my
case had a mild celebrity among the psychologists of the period. I was
lectured upon as a typical example of secondary personality—even
though I seemed to puzzle the lecturers now and then with some
bizarre symptoms or some queer trace of carefully veiled mockery.

Of real friendliness, however, I encountered little. Something in
my aspect and speech seemed to excite vague fears and aversions in
every one I met, as if I were a being infinitely removed from all that is
normal and healthful. This idea of a black, hidden horror connected
with incalculable gulfs of some sort of *distance* was oddly widespread
and persistent.

My own family formed no exception. From the moment of my
strange waking my wife had regarded me with extreme horror and
loathing, vowing that I was some utter alien usurping the body of her

husband. In 1910 she obtained a legal divorce, nor would she ever consent to see me even after my return to normality in 1913. These feelings were shared by my elder son and my small daughter, neither of whom I have ever seen since.

Only my second son, Wingate, seemed able to conquer the terror and repulsion which my change aroused. He indeed felt that I was a stranger, but though only eight years old held fast to a faith that my proper self would return. When it did return he sought me out, and the courts gave me his custody. In succeeding years he helped me with the studies to which I was driven, and today, at thirty-five, he is a professor of psychology at Miskatonic.

But I do not wonder at the horror I caused—for certainly, the mind, voice, and facial expression of the being that awakened on May 15, 1908, were not those of Nathaniel Wingate Peaslee.

I will not attempt to tell much of my life from 1908 to 1913, since readers may glean all the outward essentials—as I largely had to do—from files of old newspapers and scientific journals.

I was given charge of my funds, and spent them slowly and on the whole wisely, in travel and in study at various centers of learning. My travels, however, were singular in extreme, involving long visits to remote and desolate places.

In 1909 I spent a month in the Himalayas, and in 1911 aroused much attention through a camel trip into the unknown deserts of Arabia. What happened on those journeys I have never been able to learn.

During the summer of 1912 I chartered a ship and sailed in the Arctic, north of Spitzbergen, afterward showing signs of disappointment.

Later in that year I spent weeks alone beyond the limits of previous or subsequent exploration in the vast limestone cavern systems of western Virginia—black labyrinths so complex that no retracing of my steps could even be considered.

My sojourns at the universities were marked by abnormally rapid assimilation, as if the secondary personality had an intelligence enormously superior to my own. I have found, also, that my rate of reading and solitary study was phenomenal. I could master every detail of a book merely by glancing over it as fast as I could turn the leaves; while my skill at interpreting complex figures in an instant was veritably awesome.

At times there appeared almost ugly reports of my power to influence the thoughts and acts of others, though I seemed to have taken care to minimize displays of this faculty.

Other ugly reports concerned my intimacy with leaders of occultist groups, and scholars suspected of connection with nameless bands of abhorrent elder-world hierophants. These rumors, though never proved at the time, were doubtless stimulated by the known tenor of some of my reading—for the consultation of rare books at libraries cannot be effected secretly.

There is tangible proof—in the form of marginal notes—that I went minutely through such things as the Comte d'Erlette's *Cultes des Goules*, Ludvig Prinn's *De Vermis Mysteriis*, the *Unaussprechlichen Kulten* of von Junzt, the surviving fragments of the puzzling *Book of Eibon*, and the dreaded *Necronomicon* of the mad Arab Abdul Alhazred. Then, too, it is undeniable that a fresh and evil wave of underground cult activity set in about the time of my odd mutation.

In the summer of 1913 I began to display signs of ennui and flagging interest, and to hint to various associates that a change might soon be expected in me. I spoke of returning memories of my earlier life—though most auditors judged me insincere, since all the recollections I gave were casual, and such as might have been learned from my old private papers.

About the middle of August I returned to Arkham and reopened my long-closed house in Crane Street. Here I installed a mechanism of the most curious aspect, constructed piecemeal by different makers of scientific apparatus in Europe and America, and guarded carefully from the sight of any one intelligent enough to analyze it.

Those who did see it—a workman, a servant, and the new housekeeper—say that it was a queer mixture of rods, wheels, and mirrors, though only about two feet tall, one foot wide, and one foot thick. The central mirror was circular and convex. All this is borne out by such makers of parts as can be located.

On the evening of Friday, September 26, I dismissed the housekeeper and the maid until noon of the next day. Lights burned in the house till late, and a lean, dark, curiously foreign-looking man called in an automobile.

It was about one A.M. that the lights were last seen. At 2:15 A.M. a policeman observed the place in darkness, but the stranger's motor still at the curb. By 4 o'clock the motor was certainly gone.

It was at 6 o'clock that a hesitant, foreign voice on the telephone asked Dr. Wilson to call at my house and bring me out of a peculiar faint. This call—a long-distance one—was later traced to a public booth in the North Station in Boston, but no sign of the lean foreigner was ever unearthed.

When the doctor reached my house he found me unconscious in the sitting room—in an easy-chair with a table drawn up before it. On the polished top were scratches showing where some heavy object had rested. The queer machine was gone, nor was anything afterward heard of it. Undoubtedly the dark, lean foreigner had taken it away.

In the library grate were abundant ashes, evidently left from the burning of every remaining scrap of paper on which I had written since the advent of the amnesia. Dr. Wilson found my breathing very peculiar, but after a hypodermic injection it became more regular.

At 11:15 A.M., September 27th, I stirred vigorously, and my hitherto masklike face began to show signs of expression. Dr. Wilson remarked that the expression was not that of my secondary personality, but seemed much like that of my normal self. About 11:30 I muttered some very curious syllables—syllables which seemed unrelated to any human speech. I appeared, too, to struggle against something. Then, just after noon—the housekeeper and the maid having meanwhile returned—I began to mutter in English.

"—of the orthodox economists of that period, Jevons typifies the prevailing trend toward scientific correlation. His attempt to link the commercial cycle of prosperity and depression with the physical cycle of the solar spots forms perhaps the apex of—"

Nathaniel Wingate Peaslee had come back—a spirit in whose time scale it was still Thursday morning in 1908, with the economics class gazing up at the battered desk on the platform.

II

My reabsorption into normal life was a painful and difficult process. The loss of over five years creates more complications than can be imagined, and in my case there were countless matters to be adjusted.

What I heard of my actions since 1908 astonished and disturbed me, but I tried to view the matter as philosophically as I could. At last, regaining custody of my second son, Wingate, I settled down with him in the Crane Street house and endeavored to resume my teaching—my old professorship having been kindly offered me by the college.

I began work with the February, 1914, term, and kept at it just a year. By that time I realized how badly my experience had shaken me. Though perfectly sane—I hoped—and with no flaw in my original personality, I had not the nervous energy of the old days. Vague dreams and queer ideas continually haunted me, and when the outbreak of the World War turned my mind to history I found myself thinking of periods and events in the oddest possible fashion.

My conception of *time*—my ability to distinguish between consecutiveness and simultaneousness—seemed subtly disordered; so that I formed chimerical notions about living in one age and casting one's mind all over eternity for knowledge of past and future ages.

The War gave me strange impressions of remembering some of its far-off consequences—as if I knew how it was coming out and could look *back* upon it in the light of future information. All such quasi-memories were attended with much pain, and with a feeling that some artificial psychological barrier was set against them.

When I diffidently hinted to others about my impressions, I met with varied responses. Some persons looked uncomfortably at me, but men in the mathematics department spoke of new developments in those theories of relativity—then discussed only in learned circles—which were later to become so famous. Dr. Albert Einstein, they said, was rapidly reducing time to the status of a mere dimension.

But the dreams and disturbed feelings gained on me, so that I had to drop my regular work in 1915. Certain of the impressions were taking an annoying shape—giving me the persistent notion that my amnesia had formed some unholy sort of exchange; that the secondary personality had indeed been an intruding force from unknown regions, and that my own personality had suffered displacement.

Thus I was driven to vague and frightful speculations concerning the whereabouts of my true self during the years that another had held my body. The curious knowledge and strange conduct of my body's late tenant troubled me more and more as I learned further details from persons, papers, and magazines.

Queernesses that had baffled others seemed to harmonize terribly with some background of black knowledge which festered in the chasms of my subconsciousness. I began to search feverishly for every scrap of information bearing on the studies and travels of that other one during the dark years.

Not all of my troubles were as semi-abstract as this. There were the dreams—and these seemed to grow in vividness and concreteness. Knowing how most would regard them, I seldom mentioned them to any one but my son or certain trusted psychologists, but eventually I commenced a scientific study of other cases in order to see how typical or nontypical such visions might be among amnesia victims.

My results, aided by psychologists, historians, anthropologists, and mental specialists of wide experience, and by a study that included all records of split personalities from the days of demoniac-possession legends to the medically realistic present, at first bothered me more than they consoled me.

I soon found that my dreams had, indeed, no counterpart in the overwhelming bulk of true amnesia cases. There remained, however, a tiny residue of accounts which for years baffled and shocked me with their parallelism to my own experience. Some of them were bits of ancient folklore; others were case histories in the annals of medicine; one or two were anecdotes obscurely buried in standard histories.

It thus appeared that, while my special kind of affliction was prodigiously rare, instances of it had occurred at long intervals ever since the beginning of men's annals. Some centuries might contain one, two, or three cases, others none—or at least none whose record survived.

The essence was always the same—a person of keen thoughtfulness seized with a strange secondary life and leading for a greater or lesser period an utterly alien existence typified at first by vocal and bodily awkwardness, and later by a wholesale acquisition of scientific, historic, artistic, and anthropological knowledge; an acquisition carried on with feverish zest and with a wholly abnormal absorptive power. Then a sudden return of the rightful consciousness, intermittently plagued ever after with vague unplaceable dreams suggesting fragments of some hideous memory elaborately blotted out.

And the close resemblance of those nightmares to my own—even in some of the smallest particulars—left no doubt in my mind of their significantly typical nature. One or two of the cases had an added ring of faint, blasphemous familiarity, as if I had heard of them before through some cosmic channel too morbid and frightful to contemplate. In three instances there was specific mention of such an unknown machine as had been in my house before the second change.

Another thing that worried me during my investigation was the somewhat greater frequency of cases where a brief, elusive glimpse of the typical nightmares was afforded to persons not visited with well-defined amnesia.

These persons were largely of mediocre mind or less—some so primitive that they could scarcely be thought of as vehicles for abnormal scholarship and preternatural mental acquisitions. For a second they would be fired with alien force—then a backward lapse, and a thin, swift-fading memory of unhuman horrors.

There had been at least three such cases during the past half century—one only fifteen years before. Had something been groping blindly through time from some unsuspected abyss in nature? Were these faint cases monstrous, sinister experiments of a kind and authorship utterly beyond sane belief?

Such were a few of the formless speculations of my weaker hours—fancies abetted by myths which my studies uncovered. For I could not doubt but that certain persistent legends of immemorial antiquity apparently unknown to the victims and physicians connected with recent amnesia cases, formed a striking and awesome elaboration of memory lapses such as mine.

Of the nature of the dreams and impressions which were growing so clamorous I still almost fear to speak. They seemed to savor of madness, and at times I believed I was indeed going mad. Was there a special type of delusion afflicting those who had suffered lapses of memory? Conceivably, the efforts of the subconscious mind to fill up a perplexing blank with pseudomemories might give rise to strange imaginative vagaries.

This, indeed—though an alternative folklore theory finally seemed to me more plausible—was the belief of many of the alienists who helped me in my search for parallel cases, and who shared my puzzlement at the exact resemblances sometimes discovered.

They did not call the condition pure insanity, but classed it rather among neurotic disorders. My course in trying to track down and analyse it, instead of vainly seeking to dismiss or forget it, they heartily endorsed as correct according to the best psychological principles. I especially valued the advice of such physicians as had studied me during my possession by the other personality.

My first disturbances were not visual at all, but concerned the more abstract matters which I have mentioned. There was, too, a feeling of profound and inexplicable horror concerning myself. I developed a queer fear of seeing my own form, as if my eyes would find it something utterly alien and inconceivably abhorrent.

When I did glance down and behold the familiar human shape in quiet gray or blue clothing, I always felt a curious relief, though in order to gain this relief I had to conquer an infinite dread. I shunned mirrors as much as possible, and was always shaved at the barber's.

It was a long time before I correlated any of these disappointed feelings with the fleeting visual impressions which began to develop. The first such correlation had to do with the odd sensation of an external, artificial restraint on my memory.

I felt that the snatches of sight I experienced had a profound and terrible meaning, and a frightful connection with myself, but that some purposeful influence held me from grasping that meaning and that connection. Then came that queerness about the element of time, and with it desperate efforts to place the fragmentary dream glimpse in the chronological and spatial pattern.

The glimpses themselves were at first merely strange rather than horrible. I would seem to be in an enormous vaulted chamber whose lofty stone groinings were well nigh lost in the shadows overhead. In whatever time or place the scene might be, the principle of the arch was known as fully and used as extensively as by the Romans.

There were colossal, round windows and high, arched doors, and pedestals or tables each as tall as the height of an ordinary room. Vast shelves of dark wood lined the walls, holding what seemed to be volumes of immense size with strange hieroglyphs on their backs.

The exposed stonework held curious carvings, always in curvilinear mathematical designs, and there were chiseled inscriptions in the same characters that the huge books bore. The dark granite masonry was of a monstrous megalithic type, with lines of convex-topped blocks fitting the concave-bottomed courses which rested upon them.

There were no chairs, but the tops of the vast pedestals were littered with books, papers, and what seemed to be writing materials—oddly figured jars of a purplish metal, and rods with stained tips. Tall as the pedestals were, I seemed at times able to view them from above. On some of them were great globes of luminous crystal serving as lamps, and inexplicable machines formed of vitreous tubes and metal rods.

The windows were glazed, and latticed with stout-looking bars. Though I dared not approach and peer out them, I could see from where I was the waving tops of singular fernlike growths. The floor was of massive octagonal flagstones, while rugs and hangings were entirely lacking.

Later, I had visions of sweeping through cyclopean corridors of stone, and up and down gigantic inclined planes of the same monstrous masonry. There were no stairs anywhere, nor was any passageway less than thirty feet wide. Some of the structures through which I floated must have towered in the sky for thousands of feet.

There were multiple levels of black vaults below, and never-opened trap-doors, sealed down with metal bands and holding dim suggestions of some special peril.

I seemed to be a prisoner, and horror hung broodingly over everything I saw. I felt that the mocking curvilinear hieroglyphs on the walls would blast my soul with their message were I not guarded by a merciful ignorance.

Still later my dreams included vistas from the great round windows, and from the titanic flat roof, with its curious gardens, wide barren area, and high, scalloped parapet of stone, to which the topmost of the inclined planes led.

There were almost endless leagues of giant buildings, each in its garden, and ranged along paved roads fully two hundred feet wide. They differed greatly in aspect, but few were less than five hundred feet square or a thousand feet high. Many seemed so limitless that they must have had a frontage of several thousand feet, while some shot up to mountainous altitudes in the gray, steamy heavens.

They seemed to be mainly of stone or concrete, and most of them embodied the oddly curvilinear type of masonry noticeable in the building that held me. Roofs were flat and garden-covered, and tended to have scalloped parapets. Sometimes there were terraces and higher levels, and wide, cleared spaces amidst the gardens. The great roads held hints of motion, but in the earlier visions I could not resolve this impression into details.

In certain places I beheld enormous dark cylindrical towers which climbed far above any of the other structures. These appeared to be of a totally unique nature and showed signs of prodigious age and dilapidation. They were built of a bizarre type of square-cut basalt masonry, and tapered slightly toward their rounded tops. Nowhere in any of them could the least traces of windows or other apertures save huge doors be found. I noticed also some lower buildings—all crumbling with the weathering of aeons—which resembled these dark, cylindrical towers in basic architecture. Around all these aberrant piles of square-cut masonry there hovered an inexplicable aura of menace and concentrated fear, like that bred by the sealed trapdoors.

The omnipresent gardens were almost terrifying in their strangeness, with bizarre and unfamiliar forms of vegetation nodding over broad paths lined with curiously carven monoliths. Abnormally vast fernlike growths predominated—some green, and some of a ghastly, fungoid pallor.

Among them rose great spectral things resembling calamites, whose bamboo-like trunks towered to fabulous heights. Then there were tufted forms like fabulous cycades, and grotesque dark-green shrubs and trees of coniferous aspect.

Flowers were small, colorless, and unrecognizable, blooming in geometrical beds and at large among the greenery.

In a few of the terrace and roof-top gardens were larger and more vivid blossoms of almost offensive contours and seeming to suggest artificial breeding. Fungi of inconceivable size, outlines, and colors speckled the scene in patterns bespeaking some unknown but well-established horticultural tradition. In the larger gardens on the ground there seemed to be some attempt to preserve the irregularities of nature, but on the roofs there was more selectiveness, and more evidences of the topiary art.

The skies were almost always moist and cloudy, and sometimes I would seem to witness tremendous rains. Once in a while, though, there would be glimpses of the sun—which looked abnormally large— and of the moon, whose markings held a touch of difference from the normal that I could never quite fathom. When—very rarely—the night sky was clear to any extent, I beheld constellations which were nearly beyond recognition. Known outlines were sometimes approximated, but seldom duplicated; and from the position of the few groups I could recognize, I felt I must be in the earth's southern hemisphere, near the Tropic of Capricorn.

The far horizon was always steamy and indistinct, but I could see that great jungles of unknown tree ferns, Calamites, Lepidodendro, and Sigillaria lay outside the city, their fantastic frondage waving mockingly in the shifting vapors. Now and then there would be suggestions of motion in the sky, but these my early visions never resolved.

By the autumn of 1914 I began to have infrequent dreams of strange floatings over the city and through the regions around it. I saw interminable roads through forests of fearsome growths with mottled, fluted, and banded trunks, and past other cities as strange as the one which persistently haunted me.

I saw monstrous constructions of black or iridescent stone in glades and clearings where perpetual twilight reigned, and traversed long causeways over swamps so dark that I could tell but little of their moist, towering vegetation.

Once I saw an area of countless miles strewn with age-blasted basaltic ruins whose architecture had been like that of the few windowless, round-topped towers in the haunting city.

And once I saw the sea—a boundless, steamy expanse beyond the colossal stone piers of an enormous town of domes and arches. Great shapeless suggestions of shadow moved over it, and here and there its surface was vexed with anomalous spoutings.

III

As I have said, it was not immediately that these wild visions began to hold their terrifying quality. Certainly, many persons have dreamed intrinsically stranger things—things compounded of unrelated scraps of daily life, pictures, and reading, and arranged in fantastically novel forms by the unchecked caprices of sleep.

For some time I accepted the visions as natural, even though I had never before been an extravagant dreamer. Many of the vague anomalies, I argued, must have come from trivial sources too numerous to track down; while others seemed to reflect a common textbook knowledge of the plants and other conditions of the primitive world of a hundred and fifty million years ago—the world of the Permian or Triassic Age.

In the course of some months, however, the element of terror did figure with accumulating force. This was when the dreams began so unfailingly to have the aspect of memories, and when my mind began to link them with my growing abstract disturbances—the feeling of mnemonic restraint, the curious impressions regarding time, the sense of a loathsome exchange with my secondary personality of 1908–13, and, considerably later, the inexplicable loathing of my own person.

As certain definite details began to enter the dreams, their horror increased a thousandfold—until by October, 1915, I felt I must do something. It was then that I began an intensive study of other cases of amnesia and visions, feeling that I might thereby objectivize my trouble and shake clear of its emotional grip.

However, as before mentioned, the result was at first almost exactly opposite. It disturbed me vastly to find that my dreams had been so closely duplicated; especially since some of the accounts were too early to admit of any geological knowledge—and therefore of any idea of primitive landscapes—on the subjects' part.

What is more, many of these accounts supplied very horrible details and explanations in connection with the visions of great buildings and jungle gardens—and other things. The actual sights and vague impressions were bad enough, but what was hinted or asserted by some of the other dreamers savored of madness and blasphemy. Worst of all, my own pseudomemory was aroused to wilder dreams and hints of coming revelations. And yet most doctors deemed my course, on the whole, an advisable one.

I studied psychology systematically, and under the prevailing stimulus my son Wingate did the same—his studies leading eventually to his present professorship. In 1917 and 1918 I took special courses at Miskatonic. Meanwhile, my examination of medical, historical, and anthropological records became indefatigable, involving travels to distant libraries, and finally including even a reading of the hideous books of forbidden lore in which my secondary personality had been so disturbingly interested.

Some of the latter were the actual copies I had consulted in my altered state, and I was greatly disturbed by certain marginal notations and ostensible *corrections* of the hideous text in a script and idiom which somehow seemed oddly unhuman.

These markings were mostly in the respective languages of the various books, all of which the writer seemed to know with equal, though obviously, academic facility. One note appended to von Junzt's *Unaussprechlichen Kulten*, however, was alarmingly otherwise. It consisted of certain curvilinear hieroglyphs in the same ink as that of the German corrections, but following no recognized human pattern. And these hieroglyphs were closely and unmistakably akin to the characters constantly met with in my dreams—characters whose meaning I would sometimes momentarily fancy I knew, or was just on the brink of recalling.

To complete my black confusion, many librarians assured me that, in view of previous examinations and records of consultation of the volumes in question, all of these notations must have been made by myself in my secondary state. This despite the fact that I was and still am ignorant of three of the languages involved. Piecing together the scattered records, ancient and modern, anthropological and medical, I found a fairly consistent mixture of myth and hallucination whose scope and wildness left me utterly dazed. Only one thing consoled me: the fact that the myths were of such early existence. What lost knowledge could have brought pictures of the Paleozoic or Mesozoic landscape into these primitive fables, I could not even guess; but the pictures had been there. Thus, a basis existed for the formation of a fixed type of delusion.

Cases of amnesia no doubt created the general myth pattern—but afterward the fanciful accretions of the myths must have reacted on amnesia sufferers and colored their pseudomemories. I myself had read and heard all the early tales during my memory lapse—my quest had amply proved that. Was it not natural, then, for my subsequent dreams and emotional impressions to become colored and molded by what my memory subtly held over from my secondary state?

A few of the myths had significant connections with other cloudy legends of the prehuman world, especially those Hindu tales involving stupefying gulfs of time and forming part of the lore of modern theosophists.

Primal myth and modern delusion joined in their assumption that mankind is only one—perhaps the least—of the highly evolved and dominant races of this planet's long and largely unknown career. Things of inconceivable shape, they implied, had reared towers to the sky and delved into every secret of nature before the first amphibian forbear of man had crawled out of the hot sea three hundred million years ago.

Some had come down from the stars; a few were as old as the cosmos itself; others had arisen swiftly from terrane germs as far behind the first germs of our life cycle as those germs are behind ourselves. Spans of thousands of millions of years, and linkages of other galaxies and universes, were spoken of. Indeed, there was no such thing as time in its humanly accepted sense.

But most of the tales and impressions concerned a relatively late race, of a queer and intricate shape, resembling no life form known to science, which had lived till only fifty million years before the advent of man. This, they indicated, was the greatest race of all because it alone had conquered the secret of time.

It had learned all things that ever were known or ever would be known on the Earth, through the power of its keener minds to project themselves into the past and future, even through gulfs of millions of years, and study the lore of every age. From the accomplishments of this race arose all legends of prophets, including those in human mythology.

In its vast libraries were volumes of texts and pictures holding the whole of Earth's annals—histories and descriptions of every species that had ever been or that ever would be, with full records of their arts, their achievements, their languages, and their psychologies.

With this aeon-embracing knowledge, the Great Race chose from every era and life form such thoughts, arts, and processes as might suit its own nature and situation. Knowledge of the past, secured through a kind of mindcasting outside the recognized senses, was harder to glean than knowledge of the future.

In the latter case the course was easier and more material. With suitable mechanical aid a mind would project itself forward in time, feeling its dim, extra-sensory way till it approached the desired period. Then, after preliminary trials, it would seize on the best discoverable representative of the highest of that period's life forms. It would enter the organism's brain and set up therein its own vibrations, while the displaced mind would strike back to the period of the displacer, remaining in the latter's body till a reverse process was set up.

The projected mind, in the body of the organism of the future, would then pose as a member of the race whose outward form it wore, learning as quickly as possible all that could be learned of the chosen age and its massed information and techniques.

Meanwhile the displaced mind, thrown back to the displacer's age and body, would be carefully guarded. It would be kept from harming the body it occupied, and would be drained of all its knowledge by trained questioners. Often it could be questioned in its own language, when previous quests into the future had brought back records of that language.

If the mind came from a body whose language the Great Race could not physically reproduce, clever machines would be made, on which the alien speech could be played as on a musical instrument.

The Great Race's members were immense rugose cones ten feet high, and with head and other organs attached to foot-thick distensible limbs spreading from the apexes. They spoke by the clicking or scraping of huge paws or claws attached to the end of two of their four limbs, and walked by the expansion and contraction of a viscous layer attached to their vast, ten-foot bases.

When the captive mind's amazement and resentment had worn off, and when—assuming that it came from a body vastly different from the Great Race's—it had lost its horror at its unfamiliar, temporary form, it was permitted to study its new environment and experience a wonder and wisdom approximating that of its displacer.

With suitable precautions, and in exchange for suitable services, it was allowed to rove all over the habitable world in titan airships or on the huge boat-like atomic-engined vehicles which traversed the great roads, and to delve freely into the libraries containing the records of the planet's past and future.

This reconciled many captive minds to their lot; since none were other than keen, and to such minds the unveiling of hidden mysteries of Earth—closed chapters of inconceivable pasts and dizzying vortices of future time which include the years ahead of their own natural ages—forms always, despite the abysmal horrors often unveiled, the supreme experience of life.

Now and then certain captives were permitted to meet other captive minds seized from the future—to exchange thoughts with consciousnesses living a hundred or a thousand or a million years before or after their own ages. And all were urged to write copiously in their own languages of themselves and their respective periods such documents to be filed in the great central archives.

It may be added that there was one special type of captive whose privileges were far greater than those of the majority. These were the dying *permanent* exiles, whose bodies in the future had been seized by keen-minded members of the Great Race who, faced with death, sought to escape mental extinction.

Such melancholy exiles were not as common as might be expected, since the longevity of the Great Race lessened its love of life—especially among those superior minds capable of projection. From cases of the permanent projection of elder minds arose many of those lasting changes of personality noticed in later history—including mankind's.

As for the ordinary cases of exploration—when the displacing mind had learned what it wished in the future, it would build an apparatus like that which had started its flight and reverse the process of projection. Once more it would be in its own body in its own age while the lately captive mind would return to that body of the future to which it properly belonged.

Only when one or the other of the bodies had died during the exchange was this restoration impossible. In such cases, of course, the exploring mind had—like those of the death escapers—to live out an alien-bodied life in the future; or else the captive mind—like the dying permanent exiles—had to end its days in the form and past age of the Great Race.

This fate was less horrible when the captive mind was also of the Great Race—a not infrequent occurrence, since in all its periods that race was intensely concerned with its own future. The number of dying permanent exiles of the Great Race was very slight—largely because of the tremendous penalties attached to displacements of future Great Race minds by the moribund.

Through projection, arrangements were made to inflict these penalties on the offending minds in their new future bodies—and sometimes forced reëxchanges were effected.

Complex cases of the displacement of exploring or already captive minds by minds in various regions of the past had been known and carefully rectified. In every age since the discovery of mind projection, a minute but well-recognized element of the population consisted of Great Race minds from past ages, sojourning for a longer or shorter while.

When a captive mind of alien origin was returned to its own body in the future, it was purged by an intricate mechanical hypnosis of all it had learned in the Great Race's Age—this because of certain troublesome consequences inherent in the general carrying forward of knowledge in large quantities.

The few existing instances of clear transmission had caused, and would cause at known future times, great disorders. And it was largely in consequence of two cases of the kind—said the old myths—that mankind had learned what it had concerning the Great Race.

Of all things surviving physically and directly from that aeon-distant world, there remained only certain ruins of great stones in far places and under the sea, and parts of the text of the frightful Pnakotic Manuscripts.

Thus the returning mind reached its own age with only the faintest and most fragmentary vision of what it had undergone since its seizure. All memories that could be eradicated were eradicated, so that in most cases only a dream-shadowed blank stretched back to the time of the first exchange. Some minds recalled more than others, and the chance joining of memories had at rare times brought hints of the forbidden past to future ages.

There probably never was a time when groups or cults did not secretly cherish certain of these hints. In the *Necronomicon* the presence of such a cult among human beings was suggested—a cult that sometimes gave aid to minds voyaging down the aeons from the days of the Great Race.

And, meanwhile, the Great Race itself waxed well-nigh ominiscient, and turned to the task of setting up exchanges with the minds of other planets, and of exploring their pasts and futures. It sought likewise to fathom the past years and origin of that black, aeon-dead orb in far space whence its own mental heritage had come—for the mind of the Great Race was older than its bodily form.

The beings of a dying elder world, wise with the ultimate secrets, had looked ahead for a new world and species wherein they might have long life, and had sent their minds *en masse* into that future race best adapted to house them—the cone-shaped beings that peopled our earth a billion years ago.

Thus the Great Race came to be, while the myriad minds sent backward were left to die in the horror of strange shapes. Later the race would again face death, yet would live through another forward migration of its best minds into the bodies of others who had a longer physical span ahead of them.

Such was the background of intertwined legend and hallucination. When, around 1920, I had my researches in coherent shape, I felt a slight lessening of the tension which their earlier stages had increased. After all, and in spite of the fancies prompted by blind emotion, were not most of my phenomena readily explainable? Any chance might have turned my mind to dark studies during the amnesia—and then I read the forbidden legends and met the members of ancient and ill-regarded cults. That, plainly, supplied the material for the dreams and disturbed feelings which came after the return of memory.

As for the marginal notes in dream hieroglyphs and languages unknown to me, but laid at my door by librarians—I might easily have picked up a smattering of the tongues during my secondary state, while the hieroglyphs were doubtless coined by my fancy from descriptions in old legends, and afterward woven into my dreams. I tried to verify certain points through conversations with known cult leaders, but never succeeded in establishing the right connections.

At times the parallelism of so many cases in so many distant ages continued to worry me as it had at first, but on the other hand I reflected that the excitant folklore was undoubtedly more universal in the past than in the present.

Probably all the other victims whose cases were like mine had had a long and familiar knowledge of the tales I had learned only when in my secondary state. When these victims had lost their memory, they had associated themselves with the creatures of their household myths—the fabulous invaders supposed to displace men's minds—and had thus embarked upon quests for knowledge which they thought they could take back to a fancied, nonhuman past.

Then, when their memory returned, they reversed the associative process and thought of themselves as the former captive minds instead of as the displacers. Hence the dreams and pseudomemories following the conventional myth pattern.

Despite the seeming cumbrousness of these explanations, they came finally to supersede all others in my mind—largely because of the greater weakness of any rival theory. And a substantial number of eminent psychologists and anthropologists gradually agreed with me.

The more I reflected, the more convincing did my reasoning seem; till in the end I had a really effective bulwark against the visions and impressions which still assailed me. Suppose I did see strange things at night? These were only what I had heard and read of. Suppose I did have odd loathings and perspectives and pseudomemories? These, too, were only echoes of myths absorbed in my secondary state. Nothing that I might dream, nothing that I might feel, could be of any actual significance.

Fortified by this philosophy, I greatly improved in nervous equilibrium, even though the visions—rather than the abstract impressions—steadily became more frequent and more disturbingly detailed. In 1922 I felt able to undertake regular work again, and put my newly gained knowledge to practical use by accepting an instructorship in psychology at the university.

My old chair of political economy had long been adequately filled—besides which, methods of teaching economics had changed greatly since my heyday. My son was at this time just entering on the post-graduate studies leading to his present professorship, and we worked together a great deal.

IV

I continued however, to keep a careful record of the *outré* dreams which crowded upon me so thickly and vividly. Such a record, I argued, was of genuine value as a psychological document. The glimpses still seemed damnably like memories, though I fought off this impression with a goodly measure of success.

In writing, I treated the phantasmata as things seen; but at all other times I brushed them aside like any gossamer illusions of the night. I had never mentioned such matters in common conversation; though reports of them, filtering out as such things will, had aroused sundry rumors regarding my mental health. It is amusing to reflect that these rumors were confined wholly to laymen, without a single champion among physicians or psychologists.

Of my visions after 1914 I will here mention only a few, since fuller accounts and records are at the disposal of the serious student. It is evident that with time the curious inhibitions somewhat waned, for the scope of my visions vastly increased. They have never, though, become other than disjointed fragments seemingly without clear motivation.

Within the dreams I seemed gradually to acquire a greater and greater freedom of wandering. I floated through many strange buildings of stone, going from one to the other along mammoth underground passages which seemed to form the common avenues of transit. Sometimes I encountered those gigantic sealed trapdoors in the lowest level, around which such an aura of fear and forbiddenness clung.

I saw tremendous tessellated pools, and rooms of curious and inexplicable utensils of myriad sorts. Then there were colossal caverns of intricate machinery whose outlines and purpose were wholly strange to me, and whose sound manifested itself only after many years of dreaming. I may here remark that sight and sound are the only senses I have ever exercised in the visionary world.

The real horror began in May, 1915, when I first saw the living things. This was before my studies had taught me what, in view of the myths and case histories, to expect. As mental barriers wore down, I beheld great masses of thin vapor in various parts of the building and in the streets below.

These steadily grew more solid and distinct, till at last I could trace their monstrous outlines with uncomfortable ease. They seemed to be enormous, iridescent cones, about ten feet high and ten feet wide at the base, and made up of some ridgy, scaly, semi-elastic matter. From their apexes projected four flexible, cylindrical members, each a foot thick, and of a ridgy substance like that of the cones themselves.

These members were sometimes contracted almost to nothing, and sometimes extended to any distance up to about ten feet. Terminating two of them were enormous claws or nippers. At the end of a third were four red, trumpetlike appendages. The fourth terminated in an irregular yellowish globe some two feet in diameter and having three great dark eyes ranged along its central circumference.

Surmounting this head were four slender gray stalks bearing flower-like appendages, whilst from its nether side dangled eight greenish antennae or tentacles. The great base of the central cone was fringed with a rubbery, gray substance which moved the whole entity through expansion and contraction.

Their actions, though harmless, horrified me even more than their appearance—for it is not wholesome to watch monstrous objects doing what one had known only human beings to do. These objects moved intelligently about the great rooms, getting books from the shelves and taking them to the great tables, or *vice versa*, and sometimes writing diligently with a peculiar rod gripped in the greenish head tentacles. The huge nippers were used in carrying books and in conversation—speech consisting of a kind of clicking.

The objects had no clothing, but wore satchels or knapsacks suspended from the top of the conical trunk. They commonly carried their head and its supporting member at the level of the cone top, though it was frequently raised or lowered.

The other three great members tended to rest downward at the sides of the cone, contracted to above five feet each, when not in use. From their rate of reading, writing, and operating their machines—those on the tables seemed somehow connected with thought—I concluded that their intelligence was enormously greater than man's.

Afterward I saw them everywhere; swarming in all the great chambers and corridors, tending monstrous machines in vaulted crypts, and racing along the vast roads in gigantic, boat-shaped cars. I ceased to be afraid of them, for they seemed to form supremely natural parts of their environment.

Individual differences amongst them began to be manifest, and a few appeared to be under some kind of restraint. These latter, though showing no physical variation, had a diversity of gestures and habits which marked them off not only from the majority, but very largely from one another.

They wrote a great deal in what seemed to my cloudy vision a vast variety of characters—never the typical curvilinear hieroglyphs of the majority. A few, I fancied, used our own familiar alphabet. Most of them worked much more slowly than the general mass of the entities.

All this time my own part in the dreams seemed to be that of a disembodied consciousness with a range of vision wider than the normal, floating freely about, yet confined to the ordinary avenues and speeds of travel. Not until August, 1915, did any suggestions of bodily existence begin to harass me. I say harass, because the first phase was a purely abstract, though infinitely terrible, association of my previously noted body-loathing with the scenes of my visions.

For a while my chief concern during dreams was to avoid looking down at myself, and I recall how grateful I was for the total absence of large mirrors in the strange rooms. I was mightily troubled by the fact that I always saw the great tables—whose height could not be under ten feet—from a level not below that of their surfaces.

And then the morbid temptation to look down at myself became greater and greater, till one night I could not resist it. At first my downward glance revealed nothing whatever. A moment later I perceived that this was because my head lay at the end of a flexible neck of enormous length. Retracting this neck and gazing down very sharply, I saw the scaley, rugose, iridescent bulk of a vast cone ten feet tall and ten feet wide at the base. That was when I waked half of Arkham with my screaming as I plunged madly up from the abyss of sleep.

Only after weeks of hideous repetition did I grow half reconciled to these visions of myself in monstrous form. In the dreams I now moved bodily among the other unknown entities, reading terrible books from the endless shelves and writing for hours at the great tables with a stylus managed by the green tentacles that hung down from my head.

Snatches of what I read and wrote would linger in my memory. There were horrible annals of other worlds and other universes, and of stirrings of formless life outside of all universes. There were records of strange orders of beings which had peopled the world in forgotten pasts, and frightful chronicles of grotesque-bodied intelligences which would people it millions of years after the death of the last human being.

I learned of chapters in human history whose existence no scholar of today has ever suspected. Most of these writings were in the language of the hieroglyphs; which I studied in a queer way with the aid of droning machines, and which was evidently an agglutinative speech with root systems utterly unlike any found in human languages.

Other volumes were in other unknown tongues learned in the same queer way. A very few were in languages I knew. Extremely clever pictures, both inserted in the records and forming separate collections, aided me immensely. And all the time I seemed to be setting down a history of my own age in English. On waking, I could recall only minute and meaningless scraps of the unknown tongues which my dream self had mastered, though whole phrases of the history stayed with me.

I learned—even before my waking self had studied the parallel cases or the old myths from which the dreams doubtless sprang—that the entities around me were of the world's greatest race, which had conquered time and had sent exploring minds into every age. I knew, too, that I had been snatched from my age, while another used my body in that age, and that a few of the other strange forms housed similarly captured minds. I seemed to talk, in some odd language of claw clicking, with exiled intellects from every corner of the solar system.

There was a mind from the planet we know as Venus, which would live incalculable epochs to come, and one from an outer moon of Jupiter six million years in the past. Of earthly minds there were some from the winged, star-headed, half-vegetable race of paleogean Antarctica; one from the reptile people of fabled Valusia; three from the furry prehuman Hyperborean worshippers of Tsathoggua; one from the wholly abominable Tcho-Tchos; two from the Arachnid denizens of earth's last age; five from the hardy Coleopterous species immediately following mankind, to which the Great Race was some day to transfer its keenest minds *en masse* in the face of horrible peril; and several from different branches of humanity.

I talked with the mind of Yiang-Li, a philosopher from the cruel empire of Tsan-Chan, which is to come in 5,000 A.D.; with that of a general of the great-headed brown people who held South Africa in 50,000 B.C.; with that of a twelfth-century Florentine monk named Bartolomeo Corsi; with that of a king of Lomar who had ruled that terrible polar land one hundred thousand years before the squat, yellow Inutos came from the west to engulf it.

I talked with the mind of Nug-Soth, a magician of the dark conquerors of 16,00 A.D.; with that of a Roman named Titus Sempronius Blaesus, who had been a quaestor in Sulla's time; with that of Khephnes, an Egyptian of the 14th Dynasty, who told me the hideous secret of Nyarlathotep; with that of a priest of Atlantis' middle kingdom; with that of a Suffolk gentleman of Cromwell's day, James Woodville; with that of a court astronomer of pre-Inca Peru; with that of the Australian physicist Nevel Kingston-Brown, who will die in 2,518 A.D.; with that of an archimage of vanished Yhe in the Pacific; with that of Theodotides, a Graeco-Bactrian official of 200 B.C.; with that of an aged Frenchman of Louis XIII's time named Pierre-Louis Montagny; with that of Crom-Ya, a Cimmerian chieftain of 15,000 B.C.; and with so many others that my brain can not hold the shocking secrets and dizzying marvels I learned from them.

I awakened each morning in a fever, sometimes frantically trying to verify or discredit such information as fell within the range of modern human knowledge. Traditional facts took on new and doubtful aspects, and I marveled at the dream fancy which could invent such surprising addenda to history and science.

I shivered at the mysteries the past may conceal, and trembled at the menaces the future may bring forth. What was hinted in the speech of post-human entities of the fate of mankind produced such an effect on me that I will not set it down here.

After man there would be the mighty beetle civilization, the bodies of whose members the cream of the Great Race would seize when the monstrous doom overtook the elder world. Later, as the earth's span closed, the transferred minds would again migrate through time and space—to another stopping place in the bodies of the bulbous vegetable entities of Mercury. But there would be races after them, clinging pathetically to the cold planet and burrowing to its horror-filled core, before the utter end.

Meanwhile, in my dreams, I wrote endlessly in that history of my own age which I was preparing—half voluntarily and half through promises of increased library and travel opportunities—for the Great Race's central archives. The archives were in a colossal subterranean structure near the city's center, which I came to know well through frequent labors and consultations. Meant to last as long as the race, and to withstand the fiercest of earth's convulsions, this titan repository surpassed all other buildings in the massive, mountainlike firmness of its construction.

The records, written or printed on great sheets of a curiously tenacious cellulose fabric, were bound into books that opened from the top, and were kept in individual cases of a strange, extremely light rustless metal of grayish hue, decorated with mathematical designs and bearing the title in the Great Race's curvilinear hieroglyphs.

These cases were stored in tiers of rectangular vaults—like closed, locked shelves—wrought of the same rustless metal and fastened by knobs with intricate turnings. My own history was assigned a specific place in the vaults of the lowest or vertebrate level—the section devoted to the cultures of mankind and of the furry and reptilian races immediately preceding it in terrestrial dominance.

But none of the dreams ever gave me a full picture of daily life. All were the merest misty, disconnected fragments, and it is certain that these fragments were not unfolded in their rightful sequence. I have, for example, a very imperfect idea of my own living arrangements in the dream world; though I seem to have possessed a great stone room of my own. My restrictions as a prisoner gradually disappeared, so that some of the visions included vivid travels over the mighty jungle roads, sojourns in strange cities, and explorations of some of the vast, dark, windowless ruins from which the Great Race shrank in curious fear. There were also long sea voyages in enormous, many-decked boats of incredible swiftness, and trips over wild regions in closed projectile-airships lifted and moved by electrical repulsion.

Beyond the wide, warm ocean were other cities of the Great Race, and on one far continent I saw the crude villages of the blacksnouted, winged creatures who would evolve as a dominant stock after the Great Race had sent its foremost minds into the future to escape the creeping horror. Flatness and exuberant green life were always the keynote of the scene. Hills were low and sparse, and usually displayed signs of volcanic forces.

Of the animals I saw, I could write volumes. All were wild; for the Great Race's mechanized culture had long since done away with domestic beasts, while food was wholly vegetable or synthetic. Clumsy reptiles of great bulk floundered in steaming morasses, fluttered in the heavy air, or spouted in the seas and lakes; and among these I fancied I could vaguely recognize lesser, archaic prototypes of many forms—Dinosaurs, pterodactyls, ichthyosaurs, labyrinthodonts, plesiosaurs, and the like—made familiar through paleontology. Of birds or mammals there were none that I could discover.

The ground and swamps were constantly alive with snakes, lizards, and crocodiles, while insects buzzed incessantly among the lush vegetation. And far out at sea, unspied and unknown monsters spouted mountainous columns of foam into the vaporous sky. Once I was taken under the ocean in a gigantic submarine vessel with searchlights, and glimpsed some living horrors of awesome magnitude. I saw also the ruins of incredible sunken cities, and the wealth of crinoid, brachiopod, coral, and ichthyic life which everywhere abounded.

Of the physiology, psychology, folkways, and detailed history of the Great Race my visions preserved but little information, and many of the scattered points I here set down were gleaned from my study of old legends and other cases rather than from my own dreaming.

For in time, of course, my reading and research caught up with and passed the dreams in many phases, so that certain dream fragments were explained in advance and formed verifications of what I had learned. This consolingly established my belief that similar reading and research, accomplished by my secondary self, had formed the source of the whole terrible fabric of pseudomemories.

The period of my dreams, apparently, was one somewhat less than 150,000,000 years ago, when the Paleozoic Age was giving place to the Mesozoic. The bodies occupied by the Great Race represented no surviving—or even scientifically known—line of terrestrial evolution, but were of a peculiar, closely homogeneous, and highly specialized organic type inclining as much to the vegetable as to the animal state.

Cell action was of an unique sort almost precluding fatigue, and wholly eliminating the need of sleep. Nourishment, assimilated through the red trumpetlike appendages on one of the great flexible limbs, was always semifluid and in many aspects wholly unlike the food of existing animals.

The beings had but two of the senses which we recognize—sight and hearing, the latter accomplished through the flowerlike appendages on the gray stalks above their heads. Of other and incomprehensible senses—not, however, well utilizable by alien captive minds inhabitating their bodies—they possessed many. Their three eyes were so situated as to give them a range of vision wider than the normal. Their blood was a sort of deep-greenish ichor of great thickness.

They had no sex, but reproduced through seeds or spores which clustered on their bases and could be developed only under water. Great, shallow tanks were used for the growth of their young—which were, however, reared only in small numbers on account of the longevity of individuals—four or five thousand years being the common life span.

Markedly defective individuals were quickly disposed of as soon as their defects were noticed. Disease and the approach of death were, in the absence of a sense of touch or of physical pain, recognized by purely visual symptoms.

The dead were incinerated with dignified ceremonies. Once in a while, as before mentioned, a keen mind would escape death by forward projection in time; but such cases were not numerous. When one did occur, the exiled mind from the future was treated with the utmost kindness till the dissolution of its unfamiliar tenement.

The Great Race seemed to form a single, loosely knit nation or league, with major institutions in common, though there were four definite divisions. The political and economic system of each unit was a sort of fascistic socialism, with major resources rationally distributed, and power delegated to a small governing board elected by the votes of all able to pass certain educational and psychological tests. Family organization was not overstressed, though ties among persons of common descent were recognized, and the young were generally reared by their parents.

Resemblances to human attitudes and institutions were, of course, most marked in those fields where on the one hand highly abstract elements were concerned, or, where on the other hand there was a dominance of the basic, unspecialized urges common to all organic life. A few added likenesses came through conscious adoption as the Great Race probed the future and copied what it liked.

Industry, highly mechanized, demanded but little time from each citizen; and the abundant leisure was filled with intellectual and aesthetic activities of various sorts.

The sciences were carried to an unbelievable height of development, and art was a vital part of life, though at the period of my dreams it had passed its crest and meridian. Technology was enormously stimulated through the constant struggle to survive, and to keep in existence the physical fabric of great cities, imposed by the prodigious geologic upheavals of those primal days.

Crime was surprisingly scant, and was dealt with through highly efficient policing. Punishments ranged from privilege deprivation and imprisonment to death or major emotion wrenching, and were never administered without a careful study of the criminal's motivations.

Warfare, largely civil for the last few millennia though sometimes waged against the winged, star-headed Old Ones who centered in the antarctic, was infrequent though infinitely devastating. An enormous army, using cameralike weapons which produced tremendous electrical effects, was kept on hand for purposes seldom mentioned, but obviously connected with the ceaseless fear of the dark, windowless elder ruins and of the great sealed trapdoors in the lowest subterranean levels.

This fear of the basalt ruins and trapdoors was largely a matter of unspoken suggestion—or, at most, of furtive quasi-whispers. Everything specific which bore on it was significantly absent from such books as were on the common shelves. It was the one subject lying altogether under a taboo among the Great Race, and seemed to be connected alike with horrible bygone struggles, and with that future peril which would some day force the race to send its keener minds ahead *en masse* in time.

Imperfect and fragmentary as were the other things presented by dreams and legends, this matter was still more bafflingly shrouded. The vague old myths avoided it—or perhaps all allusions had for some reason been excised. And in the dreams of myself and others, the hints were peculiarly few. Members of the Great Race never intentionally referred to the matter, and what could be gleaned came only from some of the more sharply observant captive minds.

According to these scraps of information, the basis of the fear was a horrible elder race of half polypous, utterly alien entities which had come through space from immeasurably distant universes and had dominated the earth and three other solar planets about six hundred million years ago. They were only partly material—as we understand matter—and their type of consciousness and media of perception differed widely from those of terrestrial organisms. For example, their senses did not include that of sight; their mental world being a strange, nonvisual pattern of impressions.

They were, however, sufficiently material to use implements of normal matter when in cosmic areas containing it; and they required housing—albeit of a peculiar kind. Though their senses could penetrate all material barriers, their substance could not; and certain forms of electrical energy could wholly destroy them. They had the power of aërial motion, despite the absence of wings or any other visible means of levitation. Their minds were of such texture that no exchange with them could be effected by the Great Race.

When these things had come to the Earth they had built mighty basalt cities of windowless towers, and had preyed horribly upon the beings they found. Thus it was when the minds of the Great Race sped across the void from that obscure, transgalactic world known in the disturbing and debatable Eltdown Shards as Yith.

The newcomers, with the instruments they created, had found it easy to subdue the predatory entities and drive them down to those caverns of inner earth which they had already joined to their abodes and begun to inhabit.

Then they had sealed the entrances and left them to their fate, afterward occupying most of their great cities and preserving certain important buildings for reasons connected more with superstition than with indifference, boldness, or scientific and historical zeal.

But as the aeons passed, there came vague, evil signs that the elder things were growing strong and numerous in the inner world. There were sporadic irruptions of a particularly hideous character in certain small and remote cities of the Great Race, and in some of the deserted elder cities which the Great Race had not peopled—places where the paths to the gulfs below had not been properly sealed or guarded.

After that greater precautions were taken, and many of the paths were closed forever—though a few were left with sealed trapdoors for strategic use in fighting the elder things if ever they broke forth in unexpected places.

The irruptions of the elder things must have been shocking beyond all description, since they had permanently colored the psychology of the Great Race. Such was the fixed mood of horror that the very aspect of the creatures was left unmentioned. At no time was I able to gain a clear hint of what they looked like.

There were veiled suggestions of a monstrous plasticity, and of temporary lapses of visibility, while other fragmentary whispers referred to their control and military use of great winds. Singular whistling noises, and colossal footprints made up of five circular toe marks, seemed also to be associated with them.

It was evident that the coming doom so desperately feared by the Great Race—the doom that was one day to send millions of keen minds across the chasm of time to strange bodies in the safer future—had to do with a final successful irruption of the elder beings.

Mental projections down the ages had clearly foretold such a horror, and the Great Race had resolved that none who could escape should face it. That the foray would be a matter of vengeance, rather than an attempt to reoccupy the outer world, they knew from the planet's later history—for their projections showed the coming and going of subsequent races untroubled by the monstrous entities.

Perhaps these entities had come to prefer Earth's inner abysses to the variable, storm-ravaged surface, since light meant nothing to them. Perhaps, too, they were slowly weakening with the aeons. Indeed, it was known that they would be quite dead in the time of the post-human beetle race which the fleeing minds would tenant.

Meanwhile, the Great Race maintained its cautious vigilance, with potent weapons ceaselessly ready despite the horrified banishing of the subject from common speech and visible records. And always the shadow of nameless fear hung about the sealed trapdoors and the dark, windowless elder towers.

V

That is the world of which my dreams brought me dim, scattered echoes every night. I cannot hope to give any true idea of the horror and dread contained in such echoes, for it was upon a wholly intangible quality—the sharp sense of pseudomemory—that such feelings mainly depended.

As I have said, my studies gradually gave me a defense against these feelings in the form of rational psychological explanations; and this saving influence was augmented by the subtle touch of accustomedness which comes with the passage of time. Yet in spite of everything the vague, creeping terror would return momentarily now and then. It did not, however, engulf me as it had before; and after 1922 I lived a very normal life of work and recreation.

In the course of years I began to feel that my experience—together with the kindred cases and the related folklore—ought to be definitely summarized and published for the benefit of serious students; hence, I prepared a series of articles briefly covering the whole ground and illustrated with crude sketches of some of the shapes, scenes, decorative motifs, and hieroglyphs remembered from the dreams.

These appeared at various times during 1928 and 1929 in the *Journal of the American Psychological Society*, but did not attract much attention. Meanwhile, I continued to record my dreams with the minutest care, even though the growing stack of reports attained troublesomely vast proportions.

On July 10, 1934, there was forwarded to me by the Psychological Society the letter which opened the culminating and most horrible phase of the whole mad ordeal. It was postmarked Pilbarra, Western Australia, and bore the signature of one whom I found, upon inquiry, to be a mining engineer of considerable prominence. Inclosed were some very curious snapshots. I will reproduce the text in its entirety, and no reader can fail to understand how tremendous an effect it and the photographs had upon me.

I was, for a time, almost stunned and incredulous; for, although I had often thought that some basis of fact must underlie certain phases of the legends which had colored my dreams, I was none the less unprepared for anything like a tangible survival from a lost world remote beyond all imagination. Most devastating of all were the photographs—for here, in cold, incontrovertible realism, there stood out against a background of sand certain worn-down, water-ridged, storm-weathered blocks of stone whose slightly convex tops and slightly concave bottoms told their own story.

And when I studied them with a magnifying glass I could see all too plainly, amidst the batterings and pittings, the traces of those vast curvilinear designs and occasional hieroglyphs whose significance had become so hideous to me. But here is the letter, which speaks for itself:

> 49 Dampier St.,
> Pilbarra, W. Australia,
> May 18, 1934.

Prof. N. W. Peaslee,
c-o Am. Psychological Society,
30 E. 41st St.,
New York City, U.S.A.

My Dear Sir:

A recent conversation with Dr. E. M. Boyle of Perth, and some papers with your articles which he has just sent me, make it advisable for me to tell you about certain things I have seen in the Great Sandy Desert east of our gold field here. It would seem, in view of the peculiar legends about old cities with huge stonework and strange designs and hieroglyphs which you describe, that I have come upon something very important.

The blackfellows have always been full of talk about "great stones with marks on them," and seem to have a terrible fear of such things. They connect them in some way with their common racial legends about Buddai, the gigantic old man who lies asleep for ages underground with his head on his arm, and who will some day awake and eat up the world.

There are some very old and half-forgotten tales of enormous underground huts of great stones, where passages lead down and down, and where horrible things have happened. The blackfellows claim that once some warriors, fleeing in battle, went down into one and never came back, but that frightful winds began to blow from the place soon after they went down. However, there usually isn't much in what these natives say.

But what I have to tell is more than this. Two years ago, when I was prospecting about five hundred miles east in the desert, I came on a lot of queer pieces of dressed stone perhaps 3 × 2 × 2 feet in size, and weathered and pitted to the very limit.

At first I couldn't find any of the marks the blackfellows told about, but when I looked close enough I could make out some deeply carved lines in spite of the weathering. There were peculiar curves, just like what the blackfellows had tried to describe. I imagine there must have been thirty or forty blocks, some nearly buried in the sand, and all within a circle perhaps a quarter of a mile in diameter.

When I saw some, I looked around closely for more, and made a careful reckoning of the place with my instruments. I also took pictures of ten or twelve of the most typical blocks, and will inclose the prints for you to see.

I turned my information and pictures over to the government at Perth, but they have done nothing about them.

Then I met Dr. Boyle, who had read your articles in the *Journal of the American Psychological Society*, and, in time, happened to mention the stones. He was enormously interested and became quite excited when I showed him my snapshots, saying that the stones and the markings were just like those of the masonry you had dreamed about and seen described in legends.

He meant to write you, but was delayed. Meanwhile, he sent me most of the magazines with your articles and I saw at once, from your drawings and descriptions, that my stones are certainly the kind you mean. You can appreciate this from the inclosed prints. Later on you will hear directly from Dr. Boyle.

Now I can understand how important all this will be to you. Without question we are faced with the remains of an unknown civilization older than any dreamed of before, and forming a basis for your legends.

As a mining engineer I have some knowledge of geology, and can tell you that these blocks are so ancient they frighten me. They are mostly sandstone and granite, though one is almost certainly made of a queer sort of cement or concrete.

They bear evidence of water action, as if this part of the world had been submerged and come up again after long ages—all since those blocks were made and used. It is a matter of hundreds of thousands of years—or Heaven knows how much more. I don't like to think about it.

In view of your previous diligent work in tracking down the legends and everything connected with them, I cannot doubt but that you will want to lead an expedition to the desert and make some archaeological excavations. Both Dr. Boyle and I are prepared to coöperate in such work if you—or organizations known to you—can furnish the funds.

I can get together a dozen miners for the heavy digging—the blackfellows would be of no use, for I've found that they have an almost maniacal fear of this particular spot. Boyle and I are saying nothing to others, for you very obviously ought to have precedence in any discoveries or credit.

The place can be reached from Pilbarra in about four days by motor tractor—which we'd need for our apparatus. It is somewhat west and south of Warburton's path of 1873, and one hundred miles southeast of Joanna Spring. We could float things up the De Grey River instead of starting from Pilbarra—but all that can be talked over later.

Roughly the stones lie at a point about 22° 3' 14" South Latitude, 125° 0' 39" East Longitude. The climate is tropical, and the desert conditions are trying.

I shall welcome further correspondence upon this subject, and am indeed keenly eager to assist in any plan you may devise. After studying your articles I am deeply impressed with the profound significance of the whole matter. Dr. Boyle will write later. When rapid communication is needed, a cable to Perth can be relayed by wireless. Hoping profoundly for an early message,

Believe me,
Most faithfully yours,
ROBERT B. F. MACKENZIE

Of the immediate aftermath of this letter, much can be learned from the press. My good fortune in securing the backing of Miskatonic University was great, and both Mr. Mackenzie and Dr. Boyle proved invaluable in arranging matters at the Australian end. We were not too specific with the public about our objects, since the whole matter would have lent itself unpleasantly to sensational and jocose treatment by the cheaper newspapers. As a result, printed reports were sparing; but enough appeared to tell of our quest for reported Australian ruins and to chronicle our various preparatory steps.

Professor William Dyer of the college's geology department—leader of the Miskatonic Antarctic Expedition of 1930–31—Ferdinand C. Ashley of the department of ancient history, and Tyler M. Freeborn of the department of anthropology—together with my son Wingate—accompanied me.

My correspondent, Mackenzie, came to Arkham early in 1935 and assisted in our final preparations. He proved to be a tremendously competent and affable man of about fifty, admirably well-read, and deeply familiar with all the conditions of Australian travel.

He had tractors waiting at Pilbarra, and we chartered a tramp steamer sufficiently small to get up the river to that point. We were prepared to excavate in the most careful and scientific fashion, sifting every particle of sand, and disturbing nothing which might seem to be in or near its original situation.

Sailing from Boston aboard the wheezy *Lexington* on March 28, 1935, we had a leisurely trip across the Atlantic and Mediterranean, through the Suez Canal, down the Red Sea, and across the Indian Ocean to our goal. I need not tell how the sight of the low, sandy West Australian coast depressed me, and how I detested the crude mining town and dreary gold fields where the tractors were given their last loads.

Dr. Boyle, who met us, proved to be elderly, pleasant and intelligent—and his knowledge of psychology led him into many long discussions with my son and me.

Discomfort and expectancy were oddly mingled in most of us when at length our party of eighteen rattled forth over the arid leagues of sand and rock. On Friday, May 31, we forded a branch of the De Grey and entered the realm of utter desolation. A certain positive terror grew on me as we advanced to this actual site of the elder world behind the legends—a terror, of course, abetted by the fact that my disturbing dreams and pseudomemories still beset me with unabated force.

It was on Monday, June 3, that we saw the first of the half-buried blocks. I cannot describe the emotions with which I actually touched—in objective reality—a fragment of cyclopean masonry in every respect like the blocks in the walls of my dream buildings. There was a distinct trace of carving—and my hands trembled as I recognized part of a curvilinear decorative scheme made hellish to me through years of tormenting nightmare and baffling research.

A month of digging brought a total of some 1250 blocks in varying stages of wear and disintegration. Most of these were carven megaliths with curved tops and bottoms. A minority were smaller, flatter, plain-surfaced, and square or octagonally cut—like those of the floors and pavements in my dreams—while a few were singularly massive and curved or slanted in such a manner as to suggest use in vaulting or groining, or as parts of arches or round window casings.

The deeper—and the farther north and east—we dug, the more blocks we found—though we still failed to discover any trace of arrangement among them. Professor Dyer was appalled at the measureless age of the fragments, and Freeborn found traces of symbols which fitted darkly into certain Papuan and Polynesian legends of infinite antiquity. The condition and scattering of the blocks told mutely of vertiginous cycles of time and geologic upheavals of cosmic savagery.

We had an aeroplane with us, and my son Wingate would often go up to different heights and scan the sand-and-rock waste for signs of dim, large-scale outlines—either differences of level or trails of scattered blocks. His results were virtually negative; for whenever he would one day think he had glimpsed some significant trend, he would on his next trip find the impression replaced by another equally insubstantial—a result of the shifting, wind-blown sand.

One or two of these ephemeral suggestions, though, affected me queerly and disagreebly. They seemed, after a fashion, to dovetail horribly with something I had dreamed or read, but which I could no longer remember. There was a terrible familiarity about them—which somehow made me look furtively and apprehensively over the abominable, sterile terrain.

Around the first week in July I developed an unaccountable set of mixed emotions about that general northeasterly region. There was horror, and there was curiosity—but more than that, there was a persistent and perplexing illusion of memory.

I tried all sorts of psychological expedients to get these notions out of my head, but met with no success. Sleeplessness also gained upon me, but I almost welcomed this because of the resultant shortening of my dream periods. I acquired the habit of taking long, lone walks in the desert late at night—usually to the north or northeast, whither the sum of my strange new impulses seemed subtly to pull me.

Sometimes, on these walks, I would stumble over nearly buried fragments of the ancient masonry. Though there were fewer visible blocks here than where we had started, I felt sure that there must be a vast abundance beneath the surface. The ground was less level than at our camp, and the prevailing high winds now and then piled the sand into fantastic temporary hillocks—exposing low traces of the elder stones while it covered other traces.

I was queerly anxious to have the excavations extend to this territory, yet at the same time dreaded what might be revealed. Obviously, I was getting into a rather bad state—all the worse because I could not account for it.

An indication of my poor nervous health can be gained from my response to an odd discovery which I made on one of my nocturnal rambles. It was on the evening of July 11, when the moon flooded the mysterious hillocks with a curious pallor.

Wandering somewhat beyond my usual limits, I came upon a great stone which seemed to differ markedly from any we had yet encountered. It was almost wholly covered, but I stooped and cleared away the sand with my hands, later studying the object carefully and supplementing the moonlight with my electric torch.

Unlike the other very large rocks, this one was perfectly square-cut, with no convex or concave surface. It seemed, too, to be of a dark basaltic substance, wholly dissimilar to the granite and sandstone and occasional concrete of the now familiar fragments.

Suddenly I rose, turned, and ran for the camp at top speed. It was a wholly unconscious and irrational flight, and only when I was close to my tent did I fully realize why I had run. Then it came to me. The queer dark stone was something which I had dreamed and read about, and which was linked with the uttermost horrors of the aeon-old legendry.

It was one of the blocks of that basaltic elder masonry which the fabled Great Race held in such fear—the tall, windowless ruins left by those brooding, half-material, alien things that festered in earth's nether abysses and against whose windlike, invisible forces the trap-doors were sealed and the sleepless sentinels posted.

I remained awake all night, but by dawn realized how silly I had been to let the shadow of a myth upset me. Instead of being frightened, I should have had a discoverer's enthusiasm.

The next forenoon I told the others about my find, and Dyer, Freeborn, Boyle, my son, and I set out to view the anomalous block. Failure, however, confronted us. I had formed no clear idea of the stone's location and a late wind had wholly altered the hillocks of shifting sand.

VI

I come now to the crucial and most difficult part of my narrative—all the more difficult because I cannot be quite certain of its reality. At times I feel uncomfortably sure that I was not dreaming or deluded; and it is this feeling—in view of the stupendous implications which the objective truth of my experience would raise—which impels me to make this record.

My son—a trained psychologist with the fullest and most sympathetic knowledge of my whole case—shall be the primary judge of what I have to tell.

First let me outline the externals of the matter, as those at the camp know them: On the night of July 17–18, after a windy day, I retired early but could not sleep. Rising shortly before eleven and afflicted as usual with that strange feeling regarding the northeastward terrain, I set out on one of my typical nocturnal walks, seeing and greeting only one person—an Australian miner named Tupper—as I left our precincts.

The moon, slightly past full, shone from a clear sky, and drenched the ancient sands with a white, leprous radiance which seemed to me somehow infinitely evil. There was no longer any wind, nor did any return for nearly five hours, as amply attested by Tupper and others who saw me walking rapidly across the pallid, secret-guarding hillocks toward the northeast.

About 3:30 A.M., a violent wind blew up, waking every one in camp and felling three of the tents. The sky was unclouded, and the desert still blazed with that leprous moonlight. As the party saw to the tents my absence was noted, but in view of my previous walks this circumstance gave no one alarm. And yet, as many as three men—all Australians—seemed to feel something sinister in the air.

Mackenzie explained to Professor Freeborn that this was a fear picked up from blackfellow folklore—the natives having woven a curious fabric of malignant myth about the high winds which at long intervals sweep across the sands under a clear sky. Such winds, it is whispered, blow out of the great stone huts under the ground, where terrible things have happened—and are never felt except near places where the big marked stones are scattered. Close to four the gale subsided as suddenly as it had begun, leaving the sand hills in new and unfamiliar shapes.

It was just past five, with the bloated, fungoid moon sinking in the west, when I staggered into camp—hatless, tattered, features scratched and ensanguined, and without my electric torch. Most of the men had returned to bed, but Professor Dyer was smoking a pipe in front of his tent. Seeing my winded and almost frenzied state, he called Dr. Boyle, and the two of them got me on my cot and made me comfortable. My son, roused by the stir, soon joined them, and they all tried to force me to lie still and attempt sleep.

But there was no sleep for me. My psychological state was very extraordinary—different from anything I had previously suffered. After a time I insisted upon talking—nervously and elaborately explaining my condition.

I told them I had become fatigued, and had lain down in the sand for a nap. There had, I said, been dreams even more frightful than usual—and when I was awaked by the sudden high wind my overwrought nerves had snapped. I had fled in panic, frequently falling over half-buried stones and thus gaining my tattered and bedraggled aspect. I must have slept long—hence the hours of my absence.

Of anything strange either seen or experienced I hinted absolutely nothing—exercising the greatest self-control in that respect. But I spoke of a change of mind regarding the whole work of the expedition, and urged a halt in all digging toward the northeast.

My reasoning was patently weak—for I mentioned a dearth of blocks, a wish not to offend the superstitious miners, a possible shortage of funds from the college, and other things either untrue or irrelevant. Naturally, no one paid the lest attention to my new wishes—not even my son, whose concern for my health was obvious.

The next day I was up and around the camp, but took no part in the excavations. I decided to return home as soon as possible for the sake of my nerves, and my son promised to fly me in the plane to Perth—a thousand miles to the southwest—as soon as he had surveyed the region I wished let alone.

If, I reflected, the thing I had seen was still visible, I might decide to attempt a specific warning even at the cost of ridicule. It was just conceivable that the miners who knew the local folklore might back me up. Humouring me, my son made the survey that very afternoon, flying over all the terrain my walk could possibly have covered. Yet nothing of what I had found remained in sight.

It was the case of the anomalous basalt block all over again—the shifting sand had wiped out every trace. For an instant I half regretted having lost a certain awesome object in my stark fright—but now I know that the loss was merciful. I can still believe my whole experience an illusion—especially if, as I devoutly hope, that hellish abyss is never found.

Wingate took me to Perth on July 20, though declining to abandon the expedition and return home. He stayed with me until the 25th, when the steamer for Liverpool sailed. Now, in the cabin of the

Empress, I am pondering long and frantically upon the entire matter, and have decided that my son, at least, must be informed. It shall rest with him whether to diffuse the matter more widely.

In order to meet any eventuality I have prepared this summary of my background—as already known in a scattered way to others—and will now tell as briefly as possible what seemed to happen during my absence from the camp that hideous night.

Nerves on edge, and whipped into a kind of perverse eagerness by that inexplicable, dread-mingled, mnemonic urge toward the northeast, I plodded on beneath the evil, burning moon. Here and there I saw, half shrouded by sand, those primal cyclopean blocks left from nameless and forgotten aeons.

The incalculable age and brooding horror of this monstrous waste began to oppress me as never before, and I could not keep from thinking of my maddening dreams, of the frightful legends which lay behind them, and of the present fears of natives and miners concerning the desert and its carven stones.

And yet I plodded on as if to some eldritch rendezvous—more and more assailed by bewildering fancies, compulsions, and pseudo-memories. I thought of some of the possible contours of the lines of stones as seen by my son from the air, and wondered why they seemed at once so ominous and so familiar. Something was fumbling and rattling at the latch of my recollection, while another unknown force sought to keep the portal barred.

The night was windless, and the pallid sand curved upward and downward like frozen waves of the sea. I had no goal, but somehow plowed along as if with fate-bound assurance. My dreams welled up into the waking world, so that each sand-embedded megalith seemed part of endless rooms and corridors of prehuman masonry, carved and hieroglyphed with symbols that I knew too well from years of custom as a captive mind of the Great Race.

At moments I fancied I saw those omniscient, conical horrors moving about at their accustomed tasks, and I feared to look down lest I find myself one with them in aspect. Yet all the while I saw the sand-covered blocks as well as the rooms and corridors; evil, burning moon as well as the lamps of luminous crystal; the endless desert as well as the waving ferns beyond the windows. I was awake and dreaming at the same time.

I do not know how long or how far—or indeed, in just what direction—I had walked when I first spied the heap of blocks bared by the day's wind. It was the largest group in one place that I had seen so far, and so sharply did it impress me that the visions of fabulous aeons faded suddenly away.

Again there were only the desert and the evil moon and the shards of an unguessed past. I drew close and paused, and cast the added light of my electric torch over the tumbled pile. A hillock had blown away, leaving a low, irregularly round mass of megaliths and smaller fragments some forty feet across and from two to eight feet high.

From the very outset I realized that there was some utterly unprecedented quality about those stones. Not only was the mere number of them quite without parallel, but something in the sandworn traces of design arrested me as I scanned them under the mingled beams of the moon and my torch.

Not that any one differed essentially from the earlier specimens we had found. It was something subtler than that. The impression did not come when I looked at one block alone, but only when I ran my eye over several almost simultaneously.

Then, at last, the truth dawned upon me. The curvilinear pattens on many of those blocks were closely related—parts of one vast decorative conception. For the first time in this aeon-shaking waste I had come upon a mass of masonry in its old position—tumbled and fragmentary, it is true, but none the less existing in a very definite sense.

Mounting at a low place, I clambered laboriously over the heap; here and there clearing away the sand with my fingers, and constantly striving to interpret varieties of size, shape, and style, and relationships of design.

After a while I could vaguely guess at the nature of the bygone structure, and at the designs which had once stretched over the vast surfaces masonry. The perfect identity of the whole with some of my dream glimpses appalled and unnerved me.

This was once a cyclopean corridor thirty feet wide and thirty feet tall, paved with octagonal blocks and solidly vaulted overhead. There would have been rooms opening off on the right, and at the farther end one of those strange inclined planes would have wound down to still lower depths.

I started violently as these conceptions occurred to me, for there was more in them than the blocks themselves had supplied. How did I know that this level should have been far underground? How did I know that the plane leading upward should have been behind me? How did I know that the long subterrene passage to the Square of Pillars ought to lie on the left one level above me?

How did I know that the room of machines and the rightward-leading tunnel to the central archives ought to lie two levels below? How did I know that there would be one of those horrible metal-banded trapdoors at the very bottom four levels down? Bewildered by this intrusion from the dream world, I found myself shaking and bathed in a cold perspiration.

Then, as a last, intolerable touch, I felt that faint, insidious stream of cool air trickling upward from a depressed place near the center of the huge heap. Instantly, as once before, my visions faded, and I saw again only the evil moonlight, the brooding desert, and the spreading tumulus of paleogean masonry. Something real and tangible, yet fraught with infinite suggestions of nighted mystery, now confronted me. For that stream of air could argue but one thing—a hidden gulf of great size beneath the disordered blocks on the surface.

My first thought was of the sinister blackfellow legends of vast underground huts among the megaliths where horrors happen and great winds are born. Then thoughts of my own dreams came back, and I felt dim pseudomemories tugging at my mind. What manner of place lay below me? What primal, inconceivable source of age-old myth cycles and haunting nightmares might I be on the brink of uncovering?

It was only for a moment that I hestitated, for more than curiosity and scientific zeal was driving me on and working against my growing fear.

I seemed to move almost automatically, as if in the clutch of some compelling fate. Pocketing my torch, and struggling with a strength that I had not thought I possessed, I wrenched aside first one titan fragment of stone and then another, till there welled up a strong draft whose dampness contrasted oddly with the desert's dry air. A black rift began to yawn, and at length—when I had pushed away every fragment small enough to budge—the leprous moonlight blazed on an aperture of ample width to admit me.

I drew out my torch and cast a brilliant beam into the opening. Below me was a chaos of tumbled masonry, sloping roughly down toward the north at an angle of about forty-five degrees, and evidently the result of some bygone collapse from above.

Between its surface and the ground level was a gulf of impenetrable blackness at whose upper edge were signs of gigantic, stress-heaved vaulting. At this point, it appeared, the desert's sands lay directly upon a floor of some titan structure of earth's youth—how preserved through aeons of geologic convulsion I could not then and cannot now even attempt to guess.

In retrospect, the barest idea of a sudden lone descent into such a doubtful abyss—and at a time when one's whereabouts were unknown to any living soul—seems like the utter apex of insanity. Perhaps it was—yet that night I embarked without hesitancy upon such a descent.

Again there was manifest that lure and driving of fatality which had all along seemed to direct my course. With torch flashing intermittently to save the battery, I commenced a mad scramble down the sinister, cyclopean incline below the opening—sometimes facing forward as I found good hand and foot holds, and at other times turning to face the heap of megaliths as I clung and fumbled more precariously.

In two directions beside me, distant walls of carven, crumbling masonry loomed dimly under the direct beams of my torch. Ahead, however, was darkness.

I kept no track of time during my downward scramble. So seething with baffling hints and images was my mind that all objective matters seemed withdrawn to incalculable distances. Physical sensation was dead, and even fear remained as a wraith-like, inactive gargoyle leering impotently at me.

Eventually I reached a level floor strewn with fallen blocks, shapeless fragments of stone, and sand and detritus of every kind. On either side—perhaps thirty feet apart—rose massive walls culminating in huge groinings. That they were carved I could just discern, but the nature of the carvings was beyond my perception.

What held me most was the vaulting overhead. The beam from my torch could not reach the roof, but the lower parts of the monstrous arches stood out distinctly. And so perfect was their identity with what I had seen in countless dreams of the elder world, that I trembled actively for the first time.

Behind and high above, a faint luminous blur told of the distant moonlight world outside. Some vague shred of caution warned me that I should not let it out of my sight, lest I have no guide for my return.

I now advanced toward the wall at my left, where the traces of carving were plainest. The littered floor was nearly as hard to traverse as the downward heap had been, but I managed to pick my difficult way.

At one place I heaved aside some blocks and kicked away the detritus to see what the pavement was like, and shuddered at the utter, fateful familiarity of the great octagonal stones whose buckled surface still held roughly together.

Reaching a convenient distance from the wall, I cast the searchlight slowly and carefully over its worn remnants of carving. Some bygone influx of water seemed to have acted on the sandstone surface, while there were curious incrustations which I could not explain.

In places the masonry was very loose and distorted, and I wondered how many aeons more this primal, hidden edifice could keep its remaining traces of form amidst earth's heavings.

But it was the carvings themselves that excited me most. Despite their time-crumbled state, they were relatively easy to trace at close range; and the complete, intimate familiarity of every detail almost stunned my imagination. That the major attributes of this hoary masonry should be familiar, was not beyond normal credibility.

Powerfully impressing the weavers of certain myths, they had become embodied in a stream of cryptic lore which, somehow, coming to my notice during the amnesiac period, had evoked vivid images in my subconscious mind.

But how could I explain the exact and minute fashion in which each line and spiral of these strange designs tallied with what I had dreamed for more than a score of years? What obscure, forgotten oconography could have reproduced each subtle shading and *nuance* which so persistently, exactly, and unvaryingly beseiged my sleeping vision night after night?

For this was no chance or remote resemblance. Definitely and absolutely, the millennially ancient, aeon-hidden corridor in which I stood was the original of something I knew in sleep as intimately as I knew my own house in Crane Street, Arkham. True, my dreams showed the place in its undecayed prime; but the identity was no less real on that account. I was wholly and horribly oriented.

The particular structure I was in was known to me. Known, too, was its place in that terrible elder city of dream. That I could visit unerringly any point in that structue or in that city which had escaped the changes and devastations of uncounted ages, I realized with hideous and instinctive certainty. What in Heaven's name could all this mean? How had I come to know what I knew? And what awful reality could lie behind those antique tales of the beings who had dwelt in this labyrinth of primordial stone?

Words can convey only fractionally the welter of dread and bewilderment which ate at my spirit. I knew this place. I knew what lay below me, and what had lain overhead before the myriad towering stories had fallen to dust and debris and the desert. No need now, I thought with a shudder, to keep that faint blur of moonlight in view.

I was torn betwixt a longing to flee and a feverish mixture of burning curiosity and driving fatality. What had happened to this monstrous megalopolis of old in the millions of years since the time of my dreams? Of the subterrene mazes which had underlain the city and linked all the titan towers, how much had still survived the writhings of earth's crust?

Had I come upon a whole buried world of unholy archaism? Could I still find the house of the writing master, and the tower where S'gg'ha, the captive mind from the star-headed vegetable carnivores of Antarctica, had chiseled certain pictures on the blank spaces of the walls?

Would the passage at the second level down to the hall of the alien minds, be still unchoked and traversable? In that hall the captive mind of an incredible entity—a half-plastic denizen of the hollow interior of an unknown trans-Plutonian planet eighteen million years in the future—had kept a certain thing which it had modeled from clay.

I shut my eyes and put my hand to my head in a vain, pitiful effort to drive these insane dream fragments from my consciousness. Then, for the first time I felt acutely the coolness, motion, and dampness of the surrounding air. Shuddering, I realized that a vast chain of aeon-dead black gulfs must indeed be yawning somewhere beyond and below me.

I thought of the frightful chambers and corridors and inclines as I recalled them from my dreams. Would the way to the central archives still be open? Again that driving fatality tugged insistently at my brain as I recalled the awesome records that once lay cased in those rectagular vaults of rustless metal.

There, said the dreams and legends, had reposed the whole history, past and future, of the cosmic space-time continuum—written by captive minds from every orb and every age in the solar system. Madness, of course—but had I not now stumbled into a nighted world as mad as I?

I thought of the locked metal shelves, and of the curious knob twistings needed to open each one. My own came vividly into my consciousness. How often had I gone through that intricate routine of varied turns and pressures in the terrestrial vertebrate section on the lowest level! Every detail was fresh and familiar.

If there were such a vault as I had dreamed of, I could open it in a moment. It was then that madness took me utterly. An instant later, and I was leaping and stumbling over the rocky debris toward the well-remembered incline to the depths below.

VII

From that point forward my impressions are scarcely to be relied on—indeed, I still possess a final, desperate hope that they all form parts of some demoniac dream or illusion born of delirium. A fever raged in my brain, and everything came to me through a kind of haze—sometimes only intermittently.

The rays of my torch shot feebly into the engulfing blackness, bringing phantasmal flashes of hideously familiar walls and carvings, all blighted with the decay of ages. In one place a tremendous mass of vaulting had fallen, so that I had to clamber over a mighty mound of stones reaching almost to the ragged, grotesquely stalactited roof.

It was all the ultimate apex of nightmare, made worse by that blasphemous tug of pseudomemory. One thing only was unfamiliar, and that was my own size in relation to the monstrous masonry. I felt oppressed by a sense of unwonted smallness, as if the sight of these towering walls from a mere human body was something wholly new and abnormal. Again and again I looked nervously down at myself, vaguely disturbed by the human form I possessed.

Onward through the blackness of the abyss I leaped, plunged and staggered—often falling and bruising myself, and once nearly shattering my torch. Every stone and corner of that demoniac gulf was known to me, and at many points I stopped to cast beams of light through choked and crumbling, yet familiar, archways.

Some rooms had totally collapsed; others were bare, or debris-filled. In a few I saw masses of metal—some fairly intact, some broken, and some crushed or battered—which I recognized as the colossal pedestals or tables of my dreams. What they could in truth have been, I dared not guess.

I found the downward incline and began its descent—though after a time halted by a gaping, ragged chasm whose narrowest point could not be much less than four feet across. Here the stone-work had fallen through, revealing incalculable inky depths beneath.

I knew there were two more cellar levels in this titan edifice, and trembled with fresh panic as I recalled the metal-clamped trapdoor on the lowest one. There could be no guards now—for what had lurked beneath had long since done its hideous work and sunk into its long decline. By the time of the posthuman beetle race it would be quite dead. And yet, as I thought of the native legends, I trembled anew.

It cost me a terrible effort to vault that yawning chasm, since the littered floor prevented a running start—but madness drove me on. I chose a place close to the left-hand wall—where the rift was least wide and the landing spot reasonably clear of dangerous debris—and after one frantic moment reached the other side in safety.

At last, gaining the lower level, I stumbled on past the archway of the room of machines, within which were fantastic ruins of metal, half buried beneath fallen vaulting. Everything was where I knew it would be, and I climbed confidently over the heaps which barred the entrance of a vast transverse corridor. This, I realized, would take me under the city to the central archives.

Endless ages seemed to unroll as I stumbled, leaped, and crawled along that debris-cluttered corridor. Now and then I could make out carvings on the age-stained walls—some familiar, others seemingly added since the period of my dreams. Since this was a subterrene house-connecting highway, there were no archways save when the route led through the lower levels of various buildings.

At some of these intersections I turned aside long enough to look down well-remembered rooms. Twice only did I find any radical changes from what I had dreamed of—and in one of these cases I could trace the sealed-up outlines of the archway I remembered.

I shook violently, and felt a curious surge of retarding weakness as I steered a hurried and reluctant course through the crypt of one of those great windowless, ruined towers whose alien, basalt masonry bespoke a whispered and horrible origin.

This primal vault was round and fully two hundred feet across, with nothing carved upon the dark-hued stonework. The floor was here free from anything save dust and sand, and I could see the apertures leading upward and downward. There were no stairs nor inclines—indeed, my dreams had pictured those elder towers as wholly untouched by the fabulous Great Race. Those who had built them had not needed stairs or inclines.

In the dreams, the downward aperture had been tightly sealed and nervously guarded. Now it lay open—black and yawning, and giving forth a current of cool, damp air. Of what limitless caverns of eternal night might brood below, I would not permit myself to think.

Later, clawing my way along a badly heaped section of the corridor, I reached a place where the roof had wholly caved in. The debris rose like a mountain, and I climbed up over it, passing through a vast, empty space where my torchlight could reveal neither walls nor vaulting. This, I reflected, must be the cellar of the house of the metal purveyors, fronting on the third square not far from the archives. What had happened to it I could not conjecture.

I found the corridor again beyond the mountain of detritus and stone, but after a short distance encountered a wholly choked place where the fallen vaulting almost touched the perilously sagging ceiling. How I managed to wrench and tear aside enough blocks to afford a passage, and how I dared disturb the tightly packed fragments when the least shift of equilibrium might have brought down all the tons of superincumbent masonry to crush me to nothingness, I do not know.

It was sheer madness that impelled and guided me—if, indeed, my whole underground adventure was not—as I hope—a hellish delusion or phase of dreaming. But I did make—or dream that I made—a passage that I could squirm through. As I wriggled over the mound of debris—my torch, switched continuously on, thrust deeply in my mouth—I felt myself torn by the fantastic stalactites of the jagged floor above me.

I was now close to the great underground archival structure which seemed to form my goal. Sliding and clambering down the farther side of the barrier, and picking my way along the remaining stretch of corridor with handheld, intermittently flashing torch, I came at last to a low, circular crypt with arches—still in a marvelous state of preservation—opening off on every side.

The walls, or such parts of them as lay within reach of my torch-light, were densely hieroglyphed and chiseled with typical curvilinear symbols—some added since the period of my dreams.

This, I realized, was my fated destination, and I turned at once through a familiar archway on my left. That I could find clear passage up and down the incline to all the surviving levels, I had, oddly, little doubt. This vast, earth-protected pile, housing the annals of all the solar system, had been built with supernal skill and strength to last as long as the system itself.

Blocks of stupendous size poised with mathematical genius and bound with cements of incredible toughness had combined to form a mass as firm as the planet's rocky core. Here, after ages more prodigious than I could sanely grasp, its buried bulk stood in all its essential contours, the vast, dust-drifted floors scarce sprinkled with the litter elsewhere so dominant.

The relatively easy walking from this point onward went curiously to my head. All the frantic eagerness hitherto frustrated by obstacles now took itsef out in a kind of febrile speed, and I literally raced along the low-roofed, monstrously well-remembered aisles beyond the archway.

I was past being astonished by the familiarity of what I saw. On every hand the great hieroglyphed metal shelf doors loomed monstrously; some yet in place, others sprung open, and still others bent and buckled under bygone geological stresses not quite strong enough to shatter the titan masonry.

Here and there a dust-covered heap beneath a gaping, empty shelf seemed to indicate where cases had been shaken down by earth tremors. On occasional pillars were great symbols and letters proclaiming classes and subclasses of volumes.

Once I paused before an open vault where I saw some of the accustomed metal cases still in position amidst the ominipresent gritty dust. Reaching up, I dislodged one of the thinner specimens with some difficulty, and rested it on the floor for inspection. It was titled in the prevailing curvilinear hieroglyphs, though something in the arrangement of the characters seemed subtly unusual.

The odd mechanism of the hooked fastener was perfectly well known to me, and I snapped up the still rustless and workable lid and drew out the book within. The latter, as expected, was some twenty by fifteen inches in area, and two inches thick; the thin metal covers opening at the top.

Its tough cellulose pages seemed unaffected by the myriad cycles of time they had lived through, and I studied the queerly pigmented, brush-drawn letters of the text—symbols unlike either the usual curved hieroglyphs or any alphabet known to human scholarship—with a haunting, half-aroused memory.

It came to me that this was the language used by a captive mind I had known slightly in my dreams—a mind from a large asteroid on which had survived much of the archaic life and lore of the primal planet whereof it formed a fragment. At the same time I recalled that this level of the archives was devoted to volumes dealing with the non-terrestrial planets.

As I ceased poring over this incredible document, I saw that the light of my torch was beginning to fail, hence quickly inserted the extra battery I always had with me. Then, armed with the stronger radiance, I resumed my feverish racing through unending tangles of aisles and corridors—recognizing now and then some familiar shelf, and vaguely annoyed by the acoustic conditions which made my footfalls echo incongruously in these catacombs.

The very prints of my shoes behind me in the millennially untrodden dust made me shudder. Never before, if my mad dreams held anything of truth, had human feet pressed upon those immemorial pavements.

Of the particular goal of my insane racing, my conscious mind held no hint. There was, however, some force of evil potency pulling at my dazed will and buried recollection, so that I vaguely felt I was not running at random.

I came to a downward incline and followed it to profound depths. Floors flashed by me as I raced, but I did not pause to explore them. In my whirling brain there had begun to beat a certain rhythm which set my right hand twitching in unison. I wanted to unlock something, and felt that I knew all the intricate twists and pressures needed to do it. It would be like a modern safe with a combination lock.

Dream or not, I had once known and still knew. How any dream—or any scrap of unconsciously absorbed legend—could have taught me a detail so minute, so intricate, and so complex, I did not attempt to explain to myself. I was beyond all coherent thought. For was not this whole experience—this shocking familiarity with a set of unknown ruins, and this monstrously exact identity of everything before me with what only dreams and scraps of myth could have suggested—a horror beyond all reason?

Probably it was my basic conviction then—as it is now during my saner moments—that I was not awake at all, and that the entire buried city was a fragment of febrile hallucination.

Eventually, I reached the lowest level and struck off to the right of the incline. For some shadowy reason I tried to soften my steps, even though I lost speed thereby. There was a space I was afraid to cross on this last, deeply buried floor.

As I drew near it I recalled what thing in that space I feared. It was merely one of the metal-barred and closely guarded trapdoors. There would be no guards now, and on that account I trembled and tiptoed as I had done in passing through that black basalt vault where a similar trapdoor had yawned.

I felt a current of cold damp air, as I had felt there, and wished that my course led in another direction. Why I had to take the particular course I was taking, I did not know.

When I came to the space I saw that the trapdoor yawned wildly open. Ahead, the shelves began again, and I glimpsed on the floor before one of them a heap very thinly covered with dust, where a number of cases had recently fallen. At the same moment a fresh wave of panic clutched me, though for some time I could not discover why.

Heaps of fallen cases were not uncommon, for all through the aeons this lightless labyrinth had been racked by the heavings of earth and had echoed at intervals to the deafening clatter of toppling objects. It was only when I was nearly across the space that I realized why I shook so violently.

Not the heap, but something about the dust of the level floor, was troubling me. In the light of my torch it seemed as if that dust were not as even as it ought to be—there were places where it looked thinner, as if it had been disturbed not many months before. I could not be sure, for even the apparently thinner places were dusty enough; yet a certain suspicion of regularity in the fancied unevenness was highly disquieting.

When I brought the torchlight close to one of the queer places I did not like what I saw—for the illusion of regularity became very great. It was as if there were regular lines of composite impressions—impressions that went in threes, each slightly over a foot square, and consisting of five nearly circular three-inch prints, one in advance of the other four.

These possible lines of foot-square impressions appeared to lead in two directions, as if something had gone somewhere and returned. They were, of course, very faint, and may have been illusions or accidents; but there was an element of dim, fumbling terror about the way I thought they ran. For at one end of them was the heap of cases which must have clattered down not long before, while at the other end was the ominous trapdoor with the cool, damp wind, yawning unguarded down to abysses past imagination.

VIII

That my strange sense of compulsion was deep and overwhelming is shown by its conquest of my fear. No rational motive could have drawn me on after that hideous suspicion of prints and the creeping dream memories it excited. Yet my right hand, even as it shook with fright, still twitched rhythmically in its eagerness to turn a lock it hoped to find. Before I knew it I was past the heap of lately fallen cases and running on tiptoe through aisles of utterly unbroken dust toward a point which I seemed to know morbidly, horribly well.

My mind was asking itself questions whose origin and relevancy I was only beginning to guess. Would the shelf be reachable by a human body? Could my human hand master all the aeon-rememberd motions of the lock? Would the lock be undamaged and workable? And what would I do—what dare I do—with what—as I now commenced to realize—I both hoped and feared to find? Would it prove the awesome, brain-shattering truth of something past normal conception, or show only that I was dreaming?

The next I knew I had ceased my tiptoed racing and was standing still, staring at a row of maddeningly familiar hieroglyphed shelves. They were in a state of almost perfect preservation, and only three of the doors in this vicinity had sprung open.

My feelings toward these shelves cannot be described—so utter and insistent was the sense of old acquaintance. I was looking high up at a row near the top and wholly out of my reach, and wondering how I could climb to best advantage. An open door four rows from the bottom would help, and the locks of the closed doors formed possible holds for hands and feet. I would grip the torch between my teeth, as I had in other places where both hands were needed. Above all I must make no noise.

How to get down what I wished to remove would be difficult, but I could probably hook its movable fastener in my coat collar and carry it like a knapsack. Again I wondered whether the lock would be undamaged. That I could repeat each familiar motion I had not the least doubt. But I hoped the thing would not scrape or creak—and that my hand could work it properly.

Even as I thought these things I had taken the torch in my mouth and began to climb. The projecting locks were poor supports; but, as I had expected, the opened shelf helped greatly. I used both the swinging door and the edge of the aperture itself in my ascent, and managed to avoid any loud creaking.

Balanced on the upper edge of the door, and leaning far to my right, I could just reach the lock I sought. My fingers, half numb from climbing, were very clumsy at first; but I soon saw that they were anatomically adequate. And the memory rhythm was strong in them.

Out of unknown gulfs of time the intricate, secret motions had somehow reached my brain correctly in every detail—for after less than five minutes of trying there came a click whose familiarity was all the more startling because I had not consciously anticipated it. In another instant the metal door was slowly swinging open with only the faintest grating sound.

Dazedly I looked over the row of grayish case ends thus exposed, and felt a tremendous surge of some wholly inexplicable emotion. Just within reach of my right hand was a case whose curving hieroglyphs made me shake with a pang infinitely more complex than one of mere fright. Still shaking, I managed to dislodge it amidst a shower of gritty flakes, and ease it over toward myself without any violent noise.

Like the other case I had handled, it was slightly more than twenty by fifteen inches in size, with curved mathematical designs in low relief. In thickness it just exceeded three inches.

Crudely wedging it between myself and the surface I was climbing, I fumbled with the fastener and finally got the hook free. Lifting the cover, I shifted the heavy object to my back, and let the hook catch hold of my collar. Hands now free, I awkwardly clambered down to the dusty floor and prepared to inspect my prize.

Kneeling in the gritty dust, I swung the case around and rested it in front of me. My hands shook, and I dreaded to draw out the book within almost as much as I longed—and felt compelled—to do so. It had very gradually become clear to me what I ought to find, and this realization nearly paralyzed my faculties.

If the thing were there—and if I were not dreaming—the implications would be quite beyond the power of the human spirit to bear. What tormented me most was my momentary inability to feel that my surroundings were a dream. The sense of reality was hideous—and again becomes so as I recall the scene.

At length I tremblingly pulled the book from its container and stared fascinatedly at the well-known hieroglyphs on the cover. It seemed to be in prime condition, and the curvilinear letters of the title held me in almost as hypnotized a state as if I could read them. Indeed, I cannot swear that I did not actually read them in some transient and terrible access of abnormal memory.

I do not know how long it was before I dared to lift that thin metal cover. I temporized and made excuses to myself. I took the torch from my mouth and shut it off to save the battery. Then, in the dark, I collected my courage—finally lifting the cover without turning on the light. Last of all, I did indeed flash the torch upon the exposed page—steeling myself in advance to suppress any sound no matter what I should find.

I looked for an instant, then collapsed. Clenching my teeth, however, I kept silent. I sank wholly to the floor and put a hand to my forehead amidst the engulfing blackness. What I dreaded and expected was there. Either I was dreaming, or time and space had become a mockery.

I must be dreaming—but I would test the horror by carrying this thing back and showing it to my son if it were indeed a reality. My head swam frightfully, even though there were no visible objects in the unbroken gloom to swirl about me. Ideas and images of the starkest terror—excited by the vistas which my glimpse had opened up—began to throng in upon me and cloud my senses.

I thought of those possible prints in the dust, and trembled at the sound of my own breathing as I did so. Once again I flashed on the light and looked at the page as a serpent's victim may look at his destroyer's eyes and fangs.

Then, with clumsy fingers, in the dark, I closed the book, put it in its container, and snapped the lid and the curious, hooked fastener. This was what I must carry back to the outer world if it truly existed—if the whole abyss truly existed—if I, and the world itself, truly existed.

Just when I tottered to my feet and commenced my return I cannot be certain. It comes to me oddly—as a measure of my sense of separation from the normal world—that I did not even once look at my watch during those hideous hours underground.

Torch in hand, and with the ominous case under one arm, I eventually found myself tiptoeing in a kind of silent panic past the draft-giving abyss and those lurking suggestions of prints. I lessened my precautions as I climbed up the endless inclines, but could not shake off a shadow of apprehension which I had not felt on the downward journey.

I dreaded having to repass through that black basalt crypt that was older than the city itself, where cold drafts welled up from unguarded depths. I thought of that which the Great Race had feared, and of what might still be lurking—be it ever so weak and dying—down there. I thought of those five-circle prints and of what my dreams had told me of such prints—and of strange winds and whistling noises associated with them. And I thought of the tales of the modern black-fellows, wherein the horror of great winds and nameless ruins was dwelt upon.

I knew from a carven wall symbol the right floor to enter, and came at last—after passing that other book I had examined—to the great circular space with the branching archways. On my right, and at once recognizable, was the arch through which I had arrived. This I now entered, conscious that the rest of my course would be harder because of the tumbled state of the masonry outside the archive building. My new metal-cased burden weighed upon me, and I found it harder and harder to be quiet as I stumbled among debris and frag-ments of every sort.

Then I came to the ceiling-high mound of debris through which I had wrenched a scanty passage. My dread at wriggling through again was infinite, for my first passage had made some noise, and I now—after seeing those possible prints—dreaded sound above all things. The case, too, doubled the problem of traversing the narrow crevice.

But I clambered up the barrier as best I could, and pushed the case through the aperture ahead of me. Then, torch in mouth, I scrambled through myself—my back torn as before by stalactites.

As I tried to grasp the case again, it fell some distance ahead of me down the slope of the debris, making a disturbing clatter and arous-ing echoes which sent me into a cold perspiration. I lunged for it at once, and regained it without further noise—but a moment afterward the slipping of blocks under my feet raised a sudden and unprece-dented din.

That din was my undoing. For, falsely or not, I thought I heard it answered in a terrible way from spaces far behind me. I thought I heard a shrill, whistling sound, like nothing else on Earth, and be-yond any adequate verbal description. If so, what followed has grim irony—save for the panic of this thing, the second thing might never have happened.

As it was, my frenzy was absolute and unrelieved. Taking my torch in my hand and clutching feebly at the case, I leaped and bounded wildly ahead with no idea in my brain beyond a mad desire to race out of these nightmare ruins to the waking world of desert and moonlight which lay so far above.

I hardly knew it when I reached the mountain of debris which towered into the vast blackness beyond the caved-in roof, and bruised and cut myself repeatedly in scrambling up its steep slope of jagged blocks and fragments.

Then came the great disaster. Just as I blindly crossed the summit, unprepared for the sudden dip ahead, my feet slipped utterly and I found myself involved in a mangling avalanche of sliding masonry whose cannon-loud uproar split the black, cavern air in a deafening series of earth-shaking reverberations.

I have no recollection of emerging from this chaos, but a momentary fragment of consciousness shows me as plunging and tripping and scrambling along the corridor amidst the clangor—case and torch still with me.

Then, just as I approached that primal basalt crypt I had so dreaded, utter madness came. For as the echoes of the avalanche died down, there became audible a repetition of that frightful alien whistling I thought I had heard before. This time there was no doubt about it—and what was worse, it came from a point not behind but *ahead of me.*

Probably I shrieked aloud then. I have a dim picture of myself as flying through the hellish basalt vault of the elder things, and hearing that damnable alien sound piping up from the open, unguarded door of limitless nether blacknesses. There was wind, too—not merely a cool, damp draft, but a violent, purposeful blast belching savagely and frigidly from that abominable gulf whence the obscene whistling came.

There are memories of leaping and lurching over obstacles of every sort, with that torrent of wind and shrieking sound growing moment by moment, and seeming to curl and twist purposefully around me as it struck out wickedly from the spaces behind and beneath.

Though in my rear, that wind had the odd effect of hindering instead of aiding my progress; as if it acted like a noose or lasso thrown around me. Heedless of the noise I made, I clattered over a great barrier of blocks and was again in the structure that led to the surface.

I recall glimpsing the archway to the room of machines and almost crying out as I saw the incline leading down to where one of those blasphemous trapdoors must be yawning two levels below. But instead of crying out I muttered over and over to myself that this was all a dream from which I must soon awake. Perhaps I was in camp—perhaps I was at home in Arkham. As these hopes bolstered up my sanity I began to mount the incline to the higher level.

I knew, of course, that I had the four-feet cleft to recross, yet was too racked by other fears to realize the full horror until I came almost upon it. On my descent, the leap across had been easy—but could I clear the gap as readily when going uphill, and hampered by fright, exhaustion, the weight of the metal case, and the anomalous backward tug of that demon wind? I thought of these things at the last moment, and thought also of the nameless entities which might be lurking in the black abysses below the chasm.

My wavering torch was growing feeble, but I could tell by some obscure memory when I neared the cleft. The chill blasts of wind and the nauseous whistling shrieks behind me were for the moment like a merciful opiate, dulling my imagination to the horror of the yawning gulf ahead. And then I became aware of the added blasts and whistling in front of me—tides of abomination surging up through the cleft itself from depths unimagined and unimaginable.

Now, indeed, the essence of pure nightmare was upon me. Sanity departed—and, ignoring everything except the animal impulse of flight, I merely struggled and plunged upward over the incline's debris as if no gulf had existed. Then I saw the chasm's edge, leaped frenziedly with every ounce of strength I possessed, and was instantly engulfed in a pandemoniac vortex of loathsome sound and utter, materially tangible blackness.

That is the end of my experience, so far as I can recall. Any further impressions belong wholly to the domain of phantasmagoric delirium. Dream, madness, and memory merged wildly together in a series of fantastic, fragmentary delusions which can have no relation to anything real.

There was a hideous fall through incalculable leagues of viscous, sentient darkness, and a babel of noises utterly alien to all that we know of the Earth and its organic life. Dormant, rudimentary senses seemed to start into vitality within me, telling of pits and voids peopled by floating horrors and leading to sunless crags and oceans and teeming cities of windowless, basalt towers upon which no light ever shone.

Secrets of the primal planet and its immemorial aeons flashed through my brain without the aid of sight or sound, and there were known to me things which not even the wildest of former dreams had ever suggested. And all the while cold fingers of damp vapor clutched and picked at me, and that eldritch, damnable whistling shrieked fiendishly above all the alternations of babel and silence in the whirlpools of darkness around.

Afterward there were visions of the cyclopean city of my dreams—not in ruins, but just as I had dreamed of it. I was in my conical, non-human body again, and mingled with crowds of the Great Race and the captive minds who carried books up and down the lofty corridors and vast inclines.

Then, superimposed upon these pictures, were frightful, momentary flashes of a nonvisual consciousness involving desperate struggles, a writhing free from clutching tentacles of whistling wind, an insane, batlike flight through half-solid air, a feverish burrowing through the cyclone-whipped dark, and a wild stumbling and scrambling over fallen masonry.

Once there was a curious, intrusive flash of half sight—a faint, diffuse suspicion of bluish radiance far over head. Then there came a dream of wind-pursued climbing and crawling—of wriggling into a blaze of sardonic moonlight through a jumble of debris which slid and collapsed after me amidst a morbid hurricane. It was the evil, monotonous beating of that maddening moonlight which at last told me of the return of what I had once known as the objective, waking world.

I was clawing prone through the sands of the Australian desert, and around me shrieked such a tumult of wind as I had never before known on our planet's surface. My clothing was in rags, and my whole body was a mass of bruises and scratches.

Full consciousness returned very slowly, and at no time could I tell just where delirious dream left off and true memory began. There had seemed to be a mound of titan blocks, an abyss beneath it, a monstrous revelation from the past, and a nightmare horror at the end—but how much of this was real?

My flashlight was gone, and likewise my metal case I may have discovered. Had there been such a case—or any abyss—or any mound? Raising my head, I looked behind me, and saw only the sterile, undulant sands of the desert.

The demon wind died down, and the bloated, fungoid moon sank reddeningly in the west. I lurched to my feet and began to stagger southwestward toward the camp. What in truth had happened to me? Had I merely collapsed in the desert and dragged a dream-racked body over miles of sand and buried blocks? If not, how could I bear to live any longer?

For, in this new doubt, all my faith in the myth-born unreality of my visions dissolved once more into the hellish older doubting. If that abyss was real, then the Great Race was real—and its blasphemous reachings and seizures in the cosmos-wide vortex of time were no myths or nightmares, but a terrible, soul-shattering actuality.

Had I, in full, hideous fact, been drawn back to a prehuman world of a hundred and fifty million years ago in those dark, baffling days of the amnesia? Had my present body been the vehicle of a frightful alien consciousness from paleogean gulfs of time?

Had I, as the captive mind of those shambling horrors, indeed known that accursed city of stone in its primordial heyday, and wriggled down those familiar corridors in the loathsome shape of my captor? Were those tormenting dreams of more than twenty years the offspring of stark, monstrous memories?

Had I once veritably talked with minds from reachless corners of time and space, learned the universe's secrets, past and to come, and written the annals of my own world for the metal cases of those titan archives? And were those others—those shocking elder things of the mad winds and demon pipings—in truth a lingering, lurking menace, waiting and slowly weakening in black abysses while varied shapes of life drag out their multimillennial courses on the planet's age-racked surface?

I do not know. If that abyss and what it held were real, there is no hope. Then, all too truly, there lies upon this world of man a mocking and incredible shadow out of time. But, mercifully there is no proof that these things are other than fresh phases of my myth-born dreams. I did not bring back the metal case that would have been a proof, and so far those subterrene corridors have not been found.

If the laws of the universe are kind, they will never be found. But I must tell my son what I saw or thought I saw, and let him use his judgment as a psychologist in gauging the reality of my experience, and communicating this account to others.

I have said that the awful truth behind my tortured years of dreaming hinges absolutely upon the actuality of what I thought I saw in those cyclopean, buried ruins. It has been hard for me, liter-ally, to set down that crucial revelation, though no reader can have failed to guess it. Of course, it lay in that book within the metal case—the case which I pried out of its lair amidst the dust of a mil-lion centuries.

No eye had seen, no hand had touched that book since the advent of man to this planet. And yet, when I flashed my torch upon it in that frightful abyss, I saw that the queerly pigmented letters on the brittle, aeon-browned cellulose pages were not indeed any nameless hieroglyphs of earth's youth. They were, instead, the letters of our fa-miliar alphabet, spelling out the words of the English language in my own handwriting.